STORIES FROM
THE
NEW YORKER
1950—1960

19 60

SIMON AND SCHUSTER · NEW YORK

LIBRARY OF CONGRESS CATALOG CARD NUMBER: 60-12590
MANUFACTURED IN THE UNITED STATES OF AMERICA
BY AMERICAN BOOK–STRATFORD PRESS, INC., NEW YORK

CONTENTS

❖

FOREWORD

❖

The stories in this book were selected from those appearing in THE NEW YORKER *during the past ten years. Many favorites are missing, of course (our own as well as our readers'), because of restrictions of space or duplication of theme, and because of the limitations of scope that we were obliged to set. We have ruled out casual or humorous essays, stories that later became chapters of novels, and, so far as possible, stories that formed part of a series. Narrative writers of the present generation have so often drawn upon the material of their own past that there is no longer a hard and fast line between fiction and autobiography, but we have included here autobiographical stories only where the facts are dealt with freely and imaginatively—in short, where the method used is the method of fiction, not of pure reminiscence. None of the stories in the volume requires a dateline, but we think it might be of interest to note that Vladimir Nabokov's prophetic fantasy, "Lance," was published in February, 1952, some years before "astronaut" became a household word.*

—THE EDITORS

STORIES FROM

THE

NEW YORKER

1950—1960

THE MAN OF THE WORLD

❖

FRANK O'CONNOR

WHEN I was a kid, there were no such things as holidays for me, and I have no feeling of grievance about it because, in the way of kids, I simply played that I had them. One year, my summer holiday was a couple of nights I spent at the house of a friend of mine called Jimmy Leary, who lived on the other side of the road at the end of our lane. His parents sometimes went away for a couple of days to visit a sick relative in Bantry, and he was given permission to have a friend in to keep him company. I took my holiday with great gravity, insisted on the loan of Father's old travelling bag, and dragged it myself down the lane, past the neighbors standing at their doors.

"Are you off somewhere, Larry?" asked one.

"Yes, Mrs. Rooney. Off for my holidays to the Learys'," I said cheerfully.

"Wisha, aren't you lucky?"

Lucky? I felt made for life. The Learys' house was a big one, with a long flight of steps up to the front door, which was always kept shut. They had a piano in the sitting room, a pair of binoculars on a table near the window, furniture in the bedrooms, and an indoor toilet, on the stairs, which struck me as the last word in immodesty. From the window of the bedroom where Jimmy and I slept, you could see the whole road up and down, from the quarry at the foot, with the tiny houses perched on the edge of it, to the open fields at the other end, where the last gas lamp rose against the sky. I was up each morning at the first light, leaning out the window in my nightshirt and watching, through the binoculars, all the mysterious figures you never saw from our lane—policemen, railway men, and farmers on their way to market.

I admired Jimmy almost as much as I admired his house and for much the same sort of reasons. He was a year older than I, and

1

was well mannered and well dressed, and he would not associate
with most of the kids on the road at all. He had a way when any
of them joined us of resting against a wall with his hands in his
trousers pockets and listening to them with a sort of well-bred smile,
a knowing smile, that seemed to me the height of elegance. And it
was not that he was a softy, because he was an excellent boxer and
wrestler, and could easily have held his own with any of them had
he wished to. But he didn't. He was superior to them. He was—there
is only one word that still describes it for me—sophisticated.

I envied him his sophistication, for I knew that I was always
taken in by the world of appearances. I would take a sudden violent
liking to some boy and, when I went to his house, would like his
parents and his sisters as well, and think how wonderful it must be
to have such a home; but when I told Jimmy, he would smile in
that knowing way of his and say quietly, "I believe they had the
bailiffs in a few weeks ago." And even though I didn't know what
bailiffs were, I would see that I had been deceived again.

It was the same with fellows and girls, too. Seeing some bigger
chap we knew walking out with a girl for the first time, Jimmy
would say, "He'd better mind himself; that one is dynamite." And
even though I knew as little of girls who were dynamite as I did of
bailiffs, his tone was sufficient to indicate that I had again been
taken in by sweet voices and broad-brimmed hats, gaslight and
evening smells from gardens.

Forty years later, I can still measure the extent of my admiration,
for though my own handwriting is almost illegible, I sometimes
find myself scribbling idly on a pad in a small, stiff, perfectly legible
hand that I recognize with amusement as a reasonably good forgery
of Jimmy's. My admiration still lies there somewhere, a fossil in my
memory, but Jimmy's knowing smile is something I have never
managed to acquire.

And it all goes back to my curiosity about fellows and girls. As
I say, I only imagined things about them but Jimmy knew. I was
excluded from knowledge by the world of appearances, that blinded
and deafened me with emotion. The least thing could excite or
depress me. The trees in the morning when I went to early Mass,
the stained-glass windows in the church, the blue streets at evening,
with the green flare of the gas lamps, the smells of cooking and of
perfume, and even the smell of a cigarette packet that I had picked
up from the gutter and crushed to my nose—all kept me on this
side of the world of appearances. Jimmy, by some right of birth

or breeding, was always at the other, and I wanted him to take me there.

One evening, he was listening to me talk while he leaned against the pillar of his gate, his pale neat hair framing his pale, good-humored face.

"Why don't you come over some night the family is away, and I'll show you a few things?" he asked lightly.

"What'll you show me, Jimmy?" I asked eagerly.

"Noticed the new couple that's come to live next door?" he asked.

"No," I replied in disappointment. It wasn't only that I never knew anything; I never noticed anything. And when he described the new family who had taken rooms in the house above the Learys', I realized with chagrin that I didn't know the old family, either.

"Oh, they're a newly married couple," he said. "They don't know that they can be seen from our house."

"But how, Jimmy?"

"Don't look up now," he said with a dreamy smile while his eyes strayed past my shoulder in the direction of the lane. "Wait till you're going. Their end wall is only a couple of feet from ours. You can see right into the bedroom from our attic."

"And what do they do, Jimmy?"

"Oh," he said with a pleasant laugh, "everything. You really should come."

"You bet I'll come!" I said, trying to sound tougher than I felt.

For three evenings I stood under the gas lamp at the foot of our lane, till I had identified the new couple. It was not enough for me to get behind the world of appearances. I also had to study the appearances themselves. The husband was the first I spotted. He came from his work at a regular hour, usually accompanied from the bus stop by an older man. He was tall, with jet-black hair and a big black guardsman's mustache that somehow failed to conceal the youthfulness of his face. Usually he stood for a few minutes outside his door, chatting—a black-coated, bowler-hatted figure who made large, sweeping gestures with his evening paper and some-times doubled up in an explosion of loud laughter.

On the third evening, I saw his wife. She had obviously been waiting for him, looking from behind the parlor curtains, and when she saw him she scurried down the steps to join in the conversation. She had thrown an old jacket about her shoulders, and stood there, her arms folded as though to protect herself from the cold wind that blew down the road from the open country, while her husband rested one hand fondly on her shoulder.

For the first time, I began to feel qualms about what I had promised to do. It was one thing to do it to people you didn't know or care about, but for me even to recognize people like that was to adopt an emotional attitude toward them. That night I remained awake, thinking out the terms of an anonymous letter that would put them on their guard, till I had worked myself up into a fever of eloquence and indignation.

But I knew that they would recognize the villain of the letter and that the villain would recognize me, so I did not write it. Instead, I gave way to fits of anger and moodiness against my parents. Yet even these emotions were unreal, because on Saturday night when Mother made a parcel of my nightshirt—I had now become sufficiently self-conscious not to take a bag—I nearly broke down and said I wouldn't go. There was something about my own house that night that upset me all over again. Father was sitting under the wall lamp, reading aloud from the paper, and Mother, with a shawl about her shoulders, was crouched over the fire in her little wickerwork chair, listening, and I suddenly realized that they, too, were part of the world of appearances that I had plotted to destroy, and as I said good night, I almost felt that I was saying goodbye to them as well.

But, once inside Jimmy's house, I did not care so much. It always had that effect on me, of blowing me up to twice the size. I tried to pick out a tune on the piano with one hand, and Jimmy, having listened to me with amusement for some time, sat down and played it himself as I felt it should be played, and this, too, seemed to be part of his superiority.

"I suppose we'd better put on a show of going to bed," he said. "Someone across the road may notice and tell. *They*'re in town. I don't suppose they'll be back till late."

We had a glass of milk in the kitchen, went upstairs, and undressed and lay down, though we put our overcoats by the bed. Jimmy had a packet of sweets, but he insisted on keeping them till later. "We may need them before we're done," he said with a smile. I noticed again, with admiration, what an orderly sort of chap he was. We talked in bed for a quarter of an hour, then put out the light, got up again, put on our overcoats and socks, and tiptoed upstairs to the attic, Jimmy leading the way with an electric torch.

Everything had been planned as if for a ceremony. Two trunks had been drawn up to the little window to act as seats, and there were even cushions on them. Looking out, you could at first see nothing but an expanse of blank end wall topped with chimney stacks, but gradually you could make out the outline of a single window, eight or ten feet below. Jimmy sat beside me and opened his packet of sweets.

"Of course, we could have stayed in bed until we heard them come in," he whispered. "You can usually hear them at the front door, but we might have fallen asleep or they might have come in quietly. It's best to make sure."

"But why don't they draw the blind?" I asked, my heart beginning to beat uncomfortably.

"Because there isn't a blind," he said with a chuckle. "Old Mrs. MacCarthy never had one, and she's not going to put one in for lodgers."

I envied him his nonchalance as he sat back with his legs crossed, sucking a sweet, as though he were waiting in the cinema for the show to begin. I was scared by the darkness and the mystery, and by the sounds that came to us from the road with such extraordinary clarity. Besides, it wasn't my house, and I didn't feel at home there. At any moment I expected the front door to open and his parents to come in and catch us.

We must have been waiting for half an hour before we heard voices in the roadway, the sound of a key in the lock, and a door opened and shut softly. Jimmy reached out and touched my arm. "I think that's our pair," he whispered. "Better not speak any more. They might hear us." I nodded, wishing I had never come. At that moment a faint light became visible in the great expanse of black wall: a faint, yellow stair light that was just sufficient to silhouette the window frame below us. Suddenly the whole room lit up. The man I had seen in the street stood by the doorway, his hand still on the switch. I could see it all plainly now—an ordinary small, suburban bedroom with flowery wallpaper, a colored picture of the Sacred Heart over the double bed with the big brass knobs, a wardrobe, and a dressing table.

He stood there till the woman came in, removing her hat in a single gesture and tossing it from her into a corner of the room. The man still stood by the door. He took off his tie and struggled with his collar, his head uplifted as he made an agonized face. His wife kicked off her shoes, and then sat on a chair by the bed and began to take off her stockings. She seemed to be talking all the time, because her head was raised, looking at him, but you couldn't hear a word she said. I glanced at Jimmy. The light from the window below softly illuminated his face as he sucked with tranquil enjoyment.

The woman rose as her husband sat on the bed, with his back to us, and began to take off his shoes and socks in the same slow, agonized way. At one point he held up his left foot and looked at it with what might have been concern. She undressed in swift, jerky movements, twisting and turning and apparently talking all the time. She crouched as she took off her slip, and then pulled her nightdress over her head and finished her undressing beneath it. As she removed her underclothes, she seemed to throw them anywhere at all, and I had the feeling that she was haphazard and disorderly, while the articles of clothing her husband took off seemed to be removed in order and put where he could find them most readily in the morning. I saw him take out his watch, look at it carefully, wind it, and hang it neatly on a nail over the bed.

Then, to my surprise, she knelt by the bed, facing out toward the window, glanced up at the picture of the Sacred Heart, made a large, swift sign of the Cross, and then put her face in her hands and buried her head in the bedclothes. I looked at Jimmy in dismay, but he did not seem to be disturbed by the sight. The husband, his folded trousers in his hand, moved about the room slowly and carefully, as though out of respect for his wife's devotions, and when he pulled on the trousers of his pajamas, he turned away. Then he put on his pajama jacket and knelt beside her. He, too, glanced at the picture over the bed and crossed himself, but he did not bury his face and head, as she had done. He knelt upright, with nothing of the abandonment suggested by her pose, and with a composed expression that managed, in a curious way, to combine reverence with self-respect. It was the expression of an employee who knew that he might, like the rest of humanity, have a few little weaknesses but recognized that he was somebody who deserved well of the management. He finished his prayers before his wife, and he crossed himself again slowly, rose, and climbed into bed, glancing again at his watch as he did so.

Several minutes passed before she drew herself up, blessed herself in her wide, sweeping way, and rose. She crossed the room in a swift movement that almost escaped me, and next moment the light went out, and it was as if the window through which we had watched the scene had disappeared with it and there was nothing but a blank black wall mounting to the chimney pots.

Jimmy rose slowly and pointed the way out to me with his flashlight.

When we got downstairs, we put on the bedroom light, and I saw on his face the virtuous and sophisticated air of a collector who has shown you all his treasures in the best possible light. Faced with that look, I could not bring myself to talk of the woman at prayer. I could not have explained to him how at that moment everything had changed for me—how, beyond us, watching the young married couple from ambush, I had felt someone else, watching us, and we had at once ceased to be observers and become the observed, and the observed in such an ignominious position! I wanted to pray myself, but I found I couldn't. Instead, I lay in bed in the darkness, covering my eyes with my hand, and I think that even then I knew that I should never be sophisticated like Jimmy, never able to put on a knowing smile, because always beyond the world of appearances I would see only eternity watching.

"Sometimes, of course, it's better than that," Jimmy's drowsy voice said from the darkness. "You shouldn't judge it by tonight."

LANCE

❖

VLADIMIR NABOKOV

THE NAME of the planet, presuming it has already received one, is immaterial. At its most favorable opposition, it may very well be separated from the earth by only as many miles as there are years between last Friday and the rise of the Himalayas—a million times the reader's average age. In the telescopic field of one's fancy, through the prism of one's tears, any particularities it presents should be no more striking than those of existing planets. A rosy globe, marbled with dusky blotches, it is one of the countless objects diligently revolving in the infinite and gratuitous awfulness of fluid space.

My planet's *maria* (which are not seas) and its *lacus* (which are not lakes) have also, let us suppose, received names; some less pedestrian, perhaps, than those of garden roses; others more pointless than the surnames of their observers (for, to take actual cases, that an astronomer should have been called Lampland is as marvellous as that an entomologist should have been called Krautwurm); but most of them of so antique a style as to vie in sonorous and corrupt enchantment with place names pertaining to romances of chivalry.

Just as our Pinedales, down here on our own planet, have often little to offer beyond a shoe factory on one side of the tracks and the rusty inferno of an automobile dump on the other, so those seductive Arcadias and Icarias and Zephyrias on planetary maps may quite likely turn out to be dead deserts lacking even the milkweed that graces our dumps. Selenographers will confirm this, but then, their lenses serve them better than ours do. In the present instance, the greater the magnification, the more the mottling of the planet's surface looks as if it were seen by a submerged swimmer peering up through semitranslucent water. And if certain connected markings resemble in a shadowy way the line-and-hole pattern of a Chinesecheckers board, let us consider them geometrical hallucinations.

I not only debar a too definite planet from any role in my story—from the role every dot and full stop should play in my story (which I see as a kind of celestial chart)—I also refuse to have anything to do with those technical prophecies that scientists are reported to make to reporters. Not for me is the rocket racket. Not for me are the artificial little satellites that the earth is promised: landing star strips for space ships ("spacers")—one, two, three, four, and then thousands of strong castles in the air, each complete with cookhouse and keep, set up by terrestrial nations in a frenzy of competitive confusion, phony gravitation, and savagely flapping flags.

Another thing I have not the slightest use for is the special-equipment business—the airtight suit, the oxygen apparatus, suchlike contraptions. Like old Mr. Boke, of whom we shall hear in a minute—if my watch is not fast, as it generally is—I am eminently qualified to dismiss these practical matters (which anyway are doomed to seem absurdly impractical to future space-ship men, such as old Boke's only son), since the emotions that gadgets provoke in me range from dull distrust to morbid trepidation. Only by a heroic effort can I make myself unscrew a bulb that has died an inexplicable death and screw in another, which will light up in my face with the hideous instancy of a dragon's egg hatching in one's bare hand.

Finally, I utterly spurn and reject so-called "science fiction." I have looked into it, and found it as boring as the mystery-story magazines—the same sort of dismally pedestrian writing with oodles of dialogue and loads of commutational humor. The clichés are, of course, disguised; essentially, they are the same throughout all cheap reading matter, whether it spans the universe or the living room. They are like those "assorted" cookies that differ from one another only in shape and shade, whereby their shrewd makers ensnare the salivating consumer in a mad Pavlovian world where, at no extra cost, variations in simple visual values influence and gradually replace flavor, which thus goes the way of talent and truth.

So the good guy grins, and the villain sneers, and a noble heart sports a slangy speech. Star czars, directors of Galactic Unions, are practically replicas of those peppy, red-haired executives in earthy earth jobs who illustrate with their little crinkles the human-interest stories of well-thumbed slicks in beauty parlors. Invaders of Denebola and Spica, Virgo's finest, bear names beginning with

Mac; cold scientists are usually found under names like Stein; some share with the super-galactic gals such abstract labels as Biola and Vala. Inhabitants of foreign planets, "intelligent" beings, humanoid or of various mythic makes, have one remarkable trait in common: their intimate structure is never depicted. In a supreme concession to biped propriety, not only do centaurs wear loincloths; they wear them about their forelegs.

This seems to complete the elimination—unless anybody wants to discuss the question of time? Here again, in order to focalize young Emery L. Boke, that more or less remote descendant of mine who is to be a member of the first interplanetary expedition (which, after all, is the one humble postulate of my tale), I gladly leave the replacement by a pretentious "2" or "3" of the honest "1" in our "1900" to the capable paws of *Starzan* and other comics and atomics. Let it be 2145 A.D. or 200 A.A., it does not matter. I have no desire to barge into vested interests of any kind. This is strictly an amateur performance, with quite casual stage properties and a minimum of scenery, and the quilled remains of a dead porcupine in a corner of the old barn. We are here among friends, the Browns and the Bensons, the Whites and the Wilsons, and when somebody goes out for a smoke, he hears the crickets, and a distant farm dog (who waits, between barks, to listen to what we cannot hear). The summer night sky is a mess of stars. Emery Lancelot Boke, at twenty-one, knows immeasurably more about them than I, who am fifty and terrified.

Lance is tall and lean, with thick tendons and greenish veins on his sun-tanned forearms and a scar on his brow. When doing nothing—when sitting ill at ease as he sits now, leaning forward from the edge of a low armchair, his shoulders hunched up, his elbows propped on his big knees—he has a way of slowly clasping and unclasping his handsome hands, a gesture I borrow for him from one of his ancestors. An air of gravity, of uncomfortable concentration (all thought is uncomfortable, and young thought especially so), is his usual expression; at the moment, however, it is a manner of mask, concealing his furious desire to get rid of a long-drawn tension. As a rule, he does not often smile, and besides "smile" is too smooth a word for the abrupt, bright contortion that now suddenly illumes his mouth and eyes as his shoulders hunch higher, his moving hands stop in a clasped position, and he lightly taps one foot. His parents are in the room, and also a chance visitor, a fool and a bore, who is not aware of what is happening—

for this is an awkward moment in a gloomy house on the eve of a fabulous departure.

An hour goes by. At last the visitor picks up his top hat from the carpet and leaves. Lance remains alone with his parents, which only serves to increase the tension. Mr. Boke I see plainly enough. But I cannot visualize Mrs. Boke with any degree of clarity, no matter how deep I sink into my difficult trance. I know that her cheerfulness—small talk, quick beat of eyelashes—is something she keeps up not so much for the sake of her son as for that of her husband and his aging heart, and this Lance realizes only too well and, on top of his own monstrous anguish, he has to cope with her feigned levity, which disturbs him more than would an utter and unconditional collapse. I am somewhat disappointed that I cannot make out her features. All I manage to glimpse is an effect of melting light on one side of her misty hair, and in this, I suspect, I am insidiously influenced by the standard artistry of modern photography and I feel how much easier writing must have been in former days when one's imagination was not hemmed in by innumerable visual aids, and a frontiersman looking at his first giant cactus or his first high snows was not necessarily reminded of a tire company's pictorial ad.

In the case of Mr. Boke, I find myself operating with the features of an old professor of history, a brilliant medievalist, whose white whiskers, pink pate, and black suit are famous on a certain sunny campus in the Deep South, but whose sole asset in connection with this story (apart from a slight resemblance to a long-dead great-uncle of mine) is that his appearance is out of date. Now if one is perfectly honest with oneself, there is nothing extraordinary in the tendency to give to the manners and clothes of a distant day (which happens to be placed in the future) an old-fashioned tinge, a badly pressed, badly groomed, dusty something, since the terms "out of date," "not of our age," and so on, are, in the long run, the only ones in which we are able to imagine and express a strangeness no amount of research can foresee. The future is but the obsolete in reverse.

In that shabby room, in the tawny lamplight, Lance talks of some last things. He has recently brought from a desolate spot in the Andes, where he has been climbing some as yet unnamed peak, a couple of adolescent chinchillas—cinder-gray, phenomenally furry, rabbit-size rodents (*Hystricomorpha*), with long whiskers, round rumps, and petallike ears. He keeps them indoors in a wire-screened

pen and gives them peanuts, puffed rice, raisins to eat, and, as a
special treat, a violet or an aster. He hopes they will breed in the
fall. He now repeats to his mother a few emphatic instructions—to
keep his pets' food crisp and their pen dry, and never forget their
daily dust bath (fine sand mixed with powdered chalk), in which
they roll and kick most lustily. While this is being discussed, Mr.
Boke lights and relights a pipe and finally puts it away. Every now
and then, with a false air of benevolent absent-mindedness, the old
man launches upon a series of sounds and motions that deceive
nobody; he clears his throat and, with his hands behind his back,
drifts toward a window; or he begins to produce a tight-lipped
tuneless humming. At last, seemingly driven by that small nasal
motor, he wanders out of the parlor. No sooner has he left the
stage than he throws off, with a dreadful shiver, the elaborate
structure of his gentle, bumbling impersonation act. In a bedroom or bathroom, he stops as if to take, in abject solitude, a deep
spasmodic draught from some secret flask, and presently staggers
out again, drunk with grief.

The stage has not changed when he quietly returns to it, buttoning his coat and resuming that little hum. It is now a matter of
minutes. Lance inspects the pen before he goes, and leaves Chin and
Chilla sitting on their haunches, each holding a flower. The only
other thing that I know about these last moments is that any such
talk as "Sure you haven't forgotten the silk shirt that came from the
wash?" or "You remember where you put those new slippers?" is
excluded. Whatever Lance takes with him is already collected at the
mysterious and unmentionable and absolutely awful place of his
zero-hour departure; he needs nothing of what we need, and he
steps out of the house, empty-handed and hatless, with the casual
lightness of one walking to the newsstand—or to a glorious scaffold.

Terrestrial space loves concealment. The most it yields to the
eye is a panoramic view. The horizon closes upon the receding
traveller like a trapdoor in slow motion. To those who remain, any
town a day's journey from here is invisible, whereas you can easily
see such transcendencies as, say, a lunar amphitheatre and the
shadow cast by its circular ridge. The conjurer who displays
the firmament has rolled up his sleeves and performs in full view
of the little spectators. Planets may dip out of sight (just as objects
are obliterated by the blurry curve of one's own cheekbone), but
they are back when the earth turns its head. The nakedness of the

night is appalling. Lance has left; the fragility of his young limbs grows in direct ratio to the distance he covers. From their balcony, the old Bokes look at the infinitely perilous night sky and wildly envy the lot of fishermen's wives.

If Boke's sources are accurate, the name "Lanceloz del Lac" occurs for the first time in Verse 3676 of the twelfth-century "Roman de la Charrete." Lance, Lancelin, Lancelotik—diminutives murmured at the brimming, salty, moist stars. Young knights in their teens learning to harp, hawk, and hunt; the Forest Dangerous and the Dolorous Tower; Aldebaran, Betelgeuse—the thunder of Saracenic war cries. Marvellous deeds of arms, marvellous warriors, sparkling within the awful constellations above the Bokes' balcony: Sir Percard the Black Knight, and Sir Perimones the Red Knight, and Sir Pertolepe the Green Knight, and Sir Persant the Indigo Knight, and that bluff old party Sir Grummore Grummursum, muttering northern oaths under his breath. The field glass is not much good, the chart is all crumpled and damp, and "You do not hold the flashlight properly"—this to Mrs. Boke.

Draw a deep breath. Look again.

Lancelot is gone; the hope of seeing him in life is about equal to the hope of seeing him in eternity. Lancelot is banished from the country of L'Eau Grise (as we might call the Great Lakes) and now rides up in the dust of the night sky almost as fast as our local universe (with the balcony and the pitch-black, optically spotted garden) speeds toward King Arthur's Harp, where Vega burns and beckons—one of the few objects that can be identified by the aid of this goddam diagram. The sidereal haze makes the Bokes dizzy—gray incense, insanity, infinity-sickness. But they cannot tear themselves away from the nightmare of space, cannot go back to the lighted bedroom, a corner of which shows in the glass door. And presently *the* planet rises, like a tiny bonfire.

There, to the right, is the Bridge of the Sword, leading to the Other World (*"dont nus estranges ne retorne"*). Lancelot crawls over it in great pain, in ineffable anguish. "Thou shalt not pass a pass here that is called the Pass Perilous." But another enchanter commands, "You shall. You shall even acquire a sense of humor that will tide you over the trying spots." The brave old Bokes think they can distinguish Lance scaling, on crampons, the verglased rock of the sky or silently breaking trail through the soft snows of nebulae. Boötes, somewhere between Camps X and XI, is a great glacier, all rubble and icefall. We try to make out the serpentine route of ascent, seem to distinguish the light leanness of Lance among the several roped silhouettes. Gone! Was it he or Denny (a young biologist, Lance's best friend)? Waiting in the dark valley at the foot of the vertical sky, we recall (Mrs. Boke more clearly than her husband) those special names for crevasses and Gothic structures of ice that Lance used to mouth with such professional gusto in his alpine boyhood (he is several light-years older by now), the seracs and the schrunds, the avalanche and its thud—French echoes and Germanic magic hobnail-nobbing up there as they do in medieval romances.

Ah, there he is again! Crossing through a notch between two stars, then, very slowly, attempting a traverse on a cliff face so sheer and with such delicate holds that the mere evocation of those groping fingertips and scraping boots fills one with acrophobic nausea. And through streaming tears the old Bokes see Lance now marooned on a shelf of stone and now climbing again and now, dreadfully safe, with his ice axe and pack, on a peak above peaks, his eager profile rimmed with light.

Or is he already on his way down? I assume that no news comes from the explorers and that the Bokes prolong their pathetic vigils. As they wait for their son to return, his every avenue of descent seems to run into the precipice of their despair. But perhaps he has swung over those high-angled wet slabs that fall away vertically into the abyss, has mastered the overhang, and is now blissfully glissading down steep celestial snows?

As, however, the Bokes' doorbell does not ring at the logical culmination of an imagined series of footfalls (no matter how patiently we space them as they come nearer and nearer in our mind), we have to thrust him back and have him start his ascent all over again, and then put him even farther back, so that he is still at headquarters (where the tents are, and the open latrines, and the begging, black-footed children) long after we had pictured him bending under the tulip tree to walk up the lawn to the door and the doorbell. As if tired by the many appearances he has made in his parents' minds, Lance now plows wearily through mud puddles, then up a hillside, in the haggard landscape of a distant war, slipping and scrambling up the dead grass of the slope. There is some routine rockwork ahead, and then the summit. The ridge is won. Our losses are heavy. How is one notified? By wire? By registered letter? And who is the executioner—a special messenger or the regular plodding, florid-nosed postman, always a little high (he has troubles of his own)? Sign here. Big thumb. Small cross. Weak pencil. Its dull-violet wood. Return it. The illegible signature of teetering disaster.

But nothing comes. A month passes. Chin and Chilla are in fine shape and seem very fond of each other—sleep together in the nest box, cuddled up in a fluffy ball. After many tries, Lance had discovered a sound with definite chinchillan appeal, produced by pursing the lips and emitting in rapid succession several soft, moist "surpths," as if taking sips from a straw when most of one's drink is finished and only its dregs are drained. But his parents cannot produce it—the pitch is wrong, or something. And there is such an intolerable silence in Lance's room, with its battered books, and the spotty white shelves, and the old shoes, and the relatively new tennis racket in its preposterously secure press, and a penny on the closet floor—and all this begins to undergo a prismatic dissolution, but then you tighten the screw and everything is again in focus. And presently the Bokes return to their balcony. Has he reached his goal—and if so, does he see us?

The classical ex-mortal leans on his elbow from a flowered ledge to contemplate this earth, this toy, this teetotum gyrating on slow display in its model firmament, every feature so gay and clear—the painted oceans, and the praying woman of the Baltic, and a still of the elegant Americas caught in their trapeze act, and Australia like a baby Africa lying on its side. There may be people among my coevals who half expect their spirits to look down from Heaven with a shudder and a sigh at their native planet and see it girdled with latitudes, stayed with meridians, and marked, perhaps, with the fat, black, diabolically curving arrows of global wars, or, more pleasantly, spread out before their gaze like one of those picture maps of vacational Eldorados, with a reservation Indian beating a drum here, a girl clad in shorts there, conical conifers climbing the cones of mountains, and anglers all over the place.

Actually, I suppose, my young descendant on his first night out, in the imagined silence of an unimaginable world, would have to view the surface features of our globe through the depth of its atmosphere; this would mean dust, scattered reflections, haze, and all kinds of optical pitfalls, so that continents, if they appeared at all through the varying clouds, would slip by in queer disguises, with inexplicable gleams of color and unrecognizable outlines.

But all this is a minor point. The main problem is: Will the mind of the explorer survive the shock? One tries to perceive the nature of that shock as plainly as mental safety permits. And if the mere act of imagining the matter is fraught with hideous risks, how, then, will the real pang be endured and overcome?

First of all, Lance will have to deal with the atavistic moment. Myths have become so firmly entrenched in the radiant sky that common sense is apt to shirk the task of getting at the uncommon sense behind them. Immortality must have a star to stand on if it wishes to branch and blossom and support thousands of blue-plumed angel-birds all singing as sweetly as little eunuchs. Deep in the human mind, the concept of dying is synonymous with that of leaving the earth. To escape its gravity means to transcend the grave, and a man upon finding himself on another planet has really no way of proving to himself that he is not dead—that the naïve old myth has not come true.

I am not concerned with the moron, the ordinary hairless ape, who takes everything in his stride; his only childhood memory is of a mule that bit him, his only consciousness of the future a vision of board and bed. What I am thinking of is the man of imagination and science, whose courage is infinite because his curiosity surpasses his courage. Nothing will keep him back. He is the ancient *curieux*, but of a hardier build, with a ruddier heart. When it comes to exploring a celestial body, his is the satisfaction of a passionate desire to feel with his own fingers, to stroke, and inspect, and smile at, and inhale, and stroke again—with that same smile of nameless, moaning, melting pleasure—the never-before touched matter of which the celestial object is made. Any true scientist (not, of course, the fraudulent mediocrity, whose only treasure is the ignorance he hides like a bone) should be capable of experiencing that sensuous pleasure of direct and divine knowledge. He may be twenty and he may be eighty-five, but without that tingle there is no science. And of such stuff Lance is made.

Straining my fancy to the utmost, I see him surmounting the panic that the ape might not experience at all. No doubt Lance may have landed in an orange-colored dust cloud somewhere in the middle of the Tharsis desert (if it is a desert), or near some purple pool—Phoenicis or Oti (if these are lakes after all). But, on the other hand . . . You see, as things go in such matters, something is sure to be solved at once, terribly and irrevocably, while other things come up one by one and are puzzled out gradually. When I was a boy . . .

When I was a boy of seven or eight, I used to dream a vaguely recurrent dream set in a certain environment, which I have never been able to recognize and identify in any rational manner, though I have seen many strange lands. I am inclined to make it serve now, in order to patch up a gaping hole, a raw wound in my story. There was nothing spectacular about that environment, nothing monstrous or even odd: just a bit of noncommittal stability represented by a bit of level ground and filmed over with a bit of neutral nebulosity; in other words, the indifferent back of a view rather than its face. And the nuisance of that dream was that for some reason I could not walk *around* the view to meet it on equal terms. There lurked in the mist a mass of something—mineral matter or the like—oppressively and quite meaninglessly shaped, and in the course of my dream I kept filling some kind of receptacle (which I then translated as "pail") with smaller shapes (translated as "pebbles"), and my nose was bleeding but I was too impatient and excited to do anything about it. And every time I had that dream, suddenly somebody would start screaming behind me, and I awoke screaming too, thus prolonging the initial anonymous shriek, with its initial note of rising exultation, but with no meaning attached to it any more—if there had been a meaning. Speaking of Lance, I would like to submit that something along the lines of my dream— But the funny thing is that as I reread what I have set down, its background, the factual memory, vanishes—has vanished altogether by now—and I have no means of proving to myself that there is any personal experience behind its description. What I wanted to say was that perhaps Lance and his companions, when they reached their planet, felt something akin to my dream—which is no longer mine.

And then they are back! A horseman, clappity-clap, gallops up the cobbled street to the Bokes' house through the driving rain and shouts out the tremendous news as he stops short at the gate, near the dripping liriodendron, while the Bokes come tearing out of the house like two hystricomorphic rodents. They are back! The pilots and the astrophysicists and one of the naturalists are back. (The other, Denny, is dead and has been left in Heaven, the old myth scoring a curious point there.)

On the sixth floor of a provincial hospital, carefully hidden from newspapermen, Mr. and Mrs. Boke are told that their boy is in a little waiting room, second to the right, ready to receive them;

there is something, a kind of hushed deference, about the tone of
this information, as if it referred to a fairy-tale king. They will enter
quietly; a nurse, a Mrs. Coover, will be there all the time. Oh, he's
all right, they are told—can go home next week, as a matter of fact.
However, they should not stay more than a couple of minutes, and
no questions, please—just chat about something or other. *You* know.
And then say you will be coming again tomorrow or day after
tomorrow.

Lance, gray-robed, crop-haired, tan gone, changed, unchanged,
changed, thin, nostrils stopped with absorbent cotton, sits on the
edge of a couch, his hands clasped, a little embarrassed. Gets up
wavily, with a beaming grimace, and sits down again. Mrs. Coover,
the nurse, has blue eyes and no chin.

A ripe silence. Then Lance: "It was wonderful. Perfectly wonderful. I am going back in November."

Pause.

"I think," says Mr. Boke, "that Chilla is with child."

Quick smile, little bow of pleased acknowledgment. Then, in
a narrative voice: *"Je vais dire ça en français. Nous venions
d'arriver—"*

"Show them the President's letter," says Mrs. Coover.

"We had just got there," Lance continues, "and Denny was still
alive, and the first thing he and I saw—"

In a sudden flutter, Nurse Coover interrupts, "No, Lance, no. No,
Madam, please. No contacts, doctor's orders—*please!"*

Warm temple, cold ear.

Mr. and Mrs. Boke are ushered out. They walk swiftly—although
there is no hurry, no hurry whatever—down the corridor, along
its shoddy, olive-and-ochre wall, the lower olive separated from the
upper ochre by a continuous brown line leading to the venerable
elevators. Going up (glimpse of patriarch in wheelchair). Going
back again in November (Lancelin). Going down (the old Bokes).
There are in that elevator two smiling women and, the object of
their bright sympathy, a girl with a baby, besides the gray-haired,
bent, sullen elevator man, who stands with his back to everybody.

THE GOLDEN WEST

❖

DANIEL FUCHS

A S EVERYONE KNOWS, the movie business isn't what it used to be.
For many of us who used to work at the studios, the pleasant,
oversized checks that came every Thursday have stopped. The blow
fell softly, mainly because when the crisis developed we couldn't
believe or didn't want to believe that it was upon us. Some of us
went back to the kind of work we had done before we were brought
out to Hollywood. Others, like a certain group of people I had
come to know, and saw almost every week, simply stayed on,
hanging.

The California sunshine continued to pour down. The streets,
the stucco mansions, the lawns and shrubbery sparkled with light.
These friends of mine went on visiting one another's homes, and
giving outdoor dinner parties, the ladies in their lovely frocks
scattered over the terrace at the tables, chattering and affectionate,
while their husbands stood off by themselves in small clusters,
nodding and smiling and smoking; my friends kept on their
housekeepers and gardeners and children's nurses; they still sent
their children to dancing school, to supervised play groups. "And
every month," as a man named Curtis Spogel once remarked sadly
to me, "another few Defense Bonds cashed in at the bank and
dissipated."

Spogel was a certified public accountant by profession, and he was
also in the movie business. He was in the exhibition end, the non-
creative side, but he was mixed in with the creative people through
his brother-in-law Julie Vencie, a top producer in the industry, now
no longer attached to any major studio. "If they would only awaken
to the realities. If they would only face the facts and do something,"
Spogel said. "But what?" he added immediately. His movie houses,
eight-hundred-seaters, were upstate in Kern County—in rural
communities, far from the cities, from the television stations. His

income was relatively unaffected by the debacle, and he didn't want
to seem unfeeling.

One Sunday afternoon, I drove over to his home in Beverly Hills,
high up on Angelo Drive. As I left my car in the parking space
near the garage, I could tell at once I was the first to arrive. The
garden lay fresh and still, the water was quiet in the swimming
pool, and Mrs. Vencie, Mrs. Spogel's mother, was sitting on the
terrace, in the shade, reading a foreign-language newspaper. Mrs.
Vencie lived with the Spogels.

I wanted to avoid the old lady. I knew she would fasten on to me
and talk, about the bad times, about her son Julie—her golden boy,
she used to call him.

A row of large, old oleander bushes separated the garage area
from the grounds and the house. I went up the row of oleanders
and made my way around the terrace, reached the house, and
slipped inside by the front way. Passing through the entrance
hall, I saw Edith Spogel standing alone in the living room, leaning
against the back of a couch in the dimness there, her eyes shut.
She was listening to the New York Philharmonic concert on the
radio and was lost in the music. I started to speak to her, but just
then I became aware of Spogel creeping up on her. He was wearing
a pair of tennis trunks and carrying a box of chocolates. "Boo!" he
said.

"Oh, Curtis!" she said startled.

"Have a sweet!" Spogel said, playful and eager.

"No, thanks," Edith said, and then, as he kept pressing the chocolates on her, she said, "Oh, Curtis, really! How can you, in the
middle of the day— Oh, hello, David," she said, seeing me. She
smoothed her eyebrows with her fingertips and sighed. "How are
you?" she said to me. "How's the family? Come—let's go out on the
terrace. Let's listen to the music there." She touched the switches on
the little box that controlled the various radio speakers, and went
outside.

"Everything these days is like walking on eggshells," Spogel said
to me, disappointed, the candy box still in his hands. "We seem to
exist in perpetual tension."

Auditing other people's books, working on the inside, Spogel
was able to spot good business opportunities. That was how he had
wandered into the movie field, buying that chain of theatres upstate; that was how he had met Julie Vencie, and then Julie's sister.
Edith was a year or two older than her brother, and getting on.

The marriage was one of those arranged, matchmaker's affairs. At the time, Julie was a big producer, under contract, bustling and sprightly, four thousand a week at the majors, and there was a certain atmosphere, a kind of glamour. But now the glamour was gone, and Spogel saddled with the support of his wife's mother, too. He was awed by this whole circle of movie people among whom he had, so to speak, blundered. He admired them. He thought they possessed some quality, some mystery, that he lacked. He always felt inferior and apologetic with them. He was apologetic and self-conscious over everything he did—because he showed Gene Autrys and Randolph Scotts at his movie houses, or sex-and-sands with Yvonne de Carlo, because he ate candy in the daytime and had no personality, because he neglected his reducing exercises. He wanted to reduce, he sincerely meant to do the exercises every day, but they made his stomach muscles hurt, and so he would forget and then, later, feel guilty. "I am a sybarite!" he said one day, daringly, when we came upon him with one of those thirty-cent chocolate bars in his hands. And then, when no one smiled, he said, "I don't smoke, I don't drink—so this is my vice, sweets. Everybody has a vice or two . . ." That was the way he was.

When we went out on the terrace, Mrs. Vencie was chattering at full speed, every word getting on Edith's nerves.

"Rich, rich—famous!" the old lady was saying, meaning her son Julie, of course. "He always wanted to be a big shot. I used to argue patiently with him by the hour. 'Julie,' I would say to him, 'you'll give yourself a breakdown. You'll bust a spring in your head! Julie, what do you want it for, who needs it—the ulcers, the hypertension, the Cadillacs? A trolley car won't get you there just the same?'"

"Ma," Edith said.

"When he was a boy," Mrs. Vencie went on, ignoring the interruption, "when we lived on the East Side, you know what he did? He walked! He couldn't stand the tenements—the babies crying, the dumbwaiters, the garbage. He would walk for miles and miles, making up dreams in his head, having ambitions. He would go and find a dime and ride on the Fifth Avenue bus—he couldn't live if he didn't look at the fancy stores, at the rich people!"

"Ma," Edith said again.

"Dear," Spogel said to his wife. "Why must you aggravate your-

self and take everything to heart so? What difference does it make
if Mother harmlessly—"

"Curtis, please," Edith said, and he stopped at once, turning
aside.

"I know nothing," he murmured to me. "I am a businessman,
bourgeois—sex-and-sands."

"Reaching for the stars!" Mrs. Vencie said. "They say if you
don't give them affection when they're little, it will have bad
aftereffects on them and give them scars. So it was my fault? I didn't
give him enough affection? Who had time for affection? I had
seven small little children. I had to scrub floors, cook supper, wash
the clothes—not like the modern women nowadays, believe me.
Everything the children wore, I sewed by myself on the machine—
the jumpers, the knee pants, the dresses for the girls. When I gave
birth to Edith and had to lay in bed for three whole days, naturally,
of course, I couldn't watch out, and so that's how we had the
tragedy—that's how we lost Freddie."

"Ma!" Edith cried.

"Ma!" Mrs. Vencie burst out, nettled. "What are you hollering
on me 'Ma' for? It ain't the truth? Poor little Freddie didn't go
up on the roof to play, and they didn't push him off?"

"Nobody's interested," Edith said. "You told us the whole story
a dozen times. It happened a hundred years ago. I'm trying to listen
to the Symphony!"

"Symphony!" Mrs. Vencie said. "Fancy lady! What's the matter
—I embarrass you? I didn't do enough for you? When the doctor
took out your tonsils and I gave you the wrong medicine by
mistake; didn't I hurry up quick and drink the whole bottle?"

"Oh, it's hopeless, it's hopeless," Edith said. "Again the story
with the tonsils and the medicine, again the whole repertoire!"
She turned away and went back into the house.

Mrs. Vencie's shoulders started to shake, and I saw she was laughing. "David, you could make a book!" she said, chortling, and
wiping her nose with the back of her hand. "It was a regular
Charlie Chaplin! See, innocently, I thought I poisoned her—that's
why I hurried up and drank the whole bottle. But in the excitement, in the hoorah I made, Edith vomited it up—excuse me,
David—but me, I kept my share down and I still got it in me to
this day! I was furious! Poor Papa," she said, her mood suddenly
shifting. She was thinking now, it turned out, of Freddie, of the
tragedy. Mr. Vencie had worked in fur, but he had caught the

furrier's lung disease and had been totally incapacitated. At the time of the accident, he had just been getting on his feet again—he had a small candy stand. "It took ten years off his life, that's why he died so soon," Mrs. Vencie said. "When the police officers came and they informed him, he went running home from the candy store, hitting his head with his hands and hollering in the street, 'Gevalt, gevalt!' . . . Oh, look, look, look," she said, her face lighting up. Another pair of visitors had emerged from the parking space. "Now we have the newlyweds," Mrs. Vencie said with satisfaction, settling herself.

The newcomers were the Kittershoys, Boris and Daisy. Boris was Julie's partner, the "kay" in Veeankay Pictures, an independent producing company they were trying to get started.

"Curtis! Curtis!" Daisy cried as she came scampering across the garden. "You should feel my thighs—like iron bands!" She was taking ballet and tennis lessons—that was all she meant by the reference to her thighs. She and Boris had recently been married, and although she was by no means in her first youth, she acted like a bride. "Doom, doom," she said as she joined us on the terrace, chiding her husband as well as Spogel. They both had long faces. "Smile!" she said. "Show optimism! The world is not coming to an end."

Boris Kittershoy came to the Spogels' hoping to see Julie, who was unpredictable, with a violent temper, and hard to approach. These meetings at the Spogels' parties were about the only chance Boris had to talk to his partner. I knew all this, so I knew what it meant to Boris when Julie failed to appear and, instead, his wife, Imogene, came, not long after the Kittershoys. She had an overnight bag. She and Julie were fighting again, it developed. She had left him or he had left her or had driven her away.

"He is an *enfant terrible*," Boris said. The Spogels and I were huddled around Imogene in the living room—away from Mrs. Vencie, on the terrace. "We are going under, perishing," Boris said, "and he must pick this time to fight with his wife! He is clinical."

"How irresponsible they are," Spogel whispered to me. "How temperamental and undisciplined." His eyes kept wavering and he glanced constantly at Edith, to see how she was managing under the new strain.

Boris and Julie had gone ahead with their independent picture largely on assurances given to them by an executive at a major studio. He had promised, orally, to furnish them with a release, with the principal financing, with a director, with name stars. The deal had fallen through, as Hollywood deals do. The executive hadn't reneged or double-crossed them; his studio had simply decided at the last moment to withdraw. It was a change of policy, but it left Veeankay with two hundred thousand dollars hard cash, or more, sunk in the venture, and no place to go. "He is a mass of contradictions, and he poses, and nobody can get along with him," Boris said, half rocking there in the dim light, on his up-holstered chair.

"It never fails!" Daisy said. "When a man is in the dumps and business is bad, he immediately gets infatuated with his wife all over again. They put you on a pedestal, and think you are the most beautiful woman in the world, and they give you no peace!"

"I suppose," Imogene said, listless. "He's crazy."

Whenever they had their fights, she drove straight up the hill to the Spogels', because she was safe there; she knew Julie couldn't suspect her of wrongdoing while she was with Spogel and her in-laws. She was very pretty. She had been in show business, had gone to work in her teens, and you always had the feeling that she was helpless and vulnerable. Julie had been giving her a bad time the last year or so. She had been crying all morning, and her face was blurry and she still had a Frownie—those things women wear when they sleep, to avoid wrinkles—stuck on her forehead, between the eyebrows. "I don't know what he wants from me," she said. "Who am I? I'm just a person. I'm not even intelligent, like he always says when he throws it up at me, I'm common and have no background. Well, actually, you know, he's not wrong. I mean, what was I before I met him, what sort of a life did I have? I always had the blues. I was ordinary. You know, he can be awfully nice when he wants to. He's disadjusted."

The quarrel had been going on since early the previous morning. She had made a face at him—that was how it had all started. She and Julie used separate bedrooms. She had gone into his room yesterday morning, looked, and seen he was still asleep, and then —on an impulse, thoughtlessly—she had made a face at him. Only he hadn't been asleep. He had been peeking at her, through his eyelashes.

She went on talking, hopeless, tearful. Time was passing, she said, and what did she do, where did she go? All she ever did was look at the television set, switching the dial all evening from channel to channel, watching the news and the wrestling and "This Is Your Life," and it was depressing. She had a lump under her arm, she said, and everybody talked about hysterectomies and she ought to go and see the doctor, and every time she combed her hair she saw more gray. "I used to sing with a band in Atlantic City," she said. "I got a hundred a week. Only two shows a night and the rest of the time to myself. I used to sunbathe on the beach all day. I ought to have my head examined for giving that all up."

She rose. Julie always came after her at the Spogels'—to fight some more or to make up—and she had to change her clothes and be ready for him. She looked around now for her overnight bag.

"You're too good to him," Daisy said. "You're too loyal. You should have an affair!"

"That's all we need now," Boris said. "That's a fine piece of advice you're giving her. Thank you very much."

"No, I'm right!" Daisy insisted gaily. "She must make herself precious to him. She must teach him a lesson. Have an affair!"

"You think it's so easy?" Imogene said. "Try it sometime yourself and you'll see. What do you think—you can just go up to a man and confront him? Everybody can always tell you exactly what to do. It's not so simple." She saw the little suitcase on the floor and stooped to pick it up. "Once I called up Eversall and I said to him— What could I say? I didn't know what to say. So I asked him did he want to take me out to dinner. And you know Eversall, how tight he is. He refused. You'd be surprised," she said, dabbing at her eyes with her handkerchief. "They know your husband or you know their wives, or you can't stand them in the first place—there are all kinds of things that crop up."

She went off to one of the bedrooms in the back of the house. Everyone remained silent for several moments. Even Daisy.

"What is there to mourn?" she said suddenly.

"There she goes again," Boris said, hitting the arm of his chair.

"No, seriously," she said. "I mean, after all, what is there for us to get so all worked up about? In the last analysis, what do we really possess? We have our naked bodies, just ourselves. That's all that really matters. I mean—" In addition to the ballet and tennis lessons, Daisy took courses at U.C.L.A., and she was also having her teeth straightened, and at parties she would scream out how the Kittershoy wives were spirited, like race horses—but nothing helped. It was her money Boris had put into the independent company. She had owned a children's-wear factory before their marriage. Boris hadn't had a dime. He had married her; he had taken the earnings of a lifetime in the children's-wear trade and had put every penny of it into the Veeankay disaster, and at night it was an agony for her to fall asleep.

"Yes, yes, we understand—we know what you mean," Spogel said, trying to head her off, but she wouldn't stop. She couldn't stop.

"No, truth," she said. "Ultimately there is only truth. Truth and goodness and beauty—those are the only basic values!"

"Sweetheart, say nothing!" Boris roared at his wife. "When I am without you, I am without an arm. But when I am *with* you, I am without a head—shut up! You don't understand conditions. You don't know what's going on. For God's sakes, do not try to be cheerful and alleviate the situation!"

"Oh, look at her, look at her!" Daisy cried, turning, for no reason, to Edith, who had been sitting by quietly all this time. "Isn't she dainty? Isn't she darling?"

"Truth! Truth! Beauty!" Boris shouted. "Life is worth living! She don't want to hear bad news; it don't exist for her. There are lines standing all around the corner—the box office is booming!"

"Oh, I love her, I love her, I love her!" Daisy said. "Curtis, you must always be kind to her. You must never hurt her. She is my very best friend!"

She subsided abruptly. The living room became still again.

The Spogels had a pocket-billiards table in a game room that stood off by itself at the foot of the garden, not far from the garage. We were on the terrace—the Kittershoys, the Spogels, and I—when suddenly we heard the rolling of the balls, the clicks they made as they hit, and we knew it was Julie down there, shooting pool. Edith went to tell Imogene, and in a few minutes Imogene wearily crossed the garden to join her husband. We settled down to wait.

More guests were arriving. They played at the swimming pool or sat in the sun or were waylaid on the terrace by old Mrs. Vencie. Daisy Kittershoy was talking to one of the guests, a doctor, describing her symptoms to him. She had called his office, I heard her say, but then had cancelled the appointment because there was really nothing the matter with her. It was just that she couldn't seem to think clearly or energetically. It was just that she couldn't seem to enjoy anything. She was tired and not tired. If she could only do manual labor or something and get herself really exhausted, she said. She kept waiting for that morning when you wake up and feel bright and everything is sharp and fine again. She had a ringing in her ears— No, not a ringing, not a buzzing—more like telephone wires singing in the wind, a humming.

The doctor kept nodding. "It's very clear. Yes, I know," he said. "Those are the typical symptoms of mental fatigue. Do you perspire?"

"Oh, Doctor, you're so wonderful!" Daisy cried. "That's all I wanted to know—that there was nothing physically wrong with me. That's why you're so popular, Doctor—you always tell your patients exactly what they want to hear!"

"Ridiculous situation," Spogel murmured to me unhappily. "The whole thing just on account of a face she made, over a dirty look she gave him."

He took me along for company as he went walking around the grounds. He pretended to be seeing after his guests, but his real purpose was to get near the game room, to find out how Imogene and Julie were doing. "Girls are so peculiar," he mused. "To make a face at a sleeping man! Who knows what goes on in their heads? Once—naturally, long before I knew Edith—I had a lady friend. She cooked for me, we went out together, she came to my place— you know, everything. But she wouldn't marry me. Once I asked her, 'Reba, would you marry me if I asked you serious?' And she said 'No.' "

We had reached the game-room window, and he stepped up to it cautiously. We eavesdropped. "Julie, I'll get a cold," we heard Imogene saying. "Julie, it's damp here. It's chilly." She was barefoot, wearing her shorts and sun top, and she was obviously trying to get him away from the game room, into the house, where she apparently felt she could do more with him. "Julie, you know I'm allergic and always catch colds. Julie, I'm shivering," she said.

"Take an allergy pill, dear," Julie said, cheerful and matter-of-fact, going on with his game. We could hear the balls rolling and mixing.

"Anything transpire?" Boris Kittershoy whispered, coming up to us.

Spogel shook his head. "Patience," he said.

Boris started to moan, under his breath. There were industry people here, contacts, items of trade gossip to be picked up. "We could talk, we could inquire—we could try!" he said. A man named Irving Lissak had telephoned Edith, inviting himself over, and the visit might mean something, Boris said; the visit might be an approach, a feeler. There were two Lissaks, brothers. They were an independent company, actively in production, and it might very well be that they could be interested into taking over the Veeankay white elephant. "Who knows—it's a possibility!" Boris exclaimed softly. "But he is incommunicado, fighting with Imogene! Why does he always do this? It seems he was put into the world only to twist and scheme up ways to make life miserable!"

"He is an enigma," Spogel whispered, nodding.

"He is a pain in the neck!" Boris said.

Boris took himself off—to inquire, to try—and Spogel and I turned back to the game-room window. "Julie, I'm sick," Imogene was saying now. "Julie, my teeth are chattering. I'll have to go back into the house and leave you all alone. Julie, I'm leaving. Julie, I'm going back to the house."

"Yes, dear. Why don't you do that?" Julie said.

He was probably just waking up. Julie followed a peculiar twenty-four-hour cycle. During the early part of the day, he was dead to the world, groggy and glazed. As the afternoon wore on, the color would start filtering into his face. By nighttime, he was rosy and glowing again, the picture of health, full of energy. He downed a bottle of whiskey every night. He smoked ·hick, expensive cigars. He made people play cards with him and kept them up till all hours of the night. He worked up gags against his partner. Then, suddenly, unaccountably, he would turn cold sober, troubled and groping. "Why do I like you?" he once said to me, in a bewildering rush of affection. He gripped me by the shoulders. "I mean it, David. That's the best thing that's happened to me all year—my meeting you. I mean it. Listen—tell me about yourself," he said, catching himself up abruptly, joking again. "Come on, pappy, you always lay low and play possum. Tell me about your wife. What sort of a girl is she? What do you think of her? What does she think of you?" And in another moment he was throwing himself around the room, drinking and laughing and getting some friend of his at the county morgue to call up Boris, to say that he, Julie, had been killed in an auto accident.

"Tell me you told me," he was saying to Imogene now in the game room. "Tell me you didn't tell me. Tell me *you* lied, *I* lied. Deny everything. Admit everything. Dress, undress, take off your clothes—you think I don't know what you're doing?"

"Oh, my goodness, he is on the warpath," Spogel said. Spogel had begun to shuffle on his feet, out of worry. "Here it's half past four already, getting on five, and I'm still in my tennis trunks. I have to shave and take a shower!"

"You poor, pathetic broad," Julie said to Imogene, "you had me —you won out. Only you were too dumb to realize it."

"When? When did I win out?" Imogene asked.

"Yesterday—when I kicked you, when you started out for your hairdresser's appointment," Julie said. It seemed she had been taking her dress off all day, and all day he had successfully managed to resist the maneuver—up to the hairdresser's appointment, up to the moment when she had started to leave and had turned and he had seen that sweet, little, round whatsis of hers, he said. Then he had caved in. He simply had been unable to hold out any longer— that was why he had kicked her, he said. "You had me in the palm of your hand right then and there," he went on. "Only, you had to go ahead and ruin everything."

"How? Why? What did I do so terrible to spoil everything?" Imogene cried.

"You don't remember?" Julie said. "After I kicked you, you turned around and what did you say? You said, 'Oh, darling, if I could only undo the hurt that I have caused you.' Where do you pick up language like that? Is that the way they talk in the dance-band business? What kind of books do you read?"

"I'm always at fault," Imogene said, sobbing. "No matter what I do, I'm always wrong. I'm responsible for everything."

"Oh, when will be the end?" Spogel said, sighing and jiggling his feet.

Up on the terrace, the extra help had arrived and were setting the tables. The people at the swimming pool had changed back into their clothes, and here and there we could see a guest in a dinner jacket.

Spogel nudged my elbow. "Listen, listen," he said. The game room had turned oddly quiet. Julie had stopped playing pool. We couldn't hear him laughing or talking any longer—just Imogene sobbing—and Spogel thought perhaps this meant they were making up in there at last. "What do you think? David, how does it sound to you?" he said, and then "Now what?" Daisy Kittershoy and Edith were hurrying down to us from the terrace. They appeared to be having some kind of altercation.

"Sh-h-h! He'll hear!" Spogel begged when the two women came up. "Please! Don't make a commotion—he'll think we're peeking!"

It turned out Daisy had heard of the impending visit of Irving Lissak, the active independent producer, and had come hurrying down to ask Spogel what he knew about the visit. Did Spogel think it was business or pleasure? Was Lissak a frequent guest here? Did Spogel know him so very well socially, or was there really something doing? "Daisy, I told you!" Edith cried. "I met him at a party weeks ago, and I told him to drop in any Sunday! You're making a whole hullabaloo over nothing!"

But Daisy wouldn't listen. "No, no!" she said, shaking her head. "I was speaking to Curtis—let Curtis answer!"

"Sh-h-h!" Spogel whispered, gesturing. "He'll hear! You came intruding at the worst possible moment. They're just starting to reconcile!"

"We're not reconciling, don't worry," Imogene said bitterly. She had come out of the game room, her eyes and cheeks smudged with tears. "You can talk all you want—he's not inside to hear."

Daisy and Edith rushed over to her. "He got hungry," Imogene said. "I hate him. He went up to the house to get a snack. He eats and has the time of his life while all the time I'm dying. He enjoys it!"

So that was why the game room had suddenly turned quiet. Spogel was dazed with disappointment. "What will be the outcome?" he said. He meant when would they ever reconcile now, Imogene here, Julie in the house somewhere, everything up in the air? On the terrace, the tables were all set—the tablecloths gleaming, the candles lit and shining quietly. "Oh, why did you do it?" Spogel said to Imogene.

"Leave her alone!" Edith said to her husband. "Can't you see she's miserable enough?"

"Why did I do what?" Imogene said.

"Go into his bedroom yesterday," Spogel said. "Make the face. Why did you needlessly have to provoke him?"

"What should I do? Love him to death because he's so irresistible and tortures me to pieces?"

"But what good did it do?" Spogel said. "What purpose could it have accomplished? What was the *sense?*"

"I thought he was *asleep!*" Imogene wailed. "Oh, Curtis, do you think people know what they do?"

She ran off into the oleander bushes. Spogel wanted to go after her, but Edith checked him. They stood together, squabbling wretchedly. Spogel wanted to bring Imogene back. They had guests to entertain, a dinner party to live through, and it was ridiculous—all this upset, everybody going around in circles, all over a dirty look, a face. "Let her go!" Edith cried. "Didn't you bother her enough? Don't interfere! Don't make difficulties!"

"I'm making difficulties?" Spogel said.

At this moment, old Mrs. Vencie came up. She was taking a little walk. "Isn't it remarkable?" she said, looking up at the ladies in the garden, the guests. She was marvelling at their appearance, at the way they kept themselves, their figures. "Imagine!" the old woman went on, full of wonder. "They get pregnant only when they want to!"

"Ma!" Edith said.

"I give them all the credit in the world," Mrs. Vencie said. "They're smarter than my generation. What, then—they should let themselves go and become sloppy and fat like a horse? Let them make the beauty, let them diet. They're absolutely right!"

"Oh, for heaven's sake, Ma, couldn't you take a day off just once and spare us all your observations and comments?" Edith said, through her teeth.

"Look at her!" Mrs. Vencie said, wiping her nose with the back of her hand. "Somebody would think she's having a miscarriage. What's the matter—I'm killing people?"

"Oh, she comes right out with everything, no inhibitions at all," Edith said.

Just then, Boris Kittershoy came stamping down on us, panting with his news, holding up two fingers in the air. *Both* Lissaks had arrived, not just Irving. The visit definitely had to be a feeler, or else why *both?* Boris couldn't stop talking and pumping. The Lissaks had access to oil money, he said, the Lissaks had a release with U-L., they were in a position where they needed a product, and a deal was perfectly feasible!

"Good, good," Mrs. Vencie said, happy for them. "What a fool I was," she said, going on with her own thoughts. "How ignorant we all were in my time. When I had the twins, I would wash out a whole clothesline of diapers every day, and then I would stand by the window and look out and I would feel *good*—I was so simple—because the diapers came out nice and white. I even used to put in bluing!" She went off, resuming her walk, mingling with the guests.

Spogel was in agonies. He wanted to go looking for Julie immediately. He wanted to tell him about the two Lissaks. But Edith was dead set against it. "Curtis, please!" she cried. "Believe me, you don't know what it is. You just don't understand, so do me a favor and stay out of it!"

Boris, in the meanwhile, had just found out from Daisy that Julie was still incommunicado, that the reconciliation had broken down, and he was putting on a big show of despair. "I have done my best," he said. "I have eaten gall and wormwood, and now I am finished with him. This is the end!"

"But I do, I do—I do understand why he always fights with Imogene!" Spogel was saying hoarsely to Edith. "She is the symbol to him of his youth, of his hopes and dreams and aspirations, and naturally, in his downfall, he takes everything out on her. She is his Mona Lisa! You think I don't know. Don't judge a product by its container. I am not necessarily an ignoramus without sensitivity!"

Daisy urged Boris to start negotiations with the Lissaks by himself; after all, he was vice-president, a partner. But he refused. "I should initiate everything so that he can renege on me and make me out a fool again?" he said. "I had my experience once—no, thank you!" Boris was referring to something that happened with Ronnie Fitts—another independent, a man whose wife had made a fortune during the war buying Beverly Hills real estate on margin. Boris had arranged matters with Fitts, had paved the way for a possible deal, and all that had been left was a final meeting. Julie had agreed to the meeting; for once, he had appeared on time; he had promised to behave himself. But when they entered Fitts' home for the conference and Julie saw the original Impressionist paintings hanging on the walls there, he turned wild with fury. He walked straight up to Fitts and insulted him right and left; he was a slob, Julie said, and what right did he have to be owning Cézannes? "He is a madman!" Boris said now, pulling away from Daisy. "He is tactless and antagonizes people. He malingers. He makes practical jokes. Suddenly, he goes flying away on trips and runs up expenses, and let somebody else have the pleasure—I suffered with him long enough!" Boris kept trying to escape from his wife, she kept arguing and clinging to him, and now the two went off together, into the garden.

"Oh, why must you have such a sensitive nature and tremble over every least little thing?" Spogel cried out at Edith. "What harm would there be if I went and talked to him?"

"But it is not my nature!" Edith cried back at him. "You don't know what happened! Believe me, you have no understanding of the situation!"

"But I do! I do!" Spogel said, his eyes shut tight. "I just told you. I do understand—" He stopped. He listened. Edith was complaining about her mother again, saying how the old woman always had to open up her big mouth and talk, talk, talk. "Oh, why do you fix on Mother all the time?" Spogel said, exasperated. "Why must you pick on her now? Don't we have more serious problems?"

"But she made the whole trouble!" Edith said. "Julie was here yesterday. He saw her, and that's when it really started! Oh, really, it's too impossible—it's humiliating!" she said. "I'd rather not talk about it."

But, little by little, the story came out. Julie snored. It was an affliction; he had a deviated septum. That was the reason he and Imogene used separate bedrooms. But yesterday, after Imogene made the face at him, he came to see his mother and asked the old woman if it was really true that he snored. And Mrs. Vencie had told a white lie. She had said he didn't snore at all.

Spogel didn't stay to hear any more. He could see the whole picture in a flash. It was the worst possible thing Mrs. Vencie could have said. Julie, of course, had immediately gone off convinced that Imogene had been avoiding him, that the talk about his snoring had been nothing but a pretext all along.

"Wait! Don't go to him!" Edith cried, clutching at her husband, but Spogel wouldn't be held back this time. He fought free and went rushing away—to find Julie, to tell him, to clear up the whole foolish misunderstanding once for all and restore peace.

"Oh, stop him!" Edith said to me, her eyes big with alarm. "David, do something! He'll go blundering in where he doesn't belong, and it will be awful!" And now she blurted out the rest of the story. She hadn't finished. It wasn't the face, the dirty look; it wasn't Mrs. Vencie's white lie. Imogene had been unfaithful to Julie. She had had an affair, and he had found out all about it. The mischief hadn't ended with Mrs. Vencie. One thing had led to another. After Julie talked to his mother, he had gone straight back to his own home. Simmering with suspicions, furious, he had searched Imogene's room, and there had been some letters. Imogene had been at a hotel at Lake Tahoe not long ago, and she had met a man there, one of the players in the band.

"Oh, run!" Edith cried to me now as we saw Spogel weaving in and out among the guests in the garden, hurrying up to the house. "Run, David—run, or it will be too late!"

By the time I came up to the terrace, I had lost Spogel in the press of people. I looked everywhere for him, but there was too much coming and going—new arrivals crossing over to greet their friends, the extra help passing through with trays of drinks and appetizers, the guests constantly shifting as they formed into groups. I saw the Kittershoys. Off to one side, on the flagstones under the lights, Boris was playing ping-pong, and Daisy hovered nearby. She was with some people, but she kept anxiously watching the ping-pong game. Boris was playing with a Mrs. Ashton, a lady who had an extremely full bosom and wore a low-cut dress. Mrs. Ashton was an intensely serious person, and as she lunged and flung herself about, she clearly had no idea of the violent effect the game was having on her bosom.

"Boris! Boris!" I heard Daisy call out. "Boris, take care—you will overexert!"

A few moments later, making my way through the guests, I stumbled on the Kittershoys again. Daisy had contrived somehow to get her husband away from the ping-pong table, and now, standing in a corner in the shadows, she was warning him against Mrs. Ashton. "She is literal-minded. She is intellectual. She will have a heart-to-heart talk with her husband and ask him for a divorce and then come running back to you, and then what? She has been analyzed!"

"But I am only amusing myself!" Boris said. "What do you want from me? I am only doing what you always preach—smile! Enjoy life! The world isn't coming to an end!" He left her and went off into the crowd.

It occurred to me that Spogel might be in the house. I went inside, and found him right away. He was in the library, but I had spent too much time wandering around outside and listening to the Kittershoys. Julie was already in there with him. Spogel had talked, had told him all about the white lie, and the damage was done.

Julie wouldn't talk about Imogene. He passed over the whole business of the snoring and the unfortunate misunderstanding. His color was high, his eyes shone, and he looked bursting with vigor and good health. "You don't say!" he said when Spogel told him that Imogene was only thoughtless and feminine, that he, Julie, was perhaps being unduly harsh with her. Spogel sensed trouble. He knew something had gone terribly awry, but for the life of him he couldn't imagine what was wrong, and he could only go ahead. "Is that so?" Julie said, in his hearty, friendly manner when Spogel told him about the Lissaks, both brothers appearing at the party, all the signs pointing to the clear-cut possibility of a transaction in the offing. "They do, do they?" Julie said when he heard the Lissaks had connections with oil people. Then he went to work on Spogel and took him apart.

Up in Kern County, Julie said, where Spogel had his theatres, the authorities let you pop the popcorn on the premises, and Spogel worked the contraptions in his houses so that the popcorn smell was piped directly out into the auditoriums, overpowering the audiences. "Not only that," Julie said, "you purposely put too much salt into the popcorn, so all during the show the poor farmers have to keep running out into the lobby to buy drinks. You chop the credits off the Westerns and run the same godforsaken pictures all over again with new titles, and nobody knows the difference. You import burlesque dancers for live shows, raise the prices sky-high, and then you shortchange the yokels on the bumps and grinds because you're scared to death the P.-T.A.'ll kick. And every year you add to your capital. Every month you set aside a nice, tidy sum for another few shares of American Tel. & Tel. What are you yammering to me about the Lissaks for? Who asked you?"

"But they are *here!*" Spogel gasped. "They have financing—they have a release!"

"What do you expect out of the Lissaks? What do you think they're going to do?" Julie said. He wouldn't go near the Lissaks with a ten-foot pole. They were greedy. They were ragpickers, junkmen. They came around shopping for bargains, looking to take advantage of desperation cases. They'd move in and immediately start taking over the whole show. Overnight they'd become experts on script, on casting, on cutting. They'd want to hog it all— a Lissak Brothers Production Produced by Julian Vencie. What are the Lissaks—beginners, children, public benefactors? Didn't they know the score? Didn't they know he had tried the banks everywhere—downtown in Los Angeles, in New York, in Boston? Didn't the Lissaks know he was two hundred thousand dollars in the hole? "Would *you* give me the money, just like that?" Julie pounded. The notion struck his fancy. "Come on, Spogel!" he cried. "You're a sport. You're a rich man. You got capital. Why don't *you* give me the money?"

"Gladly!" Spogel said. "I would do it like a shot, only what would be the sense?" The fact of the matter was that he himself was getting out of the business, selling his houses, liquidating, and how would it be to liquidate everything and then jump right back in again, investing in a movie? "Julie, darling, the handwriting is on the wall!" Spogel pleaded.

Julie roared with laughter. He roared because Spogel looked so comical, with his arms extended, his face honest and confounded, and because Spogel was so beautifully right. Spogel had put it perfectly: The handwriting was on the wall. The industry was dead. It was all over—the years of picturemaking, the work, the rush, the all-night sessions at the studio, the whole wonderful excitement and rapture.

The library had two doors, one leading to the hall, the other to the back of the house. Now, as Julie stood shaking with his innocent glee, Edith came running in from the hall. "They're gone! They're gone!" she said to her husband, meaning the Lissaks. "Curtis, they only came in for a cocktail on their way to Malibu. It was purely social!"

Julie was perversely triumphant, enormously delighted to learn that he was so far gone that the Lissaks didn't even want to take advantage of him. Just then, the other door opened. Imogene walked in. She had borrowed one of Edith's dresses, had carefully made up her face, had carefully done her hair, and she came in smiling, and lovely, and hopeful.

"That Bartók baloney!" Julie said to her by way of greeting. "All you have to do is mention Braque and the art of Arnold Schoenberg, and they drop like flies!" Her face fell, under the fresh makeup.

It turned out that Julie was referring to the letters, to things he had read in the correspondence with the hotel-band player.

"Julie, don't—not here, not in front of everybody!" she said, but he wouldn't spare her. He kept quoting from the letters, mentioning the most delicate intimacies, merrily relishing every tender tidbit.

"Oh, Julie, how can you!" Edith said. She went up to Imogene and put her arm around her, and they moved toward the door.

"I didn't know!" Spogel protested fervently, apologizing to Imogene and Edith both. "I didn't know. Believe me, I meant only for the best!"

"You ought to read that fancy stuff!" Julie said. "They weren't going to live to make money; they would make money to live! They had it all figured out—he would play the fiddle only three days a week, and have the rest of the time for life and love. What were they going to do for four days every week—talk about Bartók?"

Imogene and the Spogels had reached the hall. The door closed behind them, and the room grew quiet. Julie paused. He was still wound up, but he had no one now to rail at. He went to the desk. He picked up the phone and dialled a number. Suddenly, he had become altogether transformed. In another moment, I heard him arguing fiercely over the phone. He was talking business now, blustering and wangling, desperately trying to make a deal. He was talking to Ronnie Fitts—the other independent producer, the one he had insulted, the man whose wife's earnings in real estate had bought him the original French paintings. "I'll let you have control!" Julie was saying. "Now wait a minute, pappy, listen. I'll let you cast the picture. You'll do it all! You'll hire and fire, you'll handle the rushes in the projection room. It'll be your name on the card, not mine!" He cajoled. He begged.

I hadn't intended to stay for the party; I was expected home for dinner. As I began walking down the hall, I heard Spogel calling to me in a stage whisper. He was standing at the door of one of the bedrooms. "David! David, quick, please, come here, help . . ." Imogene had gone in there, and Spogel didn't know what she might be doing to herself. He feared the worst. "There are pills on the dressing table—sleeping pills! Oh, I never would forgive myself! Imogene!" he whispered frantically, turning back to the door. "Imogene!" He tried the knob.

The door wasn't locked. It opened easily. Imogene was sitting at the dressing table, facing herself in the mirror. She was softly singing "Some Enchanted Evening" and trying on a sequined hair net of Edith's. She stared at Spogel. "I'm not committing suicide on his account, don't worry," she said slowly. "What did you think—" She broke off. It happened that our eyes met, Imogene's and mine, and we looked at each other for a second, suspended in silence. I noticed the curve of her cheek, and in that instant I saw her as a little girl, chubby and fresh and clear-eyed, everything yet to come. She looked at me with defiance, and then she turned away.

"Sorry," Spogel said sadly. He gently closed the door and, without a word, walked off to shave and take his shower.

In the entrance hall, I found Daisy Kittershoy—all alone there, oddly hunched over the wraps and topcoats on the table, searching away through the pile. "All the years, all the years, all the years," she was saying to herself, like a chant. "You can't know, David," she said, speaking straight at me but not really seeing me, "you don't know how much I looked forward to retiring from the business world. I thought, you see—I anticipated— What you must understand, you see, is that all my life I have been a businesswoman, my mind always taken up, every morning in the shop— I expected a paradise on earth!"

She turned back to the pile of clothing on the table. She was looking for Boris's topcoat, she told me—for the car keys in his pocket. He had left the party. She didn't know where he'd gone, and now she wanted to go home. She had a headache. Her ears throbbed. She wanted to take a bath. She wanted to lie down and rest and sleep. "Seventy-eight thousand dollars!" she said, anguish welling up in her. "Seventy-eight thousand dollars. Do you know what that means, David? All the years, all the years—fighting in the shop, fighting with the contractors, with the buyers, the returns, the rejections!" She wept. She held her face in her hands. "No," she said, making an effort, taking a grip on herself. She dropped her hands and straightened her shoulders. "I mustn't. I mustn't. That was always my trouble—I was always overpreoccupied with material values. It teaches me a lesson. It serves me right. I never had time for literature, or lectures—gardening!" she said. She found Boris's topcoat and reached into the pocket for the keys.

Out on the terrace, old Mrs. Vencie was sitting in her usual place, still going strong. She caught my arm as I passed. "Look, look!" she said, pointing to the city below us, to the thousands and thousands of lights spreading for miles all the way out to the ocean. "Isn't it remarkable, David? All the lights, all the people, each and every one a living human being, the blood in their veins just as red as you or me." On the road winding above us there were headlights moving—young people, undergraduates at the university, driving to the top of the hill on a weekend night. Edith and Spogel were always careful to tell Mrs. Vencie the youngsters went up there to see the view, to hold romantic conversations, but the old woman wasn't fooled. She knew what they did in the parked cars—they necked. "And why not?" Mrs. Vencie said.

The Spogels' dinner party was well under way. The servants bustled. The ladies in their lovely frocks chattered over the candlelight, their faces animated and affectionate, while their husbands stood by themselves, quietly smoking, quietly discussing the situation of the industry.

Mrs. Vencie was telling me how she met her husband. "So," she said, "they told me, 'Go to the shop, make believe you don't know anything, look on him, see if you like him—what will it hurt?' So I went there, to the fur shop where he worked. But, unbeknownst to me, they told him the same story. They told him to look and see, too, maybe he would be interested—so there we stood, like two big dumbbells, spying on each other, bashful and ashamed!"

"Outdoor living," I heard someone say. On the hillside below, bulldozers had scooped out level sites. Homes now lay before us in descending tiers. Most people on Angelo Drive had buffet dinners on Sunday evenings, and it made a picture—the splashes of light down there, the guests grouped on the lawns, the blue-tiled swimming pools.

"Poor Papa," Mrs. Vencie said, nodding, remembering. "You should have seen him when he was alive, David. He was elegant. He had a Kaiser Wilhelm mustache, with the points—a prince! On Sunday morning, he bought the breakfast, and if you asked him what did the whitefish cost, the carp, he never knew. He was too aristocratic to ask the storekeeper the price—he just paid the whole bill. Once, when I was in the mountains with the children, he sent me a letter—he was giving me a big surprise. I wondered to myself, what could it be? Was it a new gas range, maybe? A new icebox, even? It was a picture of himself! He went to a photographer and took a picture—with the mustache, with his Palm Beach summer suit, blowing me a kiss. Poor Papa!"

She took time out to marvel at the view. "Look! It shimmers before the eyes!" she said, pointing again, meaning the multitude of lights. She was old. She knew that nothing was out of the ordinary, that hopes were betrayed, that you always started out with illusion, and yet everything was a wonder to her. "Isn't it gorgeous?" she said to me. "It's like a fairyland, David. It's like magic!"

JUST A LITTLE MORE

❖

V. S. Pritchett

THEY WERE speaking in low voices in the kitchen.

"How is he? Has he said what he is going to do?" she asked her husband. "Is there any news?"

"None at all," the husband whispered. "He's coming down now. He says he just wants a house by the sea, in a place where the air is bracing and the water's soft and there's a good variety of fish."

"Sh-h-h! Why do we whisper like this? Here he comes. Get the plates."

A moment later, the very old gentleman, her father-in-law, was standing in the doorway, staring and smiling. He was short and very fat, and one of the things he liked to do was to pause in the doorway of a room and look it over from ceiling to floor. In the old days, his family or his workers at the factory used to stiffen nervously when he did this, wondering where his eye would stop.

"Excuse me being rude," he said at last. "What a lovely smell."

"Take your father in," the wife said. "These plates are hot. Go into the dining room, Grandpa."

"I'm just looking at your refrigerator, darling," the old gentleman said. "Very nice. It's a Pidex, I see. Is that a good make? I mean is it good—does it work well? . . . I'm glad to hear that. Did you get it from the Pidex people? . . . Ah, I thought you did. Good people."

The son, who was in his fifties, took the old gentleman by the elbow and moved him slowly into the dining room. The old gentleman blew his nose.

"No. Your mother's hands were as cold as ice when I got to her," said the old gentleman, astonished by a memory. "But she had gone. Where do I go? Do I sit here?"

He sat down very suddenly at the table. Although he weighed close to two hundred pounds, his clothes hung loosely on him, for he had once weighed much more. His nostrils had spread and reddened over a skin that was greenish and violet on the cheeks but as pale and stringy as a chicken's at the neck.

His daughter-in-law and two grandchildren brought in the joint and the vegetables. The grandchildren were called Richard and Helen. They were in their teens. Their mouths watered when they saw the food on the table, and they leaned toward it, but kept their eyes politely on the old man, like elderly listeners.

"I hope you haven't cooked anything special for me," the old man said. "I was just saying I talk too much when I come for a weekend here, and I eat too much. It's living alone—having no one to talk to, and so forth, and you can't be bothered to eat—that's the point. What a lovely piece of beef that is! Wonderful. I haven't seen a joint of beef like that for centuries. A small bit of loin of lamb we might have, but my wife can't digest it." He often forgot that his wife was dead. "And it doesn't keep. I put it in the larder and I forget and it goes wrong." His big face suddenly crinkled like an apple, with disgust.

"Well, well, I don't know, I'm sure," he went on, gazing at the beef his son was now carving. "I suppose it's all right. What do you call a joint like that?" He pointed across the table to his grandson. "We used to have beef when your father was a boy, Richard. Your father was a boy once. You can't imagine that, can you? Aitchbone, was it? I can't remember. I don't know where your mother used to get it. Bell's, I suppose. I don't know what we paid for it. Sixpence a pound, perhaps. We can't do it now; it's the price."

His son passed him a plate. The old man hesitated, not knowing whether to pass it on and not wanting to. "If this is for me, don't give me any more," he said. "I hardly eat anything nowadays. If I could have just a little fat . . ." Relieved, he kept the plate.

"Pass the vegetables to Grandpa," said his daughter-in-law to Helen.

"Grandpa, vegetables?" Helen said, looking younger now as she spoke.

"Oh," said the old gentleman. He had gone into a dream. "I was just watching you carving," he said to his son. "I was looking at your face. You've got just the expression of your Great-Grandfather Harry. I remember him when I was a little boy. Father took me to see him—it was one morning. He took me down to a warehouse, would it be?—in the docks or harbor—a factory, perhaps—and he lifted me up to a window and I saw him, just his face, it was only a minute. He was slitting up herrings; it was a curing place."

"Fish! I knew it." His daughter-in-law laughed.

"The sea is in our blood," said her husband. Everyone was laughing.

"What is this? What are you laughing at? What have I said?" the old gentleman asked, smiling. "Are you getting at me?"

"That is where you get your taste for kippers," said the daughter-in-law to her husband.

"Ah, kippers!" said the old gentleman, delighted by his strange success. "How are you for fish in this neighborhood? Do you get good fish? I sometimes feel like a piece of fish. But there doesn't seem to be the fish about, these days. I don't know why that is. No, I went up to the fishmonger on Tuesday and I looked. He came up to me, and I said, 'Good morning.' 'Good morning, Mr. Hopkins,' he said. 'What can I do for you?' 'Do for me?' I said. 'Give me a fortnight in Monte Carlo.' He exploded. I said, 'What's happened to you? What's wrong?' 'What do you mean, Mr. Hopkins?' he said. 'I mean, where's your fish?' I said. 'That's not what I call fish. Not f-i-s-h.' He knew what I meant. 'Sole,' he said. 'Dover sole,' I said. 'Mr. Hopkins,' he said, 'I haven't had a Dover sole for a fortnight. Not one I'd sell *you*. Lemon sole,' he said, and something—grayling, did he say? Well, that's the way it is. And so we go on.

"No," the old man said after a moment. "Kitty, your mother, my wife, was very fond of fish. When we were first married, and so forth, we came down from the north— How old are you, my boy? Fifty-seven? You're not fifty-seven!—it was just before you were born, and my wife said, 'I'd give anything for an oyster.' The train didn't get in till eight, but we were young and reckless in those days. I didn't care a damn for anyone. I was ready to knock the world over. I was in a good crib, five pounds a week at Weekley's— before Hollins took them over. All expenses. I thought I was Julius Caesar—marvellous, isn't it? Do I mean him? And we went across the road and your mother said, 'Come on—' "

The son interrupted, picking up the story. "And a busdriver leaned out of his cab and said, 'Watch out, lady. Babies are scarce this year.' Mother told me."

"I'm sure she didn't," said the old gentleman, blushing a little. "Your father's imagination, Richard!"

"Yes, but what happened?" asked his daughter-in-law.

"And there was a little place, a real old London fish place—sawdust on the floor, I suppose they had in those days. Crossfield . . . Cross . . . Crofty—I forget the name—and we had a dozen oysters each, maybe I had a couple of dozen; I don't remember now, I couldn't say. Frederick's—*that* was the name of the place. Frederick's. And I suppose we must have followed it with Dover sole. They used to do a wonderful Welsh rabbit."

"And that is how I was born," said the son. "Let me give you some more beef, Father."

"Me? Oh, no. I don't eat what I used to. It's living alone, and these new teeth of mine—I've had a lot of trouble with them. Don't give me any more. I don't mind a couple of slices—well, just another. And some fat. I like a piece of fat. That's what I feel. You go home and you get to the house, and it's dark. And it's empty. You go in and the boiler's low—I don't seem to get the right coke. Do you get good coke here? You look at it all and you look in the larder and you can't be bothered. There's a chop, a bit of bread and cheese, perhaps. And you think, Well, if this is all there is in life, you may as well finish it. I'm in a rut down in that place. I've got to get away. I can't breathe there. I'd like to get down to the sea."

"I think you ought to go where you have friends," said his daughter-in-law.

The old gentleman put his knife and fork down. "Friends?" he said, in a stern voice, raising his chin. "I have no friends. All my friends are dead." He said this with indignation and contempt.

"But what about your friend Rogers, in Devonshire?" said his son.

"Rogers? I was disappointed in Rogers. He's aged. He's let himself go. I hadn't seen him for twenty-five years. When I saw him, I said to him, 'Why, what's the matter with you? Trying to pretend you are an old man?' He looked at me. He'd let his mustache go long and gray. I wouldn't have known him. And there was something else. A funny thing. It upset me." The old gentleman's jolly face shrivelled up again, with horror. "The hairs in his nose had gone gray!" he said. "I couldn't bear it. He was very kind, *and* his wife was. We had lunch. Soup of some kind—tomato, or maybe oxtail—and then a piece of lamb, potatoes, and cauliflower. Oh, very nice. I've forgotten what the dessert was—some cream, I suppose, they have good cream there—and coffee, of course. Cheese . . . I don't remember. Afterward—and this is what upsets me about

old people—they wanted a rest. Every day, after lunch, they go off
and have a sleep—every day. Can you imagine that? I couldn't
stand that. Terrible."

"It's good to have a siesta," said the son.

"I couldn't. I never have. I just can't," said the old gentleman,
in a panic. "The other afternoon after lunch, I forget what I had,
a chop, I think—I couldn't be bothered to cook vegetables, well, on
your own you don't, that's the point—I dropped off. I don't know
how long, and when I woke up it was dark. I couldn't see anything.
I didn't know where I was. 'Where am I?' I said. 'What day is it?'
And I reached out for my wife. I thought I was in bed, and I called
out 'Kitty, Kitty, where are you?' and then I said, 'Oh.' It came
back to me. I'm here. In this room. I couldn't move. I got up and
put on the light. I was done up. I poured myself out a small glass
of port. I felt I had to. It was shocking. And shocking dreams."

He stared and then suddenly he turned to his daughter-in-law
and said, in another voice, "Those sandwiches I shan't forget. Egg,
wasn't it? You remember." He wagged a finger at Helen. "Helen,
your mother is a wonder at egg sandwiches. It was the first time in
my life I'd ever eaten them. The day we put Kitty away, you remember, she came down and made egg sandwiches. What is the
secret of it? She won't tell. Butter, I suppose? Richard, what is the
word I want? You know—'smashing,' I suppose you'd call them."

He paused, and his eyes grew vaguer. "No," he went on, "I don't
know what I'll do. I think I shall go to the sea and look around.
I shall get a list of houses, and put my furniture in store. I could
live with your brother John, or you. I know I could, but it would
be wrong. You have your own lives. I want my independence. Life
is beginning for me—that is what I feel. I feel I would like to go on
a cruise round the world. There was a house at Bexhill I saw. They
wanted seven thousand for it. I felt it would suit me."

"Seven thousand!" said his son, in alarm. "Where would you get
seven thousand from?"

"Oh," said the old gentleman sharply, "I should raise it."

"Raise it!" exclaimed the son. "How?"

"That's just it," said the old gentleman cheerfully. "I don't
know. The way will open up. You, perhaps, or John."

Husband and wife looked down the table at each other in
consternation.

"Shall we go upstairs and have some coffee?" she said.

"That son of yours, that Richard—did you see what he ate?" said the old gentleman as he got up from the table. "Marvellous, isn't it? Of course, things are better than when I was a boy. I feel everything is better. We used to go to school with twopence for a pie. Not every day—twice a week. The other days, we just looked at the shopwindow. Pies piled up. And once a week—Friday, I expect—it was herrings in the evening. The fisherwomen came calling them in the street, eighteen a shilling, fresh fish out of the sea. Salmon I used to be fond of. D'you ever have salmon?"

He paused in the doorway and looked at the carpet on the stairs and at the wallpaper. "I like rich things," he said, nodding to the carpet. "That gravy was good. Luscious grapes, pears, all large fruits I like. Those Christmas displays at the meat market—turkeys and geese by the thousand there used to be. I always used to bring your mother something. A few chops, two or three pairs of kippers. And so forth. I don't know what."

"Upstairs to the sitting room, Father," said the son. "I'm coming in a minute with the coffee."

The son went into the kitchen, and the whispering began again.

"Seven thousand!" he said. "Seven million wouldn't keep him!"

"Sh-h-h," said his wife. "It's a daydream."

"But what are we going to do?"

In a few minutes, he took the coffee upstairs. The old gentleman was sitting down, with his waistcoat undone and his thumbs twiddling on his stomach.

"I've been thinking about you," the old gentleman said rebukingly. "You've lost weight. You don't eat. You worry too much. My wife used to worry."

The son passed a coffee cup to him.

"Is there a lot of sugar in it? Thank you," the old man said. He gave it a stir, took a sip, and then held the cup out. "I think I'll have a couple of spoonfuls more."

RAISE HIGH THE ROOF BEAM,
CARPENTERS

❖

J. D. SALINGER

ONE NIGHT some twenty years ago, during a siege of mumps in our enormous family, my youngest sister, Franny, was moved, crib and all, into the ostensibly germfree room I shared with my eldest brother, Seymour. I was fifteen, Seymour was seventeen. Along about two in the morning, the new roommate's crying awakened me. I lay in a still, neutral position for a few minutes, listening to the racket, till I heard, or felt, Seymour stir in the bed next to mine. In those days, we kept a flashlight on the night table between us, for emergencies that, as far as I remember, never arose. Seymour turned it on and got out of bed. "The bottle's on the stove, Mother said," I told him. "I gave it to her a little while ago," Seymour said. "She isn't hungry." He went over in the dark to the bookcase and beamed the flashlight slowly back and forth along the stacks. I sat up in bed. "What are you going to do?" I said. "I thought maybe I'd read something to her," Seymour said, and took down a book. "She's ten months old, for God's sake," I said. "I know," Seymour said. "They have ears. They can hear."

The story Seymour read to Franny that night, by flashlight, was a favorite of his, a Taoist tale. To this day, Franny swears that she remembers Seymour reading it to her:

> Duke Mu of Chin said to Po Lo: "You are now advanced in years. Is there any member of your family whom I could employ to look for horses in your stead?" Po Lo replied: "A good horse can be picked out by its general build and appearance. But the superlative horse— one that raises no dust and leaves no tracks—is something evanescent and fleeting, elusive as thin air. The talents of my sons lie on a lower plane altogether; they can tell a good horse when they see one, but they cannot tell a superlative horse. I have a friend, however, one

46

Chiu-fang Kao, a hawker of fuel and vegetables, who in things apper-
taining to horses is nowise my inferior. Pray see him."

Duke Mu did so, and subsequently dispatched him on the quest
for a steed. Three months later, he returned with the news that he
had found one. "It is now in Shach'iu," he added. "What kind of a
horse is it?" asked the Duke. "Oh, it is a dun-colored mare," was the
reply. However, someone being sent to fetch it, the animal turned
out to be a coal-black stallion! Much displeased, the Duke sent for
Po Lo. "That friend of yours," he said, "whom I commissioned to
look for a horse, has made a fine mess of it. Why, he cannot even
distinguish a beast's color or sex! What on earth can he know about
horses?" Po Lo heaved a sigh of satisfaction. "Has he really got as
far as that?" he cried. "Ah, then he is worth ten thousand of me put
together. There is no comparison between us. What Kao keeps in
view is the spiritual mechanism. In making sure of the essential, he
forgets the homely details; intent on the inward qualities, he loses
sight of the external. He sees what he wants to see, and not what he
does not want to see. He looks at the things he ought to look at, and
neglects those that need not be looked at. So clever a judge of horses
is Kao, that he has it in him to judge something better than horses."

When the horse arrived, it turned out indeed to be a superlative
animal.

I've reproduced the tale here not just because I invariably go out
of my way to recommend a good prose pacifier to parents or older
brothers of ten-month-old babies but for quite another reason.
What directly follows is an account of a wedding day in 1942.
It is, in my opinion, a self-contained account, with a beginning and
an end, and a mortality, all its own. Yet, because I'm in possession
of the fact, I feel I must mention that the bridegroom is now, in
1955, no longer living. He committed suicide in 1948, while he was
on vacation in Florida with his wife. . . . Undoubtedly, though,
what I'm really getting at is this: Since the bridegroom's permanent
retirement from the scene, I haven't been able to think of anybody
whom I'd care to send out to look for horses in his stead.

In late May of 1942, the progeny—seven in number—of Les and
Bessie (Gallagher) Glass, retired Pantages Circuit vaudevillians,
were flung, extravagantly speaking, all over the United States. I, for
one, the second-eldest, was in the post hospital at Fort Benning,
Georgia, with pleurisy—a little keepsake of thirteen weeks' infantry
basic training. The twins, Walt and Waker, had been split up a
whole year earlier. Waker was in a conscientious objectors' camp

in Maryland, and Walt was somewhere in the Pacific—or on his way there—with a field-artillery unit. (We've never been altogether sure where Walt was at that specific time. He was never a great letter writer, and very little personal information—almost none—reached us after his death. He was killed in an unspeakably absurd G.I. accident in late autumn of 1945, in Japan.) My eldest sister, Boo Boo, who comes, chronologically, between the twins and me, was an ensign in the Waves, stationed, off and on, at a naval base in Brooklyn. All that spring and summer, she occupied the small apartment in New York that my brother Seymour and I had all but technically given up after our induction. The two youngest children in the family, Zooey (male) and Franny (female), were with our parents in Los Angeles, where my father was hustling talent for a motion-picture studio. Zooey was thirteen, and Franny was eight. They were both appearing every week on a children's radio quiz program called, with perhaps typically pungent Coast-to-Coast irony, "It's a Wise Child." At one time or another, I might well bring in here—or, rather, in one year or another—all the children in our family have been weekly hired "guests" on "It's a Wise Child." Seymour and I were the first to appear on the show, back in 1927, at the respective ages of ten and eight, in the days when the program "emanated" from one of the convention rooms of the old Murray Hill Hotel. All seven of us, from Seymour through Franny, appeared on the show under pseudonyms. Which may sound highly anomalous, considering that we're the children of vaudevillians, a sect not usually antipathetic to publicity, but my mother had once read a magazine article on the little crosses professional children are obliged to bear—their estrangement from normal, presumably desirable society—and she took an iron stand on the issue, and never, never wavered. (This is not the time at all to go into the question of whether most, or all, "professional" children ought to be outlawed, pitied, or unsentimentally executed as disturbers of the peace. For the moment, I'll only pass along that our combined income on "It's a Wise Child" has sent six of us through college, and is now sending the seventh.)

Our eldest brother, Seymour—with whom I'm all but exclusively concerned here—was a corporal in what, in 1942, was still called the Air Corps. He was stationed at a B-17 base in California, where, I *believe,* he was an acting company clerk. I might add, not quite parenthetically, that he was by far the least prolific letter writer in the family. I don't think I've had five letters from him in my life.

On the morning of either May 22nd or 3rd (no one in my family has ever dated a letter), a letter from my sister Boo Boo was placed on the foot of my cot in the post hospital at Fort Benning while my diaphragm was being strapped with adhesive tape (a usual medical procedure with pleurisy patients, presumably guaranteed to prevent them from coughing themselves to pieces). When the ordeal was over, I read Boo Boo's letter. I still have it, and it follows here verbatim:

DEAR BUDDY,

I'm in a terrible rush to pack, so this will be short but *penetrating*. Admiral Behind-pincher has decided that he must fly to parts unknown for the war effort and has also decided to take his secretary with him if I behave myself. I'm just sick about it. Seymour aside, it means Quonset huts in freezing air bases and boyish passes from our fighting men and those horrible paper things to get sick in on the plane. The point is, Seymour is getting married—yes, *married,* so please pay attention. I can't be there. I may be gone for anywhere from six weeks to two months on this trip. I've met the girl. She's a zero in my opinion but terrific-looking. I don't actually *know* that she's a zero. I mean she hardly said two words the night I met her. Just sat and smiled and smoked, so it isn't fair to say. I don't know anything about the romance itself at all, except that they apparently met when Seymour was stationed at Monmouth last winter. The mother is the end—a finger in all the arts, and sees a good Jungian man twice a week (she asked me twice, the night I met her, if I'd ever been analyzed). She told me she just wishes Seymour would *relate* to more people. In the same breath, said she just loves him, though, etc., etc., and that she used to listen to him religiously all the years he was on the air. That's all I know except that you've *got* to get to the wedding. I'll never forgive you if you don't. I mean it. Mother and Daddy can't get here from the Coast. Franny has the measles, for one thing. Incidentally, did you hear her last week? She went on at beautiful length about how she used to fly all around the apartment when she was four and no one was home. The new announcer is worse than Grant—if possible, even worse than Sullivan in the old days. He said she surely just *dreamt* that she was able to fly. The baby stood her ground like an angel. She said she *knew* she was able to fly because when she came down she always had dust on her fingers from touching the light bulbs. I long to see her. You, too. Anyhow, you've *got* to get to the wedding. Go A.W.O.L. if you have to, but please *go*. It's at three o'clock, June 4th. *Very* nonsectarian and Emancipated, at her grandmother's house on 63rd. Some judge is marrying them. I don't know the number of the house, but it's exactly two doors down from where Carl and Amy used to live in luxury. I'm going to wire Walt, but I think he's been shipped out already. *Please* get there, Buddy. He weighs about as much as a cat and he has that ecstatic look on his face that you can't talk to. Maybe it's going to be perfectly all right, but I hate 1942. I think I'll hate 1942 till I die, just on general principles. All my love and see you when I get back.

Boo Boo

A couple of days after the letter arrived, I was discharged from the hospital, in the custody, so to speak, of about three yards of adhesive tape around my ribs. Then began a very strenuous week's campaign to get permission to attend the wedding. I was finally able to do it by laboriously ingratiating myself with my company commander, a bookish man by his own confession, whose favorite author, as luck had it, happened to be my favorite author—L. Manning Vines. Or Hinds. Despite this spiritual bond between us, the most I could wangle out of him was a three-day pass, which would, at best, give me just enough time to travel by train to New York, see the wedding, bolt a dinner somewhere, and then return damply to Georgia.

All sit-up coaches on trains in 1942 were only nominally ventilated, as I remember, abounded with M.P.s, and smelled of orange juice, milk, and rye whiskey. I spent the night coughing and reading a copy of Ace Comics that someone was kind enough to lend me. When the train pulled into New York—at ten after two on the afternoon of the wedding—I was coughed out, generally exhausted, perspiring, unpressed, and my adhesive tape was itching hellishly. New York itself was indescribably hot. I had no time to go to my apartment first, so I left my luggage, which consisted of a rather oppressive-looking little canvas zipper bag, in one of those steel boxes at Penn Station. To make things still more provocative, as I was wandering around in the garment district trying to find an empty cab, a second lieutenant in the Signal Corps, whom I'd apparently overlooked saluting, crossing Seventh Avenue, suddenly took out a fountain pen and wrote down my name, serial number, and address while a number of civilians looked interestedly on.

I was limp when I finally got into a cab. I gave the driver directions that would take me at least as far as "Carl and Amy's" old house. As soon as we arrived in that block, however, it was very simple. One just followed the crowd. There was even a canvas canopy. A moment later, I entered an enormous old brownstone and was met by a very handsome, lavender-haired woman, who asked me whether I was a friend of the bride or the groom. I said the groom. "Oh," she said, "well, we're just bunching everybody up together." She laughed rather immoderately, and showed me to what seemed to be the last vacant folding chair in a very crowded outsize room. I have a thirteen-year-old blackout in my mind with regard to the over-all physical details of the room. Beyond the fact that it was jam-packed and stifling hot, I can remember only two things: that there was an organ playing almost directly behind me, and that the woman in the seat directly at my right turned to me and enthusiastically stage-whispered, *"I'm Helen Silsburn!"* From the location of our seats, I gathered that she was not the bride's mother, but, to play it safe, I smiled and nodded gregariously, and was about to say who *I* was, but she put a decorous finger to her lips, and we both faced front. It was then, roughly, three o'clock. I closed my eyes and waited, a trifle guardedly, for the organist to quit the incidental music and plunge into "Lohengrin."

I haven't a very clear idea of how the next hour and a quarter passed, aside from the cardinal fact that there was no plunging into "Lohengrin." I remember a little dispersed band of unfamiliar faces that surreptitiously turned around, now and then, to see who was coughing. And I remember that the woman at my right addressed me once again, in the same rather festive whisper. "There must be some delay," she said. "Have you ever seen Judge Ranker? He has the face of a *saint*." And I remember the organ music veering peculiarly, almost desperately, at one point, from Bach to early Rodgers and Hart. On the whole, though, I'm afraid, I passed the time paying little sympathetic hospital calls on myself for being obliged to suppress my coughing spells. I had a sustained, cowardly notion, the entire time I was in the room, that I was about to hemorrhage, or, at the very least, fracture a rib, despite the corset of adhesive tape I was wearing.

At twenty minutes past four—or, to put it another, blunter way, an hour and twenty minutes past what seemed to be all reasonable hope—the unmarried bride, her head down, a parent stationed on either side of her, was helped out of the building and conducted, fragilely, down a long flight of stone steps to the sidewalk. She was then deposited—almost hand over hand, it seemed—into the first of the sleek black hired cars that were waiting, double-parked, at the curb. It was an excessively graphic moment—a tabloid moment—

and, as tabloid moments go, it had its full complement of eye-witnesses, for the wedding guests (myself among them) had already begun to pour out of the building, however decorously, in alert, not to say goggle-eyed, droves. If there was any even faintly lenitive aspect to the spectacle, the weather itself was responsible for it. The June sun was so hot and so glaring, of such multi-flashbulb-like mediacy, that the image of the bride, as she made her almost invalided way down the stone steps, tended to blur where blurring mattered most.

Once the bridal car was at least physically removed from the scene, the tension on the sidewalk—especially around the mouth of the canvas canopy, at the curb, where I, for one, was loitering—deteriorated into what, had the building been a church, and had it been a Sunday, might have been taken for fairly normal congregation-dispersing confusion. Then, very suddenly, the emphasized word came—reportedly from the bride's Uncle Al—that the wedding guests were to *use* the cars standing at the curb; that is, reception or no reception, change of plans or no change of plans. If the re-action in my vicinity was any criterion, the offer was generally received as a kind of *beau geste*. It didn't quite go without saying, however, that the cars were to be "used" only after a formidable-looking platoon of people—referred to as the bride's "immediate family"—had taken what transportation *they* needed to quit the scene. And, after a somewhat mysterious and bottleneck-like delay (during which I remained peculiarly riveted to the spot), the "immediate family" did indeed begin to make its exodus, as many as six or seven persons to a car, or as few as three or four. The number, I gathered, depended upon the age, demeanor, and hip spread of the first occupants in possession.

Suddenly, at someone's parting—but markedly crisp—suggestion, I found myself stationed at the curb, directly at the mouth of the canvas canopy, attending to helping people into cars.

How I had been singled out to fill this post deserves some small speculation. So far as I know, the unidentified, middle-aged man of action who had picked me for the job hadn't a glimmer of a notion that I was the bridegroom's brother. Therefore, it seems logical that I was singled out for other, far less poetic reasons. The year was 1942. I was twenty-three, and newly drafted into the Army. It strikes me that it was solely my age, my uniform, and the unmistakably serviceable, olive-drab aura about me that had left no doubt concerning my eligibility to fill in as doorman.

I was not only twenty-three but a conspicuously retarded twenty-three. I remember loading people into cars without any degree of competence whatever. On the contrary, I went about it with a certain disingenuous, cadetlike semblance of single-mindedness, of adherence to duty. After a few minutes, in fact, I became all too aware that I was catering to the needs of a predominantly older, shorter, fleshier generation, and my performance as an arm taker and door closer took on an even more thoroughly bogus puissance. I began to conduct myself like an exceptionally adroit, wholly engaging young giant with a cough.

But the heat of the afternoon was, to say the least, oppressive, and the compensations of my office must have seemed to me increasingly tokenless. Abruptly, though the crowd of "immediate family" seemed scarcely to have begun to thin out, I myself lunged into one of the freshly loaded cars, just as it started to draw away from the curb. In doing it, I hit my head a very audible (perhaps retributive) crack on the roof. One of the occupants of the car was none other than my whispering acquaintance, Helen Silsburn, and she started to offer me her unqualified sympathy. The crack had evidently resounded throughout the car. But at twenty-three I was the sort of young man who responds to all public injury of his person, short of a fractured skull, by giving out a hollow, sub-normal-sounding laugh.

The car moved west, directly, as it were, into the open furnace of the late-afternoon sky. It continued west for two blocks, till it reached Madison Avenue, and then it right-angled sharply north. I felt as though we were all being saved from being caught up by the sun's terrible flue only by the anonymous driver's enormous alertness and skill.

The first four or five blocks north on Madison, conversation in the car was chiefly limited to remarks like "Am I giving you enough room?" and "I've never been so *hot* in my entire life." The one who had never been so hot in her entire life was, as I'd learned from a certain amount of eavesdropping at the curb, the bride's Matron of Honor. She was a hefty girl of about twenty-four or -five, in a pink satin dress, with a circlet of artificial forget-me-nots in her hair. There was a distinctly athletic ethos about her, as if, a year or two earlier, she might have majored in physical education in college. In her lap she was holding a bouquet of gardenias rather as though it were a deflated volleyball. She was seated in the back of the car, hip-pressed between her husband and a tiny elderly man in a top hat and cutaway, who was holding an unlighted clear-Havana cigar. Mrs. Silsburn and I—our respective inside knees unribaldly touching—occupied the jump seats. Twice, without any excuse whatever, out of sheer approval, I glanced around at the tiny elderly man. When I'd originally loaded the car and held the door open for him, I'd had a passing impulse to pick him up bodily and insert him gently through the open window. He was tininess itself, surely being not more than four nine or ten and without being either a midget or a dwarf. In the car, he sat staring very severely straight ahead of him. On my second look around at him, I noticed that he had what very much appeared to be an old gravy stain on the lapel of his cutaway. I also noticed that his silk hat cleared the roof of the car by a good four or five inches. . . . But for the most part, those first few minutes in the car, I was still mainly concerned with my own state of health. Besides having pleurisy and a bruised head, I had a hypochondriac's notion that I was getting a strep throat. I sat surreptitiously curling back my tongue and exploring the suspected ailing part. I was staring, as I remember, directly in front of me, at the back of the driver's neck, which was a relief map of boil scars, when suddenly my jump-seat mate addressed me: "I didn't get a chance to ask you inside. How's that darling mother of yours? Aren't you Dickie Briganza?"

My tongue, at the time of the question, was curled back exploratively as far as the soft palate. I disentangled it, swallowed, and turned to her. She was fifty, or thereabouts, fashionably and tastefully dressed. She was wearing a very heavy pancake makeup. I answered no—that I wasn't.

She narrowed her eyes a trifle at me and said I looked exactly like Celia Briganza's boy. Around the mouth. I tried to show by my expression that it was a mistake anybody could make. Then I went on staring at the back of the driver's neck. The car was silent. I glanced out of the window, for a change of scene.

"How do you like the Army?" Mrs. Silsburn asked. Abruptly, conversationally.

I had a brief coughing spell at that particular instant. When it was over, I turned to her with all available alacrity and said I'd made a lot of buddies. It was a little difficult for me to swivel in her direction, what with the encasement of adhesive tape around my diaphragm.

She nodded. "I think you're all just wonderful," she said, somewhat ambiguously. "Are you a friend of the bride's or the groom's?" she then asked, delicately getting down to brass tacks.

"Well, actually, I'm not exactly a friend of—"

"You'd better not say you're a friend of the *groom*," the Matron of Honor interrupted me, from the back of the car. "I'd like to get my hands on him for about *two minutes*. Just *two minutes*, that's all."

Mrs. Silsburn turned briefly—but completely—around to smile at the speaker. Then she faced front again. We made the round trip, in fact, almost in unison. Considering that Mrs. Silsburn had turned around for only an instant, the smile she had bestowed on the Matron of Honor was a kind of jump-seat masterpiece. It was vivid enough to express unlimited partisanship with all young people, all over the world, but most particularly with this spirited, outspoken local representative, to whom, perhaps, she had been little more than perfunctorily introduced, if at all.

"Bloodthirsty wench," said a chuckling male voice. And Mrs. Silsburn and I turned around again. It was the Matron of Honor's husband who had spoken up. He was seated directly behind me, at his wife's left. He and I briefly exchanged that blank, uncomradely look which, possibly, in the crapulous year of 1942, only an officer and a private could exchange. A first lieutenant in the Signal Corps, he was wearing a very interesting Air Corps pilot's cap—a visored hat with the metal frame removed from inside the crown, which usually conferred on the wearer a certain, presumably desired, intrepid look. In his case, however, the cap didn't begin to fill the bill. It seemed to serve no other purpose than to make my own outsize, regulation headpiece feel rather like a clown's hat that someone had nervously picked out of the incinerator. His face was sallow and, essentially, daunted-looking. He was perspiring with an almost incredible profusion—on his forehead, on his upper lip, and even at the end of his nose—to the point where a salt tablet might have been in order. "I'm married to the bloodthirstiest wench in six counties," he said, addressing Mrs. Silsburn and giving another soft, public chuckle. In automatic deference to his rank, I very nearly chuckled right along with him—a short, inane, stranger's and draftee's chuckle that would clearly signify that I was with him and everyone else in the car, against no one.

"I *mean* it," the Matron of Honor said. "Just two minutes—that's all, brother. Oh, if I could just get my two little *hands*—"

"All right, now, take it easy, take it easy," her husband said, still with apparently inexhaustible resources of connubial good humor. "Just take it easy. You'll last longer."

Mrs. Silsburn faced around toward the back of the car again, and favored the Matron of Honor with an all but canonized smile. "Did anyone see any of his people at the wedding?" she inquired softly, with just a little emphasis—no more than perfectly genteel—on the personal pronoun.

The Matron of Honor's answer came with toxic volume: "No. They're all out on the West *Coast* or someplace. I just wish I *had*."

Her husband's chuckle sounded again. "What wouldja done if you had, honey?" he asked—and winked indiscriminately at me.

"Well, I don't *know,* but I'd've done *some*thing," said the Matron of Honor. The chuckle at her left expanded in volume. "Well, I would have!" she insisted. "I'd've said *some*thing to them. I mean. My gosh." She spoke with increasing aplomb, as though perceiving that, cued by her husband, the rest of us within earshot were finding something attractively forthright—spunky—about her sense of justice, however youthful or impractical it might be. "I don't know *what* I'd have said to them. I probably would have just blabbered something idiotic. But my *gosh*. Honestly! I just can't stand to see somebody get away with absolute murder. It makes my blood boil." She suspended animation just long enough to be bolstered by a look of simulated empathy from Mrs. Silsburn. Mrs. Silsburn and I were now turned completely, supersociably, around in our jump seats. "I *mean* it," the Matron of Honor said. "You can't just *barge* through life hurting people's feelings whenever you feel like it."

"I'm afraid I know very little about the young man," Mrs. Silsburn said, softly. "As a matter of fact, I haven't even met him. The first I'd heard that Muriel was even engaged—"

"*Nobody's* met him," the Matron of Honor said, rather explosively. "*I* haven't even met him. We had two rehearsals, and both times Muriel's poor father had to take his place, just because his crazy plane couldn't take off. He was supposed to get a hop here last Tuesday night in some crazy Army plane, but it was *snowing* or something crazy in Colorado, or *Arizona,* or one of those crazy places, and he didn't get in till one o'clock in the *morn*ing, *last night. Then*—at that insane hour—he calls Muriel on the phone from way out in Long *Island* or someplace and asks her to meet him in the lobby of some horrible hotel so they can *talk*." The Matron of Honor shuddered eloquently. "And you know

Muriel. She's just darling enough to let anybody and his brother push her around. That's what gripes me. It's always those kind of people that get hurt in the end . . . . Anyway, so she gets dressed and gets in a cab and sits in some horrible lobby talking with him till quarter to *five* in the morning." The Matron of Honor released her grip on her gardenia bouquet long enough to raise two clenched fists above her lap. "*Ooo*, it makes me so mad!" she said.

"What hotel?" I asked the Matron of Honor. "Do you know?" I tried to make my voice sound casual, as though, possibly, my father might be in the hotel business and I took a certain understandable filial interest in where people stopped in New York. In reality, my question meant almost nothing. I was just thinking aloud, more or less. I'd been interested in the fact that my brother had asked his fiancée to meet him in a hotel lobby, rather than at his empty, available apartment. The morality of the invitation was by no means out of character, but it interested me, mildly, nonetheless.

"*I* don't know which hotel," the Matron of Honor said irritably. "Just some ho*tel*." She stared at me. "Why?" she demanded. "Are you a friend of his?"

There was something distinctly intimidating about her stare. It seemed to come from a one-woman mob, separated only by time and chance from her knitting bag and a splendid view of the guillotine. I've been terrified of mobs, of any kind, all my life. "We were boys together," I answered, all but unintelligibly.

"Well, lucky you!"

"Now, now," said her husband.

"Well, I'm *sorry*," the Matron of Honor said to him, but addressing all of us. "But you haven't been in a room watching that poor kid cry her eyes out for a solid hour. It's not funny—and don't you forget it. I've heard about grooms getting cold feet, and all that. But you don't do it at the *last minute*. I mean you don't do it so that you'll embarrass a lot of perfectly nice people half to death and almost break a kid's spirit and everything! If he'd changed his *mind,* why didn't he write to her and at least break it off like a gentleman, for goodness' sake? Before all the damage was done."

"All right, take it easy, just take it easy," her husband said. His chuckle was still there, but it was sounding a trifle strained.

"Well, I mean it! Why couldn't he write to her and just tell her, like a *man,* and prevent all this tragedy and everything?" She looked at me, abruptly. "Do you have any idea where he is, by any chance?" she demanded, with metal in her voice. "If you were *boyhood* friends, you should have some—"

"I just got into New York about two hours ago," I said nervously. Not only the Matron of Honor but her husband and Mrs. Silsburn as well were now staring at me. "So far, I haven't even had a chance to get to a phone." At that point, as I remember, I had a coughing spell. It was genuine enough, but I must say I did very little to suppress it or shorten its duration.

"You had that cough looked at, soldier?" the Lieutenant asked me when I'd come out of it.

At that instant, I had another coughing spell—a perfectly genuine one, oddly enough. I was still turned a sort of half or quarter right in my jump seat, with my body averted just enough toward the front of the car to be able to cough with all due hygienic propriety.

It seems very disorderly, but I think a paragraph ought to be wedged in right here to answer a couple of stumpers. First off, why did I go on sitting in the car? Aside from all incidental consider- ations, the car was reportedly destined to deliver its occupants to the bride's parents' apartment house. No amount of information, first- or second-hand, that I might have acquired from the prostrate, unmarried bride or from her disturbed (and, very likely, angry) parents could possibly have made up for the awkwardness of my presence in their apartment. Why, then, did I go on sitting in the car? Why didn't I get out while, say, we were stopped for a red light? And, still more salient, why had I jumped into the car in the first place? . . . There seem to me at least a dozen answers to these questions, and all of them, however dimly, valid enough. I think, though, that I can dispense with them, and just reiterate that the year was 1942, that I was twenty-three, newly drafted, newly advised in the efficacy of keeping close to the herd—and, above all, I felt lonely. One simply jumped into loaded cars, as I see it, and stayed seated in them.

To get back to the plot, I remember that while all three—the Matron of Honor, her husband, and Mrs. Silsburn—were con- junctively staring at me and watching me cough, I glanced over at the tiny elderly man in the back. He was still staring fixedly straight ahead of him. I noticed, almost with gratitude, that his feet didn't

quite touch the floor. They looked like old and valued friends of
mine.

"What's this man supposed to *do,* anyway?" the Matron of Honor
said to me when I'd emerged from my second coughing spell.

"You mean Seymour?" I said. It seemed clear, at first, from her
inflection, that she had something singularly ignominious in mind.
Then, suddenly, it struck me—and it was sheerly intuitive—that she
might well be in secret possession of a motley number of biographi-
cal facts about Seymour; that is, the low, regrettably dramatic, and
(in my opinion) basically misleading facts about him. That he'd
been Billy Black, a national radio "celebrity," for some six years
of his boyhood. Or that, for another example, he'd been a freshman
at Columbia when he'd just turned fifteen.

"Yes, *Sey*mour," said the Matron of Honor. "What'd he do before
he was in the Army?"

Again I had the same little effulgent flash of intuition that she
knew much more about him than, for some reason, she meant to
indicate. It seemed, for one thing, that she knew perfectly well that
Seymour had been teaching English before his induction—that he'd
been a professor. A *professor.* For an instant, in fact, as I looked at
her, I had a very uncomfortable notion that she might even know
that I was Seymour's brother. It wasn't a thought to dwell on. Instead, I looked her unsquarely in the eye and said, "He was a chiropodist." Then, abruptly, I faced around and looked out of my window.
The car had been motionless for some minutes, and I had just
become aware of the sound of martial drums in the distance, from
the general direction of Lexington or Third Avenue.

"It's a parade!" said Mrs. Silsburn. She had faced around, too.
We were in the upper Eighties. A policeman was stationed in
the middle of Madison Avenue and was halting all north- and southbound traffic. So far as I could tell, he was *just* halting it; that is,
not redirecting it either east or west. There were three or four cars
and a bus waiting to move southward, but our car chanced to be
the only vehicle aimed uptown. At the immediate corner, and at
what I could see of the uptown side street leading toward Fifth
Avenue, people were standing two and three deep along the curb
and on the walk, waiting, apparently, for a detail of troops, or
nurses, or Boy Scouts, or what-have-you, to leave their assembly
point at Lexington or Third Avenue and march past.

"Oh, *Lord.* Wouldn't you just know?" said the Matron of Honor.

I turned around and very nearly bumped heads with her. She was leaning forward, toward and all but into the space between Mrs. Silsburn and me. Mrs. Silsburn turned toward her, too, with a responsive, rather pained expression.

"We may be here for *weeks*," the Matron of Honor said, craning forward to see out of the driver's windshield. "I should be there *now*. I told Muriel and her mother I'd be in one of the first cars and that I'd get up to the house in about *five minutes*. Oh, God! Can't we *do* something?"

"I should be there, too," Mrs. Silsburn said, rather promptly.

"Yes, but I solemnly *prom*ised her. The apartment's gonna be loaded with all kinds of crazy aunts and uncles and absolute strangers, and I told her I'd stand *guard* with about ten bayonets and see that she got a little privacy and—" She broke off. "Oh, God. This is awful."

Mrs. Silsburn gave a small, stilted laugh. "I'm afraid I'm one of the crazy aunts," she said. Clearly, she was affronted.

The Matron of Honor looked at her. "Oh—I'm sorry. I didn't mean you," she said. She sat back in her seat. "I just meant that their apartment's so tiny, and if everybody starts pouring in by the dozens— You know what I mean."

Mrs. Silsburn said nothing, and I didn't look at her to see just how seriously she'd been affronted by the Matron of Honor's remark. I remember, though, that I was impressed, in a peculiar sense, with the Matron of Honor's tone of apology for her little slip about "crazy aunts and uncles." It had been a genuine apology, but not an embarrassed and, still better, not an obsequious one, and for a moment I had a feeling that, for all her stagy indignation and showy grit, there *was* something bayonetlike about her, something not altogether unadmirable. (I'll grant, quickly and readily, that my opinion in this instance has a very limited value. I often feel a rather excessive pull toward people who don't overapologize.) The point is, however, that right then, for the first time, a small wave of prejudice against the missing groom passed over me, a just perceptible little whitecap of censure for his unexplained absenteeism.

"Let's see if we can get a little action around here," the Matron of Honor's husband said. It was rather the voice of a man who keeps calm under fire. I felt him deploying behind me, and then, abruptly, his head craned into the limited space between Mrs. Silsburn and me. "Driver," he said peremptorily, and waited for a response. When it came with promptness, his voice became a bit more tractile, democratic: "How long do you think we'll be tied up here?"

The driver turned around. "You got me, Mac," he said. He faced front again. He was absorbed in what was going on at the intersection. A minute earlier, a small boy with a partly deflated red balloon had run out into the cleared, forbidden street. He had just been captured and was being dragged back to the curb by his father, who gave the boy two only partly openhanded punches between the shoulder blades. The act was righteously booed by the crowd.

"Did you *see* what that man did to that *child?*" Mrs. Silsburn demanded of everyone in general. No one answered her.

"What about asking that cop how long we're apt to be held up here?" the Matron of Honor's husband said to the driver. He was still leaning forward. He'd evidently not been altogether satisfied with the laconic reply to his first question. "We're all in something of a hurry, you know. Do you think you could ask him how long we're apt to be tied up here?"

Without turning around, the driver rudely shrugged his shoulders. But he turned off his ignition, and got out of the car, slamming the heavy limousine door behind him. He was an untidy, bullish-looking man in partial chauffeur's livery—a black serge suit, but no cap.

He walked slowly and very independently, not to say insolently, the few steps over to the intersection, where the ranking policeman was directing things. The two then stood talking to each other for an endless amount of time. (I heard the Matron of Honor give a groan, behind me.) Then, suddenly, the two men broke into uproarious laughter—as though they hadn't really been conversing at all but had been exchanging very short dirty jokes. Then our driver, still laughing uninfectiously, waved a fraternal hand at the cop and walked—slowly—back to the car. He got in, slammed his door shut, extracted a cigarette from a package on the ledge over the dashboard, tucked the cigarette behind his ear, and then, and then only, turned around to make his report to us. "He don't know," he said. "We gotta wait for the parade to pass by here." He gave us, collectively, an indifferent once-over. "After that we can go ahead O.K." He faced front, disengaged the cigarette from behind his ear, and lit it.

In the back of the car, the Matron of Honor sounded a voluminous little plaint of frustration and pique. And then there was silence. For the first time in several minutes, I glanced around at the tiny elderly man with the unlighted cigar. The delay didn't seem to affect him. His standard of comportment for sitting in the rear seat of cars—cars in motion, cars stationary, and even, one couldn't help imagining, cars that were driven off bridges into rivers—seemed to be fixed. It was wonderfully simple. You just sat very erect, maintaining a clearance of four or five inches between your top hat and the roof, and you stared ferociously ahead at the windshield. If Death—who was out there all the time, possibly sitting on the hood—if Death stepped miraculously through the glass and came in after you, in all probability you just got up and went along with him, ferociously but quietly. Chances were, you could take your cigar with you, if it was a clear Havana.

"What are we going to do? Just *sit* here?" the Matron of Honor said. "I'm so hot I could die." And Mrs. Silsburn and I turned around just in time to see her look at her husband directly for the first time since they'd got into the car. "Can't you move over just a tiny little bit?" she said to him. "I'm so squashed in here I can hardly breathe."

The Lieutenant, chuckling, opened his hands expressively. "I'm practically sitting on the fender now, Bunny," he said.

The Matron of Honor then looked over, with mixed curiosity and disapproval, at her other seatmate, who, as though unconsciously dedicated to cheering me up, was occupying far more space than he needed. There was a good two inches between his right hip and the base of the outside armrest. The Matron of Honor undoubtedly noticed it, too, but, for all her metal, she didn't quite have what it would have taken to speak up to that formidable-looking little personage. She turned back to her husband. "Can you reach your cigarettes?" she said irritably. "I'll never get mine out, the way we're packed in here." With the words "packed in," she turned her head again to shoot a brief, all-implicit look at the tiny guilty party who had usurped the space she thought ought rightfully to be hers. He remained sublimely out of touch. He went on glaring straight ahead of him, toward the driver's windshield. The Matron of Honor looked at Mrs. Silsburn, and raised her eyebrows expressively. Mrs. Silsburn responded with a countenance full of understanding and sympathy. The Lieutenant, meanwhile, had shifted his weight over to his left, or window-side, buttock, and from the right-hand pocket of his officer's pinks had taken out a package of cigarettes and a folder of matches. His wife picked out

a cigarette, and waited for a light, which was immediately forthcoming. Mrs. Silsburn and I watched the lighting of the cigarette
as though it were a moderately bewitching novelty.

"Oh, pardon *me*," the Lieutenant suddenly said, and extended
his cigarette pack to Mrs. Silsburn.

"No, thank you. I don't smoke," Mrs. Silsburn said quickly—
almost with regret.

"Soldier?" the Lieutenant said, extending the pack to me, after
the most imperceptible of hesitations. In all truth, I rather liked
him for putting through the offer, for the small victory of common
courtesy over caste, but I declined the cigarette.

"May I see your matches?" Mrs. Silsburn said, in an exceedingly
diffident, almost little-girlish voice.

"These?" said the Lieutenant. He handed his folder of matches
readily over to Mrs. Silsburn.

While I looked on with an expression of absorption, Mrs. Silsburn examined the match folder. On its outside cover, in gold
letters on a crimson background, were printed the words "These
Matches Were Stolen from Bob and Edie Burwick's House." "*Darling*," Mrs. Silsburn said, shaking her head. "Really darling." I
tried to show by my expression that I perhaps couldn't read the
inscription without eyeglasses; I squinted, neutrally. Mrs. Silsburn
seemed reluctant to hand the folder back to its owner. When she
had, and the Lieutenant had replaced the folder in the breast
pocket of his tunic, she said, "I don't think I've ever seen that
before." Turned almost completely around, now, in her jump seat,
she sat gazing rather fondly at the Lieutenant's breast pocket.

"We had a whole bunch of them made up last year," the Lieutenant said. "Be amazed, actually, how it keeps you from running
out of matches."

The Matron of Honor turned to him—or, rather, on him. "We
didn't do it for *that*," she said. She gave Mrs. Silsburn a you-know-
how-men-are look, and said to her, "I don't know. I just thought
it was cute. Corny, but sort of cute. You know."

"It's darling. I don't think I've ever—"

"Actually, it isn't original or anything like that. Everybody's
got them now," the Matron of Honor said. "Where I got the idea
originally, as a matter of fact, was from Muriel's mother and dad.
They always had them around the house." She inhaled deeply on
her cigarette, and as she went on talking, she released the smoke in
little syllabic drafts. "*Golly*, they're terrific people. That's what

kills me about this whole business. I mean why doesn't something like this happen to all the stinkers in the world, instead of the nice ones? That's what I can't understand." She looked to Mrs. Silsburn for an answer.

Mrs. Silsburn smiled a smile that was at once worldly, wan, and enigmatic—the smile, as I remember, of a sort of jump-seat Mona Lisa. "I've often wondered," she mused softly. She then mentioned, rather ambiguously, "Muriel's mother is my late husband's baby sister, you know."

"Oh!" the Matron of Honor said with interest. "Well, then, *you know.*" She reached out an extraordinarily long left arm, and flicked her cigarette ashes into the ashtray near her husband's window. "I honestly think she's one of the few really brilliant people I've met in my entire life. I mean she's read just about everything that's ever been printed. My gosh, if I'd read just about one-tenth of what that woman's read and for*got*ten, I'd be happy. I mean she's *taught,* she's worked on a *news*paper, she designs her own *clothes,* she does every single bit of her own *house*work. Her cooking's out of this *world.* Golly! I honestly think she's the most wonder—"

"Did she approve of the marriage?" Mrs. Silsburn interrupted. "I mean the reason I ask, I've been in Detroit for weeks and weeks. My sister-in-law suddenly passed away, and I've—"

"She's too nice to say," the Matron of Honor said flatly. She shook her head. "I mean she's too—you know—dis*cr*eet and all." She reflected. "As a matter of fact, this morning's about the only time I ever heard her say boo on the subject, really. And then it was only just because she was so upset about poor Muriel." She reached out an arm and tipped her cigarette ashes again.

"What'd she say this morning?" Mrs. Silsburn asked avidly.

The Matron of Honor seemed to reflect for a moment. "Well, nothing very much, really," she said. "I mean nothing small or really de*rog*atory or anything like that. All she said, really, was that this Seymour, in her opinion, was a latent homosexual and that he was basically afraid of marriage. I mean she didn't say it nasty or anything. She just said it—you know—intelligently. I mean she was psychoanalyzed herself for years and years." The Matron of Honor looked at Mrs. Silsburn. "That's no *secret* or anything. I mean Mrs. Fedder'll tell you that herself, so I'm not giving away any secret or anything."

"I know that," Mrs. Silsburn said quickly. "She's the last person in the—"

"I mean the point is," the Matron of Honor said, "she isn't the kind of person that comes right out and says something like that unless she knows what she's talking about. And she never, never would've said it in the *first* place if poor Muriel hadn't been so—you know—so prostrate and everything." She shook her head grimly. "Golly, you should've seen that poor kid."

I should, no doubt, break in here to describe my general reaction to the main import of what the Matron of Honor was saying. I'd just as soon let it go, though, for the moment, if the reader will bear with me.

"What else did she say?" Mrs. Silsburn asked. "Rhea, I mean. Did she say anything else?" I didn't look at her—I couldn't take my eyes off the Matron of Honor's face—but I had a passing, wild impression that Mrs. Silsburn was all but sitting in the main speaker's lap.

"No. Not really. Hardly anything." The Matron of Honor, reflecting, shook her head. "I mean, as I say, she wouldn't have said *anything*—with people standing around and all—if poor Muriel hadn't been so crazy upset." She flicked her cigarette ashes again. "About the only other thing she said was that this Seymour was a really schizoid personality and that, if you really looked at it the right way, it was really better for Muriel that things turned out the way they did. Which makes sense to *me*, but I'm not so sure it does to Muriel. He's got her so *buffaloed* that she doesn't know whether she's coming or going. That's what makes me so—"

She was interrupted at that point. By me. As I remember, my voice was unsteady, as it invariably is when I'm vastly upset.

"What brought Mrs. Fedder to the conclusion that Seymour is a latent homosexual and a schizoid personality?"

All eyes—all searchlights, it seemed—the Matron of Honor's, Mrs. Silsburn's, even the Lieutenant's, were abruptly trained on me. "What?" the Matron of Honor said to me, sharply, faintly hostilely. And again I had a passing, abrasive notion that she knew I was Seymour's brother.

"What makes Mrs. Fedder think that Seymour's a latent homosexual and schizoid personality?"

The Matron of Honor stared at me, then gave an eloquent snort. She turned and appealed to Mrs. Silsburn with a maximum of irony. "Would you say that somebody's *norm*al that pulled a stunt like the one today?" She raised her eyebrows, and waited. "Would you?" she asked quietly-quietly. "Be honest. I'm just asking. For this gentleman's benefit."

Mrs. Silsburn's answer was gentleness itself, fairness itself. "No, I certainly would not," she said.

I had a sudden, violent impulse to jump out of the car and break into a sprint, in any direction at all. As I remember, though, I was still in my jump seat when the Matron of Honor addressed me again. "Look," she said, in the spuriously patient tone of voice that a teacher might take with a child who is not only retarded but whose nose is forever running unattractively. "I don't know how much you know about people. But what man in his right mind, the night before he's supposed to get married, keeps his fiancée up all night blabbing to her all about how he's too *happy* to get married and that she'll have to post*pone* the wedding till he feels *steadier* or he won't be able to come to it? *Then,* when his fiancée explains to him like a *child* that everything's been arranged and planned out for months, and that her father's gone to incredible expense and trouble and all to have a reception and everything like that, and that her relatives and friends are coming from all over the *country—then,* after she explains all that, he says to her he's terribly sorry but he can't get married till he feels less *happy* or some crazy thing! Use your head, now, if you don't mind. Does that sound like somebody *normal?* Does that sound like somebody in their right mind?" Her voice was now shrill. "Or does that sound like somebody that should be stuck in some booby hatch?" She looked at me very severely, and when I didn't immediately speak up in either defense or surrender, she sat heavily back in her seat, and said to her husband, "Give me another cigarette, please. This thing's gonna burn me." She handed him her burning stub, and he extinguished it for her. He then took out his cigarette package again. "You light it," she said. "I haven't got the energy."

Mrs. Silsburn cleared her throat. "It sounds to me," she said, "like a blessing in disguise that everything's turned—"

"I ask *you,*" the Matron of Honor said to her with a fresh impetus, at the same time accepting a freshly lighted cigarette from her husband. "Does that sound like a normal person—a normal *man*—to you? Or does it sound like somebody that's either never *grown up* or is just an absolute raving maniac of some crazy kind?"

"Goodness. I don't know what to say, really. It just sounds to me like a blessing in disguise that every—"

The Matron of Honor sat forward suddenly, alertly, exhaling smoke through her nostrils. "All right, never mind that, drop that for a minute—I don't need that," she said. She was addressing Mrs. Silsburn, but in actuality she was addressing me through Mrs. Silsburn's face, so to speak. "Did you ever see —— ——, in the movies?" she demanded.

The name she mentioned was the professional name of a then fairly well-known—and now, in 1955, a quite famous—actress-singer.

"Yes," said Mrs. Silsburn quickly and interestedly, and waited.

The Matron of Honor nodded. "All right," she said. "Did you ever notice, by any chance, how she smiles sort of crooked? Only on one side of her face, sort of? It's very noticeable if you—"

"*Yes*—yes, I have!" Mrs. Silsburn said.

The Matron of Honor dragged on her cigarette, and glanced over —just perceptibly—at me. "Well, that happens to be a partial par*aly*sis of some kind," she said, exhaling a little gust of smoke with each word. "And do you know how she got it? This *normal* Seymour person apparently hit her and she had nine stitches taken in her face." She reached over (in lieu, possibly, of a better stage direction) and flicked her ashes again.

"May I ask where you heard that?" I said. My lips were quivering slightly, like two fools.

"You may," she said, looking at Mrs. Silsburn instead of me. "Muriel's mother happened to mention it about two hours ago, while Muriel was sobbing her eyes out." She looked at me. "Does that answer your question?" She suddenly shifted her bouquet of gardenias from her right to her left hand. It was the nearest thing to a fairly commonplace nervous gesture that I'd seen her make. "Just for your information, incidentally," she said, looking at me, "do you know who I think you are? I think you're this Seymour's brother." She waited, very briefly, and, when I didn't say anything: "You *look* like him, from his crazy picture, and I happen to know that he was supposed to come to the wedding. His sister or somebody told Muriel." Her look was fixed unwaveringly on my face. "Are you?" she asked bluntly.

My voice must have sounded a trifle rented when I answered. "Yes," I said. My face was burning. In a way, though, I felt an infinitely less furry sense of self-identification than I had since I'd got off the train earlier in the afternoon.

"I *knew* you were," the Matron of Honor said. "I'm not *stupid*, you know. I knew who you were the minute you got in this car."

She turned to her husband. "Didn't I say he was his brother the minute he got in this car? Didn't I?"

The Lieutenant altered his sitting position a trifle. "Well, you said he probably—yes, you did," he said. "You did. Yes."

One didn't have to look over at Mrs. Silsburn to perceive how attentively she had taken in this latest development. I glanced past and behind her, furtively, at the fifth passenger—the tiny elderly man—to see if his insularity was still intact. It was. No one's indifference has ever been such a comfort to me.

The Matron of Honor came back to me. "For your information, I also know that your brother's no chiropodist. So don't be so funny. I happen to know he was Billy Black on 'It's a Wise Child' for about fifty years or something."

Mrs. Silsburn abruptly took a more active part in the conversation. "The radio program?" she inquired, and I felt her looking at me with a fresh, keener interest.

The Matron of Honor didn't answer her. "Which one were you?" she said to me. "Georgie Black?" The mixture of rudeness and curiosity in her voice was interesting, if not quite disarming.

"Georgie Black was my brother Walt," I said, answering only her second question.

She turned to Mrs. Silsburn. "It's supposed to be some kind of a secret or something, but this man and his brother Seymour were on this radio program under fake names or something. The Black children."

"Take it easy, honey, take it easy," the Lieutenant suggested, rather nervously.

His wife turned to him. "I will not take it easy," she said—and again, contrary to my every conscious inclination, I felt a little pinch of something close to admiration for her metal, solid brass or no. "His brother's supposed to be so intelligent, for heaven's sake," she said. "In college when he was fourteen or something, and all like that. If what he did to that kid today is intelligent, then I'm Mahatma Gandhi! I don't care. It just makes me sick!"

Just then, I felt a minute extra added discomfort. Someone was very closely examining the left, or weaker, side of my face. It was Mrs. Silsburn. She started a bit as I turned abruptly toward her. "May I ask if you were Buddy Black?" she said, and a certain deferential note in her voice rather made me think, for a fractional moment, that she was about to present me with a fountain pen and a small, morocco-bound autograph album. The passing thought made me distinctly uneasy—considering, if nothing else, the fact that it was 1942 and some nine or ten years past my commercial bloom. "The reason I ask," she said, "my husband used to listen to that program without fail every single—"

"If you're interested," the Matron of Honor interrupted her, looking at me, "that was the one program on the air I always absolutely loathed. I loathe precocious children. If I ever had a child that—"

The end of her sentence was lost to us. She was interrupted, suddenly and unequivocally, by the most piercing, most deafening, most *impure* E-flat blast I've ever heard. All of us in the car, I'm sure, literally jumped. At that moment, a drum-and-bugle corps, composed of what seemed to be a hundred or more tone-deaf Sea Scouts, was passing. With what seemed to be almost delinquent abandon, the boys had just rammed into the sides of "The Stars and Stripes Forever." Mrs. Silsburn, very sensibly, clapped her hands over her ears.

For an eternity of seconds, it seemed, the din was all but incredible. Only the Matron of Honor's voice could have risen above it— or, for that matter, would have attempted to. When it did, one might have thought she was addressing us, obviously at the top of her voice, from some great distance away, somewhere, possibly, in the vicinity of the bleachers of Yankee Stadium.

"I can't take this!" she said. "Let's get out of here and find some place to *phone* from! I've got to phone Muriel and say we're delayed! She'll be crazy!"

With the advent of the local Armageddon, Mrs. Silsburn and I had faced front to see it in. We now turned around again in our jump seats to face the Leader. And, possibly, our deliverer.

"There's a Schrafft's on Seventy-ninth Street!" she bellowed at Mrs. Silsburn. "Let's go have a *soda*, and I can *phone* from there! It'll at least be air-conditioned!"

Mrs. Silsburn nodded enthusiastically, and pantomimed "Yes!" with her mouth.

"You come, too!" the Matron of Honor shouted at me.

With *very* peculiar spontaneity, I remember, I shouted back to her the altogether extravagant word "Fine!" (It isn't easy, to this day, to account for the Matron of Honor's having included me in her invitation to quit the ship. It may simply have been inspired by a born leader's natural sense of orderliness. She may have had some sort of remote but compulsive urge to make her landing party complete. . . . My singularly immediate acceptance of the invitation strikes me as much more easily explainable. I prefer to think it was a basically religious impulse. In certain Zen monasteries, it's a cardinal rule, if not the only serious enforced discipline, that when one monk calls out "Hi!" to another monk, the latter must call back "Hi!" without thinking.)

The Matron of Honor then turned and, for the first time, directly addressed the tiny elderly man beside her. To my undying gratification, he was still glaring straight ahead of him, as though his own private scenery hadn't changed an iota. His unlighted clear-Havana cigar was still clenched between two fingers. What with his apparent unmindfulness of the terrible din the passing drum-and-bugle corps was making, and, possibly, from a grim tenet that all old men over eighty must be either stone-deaf or very hard of hearing, the Matron of Honor brought her lips to within an inch or two of his left ear. "We're going to get out of the car!" she shouted at him—almost into him. "We're going to find a place to *phone* from, and maybe have some refreshment! Do you want to come with us?"

The elderly man's immediate reaction was just short of glorious. He looked first at the Matron of Honor, then at the rest of us, and then grinned. It was a grin that was no less resplendent for the fact that it made no sense whatever. Nor for the fact that his teeth were obviously, beautifully, transcendently false. He looked at the Matron of Honor inquisitively for just an instant, his grin wonderfully intact. Or, rather, he looked *to* her—as if, I thought, he believed the Matron of Honor, or one of us, had lovely plans to pass a picnic basket his way.

"I don't think he heard you, honey!" the Lieutenant shouted.

The Matron of Honor nodded, and once again brought the megaphone of her mouth up close to the old man's ear. With really praiseworthy volume, she repeated her invitation to the old man to join us in quitting the car. Once again, at face value, the old man seemed more than amenable to any suggestion in the world—possibly not short of trotting over and having a dip in the East River. But again, too, one had an uneasy conviction that he hadn't heard a word that was said to him. Abruptly, he proved that this was true. With an enormous grin at all of us collectively, he raised his cigar hand and, with one finger, significantly tapped first his mouth, then his ear. The gesture, as *he* made it, seemed related to a perfectly first-class joke of some kind that he fully meant to share with all of us.

At that moment, Mrs. Silsburn, beside me, gave a visible little sign—almost a jump—of comprehension. She touched the Matron of Honor's pink satin arm, and shouted, "I know who he is! He's deaf and dumb—he's a deaf-mute! He's Muriel's father's uncle!"

The Matron of Honor's lips formed the word "Oh!" She swung around in her seat, toward her husband. "You got a pencil and paper?" she bellowed to him.

I touched her arm and shouted that I had. Hastily—almost, in fact, for some reason, as though time were about to run out on all of us—I took out of my inside tunic pocket a small pad and a pencil stub that I'd recently acquisitioned from a desk drawer of my company Orderly Room at Fort Benning.

Somewhat overly legibly, I wrote on a sheet of paper, "We're held up indefinitely by the parade. We're going to find a phone and have a cold drink somewhere. Will you join us?" I folded the paper once, then handed it to the Matron of Honor, who opened it, read it, and then handed it to the tiny old man. He read it, grinning, and then looked at me and wagged his head up and down several times vehemently. I thought for an instant that this was the full and perfectly eloquent extent of his reply, but he suddenly motioned to me with his hand, and I gathered that he wanted me to pass him my pad and pencil. I did so—without looking over at the Matron of Honor, from whom great waves of impatience were rising. The old man adjusted the pad and pencil on his lap with the greatest care, then sat for a moment, pencil poised, in obvious concentration, his grin diminished only a very trifle. Then the pencil began, very unsteadily, to move. An "i" was dotted. And then both pad and pencil were returned personally to me, with a marvellously cordial extra added wag of the head. He had written, in letters that had not quite jelled yet, the single word "Delighted." The Matron of Honor, reading over my shoulder, gave a sound faintly like a snort, but I quickly looked over at the great writer and tried to show by my expression that all of us in the car knew a poem when we saw one, and were grateful.

One by one, then, from both doors, we all got out of the car—abandoned ship, as it were, in the middle of Madison Avenue, in a sea of hot, gummy macadam. The Lieutenant lingered behind a moment to inform the driver of our mutiny. As I remember very well, the drum-and-bugle corps was still endlessly passing, and the din hadn't abated a bit.

The Matron of Honor and Mrs. Silsburn led the way to Schrafft's. They walked as a twosome—almost as advance scouts—south on the east side of Madison Avenue. When he'd finished briefing the driver, the Lieutenant caught up with them. Or almost up with them. He fell a little behind them, in order to take out his wallet in privacy and see, apparently, how much money he had with him.

The bride's father's uncle and I brought up the rear. Whether he had intuited that I was his friend or simply because I was the owner of a pad and pencil, he had rather more scrambled than gravitated to a walking position beside me. The very top of his beautiful silk hat didn't quite come up as high as my shoulder. I set a comparatively slow gait for us, in deference to the length of his legs. At the end of a block or so, we were quite a good distance behind the others. I don't think it troubled either of us. Occasionally, I remember, as we walked along, my friend and I looked up and down, respectively, at each other and exchanged idiotic expressions of pleasure at sharing one another's company.

When my companion and I reached the revolving door of Schrafft's Seventy-ninth Street, the Matron of Honor, her husband, and Mrs. Silsburn had all been standing there for some minutes. They were waiting, I thought, as a rather forbiddingly integrated party of three. They had been talking, but they stopped when our motley twosome approached. In the car, just a couple of minutes earlier, when the drum-and-bugle corps blasted by, a common discomfort, almost a common anguish, had lent our small group a semblance of alliance—of the sort that can be temporarily conferred on Cook's tourists caught in a very heavy rainstorm at Pompeii. All too clearly now, as the tiny old man and I reached the revolving door of Schrafft's, the storm was over. The Matron of Honor and I exchanged expressions of recognition, not of greeting. "It's closed for alterations," she stated coldly, looking at me. Unofficially but unmistakably, she was appointing me odd-man-out again, and at that moment, for no reason worth going into, I felt a sense of isolation and loneliness more overwhelming than I'd felt all day. Somewhat simultaneously, it's worth noting, my cough reactivated itself. I pulled my handkerchief out of my hip pocket. The Matron of Honor turned to Mrs. Silsburn and her husband. "There's a Longchamps around here *some*where," she said, "but I don't know where."

"I don't either," Mrs. Silsburn said. She seemed very close to tears. At both her forehead and her upper lip, perspiration had seeped through even her heavy pancake makeup. A black patent-leather handbag was under her left arm. She held it as though it were a favorite doll, and she herself an experimentally rouged and powdered, and very unhappy, runaway child.

"We're not gonna be able to get a cab for love or money," the Lieutenant said pessimistically. He was looking the worse for wear, too. His "hot pilot's" cap appeared almost cruelly incongruous on his pale, dripping, deeply unintrepid-looking face, and I remember having an impulse to whisk it off his head, or at least to straighten it somewhat, to adjust it into a less cocked position—the same impulse, in general motive, that one might feel at a children's party, where there is invariably one small, exceedingly homely child wearing a paper hat that crushes down one or both ears.

"Oh, God, what a day!" the Matron of Honor said for all of us. Her circlet of artificial flowers was somewhat askew, and she was thoroughly damp, but, I thought, the only thing really destructible about her was her remotest appendage, so to speak—her gardenia bouquet. She was still holding it, however absent-mindedly, in her hand. It obviously hadn't stood the gaff. "What'll we *do?*" she asked, rather frantically, for her. "We can't *walk* there. They live practically in *River*dale. Does anybody have any bright ideas?" She looked first at Mrs. Silsburn, then at her husband—and then, in desperation possibly, at me.

"I have an apartment near here," I said suddenly and nervously. "It's just down the block, as a matter of fact." I have a feeling that I gave out this information a trifle too loudly. I may even have shouted it, for all I know. "It belongs to my brother and me. My sister's using it while we're in the Army, but she's not there now. She's in the Waves, and she's off on some trip." I looked at the Matron of Honor—or at some point just over her head. "You can at least phone from there, if you like," I said. "And the apartment's air-conditioned. We might all cool off for a minute and get our breaths."

When the first shock of the invitation had passed over, the Matron of Honor, Mrs. Silsburn, and the Lieutenant went into a sort of consultation, of eyes only, but there was no visible sign that any kind of verdict was forthcoming. The Matron of Honor was the first to take any kind of action. She'd been looking—in vain—at the other two for an opinion on the subject. She turned back to me and said, "Did you say you had a phone?"

"Yes. Unless my sister's had it disconnected for some reason, and I can't see why she would have."

"How do we know your *brother* won't be there?" the Matron of Honor said.

It was a small consideration that hadn't entered my overheated head. "I don't think he will be," I said. "He *may* be—it's his apartment, too—but I don't think he will. I really don't."

The Matron of Honor stared at me, openly, for a moment—and not really rudely, for a change, unless children's stares are rude. Then she turned back to her husband and Mrs. Silsburn, and said, "We might as well. At least we can phone." They nodded in agreement. Mrs. Silsburn, in fact, went so far as to remember her code of etiquette covering invitations given in front of Schrafft's. Through her sun-baked pancake makeup, a semblance of an Emily Post smile peeped out at me. It was very welcome, as I remember. "C'mon, then, let's get out of this *sun*," our leader said. "What'll I do with *this?*" She didn't wait for an answer. She stepped over to the curb and unsentimentally disengaged herself from her wilted gardenia bouquet. "O.K., lead on, Macduff," she said to me. "We'll follow you. And all I have to say is he'd better *not* be there when we get there, or I'll kill the bastard." She looked at Mrs. Silsburn. "Excuse my language—but I mean it."

As directed, I took the lead, almost happily. An instant later, a silk hat materialized in the air beside me, considerably down and at the left, and my special, only technically unassigned cohort grinned up at me—for a moment, I rather thought he was going to slip his hand into mine.

My three guests and my one friend remained outside in the hall while I briefly cased the apartment.

The windows were all closed, the two air-conditioners had been turned to "Shut," and the first breath one took was rather like inhaling deeply in someone's ancient raccoon-coat pocket. The only sound in the whole apartment was the somewhat trembling purr of the aged refrigerator Seymour and I had acquired second-hand. My sister Boo Boo, in her girlish, naval way, had left it turned on. There were, in fact, throughout the apartment, any number of little untidy signs that a seafaring lady had taken over the place. A handsome, small-size, ensign's navy-blue jacket was flung, lining down, across the couch. A box of Louis Sherry candies—half empty, and with the unconsumed candies all more or less experimentally squeezed—was open on the coffee table, in front of the couch. A framed photograph of a very resolute-looking young man I'd never seen before stood on the desk. And all the ashtrays in sight were in full blossom with crumpled facial tissues and lipsticked cigarette ends. I didn't go into the kitchen, the bedroom, or the bathroom, except to open the doors and take a quick look to see if Seymour was standing upright anywhere. For one reason, I felt enervated and lazy. For another, I was kept pretty busy raising blinds, turning on air-conditioners, emptying loaded ashtrays. Besides, the other members of the party barged in on me almost immediately. "It's hotter in here than it is on the street," the Matron of Honor said, by way of greeting, as she strode in.

"I'll be with you in just a minute," I said. "I can't seem to get this air-conditioner to work." The "On" button seemed to be stuck, in fact, and I was busily tinkering with it.

While I worked on the air-conditioner switch—with my hat still on my head, I remember—the others circulated rather suspiciously around the room. I watched them out of the corner of one eye. The Lieutenant went over to the desk and stood looking up at the three or four square feet of wall directly above it, where my brother and I, for defiantly sentimental reasons, had tacked up a number of glossy eight-by-ten photographs. Mrs. Silsburn sat down—inevitably, I thought—in the one chair in the room that my deceased Boston bull used to enjoy sleeping in; its arms, upholstered in dirty corduroy, had been thoroughly slavered and chewed on in the course of many a nightmare. The bride's father's uncle—my great friend— seemed to have disappeared completely. The Matron of Honor, too, seemed suddenly to be somewhere else. "I'll get you all something to drink in just a second," I said uneasily, still trying to force the switch button on the air-conditioner.

"I could use something cold to drink," said a very familiar voice. I turned completely around and saw that she had stretched herself out on the couch, which accounted for her noticeable vertical disappearance. "I'll use your phone in just a second," she advised me. "I couldn't open my mouth anyway to talk on the phone, in this condition, I'm so parched. My *tongue's* so dry."

The air-conditioner abruptly whirred into operation, and I came over to the middle of the room, into the space between the couch and the chair where Mrs. Silsburn was sitting. "I don't know what

there is to drink," I said. "I haven't looked in the refrigerator, but
I imagine—"

"Bring *anything*," the eternal spokeswoman interrupted from the
couch. "Just make it wet. And *cold*." The heels of her shoes were
resting on the sleeve of my sister's jacket. Her hands were folded
across her chest. A pillow was bunched up under her head. "Put ice
in it, if you have any," she said, and closed her eyes. I looked down
at her for a brief but murderous instant, then bent over and, as
tactfully as possible, eased Boo Boo's jacket out from under her
feet. I started to leave the room and go about my chores as host,
but just as I took a step, the Lieutenant spoke up from over at the
desk.

"Whereja get all these pictures?" he said.

I went directly over to him. I was still wearing my visored, over-
size garrison cap. It hadn't occurred to me to take it off. I stood
beside him at the desk, and yet a trifle behind him, and looked up
at the photographs on the wall. I said they were mostly old pictures
of the children who had been on "It's a Wise Child" in the days
when Seymour and I had been on the show.

The Lieutenant turned to me. "What was it?" he said. "I never
heard it. One of those kids' quiz shows? Questions and answers,
and like that?" Unmistakably, a soupçon of Army rank had slipped
unnoisily but insidiously into his voice. He also seemed to be looking at my hat.

I took off my hat, and said, "No, not exactly." A certain amount
of low family pride was suddenly evoked. "It *was* before my brother
Seymour was on it. And it more or less got that way again after he
went off the program. But he changed the whole format, really. He
turned the program into a kind of children's round-table discussion."

The Lieutenant looked at me with, I thought, somewhat excessive
interest. "Were you on it, too?" he said.

"Yes."

The Matron of Honor spoke up from the other side of the room,
from the invisible, dusty recesses of the couch. "I'd like to see a kid
of *mine* get on one of those crazy programs," she said. "Or *act*. Any
of those things. I'd die, in fact, before I'd let any child of mine
turn themself into a little exhibitionist before the public. It warps
their whole entire lives. The pub*lic*ity and all, if nothing else—ask
any psychiatrist. I mean how can you have any kind of a normal

*child*hood or anything?" Her head, crowned in a now lopsided circlet of flowers, suddenly popped into view. As though disembodied, it perched on the catwalk of the back of the couch, facing the Lieutenant and me. "That's probably what's the matter with that brother of yours," the Head said. "I mean you lead an absolutely freakish life like that when you're a kid, and so naturally you never learn to grow up. You never learn to relate to normal people or anything. That's exactly what Mrs. Fedder was saying in that crazy bedroom a couple of hours ago. But exactly. Your brother's never learned to relate to anybody. All he can do, apparently, is go around giving people a bunch of stitches in their faces. He's absolutely unfit for marriage, or *any*thing halfway normal, for goodness' sake. As a matter of fact, that's *exactly* what Mrs. Fedder said." The Head then turned just enough to glare over at the Lieutenant. "Am I right, Bob? Did she or didn't she say that? Tell the truth."

The next voice to speak up was not the Lieutenant's but mine. My mouth was dry, and my groin felt damp. I said I didn't give a good God damn what Mrs. Fedder had to say on the subject of Seymour. Or, for that matter, what any professional dilettante or amateur bitch had to say. I said that from the time Seymour was ten years old, every *summa-cum-laude* Thinker and intellectual men's-room attendant in the country had been having a go at him. I said it might be different if Seymour had just been some nasty little high-I.Q. showoff. I said he hadn't ever been an exhibitionist. He went down to the broadcast every Wednesday night as though he were going to his own funeral. He didn't even talk to you, for God's sake, the whole way down on the bus or subway. I said that not one God-damn person, of all the patronizing, fourth-rate critics and column writers, had ever seen him for what he really was. A poet, for God's sake. And I meant a *poet*. If he never wrote a line of poetry, he could still flash what he had at you with the back of his ear if he wanted to.

I stopped right there, thank God. My heart was banging away something terrible, and, like most hypochondriacs, I had a little passing, intimidating notion that such speeches were the stuff that heart attacks are made of. To this day, I have no idea at all how my guests reacted to my outbreak, the polluted little stream of invective I'd loosed on them. The first real exterior detail that I was aware of was the universally familiar sound of plumbing. It came from another part of the apartment. I looked around the room suddenly, between and through and past the immediate faces of my guests. "Where's the old man?" I asked. "The little old man?" Butter wouldn't have melted in my mouth.

Oddly enough, when an answer came, it came from the Lieutenant, not the Matron of Honor. "I believe he's in the bathroom," he said. The statement was issued with a special forthrightness, proclaiming the speaker to be one of those who don't mince everyday hygienic facts.

"Oh," I said. I looked rather absently around the room again. Whether or not I deliberately avoided meeting the Matron of Honor's terrible eye, I don't remember, or don't care to remember. I spotted the bride's father's uncle's silk hat on the seat of a straight chair, across the room. I had an impulse to say hello, aloud, to it. "I'll get some cold drinks," I said. "I'll just be a minute."

"May I use your phone?" the Matron of Honor suddenly said to me as I passed by the couch. She swung her feet to the floor.

"Yes—yes, of course," I said. I looked at Mrs. Silsburn and the Lieutenant. "I thought I'd make some Tom Collinses, if there are any lemons or limes. Will that be all right?"

The Lieutenant's answer startled me by its sudden conviviality. "Bring 'em on," he said, and rubbed his hands together, like a hearty drinking man.

Mrs. Silsburn left off studying the photographs over the desk to advise me, "If you're going to make Tom Collinses—please, just a teentsy, teentsy little bit of gin in mine. Almost none at all, if it isn't too much trouble." She was beginning to look a bit recuperated, even in just the short time since we'd got off the street. Perhaps, for one reason, because she was standing within a few feet of the air-conditioner I'd turned on and some cool air was coming her way. I said I'd look out for her drink, and then left her among the minor radio "celebrities" of the early thirties and late twenties, the many passé little faces of Seymour's and my boyhood. The Lieutenant seemed well able to shift for himself in my absence, too; he was already moving, hands joined behind his back, like a lone connoisseur, toward the bookshelves. The Matron of Honor followed me out of the room, yawning as she did—a cavernous, audible yawn that she made no effort to suppress or obstruct from view.

As the Matron of Honor followed me toward the bedroom, where the phone was, the bride's father's uncle came toward us from the far end of the hall. His face was in the ferocious repose

that had fooled me during most of the car ride, but as he came
closer to us in the hall, the mask reversed itself; he pantomimed
to us both the very highest salutations and greetings, and I found
myself grinning and nodding immoderately in return. His sparse
white hair looked freshly combed—almost freshly washed, as though
he might have discovered a tiny barbershop cached away at the
other end of the apartment. When he'd passed us, I felt a com-
pulsion to look back over my shoulder, and when I did, he waved
to me, vigorously—a great, *bon-voyage,* come-back-soon wave. It
picked me up no end. "What is he? Crazy?" the Matron of Honor
said. I said I hoped so, and opened the door of the bedroom.

She sat down heavily on one of the twin beds—Seymour's, as a
matter of fact. The phone was on the night table within easy reach.
I said I'd bring her a drink right away. "Don't bother—I'll be right
out," she said. "Just close the door, if you don't mind. . . . I don't
mean it that way, but I can never talk on the phone unless the
door's closed." I told her I was the exact same way, and started to
leave. But just as I'd turned to come out of the space between the
two beds, I noticed a small collapsible canvas valise over on the
window seat. At first glance, I thought it was mine, miraculously
arrived at the apartment, all the way from Penn Station, under its
own steam. My second thought was that it must be Boo Boo's. I
walked over to it. It was unzipped, and just one look at the top
layer of its contents told me who the real owner was. With another,
more inclusive look, I saw something lying on top of two laundered
suntan shirts that I thought ought not to be left alone in the room
with the Matron of Honor. I picked it out of the bag, slipped it
under one arm, waved fraternally to the Matron of Honor, who
had already inserted a finger into the first hole of the number she
intended to dial, and was waiting for me to clear out, and then I
closed the door behind me.

I stood for some little time outside the bedroom, in the gracious
solitude of the hall, wondering what to do with Seymour's diary,
which, I ought to rush to say, was the object I'd picked out of the
top of the canvas bag. My first constructive thought was to hide it
till my guests had left. It seemed to me a good idea to take it into
the bathroom and drop it into the laundry hamper. However, on a
second and much more involved train of thought, I decided to take
it into the bathroom and read parts of it and *then* drop it into the
laundry hamper.

It was a day, God knows, not only of rampant signs and symbols but of wildly extensive communication via the written word. If you jumped into crowded cars, Fate took circuitous pains, before you did any jumping, that you had a pad and pencil with you, just in case one of your fellow-passengers was a deaf-mute. If you slipped into bathrooms, you did well to look up to see if there were any little messages, faintly apocalyptical or otherwise, posted high over the washbowl.

For years, among the seven children in our one-bathroom family, it was our perhaps cloying but serviceable custom to leave messages for one another on the medicine-cabinet mirror, using a moist sliver of soap to write with. The general theme of our messages usually ran to excessively strong admonitions and, not infrequently, undisguised threats. "Boo Boo, pick up your washcloth when you're done with it. Don't leave it on the floor. Love, Seymour." "Walt, your turn to take Z. and F. to the park. I did it yesterday. Guess who." "Wednesday is their anniversary. Don't go to movies or hang around studio after broadcast or pay forfeit. This means you, too, Buddy." "Mother said Zooey nearly ate the Feenolax. Don't leave slightly poisonous objects on the sink that he can reach and eat." These, of course, are samples straight out of our childhood, but years later, when, in the name of independence or what-have-you, Seymour and I branched out and took an apartment of our own, he and I had not more than nominally departed from the old family custom. That is, we didn't just throw away our old soap fragments.

When I'd checked into the bathroom with Seymour's diary under my arm, and had carefully secured the door behind me, I spotted a message almost immediately. It was not, however, in Seymour's handwriting but, unmistakably, in my sister Boo Boo's. With or without soap, her handwriting was always almost indecipherably minute, and she had easily managed to post the following message up on the mirror: "Raise high the roof beam, carpenters. Like Ares comes the bridegroom, taller far than a tall man. Love, Irving Sappho, formerly under contract to Elysium Studios Ltd. Please be happy happy *happy* with your beautiful Muriel. This is an order. I outrank everybody on this block." The contract writer quoted in the text, I might mention, has always been a great favorite—at appropriately staggered time intervals—with all the children in our family, largely through the immeasurable impact of Seymour's taste

in poetry on all of us. I read and reread the quotation, and then I
sat down on the edge of the bathtub and opened Seymour's diary.

What follows is an exact reproduction of the pages from Seymour's diary that I read while I was sitting on the edge of the bathtub. It seems perfectly orderly to me to leave out individual date-
lines. Suffice it to say, I think, all these entries were made while he
was stationed at Fort Monmouth, in late 1941 and early 1942, some
several months before the wedding date was set.

"It was freezing cold at retreat parade this evening, and yet about
six men from our platoon alone fainted during the endless playing
of 'The Star-Spangled Banner.' I suppose if your blood circulation
is normal, you can't take the unnatural military position of attention. Especially if you're holding a leaden rifle up at Present Arms.
I have no circulation, no pulse. Immobility is my home. The tempo
of 'The Star-Spangled Banner' and I are in perfect understanding.
To me, its rhythm is a romantic waltz.

"We got passes till midnight, after the parade. I met Muriel at
the Biltmore at seven. Two drinks, two drugstore tuna-fish sandwiches, then a movie she wanted to see, something with Greer
Garson in it. I looked at her several times in the dark when Greer
Garson's son's plane was missing in action. Her mouth was open.
Absorbed, worried. The identification with Metro-Goldwyn-Mayer
tragedy complete. I felt awe and happiness. How I love and need
her undiscriminating heart. She looked over at me when the children in the picture brought in the kitten to show to their mother.
M. loved the kitten and wanted me to love it. Even in the dark,
I could sense that she felt the usual estrangement from me when I
don't automatically love what she loves. Later, when we were
having a drink at the station, she asked me if I didn't think that
kitten was 'rather nice.' She doesn't use the word 'cute' any more.
When did I ever frighten her out of her normal vocabulary? Bore
that I am, I mentioned R. H. Blyth's definition of sentimentality:
that we are being sentimental when we give to a thing more tenderness than God gives to it. I said (sententiously?) that God undoubtedly loves kittens, but not, in all probability, with Technicolor
bootees on their paws. He leaves that creative touch to script-
writers. M. thought this over, seemed to agree with me, but the
'knowledge' wasn't too very welcome. She sat stirring her drink and
feeling unclose to me. She worries over the way her love for me

comes and goes, appears and disappears. She doubts its reality simply because it isn't as steadily pleasurable as a kitten. God knows it *is* sad. The human voice conspires to desecrate everything on earth."

"Dinner tonight at the Fedders'. Very good. Veal, mashed potatoes, lima beans, a beautiful oil-and-vinegar green salad. For dessert there was something Muriel made herself: a kind of frozen cream-cheese affair, with raspberries on it. It made tears come to my eyes. Saigyo says, 'What it is I know not/But with the gratitude/My tears fall.') A bottle of ketchup was placed on the table near me. Muriel apparently told Mrs. Fedder that I put ketchup on everything. I'd give the world to have seen M. telling her mother defensively that I put ketchup even on string beans. My precious girl.

"After dinner Mrs. Fedder suggested we listen to the program. Her enthusiasm, her nostalgia for the program, especially for the old days when Buddy and I were on it, make me uneasy. Tonight it was broadcast from some naval airbase, of all places, near San Diego. Much too many pedantic questions and answers. Franny sounded as though she had a head cold. Zooey was in dreamy top form. The announcer had them off on the subject of housing developments, and the little Burke girl said she hated houses that all look alike—meaning a long row of identical 'development' houses. Zooey said they were 'nice.' He said it would be very nice to come home and be in the wrong house. To eat dinner with the wrong people by mistake, sleep in the wrong bed by mistake, and kiss everybody goodbye in the morning thinking they were your own family. He said he even wished everybody in the world looked exactly alike. He said you'd keep thinking everybody you met was your wife or your mother or father, and people would always be throwing their arms around each other wherever they went, and it would look 'very nice.'

"I felt unbearably happy all evening. The familiarity between Muriel and her mother struck me as being so beautiful when we were all sitting in the living room. They know each other's weaknesses, especially conversational weaknesses, and pick at them with their eyes. Mrs. Fedder's eyes watch over Muriel's conversational taste in 'literature,' and Muriel's eyes watch over her mother's tendency to be windy, verbose. When they argue, there can be no danger of a permanent rift, because they're Mother and Daughter.

A terrible and beautiful phenomenon to watch. Yet there are times when I sit there enchanted that I wish Mr. Fedder were more conversationally active. Sometimes I feel I need him. Sometimes, in fact, when I come in the front door, it's like entering a kind of untidy, secular, two-woman convent. Sometimes when I leave, I have a peculiar feeling that both M. and her mother have stuffed my pockets with little bottles and tubes containing lipstick, rouge, hair nets, deodorants, and so on. I feel overwhelmingly grateful to them, but I don't know what to do with their invisible gifts."

"We didn't get our passes directly after retreat this evening, because someone dropped his rifle while the visiting British general was making his inspection. I missed the 5:52 and was an hour late meeting Muriel. Dinner at Lun Far's, on 58th. M. irritable and tearful throughout dinner, genuinely upset and scared. Her mother thinks I'm a schizoid personality. Apparently she's spoken to her psychoanalyst about me, and he agrees with her. Mrs. Fedder has asked Muriel to find out discreetly if there's any insanity in the family. I gather that Muriel was naïve enough to tell her where I got the scars on my wrists, poor sweet baby. From what M. says, however, this doesn't bother her mother nearly so much as a couple of other things. Three other things. One, I withdraw from and fail to relate to people. Two, apparently there is something 'wrong' with me because I haven't seduced Muriel. Three, evidently Mrs. Fedder has been haunted for days by my remark at dinner one night that I'd like to be a dead cat. She asked me at dinner last week what I intended to do after I got out of the Army. Did I intend to resume teaching at the same college? Would I go back to teaching at all? Would I consider going back on the radio, possibly as a 'commentator' of some kind? I answered that it seemed to me that the war might go on forever, and that I was only certain that if peace ever came again I would like to be a dead cat. Mrs. Fedder thought I was cracking a joke of some kind. A sophisticated joke. She thinks I'm very sophisticated, according to Muriel. She thought my deadly-serious comment was the sort of joke one ought to acknowledge with a light, musical laugh. When she laughed, I suppose it distracted me a little, and I forgot to explain to her. I told Muriel tonight that in Zen Buddhism a master was once asked what was the most valuable thing in the world, and the master answered that a dead cat was, because no one could put a price on it. M. was relieved, but I could see she could hardly wait to get home to assure her mother of the harmlessness of my remark. She rode to the station with me in the cab. How sweet she was, and in so much better humor. She was trying to teach me to smile, spreading the muscles around my mouth with her fingers. How beautiful it is to see her laugh. Oh, God, I'm so happy with her. If only she could be happier with me. I amuse her at times, and she seems to like my face and hands and the back of my head, and she gets a vast satisfaction out of telling her friends that she's engaged to the Billy Black who was on 'It's a Wise Child' for years. And I think she feels a mixed maternal and sexual drive in my general direction. But on the whole I don't make her really happy. Oh, God, help me. My one terrible consolation is that my beloved has an undying, basically undeviating love for the institution of marriage itself. She has a primal urge to play house permanently. Her marital goals are so absurd and touching. She wants to get a very dark sun tan and go up to the desk clerk in some very posh hotel and ask if her Husband has picked up the mail yet. She wants to shop for curtains. She wants to shop for maternity clothes. She wants to get out of her mother's house, whether she knows it or not, and despite her attachment to her. She wants children—good-looking children, with her features, not mine. I have a feeling, too, that she wants her own Christmas-tree ornaments to unbox annually, not her mother's.

"A very funny letter came from Buddy today, written just after he came off K.P. I think of him as I write about Muriel. He would despise her for her marriage motives as I've put them down here. But are they despicable? In a way, they must be, but yet they seem to me so human-size and beautiful that I can't think of them even now as I write this without feeling deeply, deeply moved. He would disapprove of Muriel's mother, too. She's an irritating, opinionated woman, a type Buddy can't stand. I don't think he could see her for what she is. A person deprived, for life, of any understanding or taste for the main current of poetry that flows through things, all things. She might as well be dead, and yet she goes on living, stopping off at delicatessens, seeing her analyst, consuming a novel every night, putting on her girdle, plotting for Muriel's health and prosperity. I love her. I find her unimaginably brave."

"The whole company is restricted to the post tonight. Stood in line for a full hour to get to use the phone in the Rec Room. Muriel sounded rather relieved that I couldn't get in tonight. Which amuses and delights me. Another girl, if she genuinely wanted an evening free of her fiancé, would go through the motions of expressing regret over the phone. M. just said Oh when I told her. How I worship her simplicity, her terrible honesty. How I rely on it."

"3:30 A.M. I'm over in the Orderly Room. I couldn't sleep. I put my coat on over my pajamas and came over here. Al Aspesi is C Q. He's asleep on the floor. I can stay here if I answer the phone for him. What a night. Mrs. Fedder's analyst was there for dinner and grilled me, off and on, till about eleven-thirty. Occasionally with great skill, intelligence. Once or twice, I found myself pulling for him. Apparently he's an old fan of Buddy's and mine. He seemed personally as well as professionally interested in why I'd been bounced off the show at sixteen. He'd actually heard the Lincoln broadcast, but he had the impression that I'd said over the air that the Gettysburg Address was 'bad for children.' Not true. I told him I'd said I thought it was a bad speech for children to have to memorize in school. He also had the impression I'd said it was a dishonest speech. I told him I'd said that 51,112 men were casualties at Gettysburg, and that if someone *had* to speak at the anniversary of the event, he should simply have come forward and shaken his fist at his audience and then walked off—that is, if the speaker was an absolutely honest man. He didn't disagree with me, but he seemed to feel that I have a perfection complex of some kind. Much talk from him, and quite intelligent, on the virtues of living the imperfect life, of accepting one's own and others' weaknesses. I agree with him, but only in theory. I'll champion indiscrimination till doomsday, on the ground that it leads to health and a kind of very real, enviable happiness. *Followed purely* it's the way of the Tao, and undoubtedly the highest way. But for a discriminating man to achieve this, it would mean that he would have to dispossess himself of poetry, go *beyond* poetry. That is, he couldn't possibly learn or drive himself to *like* bad poetry in the abstract, let alone equate it with good poetry. He would have to drop poetry altogether. I said it would be no easy thing to do. Dr. Sims said I was putting it too stringently—putting it, he said, as only a perfectionist would. Can I deny that?

"Evidently Mrs. Fedder had nervously told him about Charlotte's nine stitches. It was rash, I suppose, to have mentioned that old finished business to Muriel. She passes everything along to her mother while it's hot. I should object, no doubt, but I can't. M. can only hear me when her mother is listening, too, poor baby. But I had no intention of discussing Charlotte's stitches with Sims. Not over just one drink.

"I more or less promised M. at the station tonight that I'll go to a psychoanalyst one of these days. Sims told me that the man right here on the post is very good. Evidently he and Mrs. Fedder have had a tête-à-tête or two on the subject. Why doesn't this rankle me? It doesn't. It seems funny. It warms me, for no good reason. Even stock mothers-in-law in the funny papers have always remotely appealed to me. Anyway, I can't see that I have anything to lose by seeing an analyst. If I do it in the Army, it'll be free. M. loves me, but she'll never feel really close to me, *familiar* with me, *frivolous* with me, till I'm slightly overhauled.

"If or when I do start going to an analyst, I hope to God he has the foresight to let a dermatologist sit in on consultation. A hand specialist. I have scars on my hands from touching certain people. Once, in the park, when Franny was still in the carriage, I put my hand on the downy pate of her head and left it there too long. Another time, at Loew's Seventy-second Street, with Zooey during a spooky movie. He was about six or seven, and he went under the seat to avoid watching a scary scene. I put my hand on his head. Certain heads, certain colors and textures of human hair leave permanent marks on me. Other things, too. Charlotte once ran away from me, outside the studio, and I grabbed her dress to stop her, to keep her near me. A yellow cotton dress I loved because it was too long for her. I still have a lemon-yellow mark on the palm of my right hand. Oh, God, if I'm anything by a clinical name, I'm a kind of paranoiac in reverse. I suspect people of plotting to make me happy."

I remember closing the diary—actually, slamming it shut—after the word "happy." I then sat for several minutes with the diary under one arm, until I became conscious of a certain discomfort from having sat so long on the side of the bathtub. When I stood up, I found I was perspiring more profusely than I had all day, as though I had just got out of a tub, rather than just been sitting on the side of one. I went over to the laundry hamper, raised the lid, and, with an almost vicious wrist movement, literally threw Seymour's diary into some sheets and pillowcases that were on the bottom of the hamper. Then, for want of a better, more constructive idea, I went back and sat down on the side of the bathtub again. I stared for a minute or two at Boo Boo's message on the medicine-cabinet mirror, and then I left the bathroom, closing the door excessively hard after me, as though sheer force might lock up the place forever after.

My next stop was the kitchen. Fortunately, it led off the hall, and I could get there without having to go through the living room and face my guests. On arrival, and with the swinging door closed behind me, I took off my coat—my tunic—and dropped it across the enamel table. It seemed to require all my energy just to take off my coat, and I stood for some time, in my T shirt, just resting up, as it were, before taking on the herculean task of mixing drinks. Then, abruptly, as though I were being invisibly policed through small apertures in the wall, I began to open cabinet and refrigerator doors, looking for Tom Collins ingredients. They were all there, except for lemons instead of limes, and in a few minutes I had a somewhat sugary pitcherful of Collinses made. I took down five glasses, and then looked around for a tray. It was just hard enough to find a tray, and it took me just long enough, so that by the time I did find one, I was giving out small, faintly audible whimpers as I opened and shut cabinet doors.

Just as I was starting out of the kitchen, with the pitcher and glasses loaded on the tray, and with my coat back on, an imaginary light bulb was turned on over my head—the way it is in comic strips to show that a character has a sudden very bright idea. I put down the tray on the floor. I went back over to the liquor shelf and took down a half-full fifth of Scotch. I brought my glass over and poured myself out—somewhat accidentally—at least four fingers of Scotch. I looked at the glass critically for a split second, and then, like a tried-and-true leading man in a Western movie, drank it off in one deadpan toss. A little piece of business, I might well mention, that I record here with a rather distinct shudder. Granted that I was twenty-three, and that I may have been doing only what any red-blooded twenty-three-year-old simpleton would have done under similar circumstances. I don't mean anything quite so simple as that. I mean that I am Not a Drinker, as the expression goes. On an ounce of whiskey, as a rule, I either get violently sick or I start scanning the room for unbelievers. On two ounces I've been known to pass out cold.

This was, however—by way of an unparalleled understatement— no ordinary day, and I remember that as I picked up the tray again and started to leave the kitchen, I felt none of the usual almost

immediate metamorphic changes. There seemed to be an un-
precedented degree of heat being generated in the subject's stomach, but that was all.

In the living room, as I brought in the loaded tray, there were
no auspicious changes in the deportment of my guests, beyond the
revitalizing fact that the bride's father's uncle had rejoined the
group. He was ensconced in my dead Boston bull's old chair. His
tiny legs were crossed, his hair was combed, his gravy stain was as
arresting as ever, and—lo and behold—*his cigar was lighted.* We
greeted each other even more extravagantly than usual, as though
these intermittent separations were suddenly too long and unnecessary for either of us to bear with.

The Lieutenant was still over at the bookshelves. He stood turning the pages of a book he'd taken out, apparently engrossed in it.
(I never did find out which book it was.) Mrs. Silsburn, looking
considerably pulled together, even refreshed, with her pancake
makeup, I thought, newly attended to, was seated on the couch
now, in the corner of it farthest away from the bride's father's
uncle. She was leafing through a magazine. "Oh, how lovely!" she
said, in a party voice, as she sighted the tray I'd just put down on
the coffee table. She smiled up at me convivially.

"I've put very little gin in it," I lied as I began to stir the pitcher.

"It's so lovely and cool in here now," Mrs. Silsburn said. "May
I ask you a question, incidentally?" With that, she put aside her
magazine, got up, and crossed around the couch and over to the
desk. She reached up and placed a fingertip on one of the photographs on the wall. "*Who* is this beautiful child?" she asked me.
With the air-conditioner now smoothly and steadily in operation,
and having had time to apply fresh makeup, she was no longer the
wilted, timorous child who had stood in the hot sun outside
Schrafft's Seventy-ninth Street. She was addressing me now with all
the brittle equipoise that had been at her disposal when I first
jumped into the car, outside the bride's grandmother's house, when
she asked me if I was someone named Dickie Briganza.

I left off stirring the pitcher of Collinses, and went around and
over to her. She had fixed a lacquered fingernail on the photograph
of the 1929 cast of "It's a Wise Child," and on one child in particular. Seven of us were sitting around a circular table, a microphone
in front of each child. "That's the most beautiful child I've ever
laid *eyes* on," Mrs. Silsburn said. "You know who she looks a teeny
bit like? Around the eyes and mouth?"

At about that point, some of the Scotch—roughly, a finger of it, I'd say—was beginning to affect me, and I very nearly answered, "Dickie Briganza," but a certain cautionary impulse still prevailed. I nodded, and said the name of the motion-picture actress whom the Matron of Honor, earlier in the afternoon, had mentioned in connection with nine surgical stitches.

Mrs. Silsburn stared at me. "Was *she* on 'It's a Wise Child'?" she asked.

"For about two years, yes. God, yes. Under her own name, of course. Charlotte Mayhew."

The Lieutenant was now behind me, at my right, looking up at the photograph. At the drop of Charlotte's professional name, he had stepped over from the bookshelves to have a look.

"I didn't know she was ever on the radio as a child!" Mrs. Silsburn said. "I didn't know that! Was she so brilliant as a child?"

"No, she was mostly just noisy, really. She sang as well then as she does now, though. And she was wonderful moral support. She usually arranged things so that she sat next to my brother Seymour at the broadcasting table, and whenever he said anything on the show that delighted her, she used to step on his foot. It was like a hand squeeze, only she used her foot." As I delivered this little homily, I had my hands on the top rung of the straight chair at the desk. They suddenly slipped off—rather in the way one's elbow can abruptly lose its "footing" on the surface of a table or a bar counter. I lost and regained my balance almost simultaneously, though, and neither Mrs. Silsburn nor the Lieutenant seemed to notice it. I folded my arms. "On certain nights when he was in especially good form, Seymour used to come home with a slight limp. That's really true. Charlotte didn't just step on his foot, she tramped on it. He didn't care. He loved people who stepped on his feet. He loved noisy girls."

"Well, isn't that interesting!" Mrs. Silsburn said. "I *cer*tainly never knew she was ever on the radio or anything."

"Seymour got her on, actually," I said. "She was the daughter of an osteopath who lived in our building on Riverside Drive." I replaced my hands on the rung of the straight chair, and leaned my weight forward on it, partly for support, partly in the style of an old back-fence reminiscer. The sound of my own voice was now singularly pleasing to me. "We were playing stoopball— Are either of you at all interested in this?"

"Yes!" said Mrs. Silsburn.

"We were playing stoopball on the side of the building one after-noon after school, Seymour and I, and somebody who turned out to be Charlotte started dropping marbles on us from the twelfth story. That's how we met. We got her on the program that same week. We didn't even know she could sing. We just wanted her because she had such a beautiful New Yorkese accent. She had a Dyckman Street accent."

Mrs. Silsburn laughed the kind of tinkling laugh that is, of course, death to the sensitive anecdotist, cold sober or otherwise. She had evidently been waiting for me to finish, so that she could make a single-minded appeal to the Lieutenant. "Who does she look like to you?" she said to him importunately. "Around the eyes and mouth especially. Who does she remind you of?"

The Lieutenant looked at her, then up at the photograph. "You mean the way she is in this picture? As a kid?" he said. "Or now? The way she is in the movies? Which do you mean?"

"Both, really, I think. But especially right here in this picture."

The Lieutenant scrutinized the photograph—rather severely, I thought, as though he by no means approved of the way Mrs. Sils-burn, who after all was a civilian as well as a woman, had asked him to examine it. "Muriel," he said shortly. "Looks like Muriel in this picture. The hair and all."

"But exactly!" said Mrs. Silsburn. She turned to me. "But exactly," she repeated. "Have you ever met Muriel? I mean have you ever seen her when she's had her hair tied in a lovely big—"

"I've never seen Muriel at all until today," I said.

"Well, all right, just take my word." Mrs. Silsburn tapped the photograph impressively with her index finger. "This child could double for Muriel at that age. But to a T."

The whiskey was steadily edging up on me, and I couldn't quite take in this information whole, let alone consider its many possible ramifications. I walked back over—just a trifle straight-linishly, I think—to the coffee table and resumed stirring the pitcher of Collinses. The bride's father's uncle tried to get my attention as I came back into his vicinity, to greet me on my reappearance, but I was just abstracted enough by the alleged fact of Muriel's re-semblance to Charlotte not to respond to him. I was also feeling just a trifle dizzy. I had a strong impulse, which I didn't indulge, to stir the pitcher from a seated position on the floor.

A minute or two later, as I was just starting to pour out the drinks, Mrs. Silsburn had a question for me. It all but sang its way across the room to me, so melodiously was it pitched. "Would it be very awful if I asked about that accident Mrs. Burwick happened to mention before? I mean those nine stitches she spoke of. Did your brother accidentally *push* her or something like that, I mean?"

I put down the pitcher, which seemed extraordinarily heavy and unwieldy, and looked over at her. Oddly, despite the mild dizziness I was feeling, distant images hadn't begun to blur in the least. If anything, Mrs. Silsburn as a focal point across the room seemed rather obtrusively distinct. "Who's Mrs. Burwick?" I said.

"My wife," the Lieutenant answered, a trifle shortly. He was looking over at me, too, if only as a committee of one to investigate what was taking me so long with the drinks.

"Oh. Certainly she is," I said.

"Was it an accident?" Mrs. Silsburn pressed. "He didn't *mean* to do it, did he?"

"Oh, *God*, Mrs. Silsburn."

"I beg your pardon?" she said coldly.

"I'm sorry. Don't pay any attention to me. I'm getting a little tight. I poured myself a great drink in the kitchen about five minutes—" I broke off, and turned abruptly around. I'd just heard a familiar heavy tread in the uncarpeted hall. It was coming toward us—at us—at a great rate, and in an instant the Matron of Honor jounced into the room.

She had eyes for no one. "I finally got them," she said. Her voice sounded strangely levelled off, stripped of even the ghost of italics. "After about an hour." Her face looked tense and overheated to the bursting point. "Is that cold?" she said, and came without stopping, and unanswered, over to the coffee table. She picked up the one glass I'd half filled a minute or so before, and drank it off in one greedy tilt. "That's the hottest room I've ever been in in my entire life," she said—rather impersonally—and set down her empty glass. She picked up the pitcher and refilled the glass halfway, with much clinking and plopping of ice cubes.

Mrs. Silsburn was already well in the vicinity of the coffee table. "What'd they say?" she asked impatiently. "Did you speak to Rhea?"

The Matron of Honor drank first. "I spoke to everybody," she said, putting down her glass, and with a grim but, for her, peculiarly undramatic emphasis on "everybody." She looked first at Mrs. Silsburn, then at me, then at the Lieutenant. "You can all relax," she said. "Everything's just fine and dandy."

"What do you mean? What happened?" Mrs. Silsburn said sharply.

"Just what I said. The *groom's* no longer indis*posed* by *happi*-ness." A familiar style of inflection was back in the Matron of Honor's voice.

"How come? Who'd you talk to?" the Lieutenant said to her. "Did you talk to Mrs. Fedder?"

"I said I talked to everybody. Everybody but the blushing bride. She and the groom've eloped." She turned to me. "How much sugar did you put in this thing, anyway?" she asked irritably. "It tastes like absolute—"

"*Eloped?*" said Mrs. Silsburn, and put her hand to her throat.

The Matron of Honor looked at her. "All right, just relax now," she advised. "You'll live longer."

Mrs. Silsburn sat down inertly on the couch—right beside me, as a matter of fact. I was staring up at the Matron of Honor, and I'm sure Mrs. Silsburn immediately followed suit.

"Apparently he was *at* the apartment when they got back. So Muriel just ups and packs her bag, and off the two of them go, just like that." The Matron of Honor shrugged her shoulders elaborately. She picked up her glass again and finished her drink. "Anyway, we're all invited to the reception. Or whatever you call it when the bride and groom have already *left*. From what I gathered, there's a whole mob of people over there already. Everybody sounded so *gay* on the phone."

"You said you talked to Mrs. Fedder. What'd she say?" the Lieutenant said.

The Matron of Honor shook her head, rather cryptically. "She was wonderful. My God, what a woman. She sounded absolutely normal. From what I gathered—I mean from what she said—this *Seymour's* promised to start going to an analyst and get himself straightened out." She shrugged her shoulders again. "Who knows? Maybe everything's gonna be hunky-dory. I'm too pooped to think any more." She looked at her husband. "Let's go. Where's your little hat?"

The next thing I knew, the Matron of Honor, the Lieutenant, and Mrs. Silsburn were all filing toward the front door, with me, as their host, following behind them. I was weaving now very obviously, but since no one turned around, I think my condition went unnoticed.

I heard Mrs. Silsburn say to the Matron of Honor, "Are you going to stop by there, or what?"

"I don't know," came the reply. "If we do, it'll just be for a minute."

The Lieutenant rang the elevator bell, and the three stood leadenly watching the indicator dial. No one seemed to have any further use for speech. I stood in the doorway of the apartment, a few feet away, dimly looking on. When the elevator door opened, I said goodbye, aloud, and their three heads turned in unison toward me. "Oh, good*bye*," they called over, and I heard the Matron of Honor shout "Thanks for the drink!" as the elevator door closed behind them.

I went back into the apartment, very unsteadily, trying to unbutton my tunic as I wandered along, or to yank it open.

My return to the living room was unreservedly hailed by my one remaining guest—whom I'd forgotten. He raised a well-filled glass at me as I came into the room. In fact, he literally waved it at me, wagging his head up and down and grinning, as though the supreme, jubilant moment we had both been long awaiting had finally arrived. I found I couldn't quite match grins with him at this particular reunion. I remember patting him on the shoulder, though. Then I went over and sat down heavily on the couch, directly opposite him, and finished yanking open my coat. "Don't you have a home to go to?" I asked him. "Who looks after you? The pigeons in the park?" In response to these provocative questions, my guest toasted me with increased gusto, wielding his Tom Collins at me as though it were a beer stein. I closed my eyes and lay back on the couch, putting my feet up and stretching out flat. But this made the room spin. I sat up and swung my feet around to the floor—doing it so suddenly and with such poor coördination that I had to put my hand on the coffee table to keep my balance. I sat slumped forward for a minute or two, with my eyes closed. Then, without having to get up, I reached for the Tom Collins pitcher and poured myself out a drink, spilling any amount of liquid and ice cubes onto the table and floor. I sat with the filled glass in my hands for some more minutes, without drinking, and then I put it down in a shallow puddle on the coffee table. "Would you like to know how Charlotte got those nine stitches?" I asked suddenly, in a tone of voice that sounded perfectly normal to me. "We were up at the Lake. Seymour had written to Charlotte, inviting her to come up and visit us, and her mother finally let her. What happened was, she sat down in the middle of our driveway one morning to pet Boo Boo's cat, and Seymour threw a stone at her. He was twelve. That's all there was to it. He threw it at her because she looked so beautiful sitting there in the middle of the driveway with Boo Boo's cat. Everybody knew that, for God's sake —me, Charlotte, Boo Boo, Waker, Walt, the whole family." I stared at the pewter ashtray on the coffee table. "Charlotte never said a word to him about it. Not a word." I looked up at my guest, rather expecting him to dispute me, to call me a liar. I am a liar, of course. Charlotte never did understand why Seymour threw that stone at her. My guest didn't dispute me, though. The contrary. He grinned at me encouragingly, as though anything further I had to say on the subject could go down only as the absolute truth with him. I got up, though, and left the room. I remember considering, halfway across the room, going back and picking up two ice cubes that were on the floor, but it seemed too arduous an undertaking, and I continued along to the hall. As I passed the kitchen door, I took off my tunic—peeled it off—and dropped it on the floor. It seemed, at the time, like the place where I always left my coat.

In the bathroom, I stood for several minutes over the laundry hamper, debating whether I should or shouldn't take out Seymour's diary and look at it again. I don't remember any more what arguments I advanced on the subject, either pro or con, but I did finally open the hamper and pick out the diary. I sat down with it, on the side of the bathtub again, and riffled the pages till I came to the very last entry Seymour had made:

"One of the men just called the flight line again. If the ceiling keeps lifting, apparently we can get off before morning. Oppenheim says not to hold our breaths. I phoned Muriel to tell her. It was very strange. She answered the phone and kept saying hello. My voice wouldn't work. She very nearly hung up. If only I could calm down a little. Oppenheim is going to hit the sack till the flight line calls us back. I should, too, but I'm too keyed up. I really called to ask her, to beg her for the last time to just go off alone with me and get married. I'm too keyed up to be with people. I feel as though I'm about to be born. Sacred, sacred day. The connection was so bad, and I couldn't talk at all during most of the call. How terrible it is when you say I love you and the person at the other end shouts back 'What?' I've been reading a miscellany of Vedanta

all day. Marriage partners are to serve each other. Elevate, help,
teach, strengthen each other, but above all, *serve*. Raise their children honorably, lovingly, and with detachment. A child is a guest
in the house, to be loved and respected—never possessed, since he
belongs to God. How wonderful, how sane, how beautifully difficult, and therefore true. The joy of responsibility for the first time
in my life. Oppenheim is already in the sack. I should be, too, but
I can't. Someone must sit up with the happy man."

I read the entry through just once, then closed the diary and
brought it back to the bedroom with me. I dropped it into Seymour's canvas bag, on the window seat. Then I fell, more or less
deliberately, on the nearer of the two beds. I was asleep—or, possibly, out cold—before I landed, or so it seemed.

When I wakened, about an hour and a half later, I had a splitting
headache and a parched mouth. The room was all but dark. I
remember sitting for rather a long time on the edge of the bed.
Then, in the cause of a great thirst, I got up and gravitated slowly
toward the living room, hoping there were still some cold and wet
remnants in the pitcher on the coffee table.

My last guest had evidently let himself out of the apartment.
Only his empty glass, and his cigar end in the pewter ashtray, indicated that he had ever existed. I still rather think his cigar end
should have been forwarded on to Seymour, the usual run of wedding gifts being what it is. Just the cigar, in a small, nice box.
Possibly with a blank sheet of paper enclosed, by way of explanation.

BERNADETTE

❖

Mavis Gallant

ON THE hundred and twenty-sixth day, Bernadette could no longer pretend not to be sure. She got the calendar out from her bureau drawer—a kitchen calendar, with the Sundays and saints' days in fat red figures, under a brilliant view of Alps. Across the Alps was the name of a hardware store and its address on the other side of Montreal. From the beginning of October the calendar was smudged and grubby, so often had Bernadette with moistened forefinger counted off the days: thirty-four, thirty-five, thirty-six. . . . That had been October, the beginning of fear, with the trees in the garden and on the suburban street a blaze of red and yellow. Bernadette had scrubbed floors and washed walls in a frenzy of bending and stretching that alarmed her employers, the kindly, liberal Knights.

"She's used to hard work—you can see that, of course," Robbie Knight had remarked, one Sunday, almost apologizing for the fact that they employed anyone in the house at all. Bernadette had chosen to wash the stairs and woodwork that day, instead of resting. It disturbed the atmosphere of the house, but neither of the Knights knew how to deal with a servant who wanted to work too much. He sat by the window, enjoying the warm October sunlight, trying to get on with the Sunday papers but feeling guilty because his wife was worried about Bernadette.

"She *will* keep on working," Nora said. "I've told her to leave that hard work for the char, but she insists. I suppose it's her way of showing gratitude, because we've treated her like a human being instead of a slave. Don't you agree?"

"I suppose so."

"I'm so tired," Nora said. She lay back in her chair with her eyes closed, the picture of total exhaustion. She had broken one of her nails clean across, that morning, helping Bernadette with some-

96

thing Bernadette might easily have done alone. "You're right about her being used to hard work. She's probably been working all her life." Robbie tried not answering this one. "It's so much the sort of thing I've battled," Nora said.

He gave up. He let his paper slide to the floor. Compelled to think about his wife's battles, he found it impossible to concentrate on anything else. Nora's weapons were kept sharp for two dragons: crooked politics and the Roman Catholic Church. She had battled for birth control, clean milk, vaccination, homes for mothers, homes for old people, homes for cats and dogs. She fought against censorship, and for votes for cloistered nuns, and for the provincial income tax.

"Good old Nora," said Robbie absently. Nora accepted this tribute without opening her eyes. Robbie looked at her, at the thin, nervous hand with the broken nail.

"She's not exciting, exactly," he had once told one of his mistresses. "But she's an awfully good sort, if you know what I mean. I mean, she's really a good sort. I honestly couldn't imagine not living with Nora." The girl to whom this was addressed had instantly burst into tears, but Robbie was used to that. Unreasonable emotional behavior on the part of other women only reinforced his respect for his wife.

The Knights had been married nearly sixteen years. They considered themselves solidly united. Like many people no longer in love, they cemented their relationship with opinions, pet prejudices, secret meanings, a private vocabulary that enabled them to exchange amused glances over a dinner table and made them feel a shade superior to the world outside the house. Their home held them, and their two daughters, now in boarding school. Private schools were out of line with the Knight's social beliefs, but in the case of their own children they had judged a private school essential.

"Selfish, they were," Robbie liked to explain. "Selfish, like their father." Here he would laugh a little, and so would his listeners. He was fond of assuming a boyish air of self-deprecation—a manner which, like his boyish nickname, had clung to him since school. "Nora slapped them both in St. Margaret's, and it cleared up in a year."

On three occasions, Nora had discovered Robbie in an affair. Each time, she had faced him bravely and made him discuss it, a process she called "working things out." Their talks would be formal, at first—a frigid question-and-answer period, with Robbie frightened and almost sick and Nora depressingly unreproachful. For a few nights, she would sleep in another room. She said that this enabled her to think. Thinking all night, she was fresh and ready for talk the next day. She would analyze their marriage, their lives, their childhoods, and their uncommon characters. She would tell Robbie what a Don Juan complex was, and tell him what he was trying to prove. Finally, reconciled, they were able to talk all night, usually in the kitchen, the most neutral room of the house, slowly and congenially sharing a bottle of Scotch. Robbie would begin avoiding his mistress's telephone calls and at last would write her a letter saying that his marriage had been rocked from top to bottom and that but for the great tolerance shown by his wife they would all of them have been involved in something disagreeable. He and his wife had now arrived at a newer, fuller, truer, richer, deeper understanding. The long affection they held for each other would enable them to start life again on a different basis, the letter would conclude.

The basic notion of the letter was true. After such upheavals his marriage went swimmingly. He would feel flattened, but not unpleasantly, and it was Nora's practice to treat him with tolerance and good humor, like an ailing child.

He looked at the paper lying at his feet and tried to read the review of a film. It was hopeless. Nora's silence demanded his attention. He got up, kissed her lightly, and started out.

"Off to work?" said Nora, without opening her eyes.

"Well, yes," he said.

"I'll keep the house quiet. Would you like your lunch on a tray?"

"No, I'll come down."

"Just as you like, darling. It's no trouble."

He escaped.

Robbie was a partner in a firm of consulting engineers. He had, at one time, wanted to be a playwright. It was this interest that had, with other things, attracted Nora when they had been at university together. Robbie had been taking a course in writing for the stage —a sideline to his main degree. His family had insisted on engineering; he spoke of defying them, and going to London or New York. Nora had known, even then, that she was a born struggler and fighter. She often wished she had been a man. She believed that to balance this overassertive side of her nature she should marry some-

one essentially feminine, an artist of some description. At the same
time, a burning fear of poverty pushed her in the direction of someone with stability, background, and a profession outside the arts.
Both she and Robbie were campus liberals; they met at a gathering
that had something to do with the Spanish war—the sort of party
where, as Nora later described it, you all sat on the floor and drank
beer out of old pickle jars. There had been a homogeneous quality
about the group that was quite deceptive; political feeling was a
great leveller. For Nora, who came from a poor and an ugly lower-
middle-class home, political action was a leg up. It brought her in
contact with people she would not otherwise have known. Her
snobbishness moved to a different level; she spoke of herself as
working-class, which was not strictly true. Robbie, in revolt against
his family, who were well-to-do, conservative, and had no idea of
the injurious things he said about them behind their backs, was,
for want of a gentler expression, slumming around. He drifted into
a beer-drinking Left Wing movement, where he was welcomed for
his money, his good looks, and the respectable tone he lent the
group. His favorite phrase at that time was "of the people." He
mistook Nora for someone of the people, and married her almost
before he had discovered his mistake. Nora then did an extraordinary about-face. She reconciled Robbie with his family. She encouraged him to go into his father's firm. She dampened, ever so
gently, the idea of London and New York.

Still, she continued to encourage his interest in theatre. More,
she managed to create such a positive atmosphere of playwriting in
the house that many of their casual acquaintances thought he *was*
a playwright, and were astonished to learn he was the Knight of
Turnbull, Knight & Beardsley. Robbie had begun and abandoned
many plays since college. He had not consciously studied since the
creative-writing course, but he read, and criticized, and had reached
the point where he condemned everything that had to do with the
English-language stage.

Nora agreed with everything he believed. She doggedly shared
his passion for the theatre—which had long since ceased to be real,
except when she insisted—and she talked to him about his work,
sharing his problems and trying to help. She knew that his trouble
arose from the fact that he had to spend his daytime hours in the
offices of the firm. She agreed that his real life was the theatre, with
the firm a practical adjunct. She was sensible: she did not ask that

he sell his partnership and hurl himself into uncertainty and insecurity—a prospect that would have frightened him very much
indeed. She understood that it was the firm that kept them going,
that paid for the girls at St. Margaret's and the trip to Europe every
second summer. It was the firm that gave Nora leisure and scope
for her tireless battles with the political and ecclesiastical authorities of Quebec. She encouraged Robbie to write in his spare time.
Every day, or nearly, during his "good" periods, she mentioned his
work. She rarely accepted an invitation without calling Robbie at
his office and asking if he wanted to shut himself up and work that
particular night. She could talk about his work, without boredom
or exhaustion, just as she could discuss his love affairs. The only
difference was that when they were mutually explaining Robbie's
infidelity, they drank whiskey. When they talked about his play
and his inability to get on with it, Nora would go to the refrigerator
and bring out a bottle of milk. She was honest and painstaking; she
had at the tip of her tongue the vocabulary needed to turn their
relationship and marriage inside out. After listening to Nora for a
whole evening, agreeing all the way, Robbie would go to bed
subdued with truth and totally empty. He felt that they had
drained everything they would ever have to say. After too much
talk, he would think, a couple should part; just part, without another word, full of kind thoughts and mutual understanding. He
was afraid of words. That was why, that Sunday morning toward
the end of October, the simple act of leaving the living room took
on the dramatic feeling of escape.

He started up the stairs, free. Bernadette was on her knees, washing the painted baseboard. Her hair, matted with a cheap permanent, had been flattened into curls that looked like snails, each
snail held with two crossed bobby pins. She was young, with a
touching attractiveness that owed everything to youth.

"Bonjour, Bernadette."

"'Jour."

Bending, she plunged her hands into the bucket of soapy water.
A moment earlier, she had thought of throwing herself down the
stairs and making it seem an accident. Robbie's sudden appearance
had frightened her into stillness. She wiped her forehead, waiting
until he had closed the door behind him. Then she flung herself
at the baseboard, cloth in hand. Did she feel something—a tugging,
a pain? "Merci, mon Dieu," she whispered. But there was nothing

to be thankful for, in spite of the walls and the buckets of water and the bending and the stretching.

Now it was late December, the hundred and twenty-sixth day, and Bernadette could no longer pretend not to be certain. The Knights were giving a party. Bernadette put the calendar back in the drawer, under her folded slips. She had counted on it so much that she felt it bore witness to her fears; anyone seeing it would know at once.

For weeks she had lived in a black sea of nausea and fear. The Knights had offered to send her home to Abitibi for Christmas, had even wanted to pay her fare. But she knew that her father would know the instant he saw her, and would kill her. She preferred going on among familiar things, as if the normality, the repeated routine of getting up in the morning and putting on Mr. Knight's coffee and Mrs. Knight's tea would, by force of pattern, cause things to be the way they had been before October. So far, the Knights had noticed nothing, although the girls, home for Christmas, teased her about getting fat. Thanks to St. Joseph, the girls had now been sent north to ski with friends, and there was no longer any danger of their drawing attention to Bernadette's waist.

Because of the party, Bernadette was to wear a uniform, which she had not done for some time. She pressed it and put it back on its hanger without trying it on, numb with apprehension, frightened beyond all thought. She had spent the morning cleaning the living room. Now it was neat, unreal, like a room prepared for a color photo in a magazine. There were flowers and plenty of ashtrays. It was a room waiting for disorder to set in.

"Thank you, Bernadette," Nora had said, taking, as always, the attitude that Bernadette had done her an unexpected service. "It looks lovely."

Nora liked the room; it was comfortable and fitted in with her horror of ostentation. Early in her marriage she had decided that her taste was uncertain; confusing elegance with luxury, she had avoided both. Later, she had discovered French-Canadian furniture, which enabled her to refer to her rooms in terms of the simple, the charming, even the amusing. The bar, for example, was a *prie-dieu* Nora had discovered during one of her forays into rural Quebec just after the war, before American tourists with a nose for a bargain had (as she said) cleaned out the Province of its greatest heritage. She had found the *prie-dieu* in a barn and had bought it for three dollars. Sandpapered, waxed, its interior recess deepened to hold bottles, it was considered one of Nora's best *trouvailles*. The party that evening was being given in honor of a priest—a liberal priest from Belgium, a champion of modern ecclesiastical art, and another of Nora's finds. (Who but Nora would have dreamed of throwing a party for a priest?)

Robbie wondered if the *prie-dieu* might not offend him. "Maybe you ought to keep the lid up, so he won't see the cross," he said.

But Nora felt that would be cheating. If the priest accepted her hospitality, he must also accept her views.

"He doesn't know your views," Robbie said. "If he did, he probably wouldn't come." He had a cold, and was spending the day at home, in order to be well for the party. The cold made him interfering and quarrelsome.

"Go to bed, Robbie," said Nora kindly. "Haven't you anything to read? What about all the books you got for Christmas?"

Considering him dismissed, she coached Bernadette for the evening. They rehearsed the handing around of the tray, the unobtrusive clearing of ashtrays. Nora noticed that Bernadette seemed less shy. She kept a blank, hypnotized stare, concentrating hard. After a whole year in the household, she was just beginning to grasp what was expected. She understood work, she had worked all her life, but she did not always understand what these terrifying, well-meaning people wanted. If, dusting a bookcase, she slowed her arm, lingering, thinking of nothing in particular, one of them would be there, like a phantom, frightening her out of her wits.

"Would you like to borrow one of these books, Bernadette?"

Gentle, tolerant, infinitely baffling, Mr. or Mrs. Knight would offer her a book in French.

"For me?"

"Yes. You can read in the afternoon, while you are resting."

Read while resting? How could you do both? During her afternoon rest periods, Bernadette would lie on the bed, looking out the window. When she had a whole day to herself, she went downtown in a bus and looked in the windows of stores. Often, by the end of the afternoon, she had met someone, a stranger, a man who would take her for a drive in a car or up to his room. She accepted these adventures as inevitable; she had been so overwarned before leaving home. Cunning prevented her giving her address or name, and if one of her partners wanted to see her again, and named a time and a street number, she was likely to forget or to meet someone else on the way. She was just as happy in the cinema, alone, or looking at displays of eau de cologne in shops.

Reduced to perplexity, she would glance again at the book. Read?

"I might get it dirty."

"But books are to be read, Bernadette."

She would hang her head, wondering what they wanted, wishing they would go away. At last she had given in. It was in the autumn, the start of her period of fear. She had been dusting in Robbie's room. Unexpectedly, in that ghostly way they had, he was beside her at the bookcase. Blindly shy, she remembered what Mrs. Knight, all tact and kindness and firm common sense, had said that morning: that Bernadette sometimes smelled of perspiration, and that this was unpleasant. Probably Mr. Knight was thinking this now. In a panicky motion her hand flew to "L'Amant de Lady Chatterley," which Nora had brought from Paris so that she could test the blundering ways of censorship. (The English version had been held at customs, the French let through, which gave Nora ammunition for a whole winter.)

"You won't like that," Robbie had said. "Still . . ." He pulled it out of the bookcase. She took the book to her room, wrapped it carefully in newspaper, and placed it in a drawer. A few days later she knocked on the door of Robbie's room and returned "L'Amant de Lady Chatterley."

"You enjoyed it?"

"Oui. Merci."

He gave her "La Porte Etroite." She wrapped it in newspaper and placed it in a drawer for five days. When she gave it back, he chose for her one of the Claudine series, and then, rather doubtfully, "Le Rouge et le Noir."

"Did you like the book by Stendhal, Bernadette?"

"Oui. Merci."

To dinner guests, Nora now said, "Oh, our Bernadette! Not a year out of Abitibi, and she was reading Gide and Colette. She knows more about French literature than we do. She goes through Stendhal like a breeze. She adores Giraudoux." When Bernadette, grim with the effort of remembering what to do next, entered the room, everyone would look at her and she would wonder what she had done wrong.

During the party rehearsal, Robbie, snubbed, went up to bed.

He knew that Nora would never forgive him if he hadn't recovered by evening. She regarded a cold in the head as something that could be turned off with a little effort; indeed, she considered any symptom of illness in her husband an act of aggression directed against herself. He sat up in bed, bitterly cold in spite of three blankets and a bathrobe. It was the chill of grippe, in the center of his bones; no external warmth could reach it. He heard Nora go out for some last-minute shopping, and he heard Bernadette's radio in the kitchen.

"Sans amour, on est rien du tout," Edith Piaf sang. The song ended and a commercial came on. He tried not to hear.

On the table by his bed were books Nora had given him for Christmas. He had decided, that winter, to reread some of the writers who had influenced him as a young man. He began this project with the rather large idea of summing himself up as a person, trying to find out what had determined the direction of his life. In college, he remembered, he had promised himself a life of action and freedom and political adventure. Perhaps everyone had then. But surely he, Robbie Knight, should have moved on to something other than a pseudo-Tudor house in a suburb of Montreal. He had been considered promising—an attractive young man with a middling-good brain, a useful background, unexpected opinions, and considerable charm. He did not consider himself unhappy, but he was beginning to wonder what he was doing, and why. He had decided to carry out his reassessment program in secret. Unfortunately, he could not help telling Nora, who promptly gave him the complete Orwell, bound in green.

He read with the conviction of habit. There was Orwell's Spain, the Spain of action and his university days. There was also the Spain he and Nora knew as tourists, a poor and dusty country where tourists became colicky because of the oil. For the moment, he forgot what he had seen, just as he could sometimes forget he had not become a playwright. He regretted the Spain he had missed, but the death of a cause no longer moved him. So far, the only result of his project was a feeling of loss. Leaving Spain, he turned to an essay on England. It was an essay he had not read until now. He skipped about, restless, and suddenly stopped at this: "I have often been struck by the peculiar easy completeness, the perfect symmetry as it were, of a working-class interior at its best. Especially on winter evenings after tea, when the fire glows in the open range and dances mirrored in the steel fender, when

Father, in shirt-sleeves, sits in the rocking chair at one side of the fire reading the racing finals, and Mother sits on the other with her sewing, and the children are happy with a penn'orth of mint humbugs, and the dog lolls roasting himself on the rag mat. . . ."

Because he had a cold and Nora had gone out and left him on a snowy miserable afternoon, he saw in this picture everything missing in his life. He felt frozen and left out. Robbie had never been inside the kitchen of a working-class home; it did not occur to him that the image he had just been given might be idyllic or sentimental. He felt only that he and Nora had missed something, and that he ought to tell her so; but he knew that it would lead to a long bout of analytical talk, and he didn't feel up to that. He blew his nose, pulled the collar of his dressing gown up around his ears, and settled back on the pillows.

Bernadette knocked at the door. Nora had told her to prepare a tray of tea, rum, and aspirin at four o'clock. It was now half past four, and Bernadette wondered if Mr. Knight would betray her to Mrs. Knight. Bernadette's sleeves were rolled up, and she brought with her an aura of warmth and good food. She had, in fact, been cooking a ham for the party. Her hair was up in the hideous snails again, but it gave her, Robbie thought, the look of a hard-working woman—a look his own wife achieved only by seeming totally exhausted.

"*Y a un* book, too," said Bernadette, in her coarse, flat little voice. She put the tray down with care. "*Je l'ai mis sur le* tray." She indicated the new Prix Goncourt, which Robbie had lent her the day it arrived. He saw at once that the pages were still uncut.

"You didn't like it?"

"Oh, *oui*," she said automatically. "*Merci*."

Never before had a lie seemed to him more pathetic, or more justified. Instead of taking the book, or his tea, he gripped Bernadette's plump, strong forearm. The room was full of warmth and comfort. Bernadette had brought this atmosphere with her; it was her native element. She was the world they had missed sixteen years before, and they, stupidly, had been trying to make her read books. He held her arm, gripping it. She stared back at him, and he saw that she was frightened. He let her go, furious with himself, and said, rather coldly, "Do you ever think about your home in Abitibi?"

"*Oui*," she said flatly.

"Some of the farms up there are very modern now, I believe," he said, sounding as if he were angry with her. "Was yours?"

She shrugged. *"On a pas la* television, *nous,"* she said.

"I didn't think you had. What about your kitchen? What was your kitchen like at home, Bernadette?"

"Sais pas," said Bernadette, rubbing the released arm on the back of her dress. "It's big," she offered, after some thought.

"Thank you," said Robbie. He went back to his book, still furious, and upset. She stood still, uncertain, a fat dark little creature not much older than his own elder daughter. He turned a page, not reading, and at last she went away.

Deeply bewildered, Bernadette returned to the kitchen and contemplated the cooling ham. She seldom thought about home. Now her memory, set in motion, brought up the image of a large, crowded room. The prevailing smell was the odor of the men's boots as they came in from the outbuildings. The table, masked with oilcloth, was always set between meals, the thick plates turned upside down, the spoons in a glass jar. At the center of the table, never removed, were the essentials: butter, vinegar, canned jam with the lid of the can half opened and wrenched back, ketchup, a tin of molasses glued to its saucer. In winter, the washing hung over the stove. By the stove, every year but the last two or three, had stood a basket containing a baby—a wailing, swaddled baby, smelling sad and sour. Only a few of Bernadette's mother's children had straggled up past the infant stage. Death and small children were inextricably knotted in Bernadette's consciousness. As a child she had watched an infant brother turn blue and choke to death. She had watched two others die of diphtheria. The innocent dead became angels; there was no reason to grieve. Bernadette's mother did all she could; terrified of injections and vaccines, she barred the door to the district nurse. She bound her infants tightly to prevent excess motion, she kept them by the flaming heat of the stove, she fed them a bouillon of warm water and cornstarch to make them fat. When Bernadette thought of the kitchen at home, she thought of her mother's pregnant figure, and her swollen feet, in unlaced tennis shoes.

Now she herself was pregnant. Perhaps Mr. Knight knew, and that was why he had asked about her mother's kitchen. Sensing a connection between her mother and herself, she believed he had seen it as well. Nothing was too farfetched, no wisdom, no perception, for these people. Their mental leaps and guesses were as mysterious to her as those of saints, or of ghosts.

Nora returned and, soon afterward, Robbie wandered downstairs. His wife had told him to get up (obviously forgetting that it was she who had sent him to bed) so that she could tidy the room. She did not ask how he felt and seemed to take it for granted that he had recovered. He could not help comparing her indifference with the solicitude of Bernadette, who had brought him tea and rum. He began comparing Bernadette with other women he had known well. His mistresses, *faute de mieux,* had been girls with jobs and little apartments. They had in common with Nora a desire to discuss the situation; they were alarmingly likely to burst into tears after lovemaking because Robbie didn't love them enough or because he had to go home for dinner. He had never known a working-class girl, other than the women his wife employed. (Even privately, he no longer used the expression "of the people.") As far as he could determine now, girls of Bernadette's sort were highly moral, usually lived with their parents until marriage, and then disappeared from sight, like Moslem women. He might have achieved an interesting union, gratifying a laudable social curiosity, during his college days, but he had met Nora straightaway. He had been disappointed to learn that her father did not work in a factory. There was an unbridgeable gap, he had since discovered, between the girl whose father went off to work with a lunch pail and the daughter of a man who ate macaroni-and-cheese in the company cafeteria. In the midst of all her solicitude for the underprivileged, Nora never let him forget it. On the three occasions when she had caught him out in a love affair, among her first questions had been "Where does she come from? What does she do?"

Robbie decided to apologize to Bernadette. He had frightened her, which he had no right to do. He no longer liked the classic role he had set for himself, the kindly educator of young servant girls. It had taken only a glimpse of his thin, busy wife to put the picture into perspective. He allowed himself one last, uncharitable thought, savoring it: Compared with Bernadette, Nora looked exactly like a furled umbrella.

Bernadette was sitting at the kitchen table. The ham had been put away, the room aired. She was polishing silver for the party, using a smelly antiseptic pink paste. He no longer felt the atmosphere of warmth and food and comfort Bernadette had brought up to his room. She did not look up. She regarded her own upside-down image in the bowl of a spoon. Her hands moved slowly, then stopped. What did he want now?

Before coming to Montreal, Bernadette had been warned about the licentious English—reserved on the surface, hypocritical, infinitely wicked underneath—and she had, in a sense, accepted it as inevitable that Mr. Knight would try to seduce her. When it was over, she would have another sin to account for. Mr. Knight, a Protestant, would not have sinned at all. Unique in her sin, she felt already lonely. His apology sent her off into the strange swamp world again, a world in which there was no footing; she had the same feeling as when they tried to make her read books. What was he sorry about? She looked dumbly around the kitchen. She could hear Nora upstairs, talking on the telephone.

Robbie also heard her and thought: Bernadette is afraid of Nora. The idea that the girl might say something to his wife crossed his mind, and he was annoyed to realize that Nora's first concern would be for Bernadette's feelings. His motives and his behavior they would discuss later, over a drink. He no longer knew what he wanted to say to Bernadette. He made a great show of drinking a glass of water and went out.

By evening, Robbie's temperature was over ninety-nine. Nora did not consider it serious. She felt that he was deliberately trying to ruin the party, and said so. "Take one good stiff drink," she said. "That's all you need."

He saw the party through a feverish haze. Nora was on top of the world, controlling the room, clergy-baiting, but in the most charming manner. No priest could possibly have taken offense, particularly a nice young priest from Belgium, interested in modern art and preceded by a liberal reputation. He could not reply; his English was limited. Besides, as Nora kept pointing out, he didn't know the situation in Quebec. He could only make little grimaces, acknowledging her thrusts, comically chewing the stem of a cold pipe.

"Until you know this part of the world, you don't know your own Church," Nora told him, smiling, not aggressive.

The English-Canadians in the room agreed, glancing nervously at the French. French Canada was represented by three journalists huddled on a couch. (Nora had promised the priest, as if offering hors d'oeuvres, representatives of what she called "our chief ethnic groups.") The three journalists supported Nora, once it was made plain that clergy-baiting and French-baiting were not going to be combined. Had their wives been there, they might not have concurred so brightly; but Nora could seldom persuade her French-Canadian finds to bring their wives along. The drinking of Anglo-Saxon women rather alarmed them, and they felt that their wives, genteel, fluffy-haired, in good little dresses and strings of pearls, would disappoint and be disappointed. Nora never insisted. She believed in emancipation, but no one was more vocal in deploring the French-Canadian who spoke hard, flat English and had become Anglicized out of all recognition. Robbie, feverish and disloyal, almost expected her to sweep the room with her hand and, pointing to the trio of journalists, announce, "I found them in an old barn and bought them for five dollars each. I've sandpapered and waxed them, and there they are."

From the Church she went on to Bernadette. She followed the familiar pattern, explaining how environment had in a few months overcome generations of intellectual poverty.

"Bernadette reads Gide and Lawrence," she said, choosing writers the young priest was bound to disapprove of. "She adores Colette."

"Excellent," he said, tepid.

Bernadette came in, walking with care, as if on a tightrope. She had had difficulty with her party uniform and she wondered if it showed.

"Bernadette," Nora said, "how many children did your mother have?"

"Thirteen, Madame," said the girl. Accustomed to this interrogation, she continued to move around the room, remembering Nora's instructions during the rehearsal.

"In how many years?" Nora said.

"Fifteen."

"And how many are living?"

"Six, Madame."

The young priest stopped chewing his pipe and said quietly, in French, "Are you sorry that your seven brothers and sisters died, Bernadette?"

Jolted out of her routine, Bernadette replied at once, as if she had often thought about it, "Oh, no. If they had lived, they would have had to grow up and work hard, and the boys would have to go to war, when there is war, to fight—" About to say, "fight for the

English," she halted. "Now they are little angels, praying for their mother," she said.

"Where?" said the priest.

"In Heaven."

"What does an angel look like, Bernadette?" he said.

She gave him her hypnotized gaze and said, "They are very small. They have small golden heads and little wings. Some are tall and wear pink and blue dresses. You don't see them because of the clouds."

"I see. Thank you," said Nora, cutting in, and the student of Gide and Colette moved off to the kitchen with her tray.

It ruined the evening. The party got out of hand. People stopped talking about the things Nora wanted them to talk about, and the ethnic groups got drunk and began to shout. Nora heard someone talking about the fluctuating dollar, and someone else said to her, of television, "Well, Nora, still holding out?"—when only a few months ago anyone buying a set had been sheepish and embarrassed and had said it was really for the maid.

When it was all over and Nora was running the vacuum so that there would be less for Bernadette to do the next day, she frowned and looked tired and rather old. The party had gone wrong. The guest of honor had slipped away early. Robbie had gone to bed before midnight without a word to anybody. Nora had felt outside the party, bored and disappointed, wishing to God they would all clear out. She had stood alone by the fireplace, wondering at the access of generosity that had led her to invite these ill-matched and noisy people to her home. Her parties in the past had been so different: everyone had praised her hospitality, applauded her leadership, exclaimed at her good sense. Indignant with her over some new piece of political or religious chicanery, they had been grateful for her combativeness, and had said so—more and more as the evening wore on. Tonight, they seemed to have come just as they went everywhere else, for the liquor and good food. A rot, a feeling of complacency, had set in. She had looked around the room and thought, with an odd little shock: How old they all seem! Just then one of her ethnic treasures—a recently immigrated German doctor—had come up to her and said, "That little girl is pregnant."

"What?"

"The little servant girl. One has only to look."

Afterward, she wondered how she could have failed to notice.

Everything gave Bernadette away: her eyes, her skin, the characteristic thickening of her waist. There were the intangible signs,
too, the signs that were not quite physical. In spite of her own
motherhood, Nora detested, with a sort of fastidious horror, any
of the common references to pregnancy. But even to herself, now,
she could think of Bernadette only in terms of the most vulgar
expressions, the terminology her own family (long discarded, never
invited here) had employed. Owing to a "mistake," Bernadette was
probably "caught." She was beginning to "show." She was at least
four months "gone." It seemed to Nora that she had better go
straight to the point with Bernadette. The girl was under twenty-
one. It was quite possible that the Knights would be considered
responsible. If the doctor had been mistaken, then Bernadette
could correct her. If Bernadette were to tell Nora to mind her own
business, so much the better, because it would mean that Bernadette had more character than she seemed to have. Nora had no
objection to apologizing in either instance.

Because of the party and the extra work involved, Bernadette
had been given the next afternoon off. She spent the morning
cleaning. Nora kept out of the way. Robbie stayed in bed, mulishly
maintaining that he wasn't feeling well. It was after lunch, and
Bernadette was dressed and ready to go downtown to a movie, when
Nora decided not to wait any longer. She cornered Bernadette in
the kitchen and, facing her, suddenly remembered how, as a child,
she had cornered field mice with a flashlight and then drowned
them. Bernadette seemed to know what was coming; she exuded
fear. She faced her tormentor with a beating, animal heart.

Nora sat down at the kitchen table and began, as she frequently
had done with Robbie, with the words "I think we ought to talk
about a certain situation." Bernadette stared. "Is there anything
you'd like to tell me?" Nora said.

"No," said Bernadette, shaking her head.

"But you're worried about something. Something is wrong. Isn't
that true?"

"No."

"Bernadette, I want to help you. Sit down. Tell me, are you
pregnant?"

"I don't understand."

"Yes, you do. *Un enfant. Un bébé.* Am I right?"

"Sais pas," said Bernadette. She looked at the clock over Nora's head.

"Bernadette."

It was getting late. Bernadette said, "Yes. I think so. Yes."

"You poor little mutt," said Nora. "Don't keep standing there like that. Sit down here, by the table. Take off your coat. We must talk about it. This is much more important than a movie." Bernadette remained standing, in hat and coat. "Who is it?" said Nora. "I didn't know you had . . . I mean, I didn't know you knew anyone here. Tell me. It's most important. I'm not angry." Bernadette continued to look up at the clock, as if there were no other point in the room on which she dared fix her eyes. "Berna*dette!*" Nora said. "I've just asked you a question. Who is the boy?"

"Un monsieur," said Bernadette.

Did she mean by that an older man, or was Bernadette, in using the word *"monsieur,"* implying a social category? *"Quel monsieur?"* said Nora.

Bernadette shrugged. She stole a glance at Nora, and something about the oblique look suggested more than fear or evasiveness. A word came into Nora's mind: sly.

"Can you . . . I mean, is it someone you're going to marry?" But no. In that case, he would have been a nice young boy, someone of Bernadette's own background. Nora would have met him. He would have been caught in the kitchen drinking Robbie's beer. He would have come every Sunday and every Thursday afternoon to call for Bernadette. "Is it someone you *can* marry?" Nora said. Silence. "Don't be afraid," said Nora, deliberately making her voice kind. She longed to shake the girl, even slap her face. It was idiotic; here was Bernadette in a terrible predicament, and all she could do was stand, shuffling from one foot to the other, as if a movie were the most important thing in the world. "If he isn't already married," Nora said, "which I'm beginning to suspect is the case, he'll marry you. You needn't worry about that. I'll deal with it, or Mr. Knight will."

"Pas possible," said Bernadette, low.

"Then I was right. He *is* married." Bernadette looked up at the clock, desperate. She wanted the conversation to stop. "A married man," Nora repeated. *"Un monsieur."* An unfounded and wholly outrageous idea rushed into her mind. Dismissing it, she said, "When did it happen?"

"Sais pas."

"Don't be silly. That really is a very silly reply. Of course you know. You've only had certain hours out of this house."

The truth of it was that Bernadette did not know. She didn't know his name or whether he was married or even where she could find him again, even if she had desired such a thing. He seemed the least essential factor. Lacking words, she gave Nora the sidelong glance that made her seem coarse and deceitful. She is so un-innocent, Nora thought, surprised and a little repelled. It occurred to her that in spite of her long marriage and her two children, she knew less than Bernadette. While she was thinking about Berna-dette and her lover, there came into her mind the language of the street. She remembered words that had shocked and fascinated her as a child. That was Bernadette's fault. It was Bernadette's atmos-phere, Nora thought, excusing herself to an imaginary censor. She said, "We must know when your baby will be born. Don't you think so?" Silence. She tried again: "How long has it been since you . . . I mean, since you missed . . ."

"One hundred and twenty-seven days," said Bernadette. She was so relieved to have, at last, a question that she could answer that she brought it out in a kind of shout.

"My God. What are you going to do?"

"Sais pas."

"Oh, Bernadette!" Nora cried. "But you must think." The naming of a number of days made the whole situation so much more immediate. Nora felt that they ought to be doing something —telephoning, writing letters, putting some plan into motion. "We shall have to think for you," she said. "I shall speak to Mr. Knight."

"No," said Bernadette, trembling, suddenly coming to life. "Not Mr. Knight."

Nora leaned forward on the table. She clasped her hands to-gether, hard. She looked at Bernadette. "Is there a special reason why I shouldn't speak to Mr. Knight?" she said.

"Oui." Bernadette had lived for so many days now in her sea of nausea and fear that it had become a familiar element. There were greater fears and humiliations, among them that Mr. Knight, who was even more baffling and dangerous than his wife, should try to discuss this thing with Bernadette. She remembered what he had said the day before, and how he had held her arm. "He must know," said Bernadette. "I think he must already know."

"You had better go on," said Nora, after a moment. "You'll miss your bus." She sat quite still and watched Bernadette's progress down the drive. She looked at the second-hand imitation-seal coat that had been Bernadette's first purchase (and Nora's despair) and the black velveteen snow boots trimmed with dyed fur and tied with tasselled cords. Bernadette's purse hung over her arm. She had the walk of a fat girl—the short steps, the ungainly little trot.

It was unreasonable, Nora knew it was unreasonable; but there was so much to reinforce the idea—"*Un monsieur,*" and the fact that he already knew ("He must know," Bernadette had said)—and then there was Bernadette's terror when she said she was going to discuss it with him. She thought of Robbie's interest in Bernadette's education. She thought of Robbie in the past, his unwillingness to remain faithful, his absence of courage and common sense. Recalling Bernadette's expression, prepared now to call it corrupt rather than sly, she felt that the girl had considered herself deeply involved with Nora; that she knew Nora much better than she should.

Robbie had decided to come downstairs, and was sitting by the living-room fire. He was reading a detective novel. Beside him was a drink.

"Get you a drink?" he said, without lifting his eyes, when Nora came in.

"Don't bother."

He went on reading. He looked so innocent, so unaware that his life was shattered. Nora remembered how he had been when she had first known him, so pleasant and dependent and good-looking and stupid. She remembered how he had been going to write a play, and how she had wanted to change the world, or at least Quebec. Tears of fatigue and strain came into her eyes. She felt that the failure of last night's party had been a symbol of the end. Robbie had done something cheap and dishonorable, but he reflected their world. The world was ugly, Montreal was ugly, the street outside the window contained houses of surpassing ugliness. There was nothing left to discuss but television and the fluctuating dollar; that was what the world had become. The children were in boarding school because Nora didn't trust herself to bring them up. The living room was full of amusing peasant furniture because she didn't trust her own taste. Robbie was afraid of her and liked humiliating her by demonstrating again and again that he preferred nearly any other woman in bed. That was the truth of things. Why had she never faced it until now?

She said, "Robbie, can I talk to you?" Reluctant, he looked away from his book. She said, "I just wanted to tell you about a dream. Last night I dreamed you died. I dreamed that there was nothing I could do to bring you back, and that I had to adjust all my thoughts to the idea of going on without you. It was a terrible, shattering feeling." She intended this to be devastating, a prelude to the end. Unfortunately, she had had this dream before, and Robbie was bored with it. They had already discussed what it might mean, and he had no desire to go into it now.

"I wish to God you wouldn't keep on dreaming I died," he said.

She waited. There was nothing more. She blinked back her tears and said, "Well, listen to this, then. I want to talk about Bernadette. What do you know, exactly, about Bernadette's difficulties?"

"Has Bernadette got difficulties?" The floor under his feet heaved and settled. He had never been so frightened in his life. Part of his mind told him that nothing had happened. He had been ill, a young girl had brought warmth and comfort into his room, and he wanted to touch her. What was wrong with that? Why should it frighten him so much that Nora knew? He closed his eyes. It was hopeless; Nora was not going to let him get on with the book. Nora looked without any sentiment at all at the twin points where his hairline was moving back. "Does she seem sort of unsettled?" he asked.

"That's a way of putting it. Sometimes you have a genuine talent for irony."

"Oh, hell," said Robbie, suddenly fed up with Nora's cat-and-mouse. "I don't feel like talking about anything. Let's skip it for now. It's not important."

"Perhaps you'd better tell me what you consider important," Nora said. "Then we'll see what we can skip." She wondered how he could sit there, concerned with his mild grippe, or his hangover, when the whole structure of their marriage was falling apart. Already, she saw the bare bones of the room they sat in, the rugs rolled, the cracks that would show in the walls when they took the pictures down.

He sighed, giving in. He closed his book and put it beside his drink. "It was just that yesterday when I was feeling so lousy she brought me—she brought me a book. One of those books we keep lending her. She hadn't even cut the pages. The whole thing's a farce. She doesn't even look at them."

"Probably not," said Nora. "Or else she does and that's the whole trouble. To get straight to the point, which I can see you don't want to do, Bernadette has told me she's having a baby. She takes it for granted that you already know. She's about four months under way, which makes yesterday seem rather pointless."

Robbie said impatiently, "We're not talking about the same thing." He had not really absorbed what Nora was saying; she spoke so quickly, and got so many things in all at once. His first reaction was astonishment, and a curious feeling that Bernadette had deceived him. Then the whole import of Nora's speech entered his mind and became clear. He said, "Are you crazy? Are you out of your mind? Are you completely crazy?" Anger paralyzed him. He was unable to think of words or form them on his tongue. At last he said, "It's too bad that when I'm angry I can't do anything except feel sick. Or maybe it's just as well. You're crazy, Nora. You get these— I don't know— You get these ideas." He said, "If I'd hit you then, I might have killed you."

It had so seldom occurred in their life together that Robbie was in the right morally that Nora had no resources. She had always triumphed. Robbie's position had always been indefensible. His last remark was so completely out of character that she scarcely heard it. He had spoken in an ordinary tone of voice. She was frightened, but only because she had made an insane mistake and it was too late to take it back. Bravely, because there was nothing else to do, she went on about Bernadette. "She doesn't seem to know what to do. She's a minor, so I'm afraid it rather falls on us. There is a place in Vermont, a private place, where they take these girls and treat them well, rather like a boarding school. I can get her in, I think. Having her admitted to the States could be your end of it."

"I suppose you think that's going to be easy," Robbie said bitterly. "I suppose you think they admit pregnant unmarried minors every day of the year."

"None of it is easy!" Nora cried, losing control. "Whose fault is it?"

"It's got nothing to do with me!" said Robbie, shouting at her. "Christ Almighty, get that through your head!"

They let silence settle again. Robbie found that he was trembling. As he had said, it was physically difficult for him to be angry.

Nora said, "Yes, Vermont," as if she were making notes. She was determined to behave as if everything were normal. She knew that unless she established the tone quickly, nothing would ever be normal again.

"What will she do with it? Give it out for adoption?" said Robbie, in spite of himself diverted by details.

"She'll send it north, to her family," said Nora. "There's always room on a farm. It will make up for the babies that died. They look on those things, on birth and on death, as acts of nature, like the changing of the seasons. They don't think of them as catastrophes."

Robbie wanted to say, You're talking about something you've read, now. They'll be too ashamed to have Bernadette or the baby around; this is Quebec. But he was too tired to offer a new field of discussion. He was as tired as if they had been talking for hours. He said, "I suppose this Vermont place, this school or whatever it is, has got to be paid for."

"It certainly does." Nora looked tight and cold at this hint of stinginess. It was unnatural for her to be in the wrong, still less to remain on the defensive. She had taken the position now that even if Robbie were not responsible, he had somehow upset Bernadette. In some manner, he could be found guilty and made to admit it. She would find out about it later. Meanwhile, she felt morally bound to make him pay.

"Will it be expensive, do you think?"

She gave him a look, and he said nothing more.

Bernadette sat in the comforting dark of the cinema. It was her favorite kind of film, a musical comedy in full color. They had reached the final scene. The hero and heroine, separated because of a stupid quarrel for more than thirty years, suddenly found themselves in the same night club, singing the same song. They had gray hair but youthful faces. All the people around them were happy to see them together. They clapped and smiled. Bernadette smiled, too. She did not identify herself with the heroine, but with the people looking on. She would have liked to have gone to a night club in a low-cut dress and applauded such a scene. She believed in love and in uncomplicated stories of love, even though it was something she had never experienced or seen around her. She did not really expect it to happen to her, nor to anyone she knew.

For the first time, her child moved. She was so astonished that she looked at the people sitting on either side of her, wondering if they had noticed. They were looking at the screen. For the first time, then, she thought of it as a child, here, alive—not a state of terror but something to be given a name, clothed, fed, and baptized. Where and how and when it would be born she did not question. Mrs. Knight would do something. Somebody would. It would be born, and it would die. That it would die she never doubted. She was uncertain of so much else: her own body was a mystery, nothing had ever been explained. At home, in spite of her mother's pregnancies, the birth of the infants was shrouded in secrecy and, like their conception, suspicion of sin. This baby was Bernadette's own; when it died, it would pray for her, and her alone, for all of eternity. No matter what she did with the rest of her life, she would have an angel of her own, praying for her. Oddly secure in the dark, the dark of the cinema, the dark of her personal fear, she felt protected. She thought: *Il prie pour moi.* She saw, as plainly as if it had been laid in her arms, her child, her personal angel, white and swaddled, baptized, innocent, ready for death.

THE BELL OF CHARITY

❖

CALVIN KENTFIELD

EARLY in the morning, my mother heard the news. Someone phoned her—I don't know who—and she did not get up from her chair after she had hung up. She found a number in the telephone book and asked the operator for it. "Hello, *hello*," she said. "Is this Mrs. Pearly? Say, this is Mrs. Garrett. . . . Yes. . . . Yes."

I could see her from the kitchen table, where I was having breakfast, and I knew she was talking to someone who was not an intimate friend, for her voice had the same quality it had when she spoke in company and raised her coffee cup with her little finger sticking out. "Weren't you a friend of Mrs. Kite's, old Mrs. Fred Kite? . . . Yes, well I thought so. . . . Yes, well she died. . . . I thought probably you hadn't, I just heard a minute ago. . . . Yes, last night in Graham Hospital. . . . Well, you know she's been so awful sick, poor old soul. . . . Well, I knew she used to come up to your house when she came here to see me. She'd always say she was going on to Mrs. Liedermeyer's house or to Mrs. Pearly's. . . . Yes, I know she did, and I thought you'd like to know. Of course it'll be in the paper but . . . Well, that preacher, I suppose. He seemed to see a lot of her while she was sick. . . . Fred?" Fred was Mrs. Kite's son. "Well, yes he is. He got married, you know. . . . Yes, I certainly was, too. He lives in St. Louis—you knew that—him and his wife, so I don't suppose he'll be up here until tomorrow. . . . Well, you know, I think she must have told that preacher all the details when she felt herself failing, because he seemed to know just who to call, and all. . . . Why, he's that major or captain or something, down there at the Salvation Army. . . . Yes, I *did think* about that, and I just believe *I* will. Somebody certainly should. . . . No, no. Why, *no*, I'll be *glad* to. All right then, Mrs. Pearly. . . . Yes. . . . Yes. . . . I'll put you

down for fifty cents. . . . That's quite all right. I knew you'd like
to know, Mrs. Pearly. Goodbye."

My mother put down the receiver, brushed a white strand of hair
away from her ear, and took the receiver up again. "Four-seven-
nine-W," she said, and turned and called to me, "There's more
coffee on the stove, Ira." Then, while she waited for her party to
answer, she took a piece of paper and a pencil from a shelf under
the telephone and began to make a list. "Hello, *Minnie?*" she said.
"Ya *up?* . . . Ya *did?* My land, what were you doing up so *early?*
. . . Well, yes, it is cooler then. You aren't *washing?* . . . Well you
just better take it easy. You're just not *able* to do that kind of
thing any more. . . . Say, you know old Mrs. Kite died. . . . Last
night at the Graham. . . . Yes, well poor old soul, she's better off.
She was all alone, you know. . . . Well he certainly *did,* and went
off to St. Louis. Can you i*mag*ine any woman marrying him? Ugh!
. . . Say, would you like to give a little something for flowers? I said
I'd do it. . . . Well, I *know* I'm not, but poor old soul. I don't
suppose there'll be very many. . . . Well I'm certainly *not* going to
tire myself out. Just a few of the people she used to come see. . . .
I'll put you down, then. . . . No, no, Minnie. I certainly won't.
I'm not *able* to, any more. I'll just make a few calls, and I can get
the flowers from Alma, next door. . . . Well, *pretty* good. This heat,
you know. . . . Oh, yes, I take it easy, and I follow my diet, and I
don't overstrain myself. Well, I just *can't.* Now, just like the other
day, when I was hanging up the clothes, reaching up, you know,
I just got so *dizzy,* and cold sweat came out on my face and I felt
so *hot.* I came right in and laid down like the doctor told me, and
after a little while—well, it was several hours—I was all right. Oh,
I still *have* them. . . . Yes, I know. That sure is right. Say, Minnie,
talking of washing, don't you just miss Roy? . . . Yes, I sure do.
Poor old Roy, he was *so* good, and *such* a help." Roy Virgil had
been everyone's handyman for as long as I could remember. "Well,
Minnie, I tell you, I just don't know what we would've done without him," my mother said. "And clean, he'd clean up the tubs so
nice and leave the basement so clean. I really couldn't afford him,
but he was *such* a help, and, well, I just wasn't able. Whenever I
think of Mrs. Kite, I think of him. . . . Yes, well you know they
were all of them around down there at the Salvation Army, and
Roy's children and Fred were so thick, you know. She was awful
good to that boy, poor old soul, her troubles are over now. . . . Say,

you remember before Roy died, he gave those goats of his to Don Karmaier for his house out there on the River Road? . . . Well you know for the longest time they just kept that slope trimmed down so *clean*. You know, Minnie, I believe those goats've died. I was by there not so long ago, and Don was out there himself with a lawnmower. I just believe those goats've died. . . . Yes, well I will, Minnie. . . . Now you just be careful and don't you go lifting that heavy basket around. . . . Yes. Goodbye. . . . Well, I don't know. I expect it'll be the Potts's Funeral Home, but I haven't heard. She was a pensioner, you know. . . . Oh, yes, the state'll pay. . . . Oh, yes, they've got a *nice* lot, thank the Lord. She had to sign her house over to Fred when she took her pension, but they let her keep that. . . . Why, it's there on the corner, down the slope there by Ed Tatters'. . . . Why, *yes,* I'm sure. You know where that big black stone is, and the Ryan vault? . . . Well, it's just in back of that. There's a peony bush there, and a faucet. It's awful close to the road, but shoot! Old Fred, her husband's buried there. They say she had that violin and that Chinaman's hat of his buried with him, but I don't know. Old Fred didn't have much sense. Well, he was a little, well, goofy, you remember. That's how young Fred got like he is, but he had enough sense to buy a lot to be buried in and keep them out of potter's field. . . . My, yes, it certainly *is,* it certainly is a blessing. Poor old soul. . . . Yes. Well, goodbye."

My mother hung up, and added several names to her list, and looked up some numbers in the telephone book. I was watching her over the rim of my coffee cup. She called another number, and when she got her party, I could tell by the way she talked that it was a friend of Mrs. Kite's but not one of her own. The next lady she called was a very old friend, and they started talking about me.

"Yes, that was him you saw," my mother said. "He's home. . . . Oh, why, he came in just a couple of nights ago, Tuesday I believe it was. . . . No, he never told me he was coming but, well, I had a feeling he might. He never said, but the last letter I got was kinda, well, I had a feeling. . . . Oh, he's been working on a boat or something of that kind. He could tell you more about it than I could. . . . Well I suppose it's what he wants to do, though I don't think he's very satisfied. . . . Oh, no, no! He mentioned something about it when he was here at Christmastime, and I just laughed. I told him I couldn't imagine what woman would want to marry him. Course he don't tell me much. He's the closest young 'un I ever saw. I don't know *how* he got that way. . . . Oh, yes, don't you remember I told you he was here at Christmas, just for a couple of days? But aside from that, it's been seven years since he was home. Yes sir, seven years. He couldn't even come home when his Daddy passed away, he was out on the ocean somewhere."

I knew she was saying all of that for me to hear. I watched her, and I saw her eyes cloud up when the vastness of the ocean, which she had never seen, entered her mind.

"Say, Mabel," she resumed. "You know poor old Mrs. Kite died. . . . Oh? Who *told* you?"

She talked for a few minutes more, then hung up and began calling still other people she had listed. I poured myself another cup of coffee and stopped listening, preferring to recall the woman who had died, whom I had known only as a faithful pilgrim, one who loved to come and visit and stay all day.

For years, Mrs. Kite had lived at the foot of our hill, and visiting us had been easy, but some time—I couldn't remember when—she had moved with her family to a house a little way out of town, on the edge of the Mississippi bluff. Thereafter, the pilgrimage back to Billy Goat Hill to see her old friends—one or maybe two at a time—had become an arduous one. She was fat and her legs were swollen, but down the bluff she would come, nevertheless, crossing Soap Creek, which was the city limits, and coming the back way to our edge of town. Through the wailing aspen woods where the carcasses of old cars lay rusting among the trees she passed, through the wild rocks of the Hollow, unheeding of the creepers that tangled the lonely path there, and of the brambles that picked at her brown lisle stockings, and the black snakes and blue racers that dwelt in the grass. She looked both ways when she reached the abandoned Wabash tracks, then crossed, and went on past the row of shacks that squatted along the right of way, ignoring the churlish dogs that bayed and yapped and reared at her from the bitter ends of their chains. On she went to the foot of Billy Goat Hill.

My older brother and I often saw her coming, for in the summer we lived long, dramatic other lives in the Hollow and the auto graveyard. Likely as not, we would run ahead, keeping—like Ayrabs —to the concealments we knew, to warn our mother. But if our Arabian, or other, existence compelled us to stay where we were, we would crouch in the hot ribs of some old Plymouth, or under a certain stony ledge, drawing our mantles about us and giggling and shushing each other until she passed by.

After each step up Billy Goat Hill, she rested. Viewed from our house, she appeared over the hill's crest hat first, like a ship coming over the horizon. Her face followed her hat; her goitred neck, her shoulders, bosom, waist came after; and then her mammoth satchel bag appeared, hanging from her wrist to only a few inches above the bulging insteps of her shoes. Emerging thus—in a sense, Anadyomene—she gave warning of her coming.

Once, the summer that I was eight, my mother and I, through a portière of sweet-potato vines, watched her from our sun porch as she gained level ground and turned in to the house on the corner. "There she goes in Mrs. Birch's. Thank the Lord!" my mother exclaimed. We continued to watch for a minute or two. "She's rang four times now," my mother said, "and Mrs. Birch don't answer, and I *know* she's home. She's hiding from that poor old thing, you can just bet your bottom dollar."

Mrs. Kite stepped off Mrs. Birch's porch and turned toward our end of the street. "Here she comes!" my mother said, and hurried to the telephone. I don't know whom she called, but I heard her say, "I just thought you'd like to know."

I hid in the dining room, by the window, where I could see the street but couldn't be seen from the front door. I watched Mrs. Kite labor toward us over the broken bricks of our neighbors' unimproved sidewalks, looking ahead and a little heavenward, with a broad, faithful smile upon her ugly face, oblivious, apparently, of the commotion she was causing or of the intricate betrayals of her progress. "She's in front of Alma's!" I called to my mother, who quickly said goodbye, and called another number.

"She's coming up the steps!" I called, and I heard my mother say, "I just thought you'd like to know. I was going to town this afternoon, but of course I can't now."

The doorbell rang.

"Well, goodbye, she's here." My mother passed me on the way to the front door, and I heard her exclaim there *"Well! Mrs. Kite! This is a surprise!"* and I heard the screen door slam.

My mother called me to the sun porch, and I saw our visitor's face beam even more brightly than it had on her way to us, she was so glad to see us and be welcomed. "Surprise!" she said. She brought with her, besides her satchel, a strong smell of sweat and washrags.

"You remember little Ira," my mother said, indicating me.

"Uh-*huh,* uh-*huh,*" said Mrs. Kite, like the courting frog in the ballad.

"This is the *baby,*" my mother pursued. "Sit down, why don't you?"

"This is the baby," said Mrs. Kite, as if she were telling my mother who I was. "Sit down, uh-*huh!* Whew!" She sank into a wicker rocker and immediately began to rock, while one warted hand probed her bag and withdrew a little lawn handkerchief to wipe her brow. "Mrs., it's hot and my kid a-fishin'," she said. She was referring to Fred.

"Yes, isn't it hot, though?" my mother said. "Think of the poor gardens."

"Think of the poor gardens," said Mrs. Kite.

I slipped away. I had planned to go to town with my mother, and I was furious. I came back an hour later and hung around in the doorway between the dining room and the sun porch. As if nothing at all had been said while I was gone, my mother asked, "Why don't you take off your hat, Mrs. Kite?"

"Yes, uh-*huh,*" said Mrs. Kite. "Why don't I take off my old black hat?"

She did so, revealing another tight hat, of hair, and I was convinced, then, that she had a second head in her bag.

Beyond the screen, the murmurs of the afternoon receded, and my mother nodded in the middle of a sentence. Finally she said, "I'm sorry, Mrs. Kite, but I've just *got* to take a nap. Now, don't let me sleep very long."

"Don't let her sleep very long," said Mrs. Kite.

"Wake me up in thirty minutes."

I turned and ran as fast as I could upstairs, grabbed an alarm clock, and ran back. My mother had left her seat, and I saw her go into the living room. She sank down upon the davenport and almost instantly began to snore. I went to the sun porch and slipped into the Morris chair she had vacated. On the wide arm, I placed the clock, training its bold face on Mrs. Kite. "I've got a little boy," she said to me, and I told her she wasn't telling me anything, because I knew it.

That was all either of us said. The curtain of airy plants outside the windows let in an emerald, aqueous light. The clock ticked. Mrs. Kite rocked and rocked, and picked her nose, and smiled from ear to ear. Her goitre gave her a frog's throat. She watched me and the clock with drowsy, wide-set eyes. Finally her mouth

relaxed and dropped open, and her long, grooved tongue rolled
out and rested upon her lower lip.

Now my mother, at the telephone, said goodbye to the last person
on her list, and heaved herself out of her chair. I was still at the
kitchen table. "You remember old Mrs. Kite, don't you?" she asked.
I nodded, and she said that she had died. I remarked that I had
already heard the news, and she said, "I'm going to run over to
Alma's and tell her, and see about some flowers."

Alma lived next door, across a wide yard, the back half of which
was neatly planted with flowers. In the yard were an arbor and a
small greenhouse. Alma and her husband had a modest florist's
business and made enough, according to my mother, to keep them
in Phoenix in the winters.

In the evening, my mother often sat on a chair outside her back
door and said how nice it was to have such a pretty view to look at.
There were some other chairs on the grass there, and a table. That
evening, my sister, who is older than I, and married, and lives on
the other side of town, came to my mother's house for supper. Her
husband had gone to a stag fish fry. She brought a chicken, and my
mother made potato salad, and spread a cloth on the outside table.
After supper, when the three of us were drinking our coffee and
looking at Alma's flowers, my Aunt Shug, who lives across the
street, came over to return a clothesline she had borrowed. She
said she had to go right back home, but she agreed to sit down for
just a minute. She sat on a green wood-and-iron bench my mother
had talked the cemetery custodian out of. "Say, Nin, have you
heard when old Mrs. Kite's funeral's going to be?" she asked my
mother.

"Why, yes, it was on the door at Potts's, and it was in the paper
tonight," my mother answered. "I believe, if I remember right, it
was to be tomorrow afternoon."

"They've got her there now, I suppose," Shug said. "Poor old
soul, she never missed a funeral."

"No sir, she didn't. She and Mrs. Virgil, Roy's wife. You remember Roy, don't you, Son? He used to come help me with the washing, but I've got a big, strong boy to do it for me now."

"They came to Tom's funeral an hour ahead of time, and sat
down and stayed all through, and were the last to leave," Shug said.

"I'm not exactly a boy," I said dryly, "Being twenty-seven and a
half years of age."

"And that Mrs. O'Blenness came with them," Shug went on. "And I heard she went to another funeral afterward, and then she went home that night and died of a heart attact."

"Well Esther Virgil was already at Potts's this afternoon, long before I ever got there," my mother said.

"You mean to say, Nin, you've been down to see her so soon?" asked Shug. "I wouldn't think they could have her out yet."

"Oh, yes, and she looked nice. You know, Charley Potts is really *very* good." My mother went on to describe what Mrs. Kite had looked like, lying in her coffin, and the dress she had been wearing, and who all had been there. It was all fresh in her mind because she and I had just returned, only a short time before supper, from the funeral home. I had driven her down but had refused at first to go in with her. However, after she had gone on alone, I had changed my mind and followed her.

As I approached the front door, I noticed to one side of it a small black bulletin board, which said, in white plastic removable letters, "MRS. MARY KITE 2:30 SAT," and on the glass of the door itself was another sign, saying "FRIGIDAIRE CONDITIONED FOR YOUR COMFORT," and still another—a card—bidding me "WALK IN." I did so, passing quickly into the parlor where lay Mrs. Kite's remains.

Besides my mother, in the cool room, there were, among the living, Roy Virgil's widow, Esther, and her daughter, Esther Roy, and Son Virgil, and Fred Kite. Little Mrs. Virgil, as always at wakes and funerals, was sitting back in her chair with her hands folded in her lap, enjoying herself. She was wearing a hair net and a house dress—a faded print of cherry clusters—and she smiled grandly at me, showing the bright-orange gums of her false teeth, though I could tell she didn't remember me.

Beside her, beneath a potted palm, was Son, about thirty-five, sitting with his legs stretched out in front of him and one arm thrown over the back of his chair, causing his Hawaiian shirt to gap open and expose his navel.

Esther Roy, who was nearly six feet tall, limbed like an oak, and pregnant, stood beside my mother at the casket. They were peering in, and Esther Roy was clutching a tiny handkerchief in one hand and with the extended forefinger of the other was pointing out various aspects of the corpse as if she were trying to sell it.

"Don't she look nice, though?" my mother said.

"Yes," said Esther Roy. "They did a beautiful job on her."

My mother, turning from the casket, saw me. She came over and put her arm through mine. She introduced me to Mrs. Virgil, who said wasn't it just grand to have me back, and to Esther Roy, who said exactly the same thing, and to Son, who welcomed me with an enormous grin. Then she turned to Fred Kite, who was sitting near Mrs. Virgil. "Hello, Fred," she said. "You got here sooner than we expected."

Fred looked at her but did not speak.

"Do you remember my baby boy?" she asked.

Fred looked me up and down and said, "I never would've knowed ya."

I never would have known him, either. He was prosperously fat, his clothes were new, and fitted him—though the collar of his shirt was dirty—and he sat straight in his chair with his arms crossed over his chest, clearly detached from the whole affair.

"Well, you won't have to worry about her any more," my mother said, her eyes beginning to cloud.

Fred looked away.

My mother stepped up to the visitors' register to sign our names, and I stepped up to the casket. Esther Roy stepped up beside me. "They did a beautiful job on her," she said.

They certainly had. She looked calm and peaceful, as she was supposed to look—entirely different from the way she had looked at Christmas. I had forgotten I had seen her then, briefly, in the falling snow. I turned to ask my mother if she was ready, but she was waiting, and everyone rose to smile us out—everyone but Fred.

"So Fred got here, then?" Shug asked.

"Oh, yes, he's here," my mother said. "But, you know, there wasn't but one dinky bunch of flowers, and the church sent those."

"You remember when Mrs. Kite used to come and sit, and bring Fred with her?" my sister asked.

"She just loved to sit on that porch of ours," my mother said.

"And repeat everything you said to her," said Shug, laughing. " 'Yes, yes, uh-huh, uh-huh.' And Fred—you remember how she used to bring him along when he was little?"

"Uh-huh, uh-huh," my sister mimicked. "Little! He wasn't so little." She cocked her head and pursed her lips and rubbed the uplifted side of her face with her fingers. "Well, you know," she said, drawing out the long syllable of the verb, "I kinda think Fred used to be kinda sweet on me."

"Well, I *know old* Fred liked me," my mother broke in, "because I've heard him say to Daddy many a time—"

"He'd come with his mother and sit," my sister said. "You know, just sit, like that, and *look* at me, and *look*."

Shug laughed and said, "Why, yes," and my sister gave a low, shuddering witch's laugh.

"Many a time," my mother said, "old Fred—oh, he'd say it to *me*, too—you know he used to come up here and visit Daddy, they were old pals, you know, him and Daddy, and he'd say—"

"Oh, *yes*," my sister said.

"He'd help him sometimes in the yard, or Daddy'd give him little things to do, but I've heard old Fred say a dozen times if I heard him once, 'Burrell,' he'd say (he always called Daddy by his middle name), 'Burrell,' he'd say"—she raised her arm and held it there, with her forefinger pointing straight out, as if she were a statue with sword drawn—" 'if I'd've seen that girl first, *you'd* never got a chance at her!' "

She dropped her arm, and Shug roared, "Just think, Nin, you could've married Fred Kite, and all your life you could've been serenaded with 'The Devil's Dream.' That was the only piece he could ever play. Remember when they lived by the cooper shop at the foot of the hill, how he used to come up the alley just *covered* with dirt, like he'd spent the night in a coal shed? With that hat on? Like a tramp, except, of course, he *did* work. With his toes sticking out and scratching on that fiddle 'The Devil's Dream'? My *land*, such a cat's meow!"

"You remember old Fred Kite, don't you, Son?" my mother asked.

"No, I don't think I do," I said. "I remember young Fred coming up through the alley, though, all the time."

"He sure did," my sister said. "And he'd just *look* at me, and *look*."

"When Burrell died, you should've married him, Nin," Shug said. "He would've played 'The Devil's Dream' at your wedding."

"Oh, he was dead and gone by then," my mother said.

"Mo-ther," my sister said with a slant to her voice, cocking her head again, "if you'd've married Fred Kite, would I be me?" She laughed immoderately. "I mean, who would *I* be?"

Shug roared again, "You missed your chance, Nin, to marry a musician."

"You know, in the paper tonight," my mother said, lowering her voice, "it mentioned they had a first little girl that died at birth."

"Now that I come to think of it," Shug said, "I *remember* she had a first baby."

"Well you know when that little thing was born, it had hoofs, just like a little cow or something, or a little goat," my mother said.

"Oh, Mother!" my sister exclaimed. "That's not true."

"That's what they say. It had just sorta little hoof-feets."

There was a long hiatus in the talk, filled in with private thoughts. The sun was departing and the air was beginning to cool. The sky flared up over Shug's house, across the street, as if her shingle roof, her Indian cigar trees, and all the inflammable earth to the westward were afire. Next door, Alma was gathering flowers. Behind her, like an enormous grasshopper's eye, the mansard panes of her little greenhouse flashed back the last rays of the sun.

"I've just got to go," said Shug, not moving.

"She must have been a hundred and thirteen, wasn't she?" I asked.

"Why, *no-o-o*," my mother said.

"She wasn't much older than I am," Shug said.

"How old are you?" I asked, smiling.

"That's none of *your* affair, young man," she said. "Say, how long are you going to stay with us?"

I was about to say I didn't know for sure, that I didn't know anything for sure, but my mother spoke up ahead of me, "Oh, he's going to be here for a *little* while, anyway," she said.

I could not remember having discussed it. To change the subject, I asked what age Mrs. Kite was, since she wasn't a hundred and thirteen.

"Well now let's see," my mother said, figuring.

"It was in the paper, wasn't it?" my sister asked. "It must've been."

"Well, now, we can figure it out," said my mother. "Esther Virgil, Roy's wife, was two years younger than Roy, and Roy and you went to school together, didn't you, Shug? Well, I'm two years younger than you are, and you're sixty-six—"

"And proud of it," said Shug, placing her palms on her knees and bending forward as though she really meant to get up and go. The ball of clothesline was still in her lap.

"So Esther Virgil must be the same age," my mother concluded.

I said, "That makes you and Esther Virgil both sixty-four, but how old was Mrs. Kite?"

"Well," my mother said, "Esther Virgil had Son at the same time Mrs. Kite had Fred. They're only a couple of months apart. Of course, there's her daughter, Esther Roy, but she's older."

"Say, Nin," Shug said, settling back, "what's that boy's real name?"

"Roy, like his Daddy," my mother answered, "but everybody has always called him Son. My, but he certainly is good to her. Esther Roy, you know, is married, but Son takes *such* good care of his mother. She's such a little thing, you know, and he just *works* for her, and *carries,* and goes *here* and *there* and *everywhere.* Of course, they all work down there at the Salvation Army. They live over there in that little house Roy used to have. And Son keeps it up *so* nice."

"They're not quite right, either, are they?" I asked.

"No, but he certainly is good to her," my mother said.

"I've *got* to go," said Shug. "I haven't even done my supper dishes yet."

"Well neither have we," my mother told her. "Do like we do, and don't worry about it. You know, Minnie and me have got it all figured out that Esther Virgil is related to Mamie Eisenhower."

"Leave it to Minnie," my sister said.

"Well you know Douds up the river there—that little place above Bonaparte—well Douds was named by some of Esther Virgil's family. Esther was a Doud before she married Roy, and Mamie Eisenhower's family were Doudses from around up in there someplace, oh, way years ago . . ."

I stepped into the house and filled my coffee cup from the percolator, and called out, asking if anyone else wanted another cup. My sister said she did, and my aunt said no, she had to go home. She was still there when I returned, however, but the color had gone from the sky above her house, and the long, gradual darkening had begun. Soon, I knew, we would all fade—my mother in her garden chair, my sister and my aunt on the graveyard bench, myself astraddle a kitchen chair with my arms crossed on the high back and my chin resting on my arms. Our faces, hands, and clothes would gradually fade, the darkest first, until only Shug's and my mother's two white heads of hair would remain suspended. After they were gone, there would only be our voices.

But it was not yet dark enough for that, nor was it dark enough for lightning bugs, though the mosquitoes materialized the instant twilight began. My mother slapped at her plump arms and her already bitten legs as she finished her private grafting of Esther Virgil to Mamie Eisenhower's family tree, ending—by some circumlocution I did not follow, because I was thinking again of Mrs. Kite in the falling snow—with how good Son Virgil was to his mother.

"Well, young Fred was always good to poor old Mrs. Kite," Shug said.

"Well yes, he was," my mother agreed, with some qualification in her tone, "up until the time he got married. I haven't talked to her since then, nor seen her even—alive, I mean. I don't know how she took it, and now we'll never know."

"Come to think of it," Shug said, "I haven't seen her, either."

"*I* have," I said, but nobody heard me, because my sister asked at the same time what was the matter with her, that she died.

"Well she had a goitre," my mother said, "but that wasn't what killed her, if you ask me."

"Say, Nin, weren't you just surprised when you seen Fred at the funeral parlor?" asked Shug.

"No, I wasn't, not a bit, because I already knew he was here," my mother answered. "Mrs. Pearly called me today—you know Mrs. Pearly, down there on the corner by the cemetery, Mrs. Kite always went down there whenever she came, she was the last one on the line. I don't think *she's* seen her, either. Mrs. Kite kinda stopped coming when Fred ran off. We used to call Mrs. Pearly the Last Ditch, but she don't know that. Well, she said she'd seen Fred coming up from the depot from that afternoon train, and he was all dressed up—"

"In Louie's suit!" my sister cried, and began to giggle.

"Yes. And his wife wasn't with him," my mother finished.

"Oh, she *never* comes with him," said Shug. "Whenever he comes up here, instead of coming with him, she takes a trip someplace else. That's what I hear."

"You know, Brother," my sister said, "Fred got married in Cousin Louie's suit."

"*What* suit?" I asked.

"Well," my mother said, "we *think* he did. Nobody from here was at the wedding, but it was the only suit he had."

"And I was told—" Shug began.

"Well it was his *courting* suit, anyway," my sister said.

"But *what* suit?" I asked again.

"After Louie died," my mother said, "May was going to throw his clothes away, but I saw that suit and I said, 'May, don't throw that suit away, I think I can sell it for you.' It was a *good* serge suit, cost over sixty dollars, so May says, 'All right, Nin, I'll take five dollars for it.' So I just gets busy and calls up Mrs. Kite, and I say, 'Mrs. Kite, I've got a suit here I think will just fit Fred,' and I told her about it and all, and told her she could have it for six dollars. I figured if it was worth five, it was worth six. She said she'd sure like to see it, so I took it down to her and she bought it. And it was his courting suit, though the poor old soul had no idea then he was going to go off and get married."

"What happened to the extra dollar?" my sister asked, before I got the chance. "I hadn't heard about that."

"I gave it to May, but, oh, she wouldn't take it for the world," my mother said. "She made me keep it. Well, *I* did the work and the running around and all, and I'm not really as well as I used to be. It was worth a dollar."

"Did he have a clean shirt on when he come from the train?" asked Shug. "You know, they tell me she won't wash for him and she won't let him spend his money for a laundry to do it."

"His mother certainly never treated him like that, she always kept him so clean," said my mother.

"Well you know, Nin, he got her through an ad."

"Not exactly an ad, Shug—one of those love lost-and-found offices."

"Agencies," Shug corrected her. "It's the same thing."

"It's the same thing," my mother agreed. "He had several on the string. All last fall, he took train trips to Des Moines and Peoria and St. Louis. Looking them over, I guess. Ugh! And his poor old mother sitting home alone. And you should've seen him! I seen him two or three times last fall, when the leaves were dropping. Oh, I'd get so *lonesome* I'd think I couldn't *stand* it, and I'd get in the car and go down to the depot and watch the train come in, just to see who was coming and going. Every time I'd hear it blowing down by the bridge and I'd think, oh, maybe one of my boys is on that train, and oh, the river down there would look so sad and winter coming. Going and coming just makes me almost cry."

"And the time one of them came, you wasn't there," said Shug.

"And the time one of them come, I wasn't there, yes sir. But I used to see Fred going courting. Oh, you should've *seen* him! In Louie's suit. It fit him just real nice, and a checkered flannel shirt with a necktie hanging down, and *white* shoes, and if he wasn't spiffed up I'll tell you. His hair he had pasted down on his head with enough grease to slide me down the hill, and *he* was going *courting*. Same outfit every time."

"What was that song old Grandma Garrett used to sing?" my sister asked. "About the frog and Miss Mousie's den?"

"I used to sing that to you kids," said my mother. She started to sing:

"Froggy would a-wooin' go, uh-huh, uh-huh,
Froggy would a-wooin' go, uh-huh, uh-huh,
Froggy would a-wooin' go,
Whether his mama would let him or no,
Uh-huh, uh-huh."

My sister clapped her hands to her cheeks and moaned and almost had a fit, saying, "Imagine, imagine, imagine answering an ad and having *that* step off the train to meet you!"

My mother said, "One time, you know, the stationmaster come over to me after the train had gone, and he said, 'Mrs. Garrett, I've just said the worst thing. I said to Fred Kite, I said, "Why, Fred, you almost look like a human being," and you know Mrs. Garrett, I didn't mean a *thing* by it, but I was so *surprised.*' "

"Which woman did the poor guy take?" I asked, though I already knew.

"He must've taken the one in St. Louis, because he got on the southbound train last time he went, just after Thanksgiving," my mother said. "The stationmaster asked him where he was going, and he said he was going to get married, and he hasn't been back since—that is, until today. Poor old soul had to die to get him back."

"I just can't get over it, what a shock it would be," my sister went on. "I just wonder what the woman looks like."

"Like him," said Shug. "Don't you know she'd *have* to?"

Fred Kite was not clear in my memory of the past, as his mother was. I could remember him tagging along behind her sometimes when she came visiting, but his face escaped me. Too many faces had intervened, I suppose, too many things had happened. I had knocked around a lot, here and there, and been disappointed, though I had never said so, and had come home, not certain what I wanted to do or where I wanted to be. I was certain I didn't want to stay, but I had never said so. I had seen almost no one I used to know. I had kept pretty much to the house, except to go out for cigarettes or to the library, and except for the trip to the funeral home. I had seen Fred there, and, as I have said, I never would have known him.

I remembered him as a baggy figure tramping the alleys as his father had done, crushing the cinders and gravel of all the back ways. His clothes were clean but were hand-me-downs from bigger men. The coats were so long in the sleeves they hung over his hands as he walked, always with his arms dangling slightly in front of him. My father once cruelly and accurately referred to Fred and his mother as monkey and organ-grinder, saying Fred would dance to her tune, but then he was sorry he had said it.

I remember one summer when Fred was adolescent and he came with his mother to our house. My sister was nearly grown then, but my brother and I were small and my father was alive. They came at dinnertime, almost on the stroke of noon, taking seats in the kitchen to watch us eat. Mrs. Kite gave us her amphibian smile. Fred stared.

My mother, whose gift it was to do so, made conversation. Everything she said, Mrs. Kite repeated. Everything Mrs. Kite repeated, Fred repeated. My brother and sister began to laugh, but I didn't. I was the sober one. We had always been told to be polite to Mrs. Kite. In spite of himself, my father had to laugh, and when I saw him shaking at the head of the table, I laughed, too.

My mother tried to cover up for us by blaming our laughter on something the poodle dog, whose name was Cutie, had done. "Here now, you stop that!" my mother said, wagging her finger at the dog, which was begging around the table for Bologna skins.

"Here, now, you stop that!" Mrs. Kite said with great pleasure. "You stop that!" said Fred.

My mother began to giggle, trying to keep her face straight, saying "Kids! Kids! Stop that!"

Mrs. Kite, joining in the gaiety and grinning even wider, shook her head and wagged a finger in a mock scold, saying "Kids! Kids! Stop that!"

And Fred, bewildered and disturbed, beat his knees with his fists and shouted *"Kids, kids, kids, kids, kids!"*

I think he knew what was going on.

My mother, there in the twilight, was saying she didn't think Mrs. Kite knew what Fred was up to when he took those trips.

When she came to a pause, I asked her if she remembered the time I had just been thinking of.

"*I* remember that," my sister said.

"My, yes!" my mother said. "So do I. Poor old soul, *she* didn't know what we were laughing at."

Dark had nearly come. A chance breeze, like a cat's-paw at sea, passed softly through the locust trees and over the short grass, displacing a few strands of ghostly hair, intruding upon the tenants of Alma's garden. Alma herself had long since gone into her house, and she had a bright light in her kitchen window.

Shug stood up to go home, but before she took a step, she said in the low, dusky voice of scandal, "I'll tell you *this* now. Mrs. Liedermeyer told me his mother *thought* they were, but they *weren't* married."

In her hand she still held the ball of clothesline she had meant to return. Without a word, as if I were still the little boy who did the errands, she handed it to me. For a moment, I held it in both hands like a crystal ball, then I rose and carried it into the house. I did not turn on a light, for I knew my way in the dark. I paused, and looked down at the ball that rested like a head in my palm. It was too dark to see the face of it now, but last winter, I was certain, I had seen it.

I had gone to town, and snow was falling. I had been surprised to see Mrs. Kite, who, according to my mother, never solicited for the Salvation Army, in an Army booth. She wore the Army's bonnet on her head, and her tunic was open at the collar, revealing a muffler wound around her goitred neck. I was walking by, but I stopped to make sure it was really she. I was about to speak when she looked at me. She didn't know me. She gave me the same wild, unseeing look she was giving the shoppers and the falling snow. There was a snarl on her lips, and shaggy mittens on her hands, and one mitten held a bell the army of charity had given her. She clutched the bell as if it were a creature she had killed, and, with deliberate downward jerks of rage, she shook it.

I put away the clothesline and rejoined the others, who had neither moved nor spoken. As if my return were a signal, my mother said, "Poor old soul, she *never* knew."

The light went out in Alma's kitchen.

"Sitting down there on that porch, all alone, and not well, year in, year out. I know what it is, all alone in that house." My mother's voice was on the verge of breaking, but there was yet a touch of outrage in it when she added, "I suppose he'll sell it first thing, now that she's gone."

Shug said, "Oh but Nin, you don't have to worry, now that Ira's back."

A screen door slammed.

I hastened to explain that I did not mean to stay.

Before another word could be said, Alma appeared in the twilight, bearing above her head a huge bouquet as though it were a torch to light her path. She walked carefully across the grass, minding her feet. When she was before us, she held out the flowers for us to see and, in the closing darkness, touched each kind and named it. "Glads," she said, "and lilies, and babies'-breath."

I could tell by my mother's voice she was trying not to cry when she said, though she could barely see them, how beautiful they were.

CHOPIN

❖

Natacha Stewart

IN THE STUDY, Guy Dutour, known to the village as *"notre cher Maître,"* played the "Andante spianato," Opus 22. When he began the "Grande Polonaise brillante," his lap dog, Malachite, asleep on a cushion by the pedals, raised her heavy Pekinese head, opened her laminated idol's eyes one at a time, and wheezed appreciation. Upstairs, in the enormous bedroom Mme. de Sévigné had occupied as a girl, his young wife, Annette, examined the pale curve of her eyebrow in a magnifying mirror. She held no tweezers; she could no more touch a hair of her brow than pluck a straying blossom at the edge of the pond.

At the kitchen door, Guy Dutour's maid of fifteen years, Gertrude, heard the chef's bicycle on the gravelled path. He dismounted with the bicycle still in motion, and Gertrude caught the handle bars like a bridle. Once he was over the threshold, she took off his beret and his trench coat, and handed him his chef's hat.

It had rained for two weeks now; sometimes it cleared toward the end of an afternoon, just long enough for the sun to illuminate the landscape until it looked like a page from "Les Très Riches Heures," and then it rained again. The water screws weltered in the drowned wild-strawberry beds, a fresh downpour tumbled the pink snails off the raspberry bushes, and the frogs were in paradise. The wind always came from the east, and on the far horizon four cypresses leaned to the right, like the first diligent strokes in a child's exercise book. Annette watched them from the window as she twisted her pale hair into a fan-shaped knot, in the manner of the peasant women of the county; then she turned to her back-view mirror to secure it, high, with two gold barrettes from Cartier's. In the study, Malachite lightly snored at the crescendos in the Mazurka, Opus 24, No. 4. In the kitchen, the chef's right hand beat a rotary motion with a silver fork while his left squeezed olive oil from a medicine dropper. Then Gertrude announced lunch. *Œufs mayonnaise, escalopes de veau Maintenon, petits pois, laitue, fromage de chèvre, mousse au chocolat,* and coffee. Over coffee, Guy Dutour addressed his wife: "My dear, what are your plans for the afternoon?" And Annette answered, "A little sleep; perhaps a little read; then Gertrude is going to help me hang the full-length mirror. She is going to the post office to get my new Balenciaga. And I must supervise the dinner. Have you forgotten? We have guests tonight."

Once in the enormous bed and under the vicuña, Annette placed two small balls of hardened pink wax in the shells of her ears, to protect herself from the frogs, and fell into a sleep of fleeting, soundless visions. In the study, his slippered feet on the arm of the couch, Guy Dutour drowsed over Simenon's latest "Maigret." At the kitchen table, propped by cushions, a napkin tied around her neck, Malachite ate cold chicken on Gertrude's left, while at the farm on the estate, Eglantine, the farmer's wife, in search of a truce with the flooded afternoon, fed her small twins *vin ordinaire* from a teaspoon before putting them to the breast. Drunk in the cellar, her husband, Pierre-Emile, sang and lamented his sinking vineyards as he rubbed Baume Bengué into the joints of his knees.

Guy Dutour was awakened by a little girl who moved toward him jerkily, her eyes strained, her face wet, delicate, and green. She held an offering of sweet peas in one hand and half a goat cheese in the other. Before she attempted the poem dedicated to *"notre cher Maître,"* Guy Dutour brought her to the cushion by the pedals and prodded her hand into a crescent of perfumed sleeping fur: Malachite opened one laminated eye, wheezed, growled, barked, and, in warning, bit the air sideways.

When Gertrude took away the sobbing little girl, Guy Dutour sat down to the piano and worked a passage from the Mazurka, Opus 24, No. 4, with infinite patience, as if he were playing Czerny back in his sedulous childhood. Gertrude, her left hand on the doorknob, waited for the end of a phrase to bring in the camomile tea. As she was about to set the cup and saucer on the rim of the piano, the teaspoon wavered, rattled, and fell to the carpetless floor. Gertrude laughed, and her direct laughter, urgent and uniting, settled between them like a conspiracy. For Guy Dutour, the moment (sprung from the fluid mazurka and his right shoulder blade, which ached from playing in the dampness) converged on Gertrude's back and her smell (fresh-chopped tarragon, delicate sweat, and a drop of *eau de Javel*). He watched her wide back stretching the blue lawn house dress as she bent to pick up the spoon, and he remembered and saw her, climbing aboard trains with the mute practice keyboard—Gertrude, who never interrupted a phrase, and saved his leftover camomile to rinse her hair! The chilled longing, the stilled sadness, of the mazurka still held to his fingertips as his hand gently went out to her; his insured hand, kissed so often, came down the length of her spine and—as she straightened, gripping her spoon —over the lenient flesh of her buttock.

Through it all, dressed in her new Balenciaga, Annette had stood in the doorway like one of those absurd apparitions summoned by Simenon to force an improbable dénouement.

Gertrude, who saw her in Guy Dutour's eyes, walked out of the room and made her way to the kitchen carefully, like a patient after adrenalin. Annette ran upstairs, combed out her pale hair, and put in a phone call to her lover in Paris. While waiting, she thought of her black sealskin coat, and decided that for the coming season its shoulders should be taken in a little. She imagined her other furs, labelled, hibernating in cold storage. She catalogued them, simultaneously wrapping the image of her husband in infinite tenderness. And she finished the list with the private little smile she had, at times, smiled against the lapel of a dinner jacket when a man, at a charity ball, complimented her on the skin of her back and shoulders. She cancelled her call.

Guy Dutour had thrown a raincoat over his shoulders, tucked Malachite under his arm, and run slowly to the farmhouse, where he now sat drinking his third glass of Anjou *rosé* with Pierre-Emile, while Eglantine rocked the twins, who slept, flushed and fitful, grasping for air with small mottled hands. In spite of her curiosity —she sniffed intrigue behind the unexpected visit—Eglantine often deserted the men's conversation to dream a set of dentures patterned on Annette's small and delectable teeth.

Guy Dutour left them to run his long black Chrysler through the mud of the village; he crossed the swollen river, grazed and splashed the length of wall by the Manoir de Vivefontaine, drove through the brown countryside, into the forest, until he saw, posed like a white nest in a clearing, the Château de Cybèle. Malachite whined and trembled by the doorstep as Guy Dutour hesitated, then recognized the loose stone that the gatekeeper had shown him. Underneath it was a key. The door opened silently, and in spite of her wheeze, which had amplified with the damp drive and the new dust,

Malachite followed Guy Dutour as he tried the easy marble staircase and haunted the forsaken rooms with the idea of renting, perhaps, for the following summer.

When he returned, Annette and her two guests, the lisping conductor and the New York impresario who never spoke, were sitting
down to dinner. Gertrude served *asperges sauce mousseline, poulet
à l'estragon, carottes au beurre noir,* and *chicorée à l'ail.* Eglantine,
still in search of intrigue, made her daily delivery in person. "Good
evening, ladies and gentlemen," she said as she slowly crossed the
dining room, balancing a wet copy of *France-Soir* on her head; she
carried the fresh goat cheese to the kitchen, that Gertrude might
bring it back in. They had *crème renversée.* Throughout dinner, the
conductor who lisped spoke: "My beat . . ." he said. "My baton
. . ." "The way *I* handle a musician . . ." "My sinus will disappear,
God forbid," he said, "the day I die." They took their coffee into
the study, and Guy Dutour sat down to the piano. Malachite slept
through the "Andante spianato," Opus 22, the "Grande Polonaise
brillante," and the Etude, Opus 10, No. 4. "Marvellous!" said the
New York impresario, over a large cup of *tilleul.* "Stupendous and
stupefying!" said the lisping conductor, and, waving Guy Dutour
aside, he got up, rubbed his jewelled hands together, walked toward
the Pleyel, and sat down.

Annette excused herself and went upstairs. She called Gertrude to
the enormous bedroom and asked for a pail of hot water. She took
her habitual cool bath. Alone in the bed, having found with her
feet the heat of one of three hot-water bottles, Annette lay still
among the cornflowers of her printed linen sheets. But she did not
sleep. There was an unexpected crescendo in the Etude, Opus 10,
No. 4, and the customary decrescendo of the chef's bicycle on the
gravelled path. There was the rain. There were frogs. There was
the old beaver coat she wore in bad weather, which she would give
Gertrude as a gesture. There was the dark mink she need no longer
keep for the evenings, because now she would have the sables—the
outrageous, snuff-colored sables, wild and more tender to the skin
of her back than a man's dark love; the sable coat would now be
hers because she had forgiven.

IMMORTALITY

❖

ROBERT HENDERSON

O N a Wednesday morning in February, a man by the name of Martin Gaines left his sprawling apartment on Murray Hill, stopped at his office on West Forty-fifth Street, and went on a business trip. Between then and the time he returned home on Friday evening, several things took place more or less at random, and settled down to lie in wait for him.

On Wednesday afternoon, Ellen, his wife—a composed, habitually smiling woman of fifty—picked up at her hairdresser's a magazine abandoned there by a girl who had bought it to read an article about Swedish glass. In it, Mrs. Gaines read an article about pernicious anemia. Her secret and baseless conviction had long been that her body, round and firm as it was, could never last out the natural term of a life as wonderful as hers. Compensation would surely set in. By nightfall, symptoms were at her, and by Friday, though still smiling, she was stiff with fear. On Wednesday night, Martin's son Steven quarrelled with his girl (who had just finished quarrelling with her sister) and stayed out in sorrow until four o'clock, cruising the city in the family car. In the morning, his mother forbade him the use of the car for a week. Being seventeen years old, he found his fate unacceptable, and, after lying elaborately about where he was going, took the car out again that night and banged it up. And on Friday afternoon Martin's married daughter, Leora—pregnant, and anxious for the sake of her child to have what belonged to her—called on an aunt, her father's sister, to claim a pair of candlesticks she believed her grandmother had left her. The aunt, who believed, or wished to believe, that they had been left to her, refused Leora, who grew angry, and promised to appeal to her father for justice that very night.

Of course, Martin Gaines knew of none of these matters when, returning, he reached his office toward dark on Friday. Even so, he was reluctant to go home; what he did know was that his father would be there overnight. His father was lame from a broken knee suffered the year before, his blood pressure was a standing cause of family alarm, and he had no business on earth living alone in his old house in New Jersey. This Martin was going to have to say to him, as he had said it before, being duty bound. He would have to insist that his father sell the house and move to the city, where his children could keep an eye on him. There would be an argument.

So Martin stayed longer in his office than he need have. He telephoned his wife, and was struck by the dull tone of a voice that habitually welcomed him home from a two-day trip with the gladness owed to someone back from war. When he questioned her, she told him only about Steven and about Leora. Martin shook his head, knowing that that was not all that was the trouble. He washed, still delaying, but accepting the whole responsibility for putting things in order when he did go home. It had never in his adult life occurred to him that he was not answerable for everything that came to his attention. He was a tall, lumbering, sombre man, lit by occasional gleams of hopeful humor, and he lived, in a way, a little apart from his wife and children, whom he cared for deeply. He longed for them to be reasonable, honest, fair, and, above all, safe. To these ends, he was somewhat of a justice of the peace with them; if he had not been, he would have indulged them wildly.

He waited a few minutes more, staring out the window at the sky turning purple as night came. It was an effect of clouds and city that he loved. Then he saw that the rain that had been falling earlier had stopped. He rolled his umbrella into a neat foil. He emptied his briefcase and put into it papers he would not read that evening because he would be explaining to his father the hazards of age. And, having delayed that long, he reached the sidewalk outside his building in time to see a man, who had just been struck by a car, lying out in the middle of Forty-fifth Street.

The man lay on his side on the wet, glistening pavement, near the cover of a steaming manhole. A policeman bent over him. A doorman directed passing cars to the far side of the street. People had begun to gather. The man's hat and glasses had fallen off, and his overcoat lay bunched across his hips like a lifted skirt. His hair was short, neat, and lightly gray. A foot in a polished shoe was thrown out crookedly. One trouser leg was pulled up, showing a few inches of white skin. In the distorted moment, this seemed distressing to Martin; he was immensely sorry for the man who was helpless to correct it. The man was of indeterminable age—forty, fifty, no age in particular—a commuter sort of man, in tweed jacket and dark slacks, on his way to his train, going home. Blood was spreading out slowly from underneath him. The policeman took his wallet from his jacket and dug through it. One of the onlookers picked up the man's briefcase and umbrella and stood holding them uncertainly. An ambulance siren screamed far away, and then screamed nearer. Steam from the manhole blew across the man's face. Martin, who had already seen more than he wanted to see, walked away.

He put the thought and sight of the man out of his mind as well as he could, but the man persisted in returning. His briefcase had become Martin's briefcase, and his umbrella Martin's also—or perhaps it was the other way around. Martin crossed Fifth Avenue among swarms of people, thinking it incredible that all of them should be unaware that half a block away from them a man lay alone—absolutely alone, for all the gathering crowd—in the wet street. He tried to rehearse what he would say to his father, but he could not find cheerful words. He wanted to paint the picture of a small, bright, safe apartment in the city, with the old man in it, safe from vertigo and falls. But though the picture had come to him often and clearly in the past, he could see nothing now but the man there in the street and his quiet face—the face, he thought, of an established, educated man, well groomed, a husband and father— and the steam, and the shining pavement. The man was the sort of man to whom, surely, such things are expected not to happen. Death (and Martin was sure this was death) comes to such people in prescribed and manageable ways. It comes dishevelled in the street only to the faceless, bodiless ones, the people whose paths one has never imaginably crossed, whose addresses are on strange avenues of their own, where one has never walked—not to men just leaving the office, as on all Friday evenings of their lives, dressed like oneself and on their way to dinner.

He walked another block among commuters funnelling into Grand Central. A tall, red-faced man, topcoat flying, clutching under one arm a package merry with valentine hearts, drove himself zigzag toward some train; clearly he would be ruined if he missed it. (The man lying in the street had been tall, too, or had seemed so: this man's height, perhaps—Martin's height.) Who was waiting for the man in the open topcoat at the far end of his train ride? Probably—and Martin now found the idea both astonishing and heart-rending—it had not even dawned on him that he could conceivably not get there. And the whole station, Martin knew, was at that moment full of breakable people who were not thinking of themselves as such. Breakable people were in the stories in the newspapers they were carrying. They themselves were only going home.

Martin turned south toward his own home, as aware as he had been only once or twice in his life that he was mortal. The fact, as a simple fact, was an old, unquestioned one; mortality had always been lurking, out there at the far end. But it had seldom quietly stood by in the near distance.

Steven Gaines was in his room—a fort where he immured himself much of the time. He was making pencil sketches of his left hand when he heard his father open the front door. Steven selected two of the sketches and threw the rest away, first tearing them into minute pieces, then stirring them in among the other trash in his wastebasket. He dated and initialled the two, and put them in a folder of drawings that had a title page reading, "The Sketchbooks of Steven Gaines, Museum of Modern Art, New York, New York, 1967." He put the book in his suitcase, which he kept, locked, in a padlocked compartment under a window seat. Then he set out to see his father and get it over with.

His father, too, was anxious to have it over with. He had kissed his wife, and had gone into the living room—a room that had not changed very much in twenty-five years, and one that Martin had never imagined looking otherwise than as it always did. But it occurred sharply to him now that the pictures were sure sometime to come down from the walls and not go up again, the windowpanes would sometime, somehow, be broken and not replaced. Steven came in, braced for judgment, and Martin wondered for a moment what to say—what was important enough to say. Then his mind reliably supplied the answers: It was not so much the damaged car that mattered as the lying. The car called for a penalty—a curtailed allowance. Deceit called for discussion. Martin began to discuss. The required words came, but they struck him as being almost entirely weightless.

They struck him, in fact, as being quite stupid and irrelevant, though the idea that they could be so was preposterous. He had never doubted the importance of honesty, and he did not doubt it now. What he was saying was only what was expected of him—by Steven and by himself—but that was the very trouble. He did not want to say it. He felt as if he were speaking ponderously to an inconsequential misdeed, not talking to his son. He wanted to reassure himself on the point, but he did not know exactly how to go about it. Still discussing, he put his left hand on Steven's shoulder, striking a pose that he recognized at once as condescending, though he had by no means meant it so. He had not considered at all what Steven would think; he had merely wanted to touch him, here, in their room that would sometime cease to exist. A dozen seconds went by, and then there was a tiny movement of the shoulder. Martin dropped his hand, and went on listening to his own words justly deploring falsehood.

When the lecture was finished ("We'll say no more about it," Martin said, in conclusion), Steven went to clean up, and Martin stayed where he was. He thought that Steven was a distant boy, a secret boy, who kept things to himself. Then the telephone rang, like a portent, and as Martin went down the hall to answer it, he thought again of the man lying in the street. Would the man's wife be setting the table, or would she know by now that he was dead? If she did not, was a telephone ringing, this minute, in the dark, high up in some echoing office (an office with a desk in it exactly like Martin's desk, chairs like his chairs)—ringing and stopping, and almost at once beginning to ring again? Martin picked up his own telephone. His angry daughter was calling. He said yes, of course she could come and talk to him in an hour or so.

And in her apartment in Cooper Village, Leora Gaines Downey (by her married name) hung up the phone and went back to the table where she and her husband were finishing an early dinner; it was early because her husband studied at night. She was a slight, graceful girl, with glasses that enhanced the seriousness of her small face. While she ate her cheese and fruit, she marshalled arguments in favor of her child, who would need a few modest heirlooms, and against her aunt, who had everything a lone woman could want, including candlesticks that did not belong to her, and—now that Leora thought of it—a seashore cottage she never used and certainly never lent. To Leora, justice was far from blind; it saw clearly through her eyes. When dinner was over, she stacked the dishes, and told her husband, to his relief, that he must not think of going with her to see her father. She put on coat and boots and a red stocking cap, and, before she left, saw that her husband was com-

fortably arranged with books and pencils and pipe at the cleared
dining table. She kissed his bald spot, which she regarded as a foreshadowing of eminence, and went out.

So now it was Martin's daughter who was talking earnestly about
affairs that three hours before would have been of weight, and he
who was listening silently. And again the whole familiar process of
establishing what was right and what was wrong seemed to have
gone off balance, and words were being spent on trivialities. Leora
had come as the family were having coffee, and while she filed her
brief for the candlesticks, Martin looked around at them all—his
discursive (and, he thought, rather greedy) daughter, his distant son,
his troubled wife (*something* was troubling her), his stubborn father
—seeing them in a strange double perspective, as if he were at the
same time there in his chair and somewhere outside the room or
beyond the window.

Then Leora paused and took off her glasses, and put them on
again and looked at him, and in that instant Martin saw her as
she had once stood looking at him when she was seven—tiny and
owlish and dubious, but severe—showing him her first glasses. The
glimpse vanished, but it left Martin filled with love for her, and
with pity for her shortcomings, which did not seem to matter as
much tonight as they often did. He ached at the thought that people
besides himself might be aware of them, and he wanted her to have
the candlesticks. But what he said to her, as if by rote, was that he
would discuss the whole question with her aunt, and sort out what
the case was. Whoever was fairly entitled to the candlesticks should
have them. And as he said this, a queer thought ran into his head—
that not only had Leora always needed him, if only to settle her
disputes, but he had always needed her to bring them to him.

Ellen Gaines, her hands steady, her smile serene and fixed, cleared
the dinner table, walking with the light stateliness she had early
learned to walk with. But she felt as if she were in a tight case—an
invisible garment that cramped and suffocated her, and shut out
all but the mere sight of her surroundings. Through it neither love
for nor pride in her silver and her Wedgwood managed to seep.
Out of it, when she smiled at her father-in-law, she was sure her
smile emerged a ghastly grin. From inside it, she absently waved
Leora home to her husband, though Leora's husband signified little
to Ellen at the moment. Inside, with her, were thoughts of hospitals

and pain, and bills—enormous bills for her husband to spend his good years paying. And, to be sure, the tips of her fingers were cold, and tingling constantly, and the base of her spine felt hollow. She looked in a mirror for ravages, or at least for the bedragglement of the sick, and saw, mocking her, her clear skin, her clear eyes, the soft, perfect waves of her gray hair. She told herself brusquely that her fears were imagination, and then, weakly and ruefully, she laughed at herself for the folly of trying to pretend that she was well. And all the time she was dreading, and longing for, the moment when she would tell her husband of her fears, as she always did. He would be scornful, and would talk about hobgoblins. He would tell her to be reasonable. He would point out that she had been examined only lately and found to be blooming. He would restrain his evident impatience, though giving her selected glimpses of it, while explaining that her symptoms were pure nerves. And at last, whether because he had said and done these things or merely because she had come out into the open with her fear and talked about it, the fear would begin to ebb, and she would feel abashed and relieved, and life and her silver would look lovely to her again.

Meanwhile, Martin had lit a cigarette and gone into his study. It was time for a television roundup of the news, and he turned it on, then turned it off. It was foolish to wonder if any notice would be taken of one man killed by a car. That was a commonplace, not a piece of news. And yet the man's life had ended there, by the steaming manhole; it had all been bound for that spot. It seemed to Martin that the block might have been shut off for a while—kept quiet—but of course such a thing was ridiculous. People were swarming along it this very minute—noisy, bound for theatres. But he hoped it would not occur to the man's wife, wherever she was, to think how quickly his death could vanish from the street. Then Martin, putting out his cigarette, went to the kitchen to help his own wife, whom he did not want to leave by herself any longer.

He walked through the swinging door into the bright kitchen, and took a towel from a rack, and for a short while, in the warm kitchen world, his own world looked like itself again. True, he had a peculiar, a senseless moment when he saw his wife visibly there beside the sink and in the same second was stormed by a longing for her, as if she were far away. But then she told him about her tingling fingertips, and he recognized, and climbed onto, what he thought was solid ground. He spoke about morbid spells and fancies, and not giving way. She mentioned vague, terrible diseases of the blood. He went on with his curative discussion. But presently, looking tired, she dropped her work and sat on a stool, her hands folded in her lap, like a large but wholly biddable child waiting to be told what to think, and at once his sound common sense and his balance collapsed again, and he was not sure of himself. He heard himself reminding her of all the good things the doctors had said, but the indulgent, scoffing note he tried to strike was missing. She nodded with no conviction whatever, and alarm grew up in him. He told himself that there was not a chance in a thousand that she was right, and then that there was indeed just that.

So the hobgoblins crossed over into Martin, and the man in Forty-fifth Street, who had reduced the importance of other things tonight, had now reduced that of reason and common sense. It seemed to Martin that he and Ellen were standing there alone in a small pocket of light and comfort encircled and crowded by loss— not his loss of her, or hers of him (though he was appalled at the thought of ever being out of reach of her if she should need him), but all loss, all ending. And there was no time, in a mortal moment, to be reasonable. He said dutifully, hopefully, that her symptoms were pure nerves, but still he could not bring the necessary—the unanswerable—impatience into his voice. She listened, and nodded again, and went back to the sink, and Martin was sure that he had failed her.

Perhaps he had failed them all, he thought a little later, but he could not say in what way, or why he thought so. He felt perplexed and thwarted. Right was right, fairness was fairness, honesty was honesty, sense was sense, and yet all these old, dependable companions seemed to be standing guard between him and his family tonight. They would not let him go close, which was all he wanted, and he guessed with a shock that perhaps they seldom had. Now it was nearly nine of this queer evening. The dishes were done. His father was in the study watching television and waiting. There were not many places for Martin to go, many things to do—many excuses for delay—in even a large apartment.

He went into the living room and tried to think of his father's house, and his father endangered in it. Nowadays, the old man forgot things, and this exasperated him, and when he found he had forgotten something, he would stamp away intemperately, upstairs or down, to do or get whatever he had forgotten. He had set up a workshop in the basement, and he was repairing half the furniture in the house. The basement stairs were steep and dim. The furniture he dragged down was cumbersome.

The house was too big; the house was too old. But the more persistently Martin tried to reason against it, the more persistently a memory kept pressing to be recalled. In front of the house was a tree that one night long ago had been sheathed in ice and had bewitched him. It had, in fact, caused him to feel a good deal as he felt now, and when he let the memory come, he did so reluctantly, not wanting it to make him compound the evening's heresies.

He and Ellen had come back from their honeymoon that night. Their apartment was not finished. They were staying in Martin's old room, and Ellen was already asleep when, past the edge of the drawn blind, Martin caught a glimpse of the tree sparkling in the light of the street lamp under it. And he did something foreign to a nature that did little on impulse and was designed, on the whole, to see icy trees as merely trees in danger of cracking. He got up and raised the blind, and the tree blazed in at him, glittering and still, and more beautiful than any tree—or anything else—had seemed to him before. He went back to bed and lay a long time looking at it, while it entangled itself in his life. Ellen beside him, and his parents in the next room, and his childhood and his hopes, and the old house and the tree became part of one another, and all of them were suddenly, for the first time, capable of ending. The past was already gone, and the future—bright though it was, and varicolored and lovely as the tree—now also had a treasonable look of brevity. But in spite of transience and loss, the spell of a moment of light that would never come again enclosed and gently, sweetly exalted him. The tree would lose its enchantment, and presently grow green again, and later storms would ice it, but he knew that that night would be unique among the nights of his life.

Now Martin went into the study and saw that, though the set was on, his father was not looking at television. He was gazing blankly down the length of his legs, stretched out in front of him. When he heard Martin come in, he heaved himself up and limped to the set and turned it off. He sat down and smiled hesitantly at Martin, who realized that it might not be necessary to argue, after all. The realization undid him. He knew—he allowed himself to know, though he had spent a year keeping the demoralizing knowledge at arm's length—that his father wanted beyond anything else in the world to spend the rest of his life in his own house. And Martin suddenly wanted overwhelmingly to stop trying to do the prim, trifling things he would have done on any ordinary night, and to give a gift, however foolish, however risky, to one of the people he loved.

"Well, Papa," he said. "I think we ought to have a talk about the house."

"I know how you feel about it," his father said. "I suppose you're right."

"I don't think you'd be happy in an apartment, or in the city," Martin said, while his mind, in its rectitude, protested and retreated and protested. "I don't think I'd consider it, if I were you."

"What's that?" his father asked.

"You want to stay at home," Martin said, "so why don't you?"

"I would like that," his father said slowly. "I think I will. You're positive you don't mind?"

"No," Martin said, already dismayed. "You stay at home."

Steven Gaines, leaving the dinner table, had seen his father look at his sister with an expression that brought into relief a wonderfully fluent line of forehead, nose, and jaw. He went to his room, and, after a few tries, jubilantly decided that he had caught it. He put the sketch in his folder, and set out to visit his girl. He considered asking her to marry him. He yearned to take the sketch along, but he did not; it was something to be revealed only when the time came.

Ellen Gaines, in her kitchen, had finished the dishes in panic. It seemed plain enough to her that Martin knew how ill she was; she had heard it in his voice. Then she watched his back as he went out the door, and abruptly she knew that he knew nothing—nothing at all. He was only afraid. He was afraid, without reason, for her. The panic lifted. What became plain to her now was that he needed her solace, and she felt glad and guilty. The fear of the last three days began to drain away. She wanted only to reassure him, to protect him. She resolved that she would not be so foolish again—so childish. She thought fondly that she must take better care of her husband.

Steven came hurrying through the kitchen on his way out. He kissed his mother as he passed, astonishing her; it was not exactly a thing he did every day. Heartened, she decided that she would save Martin a chore. She went into their room and called her sister-in-law. The sister-in-law laughed, and said that of course she would gladly give the candlesticks to Leora. The trouble was only that Leora had insisted that they belonged to her.

The goodness of Ellen Gaines' life flowed over and through her once more. She called Leora and told her that she could have the candlesticks at the price of a small retreat. Seeing her child already passing the candlesticks on, with grace, to new generations, Leora planned a handsome retreat, intended so to propitiate her aunt that when summer came she would offer her the beach house. Then, looking ahead as her habit was, Leora saw herself inheriting it.

Martin's father was, by this time, on his way to bed. He reflected that if Martin had not changed his mind, he would have had to give in. Later, secretly, in the dark, he confessed to the darkness that he was not certain how long he could keep the house up. Still, he was excited—too excited to sleep. He thought that one minute you could be about to live your life out in a place you'd rather be dead than live in, and the next you could be on your way home, where you belonged. Silently, he promised Martin that he would be careful on the stairs. One had to slow down a little as one grew older. But, by and large, it seemed to him that now he had all he was prepared to ask of life. He could not make out what had got into Martin, but whatever it was, he would always be grateful that it had.

It was now just past eleven. On a short, winding county road leading from Route 22 a few miles north of Armonk, there were three houses, well apart. In the one nearest the highway, a single bedroom light was shining, back of slanted Venetian blinds. In the second, there were no lights. In the third—a half-timbered house set on a knoll and surrounded by rhododendron and small firs—all the lights were burning. At eleven-ten, an enclosed black car—a small hearse—turned off Route 22, wound along the short road, and turned in at the driveway of the third house.

THE HAPPIEST I'VE BEEN

❖

John Updike

Neil Hovey came for me wearing a good suit. He parked his
father's blue Chrysler on the dirt ramp by our barn and got
out and stood by the open car door in a double-breasted tan gabar-
dine suit, his hands in his pockets and his hair combed with water,
squinting up at a lightning rod an old hurricane had knocked
crooked. We were driving to Chicago, so I had packed my good
clothes and dressed in worn-out slacks and an outgrown corduroy
shirt. But Neil, though not my closest friend, was the one I had
always been most relaxed with, so I wasn't very disturbed. My
parents and I walked out from the house, across the low stretch of
lawn that was mostly mud after the thaw that had come on Christmas Day, and my grandmother, though I had kissed her goodbye
inside the house, came out onto the porch, stooped and rather angry-
looking, her head haloed by wild old woman's white hair and the
hand more severely afflicted by arthritis waggling at her breast in a
worried way. It was growing dark, and my grandfather had gone to
bed. "Nev-er trust the man who wears the red necktie and parts his
hair in the middle" had been his final advice to me.

We had expected Neil since the middle of the afternoon. Nineteen almost twenty, I was a college sophomore home on vacation;
that fall I had met in a fine-arts course a girl I had decided I loved,
and she had invited me to the New Year's party her parents always
gave and to stay at her house a few days. She lived in Chicago and
so did Neil now, though he had gone to our high school. His father
did something—sold steel was my impression, a huge man opening
a briefcase and saying "The I-beams are very good this year"—that
required him to be always on the move, so that at about thirteen
Neil had been left with Mrs. Hovey's parents. They had lived in
Olinger since the town was incorporated; indeed, old Jesse Lan-
caster, whose sick larynx whistled when he breathed to us boys his

shocking and uproarious thoughts on the girls that walked by his porch all day long, had twice been burgess. Meanwhile Neil's father got a stationary job, in Chicago, but he let Neil stay in Olinger until he finished high school. From Chicago to this part of Pennsylvania was a drive of seventeen hours. In the twenty months Neil had been gone, he had come east fairly often; he loved driving, and Olinger was the one thing he had that was close to a childhood home. In Chicago he was working in a garage and getting his teeth straightened by the Army so they could draft him. The Korean War was on. He had to go back, and I wanted to go to Chicago, so it was a happy arrangement. "You're all dressed up," I accused him immediately.

"I've been saying goodbye."

The knot of his necktie was low and the corners of his mouth were rubbed with pink. Years later my mother recalled how that evening his breath stank so strongly of beer she was frightened to let me go with him. "*Your* grandfather always thought *his* grandfather was a very dubious character," she said.

My father and Neil put my suitcases into the trunk; they contained all the clothes I had brought with me from school, for the girl and I were going back to college on the train together, and I would not see my home again until spring.

"Well, goodbye, boys," my mother said. "I think you're both very brave." In regard to me she meant the girl as much as the roads.

"Don't you worry, Mrs. Nordholm," Neil told her quickly. "He'll be safer than in his own bed. I bet he sleeps from here to Indiana." He looked at me with an irritating imitation of her own fond gaze. When they shook hands goodbye it was with an equality established on the base of my helplessness. His being so slick startled me, but you can have a friend for years and never see how he operates with adults.

I embraced my mother and over her shoulder with the camera of my head tried to take a snapshot I could keep of the house, the woods behind it and the sunset behind them, the bench beneath the walnut tree where my grandfather cut apples into skinless bits and fed them to himself, and the ruts the bakery truck had made in the soft lawn that morning.

We started down the half mile of dirt road to the highway that, one way, went through Olinger to the city of Alton and, the other way, led through farmland to the Turnpike. It was luxurious after the stress of farewell to finger a cigarette out of the pack squaring my shirt pocket. My family knew I smoked but I didn't do it in front of them; we were all too sensitive to bear the awkwardness. I lit mine and held the match for Hovey. It was a relaxed friendship. We were about the same height and had the same degree of athletic incompetence and the same curious lack of whatever force it was that aroused loyalty and compliance in beautiful girls. There was his bad teeth and my skin allergy; these were being remedied now, when they mattered less. But it seemed to me that the most important thing—about both our friendship and our failures to become, for all the love we felt for women, actual lovers—was that he and I lived with grandparents. This improved both our backward and forward vistas; we knew about the midnight coughing fits and bedside commodes that awaited most men, and we had a sense of childhoods before 1900, when the farmer ruled the land and America faced west. We had gained a humane dimension that made us gentle and humorous among peers but diffident at dances and hesitant in cars. Girls hate boys' doubts; they amount to insults. Gentleness is for married women to appreciate. (This is my thinking then.) A girl who has received out of nowhere a gift worth all Africa's ivory and Asia's gold wants more than just humanity to bestow it on.

When he came to the highway Neil turned right, toward Olinger, instead of left toward the Turnpike. My reaction was to twist and assure myself through the rear window that, though a pink triangle of sandstone stared through the bare treetops, nobody at my house could possibly see.

When he was again in third gear, Neil asked, "Are you in a hurry?"

"No. Not especially."

"Schuman's having his New Year's party two days early so we can go. I thought we'd go for a couple hours and miss the Friday-night stuff on the Pike." His mouth moved and closed carefully over the dull, silver, painful braces.

"Sure," I said. "I don't care." In everything that followed there was this sensation of my being picked up and carried somewhere.

It was four miles from the farm to Olinger; we entered by Buchanan Road, driving past the tall white brick house I had lived in until I was fifteen. My grandfather had bought it before I was born and his stocks went bad, which had happened in the same year. The new owners had strung colored bulbs all along the front doorframe and the edges of the porch roof. Downtown the cardboard Santa

Claus still nodded in the drugstore window, but the loudspeaker on the undertaker's lawn had stopped broadcasting carols. It was quite dark now, so the arches of red and green lights above Grand Avenue seemed miracles of life; in daylight you saw the bulbs were just hung from a straight cable by cords of different lengths. Larry Schuman lived on the other side of town, the newer side. Lights ran all the way up the front edges of his house and across the rain gutter. The next-door neighbor had a plywood reindeer-and-sleigh floodlit on his front lawn and a snowman of papier-mâché leaning tipsily (his eyes were x's) against the corner of the house. No real snow had fallen yet that winter. The air this evening, though, hinted that harder weather was coming.

The Schumans' living room felt warm. In one corner a blue spruce drenched with tinsel reached to the ceiling; around its pot surged a drift of wrapping paper and ribbon and boxes, a few still containing presents—gloves and diaries and other small properties that hadn't yet been absorbed into the main stream of affluence. The ornamental balls were big as baseballs and all either crimson or indigo; the tree was so well dressed I felt self-conscious in the same room with it, without a coat or tie and wearing an old green shirt too short in the sleeves. Everyone else was dressed for a party. Then Mr. Schuman stamped in comfortingly, crushing us all into one underneath his welcome—Neil and me and the three other boys who had shown up so far. He was dressed to go out on the town, in a vanilla topcoat and silvery silk muffler, and smoking a cigar with the band still on. You could see, in Mr. Schuman, where Larry got the red hair and pale eyelashes and the self-confidence, but what in the son was smirking and pushy was in the father shrewd and masterful. What the one used to make you nervous the other used to put you at ease. While Mr. was jollying us, Zoe Loessner, Larry's probable fiancée and the only girl at the party so far, was talking nicely to Mrs., nodding with her entire neck and fingering her Kresge pearls and blowing cigarette smoke through the corners of her mouth, to keep it away from the middle-aged woman's face. Each time Zoe spat out a plume, the shelf of blond hair overhanging her temple lifted slightly, so emphatic was her politeness. Mrs. Schuman beamed serenely above her fur coat and rhinestone pocketbook. It was odd to see her dressed in the trappings of the prosperity which usually supported her good nature invisibly, like a firm mattress under a homely bright quilt. She was a prime product of the country, a Pennsylvania Dutch woman, who loved feeding her sons, and imagined that the entire world, like her life, was going well. I never saw her not smile, except at her husband. At last she moved him into the outdoors. He turned at the threshold and did a trick with his knees and called in to us, "Be good and if you can't be good, be careful."

With them out of the way, the next item was getting liquor. It was a familiar business. Did anybody have a forged driver's license? If not, who would dare to make one? Larry could provide India ink. Then again, Larry's older brother Dale might be home and would go if it didn't take too much time. However, on weekends he often went straight from work to his fiancée's apartment and stayed until Sunday. If worst came to worst, Larry knew an illegal place in Alton, but they really soaked you. The problem was solved strangely. More people were arriving all the time, and one of them, Cookie Behn, who had been held back one year and hence was deposited in our grade, announced that last November he had become in honest fact twenty-one. I, at least, gave Cookie my share of the money feeling a little queasy, vice had become so handy.

The party was the party I had been going to all my life, beginning with Ann Mahlon's first Halloween party, that I attended as a hot, lumbering, breathless, and blind Donald Duck. My mother had made the costume, and the eyes kept slipping, and were farther apart than my eyes, so that even when the clouds of gauze parted, it was to reveal the frustrating depthless world seen with one eye. Ann, who because her mother loved her so much as a child had remained somewhat childish, and I and another boy and girl who were not involved in any romantic crisis went down into the Schumans' basement to play circular ping-pong. Armed with paddles, we stood each at a side of the table and when the ball was stroked ran around it counterclockwise, slapping the ball and laughing. To run better the girls took off their high-heeled shoes and ruined their stockings on the cement floor. Their faces and arms and shoulder sections became flushed, and when either of the girls lunged forward toward the net the stiff neckline of her semi-formal dress dropped away and the white cups of her brassière could be glimpsed holding in fat, and when one of them reached high her shaved armpit gleamed like a bit of chicken skin. An earring of Ann's flew off and the two connected rhinestones skidded to lie near the wall, among the Schumans' power mower and badminton poles and empty bronze motor-oil cans twice punctured by triangles. All these images were immediately lost in the whirl of our running; we were dizzy before we stopped. Ann leaned on me getting back into her shoes.

When we pushed the cellar door open it banged against the newel post of the carpeted stairs going to the second floor; a third of the way up, a couple sat discussing. The girl, Jacky Iselin, cried without emotion—the tears and nothing else, like water flowing over wood. Some people were in the kitchen, mixing drinks and making noise. In the living room others danced to records: 78s then—stiff discs stacked in a ponderous leaning cylinder on the spindle of the Schumans' console. Every three minutes, with a click and a crash, another dropped and the mood abruptly changed. One moment it would be "Stay As Sweet As You Are": Clarence Lang with the absolute expression of an idiot standing and rocking monotonously with June Kaufmann's boneless sad brown hand trapped in his and their faces, staring in the same direction, pasted together like the facets of an idol. The music stopped; when they parted, a big squarish dark patch stained the cheek of each. Then the next moment it would be Goodman's "Loch Lomond" or "Cherokee" and nobody but Margaret Lento wanted to jitterbug. Mad, she danced by herself, swinging her head recklessly and snapping her backside; a corner of her skirt flipped a Christmas ball onto the rug, where it collapsed into a hundred convex reflectors. Female shoes were scattered in innocent pairs about the room. Some were flats, resting under the sofa shyly toed in; others were high heels lying askew, the spike of one thrust into its mate. Sitting alone and ignored in a great armchair, I experienced within a warm keen dishevelment, as if there were real tears in my eyes. Had things been less unchanged, they would have seemed less tragic. But the girls who had stepped out of these shoes were, with few exceptions, the ones who had attended my life's party. The alterations were so small: a haircut, an engagement ring, a tendency toward plumpness more frankly confessed. While they wheeled above me I sometimes caught from their faces an unfamiliar glint, off of a hardness I did not remember, as if beneath their skins these girls were growing more dense. The brutality added to the features of the boys I knew seemed a more willed effect, more desired and so less grievous. Considering that there was a war, surprisingly many were present—4-F or at college or simply waiting to be called. Shortly before midnight the door rattled, and there, under the porch light, looking forlorn and chilled in their brief athletic jackets, stood three members of the class ahead of ours who in the old days always tried to crash Schuman's parties. At

Olinger High they had been sports stars, and they still stood with that well-coördinated looseness, a look of dangling from strings. The three of them had enrolled together at Melanchthon, a small Lutheran college on the edge of Alton, and in this season played on the Melanchthon basketball team. That is, two did; the third hadn't been good enough. Schuman, out of cowardice more than mercy, let them in, and they hid immediately in the basement, and didn't bother us, having brought their own bottle.

There was one novel awkwardness. Darryl Bechtel had married Emmy Johnson, and the couple came. Darryl had worked in his father's greenhouse and had been considered dull; it was Emmy that we knew. At first no one danced with her, and Darryl didn't know how, but then Schuman, perhaps as host, dared. Others followed, but Schuman had her in his arms most often, and at midnight, when we were pretending the new year began, he kissed her; a wave of kissing swept the room now, and everyone struggled to kiss Emmy. Even I did. There was something about her being married that made it extraordinary. Her cheeks burning, she kept glancing around for rescue, but Darryl, embarrassed to see his wife dance, had gone into old man Schuman's den, where Neil sat brooding, sunk in mysterious sorrow.

When the kissing subsided and Darryl emerged, I went in to see Neil. He was holding his face in his hands and tapping his foot to a record playing on Mr. Schuman's private phonograph: Krupa's "Dark Eyes." The arrangement was droning and circular and Neil had kept the record going for hours. He loved saxophones; most of us children of that depression vintage did. I asked him, "Do you think the traffic on the Turnpike has died down by now?"

He took down the tall glass on the cabinet beside him and took a studied swallow. From the side, his face seemed lean and somewhat blue. "Maybe," he said, staring at the ice cubes submerged in the ochre liquid. "The girl in Chicago's expecting you?"

"Well, yeah, but we can call and let her know, once *we* know."

"You think she'll spoil?"

"How do you mean?"

"I mean, won't you be seeing her all the time after we get there? Aren't you going to marry her?"

"I have no idea. I might."

"Well then you'll have the rest of Kingdom Come to see her." He looked directly at me, and it was plain in the blur of his eyes that he was sick-drunk. "The trouble with you guys that have all the luck," he said slowly, "is that you don't give a damn about us that don't have any." Such melodramatic rudeness, coming from Neil, surprised me, as had his blarney with my mother hours before. In trying to evade his steady, wounded stare, I discovered there was another person in the room: a girl sitting with her shoes on, reading *Holiday*. Though she held the magazine in front of her face, I knew from the gaudy air of her clothes and from her unfamiliar legs that she was the girl friend Margaret Lento had brought.

Margaret didn't come from Olinger but from Riverside, a section of Alton. She had met Larry Schuman at a summer job in a restaurant, and for the rest of high school they had more or less gone together. Since then, though, it had dawned on Mr. and Mrs. Schuman that even in a democracy distinctions exist: probably welcome news to Larry. In the cruelest and most prolonged way he could manage, he had been breaking off with her throughout the year now nearly ended. I had been surprised to find her at this party. Obviously she had felt shaky about attending and had brought the friend as the only kind of protection she could afford. The other girl was acting just like a guard.

There being no answer to Neil, I went into the living room, where Margaret, insanely drunk, was throwing herself around as if wanting to break a bone. Somewhat in time to the music she would run a few steps, then snap her body like a whip, her chin striking her chest and her hands flying backward, fingers fanned, as her shoulders pitched forward. In her state her body was childishly plastic; unharmed, she would bounce back from this jolt and begin to clap and kick and hum. Schuman stayed away from her. Margaret was small, not more than five three, with the smallness ripeness comes to early. She had bleached a section of her black hair platinum, cropped her head all over, and trained the stubble into short hyacinthine curls like those on antique statues of boys. Her face seemed quite coarse from the front, so her profile was classical unexpectedly. She might have been Portia. When she was not putting on her savage, pointless dance, she was in the bathroom being sick. The pity and the vulgarity of her exhibition made everyone who was sober uncomfortable; our common guilt in witnessing this girl's rites brought us so close together in that room that it seemed never, not in all time, could we be parted. I myself was perfectly sober. I had the impression people only drank to stop being unhappy and I nearly always felt at least fairly happy.

Luckily, Margaret was in a sick phase around one o'clock, when the elder Schumans came home. They looked in at us briefly. It was a pleasant joke to see in their smiles that, however corrupt and unwinking we felt, to them we looked young and sleepy: Larry's friends. Things quieted after they went up the stairs. In half an hour, people began coming out of the kitchen balancing cups of coffee. By two o'clock, four girls stood in aprons at Mrs. Schuman's sink, and others were padding back and forth carrying glasses and ashtrays. Another blameless racket pierced the clatter in the kitchen. Out on the cold grass the three Melanchthon athletes had set up the badminton net and in the faint glow given off by the house were playing. The bird, ascending and descending through uneven bars of light, glimmered like a firefly. Now that the party was dying, Neil's apathy seemed deliberately exasperating, even vindictive. For at least another hour, he persisted in hearing "Dark Eyes" over and over again, holding his head and tapping his foot. The entire scene in the den had developed a fixity that was uncanny; the girl remained in the chair and read magazines, *Holiday* and *Esquire*, one after another. In the meantime, cars came and went and raced their motors out front; Schuman took Ann Mahlon home and didn't come back; and the athletes carried the neighbor's artificial snowman into the center of the street and disappeared. Somehow in the arrangements shuffled together at the end, Neil had agreed to take Margaret and the other girl home. Margaret convalesced in the downstairs bathroom for most of that hour. I unlocked a little glass bookcase ornamenting a desk in the dark dining room and removed a volume of Thackeray's Works. It turned out to be Volume II of "Henry Esmond." I began it, rather than break another book out of the set, which had been squeezed in there so long the bindings had sort of interpenetrated.

Esmond was going off to war again when Neil appeared in the archway and said, "O.K., Norseman. Let's go to Chicago." "Norseman" was a variant of my name he used only when he was feeling special affection.

We turned off all the lamps and left the hall bulb burning against Larry's return. Margaret Lento seemed chastened. Neil gave her his arm and helped her into the back seat of his father's car; I stood aside to let the other girl get in with her, but Neil indicated that I should. I supposed he realized this left only the mute den-girl to go up front with him. She sat well over on her side, was all I noticed. Neil backed into the street and with unusual care steered past the snowman. Our headlights made vivid the fact that the snowman's back was a hollow right-angled gash; he had been built up against the corner of the house.

From Olinger, Riverside was diagonally across Alton. The city was sleeping as we drove through it. Most of the stop lights were blinking green. Among cities Alton had a bad reputation; its graft and gambling and easy juries and bawdyhouses were supposedly notorious throughout the Middle Atlantic states. But to me it always presented an innocent face: row after row of houses built of a local dusty-red brick, the color of flowerpots, each house fortified with a tiny, intimate, balustraded porch, and nothing but the wealth of movie houses and beer signs along its main street to suggest that its citizens loved pleasure more than the run of mankind. Indeed, as we moved at moderate speed down these hushed streets bordered with parked cars, a limestone church bulking at every corner and the hooded street lamps keeping watch from above, Alton seemed less the ultimate center of an urban region than itself a suburb of some vast mythical metropolis, like Pandemonium or Paradise. I was conscious of evergreen wreaths on door after door and of fanlights of stained glass in which the house number was embedded. I was also conscious that every block was one block farther from the Turnpike.

Riverside, fitted into the bends of the Schuylkill, was not so regularly laid out. Margaret's house was one of a short row, composition-shingled, which we approached from the rear, down a tiny cement alley speckled with drains. The porches were a few inches higher than the narrow pavement. Margaret asked us if we wanted to come in for a cup of coffee, since we were going to Chicago; Neil accepted by getting out of the car and slamming his door. The noise filled the alley, alarming me. I wondered at the easy social life that evidently existed among my friends at three-thirty in the morning. Margaret did, however, lead us in stealthily, and she turned on only the kitchen switch. The kitchen was divided from the living room by a large sofa, which faced into littered gloom where distant light from beyond the alley spilled over a window sill and across the spines of a radiator. In one corner the glass of a television set showed; the screen would seem absurdly small now, but then it seemed disproportionately elegant. The shabbiness everywhere would not have struck me so much if I hadn't just come from Schuman's place. Neil and the other girl sat on the sofa; Margaret held a match to a gas burner and, as the blue flame licked an old kettle, doled instant coffee into four flowered cups.

By the kitchen's solitary window, overlooking a drab Alton street, someone who had once lived in this house had built a breakfast nook like a luncheonette booth, a yellow table between two high-backed benches. I sat in it and read all the words I could see: "Salt," "Pepper," "Have some LUMPS," "December," "Mohn's Milk Inc.— A Very Merry Christmas and Joyous New Year—Mohn's Milk is *Safe* Milk—'Mommy, Make It Mohn's!' " "Matches," "Hotpoint," "PRESS," "Magee Stove FEDERAL & Furnace Corp.," "God Is in This House," "Ave Maria Gratia Plena," "SHREDDED WHEAT Benefits— Exciting New Pattern KUNGSHOLM." After serving the two on the sofa, Margaret came to me with coffee and sat down opposite me in the booth. Fatigue had raised two blue welts beneath her eyes.

"Well," I asked her, "did you have a good time?"

She smiled and glanced down and made the small sound "Ch," vestigial of "Jesus." With absent-minded delicacy she stirred her coffee, lifting and replacing the spoon without a ripple.

"Rather odd at the end," I said. "Not even the host there."

"He took Ann Mahlon home."

"I know." I was surprised that she did, having been sick in the bathroom for that hour.

"You sound jealous," she added.

"Who does? I do? I don't."

"You like her, John, don't you?" Her using my first name and the quality of the question did not, though we had really—not counting parties—just met, seem forward, considering the hour and that she had brought me coffee. There is little further to go with a girl who has brought you coffee.

"Oh, I like everybody," I told her, "and the longer I've known them the more I like them, because the more they're me. The only people I like better are ones I've just met. Now Ann Mahlon I've known since kindergarten. Every day her mother used to bring her to the edge of the schoolyard for months after all the other mothers had stopped." I wanted to cut a figure in Margaret's eyes, but they were too dark. Stoically she had got on top of her weariness, but it was growing bigger under her.

"Did you like her then?"

"I felt sorry for her being embarrassed by her mother."

She asked me, "What was Larry like when he was little?"

"Oh, bright. Kind of mean."

"Was he mean?"

"I'd say so. Yes. In some grade or other he and I began to play chess together. I always won until secretly he took lessons from a man his parents knew and read strategy books."

Margaret laughed, genuinely pleased. "Then did he win?"

"Once. After that I really tried, and after *that* he decided chess was kid stuff. Besides, he'd used me up. He'd have these runs on people where you'd be down at his house every afternoon, then in a couple months he'd get a new pet and that'd be that."

"He's funny," she said. "He has a kind of cold mind. He decides on what he wants, then he does what he has to do, you know, and nothing anybody says can change him."

"He does tend to get what he wants," I told her guardedly, realizing that to her this meant her. Poor bruised little girl, in her mind he was all the time cleaving with rare cunning through his parents' objections straight to her.

My coffee was nearly gone, so I glanced toward the sofa in the other room. Neil and the girl had sunk out of sight behind its back. Before this it had honestly not occurred to me that they had a relationship, but now that I saw, it seemed plausible, and, at this time of night, good news, though it meant we would not be going to Chicago quite yet.

So I talked to Margaret about Larry, and she responded, showing really quite an acute sense of him. To me, considering the personality of a childhood friend so seriously, as if overnight he had become a factor in the world, seemed absurd; I couldn't even deeply believe that in her world he mattered much. Larry Schuman, in little more than a year, had become nothing to me. The important thing, rather than the subject, was the conversation itself, the quick agreements, the slow nods, the weave of different memories; it was like one of those Panama baskets shaped underwater around a worthless stone.

She offered me more coffee. When she returned with it, she sat down not opposite but beside me, lifting me to such a pitch of gratitude and affection that the only way I could think to express it was by *not* kissing her, as if a kiss were another piece of abuse women suffered. She said, "Cold. Cheap bastard turns the thermostat down to sixty," meaning her father. She drew my arm around her shoulders and folded my hand about her bare forearm, to warm it. The back of my thumb fitted against the curve of one breast. Her head went into the hollow where my arm and chest joined; she was ter-

ribly small, measured against your own body. Perhaps she weighed
a hundred pounds. Her lids lowered and I kissed her two beautiful
eyebrows and then the spaces of skin between the rough curls, some
black and some bleached, that fringed her forehead. Other than this
I tried to keep as still as a bed would be. It *had* grown cold. A shiver
starting on the side away from her would twitch my shoulders when
I tried to repress it; she would frown and unconsciously draw my
arm tighter. No one had switched the kitchen light off. On Margaret's foreshortened upper lip there seemed to be two pencil
marks; the length of wrist my badly fitting sleeve exposed looked
pale and naked against the spiralling down of the smaller arm held
beneath it.

Outside on the street the house faced there was no motion. Only
once did a car go by—around five o'clock, with twin mufflers, the
radio on, and a boy yelling. Neil and the girl murmured together
incessantly; some of what they said I could overhear.

"No. Which?" she asked.

"I don't care."

"Wouldn't you want a boy?"

"I'd be happy whatever I got."

"I know, but which would you *rather* have? Don't men want
boys?"

"I don't care. You."

Somewhat later, Mohn's truck passed on the other side of the
street. The milkman, well bundled, sat behind headlights in a warm
orange volume the size of a phone booth, steering one-handed and
smoking a cigar that he set on the edge of the dashboard when, his
wire carrier vibrant, he ran out of the truck with bottles. His passing led Neil to decide the time had come. Margaret woke up frightened of her father; we hissed our farewells and thanks to her
quickly. Neil dropped the other girl off at her house a few blocks
away; he knew where it was. Sometime during that night I must
have seen this girl's face, but I have no memory of it. She is always
behind a magazine or in the dark or with her back turned. Neil
married her years later, I know, but after we arrived in Chicago I
never saw him again, either.

Red dawn light touched the clouds above the black slate roofs
as, with a few other cars, we drove through Alton. The moon-sized
clock of a beer billboard said ten after six. Olinger was deathly still.

The air brightened as we moved along the highway; the glowing wall of my home hung above the woods as we rounded the long curve by the Mennonite dairy. With a .22 I could have had a pane of my parents' bedroom window, and they were dreaming I was in Indiana. My grandfather would be up, stamping around in the kitchen for my grandmother to make him breakfast, or outside walking to see if any ice had formed on the brook. For an instant I genuinely feared he might hail me from the peak of the barn roof. Then trees interceded and we were safe in a landscape where no one cared.

At the entrance to the Turnpike Neil did a strange thing; he stopped the car and had me take the wheel. He had never trusted me to drive his father's car before; he had believed my not knowing where the crankshaft or fuel pump was handicapped my competence to steer. But now he was quite complacent. He hunched under an old mackinaw and leaned his head against the metal of the window frame and soon was asleep. We crossed the Susquehanna on a long smooth bridge below Harrisburg, then began climbing toward the Alleghenies. In the mountains there was snow, a dry dusting like sand that waved back and forth on the road surface. Farther along, there had been a fresh fall that night, about two inches, and the plows had not yet cleared all the lanes. I was passing a Sunoco truck on a high curve when without warning the scraped section gave out and I realized I might skid into the fence, if not over the edge. The radio was singing "Carpets of clover, I'll lay right at your feet," and the speedometer said 81. Nothing happened; the car stayed firm in the snow, and Neil slept through the danger, his face turned skyward and his breath struggling in his nose. It was the first time I heard a contemporary of mine snore.

When we came into tunnel country, the flicker and hollow amplification stirred Neil awake. He sat up, the mackinaw dropping to his lap, and lit a cigarette. A second after the scratch of his match the moment occurred of which each following moment was a slight diminution, as we made the long irregular descent toward Pittsburgh. There were many reasons for my feeling so happy. We were on our way. I had seen a dawn. This far, Neil could appreciate, I had brought us safely. Ahead, a girl waited who, if I asked, would marry me, but first there was a long trip; many hours and towns interceded between me and that encounter. There was the quality of the 10 A.M. sunlight as it existed in the air ahead of the windshield, filtered by the thin overcast, blessing irresponsibility—you felt you could slice forever through such a cool pure element—and springing, by implying how high these hills had become, a wide-spreading pride: Pennsylvania, your state—as if you had made your life. And there was knowing that twice since midnight a person had trusted me enough to fall asleep beside me.

THE FRENCH SCARECROW

❖

WILLIAM MAXWELL

I spied John Mouldy in his cellar
Deep down twenty steps of stone;
In the dusk he sat a-smiling,
Smiling there alone.
    —*Walter de la Mare.*

DRIVING past the Fishers' house on his way out to the public
road, George Martin said to himself absent-mindedly, "There's
Edmund working in his garden," before he realized that it was a
scarecrow. And two nights later he woke up sweating from a dream,
a nightmare, which he related next day, lying tense on the analyst's
couch.

"I was in this house, where I knew I oughtn't to be, and I looked
around and saw there was a door, and in order to get to it I had
to pass a dummy—a dressmaker's dummy without any head."

After a considerable silence the disembodied voice with a German accent said, "Any day remnants?"

"I can't think of any," George Martin said, shifting his position
on the couch. "We used to have a dressmaker's dummy in the sewing room when I was a child, but I haven't thought of it for years.
The Fishers have a scarecrow in their garden, but I don't think it
could be that. The scarecrow looks like Edmund. The same thin
shoulders, and his clothes, of course, and the way it stands looking
sadly down at the ground. It's a caricature of Edmund. One of those
freak accidents. I wonder if they realize it. Edmund is not sad, exactly, but there was a period in his life when he was neither as
happy or as hopeful as he is now. Dorothy is a very nice woman. Not
at all maternal, I would say. At least, she doesn't mother Edmund.
And when you see her with some woman with a baby, she always
seems totally indifferent. Edmund was married before, and his first
wife left him. Helena was selfish but likable, the way selfish people

sometimes are. And where Edmund was concerned, completely heartless. I don't know why. She used to turn the radio on full blast at two o'clock in the morning, when he had to get up at six-thirty to catch a commuting train. And once she sewed a ruffle all the way around the bed he was trying to sleep in. Edmund told me once that her mother preferred her older sister, and that Helena's whole childhood had been made miserable because of it. He tried every way he could think of to please her and make her happy, and with most women that would have been enough, I suppose, but it only increased her dissatisfaction. Maybe if there had been any children . . . She used to walk up and down the road in a long red cloak, in the wintertime when there was snow on the ground. And she used to talk about New York. And it was as if she was under a spell and waiting to be delivered. Now she blames Edmund for the divorce. She tells everybody that he took advantage of her. Perhaps he did, unconsciously. Consciously, he wouldn't take advantage of a fly. I think he needs analysis, but he's very much opposed to it. Scared to death of it, in fact . . ."

Step by step, George Martin had managed to put a safe distance between himself and the dream, and he was beginning to breathe easier in the complacent viewing of someone else's failure to meet his problems squarely when the voice said, "Well—see you again?"

"I wish to Christ you wouldn't say that! As if I had any choice in the matter."

His sudden fury was ignored. A familiar hypnotic routine obliged him to sit up and put his feet over the side of the couch. The voice became attached to an elderly man with thick glasses and a round face that George would never get used to. He got up unsteadily and walked toward the door. Only when he was outside, standing in front of the elevator shaft, did he remember that the sewing room had a door opening into his mother and father's bedroom, and at one period of his life he had slept there, in a bed with sides that could be let down, a child's bed. This information was safe from the man inside—unless he happened to think of it while he was lying on the couch next time.

That evening he stopped when he came to the Fishers' vegetable garden and turned the engine off and took a good look at the scarecrow. Then, after a minute or two, afraid that he would be seen from the house, he started the car and drove on.

The Fishers' scarecrow was copied from a scarecrow in France. The summer before, they had spent two weeks as paying guests in a country house in the Touraine, in the hope that this would improve their French. The improvement was all but imperceptible to them afterward, but they did pick up a number of ideas about gardening. In the *potager,* fruit trees, tree roses, flowers, and vegetables were mingled in a way that aroused their admiration, and there was a more than ordinarily fanciful scarecrow, made out of a blue peasant's smock, striped morning trousers, and a straw hat. Under the hat the stuffed head had a face painted on it; and not simply two eyes, a nose, and a mouth but a face with a sly expression. The scarecrow stood with arms upraised, shaking its white-gloved fists at the sky. Indignant, self-centered, half crazy, it seemed to be saying: *This is what it means to be exposed to experience.* The crows were not taken in.

Effects that had needed generations of dedicated French gardeners to bring about were not, of course, to be imitated successfully by two amateur gardeners in Fairfield County in a single summer. The Fishers gave up the idea of marking off the paths of their vegetable garden with espaliered dwarf apple and pear trees, and they could see no way of having tree roses without also having to spray them, and afterward having to eat the spray. But they did plant zinnias, marigolds, and blue pansies in with the lettuce and the peas, and they made a very good scarecrow. Dorothy made it, actually. She was artistic by inclination, and threw herself into all such undertakings with a childish pleasure.

She made the head out of a dish towel stuffed with hay, and was delighted with the blue stripe running down the face. Then she got out her embroidery thread and embroidered a single eye, gathered the cloth in the middle of the face into a bulbous nose, made the mouth leering. For the body she used a torn pair of Edmund's blue jeans she was tired of mending, and a faded blue workshirt. When Edmund, who was attached to his old clothes, saw that she had also helped herself to an Army fatigue hat from the shelf in the hall closet, he exclaimed, "Hey, don't use that hat for the scarecrow! I wear it sometimes."

"*When* do you wear it?"

"I wear it to garden in."

"You can wear some other old hat to garden in. He's got to have something on his head," she said lightly, and made the hat brim dip down over the blank eye.

"When winter comes, I'll wear it again," Edmund said to himself, "if it doesn't shrink too much, or fall apart in the rain."

The scarecrow stood looking toward the house, with one arm

limp and one arm extended stiffly, ending in a gloved hand holding
a stick. After a few days the head sank and sank until it was resting
on the straw breastbone, and the face was concealed by the brim of
the hat. They tried to keep the head up with a collar of twisted
grass, but the grass dried, and the head sank once more, and in that
attitude it remained.

The scarecrow gave them an eerie feeling when they saw it from
the bedroom window at twilight. A man standing in the vegetable
garden would have looked like a scarecrow. If he didn't move.
Dorothy had never lived in the country before she married Edmund, and at first she was afraid. The black windows at night made
her nervous. She heard noises in the basement, caused by the steam
circulating through the furnace pipes. And she would suddenly
have the feeling—even though she knew it was only her imagination
—that there was a man outside, looking through the windows at
them. "Shouldn't we invite him in?" Edmund would say when her
glance strayed for a second. "Offer him a drink and let him sit by
the fire? It's not a very nice night out."

He assumed that The Man Outside represented for her all the
childish fears—the fear of the dark, of the burglar on the stairs, of
what else he had no way of knowing. Nor she either, probably. The
Man Outside was simply there, night after night, for about six
weeks, and then he lost his power to frighten, and finally went away
entirely, leaving the dark outside as familiar and safe to her as the
lighted living room. It was Edmund, strangely, who sometimes, as
they were getting ready for bed, went to the front and back doors
and locked them. For he was aware that the neighborhood was
changing, and that things were happening—cars stolen, houses
broken into in broad daylight—that never used to happen in this
part of the world.

The Fishers' white clapboard house was big and rambling, much
added onto at one time or another, but in its final form still plain
and pleasant-looking. The original house dated from around 1840.
Edmund's father, who was a New York banker until he retired at
the age of sixty-five, had bought it before the First World War. At
that time there were only five houses on this winding country road,
and two of them were farmhouses. When the Fishers came out from
town for the summer, they were met at the railroad station by a man
with a horse and carriage. The surrounding country was hilly and
offered many handsome views, and most of the local names were to

be found on old tombstones in the tiny Presbyterian churchyard. Edmund's mother was a passionate and scholarly gardener, the founder of the local garden club and its president for twenty-seven years. Her regal manner was quite unconscious, and based less on the usual foundations of family, money, etc. than on the authority with which she could speak about the culture of delphinium and lilies, or the pruning of roses. The house was set back from the road about three hundred yards, and behind it were the tennis courts, the big three-story barn, a guesthouse overlooking the pond where all the children in the neighborhood skated in winter, and, eventually, a five-car garage. Back of the pond, a wagon road went off into the woods and up onto higher ground. In the late twenties, when Edmund used to bring his school friends home for spring and fall weekends and the Easter vacation, the house seemed barely large enough to hold them all. During the last war, when the taxes began to be burdensome, Edmund's father sold off the back land, with the guesthouse, the barn, and the pond, to a Downtown lawyer, who shortly afterward sold it to a manufacturer of children's underwear. The elder Mr. and Mrs. Fisher started to follow the wagon road back into the woods one pleasant Sunday afternoon, and he ordered them off his property. He was quite within his rights, of course, but nevertheless it rankled. "In the old days," they would say whenever the man's name was mentioned, "you could go anywhere, on anybody's land, and no one ever thought of stopping you."

Edmund's father, working from his own rough plans and supervising the carpenters and plumbers and masons himself, had converted the stone garage into a house, and he had sold it to George Martin, who was a bachelor. The elder Fishers were now living in the Virgin Islands the year round, because of Mrs. Fisher's health. Edmund and Dorothy still had ten acres, but they shared the cinder drive with George and the clothing manufacturer, and, of course, had less privacy than before. The neighborhood itself was no longer the remote place it used to be. The Merritt Parkway had made all the difference. Instead of five houses on the two-and-a-half-mile stretch of dirt road, there were twenty-five, and the road was macadamized. Cars and delivery trucks cruised up and down it all day long.

In spite of all these changes, and in spite of the considerable difference between Edmund's scale of living and his father's—Dorothy managed with a part-time cleaning woman where in the old days there had been a cook, a waitress, an upstairs maid, a chauffeur, and

two gardeners—the big house still seemed to express the financial
stability and social confidence and belief in good breeding of the
Age of Trellises. Because he had lived in the neighborhood longer
than anyone else, Edmund sometimes felt the impulses of a host, but
he had learned not to act on them. His mother always used to pay
a call on new people within a month of their settling in, and if she
liked them, the call was followed by an invitation to the Fishers'
for tea or cocktails, at which time she managed to bring up the
subject of the Garden Club. But in the last year or so that she had
lived there, she had all but given this up. Twice her call was not
returned, and one terribly nice young couple accepted an invitation
to tea and blithely forgot to come. Edmund was friendly when he
met his neighbors on the road or on the station platform, but he
let them go their own way, except for George Martin, who was
rather amusing, and obviously lonely, and glad of an invitation to
the big house.

"I am sewed to this couch," George Martin said. "My sleeves are
sewed to it, and my trousers. I could not move if I wanted to. Oedi-
pus is on the wall over me, answering the spink-spank-sphinx, and
those are pussy willows, and I do not like bookcases with glass sides
that let down, and the scarecrow is gone. I don't know what they
did with it, and I don't like to ask. And today *I* might as well be
stuffed with straw. The dream I had last night did it. I broke two
plates, and woke up unconfident and nervous and tired. I don't
know what the dream means. I had three plates and I dropped two
of them, and it was so vivid. It was a short dream but very vivid. I
thought at first that the second plate—why *three* plates?—was all
right, but while I was looking at it, the cracks appeared. When I
picked it up, it gave; it came apart in my hands. It was planted with
flowers, and it had openwork, and I was in a hurry, and in my
hurry I dropped the plates. And I was upset. I hardly ever break
anything. Last night while I was drying the glasses, I thought how I
never break any of them. They're Swedish and very expensive. The
plates I dreamed about were my mother's. Not actually; I *dreamed*
that they were my mother's plates. I broke two things of hers when
I was little. And both times it was something she had warned me
about. I sat in the teacart playing house, and forgot and raised my
head suddenly, and it went right through the glass tray. And the
other was an etched-glass hurricane lamp that she prized very highly.
I climbed up on a chair to reach it. And after she died, I could

have thought—I don't ever remember thinking this, but I could have thought that I did something I shouldn't have, and she died. . . . Thank you, I have matches. . . . I can raise my arm. I turned without thinking. I can't figure out that dream. My stepmother was there, washing dishes at the sink, and she turned into Helena Fisher, and I woke up thinking, Ah, that's it. They're *both* my stepmothers! My stepmother never broke anything that belonged to my mother, so she must have been fond of her. They knew each other as girls. And I never broke anything that belonged to my stepmother. I only broke something that belonged to my mother. . . . Did I tell you I saw her the other day?"

"You saw someone who reminded you of your mother?"

"No, I saw Helena Fisher. On Fifth Avenue. I crossed over to the other side of the street, even though I'm still fond of her, because she hasn't been very nice to Dorothy, and because it's all so complicated, and I really didn't have anything to say to her. She was very conspicuous in her country clothes." He lit another cigarette and then said, after a prolonged silence, "I don't seem to have anything to say now, either." The silence became unbearable, and he said, "I can't think of anything to talk about."

"Let's talk about you—about this dream you had," the voice said, kind and patient as always, the voice of his father (at $20 an hour).

The scarecrow had remained in the Fishers' vegetable garden, with one arm limp and one arm stiffly extended, all summer. The corn and the tomato vines grew up around it, half obscuring it during the summer months, and then, in the fall, there was nothing whatever around it but the bare ground. The blue workshirt faded still more in the sun and rain. The figure grew frail, the straw chest settled and became a middle-aged thickening of the waist. The resemblance to Edmund disappeared. And on a Friday afternoon in October, with snow flurries predicted, Edmund Fisher went about the yard carrying in the outdoor picnic table and benches, picking up stray flowerpots, and taking one last look around for the pruning shears, the trowel, and the nest of screwdrivers that had all disappeared during the summer's gardening. There were still three or four storm windows to put up on the south side of the house, and he was about to bring them out and hang them when Dorothy, on her hands and knees in the iris bed, called to him.

"What about the scarecrow?"

"Do you want to save it?" he asked.

"I don't really care."

"We might as well," he said, and was struck once more by the lifelike quality of the scarecrow, as he lifted it out of the soil. It was almost weightless. "Did the doctor say it was all right for you to do that sort of thing?"

"I didn't ask him," Dorothy said.

"Oughtn't you to ask him?"

"No," she said, smiling at him. She was nearly three months pregnant. Moonfaced, serenely happy, and slow of movement (when she had all her life been so quick about everything), she went about now doing everything she had always done but like somebody in a dream, a sleepwalker. The clock had been replaced by the calendar. Like the gardeners in France, she was dedicated to making something grow. As Edmund carried the scarecrow across the lawn and around the corner of the house, she followed him with her eyes. Why is it, she wondered, that he can never bear to part with anything, even though it has ceased to serve its purpose and he no longer has any interest in it?

It was as if sometime or other in his life he had lost something, of such infinite value that he could never think of it without grieving, and never bear to part with anything worthless because of the thing he had had to part with that meant so much to him. But what? She had no idea, and she had given some thought to the matter. She was sure it was not Helena; he said (and she believed him) that he had long since got over any feeling he once had for her. His parents were both still living, he was an only child, and death seemed never to have touched him. Was it some early love, that he had never felt he dared speak to her about? Some deprivation? Some terrible injustice done to him? She had no way of telling. The attic and the basement testified to his inability to throw things away, and she had given up trying to do anything about either one. The same with people. At the end of a perfectly pleasant evening he would say "Oh no, it's early still. You mustn't go home!" with such fervor that even though it actually was time to go home and the guests wanted to, they would sit down, confused by him, and stay a while longer. And though the Fishers knew more people than they could manage to see, he would suddenly remember somebody he hadn't thought of or written to in a long time, and feel impelled to do something about them. Was it something that happened to him in his childhood, Dorothy asked herself. Or was it something in his temperament, born in him, a flaw in his horoscope, Mercury in an unsympathetic relation to the moon?

She resumed her weeding, conscious in a way that she hadn't been before of the autumn day, of the end of the summer's gardening, of the leaf-smoke smell and the smell of rotting apples, the hickory tree that lost its leaves before all the other trees, the grass so deceptively green, and the chill that had descended now that the sun had gone down behind the western hill.

Standing in the basement, looking at the hopeless disorder ("A place for everything," his father used to say, "and nothing in its place"), Edmund decided that it was more important to get at the storm windows than to find a place for the scarecrow. He laid it on one of the picnic-table benches, with the head toward the oil burner, and there it sprawled, like a man asleep or dead-drunk, with the line of the hipbone showing through the trousers, and one arm extended, resting on a slightly higher workbench, and one shoulder raised slightly, as if the man had started to turn in his sleep. In the dim light it could have been alive. I must remember to tell Dorothy, he thought. If she sees it like that, she'll be frightened.

The storm windows were washed and ready to hang. As Edmund came around the corner of the house, with IX in one hand and XI in the other, the telephone started to ring, and Dorothy went in by the back door to answer it, so he didn't have a chance to tell her about the scarecrow. When he went indoors, ten minutes later, she was still standing by the telephone, and from the fact that she was merely contributing a monosyllable now and then to the conversation, he knew she was talking to George Martin. George was as dear as the day was long—everybody liked him—but he had such a ready access to his own memories, which were so rich in narrative detail and associations that dovetailed into further narratives, that if you were busy it was a pure and simple misfortune to pick up the telephone and hear his cultivated, affectionate voice.

Edmund gave up the idea of hanging the rest of the storm windows, and instead he got in the car and drove to the village; he had remembered that they were out of cat food and whiskey. When he walked into the house, Dorothy said, "I've just had such a scare. I started to go down in the cellar—"

"I knew that would happen," he said, putting his hat and coat in the hall closet. "I meant to tell you."

"The basement light was burnt out," she said, "and so I took the flashlight. And when I saw the scarecrow I thought it was a man."

"Our old friend," he said, shaking his head. "The Man Outside."
"And you weren't here. I knew I was alone in the house . . ."
Her fright was still traceable in her face as she described it.

On Saturday morning, Edmund dressed hurriedly, the alarm
clock having failed to go off, and while Dorothy was getting breakfast, he went down to the basement, half asleep, to get the car out
and drive to the village for the cleaning woman, and saw the scarecrow in the dim light, sprawling by the furnace, and a great clot of
fear seized him and his heart almost stopped beating. It lay there
like an awful idiot, the realistic effect accidentally encouraged by
the pair of work shoes Edmund had taken off the night before and
tossed carelessly down the cellar stairs. The scarecrow had no feet—
only two stumps where the trouser legs were tied at the bottom—
but the shoes were where, if it had been alive, they might have been
dropped before the person lay down on the bench. I'll have to do
something about it, Edmund thought. We can't go on frightening
ourselves like this. . . . But the memory of the fright was so real
that he felt unwilling to touch the scarecrow. Instead, he left it
where it was, for the time being, and backed the car out of the
garage.

On the way back from the village, Mrs. Ryan, riding beside him
in the front seat of the car, had a story to tell. Among the various
people she worked for was a family with three boys. The youngest
was in the habit of following her from room to room, and ordinarily
he was as good as gold, but yesterday he ran away, she told Edmund.
His mother was in town, and the older boys, with some of the neighbors' children, were playing outside with a football, and Mrs. Ryan
and the little boy were in the house. "Monroe asked if he could go
outside, and I bundled him up and sent him out. I looked outside
once, and saw that he was playing with the Bluestones' dog, and I
said, 'Monroe, honey, don't pull that dog's tail. He might turn and
bite you.'" While she was ironing, the oldest boy came inside for
a drink of water, and she asked him where Monroe was, and he said,
"Oh, he's outside." But when she went to the door, fifteen minutes
later, the older boys were throwing the football again and Monroe
was nowhere in sight. The boys didn't know what had happened to
him. He disappeared. All around the house was woods, and Mrs.
Ryan, in a panic, called and called.

"Usually when I call, he answers immediately, but this time there
was no answer, and I went into the house and telephoned the Blue-

stones, and they hadn't seen him. And then I called the Hayeses
and the Murphys, and they hadn't seen him either, and Mr. Hayes
came down, and we all started looking for him. Mr. Hayes said only
one car had passed in the last half hour—I was afraid he had been
kidnapped, Mr. Fisher—and Monroe wasn't in it. And I thought,
When his mother comes home and I have to tell her what I've done
. . . And just about that time, he answered, from behind the
hedge!"

"Was he there all the time?" Edmund asked, shifting into second
as he turned in to his own driveway.

"I don't know where he was," Mrs. Ryan said. "But he did the
same thing once before—he wandered off on me. Mr. Ryan thinks
he followed the Bluestones' dog home. His mother called me up last
night and said that he knew he'd done something wrong. He said
'Mummy, I was bad today. I ran off on Sadie. . . .' But Mr. Fisher.
I'm telling you, I was almost out of my mind."

"I don't wonder," Edmund said soberly.

"With woods all around the house, and as Mr. Hayes said, climbing over a stone wall a stone could fall on him and we wouldn't
find him for days."

Ten minutes later, she went down to the basement for the scrub
bucket, and left the door open at the head of the stairs. Edmund
heard her exclaim, for their benefit, "God save us, I've just had the
fright of my life!"

She had seen the scarecrow.

The tramp that ran off with the child, of course, Edmund thought.
He went downstairs a few minutes later, and saw that Mrs. Ryan
had picked the dummy up and stood it in a corner, with its de-
generate face to the wall, where it no longer looked human or
frightening.

Mrs. Ryan is frightened because of the nonexistent tramp. Dorothy is afraid of The Man Outside. What am I afraid of, he wondered. He stood there waiting for the oracle to answer, and it did,
but not until five or six hours later. Poor George Martin called,
after lunch, to say that he had the German measles.

"I was sick as a dog all night," he said mournfully. "I thought I
was dying. I wrote your telephone number on a slip of paper and
put it beside the bed, in case I *did* die."

"Well, for God's sake, why didn't you call us?" Edmund exclaimed.

"What good would it have done?" George said. "All you could have done was say you were sorry."

"Somebody could have come over and looked after you."

"No, somebody couldn't. It's very catching. I think I was exposed to it a week ago at a party in Westport."

"I had German measles when I was a kid," Edmund said. "We've both had it."

"You can get it again," George said. "I still feel terrible. . . ."

When Edmund left the telephone, he made the mistake of mentioning George's illness to Mrs. Ryan, forgetting that it was the kind of thing that was meat and drink to her.

"Has Mrs. Fisher been near him?" she asked, with quickened interest.

He shook his head.

"There's a great deal of it around," Mrs. Ryan said. "My daughter got German measles when she was carrying her first child, and she lost it."

He tried to ask if it was a miscarriage or if the child was born dead, and he couldn't speak; his throat was too dry.

"She was three months along when she had it," Mrs. Ryan went on, without noticing that he was getting paler and paler. "The baby was born alive, but it only lived three days. She's had two other children since. I feel it was a blessing the Lord took that one. If it had lived, it might have been an imbecile. You love them even so, because they belong to you, but it's better if they don't live, Mr. Fisher. We feel it was a blessing the child was taken."

Edmund decided that he wouldn't tell Dorothy, and then five minutes later he decided that he'd better tell her. He went upstairs and into the bedroom where she was resting, and sat down on the edge of the bed, and told her about George's telephone call. "Mrs. Ryan says it's very bad if you catch it while you're pregnant. . . . And she said some more."

"I can see she did, by the look on your face. You shouldn't have mentioned it to her. What did she say?"

"She said—" He swallowed. "She said the child could be born an imbecile. She also said there was a lot of German measles around. You're not worried?"

"We all live in the hand of God."

"I tell myself that every time I'm really frightened. Unfortunately that's the only time I do think it."

"Yes, I know."

Five minutes later, he came back into the room and said, "Why don't you call the doctor? Maybe there's a shot you can take."

The doctor was out making calls, and when he telephoned back, Dorothy answered, on the upstairs extension. Edmund sat down on the bottom step of the stairs and listened to her half of the conversation. As soon as she had hung up, she came down to tell him what the doctor had said.

"The shot only lasts three weeks. He said he'd give it to me if I should be exposed to the measles anywhere."

"Did he say there was an epidemic of it?"

"I didn't ask him. He said that it was commonly supposed to be dangerous during the first three months, but that the statistics showed that it's only the first two months, while the child is being formed, that you have to worry." Moonfaced and serene again, she went to put the kettle on for tea.

Edmund got up and went down to the basement. He carried the dummy outside, removed the hat and then the head, unbuttoned the shirt, removed the straw that filled it and the trousers, and threw it on the compost pile. The hat, the head, the shirt and trousers, the gloves that were hands, he rolled into a bundle and put away on a basement shelf, in case Dorothy wanted to make the scarecrow next summer. The two crossed sticks reminded him of the comfort that Mrs. Ryan, who was a devout Catholic, had and that he did not have. The hum of the vacuum cleaner overhead in the living room, the sad song of a mechanical universe, was all the reassurance he could hope for, and it left so much (it left the scarecrow, for example) completely unexplained and unaccounted for.

THE CODE

❖

RICHARD T. GILL

I

I REMEMBER, almost to the hour, when I first began to question
my religion. I don't mean that my ideas changed radically just
at that time. I was only twelve, and I continued to go to church
faithfully and to say something that could pass for prayers each
night before I went to sleep. But I never again felt quite the same.
For the first time in my life, it had occurred to me that when I grew
up I might actually leave the Methodist faith.

It all happened just a few days after my brother died. He was five
years old, and his illness was so brief and his death so unexpected
that my whole family was almost crazed with grief. My three aunts,
each of whom lived within a few blocks of our house, and my
mother were all firm believers in religion, and they turned in unison,
and without reservation, to this last support. For about a week, a
kind of religious frenzy seized our household. We would all sit in
the living room—my mother, my aunts, my two sisters, and I, and
sometimes Mr. Dodds, the Methodist minister, too—saying prayers
in low voices, comforting one another, staying together for hours at
a time, until someone remembered that we had not had dinner or
that it was time for my sisters and me to be in bed.

I was quite swept up by the mood that had come over the house.
When I went to bed, I would say the most elaborate, intricate
prayers. In the past, when I had finished my "Now I lay me down
to sleep," I would bless individually all the members of my immediate family and then my aunts, and let it go at that. Now, however,
I felt that I had to bless everyone in the world whose name I could
remember. I would go through all my friends at school, including
the teachers, the principal, and the janitor, and then through the
names of people I had heard my mother and father mention, some
of whom I had never even met. I did not quite know what to do

about my brother, whom I wanted to pray for more than for anyone else. I hesitated to take his name out of its regular order, for
fear I would be committed to believing that he had really died. But
then I *knew* that he had died, so at the end of my prayers, having
just barely mentioned his name as I went along, I would start blessing him over and over again, until I finally fell asleep.

The only one of us who was unmoved by this religious fervor
was my father. Oddly enough, considering what a close family we
were and how strongly my mother and aunts felt about religion, my
father had never shown the least interest in it. In fact, I do not
think that he had ever gone to church. Partly for this reason, partly
because he was a rather brusque, impatient man, I always felt that
he was something of a stranger in our home. He spent a great deal
of time with us children, but through it all he seemed curiously
unapproachable. I think we all felt constrained when he played
with us and relieved when, at last, we were left to ourselves.

At the time of my brother's death, he was more of a stranger
than ever. Except for one occasion, he took no part in the almost
constant gatherings of the family in the living room. He was not
going to his office that week—we lived in a small town outside
Boston—and he was always around the house, but no one ever
seemed to know exactly where. One of my aunts—Sarah, my
mother's eldest sister—felt very definitely that my father should not
be left to himself, and she was continually saying to me, "Jack, go
upstairs and see if you can find him and talk to him." I remember
going timidly along the hallway of the second floor and peeking into
the bedrooms, not knowing what I should say if I found him and
half afraid that he would scold me for going around looking into
other people's rooms. One afternoon, not finding him in any of
the bedrooms, I went up into the attic, where we had a sort of playroom. I remember discovering him there by the window. He was
sitting absolutely motionless in an old wicker chair, an empty pipe
in his hands, staring out fixedly over the treetops. I stood in the
doorway for several minutes before he was aware of me. He turned
as if to say something, but then, looking at me or just above my
head—I was not sure which—he seemed to lose himself in his
thoughts. Finally, he gave me a strangely awkward salute with his
right hand and turned again to the window.

About the only times my father was with the rest of us were
when we had meals or when, in the days immediately following the

funeral, we all went out to the cemetery, taking fresh flowers or wreaths. But even at the cemetery he always stood slightly apart— a tall, lonely figure. Once, when we were at the grave and I was nearest him, he reached over and squeezed me around the shoulders. It made me feel almost embarrassed, as though he were breaking through some inviolable barrier between us. He must have felt as I did, because he at once removed his arm and looked away, as though he had never actually embraced me at all.

It was the one occasion when my father was sitting in the living room with us that started me to wondering about my religion. We had just returned from the cemetery—two carloads of us. It was three or four days after the funeral and just at the time when, the shock having worn off, we were all experiencing our first clear realization of what had happened. Even I, young as I was, sensed that there was a new air of desolation in our home.

For a long time, we all sat there in silence. Then my aunts, their eyes moist, began talking about my brother, and soon my mother joined in. They started off softly, telling of little things he had done in the days before his illness. Then they fell silent and dried their eyes, and then quickly remembered some other incident and began speaking again. Slowly the emotion mounted, and before long the words were flooding out. "God will take care of him!" my Aunt Sarah cried, almost ecstatically. "Oh, yes, He will! He will!" Presently, they were all talking in chorus—saying that my brother was happy at last and that they would all be with him again one day.

I believed what they were saying and I could barely hold back my tears. But swept up as I was, I had the feeling that they should not be talking that way while my father was there. The feeling was one that I did not understand at all at the moment. It was just that when I looked over to the corner where he was sitting and saw the deep, rigid lines of his face, saw him sitting there silently, all alone, I felt guilty. I wanted everyone to stop for a while—at least until he had gone upstairs. But there was no stopping the torrent once it had started.

"Oh, he was too perfect to live!" Aunt Agnes, my mother's youngest sister, cried. "He was never a bad boy. I've never seen a boy like that. I mean he was never even naughty. He was just too perfect."

"Oh, yes. Oh, yes," my mother sighed.

"It's true," Aunt Sarah said. "Even when he was a baby, he never really cried. There was never a baby like him. He was a saint."

"He *was* a saint!" Aunt Agnes cried. "That's why he was taken from us!"

"He was a perfect baby," my mother said.

"He was taken from us," Aunt Agnes went on, "because he was too perfect to live."

All through this conversation, my father's expression had been growing more and more tense. At last, while Aunt Agnes was speaking, he rose from his chair. His face was very pale, and his eyes flashed almost feverishly. "Don't talk like that, Agnes!" he exclaimed, with a strange violence that was not anger but something much deeper. "I won't have you talking like that any more. I don't want anybody talking like that!" His whole body seemed to tremble. I had never seen him so worked up before. "Of course he was a bad boy at times!" he cried. "Every boy's bad once in a while. What do you have to change him for? Why don't you leave him as he was?"

"But he was such a perfect baby," Aunt Sarah said.

"He *wasn't* perfect!" my father almost shouted, clenching his fist. "He was no more perfect than Jack here or Betty or Ellen. He was just an ordinary little boy. He wasn't perfect. And he wasn't a saint. He was just a little boy, and I won't have you making him over into something he wasn't!"

He looked as though he were going to go on talking like this, but just then he closed his eyes and ran his hand up over his forehead and through his hair. When he spoke again, his voice was subdued. "I just wish you wouldn't talk that way," he said. "That's all I mean." And then, after standing there silently for a minute, he left the living room and walked upstairs.

I sat watching the doorway through which he had gone. Suddenly, I had no feeling for what my mother and my aunts had been saying. It was all a mist, a dream. Out of the many words that had been spoken that day, it was those few sentences of my father's that explained to me how I felt about my brother. I wanted to be with my father to tell him so.

I went upstairs and found him once again in the playroom in the attic. As before, he was silent and staring out the window when I entered, and we sat without speaking for what seemed to me like half an hour or more. But I felt that he knew why I was there, and I was not uncomfortable with him.

Finally, he turned to me and shook his head. "I don't know what I can tell you, Jack," he said, raising his hands and letting them drop into his lap. "That's the worst part of it. There's just nothing I can say that will make it any better."

Though I only half understood him then, I see now that he was telling me of a drawback—that he had no refuge, no comfort, no support. He was telling me that you were all alone if you took the path that he had taken. Listening to him, I did not care about the drawback. I had begun to see what a noble thing it was for a man to bear the full loss of someone he had loved.

II

BY THE TIME I was thirteen or fourteen I was so thoroughly committed to my father's way of thinking that I considered it a great weakness in a man to believe in religion. I wanted to grow up to face life as he did—truthfully, without comfort, without support.

My attitude was never one of rebellion. Despite the early regimen of Sunday school and church that my mother had encouraged, she was wonderfully gentle with me, particularly when I began to express my doubts. She would come into my room each night after the light was out and ask me to say my prayers. Determined to be honest with her, I would explain that I could not say them sincerely, and therefore should not say them at all. "Now, Jack," she would reply, very quietly and calmly, "you mustn't talk like that. You'll really feel much better if you say them." I could tell from the tone of her voice that she was hurt, but she never tried to force me in any way. Indeed, it might have been easier for me if she *had* tried to oppose my decision strenuously. As it was, I felt so bad at having wounded her that I was continually trying to make things up— running errands, surprising her by doing the dishes when she went out shopping—behaving, in short, in the most conscientious, considerate fashion. But all this never brought me any closer to her religion. On the contrary, it only served to free me for my decision *not* to believe. And for that decision, as I say, my father was responsible.

Part of his influence, I suppose, was in his physical quality. Even at that time—when he was in his late forties and in only moderately good health—he was a most impressive figure. He was tall and heavy-chested, with leathery, rough-cast features and with an easy, relaxed rhythm in his walk. He had been an athlete in his youth, and, needless to say, I was enormously proud of his various feats and told about them, with due exaggeration, all over our neighborhood. Still, the physical thing had relatively little to do with the matter. My father, by that time, regarded athletes and athletics with contempt. Now and again, he would take me into the back yard to fool around with boxing gloves, but when it came to something serious, such as my going out for football in high school, he invariably put his foot down. "It takes too much time," he would tell me. "You ought to be thinking of college and your studies. It's nonsense what they make of sports nowadays!" I always wanted to remind him of *his* school days, but I knew it was no use. He had often told me what an unforgivable waste of time he considered his youth to have been.

Thus, although the physical thing was there, it was very much in the background—little more, really, than the simple assumption that a man ought to know how to take care of himself. The real bond between us was spiritual, in the sense that courage, as opposed to strength, is spiritual. It was this intangible quality of courage that I wanted desperately to possess and that, it seemed to me, captured everything that was essential about my father.

We never talked of this quality directly. The nearest we came to it was on certain occasions during the early part of the Second World War, just before I went off to college. We would sit in the living room listening to a speech by Winston Churchill, and my father would suddenly clap his fist against his palm. "My God!" he would exclaim, fairly beaming with admiration. "That man's got the heart of a tiger!" And I would listen to the rest of the speech, thrilling to every word, and then, thinking of my father, really, I would say aloud that, of all men in the world, the one I would most like to be was Churchill.

Nor did we often talk about religion. Yet our religion—our rejection of religion—was the deepest statement of the bond between us. My father, perhaps out of deference to my mother and my sisters and aunts, always put his own case very mildly. "It's certainly a great philosophy," he would say of Christianity. "No one could question that. But for the rest . . ." Here he would throw up his hands and cock his head to one side, as if to say that he had tried, but simply could not manage the hurdle of divinity. This view, however mildly it may have been expressed, became mine with absolute clarity and certainty. I concluded that religion was a refuge, without the least foundation in fact. More than that, I positively objected to those— I should say those *men,* for to me it was a peculiarly masculine matter—who turned to religion for support. As I saw it, a man ought to face life as it really is, on his own two feet, without a crutch, as my father did. That was the heart of the matter. By the time I left home for college, I was so deeply committed to this view that I would have considered it a disloyalty to him, to myself, to the code we had lived by, to alter my position in the least.

I did not see much of my father during the next four years or so. I was home during the summer vacation after my freshman year, but then, in the middle of the next year, I went into the Army. I was shipped to the Far East for the tail end of the war, and was in Japan at the start of the Occupation. I saw my father only once or twice during my entire training period, and, naturally, during the time I was overseas I did not see him at all.

While I was away, his health failed badly. In 1940, before I went off to college, he had taken a job at a defense plant. The plant was only forty miles from our home, but he was working on the night shift, and commuting was extremely complicated and tiresome. And, of course, he was always willing to overexert himself out of a sense of pride. The result was that late in 1942 he had a heart attack. He came through it quite well, but he made no effort to cut down on his work and, as a consequence, suffered a second, and more serious, attack, two years later. From that time on, he was almost completely bedridden.

I was on my way overseas at the time of the second attack, and I learned of it in a letter from my mother. I think she was trying to spare me, or perhaps it was simply that I could not imagine so robust a man as my father being seriously ill. In any event, I had only the haziest notion of what his real condition was, so when, many months later, I finally did realize what had been going on, I was terribly surprised and shaken. One day, some time after my arrival at an American Army post in Japan, I was called to the orderly room and told that my father was critically ill and that I was to be sent home immediately. Within forty-eight hours, I was standing in the early-morning light outside my father's bedroom, with my mother and sisters at my side. They had told me, as gently as they could, that he was not very well, that he had had another attack. But it was impossible to shield me then. I no sooner stepped into the room and saw him than I realized that he would not live more than a day or two longer.

From that moment on, I did not want to leave him for a second. Even that night, during the periods when he was sleeping and I was of no help being there, I could not get myself to go out of the room for more than a few minutes. A practical nurse had come to sit up with him, but since I was at the bedside, she finally spent the night in the hallway. I was really quite tired, and late that night my mother and my aunts begged me to go to my room and rest for a while, but I barely heard them. I was sure he would wake up soon, and when he did, I wanted to be there to talk to him.

We did talk a great deal that first day and night. It was difficult for both of us. Every once in a while, my father would shift position in the bed, and I would catch a glimpse of his wasted body. It was a knife in my heart. Even worse were the times when he would reach out for my hand, his eyes misted, and begin to tell me how he felt about me. I tried to look at him, but in the end I always looked down. And, knowing that he was dying, and feeling desperately guilty, I would keep repeating to myself that he knew how I felt, that he would understand why I looked away.

There was another thing, too. While we talked that day, I had a vague feeling that my father was on the verge of making some sort of confession to me. It was, as I say, only the vaguest impression, and I thought very little about it. The next morning, however, I began to sense what was in the air. Apparently, Mr. Dodds, the minister, whom I barely knew, had been coming to the house lately to talk to my father. My father had not said anything about this, and I learned it only indirectly, from something my mother said to my eldest sister at the breakfast table. At the moment, I brushed the matter aside. I told myself it was natural that Mother would want my father to see the minister at the last. Nevertheless, the very mention of the minister's name caused something to tighten inside me.

Later that day, the matter was further complicated. After lunch, I finally did go to my room for a nap, and when I returned to my father's room, I found him and my mother talking about Mr. Dodds. The conversation ended almost as soon as I entered, but I was left with the distinct impression that they were expecting the minister to pay a visit that day, whether very shortly or at supper-time or later in the evening, I could not tell. I did not ask. In fact, I made a great effort not to think of the matter at all.

Then, early that evening, my father spoke to me. I knew before he said a word that the minister *was* coming. My mother had straightened up the bedroom, and fluffed up my father's pillows so that he was half sitting in the bed. No one had told me anything, but I was sure what the preparations meant. "I guess you probably know," my father said to me when we were alone, "we're having a visitor tonight. It's—ah—Mr. Dodds. You know, the minister from your mother's church."

I nodded, half shrugging, as if I saw nothing the least unusual in the news.

"He's come here before once or twice," my father said. "Have I mentioned that? I can't remember if I've mentioned that."

"Yes, I know. I think Mother said something, or perhaps you did. I don't remember."

"I just thought I'd let you know. You see, your mother wanted me to talk to him. I— I've talked to him more for her sake than anything else."

"Sure. I can understand that."

"I think it makes her feel a little better. I think—" Here he broke off, seemingly dissatisfied with what he was saying. His eyes turned to the ceiling, and he shook his head slightly, as if to erase the memory of his words. He studied the ceiling for a long time before he spoke again. "I don't mean it was all your mother exactly," he said. "Well, what I mean is he's really quite an interesting man. I think you'd probably like him a good deal."

"I know Mother has always liked him," I replied. "From what I gather, most people seem to like him very much."

"Well, he's that sort," my father went on, with quickening interest. "I mean, he isn't what you'd imagine at all. To tell the truth, I wish you'd talk to him a little. I wish you'd talk things over with him right from scratch." My father was looking directly at me now, his eyes flashing.

"I'd be happy to talk with him sometime," I said. "As I say, everybody seems to think very well of him."

"Well, I wish you would. You see, when you're lying here day after day, you get to thinking about things. I mean, it's good to have someone to talk to." He paused for a moment. "Tell me," he said, "have you ever . . . have you ever wondered if there wasn't some truth in it? Have you ever thought about it that way at all?"

I made a faint gesture with my hand. "Of course, it's always possible to wonder," I replied. "I don't suppose you can ever be completely certain one way or the other."

"I know, I know," he said, almost impatiently. "But have you ever felt—well, all in a sort of flash—that it *was* true? I mean, have you ever had that feeling?"

He was half raised up from the pillow now, his eyes staring into me with a feverish concentration. Suddenly, I could not look at him any longer. I lowered my head.

"I don't mean permanently or anything like that," he went on. "But just for a few seconds. The feeling that you've been wrong all along. Have you had that feeling—ever?"

I could not look up. I could not move. I felt that every muscle in my body had suddenly frozen. Finally, after what seemed an eternity, I heard him sink back into the pillows. When I glanced up a moment later, he was lying there silent, his eyes closed, his lips parted, conveying somehow the image of the death that awaited him.

Presently, my mother came to the door. She called me into the hall to tell me that Mr. Dodds had arrived. I said that I thought my father had fallen asleep but that I would go back and see.

It was strangely disheartening to me to discover that he was awake. He was sitting there, his eyes open, staring grimly into the gathering shadows of the evening.

"Mr. Dodds is downstairs," I said matter-of-factly. "Mother wanted to know if you felt up to seeing him tonight."

For a moment, I thought he had not heard me; he gave no sign of recognition whatever. I went to the foot of the bed and repeated myself. He nodded, not answering the question but simply indicating that he had heard me. At length, he shook his head. "Tell your mother I'm a little tired tonight," he said. "Perhaps—well, perhaps some other time."

"I could ask him to come back later, if you'd like."

"No, no, don't bother. I—I could probably use the rest."

I waited a few seconds. "Are you sure?" I asked. "I'm certain he could come back in an hour or so."

Then, suddenly, my father was looking at me. I shall never forget his face at that moment and the expression burning in his eyes. He was pleading with me to speak. And all I could say was that I would be happy to ask Mr. Dodds to come back later, if he wanted it that way. It was not enough. I knew, instinctively, at that moment that it was not enough. But I could not say anything more.

As quickly as it had come, the burning flickered and went out. He sank back into the pillows again. "No, you can tell him I won't be needing him tonight," he said, without interest. "Tell him not to bother waiting around." Then he turned on his side, away from me, and said no more.

So my father did not see Mr. Dodds that night. Nor did he ever see him again. Shortly after midnight, just after my mother and sisters had gone to bed, he died. I was at his side then, but I could not have said exactly when it occurred. He must have gone off in his sleep, painlessly, while I sat there awake beside him.

In the days that followed, our family was together almost constantly. Curiously enough, I did not think much about my father just then. For some reason, I felt the strongest sense of responsibility toward the family. I found myself making the arrangements for the funeral, protecting Mother from the stream of people who came to the house, speaking words of consolation to my sisters and even to my aunts. I was never alone except at night, when a kind of oblivion seized me almost as soon as my head touched the pillow. My sleep was dreamless, numb.

Then, two weeks after the funeral, I left for Fort Devens, where I was to be discharged from the Army. I had been there three days when I was told that my terminal leave would begin immediately and that I was free to return home. I had half expected that when I was at the Fort, separated from the family, something would break inside me. But still no emotion came. I thought of my father often during that time, but, search as I would, I could find no sign of feeling.

Then, when I had boarded the train for home, it happened. Suddenly, for no reason whatever, I was thinking of the expression on my father's face that last night in the bedroom. I saw him as he lay there pleading with me to speak. And I knew then what he had wanted me to say to him—that it was really all right with me, that it wouldn't change anything between us if he gave way. And then I was thinking of myself and what I had said and what I had *not* said. Not a word to help! Not a word!

I wanted to beg his forgiveness. I wanted to cry out aloud to him. But I was in a crowded train, sitting with three elderly women just returning from a shopping tour. I turned my face to the window. There, silent, unnoticed, I thought of what I might have said.

WHAT YOU HEAR FROM 'EM?

❖

PETER TAYLOR

WHENEVER someone misunderstood Aunt Munsie's question, she didn't bother to clarify it. She might repeat it two or three times, in order to drown out some fool answer she was getting from some fool white woman, or man, either. "What you hear from 'em?" she'd ask. "What you hear from 'em? *What you hear from 'em?*" She was so deaf that anyone whom she thoroughly drowned out only laughed and said Aunt Munsie had got so deaf she couldn't hear it thunder. It was, of course, only the most utterly fool answers that ever received the drowning-out treatment. For a number of years, Aunt Munsie was willing to listen to those who mistook her " 'em" to mean any and all of the Dr. Tolliver children. And for more years than that she would listen to those who thought she wanted just *any* news of her two favorites among the Tolliver children—Thad and Will. But later on she stopped putting the question to all insensitive and frivolous souls who didn't understand that what she was interested in hearing —and *all* she was interested in hearing—was when Mr. Thad and Mr. Will Tolliver were going to pack up their families and come back to Thornton for good.

They had always promised her to come back—to come back sure enough, that is. On separate occasions, both Thad and Will had promised her. For ten years, she hadn't seen them together, but each of them had made visits to Thornton now and then with his own family. She would see a big car stopping in front of her house on a Sunday afternoon and see either Will or Thad with his wife and children piling out into the dusty street—it was nearly always summer when they came—and then see them filing across the street, jumping the ditch, and unlatching the gate to her yard. She always met them in that pen of a yard, but long before they had jumped the ditch she was clapping her hands and calling out, "Hai-ee!

191

Hai-ee, now! Look-a-here! Whee! Whee! Look-a-here!" She had got
so blind that she was never sure whether it was Mr. Thad or Mr.
Will until she had her arms about his waist. They had always looked
a good deal alike, and their city clothes made them look even more
alike nowadays. Aunt Munsie's eyes were so bad, besides being so
full of moisture on those occasions, that she really recognized them
by their girth. Will had grown a regular washpot of a stomach and
Thad was still thin as a rail. They would sit on her porch for twenty
or thirty minutes—whichever one it was and his family—and then
they would be gone again.

Aunt Munsie wouldn't try to detain them—not seriously. Those
short little old visits didn't mean a thing to her. He—Thad or Will—
would lean against the banister rail and tell her how well his children were doing in school or college, and she would make each
child in turn come and sit beside her on the swing for a minute and
receive a hug about the waist or shoulders. They were timid with
her, not seeing her any more than they did, but she could tell from
their big Tolliver smiles that they liked her to hug them and make
over them. Usually, she would lead them all out to her back yard
and show them her pigs and dogs and chickens. (She always had at
least one frizzly chicken to show the children.) They would traipse
through her house to the back yard and then traipse through again
to the front porch. It would be time for them to go when they came
back, and Aunt Munsie would look up at *him*—Mr. Thad or Mr.
Will (she had begun calling them "Mr." the day they married)—
and say, "Now, look here. When you comin' back?"

Both Thad and Will knew what she meant, of course, and whichever it was would tell her he was making definite plans to wind up
his business and that he was going to buy a certain piece of property, "a mile north of town" or "on the old River Road," and build
a jim-dandy house there. He would say, too, how good Aunt
Munsie's own house was looking, and his wife would say how grand
the zinnias and cannas looked in the yard. (The yard was all flowers
—not a blade of grass.) The visit was almost over then. There remained only the exchange of presents. One of the children would
hand Aunt Munsie a paper bag containing a pint of whiskey or a
carton of cigarettes. Aunt Munsie would go to her back porch or
to the pit in the yard and get a fern or a wandering Jew, potted in
a rusty lard bucket, and make Mrs. Thad or Mrs. Will take it along.
Then the visit was over, and they would leave. From the porch,
Aunt Munsie would wave goodbye with one hand and lay the other

hand, trembling slightly, on the banister rail. (The banisters had come off a porch of the house where Thad and Will had grown up. Dr. Tolliver had been one of the first to widen his porches and remove the gingerbread from his house.) The children and their mother would wave to Aunt Munsie from the street. Their father would close the gate, resting his hand a moment on its familiar wrought-iron frame, and wave to her before he jumped the ditch. (The iron fence, with its iron gate, had been around the yard at Dr. Tolliver's till he took it down and set out a hedge, just a few weeks before he died.)

Such paltry little visits meant nothing to Aunt Munsie. No more did the letters that came with "her things" at Christmas. She was supposed to get her daughter, Lucrecie, who lived next door, to read the letters, but in late years she had taken to putting them away unopened, and some of the presents, too. All she wanted to hear from *them* was when they were coming back for good, and she had learned that the Christmas letters never told her that. On her daily route with her slop wagon through the Square, up Jackson Street, and down Jefferson, there were only four or five houses left where she asked her question. These were houses where the amount of pig slop was not worth stopping for, houses where one old maid, or maybe two, lived, or a widow with one old bachelor son who had never amounted to anything and ate no more than a woman. And so —in the summertime, anyway—she took to calling out at the top of her lungs, when she approached the house of one of the elect, "What you hear from 'em?" Sometimes a Miss Patty or a Miss Lucille or a Mr. Ralph would get up out of a porch chair and come down the brick walk to converse with Aunt Munsie. Or sometimes one of them would just lean out over the shrubbery planted around the porch and call, "Not a thing, Munsie. Not a thing lately."

She would shake her head and call back, "Naw. Naw. Not a thing. Nobody don't hear from 'em. Too busy, they be!"

Aunt Munsie's skin was the color of a faded tow sack. She was hardly four feet tall. She was generally believed to be totally bald, and on her head she always wore a white dust cap with an elastic band. She wore an apron, too, while making her rounds with her slop wagon. Even when the weather got bad and she tied a wool scarf about her head and wore an overcoat, she put on an apron over the coat. Her hands and feet were delicately small, which made the old-timers sure she was of Guinea stock that had come

to Tennessee out of South Carolina. What most touched the hearts
of old ladies on Jackson and Jefferson Streets was her little feet.
The sight of her feet "took them back to the old days," they said,
because Aunt Munsie still wore flat-heeled, high-button shoes.
Where ever did Munsie find such shoes any more?

   She walked down the street, the very center of the street, with a
spry step and was continually turning her head from side to side,
as though looking at the old houses and trees for the first time.
If her sight was as bad as she sometimes let on it was, she probably
recognized the houses only by their roof lines against the Thornton
sky. Since this was nearly thirty years ago, most of the big Victorian
and ante-bellum houses were still standing, though with their yard
fences already gone and their lovely gingerbread work beginning to
go. (It went first from houses where there was someone, like Dr.
Tolliver, with a special eye for style and for keeping up with the
times.) The streets hadn't yet been broadened—or only Nashville
Street had—and the maples and elms met above the streets. In the
autumn, their leaves covered the high banks and filled the deep
ditches on either side. The dark macadam surfacing itself was barely
wide enough for two automobiles to pass. Aunt Munsie, pulling
her slop wagon, which was a long, low, four-wheeled vehicle about
the size and shape of a coffin, paraded down the center of the street
without any regard for, if with any awareness of, the traffic problems
she sometimes made. Grasping the wagon's decidedly sawed-off-
looking tongue, she pulled it after her with a series of impatient
jerks, as though that tongue were the arm of some very stubborn,
overgrown white child she had to nurse in her old age. Strangers
in town or trifling high-school boys would blow their horns at her,
but she was never known to so much as glance over her shoulder
at the sound of a horn. Now and then, a pedestrian on the sidewalk
would call out to the driver of an automobile, "She's so deaf she
can't hear it thunder."

   It wouldn't have occurred to anyone in Thornton—not in those
days—that something ought to be done about Aunt Munsie and her
wagon for the sake of the public good. In those days, everyone had
equal rights on the streets of Thornton. A vehicle was a vehicle,
and a person was a person, each with the right to move as slowly
as he pleased and to stop where and as often as he pleased. In the
Thornton mind, there was no imaginary line down the middle of
the street, and, indeed, no one there at that time had heard of
drawing a real line on *any* street. It was merely out of politeness

that you made room for others to pass. Nobody would have blown a horn at an old colored woman with her slop wagon—nobody but some Yankee stranger or a trifling high-school boy or maybe old Mr. Ralph Hadley in a special fit of temper. When citizens of Thornton were in a real hurry and got caught behind Aunt Munsie, they leaned out their car windows and shouted, "Aunt Munsie, can you make a little room?" And Aunt Munsie didn't fail to hear *them*. She would holler "Hai-ee, now! Whee! Look-a-here!" and jerk her wagon to one side. As they passed her, she would wave her little hand and grin a toothless, pink-gummed grin.

Yet, without any concern for the public good, Aunt Munsie's friends among the white women began to worry more and more about the danger of her being run down by an automobile. They talked among themselves and they talked to her about it. They wanted her to give up collecting slop, now she had got so blind and deaf. "Pshaw," said Aunt Munsie, closing her eyes contemptuously. "Not me." She meant by that that no one would dare run into her or her wagon. Sometimes when she crossed the Square on a busy Saturday morning or on a first Monday, she would hold up one hand with the palm turned outward and stop all traffic until she was safely across and in the alley beside the hotel.

Thornton wasn't even then what it had been before the Great World War. In every other house, there was a stranger or a mill hand who had moved up from Factory Town. Some of the biggest old places stood empty, the way Dr. Tolliver's had until it burned. They stood empty not because nobody wanted to rent them or buy them but because the heirs who had gone off somewhere making money could never be got to part with "the home place." The story was that Thad Tolliver nearly went crazy when he heard their old house had burned, and wanted to sue the town, and even said he was going to help get the Republicans into office. Yet Thad had hardly put foot in the house since the day his daddy died. It was said the Tolliver house had caught fire from the Major Pettigru house, which had burned two nights before, and no doubt it had. Sparks could have smoldered in that roof of rotten shingles for a long time before bursting into flame. Some even said the Pettigru house might have caught from the Johnston house, which had burned earlier that same fall. But Thad knew and Will knew and everybody knew the town wasn't to blame, and knew there was no firebug. Why, those old houses stood there empty year after year, and in the fall the leaves fell from the trees and settled around the porches and stoops, and who was there to rake the leaves? Maybe it was a good thing those houses burned, and maybe it would have been as well if some of the houses that still had people in them burned, too. There were houses in Thornton the heirs had never left that looked far worse than the Tolliver or the Pettigru or the Johnston house ever had. The people who lived in them were the ones who gave Aunt Munsie the biggest fool answers to her question, the people whom she soon quit asking her question of or even passing the time of day with, except when she couldn't help it, out of politeness. For, truly, to Aunt Munsie there were things under the sun worse than going off and getting rich in Nashville and Memphis and even in Washington, D.C. This was a subject she and her daughter Lucrecie mouthed at each other about across their back fence sometimes. Lucrecie was shiftless, and she liked shiftless white people like the ones who didn't have the ambition to leave Thornton. She thought their shiftlessness showed they were *quality*. "Quality?" Aunt Munsie would echo, her voice full of sarcasm. "Whee! Hai-ee! You talk like *you* was *my* mammy, Crecie. Well, if there be quality, there be quality *and* quality. There's quality and there's *has-been* quality, Crecie." There was no end to that argument Aunt Munsie had with Crecie, and it wasn't at all important to Aunt Munsie. The people who still lived in these houses—the ones she called has-been quality—meant little more to her than the mill hands, and the strangers from up North who ran the Piggly Wiggly, the five-and-ten-cent store, and the roller-skating rink.

There was this to be said, though, for the has-been quality: They knew *who* Aunt Munsie was, and in a limited, literal way they understood what she said. But those *others*—why, they thought Aunt Munsie a beggar, and she knew they did. They spoke of her as Old What You Have for Mom, because that's what they thought she was saying when she called out, "What you hear from 'em?" Their ears were not attuned to that soft "r" she put in "from" or the elision that made "from 'em" sound to them like "for Mom." Many's the time Aunt Munsie had seen, or sensed the presence of, one of those *other* people, watching from next door, when Miss Leonora Lovell, say, came down her front walk and handed her a little parcel of scraps across the ditch. Aunt Munsie knew what they thought of her —how they laughed at her and felt sorry for her and despised her all at once. But, like the has-been quality, they didn't matter, never had, never would.

Oh, they mattered in a way to Lucrecie. Lucrecie thought about them and talked about them a lot. She called them "white trash" and even "radical Republicans." It made Aunt Munsie grin to hear Crecie go on, because she knew Crecie got all her notions from her own has-been-quality people. And so it didn't matter, except that Aunt Munsie knew Crecie truly had all sorts of good sense and had only been carried away and spoiled by such folks as she had worked for, such folks as had really raised Crecie from the time she was big enough to run errands for them, fifty years back. In her heart, Aunt Munsie knew that even Lucrecie didn't matter to her the way a daughter might. It was because while Aunt Munsie had been raising a family of white children, a different sort of white people from hers had been raising her own child, Crecie. Sometimes, if Aunt Munsie was in her chicken yard or out in her little patch of cotton when Mr. Thad or Mr. Will arrived, Crecie would come out to the fence and say, "Mama, some of your chillun's out front."

Miss Leonora Lovell and Miss Patty Bean, and especially Miss Lucille Satterfield, were all the time after Aunt Munsie to give up collecting slop. "You're going to get run over by one of those crazy drivers, Munsie," they said. Miss Lucille was the widow of old Judge Satterfield. "If the Judge were alive, Munsie," she said, "I'd make him find a way to stop you. But the men down at the court-house don't listen to the women in this town any more. And I think they'd be 'most too scared of you to do what I want them to do." Aunt Munsie wouldn't listen to any of that. She knew that if Miss Lucille had come out there to her gate, she must have *something* she was going to say about Mr. Thad or Mr. Will. Miss Lucille had two brothers and a son of her own who were lawyers in Memphis, and who lived in style down there and kept Miss Lucille in style here in Thornton. Memphis was where Thad Tolliver had his Ford-and-Lincoln agency, and so Miss Lucille always had news about Thad, and, indirectly, about Will, too.

"Is they doin' any good? What you hear from 'em?" Aunt Munsie asked Miss Lucille one afternoon in early spring. She had come along just when Miss Lucille was out picking some of the jonquils that grew in profusion on the steep bank between the sidewalk and the ditch in front of her house.

"Mr. Thad and his folks will be up one day in April, Munsie," Miss Lucille said in her pleasantly hoarse voice. "I understand Mr. Will and his crowd may come for Easter Sunday."

"One day, and gone again!" said Aunt Munsie.

"We always try to get them to stay at least one night, but they're busy folks, Munsie."

"When they comin' back sure enough, Miss Lucille?"

"Goodness knows, Munsie. Goodness knows. Goodness knows when any of them are coming back to stay." Miss Lucille took three quick little steps down the bank and hopped lightly across the ditch. "They're prospering so, Munsie," she said, throwing her chin up and smiling proudly. This fragile lady, this daughter, wife, sister, mother of lawyers (and, of course, the darling of all their hearts), stood there in the street with her pretty little feet and shapely ankles close together, and holding a handful of jonquils before her as if it were her bridal bouquet. "They're *all* prospering so, Munsie. Mine *and* yours. You ought to go down to Memphis to see them now and then, the way I do. Or go up to Nashville to see Mr. Will. I understand he's got an even finer establishment than Thad. They've done well, Munsie—yours *and* mine—and we can be proud of them. You owe it to yourself to go and see how well they're fixed. They're rich men by our standards in Thornton, and they're going farther—*all* of them."

Aunt Munsie dropped the tongue of her wagon noisily on the pavement. "What I want go see 'em for?" she said angrily and with a lowering brow. Then she stooped and, picking up the wagon tongue again, she wheeled her vehicle toward the center of the street, to get by Miss Lucille, and started off toward the Square. As she turned out into the street, the brakes of a car, as so often, screeched behind her. Presently everyone in the neighborhood could hear Mr. Ralph Hadley tooting the insignificant little horn on his mama's coupé and shouting at Aunt Munsie in his own tooty voice, above the sound of the horn. Aunt Munsie pulled over, making just enough room to let poor old Mr. Ralph get by but without once looking back at him. Suddenly, before Mr. Ralph could get his car started again, Miss Lucille was running along beside Aunt Munsie, saying, "Munsie, you be careful! You're going to meet your death on the streets of Thornton, Tennessee!"

"Let 'em," said Aunt Munsie. Miss Lucille didn't know whether Munsie meant "Let 'em run over me; I don't care" or meant "Let 'em just dare!" Miss Lucille soon turned back, without Aunt Munsie's ever looking at her. And when Mr. Ralph Hadley did get his motor started, and sailed past in his mama's coupé, Aunt Munsie didn't give him a look, either. Nor did Mr. Ralph turn his face to look at Aunt Munsie. He was on his way to the drugstore, to pick up his mama's prescriptions, and he was too entirely put out, peeved, and upset to endure even the briefest exchange with that ugly, uppity old Munsie of the Tollivers'.

Aunt Munsie continued pulling her slop wagon toward the Square. There was a more animated expression on her face than usual, and every so often her lips would move rapidly and emphatically over a phrase or sentence. Why should she go to Memphis and Nashville and see how rich they were? No matter how rich they were, what difference did it make, if they didn't own any land, or none in Cameron County. She had heard the old Doctor tell them— tell both his boys and his girls, and the old lady, too, in her day— that nobody was rich who didn't own land, and nobody stayed rich who didn't see after his land first-hand. But, of course, Aunt Munsie had herself mocked the old Doctor to his face for going on about land so much. She used to tell him she hadn't ever seen *him* behind a plow. And was anybody ever more scared of a mule than Dr. Tolliver was? Mules or horses, either? Aunt Munsie had heard him say that the happiest day of his life was the day he first learned that the horseless carriage was a reality.

No, it wasn't really to own land that Thad and Will ought to come back to Thornton. It was more that if they were going to be rich, they ought to come home, where their money counted for something. How could Will or Thad ever be rich anywhere else? They could just have a lot of money in the bank, that was all—like that mill manager from Chi. The mill manager could have a yard full of big cars and a stucco house as big as you like, but who would ever take him for rich? Aunt Munsie would sometimes say all these things to Crecie, or something as nearly like them as she could find words for. Crecie might nod her head in agreement or she might be in a mood to say being rich wasn't any good for anybody and didn't matter, and that you could live on just being quality better than on being rich in Thornton. "Quality's better than land or better than money in the bank here," Crecie would say.

Aunt Munsie would sneer at her and say, "It never were."

Lucrecie could talk all she wanted about the old times! Aunt Munsie knew too much about what they were like, for both the richest white folks and the blackest field hands. Nothing about the old times was as good as these days, and there were going to be better times yet when Mr. Thad and Mr. Will came back. Everybody lived easier now than they used to, and were better off. She could never be got to reminisce about her childhood in slavery, or her life with her husband, or even about those halcyon days after the old Mizziz had died and Aunt Munsie's word had become law in the Tolliver household. Without being able to book-read or even to make numbers, she had finished raising the whole pack of tow-headed Tollivers just as the Mizziz would have wanted it done. The Doctor told her she *had* to—he didn't ever once think about getting another wife, or taking in some cousin, not after his "Molly darling" —and Aunt Munsie *did*. But, as Crecie said, when a time was past in her mama's life, it seemed to be gone and done with in her head, too.

Lucrecie would say frankly she thought her mama was "hard about people and things in the world." She talked about her mama not only to the Blalocks, for whom she had worked all her life, but to anybody else who gave her an opening. It wasn't just about her mama, though, that she would talk to anybody. She liked to talk, and she talked about Aunt Munsie not in any ugly, resentful way but as she would about the rainy season or where the fire was last night. (Crecie was twice the size of her mama, and black the way her old daddy had been, and loud and good-natured the way he was —or at least the way Aunt Munsie wasn't. You wouldn't have known they were mother and daughter, and not many of the young people in town did realize it. Only by accident did they live next door to each other; Mr. Thad and Mr. Will had bought Munsie her house, and Crecie had heired hers from her second husband.) *That* was how she talked about her mama—as she would have about any lonely, eccentric, harmless neighbor. "I may be dead wrong, but I think Mama's kind of hardhearted," she would say. "She's a good old soul, I reckon, but when something's past, it's gone and done with for Mama. She don't think about day before yestiddy—or yestiddy, either. I don't know, maybe that's the way to be. Maybe that's why the old soul's gona outlive us all." Then, obviously think-ing about what a picture of health she herself was at sixty, Crecie would throw back her head and laugh so loud you might hear her out at the fairgrounds.

Crecie, however, knew her mama wasn't honest-to-God mean and hadn't ever been mean to the Tolliver children, the way the Bla-locks liked to make out she had. All the Tolliver children but Mr. Thad and Mr. Will had quarrelled with her for good by the time they were grown, but they had quarrelled with the old Doctor, too (and as if they were the only ones who shook off their old folks this day and time). When Crecie talked about her mama, she didn't spare her anything, but she was fair to her, too. And it was in no hateful or disloyal spirit that she took part in the conspiracy that finally got Aunt Munsie and her slop wagon off the streets of Thornton. Crecie would have done the same for any neighbor. She had small part enough, actually, in that conspiracy. Her part was merely to break the news to Aunt Muncie that there was now a law against keeping pigs within the city limits. It was a small part but one that no one else quite dared to take.

"They ain't no such law!" Aunt Munsie roared back at Crecie. She was slopping her pigs when Crecie came to the fence and told her about the law. It had seemed the most appropriate time to Lucrecie. "They ain't never been such a law, Crecie," Aunt Munsie said. "Every house on Jackson and Jefferson used to keep pigs."

"It's a brand-new law, Mama."

Aunt Munsie finished bailing out the last of the slop from her wagon. It was just before twilight. The last, weak rays of the sun colored the clouds behind the mock-orange tree in Crecie's yard. When Aunt Munsie turned around from the sty, she pretended that that little bit of light in the clouds hurt her eyes, and turned away her head. And when Lucrecie said that everybody had until the first of the year to get rid of their pigs, Aunt Munsie was in a spell of deafness. She headed out toward the crib to get some corn for the chickens. She was trying to think whether anybody else inside the town still kept pigs. Herb Mallory did—two doors beyond Crecie. Then Aunt Munsie remembered Herb didn't pay city taxes. The town line ran between him and Shad Willis.

That was sometime in June, and before July came, Aunt Munsie knew all there was worth knowing about the conspiracy. Mr. Thad and Mr. Will had each been in town for a day during the spring. They and their families had been to her house and sat on the porch; the children had gone back to look at her half-grown collie dog and the two hounds, at the old sow and her farrow of new pigs, and at the frizzliest frizzly chicken Aunt Munsie had ever had. And on those visits to Thornton, Mr. Thad and Mr. Will had also made their usual round among their distant kin and close friends. Everywhere they went, they had heard of the near-accidents Aunt Munsie was causing with her slop wagon and the real danger there was of her being run over. Miss Lucille Satterfield and Miss Patty Bean

had both been to the Mayor's office and also to see Judge Lawrence
to try to get Aunt Munsie "ruled" off the streets, but the men in
the courthouse and in the Mayor's office didn't listen to the women
in Thornton any more. And so either Mr. Thad or Mr. Will—how
would which one of them it was matter to Munsie?—had been prevailed upon to stop by Mayor Lunt's office, and in a few seconds'
time had set the wheels of conspiracy in motion. Soon a general
inquiry had been made in the town as to how many citizens still
kept pigs. Only two property owners besides Aunt Munsie had been
found to have pigs on their premises, and they, being men, had been
docile and reasonable enough to sell what they had on hand to Mr.
Will or Mr. Thad Tolliver. Immediately afterward—within a matter
of weeks, that is—a city ordinance had been passed forbidding the
possession of swine within the corporate limits of Thornton. Aunt
Munsie had got the story bit by bit from Miss Leonora and Miss
Patty and Miss Lucille and others, including the constable himself,
whom she didn't hesitate to stop right in the middle of the Square
on a Saturday noon. Whether it was Mr. Thad or Mr. Will who
had been prevailed upon by the ladies she never ferreted out, but
that was only because she did not wish to do so.

The constable's word was the last word for her. The constable
said yes, it was the law, and he admitted yes, he had sold his own
pigs—for the constable was one of those two reasonable souls—to
Mr. Thad or Mr. Will. He didn't say which of them it was, or if
he did, Aunt Munsie couldn't remember it. After her interview
with the constable, Aunt Munsie never again exchanged words with
any human being about the ordinance against pigs. That afternoon,
she took a fishing pole from under her house and drove the old sow
and the nine shoats down to Herb Mallory's, on the outside of town.
They were his, she said, if he wanted them, and he could pay her
at killing time.

It was literally true that Aunt Munsie never again exchanged
words with anyone about the ordinance against pigs or about the
conspiracy she had discovered against herself. But her daughter
Lucrecie had a tale to tell about what Aunt Munsie did that afternoon after she had seen the constable and before she drove the pigs
over to Herb Mallory's. It was mostly a tale of what Aunt Munsie
said to her pigs and to her dogs and her chickens.

Crecie was in her own back yard washing her hair when her
mama came down the rickety porch steps and into the yard next

door. Crecie had her head in the pot of suds, and so she couldn't look up, but she knew by the way Mama flew down the steps that there was trouble. "She came down them steps like she was wasp-nest bit, or like some youngon who's got hisself wasp-nest bit—and her all of eighty, I reckon!" Then, as Crecie told it, her mama scurried around in the yard for a minute or so like she thought Judgment was about to catch up with her, and pretty soon she commenced slamming at something. Crecie wrapped a towel about her soapy head, squatted low, and edged over to the plank fence. She peered between the planks and saw what her mama was up to. Since there never had been a gate to the fence around the pigsty, Mama had taken the wood axe and was knocking a hole in it. But directly, just after Crecie had taken her place by the plank fence, her mama had left off her slamming at the sty and turned about so quickly and so exactly toward Crecie that Crecie thought the poor, blind old soul had managed to spy her squatting there. Right away, though, Crecie realized it was not *her* that Mama was staring at. She saw that all Aunt Munsie's chickens and those three dogs of hers had come up behind her, and were clucking and whining to know why she didn't stop that infernal racket and put out some feed for them.

Crecie's mama set one hand on her hip and rested the axe on the ground. "Just look at yuh!" she said, and then she let the chickens and the dogs—and the pigs, too—have it. She told them what a miserable bunch of creatures they were, and asked them what right they had to always be looking for handouts from her. She sounded like the boss-man who's caught all his pickers laying off before sun-down, and she sounded, too, like the preacher giving his sinners Hail Columbia at camp meeting. Finally, shouting explosively, "Now, g'wine! G'wine! G'wine! G'wine widja!," and swinging the axe wide and broad above their heads, she sent the dogs howling under the house and the chickens scattering in every direction. Only the collie pup, of the three dogs, didn't scamper to the farthest corner under-neath the house. He stopped under the steps, and not two seconds later he was poking his long head out again and showing the whites of his doleful brown eyes. Crecie's mama took a step toward him and then she halted. "You want to know what's the commotion about? I reckoned you would," she said with profound contempt, as though the collie were a more reasonable soul than the other ani-mals, and as though there were nothing she held in such thorough disrespect as reason. "I tell you what the commotion's about," she said. "They *ain't* comin' back. They ain't never comin' back. They ain't never had no notion of comin' back." She turned her head to one side, and the only explanation Crecie could find for her mama's next words was that that collie pup did look so much like Miss Lucille Satterfield.

"Why don't I go down to Memphis or up to Nashville and see 'em sometime, like *you* does?" Aunt Munsie asked the collie. "I tell you why. Becaze I ain't nothin' to 'em in Memphis, and they ain't nothin' to me in Nashville. *You* can go!" she said, advancing and shaking the big axe at the dog. "A collie dog's a collie dog anywhar. But Aunt Munsie, she's just their Aunt Munsie here in Thornton. I got sense enough to see *that*." The collie slowly pulled his head back under the steps, and Aunt Munsie watched for a minute to see if he would show himself again. When he didn't, she went and jerked the fishing pole out from under the house and headed toward the pigsty. Crecie remained squatting beside the fence until her mama and the pigs were out in the street and on their way to Herb Mallory's.

That was the end of Aunt Munsie's keeping pigs and the end of her daily rounds with her slop wagon, but it wasn't the end of Aunt Munsie. She lived on for nearly twenty years after that, till long after Lucrecie had been put away, in fine style, by the Blalocks. Ever afterward, though, Aunt Munsie seemed different to people. They said she softened, and everybody said it was a change for the better. She would take paper money from under her carpet, or out of the chinks in her walls, and buy things for up at the church, or buy her own whiskey when she got sick, instead of making somebody bring her a nip. On the Square, she would laugh and holler with the white folks the way Crecie and all the other old-timers did, and she even took to tying a bandanna about her head—took to talking old-nigger foolishness, too, about the Bell Witch, and claiming she remembered the day General N. B. Forrest rode into town and saved all the cotton from the Yankees at the depot. When Mr. Will and Mr. Thad came to see her with their families, she got so she would reminisce with them about their daddy and tease them about all the silly little things they had done when they were growing up. "Mr. Thad—him still in kilts, too—he say, 'Aunt Munsie, reach down in yo' stockin' and git me a copper cent. I want some store candy.' " She told them about how Miss Yola Ewing, the sewing woman, heard her threatening to bust Will's back wide open when he broke the lamp chimney, and how Miss Yola went to the Doctor and told him he ought to run Aunt Munsie off. Aunt Munsie and the Doctor had had a big laugh about it in the kitchen, and Miss Yola must have eavesdropped on them, because she left without finishing the girls' Easter dresses.

The visits from Mr. Thad and Mr. Will continued as long as Aunt Munsie lived, but she never asked them any more about when they were sure enough coming back. And the children, though she hugged them more than ever—and, toward the last, there were the children's children to be hugged—never set foot in her back yard again. Aunt Munsie lived on for nearly twenty years, and when they finally buried her, they put on her tombstone that she was aged one hundred years, though nobody knew how old she was. There was no record of when she was born. All anyone knew was that in her last years she had said she was a girl helping about the big house when freedom came. That would have made her probably about twelve years old in 1865, according to her statements and depictions. But all agreed that in her old age Aunt Munsie, like other old darkies, was not very reliable about such things. Her spirit softened, and she became not very reliable about facts.

SENTIMENTAL EDUCATION

❖

HAROLD BRODKEY

IT was eight o'clock on a warm September evening, and all the
bells of Harvard were striking the hour. Elgin Smith, tired of
studying, was standing on the steps of Widener Library—those wide,
Roman, inconvenient steps—blinking his eyes and staring into the
distance, because that was supposed to refresh the corneas and the
retina. He was thinking, but not of his schoolwork. He was thinking of what it would be like to fall in love, to worship a girl and to
put his life at her feet. He despised himself, because he feared he
was incapable of passion and he believed that only passionate people were worth while and all other kinds were shallow. He was taking courses in English Literature, in German Literature, in Italian
Literature, in History, ancient and medieval, and every one of them
was full of incidents that he thought mocked him, since they seemed
to say that the meaning of life, the peak of existence, the core of
events was one certain emotion, to which he was a stranger, and for
which he was very likely too rational. Therefore, he stood on the
steps of Widener, so cracked by longing that it seemed only gravity
held him together.

He was very tall, six feet three, and gangling. He had a small
head, curiously shaped (his roommate, Dimitri, sometimes accused
him of looking like a wedge of cheese), and a hooked nose. He
wanted to be a professor in the field of comparative philology, and
he believed in Beauty. He studied all the time, and there were
moments when he was appalled by how hard he worked. He was
known for his crying in movies. He was not unathletic.

Somehow, he had become convinced that he was odd and that
only odd girls liked him, pitiable girls who couldn't do any better,
and this singed his pride.

It was his fate that this particular night he should see a girl walking up the steps of Widener Library. She was of medium height and

had black hair cut short; she was wearing a light-colored coat that floated behind her because she was walking so fast, nearly running, but not quite; and the curve of her forehead and the way her eyes were set took Elgin's breath away. She was so pretty and carried herself so well and had a look of such healthy and arrogant self-satisfaction that Elgin sighed and thought here was the sort of not odd girl who could bestow indescribable benefits on any young man she liked—and on his confidence. She was that very kind of girl, that far from unhappy, that world-contented kind, he believed would never fall for him.

She carried her books next to her bosom. Elgin's eyes followed her up the steps; and then his head turned, his nostrils distended with emotion; and she was gone, vanished into Widener.

"Surely this year," he thought, looking up at the sky. "Now that I'm almost nineteen." He stretched out his arms, and the leaves on the trees, already growing dry at the approach of autumn, rustled in the breezes.

He thought about that girl once or twice in the days that followed, but the longing for her didn't really take root until he saw her again, two weeks later, at a Radcliffe Jolly-Up in Cabot Hall. It was in one of the dimly lit common rooms, where couples were indefatigably dancing in almost total darkness. Elgin was swaying in place (he was not a good dancer) with a girl who helped him on his German when he caught sight of his Widener Library vision. When the next dance began, he wound through the couples looking for her, to cut in on her, but when he drew near her, he turned and walked over to the wall, where he caught his breath and realized he was frightened.

This was the stroke that fatally wounded him. Knowing he was frightened of that girl, he longed for her, the way men who think they are cowards long for war so they can prove they're not. Or perhaps it was some other reason. The girl had a striking appearance; there was her youth and her proud, clean look to recommend her.

But whatever the reason, he did begin to think about her in earnest. She rose up in clouds of brilliant light in his head whenever he came across certain words in his reading. ("Mistress" was one, "beautiful" another; you can guess the rest.) He did a paper on "The Unpossessable Loved One in Troubadour Poetry." When he walked through the Yard on his way to classes, his eyes revolved nervously and never rested, searching all the faces on all the walks in the hope of seeing her. In fact, on his walks to classes he looked so disordered that a number of his friends asked him if he was feeling ill, and it pleased Elgin, after the first two times this happened, to reply that he was. He was ill with longing.

At night, before going to the dining hall for supper, he would put on his bathrobe and slip down to the pool in the basement of Adams House. There, under the wooden beams, he would swim angrily from one end of the pool to the other, faster and faster, until his arms ached. Then he would take a cold shower.

When he slept, he dreamed of carnage, horses, and speeding automobiles. He went to French movies and ground his knees against the seat in front of him. He laughed at himself, and decided to break this absurd habit he had got into of thinking all the time about this girl he had never met, but he didn't quite succeed. At last, he admitted to himself that he was in love with her; and one night, sleeping in his lower bunk while Dimitri breathed heavily over his head, he had tears in his eyes because he was so foolish and did desire that girl whom he had seen the two times mentioned and only twice more besides.

Having resigned himself—in imitation of Dante—to a state of perpetual longing, he felt calmer and looked at the world with sad, scholarly eyes. But his equilibrium was delicate, and in December Dimitri began having an affair with a Radcliffe girl named Felicia. Upperclassmen could have girls in their room in the afternoon if they signed them in with the campus policeman who sat in a little room near the main entrance of their house, and signed them out when they left. There was always the chance the policeman would come to the room and check up, but even so on gray December afternoons Dimitri, all bundled up, would come searching through Widener for Elgin and ask him not to come home until after six o'clock because Dimitri was taking Felicia to the room. Then Elgin would sit in front of his books, numbed, unable to read, with fine beads of sweat standing out on his upper lip and forehead.

Once he came back to the room and found Dimitri lying in front of a fire in the fireplace; the fire was being fed by Dimitri's lecture notes. "Oh God, it's you. How I hate your ugly face!" Dimitri said, but Elgin knew what he meant; at that moment, being Elgin and not Felicia was a blasphemy. He tiptoed through the room to hang up his coat and tiptoed out again.

In January, immediately after exams, Elgin came down with flu.

He was exhausted. When he was well again, it seemed to him that he had been washed clean and purified. He hardly thought about that girl at all.

But one sunny, cold morning in February Elgin saw her standing in front of Sever Hall. She was wearing long blue woollen socks, and she was talking to a pock-marked boy in a raccoon overcoat. Elgin suddenly turned and went into Sever and waited in the hall until the bell rang. The girl came in, and Elgin followed her upstairs and into a classroom; he sat three rows in back of her. It was a course given by Professor Bush on Metaphysical Poets of the Seventeenth Century. And that afternoon Elgin went and got permission to transfer from The Victorian Novel to that class.

The girl's name was Caroline Hedges and she came from Baltimore. She was a horsewoman of considerable ability. She spent a good deal of her time on clothes, not ever being quite sure where true elegance lay. She was inclined to buy pale colors, blouses one size too large for her, and tweeds. She was easily embarrassed. She read a good deal, her favorite books being "The Charterhouse of Parma," "Anna Karenina," and "Madame Bovary."

She was very proud and easily moved by appeals to her courage. She considered she'd had a happy childhood, and she liked her family (although she could not help looking down on them a little because their name was not famous in the history of America). When she was ten, she had briefly loved a cousin of hers, who was twelve, and who had taken her to the National Museum of Art in Washington and told her the names of the great painters.

At Radcliffe, her freshman year, she discovered that she had been sheltered, compared to most of the other girls, and she felt young and slightly ashamed of herself. This gave her a look of great purity, and she was something of a belle. But late in the spring of her freshman year she stayed up all one night, obsessed and genuinely moved by the fact that she was intelligent and hadn't really known it before. She had just found it out by noticing that section men and assistant professors and sometimes full professors liked to hear her talk in class. From that night on, she limited her dating and threw herself into studying.

"It is poetry that I love," she wrote in her diary. "It is hard for me to explain why. Once when I was staying with Aunt Kitty in New York I went for a walk in Central Park when it was snowing.

In the zoo I saw the Bactrian camel standing in the middle of its pen. It was holding its head straight up in the air with its mouth open and its tongue out and the snowflakes were falling on it. Perhaps he never saw snow before. I'm not exactly sure where Bactria is or what its climate is like—perhaps it was remembering snow. That is how I feel about poetry."

Another entry read, "My mother writes and asks me if I still see Louis Du Pont whom she thought such a charming boy. How can Mother think anyone so plump is charming?"

Early in April of her junior year, she wrote, "Today in Metaphysical Poetry, we discussed the tradition of Platonic Love in Jacobean England. A boy named Elgin Smith spoke brilliantly, I thought. He described the winters the young people spent in those vast country houses, twenty or so young people visiting in one house, with two or three chaperons, and snow everywhere. They sang and gave masques and such things. Because young people are so hot-blooded, it was necessary to devise a code of courtship to restrain them, for marriages of alliance had to be made later. Needless to say, it didn't work, Platonic Love, I mean, and it was much more often written about than observed. I do so admire brilliance and wish that I had some. This young man had the oddest voice; it is positively nasal and twangs and twangs. I wanted to put my hand over his mouth and tell him 'Sh-h-h.' He is terribly intense and nervous. He has borrowed a pencil from me several times, and he asked me to have coffee with him once. I said I couldn't, but next time he asks, I will accept. I long for some really intelligent friends."

When you consider the combustibility of the emotions of these two young people, it is hardly surprising that within two weeks of their first long conversation together they were trembling when they talked, and found themselves oppressed whenever silences fell. The impulse to discuss this state of affairs with each other kept recurring, but they fought it, until one afternoon when they were sitting in the Cambridge Common and having a cigarette together before separating for dinner.

All through the Common, young mothers were sitting, bored, by baby carriages, and beneath the trees, newly come to leaf, children were climbing on the old cannon. Abraham Lincoln was brooding under his canopy, and trolleys clanged on Massachusetts Avenue.

"Elgin," Caroline said, "we've talked about a hundred things, a thousand things, I bet."

"Yes."

"But we've never talked about what we think of each other."

"No," he said, twisting his fingers together. "I guess we never have."

"I—I don't approve of it, actually," Caroline said. "Analyzing things and all. Some things are better left unsaid."

"I agree," Elgin said. The words seemed to explode on his lips, leaving a faintly surprised look on his face.

"Do you?" Caroline said. For her part, she was having difficulty hanging on to her poise.

"There isn't much people can say that hasn't been said before," Elgin said with finality. Then he added, "It's my reading. I've read so much I guess I'm a little jaded."

"I see," said Caroline. "Well, it's a fascinating subject."

"Yes," said Elgin, "it is."

They sat in silence for several seconds, both of them on the verge of speaking, but Elgin was frightened and Caroline was disconcerted, as if her ideas of what could happen had been trampled on and left for dead.

"Let's get started back," Elgin said, and Caroline agreed. She rose and the two of them walked on toward Radcliffe, past the Hotel Continental. At the corner, Caroline said, "You coming by this evening?"

Elgin nodded.

Caroline reached out and shook Elgin's hand, which was a strange thing for her to do.

"Caroline!" Elgin said sharply.

"Yes."

"Let's go have dinner together."

"Where? I thought you were broke."

"The Chinese restaurant."

"All right, if I have enough money." She opened her purse and looked; she and Elgin went Dutch most places. "I've got two dollars and some change." They linked arms and walked back to the Common.

"I think Vaughan is a little bit of a bore," Caroline said. "Really, the language has deteriorated so much since Donne."

They sat down on the same bench where they had sat before.

Elgin said, "I assume since our conversation fifteen minutes ago it would be terrible if I talked about the way I feel about you."

"Oh, no," said Caroline. "Go right ahead."

"Well, they're very strong."

"I'd more or less guessed that," Caroline said, unable to make her voice sound normal.

"But I never mentioned it before," Elgin said, "because I didn't want anything to come up that might make you want to stop seeing me."

"I understand," Caroline said. "That was very subtle of you."

"Please shut up," Elgin said. "I'm trying to get some words out and it's very hard. I want you to know I'm not just chasing you or anything like that."

"Oh?"

"I saw you last fall. You were going into Widener. It was—you know—at first sight."

"Elgin!"

"It was. I only took Metaphysical Poetry because you were taking it. Caroline, I have deep feelings about you."

Caroline felt an intense sense of relief. "Well, I always thought so," she said. "But I wasn't sure." Then she realized Elgin was trembling. "Elgin, what's wrong?"

A child ran by with a red disintegrator pistol. "You're not angry?" Elgin asked.

"Of course not!" she said ringingly.

"You're not going to tell me that the most I can expect is your friendship? And if I expect more we oughtn't to see each other any more?"

There was silence. "I hadn't thought this far," Caroline said. She thought it was much more decent if she didn't have to mention her feelings; she felt trapped. "Well, Elgin, I'll tell you, I certainly don't want to stop seeing you." She moved her legs until they were spread ungracefully. "But, really, I think . . . we ought to be careful and not get, oh, I don't know, sloppy, if you know what I mean."

"I don't mind that," Elgin said. He swallowed. "But is it all right —Is it all right, Caroline, if I show how I feel a little more?" His voice rose and quivered with longing.

"I don't know what you mean."

"You do."

"Honestly, Elgin, I—"

"You do!"

"I suppose so. . . . Yes. Do show it. Let's be honest. For God's sake, who can it hurt? Yes, let's not be priggish."

To her astonishment and delight, Elgin caught her hand and pressed it to his lips.

They hadn't kissed then, nor did they kiss each other for several days afterward. It was a tacit confession that they suspected the presence of passion, and in such cases, if one is at all practical, one stands back, one dawdles, one doesn't rush in to confront the beast in its lair. Or to put it another way, one doesn't go tampering with the floodgates. What they did, after this conversation, was suddenly to become lighthearted. They made jokes; Caroline stole Elgin's notebook from his hands and made him chase her; they discussed Metaphysical Poetry. And when this lightness and gaiety had eased their suspicion and their fright was in abeyance, Caroline decided she wanted Elgin to kiss her.

She was walking up Garden Street in late afternoon, and the sunlight was clear and golden. There was a light wind that ruffled her hair, and she was striding along, passing any number of couples, Harvard boys and Radcliffe girls, some with their arms around each other's waist, some holding hands, some just walking side by side. Caroline decided then, in a single flash; and the next minute her cheeks began to glow and she pushed happily at her hair, which kept blowing across her eyes.

At seven o'clock that evening, Elgin arrived at Cabot Hall to pick her up. He was wearing his shabby tweed jacket and khaki pants and striped tie. Caroline came downstairs wearing her prettiest sweater, a pink cashmere. Her hair was carefully brushed and she wore lipstick, so Elgin knew something was up.

"I'd sort of like to go to a movie tonight," she said. "I've got enough money for both of us if you're flat."

Elgin told her he had a little cash. They settled on the U.T.—the University Theatre in Harvard Square.

"I'm in the mood for gangsters," Caroline said as they emerged from Cabot into the spring evening.

The sky between the trees was purple, a deep, stirring plum color. Caroline put her arm through Elgin's, and they strode briskly through the Quad toward Garden Street, and then through the Common—one of a number of couples, in a long, irregular procession stretching from the Radcliffe dormitories to Harvard Square.

"I finished my paper on Donne," Elgin said.

Caroline laughed inconsequently, and Elgin laughed, too, for no good reason.

They passed through the middle of the Common, by Lincoln's statue, where a lamp cast a ghostly white glare on leaves and benches and the surface of the walk. Caroline's charming face swam into the light, shadows fell across it, and Elgin closed his eyes.

Caroline pressed his hand. They hurried.

All during the movie, they sat holding both of each other's hands, and their shoulders touching. Entwined and tangled like that, they giggled together whenever the movie became particularly violent. They couldn't stop giggling after a while, as the death toll in the movie mounted. When the movie ended, they left and Elgin bought Caroline a chocolate ice-cream cone at St. Clair's and they walked down to the Charles River.

The Charles looked placid, and glimmered as it quietly flowed under the bridge; the lights of Eliot House were reflected in its surface. Caroline put her head on Elgin's shoulder. They breathed in unison, the two of them, standing on the bank of the river, and then Elgin said, "It's clumsy to ask, but Caroline, do you really . . . or . . . would I . . ." He missed her lips, kissing her cheek instead, and he was holding her so tightly that she couldn't move and correct his mistake. But a minute later he corrected his error himself. They both had difficulty breathing. "I love, I love you, I love you," he whispered.

It sounded beautiful in the moonlight, the river ran quietly beneath the bridge, and Caroline was glad she had let him kiss her.

After that they took to kissing each other a good deal. They met every afternoon at Widener. When one of them broke off work, the other would break off, too, and they would both go downstairs. Along either side of the steps rose large stone arms, which looked as if they should be surmounted by statues, but they were bare, and in spring, in the afternoons, on both of them there would usually be people sitting, sometimes alone, sometimes in pairs. Here Elgin and Caroline would sit and look out over the Yard toward the Chapel.

At four-thirty, they would go to Massachusetts Avenue and have a cup of coffee in one of the luncheonettes. Usually they separated then, Caroline to go to Cabot Hall, Elgin to Adams House, for supper, but some evenings, when they had the money, they had dinner together at a Chinese restaurant near the Square, where the food was very cheap. (Elgin didn't like taking her to Adams House on the nights when girls were allowed in the dining hall, because it reminded him that he was young and ineffectual and under the control of an institution.) In the evenings, they studied, either in the library or in one of the common rooms at Cabot, and at nine o'clock when the library closed, they would walk down to the river-bank. Elgin had an old raincoat that he wore, and they used that to spread on the grass, to sit on. They sat side by side and shared long, rather tender kisses. At first on these expeditions they talked about poetry, but after a while conversation began to seem disagreeable, and they sat in silence.

Then they began to leave off studying at Widener earlier in the afternoon, at three-thirty, or even three. Caroline liked going with Elgin to the Boston Museum of Fine Arts, and they would look at the pictures and, when their feet were tired, go and sit in the Fens, the park just behind the Museum, which has a rose garden at one end of it. Caroline wanted Elgin to lose his Middle Western pro-nunciation, and the excuse they used for these jaunts was that this was time spent in teaching Elgin how to speak. He would bring a book, Bacon's "Essays," or Montaigne's, or Jeremy Taylor's "Ser-mons," or Johnson's "Rasselas"—good, sturdy books, with sentences so rich that sometimes Elgin's voice grew fuzzy with the pleasure he felt reading them.

"Always, all-ways, not oll-wez," Caroline would say.

"Wait, Caroline, just wait a bit, listen to this," and he would read another rolling, rhetorical period. "Isn't that gorgeous?"

"Not gorgeous," Caroline would say. "That's not the right word somehow."

"Oh, it is in this case," Elgin would say. "It's absolutely exact."

And Caroline, struggling not to be moved, would say, "I suppose. I suppose, just barely."

Then Elgin started reading Colette and Boccaccio. Now, when silence fell, something seemed to be lying beside them on the grass, breathing softly. Glances, trees, the movements of people in the park suddenly split off from the commonsensical, taken-for-granted world and became strange. Caroline frowned more and more often, turned into something very like a nag. She made Elgin buy new ties and have his shoes reheeled. Often, in the afternoons, she would take him to St. Clair's and make him drink freshly squeezed orange juice. When it was raining, she still insisted they go for walks because it was good for Elgin. She took to proofreading all his papers and typ-ing them over for him because he was a poor and careless typist. One day, Elgin read to her the story in Boccaccio of the young girl who used to tell her mother that she wanted to sleep in the garden in order to hear the nightingale sing, but the girl met her lover in the garden—*he* was the nightingale. Elgin read this story to Caroline in an intense and quavering voice. For a week afterward, Caroline walked back and forth to classes hearing in her head the phrase "listening to the nightingale." Finally, the phrase came to stand for so much, it aroused such deep tumult in her and made her feel so lonely and deprived, that one night Elgin came back to his room, woke Dimitri from a sound sleep, and asked him to stay away from the room the next afternoon.

It turned out that Elgin and Caroline were both virgins.

Their first dip into sensual waters left them nonplussed. They didn't know what to make of it. They tried to persuade themselves that something had really happened, but the minute it was over, they couldn't believe they had ever done such a thing. They rushed into further experiences; they broke off in the middle of embraces and looked at each other, stunned and delighted. "Is this really happening?" they both asked at different times, and each time the other said, "No," and they would laugh. They knew that nothing they did was real, was actual. They had received a blow on the head and were prey to erotic imaginings, that was all. But at the same time they half realized it was true, they *were* doing these things, and then the fact that they, Caroline and Elgin, shared such intimacy dazed and fascinated them; and when they were together, they tried to conceal it, but this indescribable attraction they felt for each other kept making itself known and draining all the strength from their bodies. They tried to make jokes about themselves and this odd little passion they felt. "We're unskilled labor," Elgin said. "You know, I'm just giving in because you're irresistible," Caroline said. She always pretended that she was completely dispassionate about sex. It just happened that she was susceptible to Elgin's entreaties. But he was too shy to entreat unless she encouraged him, and Caroline often felt like the worst kind of hypocrite. The truth of the matter is, they were caught up in a fever of their senses.

Caroline would have her lunch in Cabot Hall, locked in an impenetrable haze of daydreaming, not even hearing the girls chattering around her. She would walk to Widener, and if boys she knew stopped her to talk, she would stare at them stonily, afraid the boy might guess her feelings for Elgin and think they applied to him. She would run up the stairs of Widener, past the Sargent murals, petrified that Elgin might not be waiting for her. Every day this fear grew worse; but every day he was there, sitting at one of the long wooden tables in the reading room, beneath the great coffered ceiling, and the look on his face when he caught sight of her would make Caroline smile giddily, because she had never known before what a miraculous power she had over men.

They managed a wry stiffness when they were in public. They spoke to each other in tones of the crudest good-fellowship. Elgin called her "Girl." "Girl, you finished with that book?" Caroline called Elgin "Cheese." "No, Cheese. Don't rush me." They didn't hold hands or touch. They thought they fooled everyone, but everyone who knew them guessed, and they both told their roommates. In fact, they wanted to talk about what was happening to them to everyone; this news was always on the tip of their tongues; and so they got into the habit of suddenly breaking off conversations with their friends when the impulse to confess grew too strong to be contained a moment longer, and all their friends thought they were becoming very queer and difficult indeed.

Each afternoon that they met in Widener started on this high level of confusion and rapidly ran downhill. The minute hand of the clock over the door of the reading room jerked every sixty seconds, marking off a whole minute in one movement, and at two-thirty they were no longer capable of speech. Elgin would be pale or flushed. He would draw breath irregularly through a mouth he couldn't quite close, or through distended nostrils, and this phenomenon would fascinate Caroline, except that she couldn't look at him for too long without feeling the most awful pain in her head. Finally, Elgin would gasp, "Well?"

"I'm finished," Caroline would say in the weakest voice imaginable.

They would walk in silence to Adams House, and Elgin would sign Caroline in at the policeman's room. In silence they would mount the stairs, and Elgin would unlock the door of his room, and then they would fall into each other's arms, sometimes giggling with relief, sometimes sombre, sometimes almost crying with the joy of this privacy and this embrace.

Then, later, both of them dressed and their faces scrubbed, Caroline, like an addict, would descend on Elgin's bureau and haul out his torn and buttonless shirts. She didn't know how to sew, but she thought she did, and she sat on Elgin's couch, smiling to herself, softly humming, and sewed buttons on wrong. Elgin tried to study, but his moods whirled and spun him around so that one minute he'd be reading quietly and the next minute he'd be striding up and down the room on the worn carpet, wringing his hands or else waving them aloft and denouncing the College and the American Educational System, full of rage, but not knowing with what or why, and forced to let it out any way he could, while Caroline, faintly bored, ignored him mostly and sewed.

Every once in a while, Caroline would cry. Then she would be unable to dress properly, and she'd drag around the room with her hair badly combed, her shoes off, looking slatternly, and say, "I don't know what's wrong with me. Actually, nothing's wrong with me." But every few minutes tears would course down her cheeks. Nor did she know why she cried; she was as innocent of understanding herself as she was of understanding Elgin.

Sometimes they quarrelled. Once, it was because Caroline wouldn't use Elgin's towel.

"If you loved me, you'd use it."

"I'd adore to use *your* towel," Caroline said, "but *this* towel is dirty."

Elgin thought her preposterous; she called Elgin a boor and slammed out of the room. She reached the bottom of the stairs and started back up and heard Elgin coming down. Neither of them said a word; they didn't apologize or mention this episode again. They went for a walk along the riverbank and talked about Metaphysical Poetry.

On Saturdays, Elgin took Caroline to the Harvard courts to play tennis. Caroline had fine ankles and legs, and while they walked to the courts, Elgin kept stealing glances at them, which made Caroline nervous. She was a good tennis player, as good as Elgin, but he could throw her off her game by charging the net and yelling at her, "I've got you now!" This would rattle her so she'd completely miss the ball, and then she would laugh with exasperation.

When he served, he made a point of calling the score in a loud, cheerful, teasing voice: "Thirty-love!" He'd say the "love" in such a way that Caroline would blush, and then she would try to drive the ball directly at him, and most of the time it went out of bounds.

One afternoon, they were in each other's arms in Elgin's room. Elgin was whispering, "I love you, Caroline. I love you so much," and someone knocked on the door. The sound seemed to blind Elgin, who squeezed his eyes closed, as tightly as he could. The knock was repeated a second time, and a third, echoing in the small room. Then the footsteps retreated.

Elgin got up and fetched cigarettes and towels for them both. They leaned back on the couch, at opposite ends, wrapped in towels, and smoked. They didn't mention the fact that they were afraid it had been the campus policeman and they would be expelled. They discussed whether or not they were depraved.

"We are," Caroline said. "Otherwise, we wouldn't be so ashamed."

"We don't have to be ashamed," Elgin said. "We only pretend we are anyway, to be polite."

"You're a rebel," Caroline said gloomily. "You can say that. But I'm a conformist. I'm basically a nice girl. I *am* ashamed."

The pressure of details, the maze of buttons, hooks, and zippers that they had to make their way through to that condition which pleased them best, kept forcing them to be self-conscious. They couldn't believe that what they were doing was real, and yet it was real, as they well knew the minute they separated, when the memory of their last encounter would descend on both of them, occupying their minds, and unfitting them for any occupation except dreaming of the next encounter. At night, lying in his bunk, Elgin would try to sleep, but he'd think of Caroline, and slowly, like a leaf curling in a salt solution, he would twist under his covers until his knees were even with his chest, and this was a tortured, involuntary movement of longing he could no more control than he could control his thoughts. He would try to do his reading for his courses: "In the early years of this century, I moved to London, feeling that Ireland and my love for Ireland were too distracting for my poetry." And then right on the printed page would appear "CAROLINE," in capital letters, and Elgin would rub his face foolishly with both hands, twisting his mouth and his cheeks and his nose.

He didn't believe that Caroline loved him as much as he loved her, or at least that she desired him as much as he did her, and this made him sullen. He picked on her. He told her she wasn't as smart as she thought she was; people treated her as if she were intelligent only because she was pretty. He would accuse her of pettiness, and she would agree with him, confess that she had an awful character, and while he was consoling her, their embraces would begin.

Elgin would be hurt whenever Caroline was the first to point out that it was time to go and have dinner. Caroline would eye the clock, but Elgin would pretend he was so entranced with Caroline he didn't know what time it was. The minutes would tick by, and

Caroline would grow gayer and gayer, trying to ignore the time, while Elgin, beetling, thin, and sardonic, refused to say the words that would release her.

Elgin became frightened. He was so frightened he couldn't eat. He was afraid of losing Caroline, of failing his courses because he couldn't study unless she was sitting beside him where he could reach out and touch her every few minutes. The thought of what it would be like if any of the quarrels they had should turn serious worried him until he was sick. Finally, looking gray and haggard, he suggested to her one afternoon that the two of them should run off and get married.

"Elgin, don't. Don't let's talk about that. You know we can't."

Elgin shrugged and looked disheartened. "I don't like self-pity," he said. "But I admit I have some. Oh, yes. I pity myself a lot. Imagine, here I am, in love with a common, ordinary, conventional girl like you."

Caroline supported her head with her hands. "Oh, Elgin," she said, "you're being cruel. You know we're awfully young. And just because we got carried away—there's no need, really, to . . . It's our animal appetites mostly, you know. . . ."

Elgin wanted to say something bitter but her last remark stopped him. "*Your* animal appetites, too?"

"Yes."

He was so happy he forgot his feelings had been hurt.

Sometimes, she and Elgin went out with Felicia and Dimitri. Caroline could not now bear girls she thought were virgins; they made her uneasy, and she would not double with Dimitri and Felicia until Elgin swore they were lovers, too. Elgin spent more than one afternoon telling her that almost all the girls at Radcliffe and all other colleges had slept with somebody. "The percentage is very high," he said.

They went boating twice at Marblehead. Dimitri had a car, which Elgin borrowed—an old, weak-lunged Ford—and they would wheeze up to Marblehead and rent a dinghy and be blown around the bay, with the sunlight bright on Caroline's hair and the salt air making them hungry and the wind whipping up small whitecaps to make the day exciting.

Caroline wrote in her diary, "His back is so beautiful. It has such a lovely shape. It's so defenseless. I like to put my ear against his back and listen to his heart—I think it's his heart I hear. It's funny he is not more handsome in his clothes, but that only makes him seem more beautiful to me, I think. I feel I would like to give birth to him. Sometimes, I want to crawl into his pocket and be carried like a pencil. I never let him see how strongly I feel. I am a dreadful person, dreadful. . . ."

Elgin wrote her a letter.

"Dear Caroline, Isn't it funny to have me writing a letter to you when I see you every day? But just imagine how it would seem later if we looked back and saw that we had never written each other how we felt.

"You, Caroline Hedges, are the greatest love of my life. just as you are the first.

"I don't suppose, you being a girl, that you know what it's like to love a girl like you, but if you knew how dependent men are on women, you might understand. Not that men can't survive alone, but they don't seem to really amount to anything until they have a woman they love.

"Reading over what I have just written, I see that everything I've said applies only to the selfish side of love. I guess that's a dead giveaway about me. But as for you, kid, just knowing you is rather awe-inspiring."

Sometimes, there would be birds singing in the ivy outside the window of Elgin's room. Sometimes, Elgin would sing to Caroline; he had a sweet, insecurely pitched voice, and his singing would give them both pleasure. Sometimes, seeing Elgin walk across the room unclothed would make all the breath leave Caroline's body, and she would not even be conscious of her gasp or that he heard her. One afternoon, Elgin went into the bathroom to get Caroline a glass of water. She was lying in the lower bunk, lapped in shadows, and she saw him come back into the room and she said weakly, "I love you, Elgin." It was the first time she had said it, that proud, stubborn girl. Elgin heard her; he stopped in his tracks and he put his head back. "God," he said. "This is the happiest moment I ever had."

Now there was no bar to their intimacy, and they talked. Elgin was relentless about asking questions: "What do you think about money? What is your father like? Are you fond of him?"

At first, Caroline was cautious. "Well, I think there's a minimum amount of money people should have. . . . My father is sort of nice. He's shallow, I guess. He doesn't seem to have very strong emotions. He works for an insurance company. I used to like him a lot; I still do. . . . I think I feel sorry for him."

"What do you mean by that?" Elgin asked. He handed her a cigarette and lit it for her. "Tell me everything about yourself. Be honest. I've never known anyone as well as I know you."

Caroline cupped her hands over her mouth. "I think he loves me, and now I love you, and I think that's sad. That he's older . . . Should we be talking like this, Elgin?"

"Why not? Who else can we talk to?"

Then it all began to come out, her feelings toward her father, toward her mother, toward money. Caroline wanted a nice house and a large family; she looked down a little on people who weren't well off. When she felt exhausted from telling Elgin these things, she asked him questions.

"My mother's very possessive," he said. "If we got married, I think we'd have in-law problems. I want to be a famous scholar. I don't disapprove of campus politics. I know I should, but I don't. Isn't that shameful?"

"This isn't dignified, talking like this," Caroline said. "I don't want to do it any more."

She was frightened. Having admitted she loved Elgin, she felt naked, and these conversations only made her feel worse. She kept hoping she and Elgin would reach some stability together, but it never came. She still was frightened when she ran up the stairs of Widener that he wouldn't be waiting for her. She wondered why she couldn't get used to this situation, why the pleasures she was drawn into didn't lose their elements of pain—indeed, why the elements of pain grew steadily worse, until she dreaded seeing Elgin and had to force herself to get out of bed in the morning and go through her day. She couldn't help thinking that what she was with comparative strangers was much pleasanter than what she was with Elgin. With him she was capricious, untruthful, often sharp-tongued, giddy with emotions that came and went, and while one emotion might be ennobling, having six or seven in the space of an hour was undignified and not decent at all. She had always believed that a woman ought to walk very straight, write a firm hand, keep house and entertain well—in short, be like those friends of her mother's whom she admired. The fact that she was young didn't seem any excuse at all for her not being like those women, and now she said to herself, "I'm wild. That's all there is to that."

She decided she was inordinately sexual. Elgin caught her in

Widener reading a book describing the great courtesans of the nineteenth century, La Belle Otero and Lola Montez. She believed that Elgin would inevitably forsake her because she had lost all her dignity and mystery, and she boasted to him that he would never forget her, even if he married some pasty-faced virgin. Elgin couldn't calm her; in fact, he was more than half persuaded that she *was* unusually passionate when she said she was, and he became uneasy with her. Caroline began to wear a little too much lipstick and to walk not in her habitual erect fashion but slouching and swaying her hips. She drank and smoked more, and when she got high, she would look at Elgin through lowered eyelids and kiss him in a knowing—a childishly knowing—way. And all of this humbled Elgin, who felt Caroline was a great enigma and that she was drawing away from him. One night, they were sitting on the riverbank and Caroline put her hands on Elgin's head and drew him to her, and Elgin pulled away desperately. "I don't want you to kiss me like that!"

"What's wrong?" Caroline asked haughtily. "Am I too much woman for you?"

Elgin's eyes grew moist. "I don't know what you do to me," he said miserably. "I'm ready to cry. I didn't think we were having *that* kind of an affair."

In the darkness, he saw Caroline's eyelids descend. Then a shudder passed over her face. He decided to stake everything rather than have Caroline frighten him into helplessness.

He grabbed her arm. "Listen, you've got to get hold of yourself. You're acting like an ass."

Caroline was motionless.

"You're ruining everything," Elgin said.

"You have too many illusions about me," Caroline said coldly. She pulled away from his grasp and lay down on his old, battered raincoat and put her hands under her head. "There are a lot of things you don't know about me. I didn't want to tell you I loved you because I wanted to hold you. There, what do you think of that?"

Elgin hit himself on the chest. "You think that's bad? Well, I always intended to seduce you, right from the beginning. God!" He lay down, too, on the damp grass, two feet away from her, and he put his hands under his head.

Lying like that, they quarrelled in this peculiar way, libelling themselves, lowering the object of love in the other's eyes.

"I think it's loathsome that we sleep together," Caroline said. "I feel like a you-know-what."

"I hate seeing you every day," Elgin said. "Not because of you but because I'm always afraid you'll see through me. Also, I miss having free time to study—that's how cold-blooded I am."

There was a full moon that night, and its light was no chillier than what these two young people said about themselves. But after a while Elgin rolled over and took Caroline in his arms. "Please don't hate me."

"I don't hate you. I love you."

"I love you, too. God, it's hell!"

They decided to be more sensible. The next day they didn't meet in Widener. Elgin stayed in his room, and at three o'clock the phone rang.

"It's me—Caroline."

"Oh God, you called. I was praying you would. Where are you?"

"In the drugstore on the corner." There was silence. "Elgin," she said at last, "did you have any orange juice today?"

He ran, down the stairs, along the sidewalk, to the drugstore, to have his orange juice.

One day, Elgin told Caroline he was going to stay home and play poker with some of the boys in his entry. Caroline said that was a good idea. She had to write her mother; for some reason, her letters home had got her mother all upset, and she wanted to take some time and calm the old biddy down. "Poor thing," said Caroline. "She's had such an empty life, and I'm so important to her." Then she smiled a thin, nervous smile. "Of course, when I think how stupid she is, I wonder what I'll find to say to her."

Elgin played poker. He lost four dollars and sixty cents. At eleven-thirty, he excused himself from the game and went out on the street. He walked hurriedly, jogging part of the distance, until he stood on the sidewalk across from Cabot Hall, looking up at the light in Caroline's room. Finally, a shadow passed over the window, and Elgin felt what he could only describe as anguish.

He looked in the gutter until he found a pebble, and then he hurled it at Caroline's window. It struck. The shadow appeared again, standing quite still. At that moment, a policeman rounded the corner. Elgin thrust his hands in his pockets and walked up the street. The policeman stopped him.

"Hey, buddy, did you just throw something at that building?"

"No, Officer." Elgin was sweating and looked so pitiable the officer said, "I guess it was a trick of the light."

When Caroline asked him if he had come by Cabot the night before, he denied it.

The next day, he and Caroline went up to his room. As Elgin closed the door, Caroline threw herself onto the couch. She looked pale and unhappy, and she was making a face, preparing herself for what was coming. But Elgin walked over and stood next to the couch and said, "Caroline, we've got to be chaste. God!" he cried. "It's not easy to say this, and if your feelings get hurt, I don't know what I'll do!"

"They're not hurt."

"I want you to be happy," he said, looking down at her. "I think we ought to get married."

"We're under age, Elgin—you know that. Our parents won't let us."

"We'll tell them you're pregnant. We'll do something."

Caroline jumped up. "But I don't want to marry you! You won't make me happy. I'm scared of you. You don't have any respect for me. I don't know how to be a good wife."

"Listen, Caroline, we haven't done the right thing. You want to have children?"

A pink, piteous flush covered Caroline's face. "Oh," she said.

"We ought to get married," he said doggedly. "It won't be easy, but otherwise we'll never be happy. You see, what we didn't figure out is the teleology of the thing. We don't have a goal. We have to have a goal, do you see?"

"Elgin, we can't be foolish. If we really love each other, we have to be very practical or else we'll just cause each other very needless pain."

They looked at each other, pure at last, haloed by an urge to sacrifice.

"I may not be right for you," Caroline whispered. "We'll wait. We'll wait until fall. We'll have the summer to think things over."

Elgin frowned, not liking to have his sacrifice ignored. "I'm willing to marry you," he said.

"No, it's not right," said Caroline. "We're too young. We couldn't have children now. We're too ignorant. We'd be terrible parents." How it pained her to say this!

"If you feel that way," Elgin said, "I think we ought to plan to break up. Nothing sudden," he added, to ease the sudden twinge that was twisting his stomach. "When school's over."

Caroline hesitated, but it seemed to her dreamlike and wonderful to be free of this febrile emotion. And atonement would be so wonderful. . . . At the same time, she was hurt. "All right," she said with dignity. "If you want."

Elgin turned away from her. "Caroline, tell me one thing," he said with his back to her. "Emotionally, would you like to marry me?"

"Yes."

"God!" he said. "You're so practical!"

"I'm not!" she cried. "I can't help it." She wrung her hands. "If you tried to carry me off, I wouldn't resist," she said. "But if you ask me, I think— I think—"

He didn't have to marry her; he wouldn't have to worry about supporting her; he hadn't lost his career. Elgin felt irrepressible relief welling up in him. "God, how we love each other."

Caroline laughed. "It's true." She laughed a little more. "It's so true!" She threw her arms around his neck and kissed him.

Of course, they didn't stick to Elgin's plan of breaking up when school ended. They decided they would take a vacation from each other, and meet in the fall, when college began again, as friends. This agreement seemed to remove a great weight from them. They had only two weeks of the reading period and three weeks of exams left to be together, but they resumed some of their old habits—the walks between classes, for instance, and the trips to the Boston Museum of Fine Arts—and they even took to reading stories aloud again, preferring Chekhov and Colette. The sweetness and the sadness of their predicament were what they loved, and they threw themselves into the role of well-disciplined lovers with all their energy. Hardly a day passed without their thinking of some new gesture toward each other. Elgin gave flowers to Caroline; she bought him cuff links and books of poetry. Elgin left off suspecting that he was being made a fool of, and was actually gentlemanly, opening doors for Caroline and lighting her cigarettes. Caroline was ladylike and concealed her moods. They engaged in rough-house; Elgin pulled her hair and she pummelled him when they sat on the riverbank. They were chaste. They referred sometimes to the times when they had listened to the nightingale, and while the chastity didn't come easily to them, the act of sacrifice did. Elgin put on weight, and his face regained its color. "My goodness," Caroline said. "I think knowing me has improved your looks." It seemed they had found the secret of being happy together, in the imminence of separation, and while they didn't understand the paradox, they knew it was true.

But as their five last weeks passed, they discovered why it was true. All the pain of the relationship was now bound up with the parting and not with the things they did to each other. "It's dreadful," Caroline said. "I have feelings. They're like heavy mice that come out of holes and sit in my stomach and weigh me down."

They had been so proud of themselves, so free and relaxed and peaceful together, and now, when they saw what this parting was going to be like, all their vivacity and happiness flagged, they lost interest in talking to each other, and all they wanted was to get it over with.

On the last day of exams, they went up to Elgin's room at six o'clock. Elgin had bought a bottle of champagne and rented two glasses. Caroline was all dressed up because she was going to catch a train for Baltimore at nine o'clock. She had on a small hat, which she kept eying in the mirror. Poor Elgin was nervous about opening the champagne. "It's imported," he said. "I don't want to sound tight, but if half of it explodes or comes out in foam, I won't be happy." Caroline laughed, but when the cork popped, she turned very serious. She was afraid of what Elgin would toast; she was afraid it would ruin her self-possession.

Elgin slowly poured the champagne into the two glasses. Then the two young people, alone in the room, picked up their glasses and held them together. "To our reunion in the fall," Elgin said. "God knows what it will be like." They drank.

Caroline put her glass down. "Let's play a record and dance," she said. Elgin put on a Cole Porter L.P., and he and Caroline circled around the room, dodging the furniture, pausing to take occasional sips of their champagne. At six-thirty, they went downstairs and ate in the dining hall.

By seven-fifteen, they were back upstairs in Elgin's room, sitting on the bunk, kissing each other with a dry, intense helplessness. At quarter of eight, Caroline said she had to go. Elgin pulled away from her; she had taken off her hat, and her dress, made of some pretty gray-blue material, was hopelessly rumpled. With his hands, he set her just so on the bunk. Then he took out his pocket comb and combed her hair. "There," he said.

"Do I look prettier now?" Caroline asked.

"Yes," Elgin said.

They walked downstairs and out the door of Adams House. When they reached the sidewalk, Caroline said, "I don't want you to come with me. I want to go back to the dorm alone. All right?"

Elgin nodded.

"I'll write you from Europe," Caroline said. "Goodbye," she said and walked away, up the sidewalk; she tried to walk crisply but her feet dragged because she felt tired. Slowly, the hoped-for sense of relief was coming; she was free of Elgin, she had herself back, but not all of herself. Elgin still held some of her, and she would never get it back except when he was beside her.

Elgin sat on the steps in front of Adams House and buried his face in his hands. "God!" he said to himself. "I love her." And he wondered what would become of them now.

DEATH OF A FAVORITE

❖

J. F. POWERS

I HAD spent most of the afternoon mousing—a matter of sport with me and certainly not of diet—in the sunburnt fields that begin at our back door and continue hundreds of miles into the Dakotas. I gradually gave up the idea of hunting, the grasshoppers convincing me that there was no percentage in stealth. Even to doze was difficult, under such conditions, but I must have managed it. At least I was late coming to dinner, and so my introduction to the two missionaries took place at table. They were surprised, as most visitors are, to see me take the chair at Father Malt's right.

Father Malt, breaking off the conversation (if it could be called that), was his usual dear old self. "Fathers," he said, "meet Fritz."

I gave the newcomers the first good look that invariably tells me whether or not a person cares for cats. The mean old buck in charge of the team did not like me, I could see, and would bear watching. The other one obviously did like me, but he did not appear to be long enough from the seminary to matter. I felt that I had broken something less than even here.

"My assistant," said Father Malt, meaning me, and thus unconsciously dealing out our fat friend at the other end of the table. Poor Burner! There was a time when, thinking of him, as I did now, as the enemy, I could have convinced myself I meant something else. But he *is* the enemy, and I was right from the beginning, when it could only have been instinct that told me how much he hated me even while trying (in his fashion!) to be friendly. (I believe his prejudice to be acquired rather than congenital, and very likely, at this stage, confined to me, not to cats as a class—there *is* that in his favor. I intend to be fair about this if it kills me.)

My observations of humanity incline me to believe that one of us —Burner or I—must ultimately prevail over the other. For myself, I should not fear if this were a battle to be won on the solid ground

229

of Father Malt's affections. But the old man grows older, the grave beckons to him ahead, and with Burner pushing him from behind, how long can he last? Which is to say: How long can *I* last? Unfortunately, it is naked power that counts most in any rectory, and as things stand now, I am safe only so long as Father Malt retains it here. Could I—this impossible thought is often with me now—could I effect a reconciliation and alliance with Father Burner? Impossible! Yes, doubtless. But the question better asked is: *How* impossible? (Lord knows I would not inflict this line of reasoning upon myself if I did not hold with the rumors that Father Burner will be the one to succeed to the pastorate.) For I do like it here. It is not at all in my nature to forgive and forget, certainly not as regards Father Burner, but it is in my nature to come to terms (much as nations do) when necessary, and in this solution there need not be a drop of good will. No dog can make that statement, or take the consequences, which I understand are most serious, in the world to come. Shifts and ententes. There is something fatal about the vocation of favorite, but it is the only one that suits me, and, all things considered—to dig I am not able, to beg I am ashamed—the rewards are adequate.

"We go through Chicago all the time," said the boss missionary, who seemed to be returning to a point he had reached when I entered. I knew Father Malt would be off that evening for a convention in Chicago. The missionaries, who would fill in for him and conduct a forty hours' devotion on the side, belonged to an order just getting started in the diocese and were anxious to make a good impression. For the present, at least, as a kind of special introductory offer, they could be had dirt-cheap. Thanks to them, pastors who'd never been able to get away had got a taste of Florida last winter.

"Sometimes we stay over in Chicago," bubbled the young missionary. He was like a rookie ballplayer who hasn't made many road trips.

"We've got a house there," said the first, whose name in religion, as they say, was—so help me—Philbert. Later, Father Burner would get around it by calling him by his surname. Father Malt was the sort who wouldn't see anything funny about "Philbert," but it would be too much to expect him to remember such a name.

"What kind of a house?" asked Father Malt. He held up his hearing aid and waited for clarification.

Father Philbert replied in a shout, "The Order owns *a house*
there!"

Father Malt fingered his hearing aid.

Father Burner sought to interpret for Father Philbert. "I think,
Father, he wants to know what it's made out of."

"Red brick—it's red brick," bellowed Father Philbert.

"*My* house is red brick," said Father Malt.

"I *noticed* that," said Father Philbert.

Father Malt shoved the hearing aid at him.

"I know it," said Father Philbert, shouting again.

Father Malt nodded and fed me a morsel of fish. Even for a
Friday, it wasn't much of a meal. I would not have been sorry to
see this housekeeper go.

"All right, all right," said Father Burner to the figure lurking
behind the door and waiting for him, always the last one, to finish.
"She stands and looks in at you through the crack," he beefed.
"Makes you feel like a condemned man." The housekeeper came
into the room, and he addressed the young missionary (Burner
was a great one for questioning the young): "Ever read any books
by this fella Koestler, Father?"

"The Jesuit?" the young one asked.

"Hell, no, he's some kind of a writer. I know the man you mean,
though. Spells his name different. Wrote a book—apologetics."

"That's the one. Very—"

"Dull."

"Well . . ."

"This other fella's not bad. He's a writer who's ahead of his time
—about fifteen minutes. Good on jails and concentration camps.
You'd think he was born in one if you ever read his books." Father
Burner regarded the young missionary with absolute indifference.
"But you didn't."

"No. Is he a Catholic?" inquired the young one.

"He's an Austrian or something."

"Oh."

The housekeeper removed the plates and passed the dessert
around. When she came to Father Burner, he asked her privately,
"What is it?"

"Pudding," she said, not whispering, as he would have liked.

"*Bread* pudding?" Now he was threatening her.

"Yes, Father."

Father Burner shuddered and announced to everybody, "No

dessert for me." When the housekeeper had retired into the kitchen, he said, "Sometimes I think he got her from a hospital and sometimes, Father, I think she came from one of *your* fine institutions"— this to the young missionary.

Father Philbert, however, was the one to see the joke, and he laughed.

"My God," said Father Burner, growing bolder. "I'll never forget the time I stayed at your house in Louisville. If I hadn't been there for just a day—for the Derby, in fact—I'd have gone to Rome about it. I think I've had better meals here."

At the other end of the table, Father Malt, who could not have heard a word, suddenly blinked and smiled; the missionaries looked to him for some comment, in vain.

"He doesn't hear me," said Father Burner. "Besides, I think he's listening to the news."

"I didn't realize it was a radio too," said the young missionary.

"Oh, hell, yes."

"I think he's pulling your leg," said Father Philbert.

"Well, I thought so," said the young missionary ruefully.

"It's an idea," said Father Burner. Then in earnest to Father Philbert, whom he'd really been working around to all the time— the young one was decidedly not his type—"You the one drivin' that new Olds, Father?"

"It's not mine, Father," said Father Philbert with a meekness that would have been hard to take if he'd meant it. Father Burner understood him perfectly, however, and I thought they were two persons who would get to know each other a lot better.

"Nice job. They say it compares with the Cad in power. What do you call that color—oxford or clerical gray?"

"I really couldn't say, Father. It's my brother's. He's a layman in Minneapolis—St. Stephen's parish. He loaned it to me for this little trip."

Father Burner grinned. He could have been thinking, as I was, that Father Philbert protested too much. "Thought I saw you go by earlier," he said. "What's the matter—didn't you want to come in when you saw the place?"

Father Philbert, who was learning to ignore Father Malt, laughed discreetly. "Couldn't be sure this was it. That house on the *other* side of the church, now—"

Father Burner nodded. "Like that, huh? Belongs to a Mason."

Father Philbert sighed and said, "It would."

"Not at all," said Father Burner. "I like 'em better than K.C.s." If he could get the audience for it, Father Burner enjoyed being broad-minded. Gazing off in the direction of the Mason's big house, he said, "I've played golf with him."

The young missionary looked at Father Burner in horror. Father Philbert merely smiled. Father Burner, toying with a large crumb, propelled it in my direction.

"Did a bell ring?" asked Father Malt.

"His P.A. system," Father Burner explained. "Better tell him," he said to the young missionary. "You're closer. He can't bring me in on those batteries he uses."

"No bell," said the young missionary, lapsing into basic English and gestures.

Father Malt nodded, as though he hadn't really thought so.

"How do you like it?" said Father Burner.

Father Philbert hesitated, and then he said, "Here, you mean?"

"I wouldn't ask you that," said Father Burner, laughing. "Talkin' about that Olds. Like it? Like the Hydramatic?"

"No kiddin', Father. It's not mine," Father Philbert protested.

"All right, all right," said Father Burner, who obviously did not believe him. "Just so you don't bring up your vow of poverty." He looked at Father Philbert's uneaten bread pudding—"Had enough?"—and rose from the table, blessing himself. The other two followed when Father Malt, who was feeding me cheese, waved them away. Father Burner came around to us, bumping my chair—intentionally, I know. He stood behind Father Malt and yelled into his ear, "Any calls for me this aft?" He'd been out somewhere, as usual. I often thought he expected too much to happen in his absence.

"There was something . . ." said Father Malt, straining his memory, which was poor.

"*Yes?*"

"Now I remember—they had the wrong number."

Father Burner, looking annoyed and downhearted, left the room.

"They said they'd call back," said Father Malt, sensing Father Burner's disappointment.

I left Father Malt at the table reading his Office under the orange light of the chandelier. I went to the living room, to my spot in the window from which I could observe Father Burner and the missionaries on the front porch, the young one in the swing with his breviary—the mosquitoes, I judged, were about to join him—

and the other two just smoking and standing around, like pool players waiting for a table. I heard Father Philbert say, "Like to take a look at it, Father?"

"Say, that's an idea," said Father Burner.

I saw them go down the front walk to the gray Olds parked at the curb. With Father Burner at the wheel they drove away. In a minute they were back, the car moving uncertainly—this I noted with considerable pleasure until I realized that Father Burner was simply testing the brakes. Then they were gone, and after a bit, when they did not return, I supposed they were out killing poultry on the open road.

That evening, when the ushers dropped in at the rectory, there was not the same air about them as when they came for pinochle. Without fanfare, Mr. Bauman, their leader, who had never worked any but the center aisle, presented Father Malt with a travelling bag. It was nice of him, I thought, when he said, "It's from all of us," for it could not have come from all equally. Mr. Bauman, in hardware, and Mr. Keller, the druggist, were the only ones well off, and must have forked out plenty for such a fine piece of luggage, even after the discount.

Father Malt thanked all six ushers with little nods in which there was no hint of favoritism. "Ha," he kept saying. "You shouldn'a done it."

The ushers bobbed and ducked, dodging his flattery, and kept up a mumble to the effect that Father Malt deserved everything they'd ever done for him and more. Mr. Keller came forward to instruct Father Malt in the use of the various clasps and zippers. Inside the bag was another gift, a set of military brushes, which I could see they were afraid he would not discover for himself. But he unsnapped a brush, and, like the veteran crowd-pleaser he was, swiped once or twice at his head with it after spitting into the bristles. The ushers all laughed.

"Pretty snazzy," said the newest usher—the only young blood among them. Mr. Keller had made him a clerk at the store, had pushed through his appointment as alternate usher in the church, and was gradually weaning him away from his motorcycle. With Mr. Keller, the lad formed a block to Mr. Bauman's power, but he was perhaps worse than no ally at all. Most of the older men, though they pretended a willingness to help him meet the problems of an

usher, were secretly pleased when he bungled at collection time
and skipped a row or overlapped one.

Mr. Keller produced a box of ten-cent cigars, which, as a *personal*
gift from him, came as a bitter surprise to the others. He was not
big enough, either, to attribute it to them too. He had anticipated
their resentment, however, and now produced a bottle of milk
of magnesia. No one could deny the comic effect, for Father Malt
had been known to recommend the blue bottle from the confessional.

"Ha!" said Father Malt, and everybody laughed.

"In case you get upset on the trip," said the druggist.

"You know it's the best thing," said Father Malt in all seriousness, and then even he remembered he'd said it too often before.
He passed the cigars. The box went from hand to hand, but, except
for the druggist's clerk, nobody would have one.

Father Malt, seeing this, wisely renewed his thanks for the bag,
insisting upon his indebtedness until it was actually in keeping with
the idea the ushers had of their own generosity. Certainly none of
them had ever owned a bag like that. Father Malt went to the
housekeeper with it and asked her to transfer his clothes from the old
bag, already packed, to the new one. When he returned, the
ushers were still standing around feeling good about the bag and
not so good about the cigars. They'd discuss that later. Father Malt
urged them to sit down. He seemed to want them near him as long
as possible. They *were* his friends, but I could not blame Father
Burner for avoiding them. He was absent now, as he usually managed to be when the ushers called. If he ever succeeded Father Malt,
who let them have the run of the place, they would be the first to
suffer—after me! As Father Malt was the heart, they were the substance of a parish that remained rural while becoming increasingly
suburban. They dressed up occasionally and dropped into St. Paul
and Minneapolis, "the Cities," as visiting firemen into Hell, though
it would be difficult to imagine any other place as graceless and
far-gone as our own hard little highway town—called Sherwood but
about as sylvan as a tennis court.

They were regular fellows—not so priestly as their urban col-
leagues—loud, heavy of foot, wearers of long underwear in wintertime and iron-gray business suits the year round. Their idea of a
good time (pilsner beer, cheap cigars smoked with the bands left
on, and pinochle) coincided nicely with their understanding of
"doing good" (a percentage of every pot went to the parish building

fund). Their wives, also active, played cards in the church basement and sold vanilla extract and chances—mostly to each other, it appeared—with all revenue over cost going to what was known as "the missions." This evening I could be grateful that time was not going to permit the usual pinochle game. (In the midst of all their pounding—almost as hard on me as it was on the dining-room table —I often felt they should have played on a meat block.)

The ushers, settling down all over the living room, started to talk about Father Malt's trip to Chicago. The housekeeper brought in a round of beer.

"How long you be gone, Father—three days?" one of them asked.

Father Malt said that he'd be gone about three days.

"Three days! This is Friday. Tomorrow's Saturday. Sunday. Monday." Everything stopped while the youngest usher counted on his fingers. "Back on Tuesday?"

Father Malt nodded.

"Who's takin' over on Sunday?"

Mr. Keller answered for Father Malt. "He's got some missionary fathers in."

"Missionaries!"

The youngest usher then began to repeat himself on one of his two or three topics. "Hey, Father, don't forget to drop in the U.S.O. if it's still there. I was in Chi during the war," he said, but nobody would listen to him.

Mr. Bauman had cornered Father Malt and was trying to tell him where that place was—that place where he'd eaten his meals during the World's Fair; one of the waitresses was from Minnesota. I'd had enough of this—the next thing would be a diagram on the back of an envelope—and I'd heard Father Burner come in earlier. I went upstairs to check on him. For a minute or two I stood outside his room listening. He had Father Philbert with him, and, just as I'd expected, he was talking against Father Malt, leading up to the famous question with which Father Malt, years ago, had received the Sherwood appointment from the Archbishop: "Have dey got dere a goot meat shop?"

Father Philbert laughed, and I could hear him sip from his glass and place it on the floor beside his chair. I entered the room, staying close to the baseboard, in the shadows, curious to know what they were drinking. I maneuvered myself into position to sniff Father Philbert's glass. To my surprise, Scotch. Here was proof that Father Burner considered Father Philbert a friend. At that moment I could not think what it was he expected to get out of a lowly missionary. My mistake, not realizing then how correct and prophetic I'd been earlier in thinking of them as two of a kind. It seldom happened that Father Burner got out the real Scotch for company, or for himself *in* company. For most guests he had nothing—a safe policy, since a surprising number of temperance cranks passed through the rectory—and for unwelcome guests who would like a drink he kept a bottle of "Scotch-type" whiskey, which was a smooth, smoky blend of furniture polish that came in a fancy bottle, was offensive even when watered, and cheap, though rather hard to get since the end of the war. He had a charming way of plucking the rare bottle from a bureau drawer, as if this were indeed an occasion for him; even so, he would not touch the stuff, presenting himself as a chap of simple tastes, of no taste at all for the things of this world, who would prefer, if anything, the rude wine made from our own grapes—if we'd had any grapes. Quite an act, and one he thoroughly enjoyed, holding his glass of pure water and asking, "How's your drink, Father? Strong enough?"

The housekeeper, appearing at the door, said there'd been a change of plans and some of the ushers were driving Father Malt to the train.

"Has he gone yet?" asked Father Burner.

"Not yet, Father."

"Well, tell him goodbye for me."

"Yes, Father."

When she had gone, he said, "I'd tell him myself, but I don't want to run into that bunch."

Father Philbert smiled. "What's he up to in Chicago?"

"They've got one of those pastors' and builders' conventions going on at the Stevens Hotel."

"Is he building?"

"No, but he's a pastor and he'll get a lot of free samples. He won't buy anything."

"Not much has been done around here, huh?" said Father Philbert.

He had fed Father Burner the question he wanted. "He built that fish pond in the back yard—for his minnows. That's the extent of the building program in his time. Of course he's only been here a while."

"How long?"

"Fourteen years," said Father Burner. *He* would be the greatest builder of them all—if he ever got the chance. He lit a cigarette and smiled. "What he's really going to Chicago for is to see a couple of ball games."

Father Philbert did not smile. "Who's playing there now?" he said.

A little irritated at this interest, Father Burner said, "I believe it's the Red Sox—or is it the Reds? Hell, how do I know?"

"Couldn't be the Reds," said Father Philbert. "The boy and I were in Cincinnati last week and it was the start of a long home stand for them."

"Very likely," said Father Burner.

While the missionary, a Cardinal fan, analyzed the pennant race in the National League, Father Burner sulked. "What's the best train out of Chicago for Washington?" he suddenly inquired.

Father Philbert told him what he could, but admitted that his information dated from some years back. "We don't make the run to Washington any more."

"That's right," said Father Burner. "Washington's in the American League."

Father Philbert laughed, turning aside the point that he travelled with the Cardinals. "I thought you didn't know about these things," he said.

"About these things it's impossible to stay ignorant," said Father Burner. "Here, and the last place, and the place before that, and in the seminary—a ball, a bat, and God. I'll be damned, Father, if I'll do as the Romans do."

"What price glory?" inquired Father Philbert, as if he smelt heresy.

"I know," said Father Burner. "And it'll probably cost me the red hat." A brave comment, perhaps, from a man not yet a country pastor, and it showed me where his thoughts were again. He did not disguise his humble ambition by speaking lightly of an impossible one. "Scratch a prelate and you'll find a second baseman," he fumed.

Father Philbert tried to change the subject. "Somebody told me Father Malt's the exorcist for the diocese."

"Used to be." Father Burner's eyes flickered balefully.

"Overdid it, huh?" asked Father Philbert—as if he hadn't heard!

"Some." I expected Father Burner to say more. He could have told some pretty wild stories, the gist of them all that Father Malt, as an exorcist, was perhaps a little quick on the trigger. He had

stuck pretty much to livestock, however, which was to his credit in
the human view.

"Much scandal?"

"Some."

"Nothing serious, though?"

"No."

"Suppose it depends on what you call serious."

Father Burner did not reply. He had become oddly morose.
Perhaps he felt that he was being catered to out of pity, or that
Father Philbert, in giving him so many opportunities to talk against
Father Malt, was tempting him.

"Who plays the accordion?" inquired Father Philbert, hearing
it downstairs.

"He does."

"Go on!"

"Sure."

"How can he hear what he's playing?"

"What's the difference—if he plays an accordion?"

Father Philbert laughed. He removed the cellophane from a
cigar, and then he saw me. And at that moment I made no attempt
to hide. "There's that damn cat."

"His assistant!" said Father Burner with surprising bitterness.
"Coadjutor with right of succession."

Father Philbert balled up the cellophane and tossed it at the
wastebasket, missing.

"Get it," he said to me, fatuously.

I ignored him, walking slowly toward the door.

Father Burner made a quick movement with his feet, which were
something to behold, but I knew he wouldn't get up, and took
my sweet time.

Father Philbert inquired, "Will she catch mice?"

She! Since coming to live at the rectory, I've been celibate, it's
true, but I daresay I'm as manly as the next one. And Father
Burner, who might have done me the favor of putting him straight,
said nothing.

"She looks pretty fat to be much of a mouser."

I just stared at the poor man then, as much as to say that I'd
think one so interested in catching mice would have heard of a
little thing called the mousetrap. After one last dirty look, I left
them to themselves—to punish each other with their company.

I strolled down the hall, trying to remember when I'd last had a mouse. Going past the room occupied by the young missionary, I smiled upon his door, which was shut, confident that he was inside hard at his prayers.

The next morning, shortly after breakfast, which I took, as usual, in the kitchen, I headed for the cool orchard to which I often repaired on just such a day as this one promised to be. I had no appetite for the sparrows hopping from tree to tree above me, but there seemed no way to convince them of that. Each one, so great is his vanity, thinks himself eminently edible. Peace, peace, they cry, and there is no peace. Finally, tired of their noise, I got up from the matted grass and left, levelling my ears and flailing my tail, in a fake dudgeon that inspired the males to feats of stunt flying and terrorized the young females most delightfully.

I went then to another favorite spot of mine, that bosky strip of green between the church and the brick sidewalk. Here, however, the horseflies found me, and as if that were not enough, visions of stray dogs and children came between me and the kind of sleep I badly needed after an uncommonly restless night.

When afternoon came, I remembered that it was Saturday, and that I could have the rectory to myself. Father Burner and the missionaries would be busy with confessions. By this time the temperature had reached its peak, and though I felt sorry for the young missionary, I must admit the thought of the other two sweltering in the confessionals refreshed me. The rest of the afternoon I must have slept something approaching the sleep of the just.

I suppose it was the sound of dishes that roused me. I rushed into the dining room, not bothering to wash up, and took my customary place at the table. Only then did I consider the empty chair next to me—the utter void. This, I thought, is a foreshadowing of what I must someday face—this, and Father Burner munching away at the other end of the table. And there was the immediate problem: no one to serve me. The young missionary smiled at me, but how can you eat a smile? The other two, looking rather wilted—to their hot boxes I wished them swift return—talked in expiring tones of reserved sins and did not appear to notice me. Our first meal together without Father Malt did not pass without incident, however. It all came about when the young missionary extended a thin sliver of meat to me.

"Hey, don't do that!" said Father Philbert. "You'll never make a mouser out of her that way."

Father Burner, too, regarded the young missionary with disapproval.

"Just this one piece," said the young missionary. The meat was already in my mouth.

"Well, watch it in the future," said Father Philbert. It was the word "future" that worried me. Did it mean that he had arranged to cut off my sustenance in the kitchen too? Did it mean that until Father Malt returned I had to choose between mousing and fasting?

I continued to think along these melancholy lines until the repast, which had never begun for me, ended for them. Then I whisked into the kitchen, where I received the usual bowl of milk. But whether the housekeeper, accustomed as she was to having me eat my main course at table, assumed there had been no change in my life, or was now acting under instructions from these villains, I don't know. I was too sickened by their meanness to have any appetite. When the pastor's away, the curates will play, I thought. On the whole I was feeling pretty glum.

It was our custom to have the main meal at noon on Sundays. I arrived early, before the others, hungrier than I'd been for as long as I could remember, and still I had little or no expectation of food at this table. I was there for one purpose—to assert myself— and possibly, where the young missionary was concerned, to incite sympathy for myself and contempt for my persecutors. By this time I knew that to be the name for them.

They entered the dining room, just the two of them.

"Where's the kid?" asked Father Burner.

"He's not feeling well," said Father Philbert.

I was not surprised. They'd arranged between the two of them to have him say the six- and eleven-o'clock Masses, which meant, of course, that he'd fasted in the interval. I had not thought of him as the hardy type, either.

"I'll have the housekeeper take him some beef broth," said Father Burner. Damned white of you, I was thinking, when he suddenly whirled and swept me off my chair. Then he picked it up and placed it against the wall. Then he went to the lower end of the table, removed his plate and silverware, and brought them to Father Malt's place. Talking and fuming to himself, he sat down in Father Malt's chair. I did not appear very brave, I fear, cowering under mine.

Father Philbert, who had been watching with interest, now greeted the new order with a cheer. "Attaboy, Ernest!"

Father Burner began to justify himself. "More light here," he said, and added, "Cats kill birds," and for some reason he was puffing.

"If they'd just kill mice," said Father Philbert, "they wouldn't be so bad." He had a one-track mind if I ever saw one.

"Wonder how many that black devil's caught in his time?" said Father Burner, airing a common prejudice against cats of my shade (though I do have a white collar). He looked over at me. "Ssssss," he said. But I held my ground.

"I'll take a dog any day," said the platitudinous Father Philbert.

"Me, too."

After a bit, during which time they played hard with the roast, Father Philbert said, "How about taking her for a ride in the country?"

"Hell," said Father Burner. "He'd just come back."

"Not if we did it right, she wouldn't."

"Look," said Father Burner. "Some friends of mine dropped a cat off the high bridge in St. Paul. They saw him go under in mid-channel. I'm talking about the Mississippi, understand. Thought they'd never lay eyes on that animal again. That's what they thought. He was back at the house before they were." Father Burner paused—he could see that he was not convincing Father Philbert—and then he tried again. "That's a fact, Father. They might've played a quick round of golf before they got back. Cat didn't even look damp, they said. He's still there. Case a lot like this. Except now they're afraid of *him*."

To Father Burner's displeasure, Father Philbert refused to be awed or even puzzled. He simply inquired: "But did they use a bag? Weights?"

"Millstones," snapped Father Burner. "Don't quibble."

Then they fell to discussing the burial customs of gangsters—poured concrete and the rest—and became so engrossed in the matter that they forgot all about me.

Over against the wall, I was quietly working up the courage to act against them. When I felt sufficiently lionhearted, I leaped up and occupied my chair. Expecting blows and vilification, I encountered only indifference. I saw then how far I'd come down in their estimation. Already the remembrance of things past—the disease of noble politicals in exile—was too strong in me, the hope of restoration unwarrantably faint.

At the end of the meal, returning to me, Father Philbert remarked, "I think I know a better way." Rising, he snatched the crucifix off the wall, passed it to a bewildered Father Burner, and, saying "Nice Kitty," grabbed me behind the ears. "Hold it up to her," said Father Philbert. Father Burner held the crucifix up to me. "See that?" said Father Philbert to my face. I miaowed. "Take that!" said Father Philbert, cuffing me. He pushed my face into the crucifix again. "See that?" he said again, but I knew what to expect next, and when he cuffed me, I went for his hand with my mouth, pinking him nicely on the wrist. Evidently Father Burner had begun to understand and appreciate the proceedings. Although I was in a good position to observe everything, I could not say as much for myself. "Association," said Father Burner with mysterious satisfaction, almost with zest. He poked the crucifix at me. "If he's just smart enough to react properly," he said. "Oh, she's plenty smart," said Father Philbert, sucking his wrist and giving himself, I hoped, hydrophobia. He scuffed off one of his sandals for a paddle. Father Burner, fingering the crucifix nervously, inquired, "Sure it's all right to go on with this thing?" "It's the intention that counts in these things," said Father Philbert. "Our motive is clear enough." And they went at me again.

After that first taste of the sandal in the dining room, I foolishly believed I would be safe as long as I stayed away from the table; there was something about my presence there, I thought, that brought out the beast in them—which is to say very nearly all that was in them. But they caught me in the upstairs hall the same evening, one brute thundering down upon me, the other sealing off my only avenue of escape. And this beating was worse than the first —preceded as it was by a short delay that I mistook for a reprieve until Father Burner, who had gone downstairs muttering something about "leaving no margin for error," returned with the crucifix from the dining room, although we had them hanging all over the house. The young missionary, coming upon them while they were at me, turned away. "I wash my hands of it," he said. I thought he might have done more.

Out of mind, bruised of body, sick at heart, for two days and nights I held on, I know not how or why—unless I lived in hope of vengeance. I wanted simple justice, a large order in itself, but I would never have settled for that alone. I wanted nothing less than my revenge.

I kept to the neighborhood, but avoided the rectory. I believed, of course, that their only strategy was to drive me away. I derived some little satisfaction from making myself scarce, for it was thus I deceived them into thinking their plan to banish me successful. But this was my single comfort during this hard time, and it was as nothing against their crimes.

I spent the nights in the open fields. I reeled, dizzy with hunger, until I bagged an aged field mouse. It tasted bitter to me, this stale provender, and seemed, as I swallowed it, an ironic concession to the enemy. I vowed I'd starve before I ate another mouse. By way of retribution to myself, I stalked sparrows in the orchard—hating myself for it but persisting all the more when I thought of those bird-lovers, my persecutors, before whom I could stand and say in self-redemption, "You made me what I am now. You thrust the killer's part upon me." Fortunately, I did not flush a single sparrow. Since *my* motive was clear enough, however, I'd had the pleasure of sinning against them and their ideals, the pleasure without the feathers and mess.

On Tuesday, the third day, all caution, I took up my post in the lilac bush beside the garage. Not until Father Malt returned, I knew, would I be safe in daylight. He arrived along about dinner-time, and I must say the very sight of him aroused a sentiment in me akin to human affection. The youngest usher, who must have had the afternoon off to meet him at the station in St. Paul, carried the new bag before him into the rectory. It was for me an act symbolic of the counter-revolution to come. I did not rush out from my hiding place, however. I had suffered too much to play the fool now. Instead I slipped into the kitchen by way of the flap in the screen door, which they had not thought to barricade. I waited under the stove for my moment, like an actor in the wings.

Presently I heard them tramping into the dining room and seating themselves, and Father Malt's voice saying, "I had a long talk with the Archbishop." (I could almost hear Father Burner praying, Did he say anything about *me?*) And then, "Where's Fritz?"

"He hasn't been around lately," said Father Burner cunningly. He would not tell the truth and he would not tell a lie.

"You know, there's something mighty funny about that cat," said Father Philbert. "We think she's possessed."

I was astonished, and would have liked a moment to think it over, but by now I was already entering the room.

"Possessed!" said Father Malt. "Aw, no!"

"Ah, yes," said Father Burner, going for the meat right away. "And good riddance."

And then I miaowed and they saw me.

"Quick!" said Father Philbert, who made a nice recovery after involuntarily reaching for me and his sandal at the same time. Father Burner ran to the wall for the crucifix, which had been, until now, a mysterious and possibly blasphemous feature of my beatings—the crucifix held up to me by the one not scourging at the moment, as if it were the will behind my punishment. They had schooled me well, for even now, at the sight of the crucifix, an undeniable fear was rising in me. Father Burner handed it to Father Malt.

"Now you'll see," said Father Philbert.

"We'll leave it up to you," said Father Burner.

I found now that I could not help myself. What followed was hidden from them—from human eyes. I gave myself over entirely to the fear they'd beaten into me, and in a moment, according to their plan, I was fleeing the crucifix as one truly possessed, out of the dining room and into the kitchen, and from there, blindly, along the house and through the shrubbery, ending in the street, where a powerful gray car ran over me—and where I gave up the old ghost for a new one.

Simultaneously, reborn, redeemed from my previous fear, identical with my former self, so far as they could see, and still in their midst, I padded up to Father Malt—he still sat gripping the crucifix —and jumped into his lap. I heard the young missionary arriving from an errand in Father Philbert's *brother's* car, late for dinner he thought, but just in time to see the stricken look I saw coming into the eyes of my persecutors. This look alone made up for everything I'd suffered at their hands. Purring now, I was rubbing up against the crucifix, myself effecting my utter revenge.

"What have we done?" cried Father Philbert. He was basically an emotional dolt and would have voted then for my canonization.

"I ran over a cat!" said the young missionary excitedly. "I'd swear it was this one. When I looked, there was nothing there!"

"Better go upstairs and rest," growled Father Burner. He sat down—it was good to see him in his proper spot at the low end of the table—as if to wait a long time, or so it seemed to me. I found myself wondering if I could possibly bring about his transfer to another parish—one where they had a devil for a pastor and several assistants, where he would be able to start at the bottom again.

But first things first, I always say, and all in good season, for now Father Malt himself was drawing my chair up to the table, restoring me to my rightful place.

IN A CAFÉ

❖

MARY LAVIN

THE café was in a back street. Mary's ankles ached and she was glad Maudie had not got there before her. She sat down at a table near the door.

It was a place she had only recently found and she dropped in often, whenever she came up to Dublin for the day. She hated to go anywhere else now. For one thing, she knew that she would be unlikely ever to have set foot in it if Richard were still alive, and this knowledge helped to give her back a semblance of the identity she had lost—once willingly, in marriage, but now, doubly and unwillingly, in widowhood. Not that Richard would have disliked the café. It was the kind of place they went to when they were students. Too much water had gone under the bridge since those days, though; say what you liked, there was something faintly snobby about a farm in Meath, and together she and Richard would have been out of place here. But it was a different matter to come here alone. There could be nothing—oh, nothing—snobby about a widow. Just by being one, she fitted into this kind of café. It was an unusual little place. She looked around.

The walls were distempered red above and the wainscoting was painted white. It was probably the wainscoting that gave it the peculiarly functional look you get in the snuggery of a public house or in the confessional of a small and poor parish church. For furniture, there were only deal tables and chairs, with black-and-white checked tablecloths that were either unironed or badly ironed. But there was a decided feeling about the place that money was not so much in short supply as dedicated to other purposes—as witness the paintings on the walls, and a notice over the fire grate to say that there were other paintings on view in a studio overhead. Those in the café were for the most part experimental in their technique.

The café was run by two students from the Art College. They often went out and left the place quite empty—as now—while they had a cup of coffee in another, quite different café across the street. Regular clients sometimes helped themselves to coffee from the pot on the gas ring behind a curtain at the back, or, if they only came in for company and found none, merely warmed themselves at the big fire always blazing in the little black grate that was the original grate when the café had been a warehouse office. Today the fire was banked up with coke. The coffee was beginning to spit on the gas ring.

Would Maudie like the place? That it might not be exactly the right place to have arranged to meet her, above all under the present circumstances, occurred vaguely to Mary, but there was nothing that could be done about it now. When Maudie got there, if she didn't like it they could go somewhere else. On the other hand, perhaps she might like it? Or perhaps she would be too upset to take notice of her surroundings? The paintings might interest her. They were certainly stimulating. There were two new ones today, which Mary had not seen before: two flower paintings, just inside the door. From where she sat, she could read the signature— "Johann Stielher." Or at least they suggested flowers. They were namable as roses, surely, in spite of being a bit angular? She knew what Richard would have said about them. But she and Richard were no longer one, so what would *she* say about them? She would say . . . she would say . . .

But whatever was keeping Maudie? It was all very well to be glad of a few minutes' time in which to gather herself together; it was a different thing entirely to be kept waiting a quarter of an hour. Mary leaned back against the boarding. She was less tired than when she came in, but she was still in no way prepared for the encounter in front of her. What had she to say to a young widow recently bereaved? Why on earth had she arranged to meet her? The incongruity of their both being widowed came forcibly upon her. Would Maudie, too, be in black with touches of white? Two widows—it was like two magpies: one for sorrow, two for joy. The absurdity of it was all at once so great she had an impulse to get up and make off out of the place. She felt herself vibrating all over with resentment at being coupled with anyone, and urgently she began to sever herself from Maudie, seeking out the disparities between them.

Maudie was only a year married. And her parents had been only too ready to take care of her child, greedily possessing themselves of it. Maudie was as free as a girl. Then—if it mattered?—she had a nice little income in her own right, apart from all Michael had left her. So?

But what was keeping her? Was she not coming at all?

Ah! The little iron bell that was above the door—also a relic from the warehouse days—tinkled to announce there was another customer coming into the café.

It wasn't Maudie, though. It was a young man—youngish, anyway —and Mary would say that he was an artist. Yet his hands, at which when he sat down he began to stare, were not like the hands of an artist. They were plump, soft-skinned hands, and there was something touching in the relaxed way in which, lightly clasped one in the other, they rested on the table. Had they a womanish look, perhaps? No, that was not the word, but she couldn't for the life of her find the right word to describe them. And her mind was teased by trying to find it. Fascinated, her eyes were drawn to those hands time and again, no matter how resolutely she tore them away. It was almost as if it were by touch, not sight, that she knew their warm fleshiness.

Even when she closed her eyes—as she did—she could still see them. And so, innocent of where she was being led, she made no real effort to free her thoughts from them, until suddenly she saw before her the familiar shape of her recurring nightmare: all at once it was Richard's hands she saw, so different from those others —wiry, supple, thin. There they were for an instant in her mind, limned by love and anguish, before they vanished.

It happened so often. In her mind she would see a part of him— his hand; his arm; his foot, perhaps, in the finely worked leather shoes he always wore—and from it frantically she would try to build up the whole man. Sometimes she succeeded better than others, built him up from foot to shoulder, seeing his hands, his gray suit, his tie—knotted always in a slightly special way—his neck, even his chin, which was rather sharp, a little less attractive than his other features. But always at that point she would be defeated. Never once since the day he died had she been able to call up his face again.

And if she could not remember him at will, what meaning had time at all? What use was it to have lived the past if behind us it fell away so sheer?

In the hour of his death, for her it was part of the pain that she knew this would happen. She was standing beside him, when outside the hospital window a bird called out with a sweet, clear whistle, and, hearing it, she knew that he was dead, because not for years had she really heard bird song or birdcall, so loud was the noise of their love in her ears. When she looked down at him, it was a strange face, the look of death itself, that lay on the pillow. And after that brief moment of silence that let in the bird song for an instant, a new noise started in her head, the noise of a nameless panic that never altogether died down.

And now, here in the little café—she caught at the table edge, for the conflagration had started again and her mind was a roaring furnace.

It was just then the man at the end of the table stood up and reached for the menu card on which she was leaning, breasts and elbows both, her face in her hands. Hastily, apologetically, she pushed it toward him, and at once the roar died down in her mind. She looked at him. Could he have known? Her heart was filled with gratitude, and she saw that his eyes were soft and gentle. But she had to admit that he didn't look as if he were much aware of her. No matter; she still was grateful to him.

"Don't you want this?" she cried, as she saw that the small slip of paper with the specialty for the day that had been clipped to the menu card had come off and was caught on the rough sleeve of her jacket. She stood up and leaned over the table with it.

"Ah, thank you!" he said, and bowed. She smiled. There was such gallantry in a bow. He was a foreigner, of course. And then, before she sat down again, she saw that he had been making little pencil sketches all over a newspaper on the table, in the margins and in the spaces between the newsprint. Such intricate, minutely involuted little figures. She was fascinated, but of course she could not stare.

Yet when she sat down she watched him covertly, and every now and then she saw that he made a particular flourish; it was his signature, she felt sure, and she tried to make it out from where she sat.

A disproportionate, ridiculous excitement rushed through her when she realized it was "Johann Stielher," the signature on the new flower paintings that had caught her attention when she first came into the place. But it's impossible, she thought. The sketches before him were so meticulous, the paintings so . . .

But the little bell had tinkled again.

"Ah! Maudie!" For all her waiting, taken by surprise in the end, she got to her feet in her embarrassment, like a man. "Maudie, my dear!" She stared fixedly in an effort to convey the sympathy that, tongue-tied, she could express in no other way.

They shook hands wordlessly.

"I'm deliberately refraining from expressing sympathy—you know that?" said Mary then, as they sat down at the checkered table.

"Oh, I do!" cried Maudie. And she seemed genuinely appreciative. "It's so awful trying to think of something to say back—isn't it? It has to come right out of yourself, and sometimes what comes is something you can't even say out loud when you do think of it!"

It was so true. Mary looked at her in surprise. So Maudie apprehended these subtleties, too? Mary looked hard at her. "I know, I know," she said. "In the end you have to say what is expected of you—and you feel so cheapened by it."

"Worse still, you cheapen the dead!" said Maudie.

Mary looked really hard at her now. Was it possible for a young girl—a simple person—to have wrung from a single experience, even though that experience was death, so much bitter knowledge? In spite of herself, she felt she was being drawn into complicity with her. She drew back resolutely. "Of course, you were more or less expecting it, weren't you?" she said, spitefully.

Unrepulsed, Maudie looked back at her. "Does that matter?" she asked, and then, unexpectedly, she herself put a rift between them. "You have the children, of course!" she said, and before Mary could say anything, she rushed on. "Oh, I know I have my baby, but there seems so little link between him and his father. I just can't believe in the past sometimes, wheeling him round the park in his pram; it's as if he was illegitimate. No! I mean it, really. I'm not just trying to be shocking. It must be so different when there has been time for a relationship to be started between children and their father, like there was in your case."

"Oh, I don't know that that matters," said Mary. "And you'll be glad to have him someday." This time she spoke with deliberate malice, for she knew so well how those same words had lacerated her. She knew what they were meant to say: the children would be better than nothing.

But the poison of her words did not penetrate Maudie. And with another stab, she knew why this was. Maudie was so young, so beautiful. There was nothing about her to suggest that she was in any way bereft or maimed.

"You'll marry again, Maudie," she said impulsively. "Don't mind my saying it," she added quickly. "It's not a criticism. It's because I know how you're suffering that I say it. Don't take offense."

Maudie didn't look offended; she only looked on the defensive. Then she relaxed. "Not coming from you," she said. "You know what it's like." Mary saw she was trying to cover up the fact that she simply could not violently refute the suggestion. "Not that I think I will," she added, but weakly. "After all, you didn't."

It was Mary who was put upon the defensive now. "After all, it's only two years—less, even," she said stiffly.

"Oh, it's not altogether a matter of time," said Maudie, seeing she had erred but not clear how or where. "It's the kind of person you are, I think. I admire you so much! It's what I'd want to be like myself if I had the strength. With remarriage it's largely the effect on oneself that matters, I think, don't you? I don't think it really matters to—to the dead. Do you? I'm sure Michael would want me to marry again if he were able to express a wish. After all, people say it's a compliment to a man if his widow marries again, did you ever hear that?"

"I did," said Mary curtly. "But I wouldn't pay much heed to it. A fat lot the dead care about compliments."

So Maudie was already thinking about remarriage? Mary's irritation was succeeded by a vague feeling of envy, and then the irritation returned tenfold. How easily it was accepted that she would not marry again. This girl regards me as too old, of course. And she's right—or she ought to be right! She remembered the way, even two years ago, people had said she "had" her children. They meant, even then, that it was unlikely, unlooked for, that she'd remarry.

Other things that had been said crowded back into her mind as well. So many people had spoken of the special quality of her marriage—hers and Richard's—their remarkable suitability one for the other, and the uniqueness of the bond between them. She was avid to hear this said at the time. But here now, in this little café, the light that had played over those words flickered and went out. Did they perhaps mean that if Richard had not appeared when he did, no one else would have been interested in her?

Whereas Maudie . . . If she looked so attractive now, when she must still be suffering from shock, what would she be like in a year from now, when she would be "out of mourning," as it would be put? Why, right now, she was so fresh and—yes, virginal; looking at her, there was no other word for it! Of course, she was only a year married. A year! You could hardly call it being married at all.

But Maudie knew a thing or two about men, for all that, and in her eyes at that moment there was a strange expression. Seeing it, Mary remembered at once that they were not alone in the café. She wondered apprehensively how much the man at the other end of the table had heard, and could hear, of what they were saying. But it was too late to stop Maudie.

"Oh, Mary," cried Maudie, leaning forward, "it's not what they give us—I've got over wanting things like a child—it's what we have to give them! It's something"—and she pressed her hands to her breasts—"something in here!"

"Maudie!" Sharply, urgently, Mary tried to make her lower her voice, and with a quick movement of her head she did manage at last to convey some caution to her. "In case you might say something," she said in a low voice.

"Oh, there was no fear," said Maudie. "I was aware all the time." She didn't speak quite so low as Mary, but did lower her voice. "I was aware of him all the time," she said. "It was him that put it into my mind—about what we have to give." She pressed her hands to her breasts again. "He looks so lonely, don't you think? He is a foreigner, isn't he? I always think it's sad for them; they don't have many friends, and even when they do, there's always a barrier, don't you agree?"

But Mary was too embarrassed to let her go on. Almost frantically, she made a diversion. "What are you going to have, Maudie?" she said loudly. "Coffee? Tea? And is there no one to take an order?"

Immediately, she felt a fool. To whom had she spoken? She looked across at Johann Stielher. As if he were waiting to meet her glance, his mild and patient eyes looked into hers.

"There is no one there," he said, nodding at the curtained gas ring, "but one can serve oneself. Perhaps you would wish that I—"

"Oh, not at all!" cried Mary. "Please don't trouble! We're in absolutely no hurry! Please don't trouble yourself," she said. "Not on our account."

But she saw at once that he was very much a foreigner, and that he was at a disadvantage, not knowing if he had made a *gaffe*. "I have intruded?" he said miserably.

"Oh, not at all!" cried Mary, and he was so serious she had to laugh.

The laugh was another mistake. His face took on a look of despair that can come upon a foreigner, it seemed, at the slightest provocation—as if, suddenly, everything was obscure to him.

"Please," she murmured, and then, vaguely, "your work," meaning that she did not wish to interrupt his sketching.

"Ah, you know my work?" he said, brightening visibly and showing a small but quite endearing vanity. "We have met before? Yes?"

"Oh, no, we haven't met," she said quickly, but, of course, after that it was impossible to go on acting as if he were a complete stranger. She turned to see what Maudie would make of the situation. It was then she felt the full force of her irritation with Maudie. She could have given her a slap. For there she sat, remotely, her face partly averted from them.

Maudie was waiting to be introduced. To be introduced! As if she, Mary, did not need any conventional preliminaries! As if it was all right that she, Mary, should begin an unprefaced conversation with a strange man in a café because it was all right for a woman of her age to strike up a conversation like that, but that it wouldn't have done for a younger woman. Yet, on her still partly averted face Mary could see the quickened look of interest. She had a good mind not to make any gesture to draw her into the conversation at all, but she had the young man to consider. She had to bring them together whether she liked or not.

"Maudie, this is . . ." She turned back and smiled at Stielher. "This is . . ." But she was confused and she had to abandon the introduction altogether. Instead, she broke into a direct question. "Those *are* your flower pictures, aren't they?" she asked.

It was enough for Maudie—more than enough, you might say. She turned to the young man, obviously greatly impressed, her lips apart, her eyes shining. My God, how attractive she was! "Oh, no, not really?" she cried. "How marvellous of you."

But Johann Stielher was looking at Mary. "You are sure we have not met before?"

"Oh, no, but you were scribbling your signature all over that newspaper." She looked around to show it to him, but it had fallen onto the floor.

"Ah, yes," he said. She couldn't be certain, of course, but she thought he was disappointed. "Ah, yes, you saw my signature," he said flatly. He looked dejected. Mary felt helpless. She turned to Maudie. It was up to her to say something now.

Just then the little warehouse bell tinkled again, and this time it was one of the proprietors who came in, casually, like a client.

"Ah, good!" said Stielher. "Coffee!" he called out. Then he turned to Mary. "Coffee for you?"

"Oh, yes, coffee for us," said Mary, but she couldn't help wondering who was going to pay for it, and simultaneously she couldn't help noticing the shabbiness of his jacket. Well—they'd see. She ignored the plate of cakes that was put down with the coffee. And she hoped Maudie would. She pushed the plate aside as a kind of hint to her, but Maudie leaned across and took a large bun filled with cream.

"Do you mind my asking you something—about your work?" Mary asked.

But Maudie interrupted. "You are living in Ireland? I mean, you aren't just here on a visit?"

There was intimacy and intimacy, and Mary felt nervous in case the young man might resent this question.

"I teach German in a college here," he said, and he did seem a little surprised, but Mary could see, all the same, that he was not at all displeased. He seemed to settle more comfortably into the conversation. "It is very good for a while to go to another country," he said, "and this country is cheap. I have a flat in the next street to here, and it is very private. If I hang myself from the ceiling, it is all right—nobody knows, nobody cares. That is a good way to live when you paint."

Mary was prepared to ponder. "Do you think so?"

Maudie was not prepared to ponder. "How odd," she said shortly, and then she looked at her watch. "I'll have to go," she said inexplicably.

Immediately, Mary's thoughts returned to the problem of who was to pay for the coffee—the unfinished coffee! It was a small affair for which to call up all one's spiritual resources, but she felt enormously courageous and determined when she heard herself ask in a loud voice for her bill. "My bill, please!" she called out, over the sound of spitting coffee on the gas stove.

Johann Stielher made no move to ask for his bill, and yet he was buttoning his jacket and folding his newspaper as if to leave, too. Would his coffee go on her bill, Mary wondered.

It was all settled in a second. The bill was for two eightpenny coffees and one bun, and there was no charge for Stielher's coffee.

As they stood up, gloved and ready to depart, the young man rose and bowed. "Perhaps we go the same way?" he asked, and they could see he was anxious to be polite.

"Oh, not at all," she and Maudie said together, as if he had offered to escort them, and Maudie even laughed openly.

There was, of course, another ridiculous situation. Stielher sat down again. Had they been too brusque? Had they hurt his feelings? Oh, if only he wasn't a foreigner, thought Mary, and she hesitated. Maudie already had her hand on the door.

"I hope I will see some more of your work sometime," said Mary. It was not a question, merely a compliment.

But Stielher sprang to his feet again. "Tonight after my classes I am bringing another picture to hang here," he said. "You would like to see it? I would be here"—he pulled out a large, old-fashioned watch—"at ten minutes past nine."

"Oh, not tonight—I couldn't come back tonight," said Mary. "I live in the country, you see," she said, explaining and excusing herself. "Another time, perhaps? It will be here for how long?"

She wasn't really listening to what he said. She was thinking that he had not asked if Maudie could come. Perhaps it was that, of the two of them, she looked the most likely to buy a picture, whereas Maudie, although in actual fact more likely to do so, looked less so. Or was it that he coupled them, so that he thought if one came both came. Or was it really Maudie he'd like to see again, and that he regarded Mary as a chaperon? Or was it— There was no knowing, and so she said goodbye again, and the next minute the little bell had tinkled over the door and they were in the street. They looked at each other.

"Well! If ever there was—" began Maudie, but she didn't get time to finish her sentence. Behind them the little bell tinkled yet again and their painter was out in the street with them.

"I forgot to give you the address of my flat—it is also my studio," he said. "I would be glad to show you my paintings at any time." He pulled out a notebook and tore out a sheet. "I will write it down," he said concisely. And he did. But when he went to hand it to them, it was Maudie who took it. "I am nearly always there, except when I am at my classes." Bowing, he turned and went back into the café.

They dared not laugh until they had walked some distance away —until they turned into the next street, in fact.

"Well, I never!" said Maudie, and she handed the paper to Mary.

"Chatham Street," Mary read. "Number 8."

"Will you go to see them?" asked Maudie.

Mary felt outraged. "What do you take me for?" she asked. "I may be a bit unconventional, but can you see me presenting myself at his place? Would you go?"

"Oh, it's different for me," said Maudie enigmatically. "And anyway, it was you he asked. But I see your point— It's a pity. Poor fellow, he must be very lonely. I wish there was something we could do for him—someone we could introduce him to."

Mary looked at her. It had never occurred to her that he might be lonely. How was it that the obvious always escaped her?

They were in Grafton Street by this time. "Well, I have some shopping to do. I suppose it's the same with you," said Maudie. "I'm glad I had that talk with you. We must have another chat soon."

"Oh, yes," said Mary, overreadily, replying to the adieus, and not, as Maudie thought, to the suggestion of their meeting again. She was anxious all at once to be rid of Maudie.

And yet, as she watched her walk away, making her passage quickly and expertly through the crowds in the street, Mary felt a sudden terrible aimlessness descend upon her like a physical paralysis. She walked alone, pausing to look in shopwindows. It was the evening hour when everyone in the streets was hurrying home, purposeful and intent. Even those who paused to look into the shopwindows did so with direction and aim, darting their bright glances keenly, like birds. Their minds were on tangibles, while her mind was straying back to the café and the strange flower pictures on the wall, to the young man who was so vulnerable in his vanity.

It was so like Maudie to laugh at him. What did she know of an artist's mind? If Maudie had not been with her, it would have been so different. She might, for one thing, have got him to talk about his work, to explain the dissimilarity between the loose style of the pictures on the wall and the exact, small sketches he'd been drawing on the margins of the paper. She might even have taken up his invitation to go and see his paintings. Why had that seemed so unconventional—so laughable? Because of Maudie, that was why!

How ridiculous their scruples would have seemed to the young man. She could only hope he had not guessed them. She looked up at the clock over her head. Supposing right now she were to slip back to the café and suggest that, after all, she found she would have time for a quick visit to his studio? Or would he have left the café? Better, perhaps, to call around to the studio? He would surely be back there now!

For a moment, she stood debating the arguments for and against going back. Would it seem odd to him? Would he be surprised? But as if it were Maudie who put the questions, she frowned them down, and all at once purposeful as anyone in the street, she turned and began to go back—headlong, you might say—toward Chatham Street.

At the point where two small streets crossed each other, she had to pause while a team of Guinness's dray horses turned with difficulty in the narrow square of the intersection. As she waited impatiently, she caught sight of herself in the gilded mirror of a public house. For a second, the familiar sight gave her a misgiving of her mission, but as the dray horses moved out of the way, she told herself that her dowdy, lumpish, and unromantic figure vouched for her spiritual integrity. She pulled herself away from the face in the glass and hurried across the street.

Between two shops, down a short alley—roofed by the second story of the premises overhead, till it was a tunnel—was his door. Away at the end of the tunnel, his door could clearly be seen, even from the middle of the street, for it was painted a bright yellow. Odd that she had never seen it in all the times she had passed that way. She crossed the street and ran down the tunnel, her footsteps echoing loud in her ears. On the door, tied to the latchet of the letter box, was a piece of white cardboard with his name on it. Grabbing the knocker, she gave three clear hammer strokes on the door.

The little alley was a sort of cul-de-sac; except for the street behind her and the door in front of her, it had no outlet. No skylight—not even an aperture that she could see. As for the premises into which the door led, there was no way of telling their size or their extent, or anything at all about them, until the door was opened.

Irresponsibly, she giggled. It was like the mystifying doors in the trunks of trees that beguiled her as a child in fairy tales and fantasies. Did this door, like those fairy doors, lead into rooms of impossible amplitude, or would it be a cramped and poky place?

As she wondered, she saw that—just as in a fairy tale—there was an aperture, after all. The letter box had lost its shutter and it gaped open, a vacant hole in the wood. Impulsively, going down on one knee, she peered in through the slit.

At first she could see only segments of objects within, but by moving her head she was able to identify things: an unfinished canvas up against the splattered white wainscot, a bicycle pump flat on the floor, the leg of a table, black iron bed legs, an iron washstand base, and, to her amusement, dangling down by the leg of the table, dripping their moisture in a pool on the floor, a pair of elongated gray wool socks. It was only possible to see the lower portion of the room, but it seemed enough for her to infer conclusively that this was indeed a little room in a tree, no bigger than the bulk of the outer trunk, leading nowhere, and—sufficient or no—itself its own end.

There was just one break in the wainscot, where a door ran down to the floor, but this was made of roughly jointed boards and so narrow that she took it to be the door of a closet. And then, as she started to rise, she saw something else—an intricate segment of fine wire spokes. It was a second before she realized that it was the wheel of a bicycle. So a bicycle, too, lived here in this little room in a tree trunk! Oh, poor young man, poor painter—poor foreigner, inept at finding the good lodgings in a strange city. Her heart went out to him.

It was just then that the boarded door—it couldn't have been a press, after all—opened into the room, and she found herself staring at two feet. They were large feet, shoved into unlaced shoes, and they were bare to the white ankles. For, of course, she thought wildly, focussing her thoughts, his socks are washed! But her power to think clearly only lasted an instant. She sprang to her feet.

"Who iss that?" asked a voice. "Did someone knock?"

It was the voice of the man in the café. But where was she to find a voice with which to reply? And who was she to say that she was? Who—to this stranger—was she? And if he opened the door, what then? All the thoughts and words that had, like a wind, blown her down this tunnel subsided suddenly, and she stood appalled at where they had brought her.

"Who iss that?" came the voice within, troubled.

Staring at those white feet thrust into the unlaced shoes, she felt that she would die on the spot if they moved an inch. She turned.

Ahead of her, bright, shining, and clear, as if it were seen at the end of a powerful telescope, was the street. Not caring if her feet were heard, volleying and echoing as if she ran through a mighty drainpipe, she kept running till she reached the street, kept running even then, jostling surprised shoppers, hitting her ankles on the wheel knobs of pushcarts and prams. Only when she came to the junction of the streets did she stop, as in the pub mirror she caught sight again of her familiar face. The face steadied her. How absurd to think that anyone would sinisterly follow this middle-aged woman!

But suppose he had been in the outer room when she knocked! Suppose he had opened the door! What would have happened then? What would she have said? A flush spread over her face. The only true words she could have uttered were those that had sunk into her mind in the café, put there by Maudie. "I'm lonely!" That was all she could have said. "I'm lonely. Are you?"

A deep shame came over her with this admission, and she began to walk quickly onward again, toward Grafton Street. If anyone had seen her there in that dark alleyway! If anyone could have looked into her mind, her heart!

And yet, was it so unnatural? So unforgivable?

As she passed the open door of the Carmelite Church, she paused. Could she rid herself of her feeling of shame in the dark of the confessional? To the sin-accustomed ears of the wise old fathers, her story would be lightweight, a tedious tale of scrupulosity. Was there no one, no one who'd understand?

She had reached Grafton Street once more, and stepped into its crowded thoroughfare. It was only a few minutes since she had left it, but in the street the evasion of light had begun. Only the bustle of people and the activity of traffic made it seem that it was yet day. Away at the top of the street, in Stephen's Green, to which she turned, although the tops of the trees were still clear, branch for branch, in the last of the light, mist muted the outline of the bushes. If one were to put a hand between the railings now, it would be with a slight shock that the fingers would feel the little branches, like fine bones, under the feathers of mist. It was the time at which she used to meet Richard.

Oh, Richard! she cried, almost out loud, as she walked along by the railings to where the car was parked. Oh, Richard, it's you I want!

And as she cried out, her mind presented him to her, as she so often saw him, coming toward her: tall, handsome, and with his curious air of apartness from those around him. He had his hat in his hand down by his side, in a way that was absolutely particular to him, trailing it at his side as on a summer day he might trail a hand in water from the side of a boat. She wanted to preserve that picture of him forever in an image, and only as she struggled to hold on to it did she realize there was no urgency in the search. She had a sense of having all the time in the world to look and look and look at him.

That was the very way he used to come to meet her, indolently trailing the old felt hat, glad to be done with the day; and when they got nearer to each other, she used to take such joy in his unsmiling face, with its happiness integral to it in all its features. It was the first time in the two years he'd been gone from her that she'd seen his face.

Not till she had taken out the key of the car and gone straight around to the driver's side, not stupidly, as so often, to the passenger seat—not till then did she realize what she had achieved. Yet she had no more than got back her rights; no more. It was not a subject for amazement. By what means exactly had she got them back, though—in that little café? That was the wonder.

DEFENDER OF THE FAITH

❖

PHILIP ROTH

I N May of 1945, only a few weeks after the fighting had ended
in Europe, I was rotated back to the States, where I spent the
remainder of the war with a training company at Camp Crowder,
Missouri. Along with the rest of the Ninth Army, I had been racing
across Germany so swiftly during the late winter and spring that
when I boarded the plane, I couldn't believe its destination lay
to the west. My mind might inform me otherwise, but there was
an inertia of the spirit that told me we were flying to a new front,
where we would disembark and continue our push eastward—
eastward until we'd circled the globe, marching through villages
along whose twisting, cobbled streets crowds of the enemy would
watch us take possession of what, up till then, they'd considered
their own. I had changed enough in two years not to mind the
trembling of the old people, the crying of the very young, the uncertainty and fear in the eyes of the once arrogant. I had been
fortunate enough to develop an infantryman's heart, which, like
his feet, at first aches and swells but finally grows horny enough
for him to travel the weirdest paths without feeling a thing.

Captain Paul Barrett was my C.O. in Camp Crowder. The day I
reported for duty, he came out of his office to shake my hand. He
was short, gruff, and fiery, and—indoors or out—he wore his polished
helmet liner pulled down to his little eyes. In Europe, he had received a battlefield commission and a serious chest wound, and he'd
been returned to the States only a few months before. He spoke
easily to me, and at the evening formation he introduced me to the
troops. "Gentlemen," he said, "Sergeant Thurston, as you know, is
no longer with this company. Your new first sergeant is Sergeant
Nathan Marx, here. He is a veteran of the European theatre, and
consequently will expect to find a company of soldiers here, and not
a company of *boys*."

I sat up late in the orderly room that evening, trying half-heartedly to solve the riddle of duty rosters, personnel forms, and morning reports. The Charge of Quarters slept with his mouth open on a mattress on the floor. A trainee stood reading the next day's duty roster, which was posted on the bulletin board just inside the screen door. It was a warm evening, and I could hear radios playing dance music over in the barracks. The trainee, who had been staring at me whenever he thought I wouldn't notice, finally took a step in my direction.

"Hey, Sarge—we having a G.I. party tomorrow night?" he asked. A G.I. party is a barracks cleaning.

"You usually have them on Friday nights?" I asked him.

"Yes," he said, and then he added, mysteriously, "That's the whole thing."

"Then you'll have a G.I. party."

He turned away, and I heard him mumbling. His shoulders were moving, and I wondered if he was crying.

"What's your name, soldier?" I asked.

He turned, not crying at all. Instead, his green-speckled eyes, long and narrow, flashed like fish in the sun. He walked over to me and sat on the edge of my desk. He reached out a hand. "Sheldon," he said.

"Stand on your feet, Sheldon."

Getting off the desk, he said, "Sheldon Grossbart." He smiled at the familiarity into which he'd led me.

"You against cleaning the barracks Friday night, Grossbart?" I said. "Maybe we shouldn't have G.I. parties. Maybe we should get a maid." My tone startled me. I felt I sounded like every top sergeant I had ever known.

"No, Sergeant." He grew serious, but with a seriousness that seemed to be only the stifling of a smile. "It's just—G.I. parties on Friday night, of all nights."

He slipped up onto the corner of the desk again—not quite sitting, but not quite standing, either. He looked at me with those speckled eyes flashing, and then made a gesture with his hand. It was very slight—no more than a movement back and forth of the wrist—and yet it managed to exclude from our affairs everything else in the orderly room, to make the two of us the center of the world. It seemed, in fact, to exclude everything even about the two of us except our hearts.

"Sergeant Thurston was one thing," he whispered, glancing at the sleeping C.Q., "but we thought that with you here things might be a little different."

"We?"

"The Jewish personnel."

"Why?" I asked, harshly. "What's on your mind?" Whether I was still angry at the "Sheldon" business, or now at something else, I hadn't time to tell, but clearly I was angry.

"We thought you—Marx, you know, like Karl Marx. The Marx Brothers. Those guys are all—M-a-r-x. Isn't that how *you* spell it, Sergeant?"

"M-a-r-x."

"Fishbein said—" He stopped. "What I mean to say, Sergeant—" His face and neck were red, and his mouth moved but no words came out. In a moment, he raised himself to attention, gazing down at me. It was as though he had suddenly decided he could expect no more sympathy from me than from Thurston, the reason being that I was of Thurston's faith, and not his. The young man had managed to confuse himself as to what my faith really was, but I felt no desire to straighten him out. Very simply, I didn't like him.

When I did nothing but return his gaze, he spoke, in an altered tone. "You see, Sergeant," he explained to me, "Friday nights, Jews are supposed to go to services."

"Did Sergeant Thurston tell you you couldn't go to them when there was a G.I. party?"

"No."

"Did he say you had to stay and scrub the floors?"

"No, Sergeant."

"Did the Captain say you had to stay and scrub the floors?"

"That isn't it, Sergeant. It's the other guys in the barracks." He leaned toward me. "They think we're goofing off. But we're not. That's when Jews go to services, Friday night. We have to."

"Then go."

"But the other guys make accusations. They have no right."

"That's not the Army's problem, Grossbart. It's a personal problem you'll have to work out yourself."

"But it's un*fair*."

I got up to leave. "There's nothing I can do about it," I said.

Grossbart stiffened and stood in front of me. "But this is a matter of *religion*, sir."

"Sergeant," I said.

"I mean 'Sergeant,' " he said, almost snarling.

"Look, go see the chaplain. You want to see Captain Barrett, I'll arrange an appointment."

"No, no. I don't want to make trouble, Sergeant. That's the first thing they throw up to you. I just want my rights!"

"Damn it, Grossbart, stop whining. You have your rights. You can stay and scrub floors or you can go to shul—"

The smile swam in again. Spittle gleamed at the corners of his mouth. "You mean church, Sergeant."

"I mean shul, Grossbart!"

I walked past him and went outside. Near me, I heard the scrunching of a guard's boots on gravel. Beyond the lighted windows of the barracks, young men in T shirts and fatigue pants were sitting on their bunks, polishing their rifles. Suddenly there was a light rustling behind me. I turned and saw Grossbart's dark frame fleeing back to the barracks, racing to tell his Jewish friends that they were right—that, like Karl and Harpo, I was one of them.

The next morning, while chatting with Captain Barrett, I recounted the incident of the previous evening. Somehow, in the telling, it must have seemed to the Captain that I was not so much explaining Grossbart's position as defending it. "Marx, I'd fight side by side with a nigger if the fella proved to me he was a man. I pride myself," he said, looking out the window, "that I've got an open mind. Consequently, Sergeant, nobody gets special treatment here, for the good or the bad. All a man's got to do is prove himself. A man fires well on the range, I give him a weekend pass. He scores high in P.T., he gets a weekend pass. He earns it." He turned from the window and pointed a finger at me. "You're a Jewish fella, am I right, Marx?"

"Yes, sir."

"And I admire you. I admire you because of the ribbons on your chest. I judge a man by what he shows me on the field of battle, Sergeant. It's what he's got here," he said, and then, though I expected he would point to his heart, he jerked a thumb toward the buttons straining to hold his blouse across his belly. "Guts," he said.

"O.K., sir. I only wanted to pass on to you how the men felt."

"Mr. Marx, you're going to be old before your time if you worry about how the men feel. Leave that stuff to the chaplain—that's his business, not yours. Let's us train these fellas to shoot straight. If the Jewish personnel feels the other men are accusing them of goldbricking—well, I just don't know. Seems awful funny that suddenly the Lord is calling so loud in Private Grossman's ear he's just got to run to church."

"Synagogue," I said.

"Synagogue is right, Sergeant. I'll write that down for handy reference. Thank you for stopping by."

That evening, a few minutes before the company gathered outside the orderly room for the chow formation, I called the C.Q., Corporal Robert LaHill, in to see me. LaHill was a dark, burly fellow whose hair curled out of his clothes wherever it could. He had a glaze in his eyes that made one think of caves and dinosaurs. "LaHill," I said, "when you take the formation, remind the men that they're free to attend church services *whenever* they are held, provided they report to the orderly room before they leave the area."

LaHill scratched his wrist, but gave no indication that he'd heard or understood.

"LaHill," I said, *"church.* You remember? Church, priest, Mass, confession."

He curled one lip into a kind of smile; I took it for a signal that for a second he had flickered back up into the human race.

"Jewish personnel who want to attend services this evening are to fall out in front of the orderly room at 1900," I said. Then, as an afterthought, I added, "By order of Captain Barrett."

A little while later, as the day's last light—softer than any I had seen that year—began to drop over Camp Crowder, I heard LaHill's thick, inflectionless voice outside my window: "Give me your ears, troopers. Toppie says for me to tell you that at 1900 hours all Jewish personnel is to fall out in front, here, if they want to attend the Jewish Mass."

At seven o'clock, I looked out the orderly-room window and saw three soldiers in starched khakis standing on the dusty quadrangle. They looked at their watches and fidgeted while they whispered back and forth. It was getting dimmer, and, alone on the otherwise deserted field, they looked tiny. When I opened the door, I heard the noises of the G.I. party coming from the surrounding barracks —bunks being pushed to the walls, faucets pounding water into buckets, brooms whisking at the wooden floors, cleaning the dirt away for Saturday's inspection. Big puffs of cloth moved round and round on the windowpanes. I walked outside, and the moment my foot hit the ground I thought I heard Grossbart call to the others,

" 'Ten-*hut!*' Or maybe, when they all three jumped to attention, I imagined I heard the command.

Grossbart stepped forward. "Thank you, sir," he said.

" 'Sergeant,' Grossbart," I reminded him. "You call officers 'sir.' I'm not an officer. You've been in the Army three weeks—you know that."

He turned his palms out at his sides to indicate that, in truth, he and I lived beyond convention. "Thank you, anyway," he said.

"Yes," a tall boy behind him said. "Thanks a lot."

And the third boy whispered, "Thank you," but his mouth barely fluttered, so that he did not alter by more than a lip's movement his posture of attention.

"For what?" I asked.

Grossbart snorted happily. "For the announcement. The Corporal's announcement. It helped. It made it—"

"Fancier." The tall boy finished Grossbart's sentence.

Grossbart smiled. "He means formal, sir. Public," he said to me. "Now it won't seem as though we're just taking off—goldbricking because the work has begun."

"It was by order of Captain Barrett," I said.

"Aaah, but you pull a little weight," Grossbart said. "So we thank you." Then he turned to his companions. "Sergeant Marx, I want you to meet Larry Fishbein."

The tall boy stepped forward and extended his hand. I shook it. "You from New York?" he asked.

"Yes."

"Me, too." He had a cadaverous face that collapsed inward from his cheekbone to his jaw, and when he smiled—as he did at the news of our communal attachment—revealed a mouthful of bad teeth. He was blinking his eyes a good deal, as though he were fighting back tears. "What borough?" he asked.

I turned to Grossbart. "It's five after seven. What time are services?"

"Shul," he said, smiling, "is in ten minutes. I want you to meet Mickey Halpern. This is Nathan Marx, our sergeant."

The third boy hopped forward. "Private Michael Halpern." He saluted.

"Salute officers, Halpern," I said. The boy dropped his hand, and, on its way down, in his nervousness, checked to see if his shirt pockets were buttoned.

"Shall I march them over, sir?" Grossbart asked. "Or are you coming along?"

From behind Grossbart, Fishbein piped up. "Afterward, they're having refreshments. A ladies' auxiliary from St. Louis, the rabbi told us last week."

"The chaplain," Halpern whispered.

"You're welcome to come along," Grossbart said.

To avoid his plea, I looked away, and saw, in the windows of the barracks, a cloud of faces staring out at the four of us. "Hurry along, Grossbart," I said.

"O.K., then," he said. He turned to the others. "Double time, *march!*"

They started off, but ten feet away Grossbart spun around and, running backward, called to me, "Good *shabbus,* sir!" And then the three of them were swallowed into the alien Missouri dusk.

Even after they had disappeared over the parade ground, whose green was now a deep blue, I could hear Grossbart singing the double-time cadence, and as it grew dimmer and dimmer, it suddenly touched a deep memory—as did the slant of the light—and I was remembering the shrill sounds of a Bronx playground where, years ago, beside the Grand Concourse, I had played on long spring evenings such as this. It was a pleasant memory for a young man so far from peace and home, and it brought so many recollections with it that I began to grow exceedingly tender about myself. In fact, I indulged myself in a reverie so strong that I felt as though a hand were reaching down inside me. It had to reach so very far to touch me! It had to reach past those days in the forests of Belgium, and past the dying I'd refused to weep over; past the nights in German farmhouses whose books we'd burned to warm us; past endless stretches when I had shut off all softness I might feel for my fellows, and had managed even to deny myself the posture of a conqueror—the swagger that I, as a Jew, might well have worn as my boots whacked against the rubble of Wesel, Münster, and Braunschweig.

But now one night noise, one rumor of home and time past, and memory plunged down through all I had anesthetized, and came to what I suddenly remembered was myself. So it was not altogether curious that, in search of more of me, I found myself following Grossbart's tracks to Chapel No. 3, where the Jewish services were being held.

I took a seat in the last row, which was empty. Two rows in front

of me sat Grossbart, Fishbein, and Halpern, holding little white
Dixie cups. Each row of seats was raised higher than the one in front
of it, and I could see clearly what was going on. Fishbein was pouring the contents of his cup into Grossbart's, and Grossbart looked
mirthful as the liquid made a purple arc between Fishbein's hand
and his. In the glaring yellow light, I saw the chaplain standing on
the platform at the front; he was chanting the first line of the
responsive reading. Grossbart's prayer book remained closed on his
lap; he was swishing the cup around. Only Halpern responded to
the chant by praying. The fingers of his right hand were spread
wide across the cover of his open book. His cap was pulled down
low onto his brow, which made it round, like a yarmulke. From
time to time, Grossbart wet his lips at the cup's edge; Fishbein, his
long yellow face a dying light bulb, looked from here to there,
craning forward to catch sight of the faces down the row, then of
those in front of him, then behind. He saw me, and his eyelids beat
a tattoo. His elbow slid into Grossbart's side, his neck inclined
toward his friend, he whispered something, and then, when the congregation next responded to the chant, Grossbart's voice was among
the others. Fishbein looked into his book now, too; his lips, however, didn't move.

Finally, it was time to drink the wine. The chaplain smiled down
at them as Grossbart swigged his in one long gulp, Halpern sipped,
meditating, and Fishbein faked devotion with an empty cup. "As I
look down amongst the congregation"—the chaplain grinned at the
word—"this night, I see many new faces, and I want to welcome you
to Friday-night services here at Camp Crowder. I am Major Leo
Ben Ezra, your chaplain." Though an American, the chaplain spoke
deliberately—syllable by syllable, almost—as though to communicate, above all, with the lip readers in his audience. "I have only a
few words to say before we adjourn to the refreshment room, where
the kind ladies of the Temple Sinai, St. Louis, Missouri, have a nice
setting for you."

Applause and whistling broke out. After another momentary
grin, the chaplain raised his hands, palms out, his eyes flicking upward a moment, as if to remind the troops where they were and
Who Else might be in attendance. In the sudden silence that followed, I thought I heard Grossbart cackle, "Let the goyim clean the
floors!" Were those the words? I wasn't sure, but Fishbein, grinning,
nudged Halpern. Halpern looked dumbly at him, then went back
to his prayer book, which had been occupying him all through the

rabbi's talk. One hand tugged at the black kinky hair that stuck out under his cap. His lips moved.

The rabbi continued. "It is about the food that I want to speak to you for a moment. I know, I know, I know," he intoned, wearily, "how in the mouths of most of you the *trafe* food tastes like ashes. I know how you gag, some of you, and how your parents suffer to think of their children eating foods unclean and offensive to the palate. What can I tell you? I can only say, close your eyes and swallow as best you can. Eat what you must to live, and throw away the rest. I wish I could help more. For those of you who find this impossible, may I ask that you try and try, but then come to see me in private. If your revulsion is so great, we will have to seek aid from those higher up."

A round of chatter rose and subsided. Then everyone sang "Ain Kelohainu;" after all those years, I discovered, I still knew the words. Then, suddenly, the service over, Grossbart was upon me. "Higher up? He means the General?"

"Hey, Shelly," Fishbein said, "he means God." He smacked his face and looked at Halpern. "How high can you go!"

"Sh-h-h!" Grossbart said. "What do you think, Sergeant?"

"I don't know," I said. "You better ask the chaplain."

"I'm going to. I'm making an appointment to see him in private. So is Mickey."

Halpern shook his head. "No, no, Sheldon—"

"You have rights, Mickey," Grossbart said. "They can't push us around."

"It's O.K.," said Halpern. "It bothers my mother, not me."

Grossbart looked at me. "Yesterday he threw up. From the hash. It was all ham and God knows what else."

"I have a cold—that was why," Halpern said. He pushed his yarmulke back into a cap.

"What about you, Fishbein?" I asked. "You kosher, too?"

He flushed. "A little. But I'll let it ride. I have a very strong stomach, and I don't eat a lot anyway." I continued to look at him, and he held up his wrist to reinforce what he'd just said; his watch strap was tightened to the last hole, and he pointed that out to me.

"But services are important to you?" I asked him.

He looked at Grossbart. "Sure, sir."

" 'Sergeant.' "

"Not so much at home," said Grossbart, stepping between us, "but away from home it gives one a sense of his Jewishness."

"We have to stick together," Fishbein said.

I started to walk toward the door; Halpern stepped back to make way for me.

"That's what happened in Germany," Grossbart was saying, loud enough for me to hear. "They didn't stick together. They let themselves get pushed around."

I turned. "Look, Grossbart. This is the Army, not summer camp."

He smiled. "So?"

Halpern tried to sneak off, but Grossbart held his arm.

"Grossbart, how old are you?" I asked.

"Nineteen."

"And you?" I said to Fishbein.

"The same. The same month, even."

"And what about him?" I pointed to Halpern, who had by now made it safely to the door.

"Eighteen," Grossbart whispered. "But like he can't tie his shoes or brush his teeth himself. I feel sorry for him."

"I feel sorry for all of us, Grossbart," I said, "but just act like a man. Just don't overdo it."

"Overdo what, sir?"

"The 'sir' business, for one thing. Don't overdo that," I said.

I left him standing there. I passed by Halpern, but he did not look at me. Then I was outside, but, behind, I heard Grossbart call, "Hey, Mickey, my *leben*, come on back. Refreshments!"

"*Leben!*" My grandmother's word for me!

One morning a week later, while I was working at my desk, Captain Barrett shouted for me to come into his office. When I entered, he had his helmet liner squashed down so far on his head that I couldn't even see his eyes. He was on the phone, and when he spoke to me, he cupped one hand over the mouthpiece. "Who the hell is Grossbart?"

"Third platoon, Captain," I said. "A trainee."

"What's all this stink about food? His mother called a goddam congressman about the food." He uncovered the mouthpiece and slid his helmet up until I could see his bottom eyelashes. "Yes, sir," he said into the phone. "Yes, sir. I'm still here, sir. I'm asking Marx, here, right now—"

He covered the mouthpiece again and turned his head back toward me. "Lightfoot Harry's on the phone," he said, between his teeth. "This congressman calls General Lyman, who calls Colonel Sousa, who calls the Major, who calls me. They're just dying to stick this thing on me. Whatsa matter?" He shook the phone at me. "I don't feed the troops? What the hell is this?"

"Sir, Grossbart is strange—" Barrett greeted that with a mockingly indulgent smile. I altered my approach. "Captain, he's a very orthodox Jew, and so he's only allowed to eat certain foods."

"He throws up, the congressman said. Every time he eats something, his mother says, he throws up!"

"He's accustomed to observing the dietary laws, Captain."

"So why's his old lady have to call the White House?"

"Jewish parents, sir—they're apt to be more protective than you expect. I mean, Jews have a very close family life. A boy goes away from home, sometimes the mother is liable to get very upset. Probably the boy mentioned something in a letter, and his mother misinterpreted."

"I'd like to punch him one right in the mouth," the Captain said. "There's a goddam war on, and he wants a silver platter!"

"I don't think the boy's to blame, sir. I'm sure we can straighten it out by just asking him. Jewish parents worry—"

"*All* parents worry, for Christ's sake. But they don't get on their high horse and start pulling strings—"

I interrupted, my voice higher, tighter than before. "The home life, Captain, is very important—but you're right, it may sometimes get out of hand. It's a very wonderful thing, Captain, but because it's so close, this kind of thing . . ."

He didn't listen any longer to my attempt to present both myself and Lightfoot Harry with an explanation for the letter. He turned back to the phone. "Sir?" he said. "Sir—Marx, here, tells me Jews have a tendency to be pushy. He says he thinks we can settle it right here in the company. . . . Yes, sir. . . . I *will* call back, sir, soon as I can." He hung up. "Where are the men, Sergeant?"

"On the range."

With a whack on the top of his helmet, he crushed it down over his eyes again, and charged out of his chair. "We're going for a ride," he said.

The Captain drove, and I sat beside him. It was a hot spring day, and under my newly starched fatigues I felt as though my armpits were melting down onto my sides and chest. The roads were dry, and by the time we reached the firing range, my teeth felt gritty with dust, though my mouth had been shut the whole trip.

The Captain slammed the brakes on and told me to get the hell out and find Grossbart.

I found him on his belly, firing wildly at the five-hundred-feet target. Waiting their turns behind him were Halpern and Fishbein. Fishbein, wearing a pair of rimless G.I. glasses I hadn't seen on him before, had the appearance of an old peddler who would gladly have sold you his rifle and the cartridges that were slung all over him. I stood back by the ammo boxes, waiting for Grossbart to finish spraying the distant targets. Fishbein straggled back to stand near me.

"Hello, Sergeant Marx," he said.

"How are you?" I mumbled.

"Fine, thank you. Sheldon's really a good shot."

"I didn't notice."

"I'm not so good, but I think I'm getting the hang of it now. Sergeant, I don't mean to, you know, ask what I shouldn't—" The boy stopped. He was trying to speak intimately, but the noise of the shooting forced him to shout at me.

"What is it?" I asked. Down the range, I saw Captain Barrett standing up in the jeep, scanning the line for me and Grossbart.

"My parents keep asking and asking where we're going," Fishbein said. "Everybody says the Pacific. I don't care, but my parents —If I could relieve their minds, I think I could concentrate more on my shooting."

"I don't know where, Fishbein. Try to concentrate anyway."

"Sheldon says you might be able to find out."

"I don't know a thing, Fishbein. You just take it easy, and don't let Sheldon—"

"*I'm* taking it easy, Sergeant. It's at home—"

Grossbart had finished on the line, and was dusting his fatigues with one hand. I called to him. "Grossbart, the Captain wants to see you."

He came toward us. His eyes blazed and twinkled. "Hi!"

"Don't point that goddam rifle!" I said.

"I wouldn't shoot you, Sarge." He gave me a smile as wide as a pumpkin, and turned the barrel aside.

"Damn you, Grossbart, this is no joke! Follow me."

I walked ahead of him, and had the awful suspicion that, behind me, Grossbart was *marching*, his rifle on his shoulder, as though he were a one-man detachment. At the jeep, he gave the Captain a rifle salute. "Private Sheldon Grossbart, sir."

"At ease, Grossman." The Captain sat down, slid over into the empty seat, and, crooking a finger, invited Grossbart closer.

"Bart, sir. Sheldon Gross*bart*. It's a common error." Grossbart nodded at me; *I* understood, he indicated. I looked away just as the mess truck pulled up to the range, disgorging a half-dozen K.P.'s with rolled-up sleeves. The mess sergeant screamed at them while they set up the chow-line equipment.

"Grossbart, your mama wrote some congressman that we don't feed you right. Do you know that?" the Captain said.

"It was my father, sir. He wrote to Representative Franconi that my religion forbids me to eat certain foods."

"What religion is that, Grossbart?"

"Jewish."

" 'Jewish, *sir*,' " I said to Grossbart.

"Excuse me, sir. Jewish, sir."

"What have you been living on?" the Captain asked. "You've been in the Army a month already. You don't look to me like you're falling to pieces."

"I eat because I have to, sir. But Sergeant Marx will testify to the fact that I don't eat one mouthful more than I need in order to survive."

"Is that so, Marx?" Barrett asked.

"I've never seen Grossbart eat, sir," I said.

"But you heard the rabbi," Grossbart said. "He told us what to do, and I listened."

The Captain looked at me. "Well, Marx?"

"I still don't know what he eats and doesn't eat, sir."

Grossbart raised his arms to plead with me, and it looked for a moment as though he were going to hand me his weapon to hold. "But, Sergeant—"

"Look, Grossbart, just answer the Captain's questions," I said sharply.

Barrett smiled at me, and I resented it. "All right, Grossbart," he said. "What is it you want? The little piece of paper? You want out?"

"No, sir. Only to be allowed to live as a Jew. And for the others, too."

"What others?"

"Fishbein, sir, and Halpern."

"They don't like the way we serve, either?"

"Halpern throws up, sir. I've seen it."

"I thought *you* throw up."

"Just once, sir. I didn't know the sausage was sausage."

"We'll give menus, Grossbart. We'll show training films about the food, so you can identify when we're trying to poison you."

Grossbart did not answer. The men had been organized into two long chow lines. At the tail end of one, I spotted Fishbein—or, rather, his glasses spotted me. They winked sunlight back at me. Halpern stood next to him, patting the inside of his collar with a khaki handkerchief. They moved with the line as it began to edge up toward the food. The mess sergeant was still screaming at the K.P.s. For a moment, I was actually terrified by the thought that somehow the mess sergeant was going to become involved in Grossbart's problem.

"Marx," the Captain said, "you're a Jewish fella—am I right?"

I played straight man. "Yes, sir."

"How long you been in the Army? Tell this boy."

"Three years and two months."

"A year in combat, Grossbart. Twelve goddam months in combat all through Europe. I admire this man." The Captain snapped a wrist against my chest. "Do you hear him peeping about the food? Do you? I want an answer, Grossbart. Yes or no."

"No, sir."

"And why not? He's a Jewish fella."

"Some things are more important to some Jews than other things to other Jews."

Barrett blew up. "Look, Grossbart. Marx, here, is a good man— a goddam hero. When you were in high school, Sergeant Marx was killing Germans. Who does more for the Jews—you, by throwing up over a lousy piece of sausage, a piece of first-cut meat, or Marx, by killing those Nazi bastards? If I was a Jew, Grossbart, I'd kiss this man's feet. He's a goddam hero, and *he* eats what we give him. Why do you have to cause trouble is what I want to know! What is it you're buckin' for—a discharge?"

"No, sir."

"I'm talking to a wall! Sergeant, get him out of my way." Barrett swung himself back into the driver's seat. "I'm going to see the chaplain." The engine roared, the jeep spun around in a whirl of dust, and the Captain was headed back to camp.

For a moment, Grossbart and I stood side by side, watching the jeep. Then he looked at me and said, "I don't want to start trouble. That's the first thing they toss up to us."

When he spoke, I saw that his teeth were white and straight, and the sight of them suddenly made me understand that Grossbart actually did have parents—that once upon a time someone had taken little Sheldon to the dentist. He was their son. Despite all the talk about his parents, it was hard to believe in Grossbart as a child, an heir—as related by blood to anyone, mother, father, or, above all, to me. This realization led me to another.

"What does your father do, Grossbart?" I asked as we started to walk back toward the chow line.

"He's a tailor."

"An American?"

"Now, yes. A son in the Army," he said, jokingly.

"And your mother?" I asked.

He winked. "A *ballabusta*. She practically sleeps with a dustcloth in her hand."

"She's also an immigrant?"

"All she talks is Yiddish, still."

"And your father, too?"

"A little English. 'Clean,' 'Press,' 'Take the pants in.' That's the extent of it. But they're good to me."

"Then, Grossbart—" I reached out and stopped him. He turned toward me, and when our eyes met, his seemed to jump back, to shiver in their sockets. "Grossbart—you were the one who wrote that letter, weren't you?"

It took only a second or two for his eyes to flash happy again. "Yes." He walked on, and I kept pace. "It's what my father *would* have written if he had known how. It was his name, though. *He* signed it. He even mailed it. I sent it home. For the New York postmark."

I was astonished, and he saw it. With complete seriousness, he thrust his right arm in front of me. "Blood is blood, Sergeant," he said, pinching the blue vein in his wrist.

"What the hell *are* you trying to do, Grossbart?" I asked. "I've seen you eat. Do you know that? I told the Captain I don't know what you eat, but I've seen you eat like a hound at chow."

"We work hard, Sergeant. We're in training. For a furnace to work, you've got to feed it coal."

"Why did you say in the letter that you threw up all the time?"

"I was really talking about Mickey there. I was talking *for* him. He would never write, Sergeant, though I pleaded with him. He'll waste away to nothing if I don't help. Sergeant, I used my name—

my father's name—but it's Mickey, and Fishbein, too, I'm watching out for."

"You're a regular Messiah, aren't you?"

We were at the chow line now.

"That's a good one, Sergeant," he said, smiling. "But who knows? Who can tell? Maybe you're the Messiah—a little bit. What Mickey says is the Messiah is a collective idea. He went to Yeshiva, Mickey, for a while. He says *together* we're the Messiah. Me a little bit, you a little bit. You should hear that kid talk, Sergeant, when he gets going."

"Me a little bit, you a little bit," I said. "You'd like to believe that, wouldn't you, Grossbart? That would make everything so clean for you."

"It doesn't seem too bad a thing to believe, Sergeant. It only means we should all *give* a little, is all."

I walked off to eat my rations with the other noncoms.

Two days later, a letter addressed to Captain Barrett passed over my desk. It had come through the chain of command—from the office of Congressman Franconi, where it had been received, to General Lyman, to Colonel Sousa, to Major Lamont, now to Captain Barrett. I read it over twice. It was dated May 14th, the day Barrett had spoken with Grossbart on the rifle range.

DEAR CONGRESSMAN:

First let me thank you for your interest in behalf of my son, Private Sheldon Grossbart. Fortunately, I was able to speak with Sheldon on the phone the other night, and I think I've been able to solve our problem. He is, as I mentioned in my last letter, a very religious boy, and it was only with the greatest difficulty that I could persuade him that the religious thing to do—what God Himself would want Sheldon to do—would be to suffer the pangs of religious remorse for the good of his country and all mankind. It took some doing, Congressman, but finally he saw the light. In fact, what he said (and I wrote down the words on a scratch pad so as never to forget), what he said was "I guess you're right, Dad. So many millions of my fellow-Jews gave up their lives to the enemy, the least I can do is live for a while minus a bit of my heritage so as to help end this struggle and regain for all the children of God dignity and humanity." That, Congressman, would make any father proud.

By the way, Sheldon wanted me to know—and to pass on to you —the name of a soldier who helped him reach this decision: SERGEANT NATHAN MARX. Sergeant Marx is a combat veteran who is Sheldon's first sergeant. This man has helped Sheldon over some of the first hurdles he's had to face in the Army, and is in part responsible for Sheldon's changing his mind about the dietary laws. I know Sheldon would appreciate any recognition Marx could receive.

Thank you and good luck. I look forward to seeing your name on the next election ballot.

Respectfully,
SAMUEL E. GROSSBART

Attached to the Grossbart communiqué was another, addressed to General Marshall Lyman, the post commander, and signed by Representative Charles E. Franconi, of the House of Representatives. The communiqué informed General Lyman that Sergeant Nathan Marx was a credit to the U.S. Army and the Jewish people.

What was Grossbart's motive in recanting? Did he feel he'd gone too far? Was the letter a strategic retreat—a crafty attempt to strengthen what he considered our alliance? Or had he actually changed his mind, via an imaginary dialogue between Grossbart *père* and Grossbart *fils?* I was puzzled, but only for a few days—that is, only until I realized that, whatever his reasons, he had actually decided to disappear from my life; he was going to allow himself to become just another trainee. I saw him at inspection, but he never winked; at chow formations, but he never flashed me a sign. On Sundays, with the other trainees, he would sit around watching the noncoms' softball team, for which I pitched, but not once did he speak an unnecessary word to me. Fishbein and Halpern retreated, too—at Grossbart's command, I was sure. Apparently he had seen that wisdom lay in turning back before he plunged over into the ugliness of privilege undeserved. Our separation allowed me to forgive him our past encounters, and, finally, to admire him for his good sense.

Meanwhile, free of Grossbart, I grew used to my job and my administrative tasks. I stepped on a scale one day, and discovered I had truly become a noncombatant; I had gained seven pounds. I found patience to get past the first three pages of a book. I thought about the future more and more, and wrote letters to girls I'd known before the war. I even got a few answers. I sent away to Columbia for a Law School catalogue. I continued to follow the war in the Pacific, but it was not my war. I thought I could see the end, and sometimes, at night, I dreamed that I was walking on the streets of Manhattan—Broadway, Third Avenue, 116th Street, where I had lived the three years I attended Columbia. I curled myself around these dreams and I began to be happy.

And then, one Saturday, when everybody was away and I was alone in the orderly room reading a month-old copy of the *Sporting News*, Grossbart reappeared.

"You a baseball fan, Sergeant?"

I looked up. "How are you?"

"Fine," Grossbart said. "They're making a soldier out of me."

"How are Fishbein and Halpern?"

"Coming along," he said. "We've got no training this afternoon. They're at the movies."

"How come you're not with them?"

"I wanted to come over and say hello."

He smiled—a shy, regular-guy smile, as though he and I well knew that our friendship drew its sustenance from unexpected visits, remembered birthdays, and borrowed lawnmowers. At first it offended me, and then the feeling was swallowed by the general uneasiness I felt at the thought that everyone on the post was locked away in a dark movie theatre and I was here alone with Grossbart. I folded up my paper.

"Sergeant," he said, "I'd like to ask a favor. It is a favor, and I'm making no bones about it."

He stopped, allowing me to refuse him a hearing—which, of course, forced me into a courtesy I did not intend. "Go ahead."

"Well, actually it's two favors."

I said nothing.

"The first one's about these rumors. Everybody says we're going to the Pacific."

"As I told your friend Fishbein, I don't know," I said. "You'll just have to wait to find out. Like everybody else."

"You think there's a chance of any of us going East?"

"Germany?" I said. "Maybe."

"I meant New York."

"I don't think so, Grossbart. Offhand."

"Thanks for the information, Sergeant," he said.

"It's not information, Grossbart. Just what I surmise."

"It certainly would be good to be near home. My parents—you know." He took a step toward the door and then turned back. "Oh, the other thing. May I ask the other?"

"What is it?"

"The other thing is—I've got relatives in St. Louis, and they say they'll give me a whole Passover dinner if I can get down there. God, Sergeant, that'd mean an awful lot to me."

I stood up. "No passes during basic, Grossbart."

"But we're off from now till Monday morning, Sergeant. I could leave the post and no one would even know."

"I'd know. You'd know."

"But that's all. Just the two of us. Last night, I called my aunt, and you should have heard her. 'Come—come,' she said. 'I got gefilte fish, *chrain*—the works!' Just a day, Sergeant. I'd take the blame if anything happened."

"The Captain isn't here to sign a pass."

"You could sign."

"Look, Grossbart—"

"Sergeant, for two months, practically, I've been eating *trafe* till I want to die."

"I thought you'd made up your mind to live with it. To be minus a little bit of heritage."

He pointed a finger at me. "You!" he said. "That wasn't for you to read."

"I read it. So what?"

"That letter was addressed to a congressman."

"Grossbart, don't feed me any baloney. You *wanted* me to read it."

"Why are you persecuting me, Sergeant?"

"Are you kidding!"

"I've run into this before," he said, "but never from my own!"

"Get out of here, Grossbart! Get the hell out of my sight!"

He did not move. "Ashamed, that's what you are," he said. "So you take it out on the rest of us. They say Hitler himself was half a Jew. Hearing you, I wouldn't doubt it."

"What are you trying to do with me, Grossbart?" I asked him. "What are you after? You want me to give you special privileges, to change the food, to find out about your orders, to give you week-end passes."

"You even talk like a goy!" Grossbart shook his fist. "Is this just a weekend pass I'm asking for? Is a Seder sacred, or not?"

Seder! It suddenly occurred to me that Passover had been celebrated weeks before. I said so.

"That's right," he replied. "Who says no? A month ago—and I was in the field eating hash! And now all I ask is a simple favor. A Jewish boy I thought would understand. My aunt's willing to go out of her way—to make a Seder a month later. . . ." He turned to go, mumbling.

"Come back here!" I called. He stopped and looked at me. "Grossbart, why can't you be like the rest? Why do you have to stick out like a sore thumb?"

"Because I'm a Jew, Sergeant. I *am* different. Better, maybe not. But different."

"This is a war, Grossbart. For the time being *be* the same."

"I refuse."

"What?"

"I refuse. I can't stop being me, that's all there is to it." Tears came to his eyes. "It's a hard thing to be a Jew. But now I understand what Mickey says—it's a harder thing to stay one." He raised a hand sadly toward me. "Look at *you*."

"Stop crying!"

"Stop this, stop that, stop the other thing! *You* stop, Sergeant. Stop closing your heart to your own!" And, wiping his face with his sleeve, he ran out the door. "The least we can do for one another—the least . . ."

An hour later, looking out of the window, I saw Grossbart headed across the field. He wore a pair of starched khakis and carried a little leather ditty bag. I went out into the heat of the day. It was quiet; not a soul was in sight except, over by the mess hall, four K.P.s sitting around a pan, sloped forward from their waists, gabbing and peeling potatoes in the sun.

"Grossbart!" I called.

He looked toward me and continued walking.

"Grossbart, get over here!"

He turned and came across the field. Finally, he stood before me. "Where are you going?" I asked.

"St. Louis. I don't care."

"You'll get caught without a pass."

"So I'll get caught without a pass."

"You'll go to the stockade."

"I'm *in* the stockade." He made an about-face and headed off.

I let him go only a step or two. "Come back here," I said, and he followed me into the office, where I typed out a pass and signed the Captain's name, and my own initials after it.

He took the pass and then, a moment later, reached out and grabbed my hand. "Sergeant, you don't know how much this means to me."

"O.K.," I said. "Don't get in any trouble."

"I wish I could show you how much this means to me."

"Don't do me any favors. Don't write any more congressmen for citations."

He smiled. "You're right. I won't. But let me do something."

"Bring me a piece of that gefilte fish. Just get out of here."

"I will!" he said. "With a slice of carrot and a little horseradish. I won't forget."

"All right. Just show your pass at the gate. And don't tell *any-body*."

"I won't. It's a month late, but a good Yom Tov to you."

"Good Yom Tov, Grossbart," I said.

"You're a good Jew, Sergeant. You like to think you have a hard heart, but underneath you're a fine, decent man. I mean that."

Those last three words touched me more than any words from Grossbart's mouth had the right to. "All right, Grossbart," I said. "Now call me 'sir,' and get the hell out of here."

He ran out the door and was gone. I felt very pleased with myself; it was a great relief to stop fighting Grossbart, and it had cost me nothing. Barrett would never find out, and if he did, I could manage to invent some excuse. For a while, I sat at my desk, comfortable in my decision. Then the screen door flew back and Grossbart burst in again. "Sergeant!" he said. Behind him I saw Fishbein and Halpern, both in starched khakis, both carrying ditty bags like Grossbart's.

"Sergeant, I caught Mickey and Larry coming out of the movies. I almost missed them."

"Grossbart—did I say tell no one?" I said.

"But my aunt said I could bring friends. That I should, in fact."

"*I'm* the Sergeant, Grossbart—not your aunt!"

Grossbart looked at me in disbelief. He pulled Halpern up by his sleeve. "Mickey, tell the Sergeant what this would mean to you."

Halpern looked at me and, shrugging, said, "A lot."

Fishbein stepped forward without prompting. "This would mean a great deal to me and my parents, Sergeant Marx."

"No!" I shouted.

Grossbart was shaking his head. "Sergeant, I could see you denying me, but how you can deny Mickey, a Yeshiva boy—that's beyond me."

"I'm not denying Mickey anything," I said. "You just pushed a little too hard, Grossbart. *You* denied him."

"I'll give him my pass, then," Grossbart said. "I'll give him my aunt's address and a little note. At least let him go."

In a second, he had crammed the pass into Halpern's pants pocket. Halpern looked at me, and so did Fishbein. Grossbart was at the door, pushing it open. "Mickey, bring me a piece of gefilte fish, at least," he said, and then he was outside again.

The three of us looked at one another, and then I said, "Halpern, hand that pass over."

He took it from his pocket and gave it to me. Fishbein had now moved to the doorway, where he lingered. He stood there for a moment with his mouth slightly open, and then he pointed to himself. "And me?" he asked.

His utter ridiculousness exhausted me. I slumped down in my seat and felt pulses knocking at the back of my eyes. "Fishbein," I said, "you understand I'm not trying to deny you anything, don't you? If it was my Army, I'd serve gefilte fish in the mess hall. I'd sell *kugel* in the PX, honest to God."

Halpern smiled.

"You understand, don't you, Halpern?"

"Yes, Sergeant."

"And you, Fishbein? I don't want enemies. I'm just like you—I want to serve my time and go home. I miss the same things you miss."

"Then, Sergeant," Fishbein said, "why don't you come, too?"

"Where?"

"To St. Louis. To Shelly's aunt. We'll have a regular Seder. Play hide-the-matzo." He gave me a broad, black-toothed smile.

I saw Grossbart again, on the other side of the screen.

"Pst!" He waved a piece of paper. "Mickey, here's the address. Tell her I couldn't get away."

Halpern did not move. He looked at me, and I saw the shrug moving up his arms into his shoulders again. I took the cover off my typewriter and made out passes for him and Fishbein. "Go," I said. "The three of you."

I thought Halpern was going to kiss my hand.

That afternoon, in a bar in Joplin, I drank beer and listened with half an ear to the Cardinal game. I tried to look squarely at what I'd become involved in, and began to wonder if perhaps the struggle with Grossbart wasn't as much my fault as his. What was I that I had to *muster* generous feelings? Who was I to have been feeling so grudging, so tight-hearted? After all, I wasn't being asked to move the world. Had I a right, then, or a reason, to clamp down on Grossbart, when that meant clamping down on Halpern, too? And Fishbein—that ugly, agreeable soul? Out of the many recollections of my childhood that had tumbled over me these past few days, I heard my grandmother's voice: "What are you making a *tsimmes?*" It was what she would ask my mother when, say, I had cut myself while doing something I shouldn't have done, and her daughter was busy bawling me out. I needed a hug and a kiss, and my mother would moralize. But my grandmother knew—mercy overrides justice. I should have known it, too. Who was Nathan Marx to be such a penny pincher with kindness? Surely, I thought, the Messiah himself—if He should ever come—won't niggle over nickels and dimes. God willing, he'll hug and kiss.

The next day, while I was playing softball over on the parade ground, I decided to ask Bob Wright, who was noncom in charge of Classification and Assignment, where he thought our trainees would be sent when their cycle ended, in two weeks. I asked casually, between innings, and he said, "They're pushing them all into the Pacific. Shulman cut the orders on your boys the other day."

The news shocked me, as though I were the father of Halpern, Fishbein, and Grossbart.

That night, I was just sliding into sleep when someone tapped on my door. "Who is it?" I asked.

"Sheldon."

He opened the door and came in. For a moment, I felt his presence without being able to see him. "How was it?" I asked.

He popped into sight in the near-darkness before me. "Great, Sergeant." Then he was sitting on the edge of the bed. I sat up.

"How about you?" he asked. "Have a nice weekend?"

"Yes."

"The others went to sleep." He took a deep, paternal breath. We sat silent for a while, and a homey feeling invaded my ugly little cubicle; the door was locked, the cat was out, the children were safely in bed.

"Sergeant, can I tell you something? Personal?"

I did not answer, and he seemed to know why. "Not about me. About Mickey. Sergeant, I never felt for anybody like I feel for him. Last night I heard Mickey in the bed next to me. He was crying so, it could have broken your heart. Real sobs."

"I'm sorry to hear that."

"I had to talk to him to stop him. He held my hand, Sergeant— he wouldn't let it go. He was almost hysterical. He kept saying if he only knew where we were going. Even if he knew it *was* the Pacific, that would be better than nothing. Just to know."

Long ago, someone had taught Grossbart the sad rule that only lies can get the truth. Not that I couldn't believe in the fact of Halpern's crying; his eyes *always* seemed red-rimmed. But, fact or not, it became a lie when Grossbart uttered it. He was entirely strategic. But then—it came with the force of indictment—so was I! There are strategies of aggression, but there are strategies of retreat as well. And so, recognizing that I myself had not been without craft and guile, I told him what I knew. "It is the Pacific."

He let out a small gasp, which was not a lie. "I'll tell him. I wish it was otherwise."

"So do I."

He jumped on my words. "You mean you think you could do something? A change, maybe?"

"No, I couldn't do a thing."

"Don't you know anybody over at C. and A.?"

"Grossbart, there's nothing I can do," I said. "If your orders are for the Pacific, then it's the Pacific."

"But Mickey—"

"Mickey, you, me—everybody, Grossbart. There's nothing to be done. Maybe the war'll end before you go. Pray for a miracle."

"But—"

"Good night, Grossbart." I settled back, and was relieved to feel the springs unbend as Grossbart rose to leave. I could see him clearly now; his jaw had dropped, and he looked like a dazed prizefighter. I noticed for the first time a little paper bag in his hand.

"Grossbart." I smiled. "My gift?"

"Oh, yes, Sergeant. Here—from all of us." He handed me the bag. "It's egg roll."

"Egg roll?" I accepted the bag and felt a damp grease spot on the bottom. I opened it, sure that Grossbart was joking.

"We thought you'd probably like it. You know—Chinese egg roll. We thought you'd probably have a taste for—"

"Your aunt served egg roll?"

"She wasn't home."

"Grossbart, she invited you. You told me she invited you and your friends."

"I know," he said. "I just reread the letter. *Next* week."

I got out of bed and walked to the window. "Grossbart," I said. But I was not calling to him.

"What?"

"What are you, Grossbart? Honest to God, what are you?"

I think it was the first time I'd asked him a question for which he didn't have an immediate answer.

"How can you do this to people?" I went on.

"Sergeant, the day away did us all a world of good. Fishbein, you should see him, he *loves* Chinese food."

"But the Seder," I said.

"We took second best, Sergeant."

Rage came charging at me. I didn't sidestep. "Grossbart, you're a liar!" I said. "You're a schemer and a crook. You've got no respect for anything. Nothing at all. Not for me, for the truth—not even for poor Halpern! You use us all—"

"Sergeant, Sergeant, I feel for Mickey. Honest to God, I do. I *love* Mickey. I try—"

"You try! You feel!" I lurched toward him and grabbed his shirt front. I shook him furiously. "Grossbart, get out! Get out and stay the hell away from me. Because if I see you, I'll make your life miserable. *You understand that?*"

"Yes."

I let him free, and when he walked from the room, I wanted to spit on the floor where he had stood. I couldn't stop the fury. It engulfed me, owned me, till it seemed I could only rid myself of it with tears or an act of violence. I snatched from the bed the bag Grossbart had given me and, with all my strength, threw it out the window. And the next morning, as the men policed the area around the barracks, I heard a great cry go up from one of the trainees, who had been anticipating only his morning handful of cigarette butts and candy wrappers. "Egg roll!" he shouted. "Holy Christ, Chinese goddam egg roll!"

A week later, when I read the orders that had come down from C. and A., I couldn't believe my eyes. Every single trainee was to be shipped to Camp Stoneman, California, and from there to the Pacific—every trainee but one. Private Sheldon Grossbart. He was to be sent to Fort Monmouth, New Jersey. I read the mimeographed sheet several times. Dee, Farrell, Fishbein, Fuselli, Fylypowycz, Glinicki, Gromke, Gucwa, Halpern, Hardy, Helebrandt, right down to Anton Zygadlo—all were to be headed West before the month was out. All except Grossbart. He had pulled a string, and I wasn't it.

I lifted the phone and called C. and A.

The voice on the other end said smartly, "Corporal Shulman, sir."

"Let me speak to Sergeant Wright."

"Who is this calling, sir?"

"Sergeant Marx."

And, to my surprise, the voice said, *"Oh!"* Then, "Just a minute, Sergeant."

Shulman's *"Oh!"* stayed with me while I waited for Wright to come to the phone. Why *"Oh!"*? Who was Shulman? And then, so simply, I knew I'd discovered the string that Grossbart had pulled. In fact, I could hear Grossbart the day he'd discovered Shulman in the PX, or in the bowling alley, or maybe even at services. "Glad to meet you. Where you from? Bronx? Me, too. Do you know So-and-So? And So-and-So? Me, too! You work at C. and A.? Really? Hey, how's chances of getting East? Could you do something? Change something? Swindle, cheat, lie? We gotta help each other, you know. If the Jews in Germany . . ."

Bob Wright answered the phone. "How are you, Nate? How's the pitching arm?"

"Good. Bob, I wonder if you could do me a favor." I heard clearly my own words, and they so reminded me of Grossbart that I dropped more easily than I could have imagined into what I had planned. "This may sound crazy, Bob, but I got a kid here on orders to Monmouth who wants them changed. He had a brother killed in Europe, and he's hot to go to the Pacific. Says he'd feel like a coward if he wound up Stateside. I don't know, Bob—can anything be done? Put somebody else in the Monmouth slot?"

"Who?" he asked cagily.

"Anybody. First guy in the alphabet. I don't care. The kid just asked if something could be done."

"What's his name?"

"Grossbart, Sheldon."

Wright didn't answer.

"Yeah," I said. "He's a Jewish kid, so he thought I could help him out. You know."

"I guess I can do something," he finally said. "The Major hasn't been around here for weeks. Temporary duty to the golf course. I'll try, Nate, that's all I can say."

"I'd appreciate it, Bob. See you Sunday." And I hung up, perspiring.

The following day, the corrected orders appeared: Fishbein, Fuselli, Fylypowycz, Glinicki, Gromke, Grossbart, Gucwa, Halpern, Hardy . . . Lucky Private Harley Alton was to go to Fort Monmouth, New Jersey, where, for some reason or other, they wanted an enlisted man with infantry training.

After chow that night, I stopped back at the orderly room to straighten out the guard-duty roster. Grossbart was waiting for me. He spoke first.

"You son of a bitch!"

I sat down at my desk, and while he glared at me, I began to make the necessary alterations in the duty roster.

"What do you have against me?" he cried. "Against my family? Would it kill you for me to be near my father, God knows how many months he has left to him?"

"Why so?"

"His heart," Grossbart said. "He hasn't had enough troubles in a lifetime, you've got to add to them. I curse the day I ever met you, Marx! Shulman told me what happened over there. There's no limit to your anti-Semitism, is there? The damage you've done here isn't enough. You have to make a special phone call! You really want me dead!"

I made the last few notations in the duty roster and got up to leave. "Good night, Grossbart."

"You owe me an explanation!" He stood in my path.

"Sheldon, you're the one who owes explanations."

He scowled. "To *you?*"

"To me, I think so—yes. Mostly to Fishbein and Halpern."

"That's right, twist things around. I owe nobody nothing, I've done all I could do for them. Now I think I've got the right to watch out for myself."

"For each other we have to learn to watch out, Sheldon. You told me yourself."

"You call this watching out for me—what you did?"

"No. For all of us."

I pushed him aside and started for the door. I heard his furious breathing behind me, and it sounded like steam rushing from an engine of terrible strength.

"You'll be all right," I said from the door. And, I thought, so would Fishbein and Halpern be all right, even in the Pacific, if only Grossbart continued to see—in the obsequiousness of the one, the soft spirituality of the other—some profit for himself.

I stood outside the orderly room, and I heard Grossbart weeping behind me. Over in the barracks, in the lighted windows, I could see the boys in their T shirts sitting on their bunks talking about their orders, as they'd been doing for the past two days. With a kind of quiet nervousness, they polished shoes, shined belt buckles, squared away underwear, trying as best they could to accept their fate. Behind me, Grossbart swallowed hard, accepting his. And then, resisting with all my will an impulse to turn and seek pardon for my vindictiveness, I accepted my own.

IN THE VILLAGE

❖

Elizabeth Bishop

A SCREAM, the echo of a scream, hangs over that Nova Scotian village. No one hears it; it hangs there forever, a slight stain in those pure blue skies, skies that travellers compare to those of Switzerland, too dark, too blue, so that they seem to keep on darkening a little more around the horizon—or is it around the rims of the eyes?—the color of the cloud of bloom on the elm trees, the violet on the fields of oats; something darkening over the woods and waters as well as the sky. The scream hangs like that, unheard, in memory—in the past, in the present, and those years between. It was not even loud to begin with, perhaps. It just came there to live, forever—not loud, just alive forever. Its pitch would be the pitch of my village. Flick the lightning rod on top of the church steeple with your fingernail and you will hear it.

She stood in the large front bedroom with sloping walls on either side, papered in wide white and dim-gold stripes. Later, it was she who gave the scream.

The village dressmaker was fitting a new dress. It was her first in almost two years and she had decided to come out of black, so the dress was purple. She was very thin. She wasn't at all sure whether she was going to like the dress or not and she kept lifting the folds of the skirt, still unpinned and dragging on the floor around her, in her thin white hands, and looking down at the cloth.

"Is it a good shade for me? Is it too bright? I don't know. I haven't worn colors for so long now. . . . How long? Should it be black? Do you think I should keep on wearing black?"

Drummers sometimes came around selling gilded red or green books, unlovely books, filled with bright new illustrations of the Bible stories. The people in the pictures wore clothes like the purple dress, or like the way it looked then.

It was a hot summer afternoon. Her mother and her two sisters were there. The older sister had brought her home, from Boston, not long before, and was staying on, to help. Because in Boston she had not got any better, in months and months—or had it been a year? In spite of the doctors, in spite of the frightening expenses, she had not got any better.

First, she had come home, with her child. Then she had gone away again, alone, and left the child. Then she had come home. Then she had gone away again, with her sister; and now she was home again.

Unaccustomed to having her back, the child stood now in the doorway, watching. The dressmaker was crawling around and around on her knees eating pins as Nebuchadnezzar had crawled eating grass. The wallpaper glinted and the elm trees outside hung heavy and green, and the straw matting smelled like the ghost of hay.

Clang.

Clang.

Oh, beautiful sounds, from the blacksmith's shop at the end of the garden! Its gray roof, with patches of moss, could be seen above the lilac bushes. Nate was there—Nate, wearing a long black leather apron over his trousers and bare chest, sweating hard, a black leather cap on top of dry, thick, black-and-gray curls, a black sooty face; iron filings, whiskers, and gold teeth, all together, and a smell of red-hot metal and horses' hoofs.

Clang.

The pure note: pure and angelic.

The dress was all wrong. She screamed.

The child vanishes.

Later they sit, the mother and the three sisters, in the shade on the back porch, sipping sour, diluted ruby: raspberry vinegar. The dressmaker refuses to join them and leaves, holding the dress to her heart. The child is visiting the blacksmith.

In the blacksmith's shop things hang up in the shadows and shadows hang up in the things, and there are black and glistening piles of dust in each corner. A tub of night-black water stands by the forge. The horseshoes sail through the dark like bloody little moons and follow each other like bloody little moons to drown in the black water, hissing, protesting.

Outside, along the matted eaves, painstakingly, sweetly, wasps go over and over a honeysuckle vine.

Inside, the bellows creak. Nate does wonders with both hands;

with one hand. The attendant horse stamps his foot and nods his
head as if agreeing to a peace treaty.

Nod.

And nod.

A Newfoundland dog looks up at him and they almost touch
noses, but not quite, because at the last moment the horse decides
against it and turns away.

Outside in the grass lie scattered big, pale granite discs, like millstones, for making wheel rims on. This afternoon they are too hot
to touch.

Now it is settling down, the scream.

Now the dressmaker is at home, basting, but in tears. It is the
most beautiful material she has worked on in years. It has been
sent to the woman from Boston, a present from her mother-in-law,
and heaven knows how much it cost.

Before my older aunt had brought her back, I had watched my
grandmother and younger aunt unpacking her clothes, her "things."
In trunks and barrels and boxes they had finally come, from Boston,
where she and I had once lived. So many things in the village came
from Boston, and even I had once come from there. But I remembered only being here, with my grandmother.

The clothes were black, or white, or black-and-white.

"Here's a mourning hat," says my grandmother, holding up
something large, sheer, and black, with large black roses on it; at
least I guess they are roses, even if black.

"There's that mourning coat she got the first winter," says my
aunt.

But always I think they are saying "morning." Why, in the morning, did one put on black? How early in the morning did one begin?
Before the sun came up?

"Oh, here are some house dresses!"

They are nicer. Clean and starched, stiffly folded. One with black
polka dots. One of fine black-and-white stripes with black grosgrain
bows. A third with a black velvet bow and on the bow a pin of
pearls in a little wreath.

"Look. She forgot to take it off."

A white hat. A white embroidered parasol. Black shoes with
buckles glistening like the dust in the blacksmith's shop. A silver
mesh bag. A silver calling-card case on a little chain. Another bag
of silver mesh, gathered to a tight, round neck of strips of silver

that will open out, like the hatrack in the front hall. A silver-framed photograph, quickly turned over. Handkerchiefs with narrow black hems—"morning handkerchiefs." In bright sunlight, over breakfast tables, they flutter.

A bottle of perfume has leaked and made awful brown stains.

Oh, marvellous scent, from somewhere else! It doesn't smell like that here; but there, somewhere, it does, still.

A big bundle of postcards. The curdled elastic around them breaks. I gather them together on the floor.

Some people wrote with pale-blue ink, and some with brown, and some with black, but mostly blue. The stamps have been torn off many of them. Some are plain, or photographs, but some have lines of metallic crystals on them—how beautiful!—silver, gold, red, and green, or all four mixed together, crumbling off, sticking in the lines on my palms. All the cards like this I spread on the floor to study. The crystals outline the buildings on the cards in a way buildings never are outlined but should be—if there were a way of making the crystals stick. But probably not; they would fall to the ground, never to be seen again. Some cards, instead of lines around the buildings, have words written in their skies with the same stuff, crumbling, dazzling and crumbling, raining down a little on little people who sometimes stand about below: pictures of Pentecost? What are the messages? I cannot tell, but they are falling on those specks of hands, on the hats, on the toes of their shoes, in their paths —wherever it is they are.

Postcards come from another world, the world of the grandparents who send things, the world of sad brown perfume, and morning. (The gray postcards of the village for sale in the village store are so unilluminating that they scarcely count. After all, one steps outside and immediately sees the same thing: the village, where we live, full size, and in color.)

Two barrels of china. White with a gold band. Broken bits. A thick white teacup with a small red-and-blue butterfly on it, painfully desirable. A teacup with little pale-blue windows in it.

"See the grains of rice?" says my grandmother, showing me the cup against the light.

Could you poke the grains out? No, it seems they aren't really there any more. They were put there just for a while and then they left something or other behind. What odd things people do with grains of rice, so innocent and small! My aunt says that she has heard they write the Lord's Prayer on them. And make them make those little pale-blue lights.

More broken china. My grandmother says it breaks her heart. "Why couldn't they have got it packed better? Heaven knows what it cost."

"Where'll we put it all? The china closet isn't nearly big enough."

"It'll just have to stay in the barrels."

"Mother, you might as well use it."

"*No,*" says my grandmother.

"Where's the silver, Mother?"

"In the vault in Boston."

Vault. Awful word. I run the tip of my finger over the rough, jewelled lines on the postcards, over and over. They hold things up to each other and exclaim, and talk, and exclaim, over and over.

"There's that cake basket."

"Mrs. Miles . . ."

"Mrs. Miles' spongecake . . ."

"She was very fond of her."

Another photograph—"Oh, that *Negro* girl! That friend."

"She went to be a medical missionary. She had a letter from her, last winter. From Africa."

"They were great friends."

They show me the picture. She, too, is black-and-white, with glasses on a chain. A morning friend.

And the smell, the wonderful smell of the dark-brown stains. Is it roses?

A tablecloth.

"She did beautiful work," says my grandmother.

"But look—it isn't finished."

Two pale, smooth wooden hoops are pressed together in the linen. There is a case of little ivory embroidery tools.

I abscond with a little ivory stick with a sharp point. To keep it forever I bury it under the bleeding heart by the crab-apple tree, but it is never found again.

Nate sings and pumps the bellows with one hand. I try to help, but he really does it all, from behind me, and laughs when the coals blow red and wild.

"Make me a ring! Make me a ring, Nate!"

Instantly it is made; it is mine.

It is too big and still hot, and blue and shiny. The horseshoe nail has a flat oblong head, pressing hot against my knuckle.

Two men stand watching, chewing or spitting tobacco, matches, horseshoe nails—anything, apparently, but with such presence; they are perfectly at home. The horse is the real guest, however. His harness hangs loose like a man's suspenders; they say pleasant things to him; one of his legs is doubled up in an improbable, affectedly polite way, and the bottom of his hoof is laid bare, but he doesn't seem to mind. Manure piles up behind him, suddenly, neatly. He, too, is very much at home. He is enormous. His rump is like a brown, glossy globe of the whole brown world. His ears are secret entrances to the underworld. His nose is supposed to feel like velvet and does, with ink spots under milk all over its pink. Clear bright-green bits of stiffened froth, like glass, are stuck around his mouth. He wears medals on his chest, too, and one on his forehead, and simpler decorations—red and blue celluloid rings overlapping each other on leather straps. On each temple is a clear glass bulge, like an eyeball, but in them are the heads of two other little horses (his dreams?), brightly colored, real and raised, untouchable, alas, against backgrounds of silver blue. His trophies hang around him, and the cloud of his odor is a chariot in itself.

At the end, all four feet are brushed with tar, and shine, and he expresses his satisfaction, rolling it from his nostrils like noisy smoke, as he backs into the shafts of his wagon.

The purple dress is to be fitted again this afternoon but I take a note to Miss Gurley to say the fitting will have to be postponed. Miss Gurley seems upset.

"Oh dear. And how is—" And she breaks off.

Her house is littered with scraps of cloth and tissue-paper patterns, yellow, pinked, with holes in the shapes of A, B, C, and D in them, and numbers; and threads everywhere like a fine vegetation. She has a bosom full of needles with threads ready to pull out and make nests with. She sleeps in her thimble. A gray kitten once lay on the treadle of her sewing machine, where she rocked it as she sewed, like a baby in a cradle, but it got hanged on the belt. Or did she make that up? But another gray-and-white one lies now by the arm of the machine, in imminent danger of being sewn into a turban. There is a table covered with laces and braids, embroidery silks, and cards of buttons of all colors—big ones for winter coats, small pearls, little glass ones delicious to suck.

She has made the very dress I have on, "for twenty-five cents." My grandmother said my other grandmother would certainly be surprised at that.

The purple stuff lies on a table; long white threads hang all about it. Oh, look away before it moves by itself, or makes a sound; before it echoes, echoes, what it has heard!

Mysteriously enough, poor Miss Gurley—I know she is poor—gives me a ten-cent piece. She leans over and drops it in the pocket of the red-and-white dress that she has made herself. It is very tiny, very shiny. King George's beard is like a little silver flame. Because they look like herring- or maybe salmon-scales, ten-cent pieces are called "fish-scales." One heard of people's rings being found inside fish, or their long-lost jackknives. What if one could scrape a salmon and find a little picture of King George on every scale?

I put my ten-cent piece in my mouth for greater safety on the way home, and swallow it. Months later, as far as I know, it is still in me, transmuting all its precious metal into my growing teeth and hair.

Back home, I am not allowed to go upstairs. I hear my aunts running back and forth and something like a tin washbasin falls bump in the carpeted upstairs hall.

My grandmother is sitting in the kitchen stirring potato mash for tomorrow's bread and crying into it. She gives me a spoonful and it tastes wonderful but wrong. In it I think I taste my grandmother's tears; then I kiss her and taste them on her cheek.

She says it is time for her to get fixed up, and I say I want to help her brush her hair. So I do, standing swaying on the lower rung of the back of her rocking chair.

The rocking chair has been painted and repainted so many times that it is as smooth as cream—blue, white, and gray all showing through. My grandmother's hair is silver and in it she keeps a great many celluloid combs, at the back and sides, streaked gray and silver to match. The one at the back has longer teeth than the others and a row of sunken silver dots across the top, beneath a row of little balls. I pretend to play a tune on it; then I pretend to play a tune on each of the others before we stick them in, so my grandmother's hair is full of music. She laughs. I am so pleased with myself that I do not feel obliged to mention the ten-cent piece. I drink a rusty, icy drink out of the biggest dipper; still, nothing much happens.

We are waiting for a scream. But it is not screamed again, and the red sun sets in silence.

Every morning I take the cow to the pasture we rent from Mr. Chisolm. She, Nelly, could probably go by herself just as well, but I like marching through the village with a big stick, directing her.

This morning it is brilliant and cool. My grandmother and I are alone again in the kitchen. We are talking. She says it is cool enough to keep the oven going, to bake the bread, to roast a leg of lamb.

"Will you remember to go down to the brook? Take Nelly around by the brook and pick me a big bunch of mint. I thought I'd make some mint sauce."

"For the leg of lamb?"

"You finish your porridge."

"I think I've had enough now . . ."

"Hurry up and finish that porridge."

There is talking on the stairs.

"No, now wait," my grandmother says to me. "Wait a minute."

My two aunts come into the kitchen. She is with them, wearing the white cotton dress with black polka dots and the flat black velvet bow at the neck. She comes and feeds me the rest of the porridge herself, smiling at me.

"Stand up now and let's see how tall you are," she tells me.

"Almost to your elbow," they say. "See how much she's grown."

"Almost."

"It's her hair."

Hands are on my head, pushing me down; I slide out from under them. Nelly is waiting for me in the yard, holding her nose just under in the watering trough. My stick waits against the door frame, clad in bark.

Nelly looks up at me, drooling glass strings. She starts off around the corner of the house without a flicker of expression.

Switch. Switch. How annoying she is!

But she is a Jersey and we think she is very pretty. "From in front," my aunts sometimes add.

She stops to snatch at the long, untrimmed grass around the gatepost.

"Nelly!"

Whack! I hit her hipbone.

On she goes without even looking around. Flop, flop, down over

the dirt sidewalk into the road, across the village green in front of
the Presbyterian church. The grass is gray with dew; the church is
dazzling. It is high-shouldered and secretive; it leans backwards a
little.

Ahead, the road is lined with dark, thin old elms; grass grows
long and blue in the ditches. Behind the elms the meadows run
along, peacefully, greenly.

We pass Mrs. Peppard's house. We pass Mrs. McNeil's house.
We pass Mrs. Geddes's house. We pass Hills' store.

The store is high, and a faded gray-blue, with tall windows, built
on a long, high stoop of gray-blue cement with an iron hitching
rail along it. Today, in one window there are big cardboard easels,
shaped like houses—complete houses and houses with the roofs
lifted off to show glimpses of the rooms inside, all in different colors
—with cans of paint in pyramids in the middle. But they are an old
story. In the other window is something new: shoes, single shoes,
summer shoes, each sitting on top of its own box with its mate
beneath it, inside, in the dark. Surprisingly, some of them appear
to be exactly the colors and texture of pink and blue blackboard
chalks, but I can't stop to examine them now. In one door, great
overalls hang high in the air on hangers. Miss Ruth Hill looks out
the other door and waves. We pass Mrs. Captain Mahon's house.

Nelly tenses and starts walking faster, making over to the right.
Every morning and evening we go through this. We are approaching
Miss Spencer's house. Miss Spencer is the milliner the way Miss
Gurley is the dressmaker. She has a very small white house with the
doorstep right on the sidewalk. One front window has lace curtains
with a pale-yellow window shade pulled all the way down, inside
them; the other one has a shelf across it on which are displayed four
summer hats. Out of the corner of my eye I can see that there is a
yellow chip straw with little wads of flamingo-colored feathers
around the crown, but again there is no time to examine anything.

On each side of Miss Spencer's door is a large old lilac bush.
Every time we go by Nelly determines to brush off all her flies on
these bushes—brush them off forever, in one fell swoop. Then Miss
Spencer is apt to come to the door and stand there, shaking with
anger, between the two bushes still shaking from Nelly's careening
passage, and yell at me, sometimes waving a hat in my direction as
well.

Nelly, leaning to the right, breaks into a cow trot. I run up with
my stick.

Whack!

"Nelly!"

Whack!

Just this once she gives in and we rush safely by.

Then begins a long, pleasant stretch beneath the elms. The Presbyterian manse has a black iron fence with openwork four-sided pillars, like tall, thin bird cages, bird cages for storks. Dr. Gillespie, the minister, appears just as we come along, and rides slowly toward us on his bicycle.

"Good day." He even tips his hat.

"Good day."

He wears the most interesting hat in the village: a man's regular stiff straw sailor, only it is black. Is there a possibility that he paints it at home, with something like stove polish? Because once I had seen one of my aunts painting a straw-colored hat navy blue.

Nelly, oblivious, makes cow flops. Smack. Smack. Smack. Smack.

It is fascinating. I cannot take my eyes off her. Then I step around them: fine dark-green and lacy and watery at the edges.

We pass the McLeans', whom I know very well. Mr. McLean is just coming out of his new barn with the tin hip roof and with him is Jock, their old shepherd dog, long-haired, black and white and yellow. He runs up barking deep, cracked, soft barks in the quiet morning. I hesitate.

Mr. McLean bellows, "Jock! You! Come back here! Are you trying to frighten her?"

To me he says, "He's twice as old as you are."

Finally I pat the big round warm head.

We talk a little. I ask the exact number of Jock's years but Mr. McLean has forgotten.

"He hasn't hardly a tooth in his head and he's got rheumatism. I hope we'll get him through next winter. He still wants to go to the woods with me and it's hard for him in the snow. We'll be lost without him."

Mr. McLean speaks to me behind one hand, not to hurt Jock's feelings: *"Deaf as a post."*

Like anybody deaf, Jock puts his head to one side.

"He used to be the best dog at finding cows for miles around. People used to come from away down the shore to borrow him to find their cows for them. And he'd always find them. The first year we had to leave him behind when we went up to the mountain to

get the cows I thought it would kill him. Well, when his teeth
started going he couldn't do much with the cows any more. Effie
used to say, 'I don't know how we'd run the farm without him.'"

Loaded down with too much black and yellow and white fur,
Jock smiles, showing how few teeth he has. He has yellow cater-
pillars for eyebrows.

Nelly has gone on ahead. She is almost up the hill to Chisolms'
when I catch up with her. We turn in to their steep, long drive,
through a steep, bare yard crowded with unhappy apple trees. From
the top, though, from the Chisolms' back yard, one always stops to
look at the view.

There are the tops of all the elm trees in the village and there,
beyond them, the long green marshes, so fresh, so salt. Then the
Minas Basin, with the tide halfway in or out, the wet red mud glazed
with sky blue until it meets the creeping lavender-red water. In the
middle of the view, like one hand of a clock pointing straight up,
is the steeple of the Presbyterian church. We are in the "Maritimes"
but all that means is that we live by the sea.

Mrs. Chisolm's pale frantic face is watching me out the kitchen
window as she washes the breakfast dishes. We wave, but I hurry
by because she may come out and ask questions. But her questions
are not as bad perhaps as those of her husband, Mr. Chisolm, who
wears a beard. One evening he had met me in the pasture and asked
me how my soul was. Then he held me firmly by both hands while
he said a prayer, with his head bowed, Nelly right beside us chewing
her cud all the time. I had felt a soul, heavy in my chest, all the way
home.

I let Nelly through the set of bars to the pasture where the brook
is, to get the mint. We both take drinks and I pick a big bunch of
mint, eating a little, scratchy and powerful. Nelly looks over her
shoulder and comes back to try it, thinking, as cows do, it might be
something especially for her. Her face is close to mine and I hold
her by one horn to admire her eyes again. Her nose is blue and as
shiny as something in the rain. At such close quarters my feelings
for her are mixed. She gives my bare arm a lick, scratchy and powerful, too, almost upsetting me into the brook; then she goes off to
join a black-and-white friend she has here, mooing to her to wait
until she catches up.

For a while I entertain the idea of not going home today at all,
of staying safely here in the pasture all day, playing in the brook

and climbing on the squishy, moss-covered hummocks in the swampy part. But an immense, sibilant, glistening loneliness suddenly faces me, and the cows are moving off to the shade of the fir trees, their bells chiming softly, individually.

On the way home there are the four hats in Miss Spencer's window to study, and the summer shoes in Hills'. There is the same shoe in white, in black patent leather, and in the chalky, sugary, unearthly pinks and blues. It has straps that button around the ankle and above, four of them, about an inch wide and an inch apart, reaching away up.

In those unlovely gilded red and green books, filled with illustrations of the Bible stories, the Roman centurions wear them, too, or something very like them.

Surely they are my size. Surely, this summer, pink or blue, my grandmother will buy me a pair!

Miss Ruth Hill gives me a Moirs' chocolate out of the glass case. She talks to me: "How is she? We've always been friends. We played together from the time we were babies. We sat together in school. Right from primer class on. After she went away, she always wrote to me—even after she got sick the first time."

Then she tells a funny story about when they were little.

That afternoon, Miss Gurley comes and we go upstairs to watch the purple dress being fitted again. My grandmother holds me against her knees. My younger aunt is helping Miss Gurley, handing her the scissors when she asks. Miss Gurley is cheerful and talkative today.

The dress is smaller now; there are narrow, even folds down the skirt; the sleeves fit tightly, with little wrinkles over the thin white hands. Everyone is very pleased with it; everyone talks and laughs.

"There. You see? It's so becoming."

"I've never seen you in anything more becoming."

"And it's so nice to see you in color for a change."

And the purple is real, like a flower against the gold-and-white wallpaper.

On the bureau is a present that has just come, from an uncle in Boston whom I do not remember. It is a gleaming little bundle of flat, triangular satin pillows—sachets, tied together with a white satin ribbon, with an imitation rosebud on top of the bow. Each is a different faint color; if you take them apart, each has a different faint scent. But tied together the way they came, they make one confused, powdery one.

The mirror has been lifted off the bureau and put on the floor against the wall.

She walks slowly up and down and looks at the skirt in it.

"I think that's about right," says Miss Gurley, down on her knees and looking into the mirror, too, but as if the skirt were miles and miles away.

But, twitching the purple skirt with her thin white hands, she says desperately, "I don't know what they're wearing any more. I have no *idea!*" It turns to a sort of wail.

"Now, now," soothes Miss Gurley. "I do think that's about right. Don't you?" She appeals to my grandmother and me.

Light, musical, constant sounds are coming from Nate's shop. It sounds as though he were making a wheel rim.

She sees me in the mirror and turns on me: "Stop sucking your thumb!"

Then in a moment she turns to me again and demands, "Do you know what I want?"

"No."

"I want some humbugs. I'm dying for some humbugs. I don't think I've had any humbugs for years and years and years. If I give you some pennies, will you go to Mealy's and buy me a bag?"

To be sent on an errand! Everything is all right.

Humbugs are a kind of candy, although not a kind I am particularly fond of. They are brown, like brook water, but hard, and shaped like little twisted pillows. They last a long time, but lack the spit-producing brilliance of cherry or strawberry.

Mealy runs a little shop where she sells candy and bananas and oranges and all kinds of things she crochets. At Christmas, she sells toys, but only at Christmas. Her real name is Amelia. She also takes care of the telephone switchboard for the village, in her dining room.

Somebody finds a black pocketbook in the bureau. She counts out five big pennies into my hand, in a column, then one more.

"That one's for you. So you won't eat up all my humbugs on the way home."

Further instructions:

"Don't run all the way."

"Don't stop on the bridge."

I do run, by Nate's shop, glimpsing him inside, pumping away with one hand. We wave. The beautiful, big Newfoundland dog is there again and comes out, bounding along with me a ways.

I do not stop on the bridge but slow down long enough to find out the years on the pennies. King George is much bigger than on a ten-cent piece, brown as an Indian in copper, but he wears the same clothes; on a penny, one can make out the little ermine trimmings on his coat.

Mealy has a bell that rings when you go in so that she'll hear you if she's at the switchboard. The shop is a step down, dark, with a counter along one side. The ceiling is low and the floor has settled well over to the counter side. Mealy is broad and fat and it looks as though she and the counter and the showcase, stuffed dimly with things every which way, were settling down together out of sight.

Five pennies buys a great many humbugs. I must not take too long to decide what I want for myself. I must get back quickly, quickly, while Miss Gurley is there and everyone is upstairs and the dress is still on. Without taking time to think, quickly I point at the brightest thing. It is a ball, glistening solidly with crystals of pink and yellow sugar, hung, impractically, on an elastic, like a real elastic ball. I know I don't even care for the inside of it, which is soft, but I wind most of the elastic around my arm, to keep the ball off the ground, at least, and start hopefully back.

But one night, in the middle of the night, there is a fire. The church bell wakes me up. It is in the room with me; red flames are burning the wallpaper beside the bed. I suppose I shriek.

The door opens. My younger aunt comes in. There is a lamp lit in the hall and everyone is talking at once.

"Don't cry!" my aunt almost shouts at me. "It's just a fire. Way up the road. It isn't going to hurt you. Don't *cry!*"

"Will! Will!" My grandmother is calling my grandfather. "Do you have to go?"

"No, don't go, Dad!"

"It looks like McLean's place." My grandfather sounds muffled.

"Oh, not their new barn!" My grandmother.

"You can't tell from here." He must have his head out the window.

"*She's* calling for you, Mother." My older aunt. "I'll go."

"No, *I'll* go." My younger aunt.

"Light that other lamp, girl."

My older aunt comes to my door. "It's way off. It's nowhere near us. The men will take care of it. Now you go to sleep." But she leaves my door open.

"Leave her door open," calls my grandmother just then. "Oh, why do they have to ring that bell like that? It's enough to terrify anybody. Will, be *careful.*"

Sitting up in bed, I see my grandfather starting down the stairs, tucking his nightshirt into his trousers as he goes.

"Don't make so much noise!" My older aunt and my grandmother seem to be quarrelling.

"Noise! I can't hear myself think, with that bell!"

"I bet Spurgeon's ringing it!" They both laugh.

"It must have been heat lightning," says my grandmother, now apparently in her bedroom, as if it were all over.

"*She's* all right, Mother." My younger aunt comes back. "I don't think she's scared. You can't see the glare so much on that side of the house."

Then my younger aunt comes into my room and gets in bed with me. She says to go to sleep, it's way up the road. The men have to go; my grandfather has gone. It's probably somebody's barn full of hay, from heat lightning. It's been such a hot summer there's been a lot of it. The church bell stops and her voice is suddenly loud in my ear over my shoulder. The last echo of the bell lasts for a long time.

Wagons rattle by.

"Now they're going down to the river to fill the barrels," my aunt is murmuring against my back.

The red flame dies down on the wall, then flares again.

Wagons rattle by in the dark. Men are swearing at the horses.

"Now they're coming back with the water. Go to sleep."

More wagons; men's voices. I suppose I go to sleep.

I wake up and it is the same night, the night of the fire. My aunt is getting out of bed, hurrying away. It is still dark and silent now, after the fire. No, not silent; my grandmother is crying somewhere, not in her room. It is getting gray. I hear one wagon, rumbling far off, perhaps crossing the bridge.

But now I am caught in a skein of voices, my aunts' and my grandmother's, saying the same things over and over, sometimes loudly, sometimes in whispers:

"Hurry. For heaven's sake, *shut the door!*"

"Sh!"

"Oh, we can't go on like this, we . . ."

"It's too dangerous. Remember that . . ."

"Sh! Don't let her . . ."

A door slams.

A door opens. The voices begin again.

I am struggling to free myself.

Wait. Wait. No one is going to scream.

Slowly, slowly it gets daylight. A different red reddens the wallpaper. Now the house is silent. I get up and dress by myself and go downstairs. My grandfather is in the kitchen alone, drinking his tea. He has made the oatmeal himself, too. He gives me some and tells me about the fire very cheerfully.

It had not been the McLeans' new barn after all, but someone else's barn, off the road. All the hay was lost but they had managed somehow to save part of the barn.

But neither of us is really listening to what he is saying; we are listening for sounds from upstairs. But everything is quiet.

On the way home from taking Nelly to the pasture I go to see where the barn was. There are people still standing around, some of them the men who got up in the night to go to the river. Everyone seems quite cheerful there, too, but the smell of burned hay is awful, sickening.

Now the front bedroom is empty. My older aunt has gone back to Boston and my other aunt is making plans to go there after a while, too.

There has been a new pig. He was very cute to begin with, and skidded across the kitchen linoleum while everyone laughed. He grew and grew. Perhaps it is all the same summer, because it is unusually hot and something unusual for a pig happens to him; he gets sunburned. He really gets sunburned, bright pink, but the strangest thing of all, the curled-up end of his tail gets so sunburned it is brown and scorched. My grandmother trims it with the scissors and it doesn't hurt him.

Sometime later this pig is butchered. My grandmother, my aunt, and I shut ourselves in the parlor. My aunt plays a piece on the piano called "Out in the Fields." She plays it and plays it; then she switches to Mendelssohn's "War March of the Priests."

The front room is empty. Nobody sleeps there. Clothes are hung there.

Every week my grandmother sends off a package. In it she puts cake and fruit, a jar of preserves, Moirs' chocolates.

Monday afternoon every week.

Fruit, cake, Jordan almonds, a handkerchief with a tatted edge.

Fruit. Cake. Wild-strawberry jam. A New Testament.

A little bottle of scent from Hills' store, with a purple silk tassel fastened to the stopper.

Fruit. Cake. "Selections from Tennyson."

A calendar, with a quotation from Longfellow for every day.

Fruit. Cake. Moirs' chocolates.

I watch her pack them in the pantry. Sometimes she sends me to the store to get things at the last minute.

The address of the sanitarium is in my grandmother's handwriting, in purple indelible pencil, on smoothed-out wrapping paper. It will never come off.

I take the package to the post office. Going by Nate's, I walk far out in the road and hold the package on the side away from him.

He calls to me. "Come here! I want to show you something."

But I pretend I don't hear him. But at any other time I still go there just the same.

The post office is very small. It sits on the side of the road like a package once delivered by the post office. The government has painted its clapboards tan, with a red trim. The earth in front of it is worn hard. Its face is scarred and scribbled on, carved with initials. In the evening, when the Canadian Pacific mail is due, a row of big boys leans against it, but in the daytime there is nothing to be afraid of. There is no one in front, and inside it is empty. There is no one except the postmaster, Mr. Johnson, to look at my grandmother's purple handwriting.

The post office tilts a little, like Mealy's shop, and inside it looks as chewed as a horse's manger. Mr. Johnson looks out through the little window in the middle of the bank of glass-fronted boxes, like an animal looking out over its manger. But he is dignified by the thick, bevelled-edged glass boxes with their solemn, upright gold-and-black-shaded numbers.

Ours is 21. Although there is nothing in it, Mr. Johnson automatically cocks his eye at it from behind when he sees me.

21.

"Well, well. Here we are again. Good day, good day," he says.

"Good day, Mr. Johnson."

I have to go outside again to hand him the package through the ordinary window, into his part of the post office, because it is too big for the little official one. He is very old, and nice. He has two fingers missing on his right hand where they were caught in a threshing machine. He wears a navy-blue cap with a black leather visor, like a ship's officer, and a shirt with feathery brown stripes, and a big gold collar button.

"Let me see. Let me see. Let me see. Hm," he says to himself, weighing the package on the scales, jiggling the bar with the two remaining fingers and thumb.

"Yes. Yes. Your grandmother is very faithful."

Every Monday afternoon I go past the blacksmith's shop with the package under my arm, hiding the address of the sanitarium with my arm and my other hand.

Going over the bridge, I stop and stare down into the river. All the little trout that have been too smart to get caught—for how long now?—are there, rushing in flank movements, foolish assaults and retreats, against and away from the old sunken fender of Malcolm McNeil's Ford. It has lain there for ages and is supposed to be a disgrace to us all. So are the tin cans that glint there, brown and gold.

From above, the trout look as transparent as the water, but if one did catch one, it would be opaque enough, with a little slick moon-white belly with a pair of tiny, pleated, rose-pink fins on it. The leaning willows soak their narrow yellowed leaves.

Clang.

Clang.

Nate is shaping a horseshoe.

Oh, beautiful pure sound!

It turns everything else to silence.

But still, once in a while, the river gives an unexpected gurgle. "*Slp*," it says, out of glassy-ridged brown knots sliding along the surface.

Clang.

And everything except the river holds its breath.

Now there is no scream. Once there was one and it settled slowly down to earth one hot summer afternoon; or did it float up, into that dark, too dark, blue sky? But surely it has gone away, forever.

Clang.

It sounds like a bell buoy out at sea.

It is the elements speaking: earth, air, fire, water.

All those other things—clothes, crumbling postcards, broken china; things damaged and lost, sickened or destroyed; even the frail almost-lost scream—are they too frail for us to hear their voices long, too mortal?

Nate!

Oh, beautiful sound, strike again!

A FATHER-TO-BE

❖

SAUL BELLOW

THE strangest notions had a way of forcing themselves into Rogin's mind. Just thirty-one and passable-looking, with short black hair, small eyes, but a high, open forehead, he was a research chemist, and his mind was generally serious and dependable. But on a snowy Sunday evening while this stocky man, buttoned to the chin in a Burberry coat and walking in his preposterous gait—feet turned outward—was going toward the subway, he fell into a peculiar state.

He was on his way to have supper with his fiancée. She had phoned him a short while ago and said, "You'd better pick up a few things on the way."

"What do we need?"

"Some roast beef, for one thing. I bought a quarter of a pound coming home from my aunt's."

"Why a quarter of a pound, Joan?" said Rogin, deeply annoyed. "That's just about enough for one good sandwich."

"So you have to stop at a delicatessen. I had no more money."

He was about to ask, "What happened to the thirty dollars I gave you on Wednesday?," but he knew that would not be right.

"I had to give Phyllis money for the cleaning woman," said Joan.

Phyllis, Joan's cousin, was a young divorcée, extremely wealthy. The two women shared an apartment.

"Roast beef," he said, "and what else?"

"Some shampoo, sweetheart. We've used up all the shampoo. And hurry, darling, I've missed you all day."

"And I've missed you," said Rogin, but to tell the truth he had been worrying most of the time. He had a younger brother whom he was putting through college. And his mother, whose annuity wasn't quite enough in these days of inflation and high taxes, needed money, too. Joan had debts he was helping her to pay, for she wasn't working. She was looking for something suitable to do.

Beautiful, well-educated, aristocratic in her attitude, she couldn't clerk in a dime store; she couldn't model clothes (Rogin thought this made girls vain and stiff, and he didn't want her to); she couldn't be a waitress or a cashier. What could she be? Well, something would turn up, and meantime Rogin hesitated to complain. He paid her bills—the dentist, the department store, the osteopath, the doctor, the psychiatrist. At Christmas, Rogin almost went mad. Joan bought him a velvet smoking jacket with frog fasteners, a beautiful pipe, and a pouch. She bought Phyllis a garnet brooch, an Italian silk umbrella, and a gold cigarette holder. For other friends, she bought Dutch pewter and Swedish glassware. Before she was through, she had spent five hundred dollars of Rogin's money. He loved her too much to show his suffering. He believed she had a far better nature than his. She didn't worry about money. She had a marvellous character, always cheerful, and she really didn't need a psychiatrist at all. She went to one because Phyllis did and it made her curious. She tried too much to keep up with her cousin, whose father had made millions in the rug business.

While the woman in the drugstore was wrapping the shampoo bottle, a clear idea suddenly arose in Rogin's thoughts: Money surrounds you in life as the earth does in death. Superimposition is the universal law. Who is free? No one is free. Who has no burdens? Everyone is under pressure. The very rocks, the waters of the earth, beasts, men, children—everyone has some weight to carry. This idea was extremely clear to him at first. Soon it became rather vague, but it had a great effect nevertheless, as if someone had given him a valuable gift. (Not like the velvet smoking jacket he couldn't bring himself to wear, or the pipe it choked him to smoke.) The notion that all were under pressure and affliction, instead of saddening him, had the opposite influence. It put him in a wonderful mood. It was extraordinary how happy he became and, in addition, clear-sighted. His eyes all at once were opened to what was around him. He saw with delight how the druggist and the woman who wrapped the shampoo bottle were smiling and flirting, how the lines of worry in her face went over into lines of cheer and the druggist's receding gums did not hinder his kidding and friendliness. And in the delicatessen, also, it was amazing how much Rogin noted and what happiness it gave him simply to be there.

Delicatessens on Sunday night, when all other stores are shut, will overcharge you ferociously, and Rogin would normally have been on guard, but he was not tonight, or scarcely so. Smells of pickle, sausage, mustard, and smoked fish overjoyed him. He pitied the people who would buy the chicken salad and chopped herring; they could do it only because their sight was too dim to see what they were getting—the fat flakes of pepper on the chicken, the soppy herring, mostly vinegar-soaked stale bread. Who would buy them? Late risers, people living alone, waking up in the darkness of the afternoon, finding their refrigerators empty, or people whose gaze was turned inward. The roast beef looked not bad, and Rogin ordered a pound.

While the storekeeper was slicing the meat, he yelled at a Puerto Rican kid who was reaching for a bag of chocolate cookies, "Hey, you want to pull me down the whole display on yourself? You, *chico,* wait a half a minute." This storekeeper, though he looked like one of Pancho Villa's bandits, the kind that smeared their enemies with syrup and staked them down on anthills, a man with toadlike eyes and stout hands made to clasp pistols hung around his belly, was not so bad. He was a New York man, thought Rogin— who was from Albany himself—a New York man toughened by every abuse of the city, trained to suspect everyone. But in his own realm, on the board behind the counter, there was justice. Even clemency.

The Puerto Rican kid wore a complete cowboy outfit—a green hat with white braid, guns, chaps, spurs, boots, and gauntlets—but he couldn't speak any English. Rogin unhooked the cellophane bag of hard circular cookies and gave it to him. The boy tore the cellophane with his teeth and began to chew one of those dry chocolate discs. Rogin recognized his state—the energetic dream of childhood. Once, he, too, had found these dry biscuits delicious. It would have bored him now to eat one.

What else would Joan like? Rogin thought fondly. Some strawberries? "Give me some frozen strawberries. No, raspberries, she likes those better. And heavy cream. And some rolls, cream cheese, and some of those rubber-looking gherkins."

"What rubber?"

"Those, deep green, with eyes. Some ice cream might be in order, too."

He tried to think of a compliment, a good comparison, an endearment, for Joan when she'd open the door. What about her complexion? There was really nothing to compare her sweet, small, daring, shapely, timid, defiant, loving face to. How difficult she was, and how beautiful!

As Rogin went down into the stony, odorous, metallic, captive air of the subway, he was diverted by an unusual confession made by a man to his friend. These were two very tall men, shapeless in their winter clothes, as if their coats concealed suits of chain mail.

"So, how long have you known me?" said one.

"Twelve years."

"Well, I have an admission to make," he said. "I've decided that I might as well. For years I've been a heavy drinker. You didn't know. Practically an alcoholic."

But his friend was not surprised, and he answered immediately, "Yes, I did know."

"You knew? Impossible! How could you?"

Why, thought Rogin, as if it could be a secret! Look at that long, austere, alcohol-washed face, that drink-ruined nose, the skin by his ears like turkey wattles, and those whiskey-saddened eyes.

"Well, I did know, though."

"You couldn't have. I can't believe it." He was upset, and his friend didn't seem to want to soothe him. "But it's all right now," he said. "I've been going to a doctor and taking pills, a new revolutionary Danish discovery. It's a miracle. I'm beginning to believe they can cure you of anything and everything. You can't beat the Danes in science. They do everything. They turned a man into a woman."

"That isn't how they stop you from drinking, is it?"

"No. I hope not. This is only like aspirin. It's super-aspirin. They call it the aspirin of the future. But if you use it, you have to stop drinking."

Rogin's illuminated mind asked of itself while the human tides of the subway swayed back and forth, and cars linked and transparent like fish bladders raced under the streets: How come he thought nobody would know what everybody couldn't help knowing? And, as a chemist, he asked himself what kind of compound this new Danish drug might be, and started thinking about various inventions of his own, synthetic albumen, a cigarette that lit itself, a cheaper motor fuel. Ye gods, but he needed money! As never before. What was to be done? His mother was growing more and more difficult. On Friday night, she had neglected to cut up his meat for him, and he was hurt. She had sat at the table motionless, with her long-suffering face, severe, and let him cut his own meat, a thing she almost never did. She had always spoiled him and made his brother envy him. But what she expected now! Oh, Lord, how he had to pay, and it had never even occurred to him formerly that these things might have a price.

Seated, one of the passengers, Rogin recovered his calm, happy, even clairvoyant state of mind. To think of money was to think as the world wanted you to think; then you'd never be your own master. When people said they wouldn't do something for love or money, they meant that love and money were opposite passions and one the enemy of the other. He went on to reflect how little people knew about this, how they slept through life, how small a light the light of consciousness was. Rogin's clean, snub-nosed face shone while his heart was torn with joy at these deeper thoughts of our ignorance. You might take this drunkard as an example, who for long years thought his closest friends never suspected he drank. Rogin looked up and down the aisle for this remarkable knightly symbol, but he was gone.

However, there was no lack of things to see. There was a small girl with a new white muff; into the muff a doll's head was sewn, and the child was happy and affectionately vain of it, while her old man, stout and grim, with a huge scowling nose, kept picking her up and resettling her in the seat, as if he were trying to change her into something else. Then another child, led by her mother, boarded the car, and this other child carried the very same doll-faced muff, and this greatly annoyed both parents. The woman, who looked like a difficult, contentious woman, took her daughter away. It seemed to Rogin that each child was in love with its own muff and didn't even see the other, but it was one of his foibles to think he understood the hearts of little children.

A foreign family next engaged his attention. They looked like Central Americans to him. On one side the mother, quite old, dark-faced, white-haired, and worn out; on the other a son with the whitened, porous hands of a dishwasher. But what was the dwarf who sat between them—a son or a daughter? The hair was long and wavy and the cheeks smooth, but the shirt and tie were masculine. The overcoat was feminine, but the shoes—the shoes were a puzzle. A pair of brown oxfords with an outer seam like a man's, but Baby Louis heels like a woman's—a plain toe like a man's, but a strap across the instep like a woman's. No stockings. That didn't help much. The dwarf's fingers were beringed, but without a wedding band. There were small grim dents in the cheeks. The eyes were puffy and concealed, but Rogin did not doubt that they could reveal strange things if they chose and that this was a creature of remarkable understanding. He had for many years owned De la Mare's "Memoirs of a Midget." Now he took a resolve; he would read it. As soon as he had decided, he was free from his consuming curiosity as to the dwarf's sex and was able to look at the person who sat beside him.

Thoughts very often grow fertile in the subway, because of the motion, the great company, the subtlety of the rider's state as he rattles under streets and rivers, under the foundations of great buildings, and Rogin's mind had already been strangely stimulated. Clasping the bag of groceries from which there rose odors of bread and pickle spice, he was following a train of reflections, first about the chemistry of sex determination, the X and Y chromosomes, hereditary linkages, the uterus, afterward about his brother as a tax exemption. He recalled two dreams of the night before. In one, an undertaker had offered to cut his hair, and he had refused. In another, he had been carrying a woman on his head. Sad dreams, both! Very sad! Which was the woman—Joan or Mother? And the undertaker—his lawyer? He gave a deep sigh, and by force of habit began to put together his synthetic albumen that was to revolutionize the entire egg industry.

Meanwhile, he had not interrupted his examination of the passengers and had fallen into a study of the man next to him. This was a man whom he had never in his life seen before but with whom he now suddenly felt linked through all existence. He was middle-aged, sturdy, with clear skin and blue eyes. His hands were clean, well-formed, but Rogin did not approve of them. The coat he wore was a fairly expensive blue check such as Rogin would never have chosen for himself. He would not have worn blue suède shoes, either, or such a faultless hat, a cumbersome felt animal of a hat encircled by a high, fat ribbon. There are all kinds of dandies, not all of them are of the flaunting kind; some are dandies of respectability, and Rogin's fellow-passenger was one of these. His straight-nosed profile was handsome, yet he had betrayed his gift, for he was flat-looking. But in his flat way he seemed to warn people that he wanted no difficulties with them, he wanted nothing to do with them. Wearing such blue suède shoes, he could not afford to have people treading on his feet, and he seemed to draw about himself a circle of privilege, notifying all others to mind their own business and let him read his paper. He was holding a *Tribune,* and perhaps it would be overstatement to say that he was reading. He was holding it.

His clear skin and blue eyes, his straight and purely Roman nose —even the way he sat—all strongly suggested one person to Rogin: Joan. He tried to escape the comparison, but it couldn't be helped. This man not only looked like Joan's father, whom Rogin detested; he looked like Joan herself. Forty years hence, a son of hers, provided she had one, might be like this. A son of hers? Of such a son, he himself, Rogin, would be the father. Lacking in dominant traits as compared with Joan, his heritage would not appear. Probably the children would resemble her. Yes, think forty years ahead, and a man like this, who sat by him knee to knee in the hurtling car among their fellow-creatures, unconscious participants in a sort of great carnival of transit—such a man would carry forward what had been Rogin.

This was why he felt bound to him through all existence. What were forty years reckoned against eternity! Forty years were gone, and he was gazing at his own son. Here he was. Rogin was frightened and moved. "My son! My son!" he said to himself, and the pity of it almost made him burst into tears. The holy and frightful work of the masters of life and death brought this about. We were their instruments. We worked toward ends we thought were our own. But no! The whole thing was so unjust. To suffer, to labor, to toil and force your way through the spikes of life, to crawl through its darkest caverns, to push through the worst, to struggle under the weight of economy, to make money—only to become the father of a fourth-rate man of the world like this, so flat-looking, with his ordinary, clean, rosy, uninteresting, self-satisfied, fundamentally bourgeois face. What a curse to have a dull son! A son like this, who could never understand his father. They had absolutely nothing, but nothing, in common, he and this neat, chubby, blue-eyed man. He was so pleased, thought Rogin, with all he owned and all he did and all he was that he could hardly unfasten his lip. Look at that lip, sticking up at the tip like a little thorn or egg tooth. He wouldn't give anyone the time of day. Would this perhaps be general forty years from now? Would personalities be chillier as the world aged and grew colder? The inhumanity of the next generation incensed Rogin. Father and son had no sign to make to each other. Terrible! Inhuman! What a vision of existence it gave him.

Man's personal aims were nothing, illusion. The life force occupied each of us in turn in its progress toward its own fulfillment, trampling on our individual humanity, using us for its own ends like mere dinosaurs or bees, exploiting love heartlessly, making us engage in the social process, labor, struggle for money, and submit to the law of pressure, the universal law of layers, superimposition!

What the blazes am I getting into? Rogin thought. To be the father of a throwback to *her* father. The image of this white-haired, gross, peevish old man with his ugly selfish blue eyes revolted Rogin. This was how his grandson would look. Joan, with whom Rogin was now more and more displeased, could not help that. For her, it was inevitable. But did it have to be inevitable for him? Well, then, Rogin, you fool, don't be a damned instrument. Get out of the way!

But it was too late for this, because he had already experienced the sensation of sitting next to his own son, his son and Joan's. He kept staring at him, waiting for him to say something, but the presumptive son remained coldly silent though he must have been aware of Rogin's scrutiny. They even got out at the same stop—Sheridan Square. When they stepped to the platform, the man, without even looking at Rogin, went away in a different direction in his detestable blue-checked coat, with his rosy, nasty face.

The whole thing upset Rogin very badly. When he approached Joan's door and heard Phyllis's little dog Henri barking even before he could knock, his face was very tense. "I won't be used," he declared to himself. "I have my own right to exist." Joan had better watch out. She had a light way of bypassing grave questions he had given earnest thought to. She always assumed no really disturbing thing would happen. He could not afford the luxury of such a carefree, debonair attitude himself, because he had to work hard and earn money so that disturbing things would *not* happen. Well, at the moment this situation could not be helped, and he really did not mind the money if he could feel that she was not necessarily the mother of such a son as his subway son or entirely the daughter of that awful, obscene father of hers. After all, Rogin was not himself so much like either of his parents, and quite different from his brother.

Joan came to the door, wearing one of Phyllis's expensive house-coats. It suited her very well. At first sight of her happy face, Rogin was brushed by the shadow of resemblance; the touch of it was extremely light, almost figmentary, but it made his flesh tremble.

She began to kiss him, saying, "Oh, my baby. You're covered with snow. Why didn't you wear your hat? It's all over its little head"— her favorite third-person endearment.

"Well, let me put down this bag of stuff. Let me take off my coat," grumbled Rogin, and escaped from her embrace. Why couldn't she wait making up to him? "It's so hot in here. My face is burning. Why do you keep the place at this temperature? And that damned dog keeps barking. If you didn't keep it cooped up, it wouldn't be so spoiled and noisy. Why doesn't anybody ever walk him?"

"Oh, it's not really so hot here! You've just come in from the cold. Don't you think this housecoat fits me better than Phyllis? Especially across the hips. She thinks so, too. She may sell it to me."

"I hope not," Rogin almost exclaimed.

She brought a towel to dry the melting snow from his short, black hair. The flurry of rubbing excited Henri intolerably, and Joan locked him up in the bedroom, where he jumped persistently against the door with a rhythmic sound of claws on the wood.

Joan said, "Did you bring the shampoo?"

"Here it is."

"Then I'll wash your hair before dinner. Come."

"I don't want it washed."

"Oh, come on," she said, laughing.

Her lack of consciousness of guilt amazed him. He did not see how it could be. And the carpeted, furnished, lamplit, curtained room seemed to stand against his vision. So that he felt accusing and angry, his spirit sore and bitter, but it did not seem fitting to say why. Indeed, he began to worry lest the reason for it all slip away from him.

They took off his coat and his shirt in the bathroom, and she filled the sink. Rogin was full of his troubled emotions; now that his chest was bare he could feel them even more distinctly inside, and he said to himself, "I'll have a thing or two to tell her pretty soon. I'm not letting them get away with it. 'Do you think,' he was going to tell her, 'that I alone was made to carry the burden of the whole world on me? Do you think I was born just to be taken advantage of and sacrificed? Do you think I'm just a natural resource, like a coal mine, or oil well, or fishery, or the like? Remember, that I'm a man is no reason why I should be loaded down. I have a soul in me no bigger or stronger than yours. Take away the externals, like the muscles, deeper voice, and so forth, and what remains? A pair of spirits, practically alike. So why shouldn't there also be equality? I can't always be the strong one.' "

"Sit here," said Joan, bringing up a kitchen stool to the sink. "Your hair's gotten all matted."

He sat with his breast against the cool enamel, his chin on the edge of the basin, the green, hot, radiant water reflecting the glass and the tile, and the sweet, cool, fragrant juice of the shampoo poured on his head. She began to wash him.

"You have the healthiest-looking scalp," she said. "It's all pink."

He answered, "Well, it should be white. There must be something wrong with me."

"But there's absolutely nothing wrong with you," she said, and pressed against him from behind, surrounding him, pouring the water gently over him until it seemed to him that the water came from within him, it was the warm fluid of his own secret loving spirit overflowing into the sink, green and foaming, and the words he had rehearsed he forgot, and his anger at his son-to-be disappeared altogether, and he sighed, and said to her from the water-filled hollow of the sink, "You always have such wonderful ideas, Joan. You know? You have a kind of instinct, a regular gift."

THREE PLAYERS OF A SUMMER GAME

❖

TENNESSEE WILLIAMS

CROQUET is a summer game that seems, in a curious way, to be composed of images, very much as a painter's abstraction of summer or one of its games would be composed of them. The delicate wire wickets set in a lawn of smooth emerald that flickers fierily at some points and rests under violet shadow in others; the wooden poles gaudily painted and like moments that stand out in a season that was a struggle for something of unspeakable importance to someone passing through it; the clean and hard wooden spheres of different colors and the strong, rigid shape of the mallets that drive the balls through the wickets; the formal design of those wickets and poles upon the croquet lawn—all this is like a painter's abstraction of a summer and a game played in it. And I cannot think of croquet without hearing a sound like the faraway booming of a cannon fired to announce a white ship coming into a harbor. The faraway booming sound is that of a green-and-white striped awning coming down over a gallery of a white frame house in Meridian, Mississippi. The house is of Victorian design carried to an extreme of improvisation, an almost grotesque pile of galleries and turrets and cupolas and eaves, all freshly painted white—so white and so fresh that it has the blue-white glitter of a block of ice in the sun. The house is like a new resolution not yet tainted by any defection from it. And I associate the summer game with players coming out of this house with the buoyant air of persons just released from a suffocating enclosure. Their clothes are as light in weight and color as the flattering clothes of dancers. There are three players—a woman, a man, and a little girl.

The voice of the woman player is not at all loud, yet it has a pleasantly resonant quality; it carries farther than most voices, and it is interspersed with peals of treble laughter. The woman player, even more than her male opponent in the game, has the grateful quickness of motion of someone let out of a suffocating enclosure; her motion has the quickness of breath released just after a moment of terror, of fingers unclenched when panic is suddenly past, or of a cry that subsides into laughter. She seems unable to speak or move about moderately; she moves convulsively in rushes, whipping her white skirts with long strides that quicken to running. Her skirts make a faint crackling sound as her pumping thighs whip them open—the sound that comes to you, greatly diminished by distance, when fitful fair-weather gusts belly out and slacken the faraway sails of a yawl. This agreeably cool summer sound is accompanied by another, which is even cooler—the ceaseless, tiny chatter of beads hung in long loops from her throat. They are not pearls but they have a milky lustre; they are small, faintly speckled white ovals—polished bird eggs turned solid and strung upon glittery filaments of silver. The woman player is never still for a moment; sometimes she exhausts herself and collapses on the grass in the conscious attitudes of a dancer. She is a thin woman, with long bones and skin of a silky sheen, and her eyes are only a shade or two darker than the blue-tinted bird's-egg beads about her long throat. She is never still—not even when she has fallen in exhaustion on the grass. The neighbors think she's gone mad, but they feel no pity for her, and that, of course, is because of her male opponent in the game. This player is Brick Pollitt, a young Delta planter, a man so tall, with such a fiery thatch of hair, that to see a flagpole on an expanse of green lawn or even a particularly brilliant weather vane or cross on a steeple is sufficient to recall that long-ago summer which his legend belongs to.

This male player of the summer game is a drinker who has not yet fallen beneath the savage axe blows of his liquor. He is not so young any more, but he has not yet lost the slim grace of his youth. He is a head taller than the tall woman player. He is such a tall man that even in those sections of the lawn dimmed under violet shadow his head continues to catch fiery rays of the descending sun, the way the heavenward-pointing index finger of a huge gilded hand atop a Protestant steeple in Meridian goes on drawing the sun's flame for a good while after the lower surfaces of the town have sunk into lingering dusk.

The third player of the summer game is the woman's daughter, a plump twelve-year-old child named Mary Louise. This little girl has made herself distinctly unpopular among the children of the neighborhood by imitating too perfectly the elegant manners and

cultivated Eastern voice of her mother. She sits in an electric automobile, on the sort of fat silk pillow that expensive lap dogs sit on,
uttering treble peals of ladylike laughter, tossing her copper curls,
using grown-up expressions such as "Oh, how delightful!" and
"Isn't that just lovely!" She sits in the electric automobile sometimes all afternoon, by herself, as if she were on display in a glass
box, only now and then raising a plaintive voice to call her mother
and ask if it is all right for her to come in now, or if she can drive
the electric around the block, which she is sometimes then permitted to do.

Our house was on the opposite corner, and I was the only child
close to her age (I was a boy of fourteen) who could put up with
her precocious refinements. For a very short time, she had had
another friend, a little girl named Dorothea, and the two of them
would get into their mothers' castoff finery and have tea parties on
the lawn, but one afternoon Dorothea took umbrage at something,
overturned the tea table, and stalked off, chanting a horrid little
verse: "Smarty, Smarty, gave a party, Nobody came but a sad old
darky!" "Common!" Mary Louise shrieked after her, and they
didn't play together any more. Sometimes she called me over to play
croquet with her, but that was only when her mother and Brick
Pollitt had disappeared into the house too early to play the game.
Mary Louise had a passion for croquet. She played it purely for
itself; it did not have for her any shadowy connotations.

What the game meant to Brick Pollitt calls for some further account of Brick's life before that summer. He had been a celebrated
athlete at Sewanee, and had married a New Orleans débutante who
was a Mardi Gras queen and whose father owned a fleet of banana
boats. It had seemed a brilliant marriage, with lots of wealth and
prestige on both sides, but only two years later Brick started falling
in love with his liquor, and Margaret, his wife, began to be praised
for her patience and loyalty to him. Brick seemed to be throwing
his life away, as if it were something disgusting that he had suddenly
found in his hands. This self-disgust came upon him with the
abruptness and violence of a crash on a highway. But what had
Brick crashed into? Nothing that anybody was able to surmise, for
he seemed to have everything that young men like Brick might
hope or desire to have. What else is there? There must have been
something that he wanted and lacked, or what reason was there for
his dropping his life and taking hold of a glass that he never let
go of for more than one waking hour? His wife, Margaret, took

hold of Brick's ten-thousand-acre plantation. She had Brick's power
of attorney, and she managed all his business affairs with astuteness.
"He'll come out of it," she would say. "Brick is passing through
something that he'll come out of." She always said the right thing,
took the conventionally right attitude, and expressed it to the world
which admired her for it. Everybody admired her as a remarkably
fine and brave little woman who had much to put up with. Two
sections of an hourglass could not drain and fill more evenly than
Brick and Margaret after he took to drink. It was as though she had
her lips fastened to some invisible wound in his body through which
drained out of him and flowed into her the assurance and vitality
that had been his before his marriage. Margaret Pollitt lost her
pale, feminine prettiness and assumed in its place something more
impressive—a firm and rough-textured sort of handsomeness. Once
very pretty but indistinct, a graceful sketch that was done with a
very light pencil, she became vivid as Brick disappeared behind
the veil of his liquor. She abruptly stopped being quiet and dainty.
She was now apt to have dirty fingernails, which she covered with
scarlet enamel. When the enamel chipped off, the gray showed underneath. Her hair was now cut short, so that she didn't have to
"mess with it." It was wind-blown and full of sparkle; she jerked
a comb through it, making it crackle. She had white teeth that
were a little too large for her thin lips, and when she threw her
head back in laughter, strong cords stood out in her smooth brown
throat. She had a booming laugh that she might have stolen from
Brick while he was drunk or asleep beside her at night. She had
a way of releasing the clutch on a car at the exact instant that her
laughter boomed out, and of not calling goodbye but of thrusting
one bare, strong arm straight out with the fingers clenched as the
car shot off in high gear and disappeared into a cloud of yellow
dust. She didn't drive her own little runabout nowadays as much
as she did Brick's Pierce-Arrow touring car, for Brick's driver's
license had been revoked. She frequently broke the speed limit on
the highway. The patrolmen would stop her, but she had such an
affability, such a disarming way with her, that they would have a
good laugh together and there would be no question of a ticket.

Somebody in her family died in Memphis that spring, and she
went there to attend the funeral and collect her inheritance, and
while she was away, Brick Pollitt slipped out from under her thumb
a bit. Another death occurred during her absence. That nice young
doctor who took care of Brick when he had to be carried to the

hospital took sick in a shocking way. An awful flower grew in his brain, like a fierce geranium—grew and grew and one day shattered its pot. All of a sudden, the wrong words came out of his mouth; he seemed to be speaking in an unknown tongue; he couldn't find things with his hands; he made troubled signs over his forehead. His wife led him about the house by one hand, yet he stumbled and fell flat; the breath was knocked out of him, and he had to be put to bed by his wife and the Negro yardman; and he lay there laughing weakly, incredulously, trying to find his wife's hand with both of his while she looked at him with eyes that she couldn't keep from blazing with terror. He lived on under drugs for a week, and it was during that time that Brick Pollitt came and sat with Isabel Grey by her dying husband's bed. She couldn't speak; she could only shake her head incessantly, like a metronome, with no lips visible in her white face but two pressed-narrow bands of a dimmer whiteness that shook as if some white liquid flowed beneath them with a rapidity and violence that made them quiver.

"God" was the only word she was able to say, but Brick Pollitt somehow understood what she meant by that word, as if it were in a language that she and he, alone of all people, could speak and understand. And when the dying man's eyes opened, as if they were being forced, on something they couldn't bear to look at, it was Brick, his hands suddenly quite sure and steady, who filled the hypodermic needle for her and pumped its contents fiercely into her husband's hard young arm. And it was over.

There was another bed at the back of the house, and he and Isabel lay beside each other on that bed for a couple of hours before they let the town know that her husband's agony was completed, and the only movement between them was the intermittent, spasmodic digging of their fingernails into each other's clenched palm while their bodies lay stiffly separate, deliberately not touching at any other points, as if they abhorred any other contact with each other.

And so you see what the summer game on the violet-shadowed lawn was—it was a running together out of something unbearably hot and bright into something obscure and cool.

The young widow was left with nothing in the way of material possessions except the house and an electric automobile. By the time Brick's wife, Margaret, had returned from her journey to Memphis, Brick had taken over the various details of the widow's life that a brother or a relative, if she had had one, would have seen to. For a week or two, people thought it was very kind of him, and then all at once they decided that Brick's reason for kindness was by no means noble. It appeared that the widow was now his mistress, and this was true. It was true in the limited way that most such opinions are true. She was his mistress, but that was not Brick's reason. His reason had something to do with that chaste interlocking of hands their first time together, after the hypodermic. It had to do with those hours, now receding and fading behind them, as all such hours must, but neither of them could have said what it was, aside from that. Neither of them was able to think very clearly. But Brick was able to pull himself together for a while and take command of the young widow's affairs.

The daughter, Mary Louise, was a plump child of twelve. She was my friend that summer. Mary Louise and I caught lightning bugs and put them in Mason jars, and we played croquet when her mother and Brick Pollitt were not inclined to play. It was Mary Louise that summer who taught me how to deal with mosquito bites. She was plagued by mosquitoes and so was I. She warned me that scratching the bites would leave scars on my skin, which was as tender as hers. I said that I didn't care. Someday you will, she told me. She carried with her constantly that summer a lump of ice in a handkerchief. Whenever a mosquito bit her, instead of scratching the bite she rubbed it gently with the handkerchief-wrapped lump of ice until the sting was frozen to numbness. Of course, in five minutes it would come back and have to be frozen again, but eventually it would disappear and leave no scar. Mary Louise's skin, where it was not temporarily mutilated by a mosquito bite or a slight rash that sometimes appeared after she ate strawberry ice cream, was ravishingly smooth and tender.

The Grey's house was very run down, but soon after Brick Pollitt started coming over to see the young widow, the house was painted. It was painted so white that it was almost a very pale blue; it had the blue-white glitter of a block of ice in the sun. In spite of his red hair, Brick Pollitt, too, had a cool appearance, because he was still young and thin, as thin as the widow, and he dressed, as she did, in clothes of light weight and color. His white shirts looked faintly pink because of his skin underneath them. Once, I saw him at an upstairs window of the widow's house just a moment before he pulled the shade down. I was in an upstairs room of my house, and I saw that Brick Pollitt was divided into two colors as distinct as two stripes of a flag, the upper part of him, which had been ex-

posed to the sun, almost crimson and the lower part of him white
as this piece of paper.

While the widow's house was being repainted, at Brick Pollitt's
expense, she and her daughter lived at the Alcazar Hotel, also at
Brick's expense. Brick drove in from his plantation every morning
to watch the house painters at work. His driving license had been
restored to him, and this was an important step forward in his
personal renovation—being able to drive his own car again. He
drove with elaborate caution and formality, coming to a dead stop
at every cross street in the town, sounding the silver trumpet at
every corner, with smiles and bows and great circular gestures of
his hands inviting pedestrians to precede him. But people did not
approve of what Brick Pollitt was doing. They sympathized with
Margaret, that brave little woman who had to put up with so much.
As for Dr. Grey's widow, she had not been very long in the town;
the Doctor had married her while he was an interne at a big hospital in Baltimore. Nobody had formed a definite opinion of her
before the Doctor died, so it was no effort now simply to condemn
her, without any qualification, as a common strumpet.

Brick Pollitt, when he talked to the house painters, shouted to
them as if they were deaf, so that all the neighbors could hear what
he had to say. He was explaining things to the world, especially the
matter of his drinking.

"It's something that you can't cut out completely right away," he
would yell up at them. "That's the big mistake that most drinkers
make—they try to cut it out completely, and you can't do that. You
can do it for maybe a month or two months, but all at once you
go back on it worse than before you went off it, and then the dis-
couragement is awful—you lose all faith in yourself and just give
up. The thing to do, the way to handle the problem is like a bull-
fighter handles a bull in a ring. Wear it down little by little, get
control of it gradually. That's how I'm handling this thing! Yep.
Now, let's say that you get up wanting a drink in the morning.
Say it's ten o'clock, maybe. Well, you say to yourself, 'Just wait
half an hour, old boy, and then you can have one.'. . . Well, at
half past ten you still want that drink and you want it a little bit
worse than you did at ten, but you say to yourself, 'Boy, you could
do without it half an hour ago, so you can do without it now.' You
see, that's how you got to argue about it with yourself, because a
drinking man is not one person. A man that drinks is two people,
one grabbing the bottle, the other one fighting him off it—not one

but two people fighting each other to get control of a bottle. Well, sir. If you can talk yourself out of a drink at ten, you can still talk yourself out of a drink at *half past* ten! But at *eleven* o'clock the need for the drink is greater. Now *here's* the important thing to remember about this struggle. You got to watch those scales, and when they tip too far against your power to resist, you got to give in a little. That's not weakness. *That's strategy!* Because don't forget what I told you. A drinking man is not one person but two, and it's a battle of wits going on between them. And so I say at eleven, 'Well, *have* your drink. *Go on* and *have* it! One drink at eleven won't hurt you!'

"What time is it now? . . . Yep! Eleven . . . All right, I'm going to have me that one drink. I could do without it, I don't crave it. But the important thing is . . ."

His voice would trail off as he entered the widow's house. He would stay in there longer than it took to have one drink, and when he came out, there would be a change in his voice as definite as a change of weather or season. The strong and vigorous tone would be a bit filmed over.

Then he would usually begin to talk about his wife. "I don't say my wife Margaret's not an intelligent woman. She is, and both of us know it, but she don't have a good head for property values. Now, you know Dr. Grey, who used to live here before that brain thing killed him. Well, he was my physician, he pulled me through some bad times when I had that liquor problem. I felt I owed him a lot. Now, that was a terrible thing the way he went, but it was terrible for his widow, too; she was left with this house and that electric automobile and that's all, and this house was put up for sale to pay off her debts, and—well, I bought it. I bought it, and now I'm giving it back to her. Now, my wife Margaret, she. And a lot of other folks, too. Don't understand about this. . . . What time is it? Twelve? High noon! . . . This ice is melted . . ."

He'd drift back into the house and stay there half an hour, and when he'd come back out, it would be rather shyly, with a sad and uncertain creaking of the screen door pushed by the hand not holding the tall glass. But after resting a little while on the steps, he would resume his talk to the house painters.

"Yes," he would say, as if he had paused only a moment before, "it's the most precious thing that a woman can give to a man—his lost respect for himself—and the meanest thing one human being can do to another human being is take his respect for himself away from him. I. I had it took away from me."

The glass would tilt slowly up and jerkily down, and he'd have to wipe his chin.

"I had it took away from me! I won't tell you how, but maybe, being men about my age, you're able to guess it. That was how. Some of them don't want it. They cut it off. They cut it right off a man, and half the time he don't even know when they cut it off him. Well, I knew it all right. I could feel it being cut off me. Do you know what I mean? . . . That's right.

"But once in a while there's one—and they don't come often— that wants for a man to keep it, and those are the women that God made and put on this earth. The other kind come out of Hell, or out of . . . I don't know what. I'm talking too much. Sure. I know I'm talking too much about private matters. But that's all right. This property is mine. I'm talking on my own property and I don't give a hoot who hears me or what they think! I'm not going to try to fool anybody about it. Whatever I do is nothing to be ashamed of. I've been through things that I would rather not mention. But I'm coming out of it now, God damn it, yes, I am! I can't take all the credit. And yet I'm proud. I'm goddam proud of myself, be- cause I was in a pitiful condition with that liquor problem of mine, but now the worst is over. I've got it just about licked. That's my car out there and I drove it up here myself. It's no short drive, it's almost a hundred miles, and I drive it each morning and drive it back each night. I've got back my driver's license, and I fired the man that was working for my wife, looking after our place. I fired that man and not only fired him but give him a kick in the britches that made him eat standing up for the next week or two. It wasn't because I thought he was fooling around. It wasn't that. But him and her both took about the same attitude toward me, and I didn't like the attitude they took. They would talk about me right in front of me, as if I wasn't there. 'Is it time for his medicine?' Yes, they were giving me dope! So one day I played possum. I was lying out there on the sofa and she said to him, 'I guess he's passed out now.' And he said, 'Jesus, dead drunk at half past one in the after- noon!' Well. I got up slowly. I wasn't drunk at that hour, I wasn't even half drunk. I stood up straight and walked slowly toward him. I walked straight up to them both, and you should of seen the eyes of them both bug out! 'Yes, Jesus,' I said, 'at half past one!' And I grabbed him by his collar and by the seat of his britches and turkey-

trotted him right on out of the house and pitched him on his face
in a big mud puddle at the foot of the steps to the front veranda.
And as far as I know or care, maybe he's still laying there and she's
still screaming, 'Stop, Brick!' But I believe I did hit her. Yes, I did.
I did hit her. There's times when you got to hit them, and that was
one of those times. I ain't been to the house since. I moved in the
little place we lived in before the big one was built, on the other
side of the bayou, and ain't crossed over there since.

"Well, sir, that's all over with now. I got back my power of attorney which I'd give to that woman and I got back my driver's
license and I bought this piece of property in town and signed my
own check for it and I'm having it completely done over to make it
as handsome a piece of residential property as you can find in this
town and I'm having that lawn out there prepared for the game
of croquet."

Then he'd look at the glass in his hand as if he had just then
noticed that he was holding it. He'd give it a look of slightly pained
surprise, as if he had cut his hand and just now noticed that it was
cut and bleeding. Then he would sigh like an old-time actor in a
tragic role. He would put the tall glass down on the balustrade with
great, great care, look back at it to make sure that it wasn't going
to fall over, and walk, very straight and steady, to the porch steps
and, just as steady but with more concentration, down them. When
he arrived at the foot of the steps, he would laugh as if someone had
made a comical remark. He would duck his head genially and shout
to the house painters something like this: "Well, I'm not making
any predictions, because I'm no fortune-teller, but I've got a strong
idea that I'm going to lick my liquor problem this summer, ha-ha,
I'm going to lick it this summer! I'm not going to take no cure and
I'm not going to take no pledge. I'm just going to prove I'm a man
again! I'm going to do it step by little step, the way that people
play the game of croquet. You know how you play that game. You
hit the ball through one wicket and then you drive it through the
next one. You hit it through that wicket and then you drive on to
another. You go from wicket to wicket, and it's a game of precision
—it's a game that takes concentration and precision, and that's
what makes it a wonderful game for a drinker. It takes a sober man
to play a game of precision. It's better than shooting pool, because
a pool hall is always next door to a gin mill, and you never see a
pool player that don't have his liquor glass on the edge of the table
or somewhere pretty near it, and croquet is also a better game than

golf, because in golf you've always got that nineteenth hole waiting for you. Nope, for a man with a liquor problem croquet may seem a little bit sissy, but let me tell you it's a game of precision. You go from wicket to wicket until you arrive at that big final pole, and then, bang, you've hit it, the game is finished, you're there! And then, and not until then, you can go up here to the porch and have you a cool gin drink, a buck or a Collins. Hey! Where did I leave that glass? Aw! Yeah, hand it down to me, will you? Ha-ha. Thanks."

He would take a birdlike sip, make a fiercely wry face, and shake his head violently as if somebody had drenched it with water. *"This God-damned stuff!"*

He would look around to find a safe place to set the glass down again. He would select a bare spot of earth between the hydrangea bushes and deposit the glass there as carefully as if he were planting a memorial tree, and then he would straighten up with a great air of relief and expand his chest and flex his arms. "Ha-ha, yep, croquet is a summer game for widows and drinkers, ha-ha!"

For a few moments, standing there in the sun, he would seem as sure and powerful as the sun itself, but then some little shadow of uncertainty would touch him again, get through the wall of his liquor; some tricky little shadow of a thought, as sly as a mouse, quick, dark, too sly to be caught, and without his moving enough for it to be noticed his still fine body would fall as violently as a giant tree crashes down beneath a final axe stroke, taking with it all the wheeling seasons of sun and stars, whole centuries of them, crashing suddenly into oblivion and rot. He would make this enormous fall without a perceptible movement of his body. At the most, it would show in the faint flicker of something across his face, whose color gave him the name people knew him by. Possibly one knee sagged a little forward. Then slowly, slowly, he would fasten one hand over his belt and raise the other one hesitantly to his head, feel the scalp and the hard round bowl of the skull underneath it, as if he dimly imagined that by feeling that dome he might be able to guess what was hidden inside it—facing now the intricate wickets of the summer to come.

For one reason or another, Mary Louise Grey was locked out of the house a great deal of the time that summer, and since she was a lonely child with little or no imagination, apparently unable to amuse herself with solitary games—except the endless one of copying her mother—the afternoons when she was excluded from the house because her mother had a headache were periods of great affliction. There were several galleries with outside stairs between them, and she would patrol the galleries and wander forlornly about the lawn or go down the front walk and sit in the glass box of the electric. She would vary her steps, sometimes walking sedately, sometimes skipping, sometimes hopping and humming, one plump hand always clutching a handkerchief that contained the lump of ice. This lump of ice to rub her mosquito bites had to be replaced at frequent intervals. "Oh, iceman!" the widow would call sweetly from an upstairs window. "Don't forget to leave some extra pieces for little Mary Louise to rub her mosquito bites with!"

From time to time, Mary Louise would utter a soft cry, and, in a voice that had her mother's trick of carrying a great distance without being loud, call, "Oh, Mother, I'm simply being devoured by mosquitoes!"

"Darling," her mother would answer from the upstairs window, "that's dreadful, but you know that Mother can't help it; she didn't create the mosquitoes and she can't destroy them for you!"

"You could let me come in the house, Mama."

"No, I can't let you come in, precious. Not yet."

"Why not, Mother?"

"Because Mother has a sick headache."

"I will be quiet."

"You say that you will, but you won't. You must learn to amuse yourself, precious; you mustn't depend on Mother to amuse you. Nobody can depend on anyone else forever. I'll tell you what you can do till Mother's headache is better. You can drive the electric out of the garage. You can drive it around the block, but don't go into the business district with it, and then you can stop in the shady part of the drive and sit there perfectly comfortably till Mother feels better and can get dressed and come out. And then I think Mr. Pollitt may come over for a game of croquet. Won't that be lovely?"

"Do you think he will get here in time to play?"

"I hope so, precious. It does him so much good to play croquet."

"Oh, I think it does all of us good to play croquet," Mary Louise would say, in a voice that trembled just at the vision of it.

Before Brick Pollitt arrived—sometimes half an hour before his coming, as though she could hear his automobile on the highway twenty miles from the house—Mary Louise would bound plumply off the gallery and begin setting up the poles and wickets. While she was doing this, her plump little buttocks and her beginning breasts and her shoulder-length copper curls would all bob up and down in unison. I would watch her from our front steps. She worked feverishly against time, for experience had taught her that the sooner she completed the preparations for the game, the greater would be the chance of getting her mother and Mr. Pollitt to play it. Frequently she was not fast enough, or they were too fast for her; by the time she had finished her perspiring job, the veranda would be deserted. Her wailing cries would begin, punctuating the dusk at intervals only a little less frequent than the passing of cars of people going out for evening drives to cool off.

"Mama! Mama! The croquet set is ready!"

Usually there would be a long, long wait for any response to come from the upstairs window toward which the calls were directed. But one time there wasn't. Almost immediately after the wailing voice was lifted, begging for the commencement of the game, Mary Louise's thin, pretty mother showed herself at the window. That was the time when I saw, between the dividing gauze of the bedroom curtains, her naked breasts, small and beautiful, shaken like two angry fists by her violent motion. She leaned between the curtains to answer Mary Louise not in her usual tone of gentle remonstrance but in a shocking cry of rage: "Oh, be still, for God's sake, you fat little monster!"

Mary Louise was shocked into a silence that must have lasted for a quarter of an hour. It was probably the word "fat" that struck her so overwhelmingly, for Mary Louise had once told me, when we were circling the block in the electric, that her mother had told her that she was *not* fat, that she was only plump, and that these cushions of flesh were going to dissolve in two or three more years and then she would be just as thin and pretty as her mother.

Though Mary Louise would call me over to play croquet with her, she was not at all satisfied with my game. I had had so little practice and she so much, and, besides, it was the company of the grown-up people she wanted. She would call me over only when they had disappeared irretrievably into the lightless house or when the game had collapsed owing to Mr. Brick Pollitt's refusal to take it seriously. When he played seriously, he was even better at it than Mary Louise, who practiced sometimes all afternoon in preparation for a game. But there were evenings when he would not leave his drink on the porch but would carry it down onto the lawn with him and play with one hand, more and more capriciously, while

in the other hand he carried a tall glass. Then the lawn would become a great stage on which he performed all the immemorial an-
tics of the clown, to the exasperation of Mary Louise and her thin,
pretty mother, both of whom would become very severe and dignified on these occasions. They would retire from the croquet lawn
and stand off at a little distance, calling softly, like a pair of
complaining doves, both in the same ladylike tones of remonstrance.
He was not a middle-aged-looking man—that is, he was not at all
big around the middle—and he could leap and run like a boy. He
could turn cartwheels and walk on his hands, and sometimes he
would grunt and lunge like a wrestler or make long, crouching
runs like a football player, weaving in and out among the wickets
and gaudily painted poles of the croquet lawn. The acrobatics and
sports of his youth seemed to haunt him. He would call out hoarsely
to invisible teammates and adversaries—muffled shouts of defiance
and anger and triumph, to which an incongruous counterpoint
was continually provided by the faint, cooing voice of the widow:
"Brick! Brick! Stop now, please stop! The child is crying! People
will think you've gone crazy!" For Mary Louise's mother knew
why the lights had gone out on all the screened porches up and
down the street and why the automobiles drove past the house at
the speed of a funeral procession while Mr. Brick Pollitt was making a circus ring of the croquet lawn.

Late one evening when he was making one of his crazy dashes
across the lawn with an imaginary football hugged against his belly,
he tripped over a wicket and sprawled on the lawn, and he pretended to be too gravely injured to get back on his feet. His groans
brought Mary Louise and her mother running from behind the
vine-screened end of the veranda and out upon the lawn to assist
him. They took him by the hands and tried to haul him up, but
with a sudden shout of laughter he pulled them both down on top
of him and held them there till both of them were sobbing. He
got up, finally, to replenish his glass of iced gin, and then returned
to the lawn. That evening was a fearfully hot one, and Brick decided to cool and refresh himself with the sprinkler while he enjoyed his drink. He turned it on and pulled it out to the center of
the lawn. There he rolled about on the grass under its leisurely
revolving arch of water, and as he rolled about, he began to wriggle
out of his clothes. He kicked off his white shoes and one of his
pale-green socks, tore off his drenched white shirt and grass-stained
linen pants, but he never succeeded in getting off his necktie.

Finally, he was sprawled, like some grotesque fountain figure, in underwear and necktie and the one remaining pale-green sock while the revolving arch of water moved with cool whispers about him. The arch of water had a faint crystalline iridescence, a mist of delicate colors, as it wheeled under the moon, for the moon had by that time begun to poke with an air of slow astonishment over the roof of the little building that housed the electric. And still the complaining doves cooed at him from various windows of the house, and you could tell their voices apart only by the fact that the mother murmured "Brick? Brick?" and Mary Louise called him Mr. Pollitt. "Oh, Mr. Pollitt, Mother is so unhappy! Mother is crying!"

That night, he talked to himself or to invisible figures on the lawn. One of them was his wife, Margaret. He kept saying, "I'm sorry, Margaret, I'm sorry, Margaret, I'm so sorry, so sorry, Margaret. I'm sorry I'm no good, I'm sorry, Margaret, I'm so sorry, so sorry I'm no good, sorry I'm drunk, sorry I'm no good, I'm so sorry it all had to turn out like this . . ."

Later on, much later, after the remarkably slow procession of touring cars had stopped passing the house, a little black sedan that belonged to the police drew up in front of the Greys' and sat there for a while. In it was the chief of police himself. He called "Brick! Brick!" almost as gently and softly as Mary Louise's mother had called from the lightless windows. "Brick! Brick, old boy! Brick, fellow?" he called, till finally the inert fountain figure in underwear and green sock and unremovable necktie staggered out from under the rotating arch of water and stumbled down to the walk and stood there negligently and quietly conversing with the chief of police, under the no longer at all astonished, now quite large and indifferent great yellow stare of the August moon. They began to laugh softly together, Mr. Brick Pollitt and the chief of police, and finally the door of the little black car opened and Mr. Brick Pollitt got in beside the chief of police while the common officer got out to collect the clothes, flabby as drenched towels, on the croquet lawn. Then they drove away, and the summer night's show was over.

It was not quite over for me, for I had been watching it all that time with unabated interest. And about an hour afterward I saw Mary Louise's mother come out onto the lawn; she stood there with an air of desolation for quite a while. Then she went into the garage and backed the electric out. The electric went sedately off into the summer night, with its buzzing no louder than an insect's, and perhaps an hour later it came back again, containing in its glass show box not only the thin, pretty widow but a quiet and chastened Mr. Pollitt. She curved an arm about his immensely tall figure as they went up the front walk, and I heard him say only one word distinctly. It was the name of his wife.

Early that autumn, which was different from summer in nothing except the quicker coming of dusk, the visits of Mr. Brick Pollitt began to take on a spasmodic irregularity. That faraway boom of a cannon at five o'clock was now the announcement that two ladies in white dresses were waiting on a white gallery for someone who was each time a little more likely to disappoint them than the time before. Disappointment was not a thing that Mary Louise was inured to; it was a country that she was passing through not as an old inhabitant but as a bewildered explorer, and each afternoon she lugged the oblong box out of the garage, ceremonially opened it upon the center of the lawn, and began to arrange the wickets in their formal pattern between the two gaudily painted poles that meant beginning, middle, and end. And the widow talked to her from the gallery, under the awning, as if there had been no important alteration in their lives or their prospects. Their almost duplicate voices as they talked back and forth between gallery and lawn rang out as clearly as if the enormous corner lot were enclosed at this hour by a still more enormous and perfectly transparent glass bell that picked up and carried through space whatever was uttered beneath it. This was true not only when they were talking to each other across the lawn but when they were seated side by side in the white wicker chairs on the gallery. Phrases from these conversations became catchwords, repeated and mocked by the neighbors, for whom the widow and her daughter and Mr. Brick Pollitt had been three players in a sensational drama. It had shocked and angered them for two acts, but now as it approached a conclusion it was declining into unintentional farce, which they could laugh at. It was not difficult to find something ludicrous in the talks between the two ladies or the high-pitched elegance of their voices.

Mary Louise would ask, "Will Mr. Pollitt get here in time for croquet?"

"I hope so, precious. It does him so much good."

"He'll have to come soon or it will be too dark to see the wickets."

"That's true, precious."

"Mother, why is it dark so early now?"

"Honey, you know why. The sun goes South."

"But why does it go South?"

"Precious, Mother cannot explain the movements of the heavenly bodies, you know that as well as Mother knows it. Those things are controlled by certain mysterious laws that people on earth don't know or understand."

"Mother, are we going East?"

"When, precious?"

"Before school starts."

"Honey, you know it's impossible for Mother to make any definite plans."

"I hope we do. I don't want to go to school here."

"Why not, precious? Are you afraid of the children?"

"No, Mother, but they don't like me. They make fun of me."

"How do they make fun of you?"

"They mimic the way I talk and they walk in front of me with their stomachs pushed out and giggle."

"That's because they're children and children are cruel."

"Will they stop being cruel when they grow up?"

"Why, I suppose some of them will and some of them won't."

"Well, I hope we go East before school opens."

"Mother can't make any plans or promises, honey."

"No, but Mr. Brick Pollitt—"

"Honey, lower your voice! Ladies talk softly."

"Oh, my goodness!"

"What is it, precious?"

"A mosquito just bit me!"

"That's too bad, but don't scratch it. Scratching can leave a permanent scar on the skin."

"I'm not scratching it. I'm just sucking it, Mother."

"Honey, Mother has told you time and again that the thing to do when you have a mosquito bite is to get a small piece of ice and wrap it up in a handkerchief and rub the bite gently with it until the sting is removed."

"That's what I do, but my lump of ice is melted!"

"Get you another piece, honey. You know where the icebox is!"

"There's not much left. You put so much in the ice bag for your headache."

"There must be some left, honey."

"There's just enough left for Mr. Pollitt's drinks."

"Never mind that."

"He needs it for his drinks, Mother."

"Yes, Mother knows what he wants the ice for, precious."

"There's only a little piece left. It's hardly enough to rub a mosquito bite with."

"Well, use it for that purpose, that purpose is better, and anyhow when Mr. Pollitt comes over as late as this, he doesn't deserve to have any ice saved for him."

"Mother?"

"Yes, precious?"

"I love ice and sugar!"

"What did you say, precious?"

"I said I loved ice and sugar!"

"Ice and sugar, precious?"

"Yes, I love the ice and sugar in the bottom of Mr. Pollitt's glass when he's through with it."

"Honey, you mustn't eat the ice in the bottom of Mr. Pollitt's glass!"

"Why not, Mother?"

"Because it's got liquor in it!"

"Oh, no, Mother. It's just ice and sugar when Mr. Pollitt's through with it."

"Honey, there's always a little liquor left in it."

"Oh, no. Not a drop's left when Mr. Pollitt's through with it!"

"But you say there's sugar left in it, and, honey, you know that sugar is very absorbent."

"It's what, Mummy?"

"It absorbs some liquor, and that's a good way to cultivate a taste for it. And, honey, you know what dreadful consequences a taste for liquor can have. It's bad enough for a man, but for a woman it's fatal. So when you want ice and sugar, let Mother know and she'll prepare some for you, but don't ever let me catch you eating what's left in Mr. Pollitt's glass!"

"Mama?"

"Yes, precious?"

"It's almost completely dark now. Everybody is turning on their lights or driving out on the river road to cool off. Can't we go out riding in the electric?"

"No, honey, we can't till we know Mr. Pollitt's not—"

"Do you still think he will come?"

"Precious, how can I say? Is Mother a fortune-teller?"

"Oh, here comes the Pierce, Mummy, here comes the Pierce!"

"Is it? Is it the Pierce?"

"Oh, no. No, it isn't. It's a Hudson Super Six. Mummy, I'm going to pull up the wickets now and water the lawn, because if Mr. Pollitt does come, he'll have people with him or won't be in a condition to play croquet. And when I've finished, I want to drive the electric around the block."

"Drive it around the block, honey, but don't go into the business district with it."

"Are you going with me, Mummy?"

"No, precious, I'm going to sit here."

"It's cooler in the electric."

"I don't think so. The electric goes too slowly to make much breeze."

If Mr. Pollitt did finally arrive those evenings, it was likely to be with a caravan of cars that came from Memphis, and then Mrs. Grey would have to receive a raffish assortment of strangers as if she herself had invited them to a party. The party would not confine itself to the downstairs rooms and galleries but would explode quickly and brilliantly in all directions, filling both floors of the house, spilling out upon the lawn, and sometimes even penetrating the little building that housed the electric automobile and the oblong box that held the packed-away croquet set. On those party nights, the fantastically balustraded and gabled and turreted white building would glitter all over, like one of those huge night-excursion boats that came downriver from Memphis, and it would be full of ragtime music and laughter. But at some point in the evening there would be, almost invariably, a disturbance. Some male guest would start cursing loudly, a woman would scream, you would hear a shattering of glass. Almost immediately afterward, the lights would go out in the house, as if it really were a boat and had run aground. From all the doors and galleries and stairs, people would come rushing forth, and the dispersion would be more rapid than the arrival had been. A little while later, the police car would pull up in front of the house. The thin, pretty widow would come out on the front gallery to receive the chief of police, and you could hear her light voice tinkling like glass chimes. "Why, it was nothing, it was nothing at all, just somebody who drank a little too much and lost his temper. You know how that Memphis crowd is, Mr. Duggan, there's always one gentleman in it who can't hold his liquor. I know it's late, but we have such a huge lawn—it occupies half the block—that I shouldn't think anybody who wasn't overcome with curiosity would have to know that a party had been going on!"

And then something happened that made no sound at all.

It wasn't an actual death, but it had nearly all the external indications of one. When there is a death in a house, the house is unnaturally quiet for a day or two. During that interval, the space that separates a house from those who watch it seems to become a translucent thickness of glass behind which whatever activity is visible goes on with the startling hush of a film when the sound track is broken. So it had been five months ago, when the pleasant young Doctor had died of that fierce flower grown in his skull. There had been an unnatural quiet for several days, and then a peculiar gray car with frosted windows had crashed through the bell of silence and the young Doctor, identifiable by the bronze gleam of hair at one end of the strapped and sheeted figure on the cot, had emerged from the house as if he were giving a public demonstration of how to go to sleep soundly in jolting motion under a blaze of lights.

That was five months ago, and it was now early October.

Mr. Pollitt had not been seen at the Greys' for more than a week when, one day, a truck pulled up before the house and a workman planted a square wooden sign at the front of the lawn. Mrs. Grey came out of the house as if it had caught fire. She ran down the steps, her white skirts making the crackling noise of flame, calling out as she descended, "You, man! What are you doing! What are you putting up there!"

"A 'For Sale' sign," he told her.

"Who told you to put that up? This house isn't for sale!"

"Yes, Ma'am, it is!"

"Who said so?"

"Mrs. Pollitt, *she* said so."

He stared at Mrs. Grey and she came no closer. Then he gave the pole of the red-lettered sign a final blow with the back of a shovel and tossed the implement crashing into the truck and drove off. The back of the sign said nothing, so presently Mrs. Grey continued her running advance to the front of the lawn, where the great red letters were visible. She stood in front of it, rapidly shaking her head, finally gasping aloud as if the import of it had just then struck her, and then she turned and went slowly and thoughtfully back to the radiant fantasy of a house just as Mary Louise appeared from behind it with the hose.

"Mother!" she called, "I'm going to water the lawn!"

"Don't!" said Mrs. Grey.

The next afternoon, a fat and pleasantly smiling man, whom I had seen times without number loitering around in front of the used-car lot next to the Paramount movie, came up the front walk of the Greys' house with the excessive nonchalance of a man who is about to commit a robbery. He pushed the bell, waited awhile, pushed it again, and then was admitted through an opening that seemed to be hardly wide enough for his figure. He came back out almost immediately with something in his closed fist. It was the key to the little building that contained the croquet set and the electric automobile. He drew its folding doors all the way open, and disclosed the electric sitting there with its usual manner of a lady putting on or taking off her gloves at the entrance to a reception. He stared at it, as if its elegance were momentarily baffling. Then he got in and drove it out of the garage, holding the polished black pilot stick with a look on his round face that was like the look of an adult who is a little embarrassed to find himself being amused by a game that was meant for children. He drove it serenely out into the wide, shady street, and at an upstairs window of the house there was some kind of quick movement, as if a figure looking out had been startled by something and then had retreated in haste.

Later, after the Greys had left town, I saw the elegant square vehicle, which appeared to be made out of glass and patent leather, standing with an air of haughty self-consciousness among a dozen or so other cars for sale in the lot next door to the Paramount movie theatre, and as far as I know, it may be still sitting there, but many degrees less glittering by now.

The Greys had come and gone all in one quick season: the young Doctor, with his understanding eyes and quiet voice, whom everyone had liked in a hesitant, early way and had said would do well in the town; the thin, pretty woman, whom no one had really known except Brick Pollitt; and the plump little girl, who might someday be as pretty and slender as her mother. They had come and gone in one season, yes, like one of these tent shows that suddenly appear in a vacant lot in a Southern town and cross the sky at night with mysteriously wheeling lights and unearthly music, and then are gone, and the summer goes on without them, as if they had never come there.

As for Mr. Brick Pollitt, I can remember seeing him only once after the Greys left town, for my time there was also coming to an end. This last time that I saw him was a brilliant fall morning. It was a Saturday morning in October. Brick's driver's license had been revoked again, and his wife, Margaret, sat in the driver's seat of the Pierce-Arrow touring car. Brick did not sit beside her. He was on the back seat of the car, pitching this way and that way with the car's jolting motion, like a loosely wrapped package being delivered somewhere. Margaret Pollitt handled the car with a wonderful male assurance, her bare arms brown and muscular, and the car's canvas top had been lowered, the better to expose on its back seat the sheepishly grinning and nodding figure of Brick Pollitt. He was immaculately clothed and barbered. The knot of his polka-dot tie was drawn as tight as strong and eager fingers could knot a tie for an important occasion. One of his large red hands protruded, clasping the door to steady his motion, and two bands of gold glittered, a small one about a finger, a large one about the wrist. His cream-colored coat was neatly folded on the seat beside him and he wore a shirt of thin white material. He was a man who had been, and even at that time still was, the handsomest you were likely to remember.

Margaret blew the car's silver trumpet at every intersection. She leaned this way and that way, elevating or thrusting out an arm as she greeted people on porches, merchants beside store entrances, people she barely knew along the walks, calling them all by their familiar names, as if she were running for office in the town, while Brick nodded and grinned with senseless amiability behind her. It was exactly the way that some ancient conqueror, such as Caesar, or Alexander the Great, or Hannibal, might have led in chains through a capital city the prince of a state newly conquered.

CAN'T YOU GET ME OUT OF HERE?

❖

JULIA STRACHEY

M Y father, whose failing eyesight prevents him from reading to himself any more, sometimes invites me to tackle our English daily newspapers with him, and to read the interesting bits aloud. The procedure goes like this: I read out one of the headlines: " '"UNFORGETTABLE!" SAYS THE QUEEN.' " I pause. No protest, so I continue: " 'The day the Queen called unforgettable ended in twenty-one-gun salutes, glistening eyes, prolonged handshakes, and that happy sense of well-being—' "

"Pass on!" interrupts my father sharply. "Next!"

I try another headline. " 'SAILORS VANISH IN CANVAS BOAT.' "

"Pass on!" says my father at once.

I try again. " 'BURIED WALLS RIDDLE. Experts are baffled by the discovery of two six-foot-wide concrete walls below the pavements in Finchley Road—' "

"Pass!" shouts my father. I look desperately for something else. I try heading after heading.

" 'THE GREATEST LIAR,' " I proclaim, and read, " 'A man went to the psychiatrist and told him—' "

"Pass away!" barks my father.

I turn the page.

" 'COLD STORE BEAUTIES.' " I pause a moment. Then read, " 'Many of the lilies on view—' "

"Pass!"

" . . . umm . . . er . . . well, how about 'MR. GAITSKELL HITS BACK. In an attempt to rescue the Socialist Party—' "

"Pass on!"

And so we seem to go on all through the paper—Pass! Pass away! Pass along! Pass!

And these words of command from my father have so hypnotized

341

me that I have fallen now into the habit of organizing my entire
life to the administrative rhythm of these commands.

Thus, seated at our country kitchen table: "No more beans to
be got out of these pods—Pass along.—Washing up next."

Or, in the sitting room: "That's just about all I can bear to read
in the parish magazine today—Pass away.—Out into the square now
to find old Mr. Field and ask him to mow the lawn."

But most often it pops up to keep my thoughts in order. To
prevent them coming round full circle too often and that sort of
thing. Pass! Pass away! Pass on!

A capacious tureen alternately full of spaghetti and of rice stood
on the table in the terrace arbor of the Pensione Bel Mare each
morning at half past twelve. To eat it, our family party—my Aunt
Emerald and Uncle Félix and their daughter, my Cousin Polly, and
myself—arranged ourselves on a circular bench round the table,
together with one or two other holidaymakers from far-distant
lands. In the hot sea winds, the vine leaves on the trellis walls of our
arbor fought each other and scuffled against our bare shoulders, as
we leaned back to watch the proprietress doling out the helpings,
and listened patiently to her diurnal singsong explanation, ladle in
hand: "*Questi si chiamano spaghetti, con una salsa di pomodoro, il
piatto preferito degli italiani.*"

One day, after my aunt had been given her helping and the ladle
had returned to hover over the spaghetti, something dark and heavy
suddenly shot out from the arbor ceiling and landed PLOP! in the
middle of the spaghetti tureen, and disappeared.

"What's that?"

"What happened?"

Everyone leaned forward. All was quiet in the spaghetti dish.

Only the Signora sat back in her chair. "Eh! *Regalo del cielo!*" A
present from Heaven! She announced it, smiling graciously round.

Suddenly three or four of the long tomato-covered *pasta* ribbons
began slowly to heave, to work about, and gyrate in the dish center.
Everyone watched. In a moment there would be an emergence,
something would appear. What?

And also when?

We sat mystified, watching the writhing spaghetti ribbons working round faster and faster, where, in the vortex, some living being
floundered, ringed greasily over and under and all about.

Leaning forward in a tense, watching circle, one could almost hear the frantic question from the hidden center of the dish: "Where am I? Can't you get me out of here?"

It was my cousin who gave the only intelligible answer. Seizing a tablespoon, she lifted the struggling vortex clear of the spaghetti and cast it out of the arbor onto a flower bed, from where, bedraggled, but none the worse, really, it leaped up and soared over the geranium heads—a small tree frog, so my uncle said. Probably, peering down from the arbor roof at our red spaghetti, it had become curious as to what sort of thing that could be, and had bounded optimistically forward to investigate.

I am a tree frog myself. And I can confirm that it is indeed a brash curiosity about queer-looking-things-far-glimpsed that starts a tree frog's nervous speckled legs to twitch. I know it all—the lunatic leap out from the scaffolding into space, the brief whiz through colored airs, then the landing down in the dark, among yielding, treacherous, slithering things. I know the seasick and obsessional floundering around tangled up in those writhing strings, the panic, and the desperation in the cries "Where am I?—Can't you get me out of here?" I know also the half-heard unintelligible ripostes from the weird circle of strangers, more sensed than seen, sitting about and watching one drown.

But for me it is the spectacle of the very Distances themselves, Long Distances (not negligible Distances), that intoxicates. Or to put it another way, the spectacle of Differences that acts like strong drink and causes the green-speckled legs to twitch. For, of course, wherever there's a difference there's a distance as well. . . . However . . . Pass Along. One doesn't want old chestnuts. Platitudes . . .

Particular instances are more the thing.

I remember (for instance) a fat and ancient golden-retriever bitch belonging to a hotel on the North Country moors of Teesdale, where my husband and I used sometimes to spend a blowy weekend.

This old thing, all grace gone, would waddle into the dank hotel dining room at every meal with thrashing, joyful tail. She would visit each table, each guest, in turn. Looking, you will say, for the odd tidbit of meat that might be coming her way. Perhaps. But looking also, it became clear, for the cordial personal welcome —the "oh-you-sweet-old-thing-you!" and the amiable spank upon the broad gold tableland behind, for never a bite to eat did she get, yet nevertheless from almost everyone a personal greeting of some kind.

My own husband, no dog-lover, and determined on this occasion to encourage no false hopes, whenever the broad, stupid, smiling head was upraised from under the tablecloth and the expectant eyes fastened to his face, even *he* (though with his gaze still fixed upon his own dinner plate and absolutely no weakening of countenance) —even *he* volunteered upon each occasion four remarks, namely, "Hallo. Hallo. Hallo. Hallo." Though he let it rest at that. And away the animal would stump again with wagging tail.

One day, amongst the motor-coach day excursionists who regularly debouched into our dining room at one o'clock, there came in one of the most clerkly and urban, seedy, and generally dried-up and unnatural-looking men—if you could call him a man—I'd ever seen. He sat down. And when the retriever came in and started upon her rounds, in the manner of a heavy yellow chest of drawers upon the move—at once cumbrous and faltering—I certainly anticipated a disappointing visit to the table where this pinched fellow sat.

But to my surprise, when the bitch put up her head to his knee, he gallantly waggled his waxed mustaches and addressed her thus (she meanwhile attending carefully, staring deep into his eyes): "Oh, you're *beautiful!!* You're a beauty! You lovely thing you. —But, good Lord, haven't you grown terribly *old,* though!! . . . Ah, no . . . I mean to say . . . well, you're not really *old*"—he pulled himself up and hesitated a moment, trying to find the word to set things right—"you're just a bit *old before your time*. That's all. And mind—you're still beautiful!"

This conclusion seemed to satisfy him. The dog also. And away she staggered well pleased, with her thwacking rope-stout tail.

Listening in to this long-distance call put through in the hotel dining room between these two beings—Clerk and Retriever—with its questions asked and answers given, so very satisfactorily on both sides, made one quite reflective. And very soon up came this question: What, then, *is* the difference or distance between an old girl from the animal world and an old girl of the human kind?

When I mention that every whisker, tail, or claw waved within my sight, all down the avenues of the years, has been narrowly observed, and conjectured upon, and filed away by me, you might imagine that I have formed some sort of opinion regarding the foregoing question. And so I have. However, Pass Away. There's first something else I want to bring up. An experience I had, so my diary tells me, on August 3, 1954.

Breakfast on the third of August, 1954, to Popsy—the youthful yellow basenji bitch belonging to our friends Vi and Rollo Anderson—seemed like breakfast on any other day. I remember I found her alone in the kitchen at Tilton Manor Farm when I got down, just before ten, to cook and eat my breakfast, as was the custom for visitors in this house.

As I returned from stove to kitchen table carrying my egg and coffee, Popsy sprang on the chair beside the window. And there she remained throughout breakfast, an upreared hound with arched neck and long, stiff paws on the kitchen window sill, looking out upon the farm *va-et-vient,* which consisted, at that hour, of a lot of reproachful ducks and hopeful kittens going the rounds of the empty pig buckets.

Heraldic! Yes. But one had to admit that Popsy, with her ever-ready meaningless grin and eyebrows wrinkled up in eternal perplexity, both looked and was a very stupid dog. It was her blank and bemused countenance, rather than her so notorious moral delinquency, which had at first put me against her. All the same, later on my attitude altered. I came to notice, in all the daily painful vicissitudes that are inevitably attendant upon such a nature—I mean the thwacks, lockings up, and other strident hostilities following upon the daily chewed and ripped-up counterpanes and the ever more and more broken-tailed chickens, etc.—I came to notice Popsy's unwavering civility to everyone, and the cordial bonhomie which she preserved throughout all these inharmonius happenings, and somehow I was melted. One realized she had the bloom of a truly hopeless innocence. After which the higher criticism came to seem out of place.

I hooked my poached egg properly on top of its toast and cut into it.

From my kitchen breakfast table I could see the two palatial greenhouses that ran along outside the windows here. Grand conservatories indeed they must once have been. In Edward VII's day, say, and even later than that. But never at any date so romantic (that is, unclassical) as now, when—their last hour so obviously at hand—they had achieved a truly epic mid-century *dégringolade* in housing beneath their dirt-clouded and fly-encrusted heights and along their cobwebbed galleries such an exotic entanglement of hens, cats, farm medical supplies, caponizing hormones, inoculating needles, dog biscuits, kettles, flowerpots, and I don't know what besides.

While drinking my coffee I could admire through one of the open greenhouse doors the most burly—because, I suppose, the oldest—fig tree I'd ever seen, whose leaves dripped down from the high roof in a green cavern of vegetable stalactites, and upon whose top branches Vi's bantam hens would crowd themselves each night to roost, to give the appearance of some kind of gray tree fairies with sparkling diamond eyes tucked into the foliage, and to sit chattering to each other like so many knives scraping upon so many dinner plates.

Of course, at this hour of the morning the bantams were outside on the gravel path pecking up grains. And with them, as usual, the white cat with the tortoise-shell patches, who—so Vi and Rollo told us—having been born and brought up in the greenhouse with the bantams, had lived out her whole subsequent life with the flock, eating and doing everything that they did, under the impression that she was a bantam too, and who was never now likely to learn that she was all the while a cat.

After breakfast, through the scullery and out at the back door we went, Popsy and I, to sniff the summer day. I wanted to look at Vi's big black hens, a flock of whom were imprisoned at the far end of this fig conservatory.

Popsy, marigold in the sunlight, stepped out high on stilt legs, prancing forward on air, and when she saw we were making for the hens she pricked high her ears, and exaggerated greatly, in the manner of a clown, her farcical grin and wild eyebrows tied in knots.

I often went over to watch this particular crowd of hens, so like a band of black-clad gentlewomen from the Cromwell Road in their gentility and affected politesse. The dumfounding thing about them was their identicalness. No Cromwell Road operatic society zealously rehearsing a crowd scene together could have produced a more drilled effect as to timing and gesture and general overactorliness.

For as soon as they saw one approach to look, these hens (who would previously be zigzagging fussily all about) would sense that the curtain had gone up, and would stop dead in their tracks, in special deferential attitudes. That is, each hen with one delicate claw upraised questioningly, and her head cocked over on one side in a stylized attentiveness. And this pose, on one leg, would be held to,

minute after minute after minute, by the whole crowd, and signified
that they were waiting courteously for one to state one's business. If
one just went on staring rudely at them without any sort of explanation, as we did this morning, they would then begin, still on one
leg, to turn and turn about their questioning heads from side to
side with an ever-increasing rapidity, and with ever more and more
energy, producing a kind of noiseless volubility, expressive of rising
amazement, pique, and, finally, general scandalization at one's
boorishness. When the pitch of emotion became such that there
was fear of a communal heart attack, I would move off a few paces.
I did so now. At once the band relaxed. Claws came to earth. Everyone scooted zigzagging off about her private business.

All the same, one only had to stand still and stare at the window-
pane to start the whole thing over again once more. And so I did
this morning. More than once.

When I finally decided to tear myself away from this pantomime,
I moved over to peer into the second glasshouse, which ran along
behind, and noticed then that Popsy was no longer with me.

This second conservatory contained—was, rather, bursting at the
seams with—a raging congestion of the most vicious-looking nettles
you ever saw in your life. Gigantic stingers, yards high, and with
great bulky boles they were, and all desperately interlocked and
fighting each other for the space to live. And though all diseased
and dying, with their ugly scabbed and tattered leaves, and carrying
along their old corpses flapping over their shoulders, they still went
on fighting each other eternally, many of them even lunging far
forward into an opposing army of loosestrife across the central aisle
and joining issue with those as well.

This morning, I saw that the loosestrife had exploded a cloud of
suffocating dirty gray powder all over their enemies and over everything. Outlines were blurred as if under lava. It made one choke
even to look at them. And in the greenhouse dimness this new
hostile fusillade of life—the gray seeds of the loosestrife, still attempting to force a footing where no further foothold could possibly
be—was a horrid sight.

I walked round outside this greenhouse, eyes glued sombrely on
the vegetable holocaust within, and only skipping aside from time
to time where some giant stinger had burst out through a broken
pane and bounded up and down in the wind, barring the pathway
and gibbering and cursing at all the passersby.

I remember that at the end of this glasshouse I spied Archie, the little boy of five who lived in the cottage of one of the farmhands, kneeling on the path and bent over a blue toy cart into which he had piled stones and gravel, from which he now appeared to be doing some kind of sorting out and throwing away.

Rollo, my host, emerged from the trees, in his faded Italian workman's shirt and trousers and carrying a hose. Without seeing me he passed by the little boy. Then he halted.

"What are you doing?" he asked Archie curiously.

"Mincing."

"*What?*"

"Mincing."

"I see," said Rollo without seeing, and passed on in the direction of his rockery. But the boy suddenly stood up and bawled after him, "We got ter do as our Lord done!"

Rollo turned in the pathway, startled.

". . . er . . . y-y-e-e-s," he said doubtfully, then resolutely turned back again and went on toward his garden. I followed him, still unobserved.

Our path met the main drive soon, and now here came Popsy hurtling over from the croquet lawn. She fairly flung herself upon her master, to whom she was devoted, as if after an absence of a lifetime. And there burst from her breast the only sound a basenji knows how to make—a stupefying chortle, part klaxon horn, part peacock, part laughing hyena, which is unmistakably a joyful greeting all the same.

Then, levitating giraffelike all around her loved one in floating circles as he crossed the drive, she accompanied him out of sight behind the house.

Giraffelike. The basenji, like the giraffe, hails from Central Africa. And certainly one could well imagine this crazy hound's ancestors racing giraffes through the simmering plains and mirages, breaching the fabulous distances like chiffon scarves outstreaming.

Rollo was very busy that morning doing some last-minute things to his rockery and clearing up his studio. Vi I did not see at all, for she was packing and giving final orders at the farm.

The fact was that Rollo and Vi were going abroad that afternoon for a long holiday. The plan being that Popsy was to be shut up while they got with their luggage into the car, and after they had gone my husband and I on our way up to London were to drive Popsy to some kennels kept by a Captain Armitage, where she was to be boarded out until they came home again.

But to return. After inspecting the hens and the nettles I went to the wooden summerhouse beside the croquet lawn. Here I sat for the rest of the morning, a yard or two from where Vi had had tethered a Jersey bull calf, almost a baby, to crop the long grass thereabouts.

I had brought out magazines to look at, and there were yellowed stacks of papers left out by the Andersons on the bamboo table.

The bull calf, cream velvet coat puffed over with smoke and enormous feminine black eyes sentimentally fringed with sweeping lashes, moved vaguely round and round its stake, munching a little and pondering.

I had noticed that Popsy had been careering round about the croquet lawn, trying in vain to get the lazy dachshunds to play with her. Now I saw that she had got hold of a teacup from somewhere. She brought it up close to my summerhouse and started tempting me to get up and wrest it away from her. She was bursting with energy this morning, needed an occupation, knew the purloining of a teacup, a strictly forbidden thing, was usually good for some sort of dramatics—so she started off the game and let the best man win. First she would press her nose into the teacup and toss it high into the air, with a side glance at me. I remained unmoved. Then, determined to be noticed, she would endeavor to get altogether inside the teacup. And finish by standing on her head, somersaulting backward, seizing the teacup by its rim again and racing with it in circles round and round among the croquet hoops. A basenji's gambols have a delightfully strange, stiff-jointed sort of elegance, and Popsy could have been a small unicorn indulging in an orgy of archaic caperings, teacup in mouth.

But no animal instinct seemed to warn her of what was to happen to her within a few short hours. And I found it sinister at this moment to see her so gay and confident with her teacup, taking utterly for granted the sunny croquet lawn and her home here. So stupidly certain that it would be like this forever. But Popsy, of course, like other animals, could not do otherwise than live in the present moment. Now she felt secure because her master and mistress were within sight. Or shall we say sound—because for the rest of that morning we heard only their voices from time to time, on the other side of the thin shrubbery that separated the summerhouse from the back door.

At one moment when we heard footsteps back there, several people evidently sauntering slowly together, I recognized the three voices of Vi, of Lewis (my husband), and of a very young man known as Baby Johnson, an elegant twentyish figure who was staying in the house at the time.

I heard Vi's voice: ". . . Flora, of course, has absolutely no idea at all what art is all about and what kind of thing artists are up to. And I must confess that *I'm* not at all sure, either."

"Beauty!" answered Baby, in a dashing, loud tone. And I could picture his languid-wafting cigarette holder. He had managed to say the shocking thing, as ever.

There was a silence. (And I knew Lewis wasn't going to break it.) Then: "Lewis! . . . *Your* turn . . ." in Vi's voice.

The kind of conversation they had evidently been having was in the nature of a busman's holiday for Lewis, whose profession is concerned with just such matters, and I wondered how he would sidestep it.

"It is by no means certain that all artists are engaged in the same activity, anyway. . . ." at last came Lewis's voice, not overcordially.

Pigs squealed in the pig houses at the farm. The footsteps had halted outside the kitchen door for some reason. Perhaps Vi was picking out weeds from the gravel pathway that caught her attention. There was another silence. Then from Vi, briskly: *"Box on, Lewis!"*

"I'm really getting rather bored stiff with all this art talk," from Lewis.

"Oh, no, Lewis! You *must* box in on it! Because it is the only way the young ever pick up or learn anything at all—by hearing people like you talk, don't you see?"

More footsteps approached. Then Rollo's voice exploded: "Oh, my God! I *was* a fool not to have put the Chablis into the refrigerator!" We had been asked to be punctual for lunch today. I looked at my wristwatch. It was five past one. I jumped up and hurried indoors to wash my hands.

Immediately after lunch Popsy was shut up in the back sitting room, so as not to see Vi and Rollo pack into the car and drive away to the airport. And when I finally let her out of there, it was not until she had raced around the passages and the kitchens, and the studio, and the rockery and the lawns, and the shrubberies, and also, finally, through all the empty bedrooms in turn, finding everywhere deserted and silent, that her intimations of disaster began to mount.

Why is it that if a dog is left alone, say, in a car on a shopping expedition, even for a bare minute, the wild fear of Calamity by Desertion at once floods over it? At once begins all that heart-broken weeping, that stricken woe. It seems to feel that some fated betrayal, which all along it had been expecting, has happened at last. *This is it.*

Before we got Popsy into the car, even, she was already wild with this primeval horror.

Then the journey to the kennels! Actually three-quarters of an hour, it seemed to last a lifetime. The hectic rush round and round from window to window, and from seat to floor, and from the floor to scramble feverishly up over the dividing barrier at my back in order to slither, panting hoarsely, down over my shoulder onto my knee; the tugging and holding of her back by main force away from Lewis, who was driving, and whom she was determined to scrabble all over—all this made one realize that one was struggling with the madness of the jungle itself. (Where am I? Can't you . . . ? etc.)

For three-quarters of an hour, her deranged nerves on fire, she kept up this incessant panting and choking and circling without a pause, round and round and round and round again.

Yet, arrived at the kennels, what was so strange, and so terrible, was the way the poor thing even then in some odd way apparently still trusted us. For she became completely docile, suffering herself to be handed over to Captain Armitage without one struggle.

For me this was the worst moment of all. As I held her in my hands, warm and silky, and passed her over to the enemy, I felt like a combination of Delilah and Judas Iscariot.

Captain Armitage immediately popped her inside a small wire enclosure fronting a dark kennel hut, to the earsplitting barks of a furious strange dog next door through the wooden partition.

We started to leave her. She plunged forward up against the enclosing wire. We turned our backs and left. It was unintelligible to her just as it is unintelligible to us—the cage which encloses the protesting life so weirdly and relentlessly. Could the helplessness of the living thing brought suddenly face to face with the magic of its prison in a wider sense have overcome her at that moment? I looked back at Popsy before getting into the car again, and my last glimpse was of her straddled low over the ground, helplessly pouring forth the contents of her guts in panic fear.

At any rate her old, familiar, beautiful life was over. She had been deserted by the ones she loved; she had been betrayed into the hands of these strangers, to live out the rest of her days in this rotten few inches of earth. That's, anyway, how it was to her.

As for me, I felt, as I lay in bed that night, as if a meat axe had been thrown into my soul and was sticking there, undislodgeable.

In no time I was out from the scaffolding and down in the darkness inside the old spaghetti tureen. I asked myself how had we ever got into this position of wielding absolute power over other animals? It was all owing, of course, to *Homo sapiens* having achieved this Extra Finger (thumb), together with a Memory, that we had been able to outmaneuver the generality of our animal brethren. Oh, yes. But now, what about our consequent responsibility toward this animal *hoi polloi?* What about paying back our debt to evolution?

On the other hand: Was it not a pipe dream, this trying to shake ourselves free from Nature Red In Tooth And Claw? This Christian humbug that man can afford to be kind? I mean to say, what was our correct attitude toward, for instance, the Kingdoms of the Flies, the Bugs, the Germs, the Virus? One must be logical.

A tree frog's legs are weak. And even if they weren't it wouldn't help among all that spongy, wheeling, springy *pasta!* Round and round I swam. Popsy, now. That was the point. (I determined to argue in a practical, a *possible* way.)

"All I'm saying is: *Am* I my friend's dog's keeper?"

It was my own voice in the darkness, calling aloud—a ludicrous sound—as if in answer to some unseen circle of accusers.

Again, a little later: "Don't you see that there's such a thing as *not* being in a position of responsibility? Such a thing as keeping, as you might say, one's proper distance? I tell you, I was merely obeying orders!"

There was an impression of a lot of shouting in my room, and I didn't really recognize, then, the answers given by the guards of Dachau and of Hola, because my father's voice interrupted at that moment—"Pass! Pass along!" it said. "Pass on. . . . Pass away!"

ASK ME NO QUESTIONS

❖

MARY McCARTHY

THERE was something strange, abnormal, about my bringing-up; only now that my grandmother is dead am I prepared to face this fact. When she died, she had not divulged her age; none of her children knew it, and whatever birth date they found in her papers has remained a secret to me. She was well over eighty, certainly, and senile when she finally "passed away," three years ago, in her tall Seattle house—under her gold taffeta puff, doubtless, with her rings on her fingers and her blue-figured diamond wristwatch on her puckered wrist. Probably she herself no longer knew how old she was; she was confused the last time I saw her, six years ago, when I flew West to be with her after she had broken her hip. Going over family photographs, which we spread out on her bed, she nodded and smiled eagerly, sitting up among her pillows like a macaw on its perch, in her plumage of black hair and rouge and eyebrow pencil and mascara. She recognized the faces—her husband, Grandpa Preston, with a mustache, her husband clean-shaven, her son in a World War I uniform, her nephews, her younger son in a sailor suit, my mother dressed as a Spanish dancer, my mother in a ball gown—but she was vague about the names. "My father," she decided after studying an obituary photograph of Grandpa, clipped out of a newspaper. "Son," "husband," and "father" were all one to her. She knew who I was, right enough, and did not mix me up with my dead mother, but this was not very flattering, since it was usually the people she had loved that she could not keep apart, melting them into a single category—father-son-husband—like the Mystery of the Trinity. One relation whom she had quarrelled with she picked out instantly, while I was still fumbling for the name. "That's Gertrude!" she proclaimed victoriously. Then she made a face—the same face she made when the cook brought her something she did not like on her tray. I reminded her that she had made up with Gertrude years ago, but she shook her head. "Bad," she said childishly. "Gertrude said bad things about me."

"You," she said one day, suddenly pointing. "You wrote bad things about me. Bad." It was not true; I had never written about her at all. But when I told her so, she would not listen, nor would she say where she had derived her notion. This was exactly like her; she collected stray grudges like bits of colored ribbon and would never tell where they came from. Nobody had ever known, for instance, the exact cause of her falling-out with Gertrude. That day, sitting by her bed, I tried to coax her into a better frame of mind. She turned her head away on the pillow and shut her eyes; long, sharp lines ran down, like rivulets of discontent, from her nose to the corners of her mouth. A hopeless silence followed. It troubled me to see her like this; those deep, bitter lines were new to me, yet it must have taken years to indent them. I did not know whether to leave or stay, and I wished the nurse would come in. "You wrote about my husband," she abruptly charged, opening her eyes and frowning over her high-bridged nose. This was a sign that she was far away; in her clear moments she spoke of him to me as "Grandpa." "Yes," I agreed. "I wrote about Grandpa."

It transpired that this had made her very angry, though she had never alluded to it in any of her letters. But why, precisely, she was angry, I could not find out from her. Certainly I had not said anything that she could call "bad" about Grandpa. It occurred to me that she was jealous because she had not been included in these writings; moreover, my grandfather had been shown with other women—a Mother Superior, a fictional aunt, myself. When she accused me of putting her in, did she really mean that she felt left out? She was capable of such a contradiction even before her mind had clouded. Or did she suppose that *she* was the aunt—a disagreeable personage? Hopeless, hopeless, I repeated to myself. It had always been like this. You could never explain anything to her or make her see you loved her. She rebuffed explanations, as she rebuffed shows of affection; they intruded on her privacy, that closely guarded preserve—as sacrosanct as her bureau drawers or the safe with a combination lock in her closet—in which she clung to her own opinion. "Look, Grandma," I began, but then I gave it up.

I was going to say that (a) I had not written about her in any shape or disguise, and (b) if I had not, it was not because I considered her unimportant but because I knew she would hate to have her likeness taken. For nearly forty years, she had refused to be photographed. The last picture made of her, a tinted photograph, stood on her chiffonier; it showed an imperious, handsome matron in a low-cut beaded evening dress and a gauzy scarf, with her hair in a pompadour and her young son at her knee. This remained her official image, and nothing would persuade her to let it be superseded. In the four-generations pictures made when my brothers and I were children—my great-grandfather, my grandfather, my mother, and the babies—my grandmother is absent. The last time I had come to visit her, with my own baby, in 1939, just before the war, I had begged her to let us take pictures of this new family group. But she would not allow it. In the snapshots I have of that summer, my grandmother again is absent; a shadow on the lawn, near the playpen, in one of them may indicate where she was standing. Yet I dared not draw these facts to her attention, for there was a story behind them, the story of her life—a story that was kept, like her age, a secret from those closest to her, though we all guessed at it and knew it in a general way, just as we all knew, in a general way, calculating from our own ages and from the laws of Nature, that she had to be over eighty when she died.

Starting to tell that story now—to publish it, so to speak, abroad— I feel a distinct uneasiness, as though her shade were interposing to forbid me. If I believed in the afterlife, I would hold my peace. I should not like to account to her in whatever place we might meet; Limbo is where I can best imagine her, waiting for me at some Victorian stairhead, with folded arms, and cold cream on her face, as she used to wait in her pink quilted Japanese bathrobe or the green one with the dragons when I turned my key softly in the front door at two or three in the morning, with a lie, which I hoped not to need, trembling on my lips. She would never forgive me for what I am about to do, and if there is an afterlife, it is God who will have to listen to my explanations.

My first recollection of her is in her gray electric, her smartly gloved hands on the steering bar, or tiller. How old I was, I am not sure, but it was long before my family left Seattle when I was six. The gray box would glide up to the curb in front of our brick house on Twenty-fourth Avenue, and we would see her step out, wearing a dressy suit, braided or spangled, and a hat with a dotted veil that was pulled tight over her high-bridged nose, so that the black furry dots against her skin looked like beauty patches. On her feet, over her shoes, were curious cloth covers fastened with pearl buttons; my father said that they were called "spats," and that some men wore them, too. She had come to see my mother, and smelled of perfume. The electric would be parked for a long time outside our house; one day my brothers and I climbed in and got it started rolling. My mother spanked us with her tortoise-shell comb, but my father boasted of the exploit. "How did the little tykes do it?" he would say, laughing; we must all have been well under six.

Next, I think I see her in our bathroom, telling my mother that we must each have our own towel with our name above it, so that we would not keep catching colds from each other. When she left that afternoon, there was a brand-new towel for each of us hanging folded on the towel rack, with our name written out on a little label pasted on the wall behind each towel: "Roy" and "Tess" for our parents, and "Mary," "Kevin," and "James Preston" for us children; my littlest brother, Sheridan, was too young to have one. I was impressed by this arrangement, which seemed to me very stylish. But the very next day my father spoiled it by using one of our towels, and soon they were all scrambled up again and the labels fell off. This was the first (and, I think, the only) time I felt critical of my debonair Irish father, for I knew that the strange lady would be cross with him if she could see our bathroom now.

On Sundays, sometimes, we were taken to lunch at her house, out by Lake Washington. Two things we loved to do there. One was to crawl under the table while the grownups were still eating and find the bulge or little mound in the carpet where there was a bell she stepped on when she wanted the maid to come in. The bulge in the carpet was rather hard to locate, with all the feet and the women's skirts in the way, but eventually we found it and made the bell ring. It was nice under there, with the white tablecloth hanging down all around us like a tent. The carpet was thick and soft and furry, and if we peered out, we could see exotic birds on the wallpaper. I don't remember anyone's telling us not to get under the table, but one Sunday, perhaps the last time we went there, we could not find the bulge at all, and I remember the strange, scary feeling this gave me, as though I had been dreaming or making up a story and there had never been any bulge or bell in the first place. It did not occur to us that the bell must have been removed to keep us from annoying the maid, and the mystery of its disappearance used to plague me, long after we had left Seattle, like some maddening puzzle. I would lie awake in my new bed, thinking about the bell and wishing I could be given another chance to look for it. Five years later, when I was brought back to that house to live, a girl of eleven (and it remained my official home until I was twenty-one), I had the great joy, the vindication, of finding the bell just where I thought it should be, between her feet and mine.

The other thing we liked to do was, after lunch, to roll down her terraces, which dropped in grassy tiers from her tall house all the way, I remembered, to Lake Washington. We rolled and rolled, almost into the water, it seemed, and nobody stopped us until it was time to go home, our white Sunday clothes smeared with green stains. The grass was like velvet, and there were flower beds all around, and a smell of roses; a sprinkler was going somewhere, and there were raspberries that we ate off bushes. Alas, when I came back, I found I had been dreaming. The grounds did not go down to the lake but only to the next block, below, and there was only one grass terrace; the second one was wild, covered with blackberry prickers, and it had always been so, they said. I rolled a few times down the bank, but it was not the same; only five or six turns and I had reached the bottom; I could not recapture the delicious dizzy sensation I remembered so well. And the raspberries, which I had been looking forward to eating, did not belong to us but to the people next door.

The strange lady was supposed to be my grandmother, but I did not think of her that way when I was little. She did not have white hair, for one thing, like my other grandmother—the real one, as I considered her. Nor did she do embroidery or tapestry work, or stare at us over her glasses. She did not have glasses—only a peculiar ornament on a chain that she put up to her eyes when she wanted to look at something. With her queer electrical car that ran sound-lessly and was upholstered inside in the softest gray, like a jewel case, her dotted veil, her gloves, which had bumps in them (made by her rings, I discovered later), her bell, and her descending ter-races, she was a fairy-tale person who lived in an enchanted house, which was full of bulges, too—two overhanging balconies, on the lake side, and four bays and a little tower. (She had a fairy-tale sister, different from herself—tall, with white hair piled on top of her head in a long, conical shape, a towering mountain peak or a vanilla ice-cream cone. We were taken to see her one day, and her house was magic also. She had a whole polar bear for a rug, and her floor shone like glass and made you slip when you walked on it; her house was like a winter palace or like the North Pole, where Santa Claus came from.) I did not love the strange lady in the electric, but I loved the things she had.

The last time I saw her, in this pristine, fairy-tale period, was in the Hotel Washington, where we were staying because our house had been sold and we were moving away from Seattle. She was riding in the elevator, wearing a funny white mask, like the one the doctor had worn when they took my tonsils out; I heard the word "epidemic," and I think she told my mother that we should have masks, too, when we rode up and down in the elevator—a thing we were fond of doing. But I did not like the masks.

We were very sick on the train and they took us off with stretchers and wheelchairs. I was still sick when I saw her again, in a place where she did not belong—a place called Minneapolis, where my other grandmother lived. Lying in an iron bed in my other grand-mother's sewing room, I watched the door open, and the strange lady came in, with a different kind of veil on—a black one, which hung all the way down over her face. She flung it back, and her face looked dreadful, as if she had been crying. Then she sat down on my bed, and her husband, Grandpa Preston, sat on a straight chair beside it. She sobbed, and her husband patted her, saying something like "Come now, Gussie," which appeared to be her name. She wiped her tears with a handkerchief; they went away on tiptoe, telling me to be a good girl. I did not understand any of this; my reason was offended by her turning up here in Minneapolis when I knew she lived in Seattle. No one enlightened me; I heard the word "flu," but it was months before it dawned on me that the occasion had been my parents' funeral. Yet when I surmised, finally, that Mama and Daddy were not coming back, I felt a certain meas-ure of relief. One mystery, at least, was cleared up; the strange lady had come and cried on my bed because her daughter was dead. I did not see her again till five years later, when she was standing in the depot in Seattle, in a hat with a black dotted veil pulled tight across her face, which was heavily rouged and powdered. By this time, I knew that she was my grandmother, that she was Jewish, and dyed her hair.

The last of these items was a canard. Her hair was naturally black, black as a raven's wing and with a fine silky gloss, like loose skeins of embroidery thread. When she was over eighty and bedridden, the first sprinkling of white hairs began to appear in her thick, shining permanent. Brushing it, the nurses used to marvel ("Wonderful, isn't it? You'd swear, at first, it was dye"), but this triumph over her calumniators came too late. The nurses could testify, my uncles and their wives could testify, I could testify, but whom were we to tell? Within the immediate family, we had always given her the benefit of the doubt, though I recall my grandfather's uneasy face when she went to have her first permanent, for in those days dyed hair did not take well to the process and was reputed to turn green or orange. It was the outsiders—the distant in-laws, the ladies who bowed to my grandmother in the shops and then turned aside to whisper something—whom I should have liked to make eat their words now, and in particular my other grandmother, with her reiterated, crushing question "Who ever saw natural hair *that* color?" But she was in her mausoleum, unavailable for comment, and the others were gone, too. My grandmother had outlived them all—an unfortunate state of affairs. Moreover, she herself was no longer in a condition to appreciate or even understand her victory; on her energetic days she would ask me to fetch her hand mirror from her bureau, and, frowning into it, would set herself to plucking out those stray white hairs, not realizing that they were the proof she had long been needing to show that her hair was truly black.

She had been a beautiful woman—"the most beautiful woman in Seattle," my friends' mothers used to tell me, adding that my mother, in her day, had been the most beautiful woman in Seattle, too. I can see it in the case of my mother, but my grandmother does not appear beautiful to me in the few photographs that exist of her as a young woman. Handsome, I would say, with a long, narrow, high-nosed, dark-eyed, proud, delicate face, the pure forehead topped by severe, somewhat boyish curls, such as the Romantic poets used to cultivate. A Biblical Jewish face that might have belonged to the young Rachel when Jacob first saw her. Her ears were pierced, and in one photograph she is wearing a pair of round, button-style earrings that lend her, somehow, a Russian appearance; in another, where she is posed with my mother as a little girl, her hair is caught in a big dark hair ribbon that gives her the air of a student. She has a gentle, open, serious mien—qualities I would never associate with the sharp, jaunty woman I knew or with the woman of the mature photograph on her chiffonier. Perhaps fashions in photography are responsible for the difference or perhaps her character changed radically during the early years of her marriage. The long, dreamy countenance became short, broad, and genial; the wide eyes narrowed and drew closer together. The change is so profound as to evoke the question "What happened?" The young woman in the photographs looks as though she could be easily hurt.

She came to Seattle from San Francisco, where her father had been what she called a "broker." Whether or not she meant a pawnbroker, I never could discover. He was a Forty-niner, having gone out to California in the gold rush, after a year in Pennsylvania. He had left Europe during the troubles of '48, and I like to think he was a political émigré, but I do not know. I do not know, though I once asked her, what part of Europe he came from. Poland, I suspect; her name, however, was German: Morganstern. Her first name was Augusta. These few sketchy facts were all she seemed to know of her early life and family history, and it puzzled her that anyone should want to find out more. "All those old things, Mary," she would say to me half grumpily. "Why do you keep asking me all those old things?" Like many great beauties, she had little curiosity; for nearly ten years she did not know the name of the family who had moved into the house next door to us.

Her parents had died when she was quite young—in her teens— and she and her younger sister, my Aunt Rosie, came to live in Seattle with an older sister, Eva, who had married a fur importer named Aronson; this was the lady with the polar-bear rug. The girls had had some private education; my grandmother, at one time, used to play the piano—rather prettily, I imagine. She had a pleasing speaking voice and a surprising knowledge of classical music. "Were you rich or poor?" I asked her once, trying to learn the source of these accomplishments. "My father had a nice business," she replied. She had read the Russian novelists; when I sought to introduce her to Tolstoy and Dostoevski, she gave her dry laugh and said they had been the popular writers of her youth. All her life, she retained a taste for long novels that went on from generation to generation, on the model of "War and Peace." She hated short stories, because, she said, just as you got to know the characters, the story ended; it was not worth the trouble. Her sister Rose was fourteen when the two arrived in Seattle; Aunt Rosie went out and inspected the University of Washington, which had just been started, and decided

she knew more than the professors did—a fact she faced up to ruefully, since she had been yearning for a higher education.

Aunt Rosie was a very different person from my grandmother,
yet they talked together on the phone for nearly an hour every day
and often went "downtown" together in the afternoon, my grandmother stopping by at her house to pick her up in the electric, later
in the Chrysler or the La Salle. Aunt Rosie was a short, bright, very
talkative, opinionated woman, something of a civic activist and
something of a bohemian. She had married an easygoing New York
Jew, Uncle Mose Gottstein, a juicy, cigar-smoking man who ran
a furniture store, subscribed to the New York *Times,* and liked to
chat about current events, his cigar tilted at a reflective angle, upward, in his cherry-red mouth. He and Aunt Rosie often sat up
all night in their first-floor bedroom, with its big walnut double
bed, Uncle Mose in his nightgown reading the newspapers, and
Aunt Rosie playing a solitaire, which she would not leave till it
came out. Uncle Mose had fond recollections of Lüchow's (Jimmy
Durante, he said, used to be a singing waiter there), and their big
bedroom, strewn with newsprint and playing cards and smelling of
cigar smoke, was like a club or a café. Aunt Rosie and her husband
and their two sons always sat there, even in the daytime, instead of
in the living room or the little parlor, which was lined with signed
photographs of opera stars and violinists and pianists. Aunt Rosie
had "known them all;" in her youth, she had been a vocal soloist,
much in demand for weddings and special services in Seattle's
Protestant churches. Later, she had managed the musical events at
Seattle's Metropolitan Theatre; the high point of her life had been
a trip she took to Vancouver with Chaliapin, about whom Uncle
Mose liked to twit her, his small, moist eyes (he later developed
cataracts) beaming behind his glasses, his apple cheeks flushed. Aunt
Rosie had met other artists besides Chaliapin and the various divas,
including Mary Garden and Galli-Curci, who had inscribed their
photographs to her; thanks to her theatre connection, she had
known Houdini and The Great Alexander and could explain the
magicians' acts by the fact that there was a trapdoor on the Metropolitan Theatre's stage. When I knew her, she was running the
Ladies' Musical Club.

Aunt Rosie was poor—compared to her sisters. Her husband was
the kind of man who is chronically unsuccessful in business—the
genial uncle nearly every Jewish family possesses who has to be

helped out by the others. Aunt Rosie had a plain "girl" to give her a hand with the housework; she dressed very unmodishly and lived in a somewhat rundown section, in a smallish frame house that needed painting. She was active in the temple as well as in the musical world. The cookbook of the Ladies' Auxiliary of the Temple de Hirsch, a volume got up for charity and much used in our family—I still own a copy—has many recipes contributed by Mrs. M. A. Gottstein. Her chicken stewed with noodles, hamburger in tomatoes, and rhubarb pie are quite unlike the recipes contributed by Mrs. S. A. Aronson, my other great-aunt, which begin with directions like this: "Take a nice pair of sweetbreads, add a cup of butter, a glass of good cream, sherry, and some foie gras." Or her recipe for baked oysters: "Pour over each caviar and cream, and dot with bits of butter. Serve hot."

Aunt Rosie, with her energy, her good heart and rattling, independent tongue, was a popular woman in Seattle, among all classes and kinds. Society ladies fond of music gushed over "the wonderful Mrs. Gottstein;" poor Jewish ladies in the temple praised her; Protestant clergymen respected her (they used to try to convert her when she was younger, she told me, because she sang their anthems with such feeling); judges, politicians, butchers, poor tailors, clerks in bookstores all knew Aunt Rosie. She had not let the Protestant ministers tempt her away from her religion, but she was a truly open person, able to cross barriers naturally because she did not notice they were there. Most of the Jews in Seattle lived a life apart, concerned with *bar mitzvahs* and weddings, and family and business affairs; a few, with German-sounding names, managed to cross into the Gentile world and get their sons pledged to regular fraternities at the University, leaving temple and observances behind them. Aunt Rosie was a unique case. Her Jewishness—that is, her bounce and volubility—was a positive asset to her in her dealings with the Gentile ascendancy. If my grandmother's marriage (to a Gentile) had made it a little easier for Aunt Rosie to get around, Aunt Rosie, I think, never suspected it; she had a lively self-conceit and no social envy or ambition. To her good-humored mind, being Jewish was simply a matter of religion.

Each of the three sisters had a different attitude toward her Jewish heritage, perhaps in each case conditioned by the man she had married. Aunt Eva—Mrs. Aronson, whose husband, Uncle Sig, had long since passed on—was a typical wealthy widow of Jewish high society. She travelled a good deal, with a rather hard, smart set who had connections in Portland, San Francisco, and New York, and even in Paris; she gambled, and went to resorts and fashionable hotels in season; when she was in Seattle, she was a habitué of the Jewish country club, where they golfed in the daytime and played bridge for very high stakes at night. The scale of living of these people—widows and widowers, bachelors and divorcees, for the most part—was far beyond anything conceived of by the local Christian *haute bourgeoisie,* which was unaware of their existence. This unawareness was mutual, at least in the case of Aunt Eva, who, gyrating with perfect aplomb on her roulette wheel of hotels, yachts, race tracks, and spas, her white hairdress always in order, seemed ignorant of the fact that there was a non-Jewish society right under her nose, whose doings were recorded in the newspapers, daily and Sunday, whose members were "seen lunching" at the Olympic Hotel on Mondays, or golfing at the Seattle Golf Club, near The Highlands, or sunning at the tennis club on the lake.

Aunt Eva, I think, hardly realized that the world contained persons who were not Jewish. She, too, never knew envy; her nature was serene and imperturbable. My grandmother's mixed marriage never seemed to give Aunt Eva a qualm; her tall unawareness was sublime, a queenly attribute. If my grandfather was not "of the tribe," as my Irish relations used to call it suggestively, she did not give any sign of perceiving it. The "unpleasant" was barred by Aunt Eva, who seldom read anything and talked in magnificent generalities. She was fond of the theatre, and when she was not travelling, she used to go every week to see the Henry Duffy stock company in Seattle. My grandmother, Aunt Rosie, and I had strong opinions about these players ("He's a perfect stick," my grandmother almost invariably complained of the leading man), but to Aunt Eva there were no distinctions. Every play she saw she pronounced "very enjoyable." And the actors "took their parts well." We used to laugh at her and try to get her to acknowledge that the play was better some weeks than others. But Aunt Eva would not cross that Rubicon; she smelled a rat. To her, all the plays and players were equal, and equally, blandly good.

Toward the end of her life, she suffered cruelly from indigestion (the foie gras and the cup of butter, doubtless), and it was an awful thing to watch her, after a Sunday luncheon at our house, majestic and erect, walk about our back living room, her lips bubbling a little and her face pale-vanilla-colored and contorting slightly from spasms of pain. "Gas," she would say, with dignity. It tortured me

to see this highly aristocratic lady reduced by her stomach to what
I felt must be a horrible embarrassment for her, but her unawareness seemed to extend to the "unpleasant" aspect of her sufferings;
she entertained them, as it were, graciously, like a hostess. My grandfather showed her great sympathy during these ordeals of hers; she
was his favorite, I think, among my grandmother's relations. Having
helped her with her business affairs, he must have come to realize
that Aunt Eva, unlike her sisters, was extremely stupid. Perhaps
this regal stupidity, like that of a stately white ox, elicited his
chivalry, for he was a gallant man, or perhaps the slow, measured
pace of her wits allowed him to forget that she was one of the
Chosen (another classic epithet dear to my Irish relations).

How did my grandfather feel about the Jews? Again, I do not
know; this was one of the many mysteries that surrounded our
family life. He almost never attended church, except to be a pall-
bearer at a funeral, but he was by birth a Presbyterian Yankee, the
son of a West Point man who was head of a military college in
Norwich, Vermont, commanded a Negro regiment during the Civil
War, and was retired as a brigadier general. Simon Manly Preston
was my great-grandfather's name (wife: Martha Sargent, born in
New Hampshire), and he lived to be ninety-nine; his last years
were passed in Seattle, where he was one of the local curiosities. All
his progeny, including Uncle Ed, another West Point man, who
died in his fifties, were eventually drawn to Seattle: my grandfather,
Harold; my Great-Uncle Clarence; and my Great-Aunt Alice, who
married a law partner of my grandfather's, Eugene H. Carr, and
lived for a time in Alaska. My grandfather first came West working
as a geodetic surveyor during his college vacation (he started at
Cornell and finished at what is now Grinnell College, in Iowa), and
when he had his A.B. degree, he decided to read law in Seattle. It
was then that he must have first met my grandmother, aged circa
seventeen, who was living in the house of the fur importer, Sigis-
mund Aronson. Did this name ring strangely in my grandfather's
Yankee ears? Possibly not. Seattle was a frontier town, where you
could expect to meet all kinds—French and Dutch and Germans,
aristocrats and plebeians. Many of our first families had aristocratic
pedigrees (the de Turennes, the von Phuls), yet it used to be said
of every first family that the great-grandfather "came here with his
pack on his back." My grandmother was courted by a number of
suitors, including one, George Preston, who had the same last

name as my grandfather. She had Jewish beaux also, I discovered, and, as far as I could make out, she did not distinguish between the two kinds. They were assorted young men who took her driving; that was all.

"As far as I could make out"—this matter was impossible to probe with my grandmother. I don't think I ever used the word "Jewish" in any connection when talking with her. I sensed she would not like it. I used to think about the word a lot myself, when I first came back to Seattle and was sent as a five-day boarder to a Sacred Heart Convent. I thought about it partly because of the ugly in-nuendoes dropped by my father's people, but chiefly because I was in love with my cousin, Aunt Rosie's tall, ravishing son Burton, who was twenty-one, ten years older than I, and I worried, being a Catholic, about the impediments to our marriage: the fact that he was my first cousin once removed, and the difference in religion —would he have to be baptized? This passion of mine was secret (or at least I hope it was), but even if it had not been, I could not have discussed the problem with my grandmother because of that unmentionable word.

I myself had a curious attitude, I now realize, in which the crudest anti-Semitism ("Ikey-Mose-Abie," I used to chant, under my breath, to myself in the convent) mingled with infatuation and with genuine tolerance and detachment. I *liked* Uncle Mose and Aunt Rosie far better than any other older people I knew, and "Ikey-Mose-Abie" represented what I supposed others would think of them. It was a sort of defiance. If I identified a little bit of myself with those others, my dead mother had gone much further; one day I found a letter she had written to my Grandmother McCarthy in which she spoke of an evening "with the Hebrews." Finding this letter was one of the great shocks of my adolescence. It destroyed my haloed image of my mother, and the thought that her mother must have read it, too (for there it was, in my desk, put away for me with other family keepsakes), nearly made me ill.

Perhaps I was too sensitive on my grandmother's behalf. No secret was ever made of the family connection with Aunt Rosie and Aunt Eva, and whenever my grandmother gave a tea, it always appeared in the paper that Mrs. M. A. Gottstein and Mrs. S. A. Aronson poured. I used to hear about some distant cousin's having a *bar mitzvah,* and once I was taken to a Jewish wedding, which fascinated me because it was held at night in a hotel ballroom. Nevertheless, there was *something,* a shying away from the subject, an aversion to naming it in words—so persistent that I was startled, one morning, when I was about sixteen, to hear my grandmother allude to "my faith." I had been talking to her about my disbelief in God, and to my surprise she grew quite agitated. She no longer practiced her faith, she declared, but she was certain that there was a kind God who understood and who watched over everything. She spoke with great feeling and emphasis—a rare thing in our relationship.

It was characteristic of her queer, oblique nature that I should have chanced to find out that she had had Jewish suitors by idly asking her the names of the young men she had driven out with. She gave them with perfect readiness, but without any indication that such a name as Schwabacher or Rosenblatt would tell a story to me. If it had been a major step to marry outside her own people, she did not seem to recall this any more, and, of course, I could not ask her.

Yet in other respects she was remarkably frank. "How did you come to marry Grandpa?" I asked her one night, when I was home on a visit after I myself had married. "Rosie and I didn't get along with Uncle Sig," she answered matter-of-factly.

So that was all; I could hardly believe my ears, and wondered whether she realized the enormity of what she was saying. "But why did you pick Grandpa instead of one of the others?" I pressed her, determined, for Grandpa's sake, that she should answer that it had been because of his eyes or his mustache or his intellect. She appeared to search her memory, in vain. "Oh, I don't know, Mary," she said, yawning. "You *must* know," I retorted. She thought he would be good to her, she finally conceded.

This archaic view of the function of a husband astonished me. But for her, as I soon learned, it was the prime, the only, consideration. "Is he good to you?" she asked me, another night, on that same visit, speaking of my new husband. I had to stop and think, because marriage had never presented itself to me in this light. "Why, yes, I suppose so," I said slowly. "Yes, of course he is." My grandmother nodded and reopened her evening newspaper. "That's all right, then." The subject of my new husband was closed. "Grandpa was always good to me," she resumed tranquilly, turning to the racing column and beginning to mark her selections for the next day's pari-mutuel.

What did these words mean? Kindness, patience, forbearance— or fur coats and jewelry? Or was it all the same thing? Love, evi-

dently, was as foreign a concept to her as this "goodness" was to
me. She did not want to hear about love; it irritated her. The words
"I love him" were meaningless sounds to her ears; if I uttered them
in her hearing, which at length I had the sense not to do, I might
as well have been talking Chinese. She did not care for love stories,
which she pronounced trash, and she used to make fun of the movie
actors who were my heroes as a young girl. "He has such thick lips,"
she used to say of Ronald Colman, mimicking his expression by
thrusting out her own upper lip. "And that mustache! Think of
kissing that bristly mustache!" Ricardo Cortez, she said, mimicking
his expression, "looked as if he had a stomach ache." Yet her own
favorite was Adolphe Menjou. My grandfather liked Lewis Stone.

She was not so much cynical as prosaic. She made fun of the young
men who used to come to take me out when I was home from college on vacations by seizing on some small detail of their appearance and relentlessly exaggerating it: curly hair, rosy cheeks, full
lips, large ears. This was not done maliciously but in high-humored
jest, as though *she* were the young girl mocking her suitors behind
their backs to her audience of sisters. I never minded it (though I
had minded about Ronald Colman), but it struck me as unfair in
the abstract; the part was always greater to her than the whole, and
some of the things she noticed would have escaped the attention of
anyone but a phrenologist.

Her marriage had been successful, and she attributed this to a
single simple recipe, like one of the Household Hints in the back
of the Temple de Hirsch cookbook, on how to clean ermine (rub
with corn meal) or how to extract grease from papered walls (flannel and spirits of wine). She had never let a quarrel continue overnight. No matter how mad she was at Grandpa, she told me, she
always kissed him good night. And, a corollary, no matter how mad
she was in the morning, she always kissed him goodbye before he
went to the office. She passed this recipe on to me gravely after I
had been divorced; if I would just follow it, I would never have
any more trouble, she was certain. This advice made me smile; it
was so remote in its application to my case. But she shook her head
reprovingly as she stood in front of her mirror, undoing her pearls
for the night. "Remember, Mary," she enjoined. "All right," I said
lightly. "I'll remember. 'Always kiss him good night.'" She had felt
the moment as a solemn one, like the time she had spoken of "my
faith," yet in an instant she, too, was smiling broadly. An anecdote
had occurred to her, and she began to tell me, acting out both parts,

of a morning when Grandpa had left for his office without the usual morning salute. . . . From one point of view, her entire married life was a succession of comic anecdotes, of which she was both butt and heroine.

These anecdotes began before her marriage, with the time the horse ran away with her and George Preston in the buggy, and Grandpa was terribly jealous. Then there was her honeymoon: how he had taken her back to Iowa to visit his family, who had settled there after the Civil War. It was winter, and before they left, my grandfather kept asking her whether she had enough clothes. She answered yes each time, but the question puzzled and offended her, for she took it as a criticism of her wardrobe. "I had very nice clothes," she explained. What he meant, it turned out, was long underwear, but he was too delicate to name it, so she went ignorantly on to Newton, Iowa, in her fine batiste-and-lace underclothing; she could never tolerate anything else next to her skin— silk was too coarse. In the barbarous Midwestern climate, she nearly froze to death, she declared, and she came out in chilblains all over. She nearly died of boredom also.

The provinciality of her in-laws horrified her. She had never met people like this, whose idea of a social evening was to stand around the stove, clad in long underwear and heavy dark clothing, the men cracking one joke after another. She could see that her in-laws, with the exception of Great-Grandpa Preston, did not like her. "They thought I was fast and stuck-up." She could not eat their food or put on the union suit they offered her. They were displeased by her elegant clothes and by her smiles and laughter. They only laughed, shortly, at the humorless jokes they told. Alone in her bedroom with her husband, she cried and cried, and finally she made him have a telegram sent to himself calling him back to Seattle. After the telegram came, her father-in-law, the General, took them to Chicago, which was supposed to be a treat. But they put up at an awful boarding house, where she could not eat the food, either. The two men stayed out all day, looking at sights like the stockyards, and the other boarders scared her, they were so rough and crude in their manners. That was the end of her honeymoon, and on the train going back she made my grandfather promise that he would never take her to Newton again.

Later, they went to Chicago for the World's Fair with my Aunt Eva, and this was the subject of another anecdote. She and Aunt

Eva were left at a stop in Montana, when the train drew out unexpectedly while they were buying postcards in the station. Another passenger, a man, seeing their predicament, jumped out of
the train and said to my grandmother, "Can I be of assistance to
you, Madam?" Somehow (I forget the details), he managed to get
the train to come back for them or to wait at the next station for
them to arrive by carriage. But my grandfather was terribly jealous;
as soon as he saw them again, he accused my grandmother of having
got off the train to be with the strange man. And she never could
convince him differently all the rest of her life.

There was the time the house caught on fire while my grandmother was downtown shopping. When she boarded the Cherry
Street trolley to go home (her house was way out, almost in the
country, then), the conductor said to her, "Mrs. Preston, your house
is on fire," and she arrived on the scene to find the fire engine there
and their one-eyed maid, Tilda (yes, so my grandmother swore),
carrying the piano out of the house balanced on one hand, like a
tray; all the little boys in the neighborhood were sitting on the lawn
reading her love letters from my grandfather, which they had found
in a bureau drawer. There was the time her riding horse ran away
with her, down in Gearhart, Oregon, and there was an incident,
I think, with a rowboat. There was the time she came to our house,
when my mother had been taken to the hospital to have our little
brother, and found the three of us sitting on the floor of the living
room making a bonfire of my father's lawbooks and pointing his
loaded revolver at each other.

My grandmother was a gifted *raconteuse* when she could be induced to tell one of her stories. She acted out all the parts zestfully,
particularly her own, and short trills of unwilling laughter proceeded from her as she spoke; when she had finished, she would
have to wipe her eyes with a handkerchief. This power of being
amused at herself, this perpetual dismay, made one see her in these
disconcerting situations, which had a classic plot—the plot of a
nightmare, really.

Someone, usually a man, laconically breaks her an untoward piece
of news, or fails to break it successfully, as in the case of the long
underwear. Or it is a runaway horse, a runaway train, a runaway
buggy, a rocking boat, a loaded revolver; my grandmother is always
helpless while some uncontrollable event unfolds before her eyes.
(There was the story of the crazy piano tuner who without a by-
your-leave walked into her parlor and took the piano apart as my

grandmother watched, unable to stop him, bewitched by his flow
of talk: "A beautiful instrument, Madam. . . . So you have neglected your lovely musical gift [an imitation of him shaking his
head]. Believe me, Madam, you owe it to the world and to your
husband and family to take up the instrument again. . . ." At the
end of the story, naturally, the dismembered piano was lying on
the floor; he had forgotten how to put it together again.) She is
always the loser in these anecdotes; she never gets the better of
the situation with a biting retort, as she often did in real life. But
because she is the heroine, she is usually rescued, in the nick of time.

In my grandmother's narratives, it is the other person who is
self-possessed, full of an almost supernatural assurance—the stranger
alighting from the moving train in a single airy bound, like an
acrobat sliding down a rope to bow at her feet. She is forever disconcerted, put out of countenance, dumb-struck. In reality, *she*
was the disconcerting one, short of speech when she was not telling
a story (and to get her to tell a story usually took a lot of coaxing),
impassive, forbidding. Most people, including all my friends, were
afraid of her.

The first thing that would have struck an outsider about her in
her later years—that is, when she was in her sixties and seventies—
was the oddity of her appearance. If you saw her downtown, shopping in Frederick's or Magnin's—and she never did anything but
shop any afternoon of her life, excluding Sundays, matinée days,
and the days of the race meetings—you would probably ask the
salesgirl who she was: a woman of medium height, a little plump
but not fat, wearing a small, high-crowned hat topped with ribbons
or feathers, pumps with Cuban heels, fabric gloves, an onyx-and-
diamond *lorgnon,* a smart dress in black or navy, printed or solid-
color, with a fur piece over it—silver fox or baum marten. This
would be in summer. In the fall, she might be wearing a dark-green
wool ensemble, or a black one trimmed with monkey, or a beige one
trimmed with beige broadtail or caracul. In the winter, she would
have on her mink or her Persian or her squirrel or her broadtail.
She would be proceeding at a stately walk through the store, stopping to finger something at a counter, smiling at the salespeople,
nodding. Her clothes in themselves should not have attracted attention. She disliked bright colors and never wore anything but black,
navy, dark green, beige, or wine. Nor were the styles youthful or

extreme. She was careful about her skirt lengths; her dresses were lavish in tucks and shirring, but the cut was simple and discreet. She wore small pearl earrings and a short string of pearls; her rings were concealed by her gloves. Underneath the gloves, her nails were natural-color, polished with a buffer. Nor did her toilet table contain a lipstick. Yet the whole effect she made was of an indescribable daring.

It was partly the black hair, so improbably black and glossy. It was partly the mascara and the eyeshadow surrounding her narrow black watchful eyes, though these aids to beauty were not applied carelessly but with an infinite discretion. It was the rouge, perhaps, most of all, the rouge and the powder and the vanishing cream underneath. When she perspired, on a warm day, the little beads of sweat on her eagle nose under her nose veil and on her long upper lip would produce a caked look that seemed sad, as though her skin were crying. Yet not even her cosmetics and the world of consummate artifice they suggested could account for the peculiarly florid impression she made as she moved across the store, peering through her *lorgnon* at the novelties and notions, and vanished into the elevator, up to the lending library or the custom-made or the hat department—her favorite purlieus—where elderly salespeople, *her* salespeople, would hurry up to greet her, throwing their arms around her, just as though they had not seen her the day before.

"Have you got anything for me?" my grandmother would demand of Mrs. Slaughter, the red-haired hat lady at Frederick's, surveying the premises with a kind of jesting coquetry, a hand on her hip. This was the same tone she took with the clerks in the circulating library or with the butcher on the telephone—a tone of challenging banter, as though she defied these people, her suitors, to please her.

On a good day, Mrs. Slaughter would bring out two or three hats she had "put away" for my grandmother in a special cupboard. "They just came in," she would whisper. "I've been saving them for you." My grandmother would try them on before the mirror, tilting her head sidewise and back in an odd way she had, at once vain and highly self-critical. If she liked one of them well enough, she would walk to the full-length mirror and assay herself, thrusting one small foot forward and balancing back and forth, seeming to weigh herself and the hat in the scales of judgment. To my disappointment, watching her, she never bought on the spot. She would set the hat or hats down on the table, as if she were through with them, and Mrs. Slaughter, who seemed to be a mind reader, would whisk them back into the special cupboard, where they would wait, out of sight of other customers, for several days or even a week, while my grandmother arrived at a decision. She was the same with her shoes and dresses; she would even coquette with a piece of meat. It was as though she would not give these things the satisfaction of letting them see that she liked them. To her, every piece of merchandise, suing for her favor, appeared to enter the masculine gender and to be subject, therefore, to rebuff. Yet the salespeople were all eager to oblige her, for she was a good customer and, more than that, underneath her badinage, always good-humored.

It pleased her to pretend to be cross with them; indeed, in all her dealings she had an air of just consenting to be mollified. Her veteran salespeople would flatter her ("You're looking younger every day, Mrs. Preston. Nobody would believe this young lady was your granddaughter. Make her pass for your daughter"), and my grandmother would hide her gratification in a short, tart, scathing laugh. Actually, they were proud of her, for she did look remarkably young, despite her blazonry of makeup; she *could* have passed for my mother. They were genuinely fond of her. "Take care of yourself," they would call after her, and some of them used to kiss her. My grandmother pretended to be suspicious of these manifestations; a muscle moved, like a protest, in her cheek while the kiss was being planted.

She was lonely. That was the thing that made her seem so garish and caused people to turn their heads when she went by. Loneliness is a garish quality, and my grandmother's wardrobe and elaborate toilette appeared flamboyant because they emphasized her isolation. An old woman trying to look young is a common enough sight, but my grandmother was something stranger and sadder—a hermit all dressed up for a gala, a recluse on stubborn parade. Tagging along, I was half conscious, even as a little girl, of the bizarre figure my grandmother cut, and if I had not known her, my imagination might have woven some story around her for a school composition—the holocaust, at the very least, of all her nearest and dearest, her husband gone to prison, her children branded as traitors. . . .

But in fact, during the years I knew her best—the years after I had left the convent and was in boarding school in Tacoma—she had a husband; two sons, whom she saw every day (one of them

lived at home and went to the University, and the other lived across
the street with an exemplary wife); two sisters, whom she saw nearly
every day; a sister-in-law, Aunt Alice Carr, who lived downtown in
the Sorrento Hotel; a granddaughter (myself) who came home from
school for vacations; a cook; and an old gardener who had been
with her twenty-five years—the original family coachman. All these
people were devoted to her. She was independent; she had her own
investments and drove her own car. Every winter, my grandfather
took her to California, where they ate at the best restaurants and
lived at the best hotels and went to the races at Tijuana, over the
border. He was a distinguished citizen, with a prosperous law practice, a reputation for immense integrity, and countless friends and
cronies. During my sophomore year in boarding school, he took her
to New York, where they saw nearly every play on the boards and
she had an outfit made by a smart new designer in a new color
called "kasha," an exact copy of an outfit worn by Katharine Cornell in "The Green Hat," and he took her to Washington, where
they had an interview with Calvin Coolidge.

She had nothing to complain of in life. There was nothing wrong
with her health, except for a mild diabetic condition, which the
best local specialist was controlling, and a high blood pressure that
was not dangerous but that gave her headaches in the afternoons.
Nor did she complain; she was a little fretful sometimes when she
was having her headaches, but she possessed an equable temper—
the result, no doubt, of self-discipline. She and I used to quarrel, and
she had much to find fault with in my conduct. She worried a good
deal about her younger son's late hours. But she was never cross or
nagging. It was only much later, when she grew senile, that she became difficult to deal with, capricious and fault-finding, sending the
cook downtown to return a mascara applier that dissatisfied her,
pushing her food away, soughing and making faces.

But until she reached her second childhood she seemed, on the
surface, a contented woman, well situated in life, self-contained, unemotional. The only blights she had suffered, so far as I knew, were
the unseasonable death of my mother and a mastoid operation that
had left her with some scars just under her ears, in her neck and
lower cheeks. If she was cold to me for a few days, or stopped speaking, abruptly, to Gertrude, or feuded with my grandfather's brother,
Uncle Clarence, these were mere quirks—the privileges of beauty—
that did nobody any harm. She was not a demonstrative person, but
neither were her sons or her husband or her daughter-in-law; they

all seemed to have been cut from the same bolt of cloth. I was the
only member of the family—not counting Aunt Rosie—who was excitable.

When I was brought back from Minneapolis to live with my
grandparents, I was impressed by our house and its appurtenances,
much as I had been as a young child—the bay-window seat in the
parlor, the cabinet with opaline Tiffany glass and little demitasse
cups, all different, the grass wallpaper, the pongee-silk curtains, the
sleeping porches upstairs, the hawthorn tree in front of the house,
the old carriage block with the name "PRESTON" carved on it, the
date "1893" over the front door, the Kelvinator in the kitchen, the
bell system, the generator in the garage that charged the electric, the
silver samovar, the Rhine-wine glasses (never used), with green
bowls and crystal stems. To me, the house was like a big toy, full
of possibilities for experiment and discovery; I was constantly
changing my sleeping quarters—out to the sleeping porch behind my
bathroom, upstairs to the little room under the eaves on the cook's
floor, back again to my green-and-violet bedroom. Once I even got
permission to sleep outdoors, in the moonlight, on the back lawn,
overlooking the lake.

The room I was given had been redone for me; I had lots of
pretty new clothes, made by my grandmother's own dressmaker; the
gardener drove me about in the electric and let me practice steering; I did not have to wear glasses any more, as I had had to in Minneapolis, and I could read anything I wanted to in my grandfather's
library: Dickens and Frank Stockton and Bulwer-Lytton and Sien-
kiewicz, and the Elsie Dinsmore books, which had belonged to my
mother. I could look through the stereoscope, or play an old record
of "Casey at the Bat" on the new Victrola. Everything we had
seemed superior to anything anyone else had—the flowers in our
garden, the vegetables on the table, which we grew ourselves in the
lower garden instead of getting them from the store, as other people
did. We had strawberry beds, too, and rows of currant bushes, a
crab-apple tree and two kinds of cherry trees, black and Royal Ann,
and—something very special for Seattle—my grandmother's favorite,
an apricot tree. At Christmas, we had our own holly, cut from a
tree in the front yard; the idea that this was better than other holly
persisted in my grandmother's mind to the very end, for every year
until she died, a box would arrive for me, just before Christmas, in
New England, from Seattle, packed full of holly from the Preston

tree. My grandmother's gardening was a distinguished, personal thing; she never joined a garden club or pored over seed catalogues, or exchanged slips or compared notes with other gardeners. Every morning after breakfast, she gave directions to the old gardener, descending from the back porch in a farmer's straw hat and a smock, with a basket over her arm, to pick flowers for the day's bouquets and supervise the new asparagus bed he was laying out or the planting of the new variety of sweet corn they were trying.

She was greedy, in a delicate way, picking daintily at her food, yet finishing off a whole bowl of fresh apricots or a dozen small buttered ears of the tenderest white corn. She had a cormorant's rapacity for the first fruits of the season: the tiniest peas, the youngest corn, baby beets cooked with their greens. This emphasis of hers on the youth of the garden's produce made her fastidious appetite seem a little indecent—cannibalistic, as though she belonged to a species that devoured its own young. "Take a spring chicken," many of her recipes began, and the phrase often salted her conversation. "She's no spring chicken," she would say of another woman. Baby beets, new potatoes, young asparagus, embryonic string beans, tiny Olympia oysters, tiny curling shrimps, lactary ears of corn—like my grandmother's clothes, our food was almost too choice, unseemly for daily use. The specialties of our table were like those of a very good hotel or club: Olympia-oyster cocktail and devilled Dungeness crabs; a salad, served as a first course, that started with a thick slice of tomato, on which was balanced an artichoke heart containing crabmeat, which in turn was covered with Thousand Island dressing and sprinkled with riced egg yolk; a young salmon served in a sherry sauce with oysters and little shrimps; eggs stuffed with chicken livers. We ate this company food every day; every meal was a surprise, aimed at pleasing some member of the family, as though we were all invalids who had to be "tempted." On Sundays, the ice cream, turned by the gardener in the freezer on the back porch, was chosen to suit me; we had strawberry (our own strawberries), peach, peppermint (made from crushed candy canes), and the one I was always begging for—bisque. Our icebox always contained a bowl of freshly made mayonnaise and a bowl of Thousand Island dressing, and usually a chicken or a turkey and a mold or *bombe* with maraschino cherries, whipped cream, and macaroons or ladyfingers in it. My grandmother's own palate was blander than the rest of the family's. I associate her with sweetbreads, with patty shells, and with a poulette sauce.

Or, if I shut my eyes, I can see her at the head of the table, on a summer morning, wearing her horn-rimmed reading glasses, the newspaper before her on a silver rack; there is a dish of fresh apricots in the middle of the table, and as she reads, her bare, plump white arm, as if absently, stretches out toward this dish; her slender, tapering fingers pinch the fruit, and she selects the choicest, ripest one. The process is repeated until the dish is empty, and she does not look up from her paper. I had a tremendous appetite myself ("If she assimilated all she ate, she'd be a mountain," my older uncle's wife used to comment after a Sunday-night supper), but my grandmother's voracity, so finical, so selective, chilled me with its mature sensuality, which was just the opposite of hunger. I conceived an aversion to apricots—a tasteless fruit anyway, I considered —from watching her with them, just as though I had witnessed what Freud calls the primal scene. Now I, too, am fond of them, and whenever I choose one from a plate, I think of my grandmother's body, full-fleshed, bland, smooth, and plump, cushioning in itself, close held—a secret, like the flat brown seed of the apricot.

This body of hers was the cult object around which our household revolved. As a young girl, I knew her shoe size and her hat size and her glove size, her height and weight, the things she ate and didn't eat, her preferences in underwear and nightgowns and stockings, the contents of her dressing table in the bathroom, down to the pumice stone that she used for removing an occasional hair from under her arms; one of her beauty attributes was that her white, shapely arms and legs were almost totally hairless, so that she never had to depend on a depilatory or a razor. No other woman has ever been known to me in such a wealth of fleshly, material detail; everything she touched became imbued for me with her presence, as though it were a relic. I still see her clothes, plumped to her shape, hanging on their velvet-covered hangers in her closet, which was permeated with the faint scents of powder and perfume, and the salty smell of her perspiration; she comes back to me in dress shields, in darned service-sheer stockings (for morning), in fagoting and hemstitching, in voile and batiste, in bouclé and monkey fur, in lace dyed écru with tea.

I never saw her undressed. Once, when she was in her seventies, I did catch a disturbing glimpse of her thighs, which were dazzling, not only in their whiteness and firmness but in the fineness of the skin's texture—closer to a delicate chiffon than to silk or satin. Disturbing because I knew she would not want to be looked at, even in admiration. She shared with my grandfather the mysteries of the big bathroom, but until she became bedridden, no one else, I think, ever saw her in less than her corset, camisole, and petticoat.

The big bathroom, which had a sofa covered with worn Oriental carpeting and an old-fashioned deep tub with claw feet, was the temple of her beauty, and I never went into it, even as a grown woman, without feeling as if I were trespassing. For me, as a young girl, it had all the attractions of the forbidden, and as soon as my grandmother left the house in the afternoon, I would fly in to examine her salves and ointments, buffers and pencils and swabs, brushes and tweezers, her jars and bottles from Elizabeth Arden, Dorothy Gray, Marie Earle, Helena Rubinstein, and Harriet Hubbard Ayer, her skin food, neck lotion, special astringent, and anti-wrinkle emollient, Hinds Honey and Almond, cucumber lotion, Murine, special eye lotion, Velva Cream, mascara, eyeshadow, dry rouge, paste rouge, vanishing cream, powders, chin strap, facial mask. One day, I found a box of something called Turkish Delight, which I took, from its name, to be a beauty preparation used in harems.

The room had a queer, potpourri smell; my grandmother seldom threw anything away, and some of her cosmetics were so old they had gone rancid. Another odor, medicinal, sometimes hung about the room in the morning; I smelled it on the days when I was allowed to have my hair washed in the basin there, by my grandmother's "woman." Actually, as I learned many years later, what I smelled was bourbon whiskey; my grandfather, though a temperate man, was accustomed to have two shots of bourbon before breakfast. The only other signs of his presence were a bottle of Eau Lilas Végétal—a purple cologne—on my grandmother's dressing table and some corn plasters in one of its drawers. He kept his shaving things, as I recall, in a small dressing room that opened off the big bathroom. You could find almost anything there: medicine, bath salts, an unopened bottle of Virginia Dare, family photographs, fishing tackle, Christmas presents that were being hidden, newspaper clippings that dated back to the time when my grandfather had been running for United States Senator. (He was defeated by Levi Ankeny, of Walla Walla.)

The temptation to try out some of my grandmother's beauty aids got the better of me when I was twelve. Unfortunately (like her Household Hint for a successful marriage), most of them had no bearing on my particular problems. "Not for the Youthful Skin," cautioned one astringent, and there was nothing in her crowded drawers for freckles. I did not need eyebrow pencil; my eyebrows were too thick already, and I had recently performed the experiment of shaving half of them off in the convent, while my grandparents were in California. My nose was my chief worry; it was too snub, and I had been sleeping with a clothespin on it to give it a more aristocratic shape. Also, I was bowlegged, and I was wondering about having an operation I had heard about that involved having your legs broken and reset. The dressing table offered no help on these scores, and, failing to find a lipstick and being timorous of the curling iron, I had to be satisfied with smearing a little paste rouge on my lips and putting dry rouge on my cheekbones (to draw attention away from the nose) and pink powder all over my face. I myself could see little change, but my grandmother could, and as soon as she came home that afternoon, a terrible scene took place, for I felt so guilty at what I had done that I would not admit I had been "into" her dressing table, even when confronted with the proof in the disarrayed drawers and the rouge that came off on the handkerchief she applied firmly to my cheek.

She did not actually, as I learned later, think that what I had done was so bad; it was the lying that offended her. But I was convinced that I had committed a real crime, so terrible that I might be sent away from home. The idea that I was not to touch my grandmother's things had impressed itself on my excitable mind like a Mosaic commandment. I had left the well-codified Catholic world in which my young childhood had been spent, and in this new world I could no longer tell what was a mortal and what a venial sin. The bathroom figured to me as the center of everything in the Preston family life from which I was excluded. I had begun to wonder about this family life a little; it was not as much fun as I had thought at first. In spite of the glamour that lay on it like a spell, I was not having as good a time, nearly, as my schoolmates had. Yet when I tried to determine what was different, the only thing I could put my finger on then was that, unlike other people, we did not have a regular lunch at home, and that at the time most people were lunching my grandmother was in the bathroom with the door shut.

This seems a small complaint, but the clue to everything was there. When I think of our house now, the strongest memory that comes back to me is of shut doors and silence. My young uncle, five years older than I was, had his own apartment, reached by a dark set of stairs that branched off the main staircase at the landing; my grandmother and grandfather had their separate chain of rooms, connected by a series of inner doors; the cook had her own, on the third floor, though she had to tiptoe down to share my bathroom; the gardener lived over the garage in rooms I never saw. There was no guest room.

During the greater part of the day, the upstairs hall was in gloom, because every door opening off it, except mine, was shut. The common rooms downstairs—the library, parlor, and living room—were seldom used in the daytime by anyone but me. The rest of the family kept to their own quarters; you would have thought the house was empty when everyone was home. I remember those summer mornings during school vacations. The mornings of the long years of my teens were so alike that they might have been one morning. The silence was profound. Every member of the family, except me, was taciturn—the cook and the gardener, too. After a wordless breakfast (my grandfather had already gone to the office), I was left to my own devices while my grandmother went out to the garden, picked flowers, then arranged them in the pantry; every vase in the house was renewed daily, but I was not allowed to help with the bouquets. Then she climbed the stairs to her bedroom; the door was shut and stayed shut for an hour or more while she talked on the telephone to her sisters and the butcher. During this period, the stillness was broken only by the hum of the vacuum cleaner and the sound of the mail dropping through the slot in the front door.

There was never any interesting mail, just the *National Geographic, Vogue,* and the *American Boy* (which my grandfather, for some reason, had subscribed to for me), some ads and charitable appeals addressed to "The Honorable Harold Preston," and perhaps a letter from Aunt Eva or Aunt Alice Carr. After a time that seemed interminable, while I lay on the sofa reading and waiting for something to happen, the door to the old nursery upstairs, where my grandfather slept and my grandmother did her sewing, would open —a signal to me that I could come up if I wanted. Then, for another hour, we would sit opposite each other in the bay window, my grandmother mending, or looking through the latest copy of *Vogue,* I staring out the window and trying to start a conversation.

"What did Aunt Rosie have to say?" I would begin. "Oh, nothing," she would answer. "Just talk. You know Rosie." Or "Uncle

Mose isn't feeling so well." Or "She had a letter from Mortie in New York." Silence. When she was finished with the magazine, she would pass it on to me, and I would study the society notices of weddings and engagements, but there was never anything from Seattle. New York, Chicago, Boston, San Francisco—that was all. You would think, to read *Vogue,* that nothing ever happened in Seattle, a supposition that, from where *I* sat, was true. Yet I never lost hope; I think I somehow expected to find my own name in those columns, just as I somehow expected that, down below, a roadster would turn the corner with a boy in it who had discovered that I existed. My interest in boys was one of the many subjects I could not discuss with my grandmother; I was not supposed to be aware of them until I was in college. Indeed, the only topics we had in common were clothes and movie actors and actresses. She disliked the kind of books I read and would have disliked the girls I saw if she had had any inkling of what they were like. She would never give her opinion of any member of the family, including those she was "mad" at. For all my fishing, I could never find out even a simple thing, such as what she thought of me.

The liveliest time we had, in all the mornings we sat opposite each other in the nursery, was when I wrote in for a Vogue pattern to make a tennis dress. If I could have learned to sew, or she had had the patience to teach me, we might have found a medium in which we could communicate. The tennis dress, thanks to her help, did not come out too badly, and, encouraged, I wrote for another pattern—a model far too old for me, in tiers of crêpe de Chine that were supposed to shade from a pale yellow, through apricot, to flame. This dress was never finished; I found the blushing remains of it in a hall cupboard on my last visit home.

The dressmaking phase, of which my grandfather entertained great hopes, was a failure. We could never be "like mother and daughter" to each other, in spite of what people said. She could not bear to watch me sewing without a thimble and with a long thread that had a slightly dirty knot on the end of it. If I started on a piece of mending, my ineptitude always drove her to finish it.

Much of my adolescent boredom and discontent sprang from the fact that I had absolutely nothing to do but read and play the Victrola. I was not allowed in the kitchen, except to fix a sandwich for my lunch, because of a historic mess I had made with a batch of marshmallows; as with the dawn-colored dress, I had been too ambitious for a beginner. All I know today of sewing I learned in boarding school and, earlier, from the nuns in the convent, and the only person who was willing to show me anything about cooking was the old gardener-chauffeur, who used to come in and make German-fried potatoes for his lunch. On the cook's day out, he would let me watch him and then try it myself. In our family now, we have a dish called, in his memory, chauffeur-fried potatoes; they are very good.

My grandmother herself did not eat lunch as a regular thing, and at twelve o'clock, or sometimes earlier, my audience was over. She would get up from her chair and retire to the bathroom, shutting the door into the hall behind her. In a minute, her bedroom door closed, the nursery door closed. From then on till a time that varied between two and three o'clock, she was invisible; no one was allowed to disturb her. She was getting ready to go downtown. This sortie was the climax of her day. Her bedroom door would open, revealing her in festive array; every outfit she wore, like every meal, was a surprise. The car would be waiting in front of the old carriage block, and we would set off, sometimes stopping for Aunt Rosie. The next two or three hours would be spent in the stores, trying on, ransacking counters. My grandmother was not much interested in bargains, though we never missed a sale at Helen Igoe's or Magnin's; what she cared about was the "latest wrinkle" in dresses or furs or notions—news from the fashion front. During these hours, she reached her highest point of laconic animation and sparkle; she shopped like an epigrammatist in top form, and the extravagance of her purchases matched her brilliant hair and bobbing feathers and turkey walk and pursy pink cheeks.

But at a quarter of five, wherever we were, my grandmother would look at her watch. It was time to pick up Grandpa in front of his club, where he always played a rubber of bridge after leaving the office. At five o'clock, punctually, he would be on the sidewalk, anxiously surveying the traffic for us. The car would draw up; he would climb in and kiss my grandmother's cheek. "Have a good day?" he would ask. "All right," she would reply, sighing a little. We would get home at five-thirty; dinner was at six, punctually. During the meal, my young uncle would be queried as to how he had passed his day, and he would answer with a few monosyllables. My grandmother would mention the names of any persons she had seen on her shopping tour. My grandfather might praise the food. "Allee samee Victor Hugo," he would say, referring to a restaurant in Los Angeles. After dinner, my married uncle would drop in with his wife, perhaps on their way out to a party. My other uncle, yawning, would retire to his quarters. The doorbell might ring. I would run to answer it, and two or three of his friends would tramp past me upstairs to his rooms. The door on the landing would shut. In a little while, he would lope down the stairs to say that he was going out. He would kiss his mother and father, and my grandfather would say to him, "Home by eleven, son." My grandfather and grandmother, having finished the evening papers, would start playing double Canfield, at which my grandmother nearly always won. "I'll have to hitch up my trousers with a safety pin," my grandfather would say to me, jesting, as he paid over her winnings; this expression signified to him the depths of poverty.

Then he might go downtown to his club for a game of poker, or he might stay in his deep chair, smoking a cigar and reading a book that always seemed to be the same book: "The Life and Letters of Walter Hines Page." My grandmother would take up her circulating-library book, I would take up mine, and silence would resume its sway over the household. The only sound would be the turning of a page or the click of the door on the kitchen landing as the cook went upstairs to bed. Rarely, the telephone would ring, and I would rush to get it, but it was never anything interesting—someone for my uncle, or a girl for me, asking what I was doing. Or my grandmother would glance over at me as I lay stretched out on the sofa with my copy (disappointing) of "Mademoiselle de Maupin": "Mary, pull your dress down." At ten o'clock, she would close her book, sighing, and start out to the front hall, on her way to bed. "Going up, Mama?" my grandfather would say if he was at home, raising his gray eyes with an invariable air of surprise. "I think so, Harry," she would reply, sighing again, from the stairs. The stairs creaked; her door closed; the bathroom door closed. Soon my grandfather would put down his book and his paper knife, offer his cheek to me for a kiss, and follow her up the stairs. The nursery door would shut.

Occasionally, we would all go to the movies, or to the theatre if a New York company was in town; my grandfather did not care for stock. We saw "The Student Prince" and "No! No! Nanette!" I remember, and "Strange Interlude," which my grandmother pronounced "talky." On Thursday nights, we might go out to dinner at my grandfather's club. On Sundays, the cook left a supper prepared for us; my married uncle and his wife always came to this meal, no matter how many invitations they had to turn down, and sometimes Aunt Eva or Aunt Alice. These suppers usually ended with our going to the movies afterward; we were always home by eleven.

About once a year, or possibly every two years, my grandmother gave a tea and we had the caterer in. That was the only entertaining we did. Except for Aunt Alice and Aunt Eva (both widows), we never gave anyone dinner outside the immediate family. We never had Uncle Mose and Aunt Rosie, or Uncle Clarence and his wife, Aunt Abbie (a vegetarian pair), or any of my cousins and their wives, or my grandfather's partners and theirs. My grandmother's brother Elkan, whom she saw rarely but was not on bad terms with, was never, to my knowledge, in our house, nor were his wife or his numerous progeny. This leads me to wonder whether it was not the Jewish connection that had put the bar on entertaining. "If we have one in the house, we'll have them all," my grandfather may have said. But we did have Aunt Eva, frequently, and once, a great exception, her daughter from Portland, to Sunday lunch. The only other exception that comes back to me was a dinner we gave for old Judge Gilman, of the Great Northern, and his wife; I remember this because the men were served whiskey before dinner, the only time this ever happened in our house. But why we had Judge and Mrs. Gilman I do not know; I think it puzzled me at the time by introducing into my head the question of why we did not have other people, since on this occasion a good time was had by all.

Up to then, it had never occurred to me that my family was remarkably inhospitable. I did not realize how strange it was that no social life was ever planned for me or my young uncle, that no young people were invited for us and no attempt made to secure invitations on our behalf. Indeed, I did not fully realize it until I was over thirty and long a mother myself. If I did not have an ordinary social set but only stray, odd friends, I blamed this on myself, thinking there was something wrong with me, like a petticoat showing, that other people could see and I couldn't. The notion that a family had responsibility for launching the younger members was more unknown to me than the theorem of Pythagoras, and if anybody had told me of it, I think I would have shut my ears, for I loved my family and did not wish to believe them remiss in any of their obligations. The fact that they would not let me go out with boys was an entirely different case. I saw their side of it, even though I disagreed violently; they were doing it for my own good, as they conceived it.

And yet I knew there was something odd about my grandmother's attitude toward outsiders. She would never go up to Lake Crescent, in the Olympic Mountains, with my grandfather and my young uncle and me in the summertime, where, amid my grandfather's circle of friends and their descendants, we had the only regular social life I ever experienced in the West. Life in the mountain hotel was very gay, even for the old people—Judge and Mrs. Battle, Colonel Blethen, Mr. Edgar Battle, Mr. Claude Ramsay, Mr. and Mrs. Boole—in my grandfather's set. They had card games on the big veranda and forest walks up to the Marymere waterfall; they went on motorboat expeditions and automobile expeditions; they watched the young people dance in the evening and sent big tips to the chef in the kitchen. I could not understand why my grandmother preferred to stay in Seattle, pursuing her inflexible routine.

She was funny that way—that was the only explanation—just as she was funny about not letting my young uncle or me ever have a friend stay to dinner. In all the years I lived with my grandmother, as a child and as a woman, I can only recall two occasions when this rule was broken. The second one was when she was bedridden and too feeble, morally, to override my determination to ask a poet who was teaching at the University to stay and have supper with me. I felt a little compunction, though the nurse and the cook assured me that it would be all right—she would forget about it the next minute. But her pretty voice, querulous, was heard from upstairs at about eight-thirty in the evening: "Mary, has that man gone home yet?" And all through the rest of my visit she kept reverting crossly to the subject of "that man" who had stayed to supper; it was no good explaining to her that he had no means of getting home, that he lived in rooms way out at the University and took his meals in diners and tearooms, that he was an old friend to whom some hospitality was due in my native city. Nor could I laugh her out of it. "Why didn't he go home for his dinner?" she reiterated, and those dark, suspicious words were very nearly the last I heard from her.

This ungraciousness of my grandmother's was a deeply confirmed trait. It was not only that she resisted offering meals to anyone outside the immediate family; she took exception to a mere caller. There was a silver tray for calling cards on the hall table, but most of the cards in it were yellow with age; my grandmother was always downtown shopping at the hour when calls were normally paid. If I had a girl in for the evening, we could not really talk until my grandmother had gone to bed, and often she would outstay the guest, sitting in a corner with her book and glancing at us from time to time as we sat on the sofa endeavoring to improvise a dialogue. We could tell she was listening, but she did not talk herself. Suddenly, looking up, she would make the gesture to me that meant "Pull your skirt down."

My uncle's situation was the same, but he had the advantage of having his own sitting room, where his friends could congregate. For the most part, my grandmother ignored their presence; she would nod to them curtly if she chanced to meet them in the hall. The girls he knew were never asked to the house; he could never give a party.

Yet she was not an unkindly woman. She was good to her servants and their families, and on some occasions, if she was persuaded to unbend and tell an anecdote, she could be positively cordial. Her house, with its big rooms and wide porches, had been built, it would seem, with a hospitable *intention*. And in my mother's day, so I was told, things had been very different; the house had been full of young people. The silver and crystal and cut glass had not always been put away in the cupboard; there had been music and dancing, and my mother's school and college friends had spent night after night on the sleeping porches without even the necessity of a permission.

My mother had been my grandmother's darling. The fact that we did not entertain, I was given to understand, was related to my mother's death. My grandmother had resented her marriage to my father; according to my Irish relations, she would not have a priest in the house, and so the ceremony had been performed on the lawn. I do not believe this story, which is contradicted by other accounts, but it is true that my grandmother resented the Catholic Church, to which my mother was eventually converted. Dr. Sharples, the family physician, had told my father, it seems, that my mother's health would not stand her repeated pregnancies, but my father went right ahead anyway, refusing to practice birth control. Actually, my mother's death had nothing to do with childbearing; she died of the flu, like so many young women, during the great epidemic. But this would not have deterred a woman like my grandmother from holding my father and the Church responsible. That was perhaps the reason she took no interest in my three brothers, who were still living with my father's people in Minneapolis; she sent them checks and gifts at birthdays and Christmas, and remembered them later in her will, but during the years I lived with her, the three little boys who had been born against her judgment were very remote from her thoughts. Possibly I was enough of a handful for a woman of her age; nevertheless, it seems odd, unfeeling, that dry lack of concern, when she well knew that their lot was not happy. But happiness, like love, was a concept she had no real patience with.

As for the impassibility or aloofness she showed sometimes toward me, this may have been due to an absence of temperamental sympathy (could she have thought I had my father's traits?), or it may have been because I reminded her painfully of my mother (I was always conscious of a resemblance that did not go far enough; everyone was always telling me how "good" my mother had been).

For three years after my mother's death, one of her friends told me, my grandmother did not go out socially. Five years, said another. And this prolonged mourning was always offered as the official explanation of any oddities in our household. My grandmother, people said, lowering their voices, had never recovered from the shock of my mother's death. As a child, I could not quite believe this; it was impossible for me to imagine this contained, self-centered woman overcome by a passion of grief. Without being a psychologist, I felt somehow that her obdurate mourning was willful and selfish.

Children generally feel this about any adult emotion that is beyond their ken, but in my grandmother's case I think I was on the track of something real. Her grief had taken a form peculiar to herself, stamped, as it were, with her monogram—the severe "AMP," in scroll lettering, that figured on her silver, her brushes and combs, her automobile. Her grief had the character of an inveterate hostility. One of my mother's friends recently wrote me a letter describing how my grandmother had hurt her feelings by refusing to speak to her for a year after my mother's death whenever they met in the stores. "Your grandmother could not stand the sight of me," she sadly decided.

And that is how I see my grandmother, bearing her loss like an affront, stubborn and angry, refusing to speak not only to individual persons but to life itself, which had wounded her by taking her daughter away. Her grief was a kind of pique, one of those nurtured *grievances* in which she specialized and which were deeply related to her coquetry. If I had only her photographs to go on, I might doubt the legend of her beauty; what confirms it for me is her manner of grieving, her mistrust of words, her refusal to listen to explanations from life or any other guilty suitor. Life itself was obliged to court her—in vain, as it appeared, for she had been mortally offended, once, twice, three times.

What the first offense was, I do not know, but I presume it had something to do with her Jewish pride and sensitiveness; some injury was dealt her early in her marriage, and it may have been a very small thing—a chance word, even—that caused her to draw back into an august silence on this topic, a silence that lasted until her death. The second one I know about. This was the tragic face-lifting that took place—in 1916 or 1917, I imagine—when she was in her forties and my mother was still living. Perhaps she really did have a mastoid operation at some later period (I rather think she must have), but the disfiguring pouchy scars I have spoken of that started on her cheeks and went down into her neck were the work of a face-lifter, who, as I understand the story, had pumped her face full of hot wax.

Such accidents were common in the early days of face-lifting, and the scars, by the time she was sixty, were not especially noticeable. It was only that her cheeks had a puffy, swollen appearance, which her makeup did not conceal—in fact, if anything, enhanced, for though she did not know it, she always looked better in the morning, before she put on the rouge and powder that made her skin's surface conspicuous. But when the scars were new, they must have been rather horrifying, and that was surely the reason for the dotted veils she wore, pulled tight across her face. The photographs break off at the time of the operation. That was when she stopped speaking to the camera, and, according to one informant, my grandmother left Seattle for a year after the tragedy.

"According to one informant"—the story of the face-lifting was well known in Seattle, and yet in the family no mention was ever made of it, at least in my hearing, and I learned of it from outsiders, my father's people, friends of my mother's, who naturally were unable to supply all the details. I was grown up when I learned it, and yet that same unnatural tact that kept me from ever using the word "Jewish" to my grandmother kept me from prying into the matter with the family. "Your grandmother's tragedy"—so I first heard the face-lifting alluded to, if I remember rightly, by one of my friends, who had heard of it from her mother. And I will not query the ap-propriateness of the word in terms of the Aristotelian canon; in this case, common usage seems right. It was a tragedy—for her and for her husband and family, who, deprived of her beauty through an act of folly, came to live in silence, like a house accursed.

My grandmother's withdrawal from society must have dated, really, from this period, and not from the time of my mother's death, which came as the crowning blow. That was why we were so peculiar, so unsocial, so, I would add, slightly inhuman; we were all devoting ourselves literally, to the cult of a relic, which was my grandmother's body, laved and freshened every day in the big bath-room, and then paraded before the public in the downtown stores.

I was living in New York when my grandfather died, of a stroke, one morning, when he was seventy-nine, in the big bathroom. My grandmother's ritual did not change. She still dressed and went downtown at the same hours, returning at the time when she would have picked him up at his club. She was cheerful when I saw her, a year or so after this. She went to the races and had a new interest, night baseball; we went to the ballpark together. Once in a great while, she would lunch and play bridge with a group of women friends, with whom she had resumed connections after twenty years. But she did not, to my knowledge, ever have them to her house; they met at the Seattle Golf Club usually, the best (non-Jewish) country club.

Like many widows, she appeared to have taken a new lease on life; I had never seen her so chatty, and she was looking very hand-some. I remember an afternoon at the races, to which she drove Aunt Rosie and me in her car, at a speed of seventy miles an hour; she herself was well over seventy. The two sisters, one a lively robin and the other a brilliant toucan, chaffed and bantered with the sporting set in the clubhouse. Conscious of their powers and their desirability, they were plainly holding court. Aunt Rosie did not bet but advised us; my grandmother, as usual, won, and I think I won, too. That night, or in the small hours of the morning, Aunt Rosie died.

It was something that she had eaten at the races, Dr. Sharples thought; an attack of indigestion caused a heart block. He believed at first that he could save her, and I had persuaded my grandmother to go to bed, confident that Aunt Rosie would be almost herself the next day. But in the middle of the night the phone rang. I ran to get it. It was Uncle Mose: "Rosie just went." My grandmother understood before I could tell her, before I had set down the telephone. A terrible scream—an unearthly scream—came from behind the closed door of her bedroom; I have never heard such a sound, neither animal nor human, and it did not stop. It went on and on, like a fire siren on the moon. In a minute, the whole household was roused; everybody came running. I got there first. Flinging open her bedroom door (even then with a sense of trepidation, of being an unwarranted intruder), I saw her, on her bed, the covers pushed back; her legs were sprawled out, and her yellow batiste nightgown, trimmed with white lace, was pulled up, revealing her thighs. She was writhing on the bed; the cook and I could hardly get hold of her. My uncle appeared in the doorway, and my first thought (and I think the cook's also) was to get that nightgown down. The spectacle was indecent, and yet of a strange boudoir beauty that contrasted in an eerie way with the awful noise she was making, more like a howl than a scream, and bearing no resemblance to sorrow. She was trying, we saw, to pull herself to her feet, to go somewhere or other, and the cook helped her up. But then, all at once, she became heavy, like a sack full of stones. The screaming stopped, and there was dead silence.

Eventually, I forget how, but thanks chiefly to the cook, we got her calmed down to the point where she was crying normally. Perhaps the doctor came and administered a sedative. I sat up with her, embracing her and trying to console her, and there was something sweet about this process, for it was the first time we had ever been close to each other. But suddenly she would remember Rosie and shriek out her name; no one could take Rosie's place, and we both knew it. Then I felt like an utter outsider. It seemed clear to me that night, as I sat stroking her hair, that she had never really cared for anyone but her sister; that was her secret. The intellectual part of my mind was aware that some sort of revelation had been made to me—of the nature of Jewish family feeling, possibly. And I wondered whether that fearful, insensate noise had been classic Jewish mourning, going back to the waters of Babylon. Of one thing I was certain: my grandmother was more different from the rest of us than I could ever have conceived.

Uncle Mose was taking it well, I learned the next morning. It was only my grandmother, so unemotional normally, who had given way to this extravagant grief, and the family, I gathered, were slightly embarrassed by her conduct, as though they, too, felt that she had revealed something—something that, as far as they were concerned, would have been better left in the dark. But what *had* she revealed, as they saw it? Her essential Jewishness? I could never find out, for I had to take the train East that very day, with my baby, and when I came back, several years later, no one seemed to remember anything unusual about the occasion of Aunt Rosie's death.

"That's my sister!" my grandmother would exclaim, eagerly pointing, when we came to a photograph of Aunt Rosie. "My sister," she would say of Aunt Eva, in a somewhat grander tone. She always brightened when one of her sisters turned up in the photograph collection, like a child when it is shown its favorite stuffed animal. I think she was a little more excited at the sight of Aunt Rosie. By that time, I imagine, she had forgotten that her sisters were dead—or, rather, the concept death no longer had any meaning for her. They had "gone away," she probably believed, just as children believe that this is what happens to their dead relations. I used to stand ready to prompt her with the names, but she did not seem to need or want this; her sisters' relationship to her was what mattered, and she always got that straight. "Aunt Rosie," I would observe, showing her a picture of a small, smiling, dark woman in a big marabou hat. "My sister," her voice would override me proudly, as if she were emending my statement.

The clothes in the old photographs amused her. She had not lost her interest in dress, and was very critical of my appearance, urging me, with impatient gestures, to pull my hair forward on my cheeks, and surveying me with pride when I had done so; it gave a "softer" look. If I did not get it right, she would pull her own black waves forward, to show me what she meant. Though she could no longer go downtown, she still kept to the same schedule. Every day at twelve o'clock, the nurse would close my grandmother's door and the doors to the nursery and the bathroom, reopening them between two and three, when the beauty preparations had been completed. "You can come in now. Your grandmother is all prettied up." One afternoon, responding to the summons, I found my grandmother frowning and preoccupied. There was something the matter, and I could not make out what it was. She wanted me to get her something, the "whatchamacallit" from her bureau. I tried nearly everything—brush, comb, handkerchief, perfume, pincushion, pocketbook, photograph of my mother. All of them were wrong, and she grew more and more impatient, as if I were behaving like an imbecile. "Not the *comb*—the whatchamacallit!" Finally, for she was getting quite wrought up, I rang for the nurse. "She wants something," I said. "But I can't make out what it is." The nurse glanced at the bureau top and then went swiftly over to the chiffonier; she picked up the hand mirror that was lying there and passed it silently to my grandmother, who at once began to beam and nod. "She's forgotten the word for mirror," the nurse said, winking at me. At that moment, the fact that my grandmother was senile became real to me.

A GAME OF CATCH

❖

RICHARD WILBUR

MONK and Glennie were playing catch on the side lawn of the firehouse when Scho caught sight of them. They were good at it, for seventh-graders, as anyone could see right away. Monk, wearing a catcher's mitt, would lean easily sidewise and back, with one leg lifted and his throwing hand almost down to the grass, and then lob the white ball straight up into the sunlight. Glennie would shield his eyes with his left hand and, just as the ball fell past him, snag it with a little dart of his glove. Then he would burn the ball straight toward Monk, and it would spank into the round mitt and sit, like a still-life apple on a plate, until Monk flipped it over into his right hand and, with a negligent flick of his hanging arm, gave Glennie a fast grounder.

They were going on and on like that, in a kind of slow, mannered, luxurious dance in the sun, their faces perfectly blank and en-tranced, when Glennie noticed Scho dawdling along the other side of the street and called hello to him. Scho crossed over and stood at the front edge of the lawn, near an apple tree, watching.

"Got your glove?" asked Glennie after a time. Scho obviously hadn't.

"You could give me some easy grounders," said Scho. "But don't burn 'em."

"All right," Glennie said. He moved off a little, so the three of them formed a triangle, and they passed the ball around for about five minutes, Monk tossing easy grounders to Scho, Scho throwing to Glennie, and Glennie burning them in to Monk. After a while, Monk began to throw them back to Glennie once or twice before he let Scho have his grounder, and finally Monk gave Scho a fast, bumpy grounder that hopped over his shoulder and went into the brake on the other side of the street.

"Not so hard," called Scho as he ran across to get it.

"You should've had it," Monk shouted.

It took Scho a little while to find the ball among the ferns and dead leaves, and when he saw it, he grabbed it up and threw it toward Glennie. It struck the trunk of the apple tree, bounced back at an angle, and rolled steadily and stupidly onto the cement apron in front of the firehouse, where one of the trucks was parked. Scho ran hard and stopped it just before it rolled under the truck, and this time he carried it back to his former position on the lawn and threw it carefully to Glennie.

"I got an idea," said Glennie. "Why don't Monk and I catch for five minutes more, and then you can borrow one of our gloves?"

"That's all right with me," said Monk. He socked his fist into his mitt, and Glennie burned one in.

"All right," Scho said, and went over and sat under the tree. There in the shade he watched them resume their skillful play. They threw lazily fast or lazily slow—high, low, or wide—and always handsomely, their expressions serene, changeless, and forgetful. When Monk missed a low backhand catch, he walked indolently after the ball and, hardly even looking, flung it sidearm for an imaginary put-out. After a good while of this, Scho said, "Isn't it five minutes yet?"

"One minute to go," said Monk, with a fraction of a grin.

Scho stood up and watched the ball slap back and forth for several minutes more, and then he turned and pulled himself up into the crotch of the tree.

"Where you going?" Monk asked.

"Just up the tree," Scho said.

"I guess he doesn't want to catch," said Monk.

Scho went up and up through the fat light-gray branches until they grew slender and bright and gave under him. He found a place where several supple branches were knit to make a dangerous chair, and sat there with his head coming out of the leaves into the sun-light. He could see the two other boys down below, the ball going back and forth between them as if they were bowling on the grass, and Glennie's crew-cut head looking like a sea urchin.

"I found a wonderful seat up here," Scho said loudly. "If I don't fall out." Monk and Glennie didn't look up or comment, and so he began jouncing gently in his chair of branches and singing "Yo-ho, heave ho" in an exaggerated way.

"Do you know what, Monk?" he announced in a few moments.

"I can make you two guys do anything I want. Catch that ball, Monk! Now you catch it, Glennie!"

"I was going to catch it anyway," Monk suddenly said. "You're not making anybody do anything when they're already going to do it anyway."

"I made you say what you just said," Scho replied joyfully.

"No, you didn't," said Monk, still throwing and catching but now less serenely absorbed in the game.

"That's what I wanted you to say," Scho said.

The ball bounded off the rim of Monk's mitt and plowed into a gladiolus bed beside the firehouse, and Monk ran to get it while Scho jounced in his treetop and sang, "I wanted you to miss that. Anything you do is what I wanted you to do."

"Let's quit for a minute," Glennie suggested.

"We might as well, until the peanut gallery shuts up," Monk said.

They went over and sat cross-legged in the shade of the tree. Scho looked down between his legs and saw them on the dim, spotty ground, saying nothing to one another. Glennie soon began abstractedly spinning his glove between his palms; Monk pulled his nose and stared out across the lawn.

"I want you to mess around with your nose, Monk," said Scho, giggling. Monk withdrew his hand from his face.

"Do that with your glove, Glennie," Scho persisted. "Monk, I want you to pull up hunks of grass and chew on it."

Glennie looked up and saw a self-delighted, intense face staring down at him through the leaves. "Stop being a dope and come down and we'll catch for a few minutes," he said.

Scho hesitated, and then said, in a tentatively mocking voice, "That's what I wanted you to say."

"All right, then, nuts to you," said Glennie.

"Why don't you keep quiet and stop bothering people?" Monk asked.

"I made you say that," Scho replied, softly.

"Shut up," Monk said.

"I made you say that, and I want you to be standing there looking sore. And I want you to climb up the tree. I'm making you do it!"

Monk was scrambling up through the branches, awkward in his haste, and getting snagged on twigs. His face was furious and foolish, and he kept telling Scho to shut up, shut up, shut up, while the other's exuberant and panicky voice poured down upon his head.

"*Now* you shut up or you'll be sorry," Monk said, breathing hard as he reached up and threatened to shake the cradle of slight branches in which Scho was sitting.

"I *want*—" Scho screamed as he fell. Two lower branches broke his rustling, crackling fall, but he landed on his back with a deep thud and lay still, with a strangled look on his face and his eyes clenched. Glennie knelt down and asked breathlessly, "Are you O.K., Scho? Are you O.K.?," while Monk swung down through the leaves crying that honestly he hadn't even touched him, the crazy guy just let go. Scho doubled up and turned over on his right side, and now both the other boys knelt beside him, pawing at his shoulder and begging to know how he was.

Then Scho rolled away from them and sat partly up, still struggling to get his wind but forcing a species of smile onto his face.

"I'm sorry, Scho," Monk said. "I didn't mean to make you fall."

Scho's voice came out weak and gravelly, in gasps. "I meant—you to do it. You—had to. You can't do—anything—unless I want—you to."

Glennie and Monk looked helplessly at him as he sat there, breathing a bit more easily and smiling fixedly, with tears in his eyes. Then they picked up their gloves and the ball, walked over to the street, and went slowly away down the sidewalk, Monk punching his fist into the mitt, Glennie juggling the ball between glove and hand.

From under the apple tree, Scho, still bent over a little for lack of breath, croaked after them in triumph and misery, "I want you to do whatever you're going to do for the whole rest of your life!"

ELEGANT ECONOMY

❖

EDITH TEMPLETON

WHEN I came into the dressing room, my mother, without looking up, acknowledged my "Good morning" with a flutter of
one hand. She picked up a nail file and proceeded to stab the letter
spread out on the table in front of her, three times over and always
in the same spot. "Tindog," she said. "That must be the word. If
the earth were to open this moment and swallow me up, I would
still say Tindog. You do agree, don't you?"

"Yes, Mama," I said, just as, two years before, upon my mother's
receipt of a similar letter, I had agreed on "Furdrag."

"Of course," said my mother, " 'dog' is easy. That's 'day.' And if
the 'T' is an 'F,' then 'Tindog' is Friday. But what if the 'T' is a
'T'? That would make it Tuesday or Thursday. That means there
are three Tindogs a week, and I can't do anything about it. Today
is Friday, and Prochazka will have to go and meet the train, and if
she doesn't arrive, he'll have to go again next Tuesday, and so on
till the right Tindog comes round. Oh God, what a nuisance! But
I do admire her, just the same."

"Yes, Mama," I said, and I cast a glance at the letter, which,
beautifully and deceptively neat, as all Aunt Leonie's letters were,
looked like a length of unravelled crochet lace. Aunt Leonie hated
all waste, and did not like to use more than one sheet of paper for
her communications. At the same time, she was convinced that it
was ill-bred to write on both sides of the letter paper. She managed
to be both well-bred and thrifty by writing first from top to bottom,
in the ordinary way, and then, after turning the sheet at right angles,
continuing across over what had already been written. This particular letter, I knew, dealt with Aunt Leonie's imminent arrival at
my grandmother's castle in Bohemia, where we were spending the
summer, as we did every year at this time, in the early 1920s. And
since Aunt Leonie knew that my grandmother was away, taking

the waters at Karlsbad, she had written to my mother, who was left in charge.

"Mama," I said, "do you admire Aunt Leonie because she is so mean?"

"Who says she is mean?" asked my mother. "Have you ever heard me say she is mean? Have you ever, for that matter, heard me say one bad word against Aunt Leonie?"

"But she only has charwomen in London," I said. "And they have to come in after eleven, so that she needn't give them elevenses, and she buys only broken biscuits, because she gets them at half price."

"You are being ridiculous," said my mother. "That's not mean. That's elegant economy. And perhaps in the future you will be good enough not to hang about in the kitchen all day long and listen to this kind of talk. At your age you are old enough to know your place. Do you think I spent all my time belowstairs when I was twelve? I always did hate backstairs gossip. Even then."

"But it's true," I said. "And she collects dead flies and boils them in sugar, and if you'd look at any of her raisins, you'd see they had lights and livers."

"If the cook didn't shoot her mouth so much," said my mother, "she might get through some work in the meantime. I had to send the coffee back to be hotted up, and, my God, she does take so long over it."

"Shall I go and ask her to hurry up, Mama?" I asked.

"For heaven's sake," said my mother, "that would be fatal. Stay right where you are."

I could not understand my mother's sudden fear of disturbing the cook, and I was still more bewildered when Emma, our own parlormaid, who, as always, had come with us from London, entered with the breakfast tray and was received with real anxiety. "What happened?" my mother asked at once, as though the heating up of the coffee had acquired a dramatic importance.

Emma lowered the tray carefully, so as not to spill the bowlful of steaming water in which the coffee jug had been set. "There is no doubt about it, Madam," she said. "Three times the cook laid out the cards, and three times they came up black and unlucky, with a journey and an unexpected lady guest. And seeing that we don't know when to expect Miss Leonie, that means she'll come today, sudden-like. At least, that's how she reads the cards."

"Naturally," said my mother. "I said all along it would be today. You do agree, Emma, don't you?"

"Indeed I do, Madam. Not that I go by anything the cook says, but seeing that today is Friday and that it's unlucky to travel on a Friday, I should imagine it's just the day Miss Leonie would choose, her being such an independent lady in more ways than one."

"Very true," said my mother. "And, of course, I do admire her for it. But you'd better see that the gong is taken away."

"Madam can rely on me. I have already hidden it where no one will find it. Dear me, it would never do, what with Mr. Frederick staying, and he being such a light sleeper and needing his rest, same as Madam does."

"Quite so," said my mother coldly, and she looked straight ahead of her with a frown. I could guess the reason for this sudden chilliness; it was because Emma had given first consideration to Uncle Frederick's comfort and had mentioned my mother only out of mere politeness. Uncle Frederick, my mother's younger brother, was a great favorite with all the servants.

"And remember, Emma," said my mother, "I don't like to be told that we are extravagant. No butter curls—that's vulgar, and besides it makes people take more butter than they really need. When you serve fruit, always a vine leaf or two tucked in between, because it looks pretty and costs nothing. With the tea, brown sugar, white sugar, and lump sugar—that's not wasteful, because it all costs the same and it looks good. And before teatime always ask if she wants China or Indian, because we haven't got China tea and she drinks Indian, and it makes a good impression."

During all this, Emma had arranged and rearranged the plates, the breadbasket, the butter dish, and the honeypot, without dislodging the napkin that she held squeezed in the crook of her elbow. Now she whipped this out, with one of her virtuoso movements, furled it round the handle of the jug, and poured the coffee. This meant that she had come to the end of her task and was unwilling to listen to any more of my mother's household litanies, which, in any case, were as ill placed as if one had lectured Uncle Frederick, who was an art dealer, on the different schools of painting.

"At Madam's service," said Emma, and she was gone.

"Did you see that?" asked my mother. "How she upped and left? She's got one of her haughty days again, and all that because I dare to take the trouble and give some thought to—"

"Mama," I said, "where did she hide the gong?"

"If you want to know, you can go and ask her yourself," said my mother. "I've had enough of Emma to last me for the morning."

I could not find Emma in the silver pantry or in the linen room or in the dining room, and when I looked into the morning room and saw her standing behind Uncle Frederick's chair, I was glad that my mother was not there to see it. Emma, who as a rule wore stiff blue-striped linen and a pleated cap until noon, had already changed into her black parlor dress with the tiny frilled apron and had crowned her head with the lace-trimmed bow. There was no doubt that she had done so to pay further homage to Uncle Frederick. I curtsied, not daring to speak, for I had arrived just at the moment when Uncle Frederick was going to have his fried egg. He had an exciting way of eating it. First, he divided the white into three sections, cut it away from the yolk, and swallowed it in three bites; then, when only the yolk remained, he lifted it whole and gulped it down in a single go. I knew nothing about Uncle Frederick's way of doing business as an art dealer, but from his way of eating eggs I imagined that he was in the habit of taking risks and that, mostly, he brought them off.

"Which one do you think, Emma?" he now asked, taking no notice of me and gazing suspiciously at the toast rack that Emma had presented to him.

"The third slice looks the likeliest to me, sir, if I may say so. The cook not being in the habit of toast at the best of times, and today even more so, seeing that Miss Leonie is due to arrive today."

"So it's today, is it?" asked Uncle Frederick while he gazed without enthusiasm at the array of liquid honey, firm honey, marmalade, and cherry jam that Emma had placed in a semicircle round his plate. "How does the cook make that out? Was it written on the wall in letters of burning toast, or what?"

"The cook knows what she knows, sir, in a manner of speaking."

"Ha," said Uncle Frederick. "Except how to make toast. Mind you put the blasted gong away, Emma—do you hear?"

"It's been attended to, sir."

"And, to make quite sure," said Uncle Frederick, "serve her breakfast in her own room. Tether her like a goat, you understand?"

"As you say, sir," said Emma.

I knew the story, but when my mother first mentioned the gong I had doubted it. Now, when I saw how serious Uncle Frederick was, I knew that what Emma called Aunt Leonie's "independence" must be true. Aunt Leonie was my grandfather's sister, and ever since her parents' death she had lived on her own in a house in London, near the river, which cost her nothing, since it was part of her inheritance. She kept no servants—she said she could not afford to pay their wages—and made do with two charwomen, who worked in shifts during the daytime. Aunt Leonie was determined, however, to continue living in the style she had always been accustomed to, no matter what thrift she practiced. Thus, she got up every morning at six, swept the forecourt, whitened the front doorsteps, and polished the bell plate and the door knocker. Then she laid the table in the dining room, cooked her breakfast in the kitchen, set the meal on the table, ran down a flight of stairs into the main hall, beat out a prolonged peal of thunder on the gong, and ran hurriedly up the stairs and sat down at table. Clearly, my mother and Uncle Frederick were afraid that Aunt Leonie would insist on the gong even when staying with us at the castle. They knew that if the castle servants did not indulge her, she was quite capable of performing the ritual herself. I also recalled being told that Aunt Leonie never threw anything away. She even made good use of bits of broken china, cementing them on the walls of her kitchen behind the stove and the sink, like a patchwork mosaic, so as to save herself the expense of tiled splash backs.

"Does Mama admire Aunt Leonie because she is so clever with her elegant economy?" I asked Uncle Frederick.

"You fascinate me," said Uncle Frederick.

"Is Aunt Leonie very poor?" I asked.

"Very poor," said Uncle Frederick. "She is so poor my heart bleeds for her all the time. Of course, I don't know what she has been up to recently, but she has some lovable ways of raking in the cash."

"But she is not richer than Grandmama?" I asked.

"But quite a bit richer."

"She can't be," I said, "because Grandmama has got the castle and the park and the estate, and Aunt Leonie has just got a house with twelve rooms and not even a gardener."

"What's wrong with that?" said Uncle Frederick. "She grubs about nicely with her own lily-white claws." He passed a hand over his head and gave me a disgusted look. "But that's neither here nor there. She owns many houses and collects the rents, while your grandmother is sitting tight on all this glory, in her feudal way, so that it's just dead capital, with money going out all the time and nothing to come in. There's your answer." He rose from the table.

Aunt Leonie arrived that day on the morning train—in order not to have to pay for her lunch, Emma said to me. Uncle Frederick joined us in the dining room just as we were sitting down to table. "I kiss your hand, Aunt Leonie," he said hurriedly. "I hope you had a pleasant journey."

My mother, who had clearly been afraid that Uncle Frederick would burst upon us with a rude remark, spread out her napkin with a look of relief and said eagerly, "Though it's been very hot and sultry all morning, I must say."

"Do you have to tell her?" said Uncle Frederick. "Do you think Aunt Leonie doesn't sweat, or what?"

"Dear boy," said Aunt Leonie. "Always so down to earth."

It always amazed me how Uncle Frederick, brimful as he was with unpleasantness, managed to make himself liked and respected by most people who knew him. I could only suppose that they thought of him as they thought of medicines, which are known to be bitter and nasty to take and yet are trusted and highly thought of, and that it was precisely Uncle Frederick's unpalatable manners that convinced people he was thoroughly sound.

There was a silence as we all watched Emma serve the soup with the dedicated bearing of a queen carrying the crown for her own coronation. "Such a hot and nasty drive," said Aunt Leonie, at last, "in that stifling coupé. And I had to close the windows and draw the curtains, because I do hate to pass all those dear little people on the road. If they greet me, I have to greet them, too, and it's such a bother looking pleasant."

"It's wonderful how you are growing more and more like the old Countess Sternborn," Uncle Frederick said. "Next time, you'll be hiding your face behind a fan, the way the Countess used to do when she was an old hag and didn't want to show her bad teeth."

"Frederick is being ridiculous," said my mother. "For one thing, fans are out of fashion, and anyway Aunt Leonie has got fine teeth."

"So I have, dear girl," said Aunt Leonie, "and I am very devoted to them."

"Good job, too," said Uncle Frederick, "the price of false teeth being what it is."

My mother drew a sharp breath.

"Dear boy," said Aunt Leonie. "Always so humorous." And, bending over her plate, she cut with her spoon through a marrow

dumpling with a remarkably gentle movement, as though to convince the dumpling that she bore no grudge.

"It's very kind of you to call him humorous," said my mother.
"If you ask me, it's nothing but sheer bad taste and being offensive,
or he would not have dragged up the whole thing in the first place.
How could Aunt Leonie ever grow to be like the Countess Sternborn, I ask you? For one thing, the Countess was a chorus girl
before she married and came floating up to the top, like the parsley
on potato soup."

"And so vulgar forever after," said Aunt Leonie. "Always trailing
about with all her pearls on, even in the fields and lanes. And such
a lot of pearls, too."

"It makes me quite sick when I think of it," said my mother,
"because it's so unfair. And all the good women about the place
with not so much as half the pearls the Countess had."

"You goose," said Uncle Frederick. "You don't get pearls for
being good. You get them for being damned good."

"So true, dear boy," said Aunt Leonie. "A single good pearl set
to advantage is all a decent woman needs." She smiled down at her
hand, on which a big black pearl shone like a clouded moon in the
night sky.

"And all those furs the Countess had," said my mother.

"Did you expect her to clothe herself in virtue, or what?" said
Uncle Frederick.

"But so many of them," said Aunt Leonie.

"That's because she was an orphan," said Uncle Frederick. "Knew
she had to look out for herself."

"Orphan, ha, ha," said my mother.

"Now you are cackling like a brainless goose," said Uncle Frederick. "But I seem to remember a certain friend of yours in London
who is bellyaching that she's got no title because of her family's
bar sinister in the sixteenth century. And I've never heard you say
'ha, ha' to her. I only mean to say, what's a bar sinister among
friends?"

"Dear boy," said Aunt Leonie. "Always so matter-of-fact. If only
his dear father had not died so young, he would have taught him
how to keep his ideals. And those tutors were never any good, of
course." And, with a smile full of pity, Aunt Leonie now glanced
at Emma, who was carrying in a roast duck and being followed by
two other maids, with new potatoes, gravy, and cucumber salad.
She looked like a queen escorted by trainbearers.

"This is too much," said my mother. "First Frederick is being disgraceful, and then, to crown it all, you are sorry for him. And besides you are quite wrong, if I may say so. Papa did die too soon, of course, but then Mama made up for it, and he had plenty of mother love. For instance—" My mother paused and watched Aunt Leonie, who had gone into a dither upon being presented with the gravy boat, which had two spouts—one set low and marked "Lean," and the other set high and marked "Fat."

"Yes, do go on about mother love, dear girl," said Aunt Leonie. "Is the bird very fat, Emma?"

Emma, resentful at being held up in her regal procession, replied, in her most unhelpful manner, "I'm sure I couldn't say, Madam."

"Oh, and I always thought you knew everything," said Aunt Leonie, and she poured some gravy first from one spout and then from the other. "Now, do go on about mother love, dear girl."

"Yes, of course," said my mother. "Now, for instance, as I was saying, when Mama got her first suspicion that Frederick might have flat feet, she took him to a specialist straightaway. She had a cast made for each foot separately, mind you, and they were given to a special shoemaker, and she always saw to it that he only wore shoes with in-built supports. So there."

"You astonish me," said Uncle Frederick. "Have you quite finished throwing my flat feet in Aunt Leonie's face, or do you want to tell her more, you ignorant goose?"

"There is no need to be insulting," said my mother, "just because I spoke the truth."

"It isn't the truth," said Uncle Frederick. "I never had flat feet."

"Never, ha, ha," said my mother.

"Did I ever? No, I never," said Uncle Frederick. "Mama was full of mother love, of course, but she was quite wrong. And the doctor was a tripehound, and the shoemaker had to make his living."

"You are being ridiculous," said my mother.

"Am I really?" said Uncle Frederick. "Then let me tell you that when I was in Vienna last year, Professor Sauerbruch happened to be there, too, for a lecturing visit. I went to see him, and he looked at my feet and photographed them and took X-rays of them, and then he told me that I had been cruelly—do you hear?—cruelly misunderstood by Mama and the rest of you. My feet had such high arches that I was as Gothic as a Gothic cathedral—do you understand? In the end, he asked me if he could keep the photographs, because he might publish them in a scientific paper of his, as examples of perfect feet."

"With your name underneath?" asked my mother. "Once I got into the *Tatler* myself."

"Ha," said Uncle Frederick. "Salad, please."

"Dear boy," said Aunt Leonie. "Such a sad childhood; I always knew it."

I thought that Uncle Frederick's story was beautiful and satisfying, like the one about the frog who turned into a prince, but my mother was still puzzled and envious about it, while Aunt Leonie gave him a broad, gentle smile, as though wishing to console him for past injustices with the sight of her fine teeth.

Emma began to offer a sweet dish the cook called "cobbler's apprentices." It was made of prunes that had been stoned and stuffed with walnut kernels and then fried in batter and dusted with powdered chocolate and sugar. After Aunt Leonie had eaten the first few apprentices, Uncle Frederick gave her a look of genuine interest, which astonished me. Following his glance, I burst into laughter. Emma turned round from the sideboard, where she had been busying herself, and an instant later she came forward with a small plate, which she put at Aunt Leonie's left with a murmur of "For the stones, Madam, begging your pardon." Aunt Leonie acknowledged it with a nod. My mother drew a deep breath and bit her lips, and swept Emma with a severely reproving glance. Then, after another deep breath to steady herself, my mother seemed to remember that this was one of Emma's haughty days. So she turned on me, instead. "Edith, how often have I told you that one does not look at other people's plates? And if Aunt Leonie does not like walnuts, there is nothing funny about it, either. And if you must go on laughing, then perhaps you will be good enough to leave us and go up to your room."

"I am sorry, Mama," I said.

"Really," said Aunt Leonie. "And I never dreamt." She had been carefully taking the walnuts out of the prunes and placing them on the edge of her plate, mistaking them for stones. "Really," she said again. "You people are leading such wasteful lives that one never knows what to expect. Not even the prunes are good enough for you as God made them. Such wicked extravagance." All this she uttered with her head bent, as though chiding the prunes, and with her fork and spoon flashing above them like signals of distress. "I might have known," she went on. "In 1905, I gave your mother a recipe for a clever cake without butter and without eggs, with grated carrots to replace them. And in 1911, when I asked her about it, she said the cook had lost it."

"Oh, my God," said my mother.

Emma now stepped in. "Will it be all right, Madam," she said, "if I serve the coffee in the Austrian Room?"

"Would you like it in the Austrian Room?" asked my mother, who was clearly anxious to make up to Aunt Leonie for the walnuts.

"That would be delightful, dear girl," said Aunt Leonie. "I do enjoy sitting there, with those painted landscapes all around me. It is as good as a holiday in Salzburg—only nicer, because you don't get the rain, and much cheaper, of course."

Emma left the room with her daintily affected step. The napkin that she draped over her hand when serving at table was flung over one shoulder in a jaunty fashion, indicating that the coronation was over. My mother watched her exit with a frown.

"I am so glad we are having coffee," said Aunt Leonie as we rose from the table. "It's not really in my life, but I know you people go in for it and I've been wondering if you could save me some for afterward. I've brought a few pairs of stockings with me. So cheap and such a nasty pink. And if that poisonous Emma of yours would boil them up in the coffee, they would turn the color of elegant flesh. Dear little Edith, here, can fetch them down from my room later on."

"Emma won't do it," I said, "because she is not a lady's maid. Mama hasn't got a lady's maid at all now—not even in London."

"That's quite true," said my mother. "Though God knows I need one badly."

"You wouldn't, dear girl, if you were in my place," said Aunt Leonie. "One evening dress at a time, and that lasts me for fifteen years. After that, I cut it up for sofa cushions. It makes a drawing room so nice and nostalgic."

"I do so agree," said my mother, with a forced smile.

"And the tiny itsy-bitsies make such pretty slipcovers for account books and timetables," said Aunt Leonie.

Uncle Frederick had been listening to all this in disgusted silence, and now, when we reached the Austrian Room, he settled himself in a corner by the third window, as though to make sure he would not be drawn into the talk. But Aunt Leonie, who had been disappointed about the plan to improve her stockings, seemed determined to get some use out of him. "I have been wanting to ask you something, dear boy," she said, "because you are so clever—finding those pretty little pictures and making people pay such high prices for them."

"You fascinate me," said Uncle Frederick. "Do you think I deal with fools, or what? Nobody has ever bought a picture from me because it was pretty. They buy as an investment or for purposes of concealment."

"Concealing what?" I asked.

"Do be quiet, Edith," said my mother, as she always did when she could not give an explanation.

"What everybody wants to conceal," said Uncle Frederick. "Income, of course. It may mean nothing to Edith, but I believe it will strike a chord in Aunt Leonie's heart."

"Dear boy. Always so understanding," said Aunt Leonie.

"What do you want to know?" asked Uncle Frederick. "Speak on."

"You know I always like to put things to good use," said Aunt Leonie, "and all waste is hateful to me. I can't help it—I am just that sort of person."

"You must be unique," said Uncle Frederick. "Do you think everybody else loves paying income tax, or what?"

"Dear boy," said Aunt Leonie. "Always so wonderfully clear-sighted."

"I'll be still more clear-sighted in a minute," said Uncle Frederick. "I don't know how you've been getting rid of some of your tenants, but I do know you have been letting those flats of yours at exorbitant rents, and now you are dancing with anxiety. If you tell me how much you've got to be salted away, I'll see if I can find a picture for you. A nice picture, a dear little picture—you understand?"

"Dear boy," said Aunt Leonie. "Always so helpful."

"I love being helpful," said Uncle Frederick, "because there's nothing like art to brighten people's lives. And nowadays more than ever, what with shares at nominal values and not a single currency that is really stable."

"What is nominal values?" I asked.

"Nominal values means," said my mother, "that you have already been staying far too long in this stuffy room and that it is high time you went out into the nice fresh air."

I curtsied and left. I wondered whether I would ever see the picture that Uncle Frederick was going to sell to Aunt Leonie, and whether it would be really large enough for her to wedge all the money she wanted to hide between the back of the canvas and the frame.

When I entered my mother's dressing room on the following morning, I found her again in a state of agitation, alternately wringing her hands over the coffee tray and fastening and unfastening the bow at the neck of her *mille-fleurs* morning gown. When she failed to notice that one of her sleeves was trailing in the coffee, I knew that she was genuinely upset.

Emma stood behind and slightly to the left of my mother's chair. "Tchk, tchk, tchk," she kept saying, shaking her head.

"This sort of thing has never happened before, has it, Emma?" asked my mother. "I mean, not here, in the castle?"

"Dear me, Madam. I should say it hasn't."

"What has happened, Mama?" I asked.

"Aunt Leonie," said my mother.

"Has she been strangled?" I asked.

"No such luck," said my mother. "I mean, she is alive and well, and for that we are duly grateful."

"Yes, Mama."

"Her ring has gone," said my mother. "The ring with the single pearl set to advantage, which is all a decent woman needs. It was out of your great-grandfather's tiepin, and it looks all right, but it is only half the pearl. The other half Aunt Leonie gave back to Mama, although Mama never wanted it, because she doesn't wear things by halves."

"Has it been stolen?" I asked.

"And then there was a row over it," said my mother, "because Aunt Leonie said that if Mama did not care for the presents she gave—presents, ha, ha, when you think it never cost her a penny in the first place—then she'd never give any presents any more to any of us. And that's why she always comes to visit when she is sure Mama isn't here and is well out of the way, if you must know."

"Has it been stolen?" I repeated.

"How should I know?" said my mother. "Stolen or lost. Anyway, it's gone."

"If I may make so bold, Madam," said Emma, "I can't see how Miss Leonie lost it, seeing that she is so careful about her things."

"You are right, Emma," said my mother. "It must be worse than lost. Besides, when the cook laid out her cards yesterday morning, they turned up black and unlucky, you remember. I thought at the time it was just because of Aunt Leonie in herself, as a guest, if you know what I mean, but now I know better."

"As Madam says," said Emma.

"But what I can't understand is how it could have disappeared," said my mother. "Because she always wears it, and she had it on last night at dinner. And then you say you took in her breakfast at seven today, to her own room, which means that no one had gone in before you, and she was already groaning and gnashing her teeth by then."

"Indeed, Madam," said Emma. "Carrying on something cruel."

"It would not be so bad in itself, because I shall write to Mama, and I am sure Mama will let her have the other half pearl to make up for it. But then Mama, too, will be most upset that anything like this should have happened under her own roof."

"Indeed, Madam. But it's still early in the day, and if I were in Madam's place, I would wait and see. It wouldn't do to upset the old lady, and she having gone to take the cure, and it may turn up, unexpected-like. There's no knowing."

"Do you really think so?" asked my mother. "Perhaps the cook could perform again with her cards. Then we might know where we stand."

"I'm afraid that's no go, Madam, the cook being very upset on account of there having been words about wasteful prunes and being contrary to God's will. There's some people who never know when to shut their traps, begging Madam's pardon, and there's times I could wring those girls' necks for them."

There was a knock at the door. "Look who is there, Edith," said my mother.

It was Uncle Frederick. "Who is going to wring whose necks?" he asked.

"You are not being funny," said my mother. "And please leave me alone. I am not in the mood to see anyone just now."

"Are you out of your mind?" said Uncle Frederick. "Do you think I come here for the pleasure of seeing you and to wish you a good morning, or what?"

"Good morning, ha, ha," said my mother.

"It's Emma I wanted to see," said Uncle Frederick. "Now, listen, Emma. You are to get Miss Leonie downstairs, and then you will wing your way to her room, clean up, turn out, and what have you. All on your own, you understand? Look under the blasted mattress and behind drawers, and so on and so forth—do you hear? I'm going to have my breakfast now, and I'll see you later."

During the next hour, I did the tour of the kitchen and the stables and the hothouses, and found that the cook and Prochazka and Kucera, the head gardener, were all in a hopeful mood. They all declared that the ring was bound to turn up. This opinion was delivered with a measure of contempt, and Kucera even went as far as to shake his fist in the direction of the castle and to say that there was always trouble with the family, as sure as there were buds in spring, and that he was sick of all of us, always excepting madam my grandmother and Mr. Frederick.

When I got back indoors, I found my mother and Aunt Leonie and Uncle Frederick in the Austrian Room. As soon as Uncle Frederick saw me, he said, "Edith will run along and tell Emma that I want some brandy in the Saints' Room."

"You are being ridiculous," said my mother. "You could have it here just as well."

"Of course I could, you goose," said Uncle Frederick. "Do you have to tell me?"

"The dear boy," said Aunt Leonie. "He is feeling the strain."

"I don't know about the strain," said Uncle Frederick, "but I feel a need for brandy. You'll excuse me, Aunt Leonie. I kiss your hand."

I followed Emma, with the brandy tray, into the Saints' Room.

"Dear me," she said upon entering. "I hope you haven't been taken queer, sir, what with the goings on. Say when, sir, begging your pardon."

"Say when yourself, Emma," said Uncle Frederick. "And put it over there. And now tell me, where is that blasted ring?"

"It's not for me to give an opinion, sir, seeing that it is not in Miss Leonie's room," said Emma.

"But you have an idea, haven't you?"

"I have, sir, in a manner of speaking. Miss Leonie must have lost it out-of-doors, seeing that last night we had a full moon."

"How do you mean?" asked Uncle Frederick. "Do you mean she is batty and gets on the go when it's full moon, or what?"

"If I may make so bold, sir, Miss Leonie did visit the orchard last night, the moon only being a convenience. Seeing that she's got a trunk full of windfalls—nasty green apples and plums, and worm-eaten into the bargain."

"Ha," said Uncle Frederick. "For baking clever cakes, or what?"

"For the making of preserves and pickles, I daresay, sir—the way the poor people do. But I would not like it to be known, because it might embarrass Miss Leonie, and also seeing that the trunk was locked."

"You bet it was," said Uncle Frederick, and he took his first gulp of brandy. "We'll draw a veil of decency over that bit. It's wonderful what one can do with a bunch of odd keys and the jolly old nail file. Now speak on."

"As I see it," said Emma, "Miss Leonie did not like to think of that fruit in the orchard wasting there on the ground and rotting away, and she went out with a string bag and an apron, because those are in the trunk, too, locked up with the rest. The apron being meant to save her dress, in the first place, and also being useful if the bag got too full. It is to be regretted that one of the undergardeners happened across her path, coming back from the village, the way they do."

"Boozed up, was he?" asked Uncle Frederick.

"To be sure, sir. And he got behind a tree and made noises. Meowed and barked, I understand, sir."

"And she barked back at him, or what?" asked Uncle Frederick.

"No, sir. But Miss Leonie looked round and did get suspicious, and hurried putting the windfalls into her apron, the string bag being full up by that time. And the man says he didn't steal the ring—it was lying there on the grass when she walked off. The way I see it, sir, she must have put the ring into her apron pocket to save it from getting scratched, and in the rush at the end it must have slipped out."

"That's what comes from saving," said Uncle Frederick. "Pour me another drop, will you?"

"At your orders, sir. The only trouble now being that the head gardener has got the ring and doesn't know what to do with it."

"I'll take it," said Uncle Frederick. "Tell him to send it up, and I'll see to it that he won't regret it—you understand? And that goes for his man, too."

"As you say, sir. It's only that the head gardener says he well knows your generosity, sir, but there's things that can't be bought for money."

"Well, what does he want?" asked Uncle Frederick. "Does he desire Aunt Leonie, or what? There's nothing she wouldn't do to get her ring back."

"Good gracious me, it isn't that, sir. It's just he wants a promise

Miss Leonie won't be after him, as she always is, to give her cuttings from his plants for her garden. He says he'll even send her up a rose if only she will leave him in peace."

"He's never sent me a rose," said Uncle Frederick, "nor Edith, here, nor her mother. Did he ever send you a rose, if it comes to that? It just goes to show it always pays to be a pest."

"As you say, sir."

Emma hurried off. About fifteen minutes later, she returned with the ring, which, like all things sent up from the garden, was wrapped in a rhubarb leaf.

"Goody, goody!" said Uncle Frederick. "We'll give her the leaf as well, because rhubarb is so relaxing."

"Begging your pardon, sir," said Emma, "it isn't the leaf that's used—only the stalk."

"Pity," said Uncle Frederick. "Now, look here. We'll let her fret a bit longer, and when you come in to say lunch is ready, you give her the ring and say it's just been found. In the washstand, where the hole is—you know, for the basin. Wedged between the marble and the basin—do you hear?"

"As you say, sir," said Emma.

"It's lucky that we haven't got any bathrooms in the castle, isn't it?" I said.

"How do you mean?" asked Uncle Frederick.

"Because," I said, "in a bathroom the ring would have been swept down the drain."

"Too true," said Uncle Frederick.

"So it's really very lucky," I said, "because in that case you'd have had to think up another story."

"It would be still luckier to have some modern bathrooms and no Aunt Leonie," said Uncle Frederick. "But I see your point."

Before luncheon, I went to my room and washed my hands all the way up to the elbows, to make sure I was perfectly clean and would not be sent away at the last minute for a wash. It would have been unbearable to miss anything at this point.

Usually, when Emma came to announce a meal, she would open the door and remain standing there until she had delivered her message. This time, she came right into the Austrian Room, where we were all assembled. She was carrying the Persian salver, which had a raised rim of pierced silver, so that one could not see whether it was empty or not. No doubt she had chosen it in order to heighten Aunt Leonie's surprise.

As it turned out, Aunt Leonie was as stingy with her emotions as she was with all her other possessions, and I was sorry for Uncle Frederick and Emma, who had taken such pains.

"My dear little ring, at last," said Aunt Leonie as she slipped it on her finger.

"Thank God for it!" cried my mother. "Now, Emma, where did you find it?"

"I believe lunch is ready," said Aunt Leonie.

"But I simply must know," said my mother.

"Dear girl," said Aunt Leonie, "all things in due course, and I should hate to let the soup go cold."

After Emma had left and while we were helping Aunt Leonie to gather her bag, her shawl, and the case with her needlework, she sat down again and made a sign for us to wait.

"As you may have observed, dear girl, I did not want to make a fuss and inquire any further. For one thing, that poisonous Emma of yours would not have told the truth, because she is very deceitful, as you may have noticed yesterday on the occasion of the gravy and the prunes. Besides, I am certain she was playing hard for a tip. Servants always do—they have those quaint little ways. That's one reason why they are not in my life. If it comes to it, I would not even be surprised if Emma herself—"

"But she isn't like that," said my mother. "You are being ridiculous, Aunt Leonie, if you will allow me to say so. I would not know what to do without Emma."

"I would know what to do without her," said Aunt Leonie, rising from her chair. "One can live in proper style without being at the mercy of all those priceless servants. Which reminds me—where is that gong you used to have in the hall?"

"You'll have to ask Emma," said my mother. "I can't think—"

"I only hope it hasn't been thrown away," said Aunt Leonie. "I know the idea seems absurd, with a gong of that size, but then, when it comes to that, where is the beef that went into the making of yesterday's soup? We didn't have it for lunch and we didn't have it for dinner, as you may have observed."

"I really can't think," said my mother.

"Dear girl," said Aunt Leonie. "Always so forgetful, just like your mother. In 1906, when I came to stay, I told your mother . . ." She swept out the door and into the passage that led to the dining room.

FIRST DARK

❖

Elizabeth Spencer

WHEN Tom Beavers started coming back to Richton, Mississippi, on weekends, after the war was over, everybody in town was surprised and pleased. They had never noticed him much before he paid them this compliment; now they could not say enough nice things. There was not much left in Richton for him to call family—just his aunt who had raised him, Miss Rita Beavers, old as God, ugly as sin, deaf as a post. So he must be fond of the town, they reasoned; certainly it was a pretty old place. Far too many young men had left it and never come back at all.

He would drive in every Friday night from Jackson, where he worked. All weekend, his Ford, dusty of flank, like a hard-ridden horse, would sit parked down the hill near Miss Rita's old wire front gate, which sagged from the top hinge and had worn a span in the ground. On Saturday morning, he would head for the drugstore, then the post office; then he would be observed walking here and there around the streets under the shade trees. It was as though he were looking for something.

He wore steel taps on his heels, and in the still the click of them on the sidewalks would sound across the big front lawns and all the way up to the porches of the houses, where two ladies might be sitting behind a row of ferns. They would identify him to one another, murmuring in their fine little voices, and say it was just too bad there was nothing here for young people. It was just a shame they didn't have one or two more old houses here, for a Pilgrimage—look how Natchez had waked up.

One Saturday morning in early October, Tom Beavers sat at the counter in the drugstore and reminded Totsie Poteet, the drugstore clerk, of a ghost story. Did he remember the strange old man who used to appear to people who were coming into Richton along the Jackson road at twilight—what they called "first dark"?

413

"Sure I remember," said Totsie. "Old Cud'n Jimmy Wiltshire used to tell us about him every time we went possum hunting. I could see him plain as I can see you, the way he used to tell it. Tall, with a top hat on, yeah, and waiting in the weeds alongside the road ditch, so'n you couldn't tell if he wasn't taller than any mortal man could be, because you couldn't tell if he was standing down in the ditch or not. It would look like he just grew up out of the weeds. Then he'd signal to you."

"Them that stopped never saw anybody," said Tom Beavers, stirring his coffee. "There were lots of folks besides Mr. Jimmy that saw him."

"There was, let me see . . ." Totsie enumerated others—some men, some women, some known to drink, others who never touched a drop. There was no way to explain it. "There was that story the road gang told. Do you remember, or were you off at school? It was while they were straightening the road out to the highway—taking the curves out and building a new bridge. Anyway, they said that one night at quitting time, along in the winter and just about dark, this old guy signalled to some of 'em. They said they went over and he asked them to move a bulldozer they had left across the road, because he had a wagon back behind on a little dirt road, with a sick nigger girl in it. Had to get to the doctor and this was the only way. They claimed they knew didn't nobody live back there on that little old road, but niggers can come from anywhere. So they moved the bulldozer and cleared back a whole lot of other stuff, and waited and waited. Not only didn't no wagon ever come, but the man that had stopped them, he was gone, too. They was right shook up over it. You never heard that one?"

"No, I never did." Tom Beavers said this with his eyes looking up over his coffee cup, as though he sat behind a hand of cards. His lashes and brows were heavier than was ordinary, and worked as a veil might, to keep you away from knowing exactly what he was thinking.

"They said he was tall and had a hat on." The screen door flapped to announce a customer, but Totsie kept on talking. "But whether he was a white man or a real light-colored nigger they couldn't say. Some said one and some said another. I figured they'd been pulling on the jug a little earlier than usual. You know why? I never heard of *our* ghost *saying* nothing. Did you, Tom?"

He moved away on the last words, the way a clerk will, talking back over his shoulder and ahead of him to his new customer at the same time, as though he had two voices and two heads. "And what'll it be today, Miss Frances?"

The young woman standing at the counter had a prescription already out of her bag. She stood with it poised between her fingers, but her attention was drawn toward Tom Beavers, his coffee cup, and the conversation she had interrupted. She was a girl whom no ordinary description would fit. One would have to know first of all who she was: Frances Harvey. After that, it was all right for her to be a little odd-looking, with her reddish hair that curled back from her brow, her light eyes, and her high, pale temples. This is not the material for being pretty, but in Frances Harvey it was what could sometimes be beauty. Her family home was laden with history that nobody but the Harveys could remember. It would have been on a Pilgrimage if Richton had had one. Frances still lived in it, looking after an invalid mother.

"What were you-all talking about?" she wanted to know.

"About that ghost they used to tell about," said Totsie, holding out his hand for the prescription. "The one people used to see just outside of town, on the Jackson road."

"But why?" she demanded. "Why were you talking about him?"

"Tom, here—" the clerk began, but Tom Beavers interrupted him.

"I was asking because I was curious," he said. He had been studying her from the corner of his eye. Her face was beginning to show the wear of her mother's long illness, but that couldn't be called change. Changing was something she didn't seem to have done, her own style being the only one natural to her.

"I was asking," he went on, "because I saw him." He turned away from her somewhat too direct gaze and said to Totsie Poteet, whose mouth had fallen open, "It was where the new road runs close to the old road, and as far as I could tell he was right on the part of the old road where people always used to see him."

"But when?" Frances Harvey demanded.

"Last night," he told her. "Just around first dark. Driving home."

A wealth of quick feeling came up in her face. "So did I! Driving home from Jackson! I saw him, too!"

For some people, a liking for the same phonograph record or for Mayan archeology is enough of an excuse to get together. Possibly, seeing the same ghost was no more than that. Anyway, a week later, on Saturday at first dark, Frances Harvey and Tom Beavers were sitting together in a car parked just off the highway, near the spot where they agreed the ghost had appeared. The season was that long, peculiar one between summer and fall, and there were so many crickets and tree frogs going full tilt in their periphery that their voices could hardly be distinguished from the background noises, though they both would have heard a single footfall in the grass. An edge of autumn was in the air at night, and Frances had put on a tweed jacket at the last minute, so the smell of mothballs was in the car, brisk and most unghostlike.

But Tom Beavers was not going to forget the value of the ghost, whether it put in an appearance or not. His questions led Frances into reminiscence.

"No, I never saw him before the other night," she admitted. "The Negroes used to talk in the kitchen, and Regina and I—you know my sister Regina—would sit there listening, scared to go and scared to stay. Then finally going to bed upstairs was no relief, either, because sometimes Aunt Henrietta was visiting us, and *she'd* seen it. Or if she wasn't visiting us, the front room next to us, where she stayed, would be empty, which was worse. There was no way to lock ourselves in, and besides, what was there to lock out? We'd lie all night like two sticks in bed, and shiver. Papa finally had to take a hand. He called us in and sat us down and said that the whole thing was easy to explain—it was all automobiles. What their headlights did with the dust and shadows out on the Jackson road. 'Oh, but Sammie and Jerry!' we said, with great big eyes, sitting side by side on the sofa, with our tennis shoes flat on the floor."

"Who were Sammie and Jerry?" asked Tom Beavers.

"Sammie was our cook. Jerry was her son, or husband, or something. Anyway, they certainly didn't have cars. Papa called them in. They were standing side by side by the bookcase, and Regina and I were on the sofa—four pairs of big eyes, and Papa pointing his finger. Papa said, 'Now, you made up these stories about ghosts, didn't you?' 'Yes, sir,' said Sammie. 'We made them up.' 'Yes, sir,' said Jerry. 'We sho did.' 'Well, then, you can just stop it,' Papa said. 'See how peaked these children look?' Sammie and Jerry were terribly polite to us for a week, and we got in the car and rode up and down the Jackson road at first dark to see if the headlights really did it. But we never saw anything. We didn't tell Papa, but headlights had nothing whatever to do with it."

"You had your own *car* then?" He couldn't believe it.

"Oh, no!" She was emphatic. "We were too young for that. Too young to drive, really, but we did anyway."

She leaned over to let him give her cigarette a light, and saw his hand tremble. Was he afraid of the ghost or of her? She would have to stay away from talking family.

Frances remembered Tommy Beavers from her childhood—a small boy going home from school down a muddy side road alone, walking right down the middle of the road. His old aunt's house was at the bottom of a hill. It was damp there, and the yard was always muddy, with big fat chicken tracks all over it, like Egyptian writing. How did Frances know? She could not remember going there, ever. Miss Rita Beavers was said to order cold ham, mustard, bread, and condensed milk from the grocery store. "I doubt if that child ever has anything hot," Frances's mother had said once. He was always neatly dressed in the same knee pants, high socks, and checked shirt, and sat several rows ahead of Frances in study hall, right in the middle of his seat. He was three grades behind her; in those days, that much younger seemed very young indeed. What had happened to his parents? There was some story, but it was not terribly interesting, and, his people being of no importance, she had forgotten.

"I think it's past time for our ghost," she said. "He's never out so late at night."

"He gets hungry, like me," said Tom Beavers. "Are you hungry, Frances?"

They agreed on a highway restaurant where an orchestra played on weekends. Everyone went there now.

From the moment they drew up on the gravelled entrance, cheerful lights and a blare of music chased the spooks from their heads. Tom Beavers ordered well and danced well, as it turned out. Wasn't there something she had heard about his being "smart"? By "smart," Southerners mean intellectual, and they say it in an almost condescending way, smart being what you are when you can't be anything else, and it is better, at least, than being nothing. Frances Harvey had been away enough not to look at things from a completely Southern point of view, and she was encouraged to discover that she and Tom had other things in common besides a ghost, though all stemming, perhaps, from the imagination it took to see one.

They agreed about books and favorite movies and longing to see

more plays. She sighed that life in Richton was so confining, but
he assured her that Jackson could be just as bad; *it* was getting to
be like any Middle Western city, he said, while Richton at least
had a sense of the past. This was the main reason, he went on,
gaining confidence in the jumble of commonplace noises—dishes,
music, and a couple of drinkers chattering behind them—that he
had started coming back to Richton so often. He wanted to keep
a connection with the past. He lived in a modern apartment,
worked in a soundproof office—he could be in any city. But Richton
was where he had been born and raised, and nothing could be more
old-fashioned. Too many people seemed to have their lives cut in
two. He was earnest in desiring that this should not happen to him.

"You'd better be careful," Frances said lightly. Her mood did
not incline her to profound conversation. "There's more than one
ghost in Richton. You may turn into one yourself, like the rest
of us."

"It's the last thing I'd think of you," he was quick to assure her.

Had Tommy Beavers really said such a thing, in such a natural,
charming way? Was Frances Harvey really so pleased? Not only
was she pleased but, feeling warmly alive amid the music and small
lights, she agreed with him. She could not have agreed with him
more.

"I hear that Thomas Beavers has gotten to be a very attractive
man," Frances Harvey's mother said unexpectedly one afternoon.

Frances had been reading aloud—Jane Austen this time. Theirs
was one house where the leather-bound sets were actually read. In
Jane Austen, men and women seesawed back and forth for two or
three hundred pages until they struck a point of balance; then they
got married. She had just put aside the book, at the end of a chapter,
and risen to lower the shade against the slant of afternoon sun.
"Or so Cud'n Jennie and Mrs. Giles Antley and Miss Fannie Staple-
ton have been coming and telling you," she said.

"People talk, of course, but the consensus is favorable," Mrs.
Harvey said. "Wonders never cease; his mother ran away with a
brush salesman. But nobody can make out what he's up to, coming
back to Richton."

"Does he have to be 'up to' anything?" Frances asked.

"Men are always up to something," said the old lady at once. She
added, more slowly, "In Thomas's case, maybe it isn't anything it

oughtn't to be. They say he reads a lot. He may just have taken up with some sort of idea."

Frances stole a long glance at her mother's face on the pillow. Age and illness had reduced the image of Mrs. Harvey to a kind of caricature, centered on a mouth that Frances could not help comparing to that of a fish. There was a tension around its rim, as though it were outlined in bone, and the underlip even stuck out a little. The mouth ate, it took medicine, it asked for things, it gasped when breath was short, it commented. But when it commented, it ceased to be just a mouth and became part of Mrs. Harvey, that witty tyrant with the infallible memory for the right detail, who was at her terrible best about men.

"And what could he be thinking of?" she was wont to inquire when some man had acted foolishly. No one could ever defend accurately the man in question, and the only conclusion was Mrs. Harvey's; namely, that he wasn't thinking, if, indeed, he could. Although she had never been a belle, never a flirt, her popularity with men was always formidable. She would be observed talking marathons with one in a corner, and could you ever be sure, when they both burst into laughter, that they had not just exchanged the most shocking stories? "Of course, *he—*" she would begin later, back with the family, and the masculinity that had just been encouraged to strut and preen a little was quickly shown up as idiotic. Perhaps Mrs. Harvey hoped by this method to train her daughters away from a lot of sentimental nonsense that was their birthright as pretty Southern girls in a house with a lawn that moonlight fell on and that was often lit also by Japanese lanterns hung for parties. "Oh, he's not like that, Mama!" the little girls would cry. They were already alert for heroes who would ride up and cart them off. "Well, then, you watch," she would say. Sure enough, if you watched, she would be right.

Mrs. Harvey's younger daughter, Regina, was a credit to her mother's long campaign; she married well. The old lady, however, never tired of pointing out behind her son-in-law's back that his fondness for money was ill-concealed, that he had the longest feet she'd ever seen, and that he sometimes made grammatical errors.

Her elder daughter, Frances, on a trip to Europe, fell in love, alas! The gentleman was of French extraction but Swiss citizenship, and Frances did not marry him, because he was already married—that much filtered back to Richton. In response to a cable, she had returned home one hot July in time to witness her father's wasted face and last weeks of life. That same September, the war began. When peace came, Richton wanted to know if Frances Harvey would go back to Europe. Certain subtly complicated European matters, little understood in Richton, seemed to be obstructing Romance; one of them was probably named Money. Meanwhile, Frances's mother took to bed, in what was generally known to be her last illness.

So no one crossed the ocean, but eventually Tom Beavers came up to Mrs. Harvey's room one afternoon, to tea.

Though almost all her other faculties were seriously impaired, in ear and tongue Mrs. Harvey was as sound as a young beagle, and she could still weave a more interesting conversation than most people who go about every day and look at the world. She was of the old school of Southern lady talkers; she vexed you with no ideas, she tried to protect you from even a moment of silence. In the old days, when a bright company filled the downstairs rooms, she could keep the ball rolling amongst a crowd. Everyone—all the men especially—got their word in, but the flow of things came back to her. If one of those twenty-minutes-to-or-after silences fell—and even with her they did occur—people would turn and look at her daughter Frances. "And what do you think?" some kind-eyed gentleman would ask. Frances did not credit that she had the sort of face people would turn to, and so did not know how to take advantage of it. What did she think? Well, to answer that honestly took a moment of reflection—a fatal moment, it always turned out. Her mother would be up instructing the maid, offering someone an ashtray or another goody, or remarking outright, "Frances is so timid. She never says a word."

Tom Beavers stayed not only past teatime that day but for a drink as well. Mrs. Harvey was induced to take a glass of sherry, and now her bed became her enormous throne. Her keenest suffering as an invalid was occasioned by the absence of men. "What is a house without a man in it?" she would often cry. From her eagerness to be charming to Frances's guest that afternoon, it seemed that she would have married Tom Beavers herself if he had asked her. The amber liquid set in her small four-sided glass glowed like a jewel, and her diamond flashed; she had put on her best ring for the company. What a pity no longer to show her ankle, that delicious bone, so remarkably slender for so ample a frame.

Since the time had flown so, they all agreed enthusiastically that

Tom should wait downstairs while Frances got ready to go out to dinner with him. He was hardly past the stair landing before the old lady was seized by such a fit of coughing that she could hardly speak. "It's been— It's been too much—too *much* for me!" she gasped out.

But after Frances had found the proper sedative for her, she was calmed, and insisted on having her say.

"Thomas Beavers has a good job with an insurance company in Jackson," she informed her daughter, as though Frances were incapable of finding out anything for herself. "He makes a good appearance. He is the kind of man"—she paused—"who would value a wife of good family." She stopped, panting for breath. It was this complimenting a man behind his back that was too much for her—as much out of character, and hence as much of a strain, as if she had got out of bed and tried to tap-dance.

"Heavens, Mama," Frances said, and almost giggled.

At this, the old lady, thinking the girl had made light of her suitor, half screamed at her "Don't be so critical, Frances! You can't be so critical of men!" and fell into an even more terrible spasm of coughing. Frances had to lift her from the pillow and hold her straight until the fit passed and her breath returned. Then Mrs. Harvey's old, dry, crooked, ineradicably feminine hand was laid on her daughter's arm, and when she spoke again she shook the arm to emphasize her words.

"When your father knew he didn't have long to live," she whispered, "we discussed whether to send for you or not. You know you were his favorite, Frances. 'Suppose our girl is happy over there,' he said. 'I wouldn't want to bring her back on my account.' I said you had to have the right to choose whether to come back or not. You'd never forgive us, I said, if you didn't have the right to choose."

Frances could visualize this very conversation taking place between her parents; she could see them, decorous and serious, talking over the fact of his approaching death as though it were a piece of property for agreeable disposition in the family. She could never remember him without thinking, with a smile, how he used to come home on Sunday from church (he being the only one of them who went) and how, immediately after hanging his hat and cane in the hall, he would say, "Let all things proceed in orderly progression to their final confusion. How long before dinner?" No, she had had to come home. Some humor had always existed between them—her father and her—and humor, of all things, cannot be betrayed.

"I meant to go back," said Frances now. "But there was the war. At first I kept waiting for it to be over. I still wake up at night sometimes thinking, I wonder how much longer before the war will be over. And then—" She stopped short. For the fact was that her lover had been married to somebody else, and her mother was the very person capable of pointing that out to her. Even in the old lady's present silence she heard the unspoken thought, and got up nervously from the bed, loosing herself from the hand on her arm, smoothing her reddish hair where it was inclined to straggle. "And then he wrote me that he had gone back to his wife. Her family and his had always been close, and the war brought them back together. This was in Switzerland—naturally, he couldn't stay on in Paris during the war. There were the children, too—all of them were Catholic. Oh, I do understand how it happened."

Mrs. Harvey turned her head impatiently on the pillow. She dabbed at her moist upper lip with a crumpled linen handkerchief; her diamond flashed once in motion. "War, religion, wife, children —yes. But men do what they want to."

Could anyone make Frances as angry as her mother could? "Believe what you like, then! You always know so much better than I do. *You* would have managed things somehow. Oh, you would have had your way!"

"Frances," said Mrs. Harvey, "I'm an old woman." The hand holding the handkerchief fell wearily, and her eyelids dropped shut. "If you should want to marry Thomas Beavers and bring him here, I will accept it. There will be no distinctions. Next, I suppose, we will be having his old deaf aunt for tea. I hope she has a hearing aid. I haven't got the strength to holler at her."

"I don't think any of these plans are necessary, Mama."

The eyelids slowly lifted. "None?"

"None."

Mrs. Harvey's breathing was as audible as a voice. She spoke, at last, without scorn, honestly. "I cannot bear the thought of leaving you alone. You, nor the house, nor your place in it—alone. I foresaw Tom Beavers here! What has he got that's better than you and this place? I knew he would come!"

Terrible as her mother's meanness was, it was not half so terrible as her love. Answering nothing, explaining nothing, Frances stood without giving in. She trembled, and tears ran down her cheeks.

The two women looked at each other helplessly across the darkening room.

In the car, later that night, Tom Beavers asked, "Is your mother trying to get rid of me?" They had passed an unsatisfactory evening, and he was not going away without knowing why.

"No, it's just the other way around," said Frances, in her candid way. "She wants you so much she'd like to eat you up. She wants you in the house. Couldn't you tell?"

"She once chased me out of the yard," he recalled.

"Not really!"

They turned into Harvey Street (that was actually the name of it), and when he had drawn the car up before the dark front steps, he related the incident. He told her that Mrs. Harvey had been standing just there in the yard, talking to some visitor who was leaving by inches, the way ladies used to—ten minutes' more talk for every forward step. He, a boy not more than nine, had been crossing a corner of the lawn where a faint path had already been worn; he had had nothing to do with wearing the path, and had taken it quite innocently and openly. "You, boy!" Mrs. Harvey's fan was an enormous painted thing. She had furled it with a clack so loud he could still hear it. "You don't cut through my yard again! Now, you stop where you are and you go all the way back around by the walk, and don't you ever do that again." He went back and all the way around. She was fanning comfortably as he passed. "Old Miss Rita Beavers' nephew," he heard her say, and though he did not speak of it now to Frances, Mrs. Harvey's rich tone had been as stuffed with wickedness as a fruitcake with goodies. In it you could have found so many things: that, of course, he didn't know any better, that he was poor, that she knew his first name but would not deign to mention it, that she meant him to understand all this and more. Her fan was probably still somewhere in the house, he reflected. If he ever opened the wrong door, it might fall from above and brain him. It seemed impossible that nowadays he could even have the chance to open the wrong door in the Harvey house. With its graceful rooms and big lawn, its camellias and magnolia trees, the house had been one of the enchanted castles of his childhood, and Frances and Regina Harvey had been two princesses running about the lawn one Saturday morning drying their hair with big white towels and not noticing when he passed.

There was a strong wind that evening. On the way home, Frances and Tom had noticed how the night was streaming, but whether with mist or dust or the smoke from some far-off fire in the dry winter woods they could not tell. As they stood on the sidewalk, the clouds raced over them, and moonlight now and again came through. A limb rubbed against a high cornice. Inside the screened area of the porch, the swing jangled its iron chains. Frances's coat blew about her, and her hair blew. She felt herself to be no different from anything there that the wind was blowing on, her happiness of no relevance in the dark torrent of nature.

"I can't leave her, Tom. But I can't ask you to live with her, either. Of all the horrible ideas! She'd make demands, take all my time, laugh at you behind your back—she has to run everything. You'd hate me in a week."

He did not try to pretty up the picture, because he had a feeling that it was all too accurate. Now, obviously, was the time she should go on to say there was no good his waiting around through the years for her. But hearts are not noted for practicality, and Frances stood with her hair blowing, her hands stuck in her coat pockets, and did not go on to say anything. Tom pulled her close to him—in, as it were, out of the wind.

"I'll be coming by next weekend, just like I've been doing. And the next one, too," he said. "We'll just leave it that way, if it's O.K. with you."

"Oh, yes, it is, Tom!" Never so satisfied to be weak, she kissed him and ran inside.

He stood watching on the walk until her light flashed on. Well, he had got what he was looking for; a connection with the past, he had said. It was right upstairs, a splendid old mass of dictatorial female flesh, thinking about him. Well, they could go on, he and Frances, sitting on either side of a sickbed, drinking tea and sipping sherry, with streaks of gray broadening on their brows, while the familiar seasons came and went. So he thought. Like Frances, he believed that the old lady had a stranglehold on life.

Suddenly, in March, Mrs. Harvey died.

A heavy spring funeral, with lots of roses and other scented flowers in the house, is the worst kind of all. There is something so recklessly fecund about a South Mississippi spring that death becomes just another word in the dictionary, along with swarms of others, and even so pure and white a thing as a gardenia has too heavy a scent and may suggest decay. Mrs. Harvey, amid such odors, sank to rest with a determined pomp, surrounded by admiring eyes.

While Tom Beavers did not "sit with the family" at this time, he was often observed with the Harveys, and there was whispered speculation among those who were at the church and the cemetery that the Harvey house might soon come into new hands, "after a decent interval." No one would undertake to judge for a Harvey how long an interval was decent.

Frances suffered from insomnia in the weeks that followed, and at night she wandered about the spring-swollen air of the old house, smelling now spring and now death. "Let all things proceed in orderly progression to their final confusion." She had always thought that the final confusion referred to death, but now she began to think that it could happen any time; that final confusion, having found the door ajar, could come into a house and show no inclination to leave. The worrisome thing, the thing it all came back to, was her mother's clothes. They were numerous, expensive, and famous, and Mrs. Harvey had never discarded any of them. If you opened a closet door, hatboxes as big as crates towered above your head. The shiny black trim of a great shawl stuck out of a wardrobe door just below the lock. Beneath the lid of a cedar chest, the bright eyes of a tippet were ready to twinkle at you. And the jewels! Frances's sister had restrained her from burying them all on their mother, and had even gone off with a wad of them tangled up like fishing tackle in an envelope, on the ground of promises made now and again in the course of the years.

("Regina," said Frances, "what else were you two talking about besides jewelry?" "I don't remember," said Regina, getting mad.

"Frances makes me so mad," said Regina to her husband as they were driving home. "I guess I can love Mama and jewelry, too. Mama certainly loved *us* and jewelry, too.")

One afternoon, Frances went out to the cemetery to take two wreaths sent by somebody who had "just heard." She drove out along the winding cemetery road, stopping the car a good distance before she reached the gate, in order to walk through the woods. The dogwood was beautiful that year. She saw a field where a house used to stand but had burned down; its cedar trees remained, and two bushes of bridal wreath marked where the front gate had swung. She stopped to admire the clusters of white bloom massing up through the young, feathery leaf and stronger now than the leaf itself. In the woods, the redbud was a smoke along shadowy ridges, and the dogwood drifted in layers, like snow suspended to give you all the time you needed to wonder at it. But why, she wondered, do they call it bridal *wreath?* It's not a wreath but a little bouquet. Wreaths are for funerals, anyway. As if to prove it, she looked down at the two she held, one in each hand. She walked on, and such complete desolation came over her that it was more of a wonder than anything in the woods—more, even, than death.

As she returned to the car from the two parallel graves, she met a thin, elderly, very light-skinned Negro man in the road. He inquired if she would mind moving her car so that he could pass. He said that there was a sick colored girl in his wagon, whom he was driving in to the doctor. He pointed out politely that she had left her car right in the middle of the road. "Oh, I'm terribly sorry," said Frances, and hurried off toward the car.

That night, reading late in bed, she thought, I could have given her a ride into town. No wonder they talk about us up North. A mile into town in a wagon! She might have been having a baby. She became conscience-stricken about it—foolishly so, she realized, but if you start worrying about something in a house like the one Frances Harvey lived in, in the dead of night, alone, you will go on worrying about it until dawn. She was out of sleeping pills.

She remembered having bought a fresh box of sedatives for her mother the day before she died. She got up and went into her mother's closed room, where the bed had been dismantled for airing, its wooden parts propped along the walls. On the closet shelf she found the shoe box into which she had packed away the familiar articles of the bedside table. Inside she found the small enamelled-cardboard box, with the date and prescription inked on the cover in Totsie Poteet's somewhat prissy handwriting, but the box was empty. She was surprised, for she realized that her mother could have used only one or two of the pills. Frances was so determined to get some sleep that she searched the entire little store of things in the shoe box quite heartlessly, but there were no pills. She returned to her room and tried to read, but could not, and so smoked instead and stared out at the dawn-blackening sky. The house sighed. She could not take her mind off the Negro girl. If she died . . . When it was light, she dressed and got into the car.

In town, the postman was unlocking the post office to sort the early mail. "I declare," he said to the rural mail carrier who arrived a few minutes later, "Miss Frances Harvey is driving herself crazy.

Going back out yonder to the cemetery, and it not seven o'clock in the morning."

"Aw," said the rural deliveryman skeptically, looking at the empty road.

"That's right. I was here and seen her. You wait there, you'll see her come back. She'll drive herself nuts. Them old maids like that, left in them old houses—crazy and sweet, or crazy and mean, or just plain crazy. They just ain't locked up like them that's down in the asylum. That's the only difference."

"Miss Frances Harvey ain't no more than thirty-two, three years old."

"Then she's just got more time to get crazier in. You'll see."

That day was Friday, and Tom Beavers, back from Jackson, came up Frances Harvey's sidewalk, as usual, at exactly a quarter past seven in the evening. Frances was not "going out" yet, and Regina had telephoned her long distance to say that "in all probability" she should not be receiving gentlemen "in." "What would Mama say?" Regina asked. Frances said she didn't know, which was not true, and went right on cooking dinners for Tom every weekend.

In the dining room that night, she sat across one corner of the long table from Tom. The useless length of polished cherry stretched away from them into the shadows as sadly as a road. Her plate pushed back, her chin resting on one palm, Frances stirred her coffee and said, "I don't know what on earth to do with all of Mama's clothes. I can't give them away, I can't sell them, I can't burn them, and the attic is full already. What can I do?"

"You look better tonight," said Tom.

"I slept," said Frances. "I slept and slept. From early this morning until just 'while ago. I never slept so well."

Then she told him about the Negro near the cemetery the previous afternoon, and how she had driven back out there as soon as dawn came, and found him again. He had been walking across the open field near the remains of the house that had burned down. There was no path to him from her, and she had hurried across ground uneven from old plowing and covered with the kind of small, tender grass it takes a very skillful mule to crop. "Wait!" she had cried. "Please wait!" The Negro had stopped and waited for her to reach him. "Your daughter?" she asked, out of breath.

"Daughter?" he repeated.

"The colored girl that was in the wagon yesterday. She was sick, you said, so I wondered. I could have taken her to town in the car, but I just didn't think. I wanted to know, how is she? Is she very sick?"

He had removed his old felt nigger hat as she approached him. "She a whole lot better, Miss Frances. She going to be all right now." Then he smiled at her. He did not say thank you, or anything more. Frances turned and walked back to the road and the car. And exactly as though the recovery of the Negro girl in the wagon had been her own recovery, she felt the return of a quiet breath and a steady pulse, and sensed the blessed stirring of a morning breeze. Up in her room, she had barely time to draw an old quilt over her before she fell asleep.

"When I woke, I knew about Mama," she said now to Tom. By the deepened intensity of her voice and eyes, it was plain that this was the important part. "It isn't right to say I *knew*," she went on, "because I had known all the time—ever since last night. I just realized it, that's all. I realized she had killed herself. It had to be that."

He listened soberly through the story about the box of sedatives. "But why?" he asked her. "It maybe looks that way, but what would be her reason for doing it?"

"Well, you see—" Frances said, and stopped.

Tom Beavers talked quietly on. "She didn't suffer. With what she had, she could have lived five, ten, who knows how many years. She was well cared for. Not hard up, I wouldn't say. Why?"

The pressure of his questioning could be insistent, and her trust in him, even if he was nobody but old Miss Rita Beavers' nephew, was well-nigh complete. "Because of you and me," she said, finally. "I'm certain of it, Tom. She didn't want to stand in our way. She never knew how to express love, you see." Frances controlled herself with an effort.

He did not reply, but sat industriously balancing a match folder on the tines of an unused serving fork. Anyone who has passed a lonely childhood in the company of an old deaf aunt is not inclined to doubt things hastily, and Tom Beavers would not have said he disbelieved anything Frances had told him. In fact, it seemed only too real to him. Almost before his eyes, that imperial, practical old hand went fumbling for the pills in the dark. But there had been much more to it than just love, he reflected. Bitterness, too, and pride, and control. And humor, perhaps, and the memory of a frightened little boy chased out of the yard by a twitch of her fan.

Being invited to tea was one thing; suicide was quite another. Times had certainly changed, he thought.

But, of course, he could not say that he believed it, either. There was only Frances to go by. The match folder came to balance and rested on the tines. He glanced up at her, and a chill walked up his spine, for she was too serene. Cheek on palm, a lock of reddish hair fallen forward, she was staring at nothing with the absorbed silence of a child, or of a sweet, silver-haired old lady engaged in memory. Soon he might find that more and more of her was vanishing beneath this placid surface.

He himself did not know what he had seen that Friday evening so many months ago—what the figure had been that stood forward from the roadside at the tilt of the curve and urgently waved an arm to him. By the time he had braked and backed, the man had disappeared. Maybe it had been somebody drunk (for Richton had plenty of those to offer), walking it off in the cool of the woods at first dark. No such doubts had occurred to Frances. And what if he told her now the story Totsie had related of the road gang and the sick Negro girl in the wagon? Another labyrinth would open before her; she would never get out.

In Richton, the door to the past was always wide open, and what came in through it and went out of it had made people "different." But it scarcely ever happens, even in Richton, that one is able to see the precise moment when fact becomes faith, when life turns into legend, and people start to bend their finest loyalties to make themselves bemused custodians of the grave. Tom Beavers saw that moment now, in the profile of this dreaming girl, and he knew there was no time to lose.

He dropped the match folder into his coat pocket. "I think we should be leaving, Frances."

"Oh, well, I don't know about going out yet," she said. "People criticize you so. Regina even had the nerve to telephone. Word had got all the way to her that you came here to have supper with me and we were alone in the house. When I tell the maid I want biscuits made up for two people, she looks like 'What would yo mama say?'"

"I mean," he said, "I think it's time we left for good."

"And never came back?" It was exactly like Frances to balk at going to a movie but seriously consider an elopement.

"Well, never is a long time. I like to see about Aunt Rita every once in a great while. She can't remember from one time to the next whether it's two days or two years since I last came."

She glanced about the walls and at the furniture, the pictures, and the silver. "But I thought you would want to live here, Tom. It never occurred to me. I know it never occurred to Mama . . . This house . . . It can't be just left."

"It's a fine old house," he agreed. "But what would we do with all your mother's clothes?"

Her freckled hand remained beside the porcelain cup for what seemed a long time. He waited and made no move toward her; he felt her uncertainty keenly, but he believed that some people should not be startled out of a spell.

"It's just as you said," he went on, finally. "You can't give them away, you can't sell them, you can't burn them, and you can't put them in the attic, because the attic is full already. So what are you going to do?"

Between them, the single candle flame achieved a silent altitude. Then, politely, as on any other night, though shaking back her hair in a decided way, she said, "Just let me get my coat, Tom."

She locked the door when they left, and put the key under the mat—a last obsequy to the house. Their hearts were bounding ahead faster than they could walk down the sidewalk or drive off in the car, and, mindful, perhaps, of what happened to people who did, they did not look back.

Had they done so, they would have seen that the Harvey house was more beautiful than ever. All unconscious of its rejection by so mere a person as Tom Beavers, it seemed, instead, to have got rid of what did not suit it, to be free, at last, to enter with abandon the land of mourning and shadows and memory.

WEDDING AT ROCIADA

❖

OLIVER LA FARGE

VISITORS to New Mexico do not go to Rociada, where my wife, Consuelo, grew up. Broadly speaking, the name Rociada covers two villages, the embracing ranch, and the valley in which they lie. The valley is high, long, and irregular, walled by the higher mountains of the Sangre de Cristo range, east of Santa Fe and the Pecos, north of Las Vegas, away from everywhere, innocent of paved roads.

Down the middle of the valley runs a clear, fast, noisy stream in which one may take trout. In the lowland along the stream and its tributaries are the farmlands; beyond them are the pastures reaching to the high-wooded knees of the mountains. Behind the crests of the first rugged walls, shaggy with spruce and fir and pine, are the main peaks, with the brown, domed, pure rock of El Ermitaño, snow-powdered until midsummer, as a monument and guardian notching the western sky. The pasture lands carry grass to tickle the belly of a calf or a colt, or to hide a young lamb. They are mountain meadows, embroidered, according to the season, with iris, columbine, Indian paintbrush, tiger lilies, or cardinal flowers.

When a man who lives and works in the arid country that is most of New Mexico, or even in the semi-green, irrigated lands along the sand-edged rivers, comes travelling through such a place as Rociada, he feels his being relax and spread out. He experiences something of what happened to the lotus-eaters, wanting to stay always a little longer, let his horses feast, smell the water, and feel the live grass. He moves on because he must, and the next night camps in lower country, where the gravelly soil shows between the single blades of grass, and dry stalks of weeds rattle in the night when the wind stirs.

In the valley of Rociada, the main river runs south from the high peaks, then turns easterly. Where it turns is the village of Rociada; a couple of miles above that is Upper Rociada. These are *placitas*, little plazas. Each consists of a score, more or less, of adobe houses,

431

a church, a store, and a dance hall, grouped inexactly around a central square. Adobe is decorated with whitewash or calcimine only where a porch protects its surface from the harsh winter snows; the rest is left plain. The settlements match the surrounding earth, from which they are built.

"*Rociada*" means, roughly, "bedewed." The main and upper settlements were made in a forgotten period by men who were not afraid of the Apache hunting bands that came drifting through that country. Gascón is newer. It was founded by Consuelo's grandfather Jean Pendaries, who came from Gascony. He built his home ranch at the south end of his domain, downstream from the village of Rociada. José Albino Baca, who married M. Pendaries' daughter Marguerite, and to whom the Pendaries' ranch eventually passed, built his house, a big, two-story adobe building with a pitched roof and porches front and back, a mile above the older place and two and a half miles from the village. On a still day when the mill on the Pendaries place was running, one could hear the dull clack of the wooden water wheel from the ranchhouse. Villages and ranches alike are strung along the stream, which has a name—Río Manuelitas—but which Consuelo, when she was a child, thought of simply as the river.

In the nineteen-twenties, dates had not much more importance to the people of the valley than they had to the river. Rociada was a clear pool into which the stream of time trickled and then stood still. Don José's three youngest children, Carmen, Consuelo, and Joséphine (Pepita), do not remember events of the period in sequence. For them, time spread out, taking on dimensions within which they wandered as they wandered within the actual area. The older children, Emilie, José, and Marie, already lightly meshed with the outside world, were beginning to feel the pull of linear, disappearing time. The little girls were a separate bunch, three little *mocas* running together. Don José was rather godlike, as a father should be—a fairly tall man, handsome, correct, slender, neat, with elegance about him. Doña Marguerite was not a person to be trifled with, but the little ones knew her more intimately than they did their father. She was small, very alive, intuitively chic. She managed to be at once perfectly French and perfectly Spanish, which is no small feat.

There was a balance between the ranch and the villages, and a balance between Don José and his wife. There have to be many balances within small groups in isolation, a tolerance and an interchange. One part does not merely support the other, but, like two slabs leaning against each other, both support, both are dependent. Don José was inclined to be severe. He had a big and busy home ranch to run, and between fifteen and twenty thousand head of sheep and some cattle to rotate safely between the summer ranges, in the high country near at hand, and the winter ranges, in the low country far to the south. He employed a throng of people—wranglers, sheepherders, cowpunchers, workmen—and, in the old New Mexico style, Don José drew these men, as Doña Marguerite did her servants, from the villages of Rociada and Upper Rociada. The people of the two villages received from them in return the multitude of services and attentions that traditionally they demanded of their *patrones*. Don José's relationship with the people was such that whenever some of his good horses were missing, he had only to tell Pascual, the official horse thief of Rociada, about it, indicating in a friendly way that he expected them back, and shortly they would appear again in his pasture.

From time to time, Don José would fire a man, usually for good cause and usually, also, with some little irritation. Then there was not much for the man to do but fish, hunt in season, and cultivate his garden. The people were freeholders and free men; there was no peonage. A man could leave the valley and try his luck in Las Vegas or even farther away, in the arid, jostling world, but there were few who left Rociada if they could help it.

Soon enough the man's wife would come to Doña Marguerite with a tale of hungry children: They were out of flour, coffee, bacon; they had no more credit at Lobato's store, in the village. One could not let the people go hungry. Doña Marguerite would get the wife supplies, taking them from the commissary or from her own kitchen. Simply to end the drain on her budget, she had to choose the moment to persuade her husband to forgive the man and hire him again.

Looking back across an abyss of change, my wife thinks of the village of Rociada first in terms of the weddings, and especially of Aurelia's wedding. Aurelia's father, Procopio Ruiz, was the most important man in the main village, so her wedding was a big affair. There was that, and then there was the business of Consuelo's and Carmen's hair, and that, in turn, was a symptom of their growing up. She was ten and Carmen twelve. They were growing up and becoming aware of grown-up matters, while Pepita, at eight, was still a baby. These things set Aurelia's wedding in Consuelo's mind.

The little girls all had black hair. Pepita's was long, with a marked natural curl at the ends. The older two wore their hair shorter, and it was, much to their regret, straight.

The afternoon before Aurelia's wedding, they gathered pieces of paper and part of an old sheet, which they tore into strips, and that night they stayed up late putting each other's hair in curls. They felt freer to do this because the older children, who would have made fun of them, were away at boarding school. Their hair curled magnificently. When they came down to breakfast, Doña Marguerite said dryly that their heads were covered with corkscrews. They did not mind. They had looked at themselves in a mirror and were more than satisfied.

In the middle of the morning, they all got into the family automobile, a big Paige touring car, with their father at the wheel and their mother in the front seat beside him, to drive to the village. The three little girls, as it happened, all had new dresses. Carmen's was apple green, with a velvet sash reaching almost to her heels. She was very conscious of the dress and of her curls. Consuelo's dress was red, her favorite color, with a white yoke, which made her think of a nun, inspiring her briefly with saintly impulses. Pepita had a blue dress, with pink bows and embroidered butterflies. The car bumped and swayed in the ruts, kicking up a brown dust. The three little girls sat straight, their eyes quick and alert. They were quiet and correct from contained excitement and the sense of their finery.

The village was gathered at the Ruizes' house, on the plaza, back of the church. The house had a pitched tin roof, with the front slope carried out to make a shelter well beyond the front of the house and supported on round posts—a *portal*. Under the *portal* at the east end, the line of the sunlight had been traced as it fell along the wall about an hour before noon. At the west end, similarly, the dividing line between sun and shadow in early afternoon had been marked. Between these inward-sloping lines the wall had been calcimined a pale blue. Across the bottom ran a two-foot strip of bright-buff clay, full of gold sparkles, which makes a sturdier coating than any lime wash. The wedding guests were standing around under the portal and just outside. Now that the *patrón* and *patrona* had arrived, the procession could form.

Most of the women wore shawls. The older women's shawls were black. Among Spanish-Americans, mourning lasts a long time, and as one grows older the deaths in one's far-reaching family crowd one upon another. The most modern of the younger women wore hats. The men were dressed in their best dark suits, their Sunday hats, smaller-brimmed than their everyday ones, and constraining collars. Some had neckties; some preferred the simple jewel-shine of a bright collar stud. Everyone was grave. The three little girls stood to one side, solemn, observant, and feeling a certain responsibility, because of their parents' role.

Then the procession started. First came Father Mueller, a very big, bearded man, in his vestments. With his bulk, his rolling processional gait had a shiplike majesty. After him came the musicians, a violin and a guitar, playing cheerful polkas. Next were Don José and Doña Marguerite, as the bride's sponsors. That was their part in every wedding; without them, everyone would have felt that something was seriously wrong. Aurelia and her father followed them, then the groom and his companions, then the immediate families of both bride and groom. The three little girls came next after these, and behind them walked the rest of the village, along with people from Upper Rociada and Gascón, and from villages as far away as Sápello and Peñasco, beyond the walls of the valley.

The procession circled the plaza before it entered the church. The children wanted to be dignified, but polka music is not the best to walk sedately to, and they had to watch out for the unevennesses of the ground and not get their best slippers scuffed. They couldn't resist making some comment on the bride's white velvet gown, her veil and wreath, and her satin slippers. Carmen asked Consuelo and Pepita if they had noticed the flash of the two gold fillings in Aurelia's front teeth when she smiled, and they had to fight off the giggles.

Consuelo found the service painfully long. The kneeling benches had been scrubbed with sand, and the sand had not been properly swept off. Her bare knees suffered. Sometimes Father Mueller enlivened Mass by saying the most outrageous things, but on this occasion he offered no entertainment. Finally, the service ended, and the procession returned to Ruiz's house, where the wedding guests formed a line, beginning at the *portal*.

It was some time before the girls' turn came to pass through the narrow doorway into the main room. Chairs lined the walls. In the middle was a table with refreshments on it. The bride and groom sat stiffly, side by side, at the back of the room. The happy couple were solemn to the point of misery. Consuelo thought that they looked as if they had taken convent vows of chastity and silence. The older people, sitting along the walls, did not look happy, either. Don José and Doña Marguerite, seated near the bride and groom, were solemn. Consuelo assumed that this was the way it was supposed to be, yet in view of all one heard beforehand, of all the plannings and anticipations, it always seemed strange. She wondered if her own wedding might be brighter.

The little girls spoke their formal congratulations and found seats. People continued to file in, greeting Don José and Doña Marguerite as well as the bridal couple and their parents. The girls studied the table in the middle of the room, which was a shimmering lake of cakes with pink, green, and yellow icing, candies, nuts, fruits, pop, wine, and whiskey. The little girls sat for a long while in the severe silence, which they dared not break, trying not to squirm. They would happily have forgone the privilege of staying in the room along with relatives and honored elders, even though it meant an early turn at the refreshments. From outside the door they could hear a buzzing of talk and occasionally a young man's laugh.

In a strictly arranged order, the bride's parents invited people, one or a couple at a time, to "pass the table." The guests took small helpings of this and that, and then sat down again and were ritually served chocolate. At last, it was the little girls' turn, the three together, and before all the delicacies their polite self-control partly broke down. They had their laps full when the chocolate was brought to them.

The hot chocolate was deliciously right, with a marshmallow in each cup, and flavored with cinnamon. That drink, the *merienda,* is a minor capsule of history. The Spaniards learned its ceremonial use from the Aztecs and left the tradition of it even in these lost valleys. A later invasion added the marshmallow. No occasion such as a wedding would be complete without it.

The musicians started again; the company, except for the bride and groom, relaxed somewhat. The less important guests and the young people, who had been standing around outside, came in or were brought in, in small groups, to congratulate the bridal couple, and to have refreshments. Some of the adults had begun to be warmed by wine or whiskey. Prohibition being in full force, the whiskey was water-clear local corn lightning; the wine was a sweet, heady red vintage from the neighborhood of Bernalillo, near Albuquerque. There were smiles here and there, a little gentle talk. After what seemed like ages to the children, the door to the next room was opened. In that room, a long table had been set up; it was covered with a white tablecloth and heavy with dishes. Again in turn, the guests were invited to the wedding breakfast, a solid meal of everything good, from chili, beans, and mutton to Spanish pie, which is twice as much pastry as fruit, and bread pudding rich with raisins. There were bright bottles of pop on the table for those who did not take coffee.

It was a vast relief to the little girls to be told to go to the breakfast, to be released from stillness. They ate beyond desire, and left the table feeling slightly dizzy. It was proper for the children to go outside now, so they walked away from the other guests and out under the *portal*, where they could draw deep breaths, take the sun on their faces, and wait for relief to set in.

After a few minutes, Carmen, who had been standing by the front door, said, "Come on, if you want to see whether Aurelia cries." They hurried into the house after her just as the bride was going to her parents' bedroom with her mother and sisters. Carmen and Consuelo tagged after them, and Pepita was right behind. Sure enough, when Aurelia was sitting on the bed and her sisters had pulled off her slippers, she cried from the sheer easing of pain.

She had prayed and prayed, she said, that her father-in-law would get slippers to fit her when he bought her trousseau; all the time he was on his trip to Las Vegas she had prayed, but it had been no good. She might have known it was useless.

The slippers had been bought not to fit a foot of flesh and bone but to fit an idea. A bride is young, beautiful, Spanish, and her foot is tiny. The dainty, costly slippers would never be worn again. They were for that day, and it was necessary not that they fit Aurelia but that she should conform to them. Consuelo wondered if fathers-in-law liked to make brides cry. In her experience, the bride always did cry.

Aurelia was pale. She said there was no blood in her feet. The children chafed them until she felt better. She got her slippers back on and returned to the reception. The little girls stayed in the bedroom to admire the fine steamer trunk in which Aurelia's trousseau had come. Señora Ruiz's trunk, a solid affair of an older period, was in a central place against the wall in the same room, with a crocheted doily on top. Doña Marguerite had said once that wives cherished their trunks more than they did their husbands. Consuelo was sure her mother did not really think this. But the trunks were

possessions for life; they were the repositories for all things of value
—heirlooms, mementos, documents, savings.

Over Señora Ruiz's trunk hung her wedding picture. In the picture, she was standing partly beside, partly behind, the chair on
which her husband sat, his legs crossed jauntily but his body rigid.
Both of them wore fixed smiles. The artist who colored the picture
had made the faces of the bride and groom so pink that they seemed
to be blushing, and he had given Señor Ruiz blue eyes. Even so,
Consuelo thought, it must have been a good likeness. Then it occurred to her that when Aurelia had her wedding picture taken, the
photographer would probably paint out the gold spots in her teeth.
Later, Consuelo learned that she had been right. She thought it
was a pity.

The wedding guests sat through the balance of the afternoon inside the house, in shifts of silence and sparse talk, nibbling and
sipping at the food and drink. Consuelo and her sisters again went
outdoors to play, as best they could under the handicap of their best
clothes. For a time, they held the blind woman, La Culacita, in
conversation, for the fascination of seeing whether a louse would
appear on her hair. She had been born blind, and she was so dirty
that Doña Marguerite would not allow her in the ranchhouse. At
intervals, the children slipped indoors for refreshment.

At eight o'clock, everyone went to the dance hall for the wedding
ball. How Aurelia managed it, the children did not know, but, in
spite of her slippers, she seemed to be able to dance forever. Consuelo thought that she looked like a white moth miller. One looked
forward to a wedding, and during it one had a sense of an event
that had a special relationship to one's own future life, but the
occasion itself became draggingly long. At the dance, things picked
up; there were movement, color, the smell of perfume and of people,
the music. The little girls sat together, taking everything in. They
noted with interest what men showed the effect of their drinks.
There was an extra titillation in knowing that sometimes dances
ended in fights, perhaps with knives or shooting, that possibly a
fight would start before their father took them home, or that at
least they might see the *bastonero* (the bouncer) put out a drunk.

Don José drove them home at nine. The children were exhausted
enough to go willingly to bed. Consuelo thought that it had been a
good wedding and a wonderful day. Her hair was straightening out
again; she knew sadly that in another day it would be as straight as

ever. Neither Aurelia's trunk nor Señora Ruiz's compared with her
mother's, which had been brought from Mexico and was magnificent, of tan leather, brass-studded, with all sorts of divided trays
inside. That was the kind of trunk Consuelo wanted to have.

That is, if she got married. It might be better to be a nun. You
might marry, and then there might be a war, and your husband
might be killed, like Tomás Romero, from Upper Rociada, in the
World War. The girls had been reading stories about wars, old ones,
and Consuelo noticed that women sent their husbands to the wars.
If you did not marry, you would not have to send a man, and so he
would not be killed. It might be better not to have either a husband or a trunk, and enter a convent and be holy.

If she did get married, she hoped that she might have a little
more fun at her wedding. She knew that, among people like her
parents, things were often done differently from the way that was
customary in the village; perhaps their weddings were not so
solemn. Then, sleepily, she remembered that all her family had
small feet; her mother's were tiny. At least, if she did get married,
the chances were that her slippers would fit her, and her father-in-
law would not be able to make her cry.

Consuelo's wedding was a small one, in Manhattan. She wore a
smart going-away dress and black pumps, which she had selected
for herself. The reception, in a small apartment on Murray Hill,
was brightly gay with champagne. The groom gave her an overnight case with her initials on it. Of all the great clan of the Bacas,
only her sister Carmen was present.

CÔTE D'AZUR

❖

ROGER ANGELL

"I'LL bet he didn't leave a will at all. Probably it'll turn out to be nothing but a charming letter. Or maybe an autographed picture of himself."

The speaker is my sister. She is sitting next to me in the club car of a north-bound Pennsylvania Railroad train. In our right hands we each hold a Scotch highball, very strong, the way the railroads serve them, and the ice clinks in our glasses with the rocking and swaying of the car. Outside the big windows opposite us, a hot June day is beginning to cool and fade. The New Jersey back yards that flash by offer up a thousand *Saturday Evening Post* covers. A housewife opens her kitchen door and puts down a dish of dog food. She is whisked away and replaced by three couples in lawn chairs, drinking beer. The women look pretty, for they are wearing shorts, and in front of the group there is a brick barbecue pit with a curl of thin smoke rising from it. Next come three boys playing catch; there is a wild throw and one of the boys leaps for the ball, but before I can see whether he catches it they are gone and I discover a forest of low metal trees ranged before a giant white box—a drive-in theatre. It is too early for the first customers there, but they are expected; the lights are on in the booths by the entrance gate, and two ticket venders—young girls in visored military caps— have moved their stools out into the driveway, where they sit side by side, smiling and waving at us. It is the present streaming by out there—faces, windows, gestures, cars stopped at crossings, trees heavy with new leaves—a landscape without history or meaning, but alive for an instant before us in the long light of early evening.

Inside the train, it is the past. It has been years since I have sat in a club car, and nothing has changed. Down the faded carpet of the center aisle comes the Negro attendant, a courtly smile on his old face, his knees bent against the motion of the train. He snaps a switch at the far end of the car, and the lights come on. The lamp on the wall behind my sister's head is covered with a mosaic shade made of sections of leaded green glass. She and I are in the past, too —much as we hate it—for we are travelling back from Wilmington, Delaware, where we have just buried our father.

Maude is watching me over her glass. She is elegant company. Thin, rather tall, with good legs and a straight back, she is a handsome, citified woman of thirty-eight. She has been a divorcée for eleven years, and she works on fashion accounts in a big New York advertising agency. Her reddish-brown hair is cut short, in a mass of soft curls, and no one looking at her now would guess that her expensive, slender black dress with the single gold pin in the collar, her short white gloves, and her narrow, stylish shoes constitute mourning. Only her eyes look weary. She is three years older than I, and I realize that I am a little afraid of her.

"What do you think, Chris?" she says, with a small, knowing smile. "What do you suppose he left us? Two dozen golf balls for you. Fifty shares of stock in a played-out gold mine for me? Or maybe some unpaid chits from the bar of some first-rate club in Florida. This is an important time for us; we've come into our inheritance."

"Oh, I don't know, Maude," I say, waving my hand. "I don't see why you have to talk like this. I didn't expect anything from him."

"You never expect anything from people, do you, Chris?"

"Oh, are we going to talk about *me* now?"

"No—not unless you want to." She smiles at me again, more gently this time. "But we should have something to say to each other, shouldn't we? Having lost our esteemed sire. But I don't care. I know what I'm going to do. I'm going to ask you to order me another drink."

I must explain that this nervous, unhappy talk is not usual between Maude and me. We are fond of each other, even though we don't show it. We see each other perhaps ten times a year. She always comes to our house in Dobbs Ferry on Christmas Day; the gifts she brings for Louisa and me and our three children are expensive and beautifully wrapped and, without fail, exactly right— the kind of present that instantly astonishes and delights. I am a trout fisherman, and two years ago she gave me a fantastically light bamboo rod that had been handmade in Chile. She comes to visit us for one or two weekends in the summer, and she and I have lunch together in town every few weeks. Perhaps once a year, Louisa and I take her to the theatre with us. I was proud of Maude when she won a part-scholarship at Mount Holyoke; I grieved over her short, miserable marriage. I am still proud of her, and perhaps I still regard her just as I did when we were children and her greater age and wisdom awed me. I love Maude, for she is my sister, and families must stay together, but we have little to say to each other. When we have lunch, she relates two or three amusing stories about her office, and asks about the children; I tell her our plans for the summer; we discuss books and plays. We stick to the present, two admiring strangers.

Funerals are grotesque enough when they are on safe home grounds—the commonplace, respectable affair in a church, with the widow looking too controlled, the grandchildren curious and a little frightened, the crazy old female cousin from Virginia who turns up in a back pew even though no one has remembered to write her, and afterward, the friends being determinedly convivial over the highballs and plates of sliced turkey. What Maude and I shared in Wilmington was worse—certainly bad enough to make us snap at each other on the train going home. Our father had died on a Tuesday morning, in the locker room of a country club just outside Wilmington; it was a quick, final stroke. I knew nothing about it until after eleven that night, for it had taken that long for them to find the name and address of a relative. Maude and I went down on the train together Wednesday morning, and the funeral—if you could call it that—was the next day. My wife wanted to come with us, but I didn't know what we would find when we got there, so I told her not to come. On the train going down, Maude and I agreed that he should be buried right there in Wilmington, though neither of us had ever been in that city. There was no other place that made sense to take him. Our mother died in 1954, and, anyway, they had been divorced for years. I hadn't seen him myself for more than two years before he died.

In Wilmington, we went to our hotel and then to the funeral parlor, where, in time, we were joined by a Mr. Summersby, the business associate of my father who had telephoned me the night before. He was a pale, apologetic man in a shimmering cocoa-colored suit and two-toned loafers. "Honored, honored," he said when I introduced him to Maude. "Though grieved to meet, Ma'am, with things the way they are. This is a terrible thing. A terrible, terrible thing." He looked anxiously back and forth at

Maude and me, as if he feared that one of us might begin to cry or ask him whether our father had had any last words for us.

The funeral director's office was air-conditioned, but the day was so heavy that his neat, shiny desk sweated between us while we discussed the endless arrangements and I signed certificates and contracts. In the end, I had to bargain the man down four hundred dollars on the price of a coffin. When Maude and I and Mr. Summersby emerged on the street at two in the afternoon, the sun hit us like a fist.

"I'd be proud to have you to lunch at the club," Summersby said, gesturing toward a large pale-blue convertible. "As my guests, you understand. It'll be cooler there, I can promise you."

A peculiar suspicion began to grow in me when we came in sight of a golf course, some ten miles outside of the city. Summersby swung between two white gateposts and drove up a winding drive-way, past fairways and old trees and shining greens, to the big stone clubhouse on the top of a rise. I was right; he was taking us to see where our father had died. In the high, shadowy front hall, with its glass-encased silver trophies and carved rosters of club champions, Summersby removed his coconut straw hat and held it in the vicinity of his heart. "It was in there," he whispered to us, nodding toward a door.

"But my God!" Maude cried, turning on him. "Do you think we want to inspect the scene, or something?"

"No, no, no," Summersby said agitatedly. "Of course not. Quite understand. I just thought maybe you'd like to visit his room."

Maude and I looked at each other. "His room?" I said to Summersby. "I don't understand. You mean there's a room here where he sometimes spent the night?"

"Spent the night?" Summersby said, equally confused. "But he *lived* here."

"He lived in a golf club?" Maude said. She turned to me, shrugging and starting to grin. "Maybe he was the caddie master."

"Oh, no!" said Summersby indignantly. "I thought you knew. He was the assistant manager. He was my right-hand man—I'm the manager. I don't know what we're going to do without him. How can I replace him? He was a gentleman through and through."

That night, while Maude and I sat in her bedroom in the hotel and had a nightcap together, she began to laugh angrily. "Assistant manager of a golf club!" she said, snorting. "Mr. Pieface's right-hand man! Oh, God, Chris, isn't it all just too perfect? The dashing end of our dashing Papa. We should bury him in the eighth bunker, or something. What did you think he did for a living?"

"I don't know," I said uncomfortably. "Estate management—that was what I always thought. That's what he wrote me when he moved here from Phoenix last year. He said it was the same work he'd been in out there, but that this was with a bigger company. But I thought—you know—an office, and looking after people's money. That sort of thing."

"Me, too," she said. "It all depends what you call it. No wonder he was always so tan."

"I still don't understand it all. I used to write him once in a while, and his address was here in the city. Some company—"

"A letter drop," she said. "He had his mail sent to some friend of his, I suppose. He didn't want us to know. But don't you see that it's *funny?*"

"No, I guess I don't."

"Poor Chris," she said, pulling back her negligee and holding one bare leg out toward the stream of cool air from the air-conditioner. "Poor baby. Do you know that while you and that man went up to see his room, the golf pro came into the dining room and introduced himself to me? His name is Verrazano, or something. He wanted me to know how much they'd all miss Daddy. He said he was coming to the funeral tomorrow. 'That Mr. Drexler was a sport,' he kept saying. 'A real sporting gentleman. All the members liked him so much. He was what you'd call a likable man.' He gave me the idea somehow that playing golf was part of Daddy's job—that he was always on tap to help make up a foursome, or whatever you call them. He said, 'You know, Miss, your father shot a seventy-eight just last Friday. Sixty-three years old, and he shoots a seventy-eight.' He wanted me to be proud of that. Is seventy-eight good, Chris?"

"Yes, it's good," I said.

"What was his room like?"

"Oh, nothing much. What you might expect."

My father's room was over the caddie shop. There had been one business suit in the closet, and fifteen or twenty sports jackets and pairs of slacks. There was a narrow bed, a dresser with a half-empty bottle of bourbon on it, a small bookcase, a desk, and one worn easy chair. Nothing more. I had gone through the desk drawers quickly. There was a checkbook from a local bank, showing a balance of two hundred and eighty-four dollars, a copy of the club regulations, some letters from a woman in Santa Barbara, and more letters, which I did not open, postmarked from places like Mexico City and Miami and Cannes. In the back of one drawer, I found a loose heap of photographs, including several snapshots of my children that I had sent him over the years. There was a faded photograph of me and Maude and a donkey, taken in France in the summer of 1933, and this I put into my pocket. Before I left the room, I glanced at the fifteen or twenty books in the shelves. One of them looked older than the others, and I took it out. It was "The Ordeal of Richard Feverel," and the bookplate inside said, "Williams College Library." My father had gone to Williams. The slip in the back showed that the book had been overdue since May 3, 1919.

It was dark by the time our train entered the tunnel that leads under the river. I took out my commuting timetable and began to estimate how long it would take me to get across town to Grand Central. But then under Penn Station, when we were waiting with the other passengers in the little hall at the end of our Pullman car and the train was creaking slowly along the platform, Maude turned to me and said, "Chris, would you mind horribly seeing me home?"

"No," I said, surprised. "I was just going to put you in a cab, or have you drop me at Grand Central. But I'll take you home."

"You can catch a later train, can't you?" The porter opened the door, admitting a cloud of damp, fetid air upon us, and she turned away. "I'm sorry, Chris," she said quietly over her shoulder. "It's silly of me. It's just that today has been— And I never see you."

"No, it's fine," I said. "Perfectly fine. I can get a train any time." I had been selfish, trying to rush off like that.

Maude lives in a dingy, comfortable old apartment house in the East Sixties, near the river. When we got there, I paid off the cabby and carried our two suitcases in. In her apartment, Maude went around turning on lamps, opening windows, and drawing the curtains. "It'll be cooler in a minute," she said. "I always get a breeze up here, and that's nicer than the air-conditioner."

I looked at my watch. "Look, Maude," I said. "It's silly for me to try to get home tonight. It's after nine, and I'd just have to turn right around and come back again in the morning. Louisa won't mind. Why don't you let me take you to dinner somewhere, and then I'll check into a hotel for the night?"

"Oh, Chris, it would be wonderful," she said. "But I won't have you staying in a hotel. You can sleep right here in the living room. That couch makes a bed, of sorts. And we can eat here. I'm sick of restaurants. I'm sure I can rustle up something for us. Let's have a cocktail, and then you can call Louisa."

Sitting on the edge of Maude's bed and sipping a Martini, I talked to my wife. Her voice, low and concerned for me, made me wish I were at home. I could see her sitting by the telephone table in the hall, with the front door open and the smell of the summer night all through the house. Then my sons talked to me, one after the other, and told me the score of the ball game they were watching, and then my fourteen-year-old daughter, Eliza. She sounded preoccupied and upset. "Is anything the matter?" I asked, suddenly anxious.

"No, but tomorrow's my history final and I've *got* to keep studying. I just can't waste any more time gossiping like this."

I laughed and wished her luck, and hung up.

I found Maude in the kitchen, stirring something in a bowl. "I'm going to make you a fabulous soufflé," she said. "I *hope*. That and a salad. And I found a bottle of white wine on the ice. We'll have a party, Chris."

She was barefooted and she had tied an apron around her waist. She suddenly looked very young, and I realized that she must be lonely a great deal of the time. I thought of her cooking in the evenings like this, alone in the neat, silent apartment. "Do you always cook for yourself, Maude?" I asked.

"Sure," she said, bending to light the oven. "I'm a master of heat-and-serve. I'm famous for my instant chow mein."

"You should get married, Maude."

"Fat chance," she said. "I wouldn't be any good at it. And besides, there aren't any men." She glanced at me almost angrily. "Don't get soft about me, Chris," she said. "I get along."

Our dinner did seem almost like a party. Relieved of the solemnities and degrading surprises of the past two days—the handful of perspiring strangers at the cemetery, and the man who had taken me aside after the ceremony, stammering with embarrassment, to present me with a small bill of my father's from a local tailoring and dry-cleaning establishment—Maude and I sat opposite each other at a little table in her living room, with the lights turned out and candles flickering between us in the warm breeze from the window. We could hear the cries of boats on the East River. We stayed there after our coffee and slowly finished the bottle of wine. We laughed and yawned, and, for once, we talked about our childhood. We tried to remember the names of the long succession of cleaning women and part-time maids who had worked for my mother through the years when the three of us had lived in a small apartment on Riverside Drive.

"And then there was—oh, *God*, what was her name, Chris?" Maude said, her face alive with warm candlelight. "The one who came just after Christmas that year? It was the time when I was sick in bed with the ear abscess. She was Irish, and she quit the day you brought me that garter snake from school. What *was* her name?"

"I don't know," I said. "I can't remember."

"Oh, you know, Chris. Remember she found the snake in the Slater's shoe box in the bathroom, where you'd left it, and she came out screeching? *Lily!*—that was it. Lily O'Something." She began to laugh. " 'Oh, Jesus, a ser-pint!' she yelled, and she ran right out of the house. You made me promise not to tell Mummy."

The telephone rang, and Maude went off to the bedroom to answer it. She was gone a long time. I cleared the dishes and stacked them in the sink, and then I stood by the window and smoked and stared down into the street. Then I remembered the snapshot I had found in my father's desk and I went to my jacket, hanging on the back of my chair, and took it out of the pocket. In the picture, Maude is about eleven years old. She has thick hair that falls just to her shoulders, her arms and legs are tan and thin, and her cotton dress looks too small for her. She faces the camera with a small, grave smile, but the photograph has faded and it is impossible to see the expression in her eyes. I stand beside her, my head reaching the level of her chin, and the donkey is between us, his long, foolish face peering over our shoulders and his ears forming the apex of the composition. My right hand is caressing his nose. I am wearing a striped jersey, abbreviated shorts, and sandals. There is a bandage on my knee, where I had cut myself on the rocks at the *plage,* and eventually, I remember, the cut became infected and had to be opened by a doctor in Nice. Looking at the snapshot that night, I found that I could not recall the name of the donkey, or even remember who had taken the snapshot. All I could add to the picture was the look in Maude's eyes. Her eyes had been large and very dark, with deep, winglike shadows beneath them; she had watched the world with a solemn, unblinking stare. Those eyes had frightened me, for that summer I believed that they saw more than mine did—down corridors at night, through closed doors, through lies, and through the false smiles of adults who are talking to children.

Maude came back into the living room and sat down. "Sorry," she said. "A friend. He wanted to console me on our great loss. I told him you were here."

"He can come up, Maude," I said, feeling in the way. "I don't mind at all."

"As a matter of fact, he *can't* come up," she said. "He's married." She shrugged. "Another hopeless cause. What do you have there?"

I handed her the photograph and told her where I had found it. She drew in her breath and then turned on the lamp beside the sofa and held the picture in the light. "That was the summer it all happened," she said. "This was just after Daddy went off. It's you and me and Beppo."

"I couldn't remember his name," I said.

"I guess you were too young to remember much. His name was Beppo. He lived right next door to the Cossarts. I doted on him."

"Maude," I said, sitting down beside her, "why did Father leave that summer? I asked Mother a couple of times, but she never said. Why did he go off like that?"

"He didn't love us enough," she said.

"What?" I said. I was startled.

"He didn't love us enough," she repeated loudly.

"Oh, come on, Maude," I said. "That's no kind of answer. I mean, where did he go when he disappeared like that?" I was annoyed; I had a feeling she was putting me off.

"Oh, who *cares?*" she cried. "He didn't love us enough. That's the only answer. It's just like you to want an explanation, Chris."

"What does that mean?"

"Oh, I know you! You just want to understand him. You want all the facts, and then you think you'll know what kind of a man he was. You're so damned understanding, Chris. You're so safe."

"I see," I said curtly.

"Oh, Chris, just look at yourself!" she said, the words bursting out of her. There were tears in her eyes. "You *are* safe, you poor baby. You're thirty-three or thirty-four years old, and you're an old man. You might as well be sixty. You've got everything—a nice, safe house in the country, safe wife, safe children, a safe, fat job. Chris, what are you *doing* as assistant regional almighty Pooh-Bah in a tools company, anyway? You could have done better for yourself.

You could have been anything, Chris—anything in the world—and just look at yourself. Me, I'm not bright enough and I don't care enough about the damned career thing to do more than the silly work I do, but you, Chris, you're a man!"

"Why don't you just stop about me?" I said. I was shaking.

"All right, I'll stop. I'll stop in a minute, dear Chris. Dear brother that I love." She put her hand on my arm. "But damn it, just once —just this one time—*look* at yourself. Why didn't you go away to college like everybody else, instead of living at home with Mummy and just going to Columbia? Why did you get married when you were twenty? Why did you have a baby right away?"

"I was in love," I said. "But maybe you don't know about that."

"All *right!* Maybe I had that coming. But Chris, look at the way you live! Look at those silly friends of yours at home. I know—I've met them. Those golfers, those bridge players. Those plump wives at dinner parties all talking to each other instead of to the men. What are you doing in a place like that, you poor booby? Have you ever once taken a chance—had a real love affair, punched somebody in the nose, gotten drunk for three days? Don't you think maybe you've missed something? Didn't you ever want to run away to sea?"

"*Now* I get it," I said. "You want me to be like Father. Is that it?"

She looked at me and then she gave an angry little laugh and wiped the tears from her face with the back of one hand. "Just listen to us," she said. "What cheap talk." She got up and found a handkerchief in her pocketbook and blew her nose. "Now I *have* stopped," she said. "Try to forgive me. I don't know—maybe I'm a bit drunk."

She went out, and I could hear the water running in the bathroom. When she came back, she was wearing a bathrobe and carrying some clean sheets over her arm. She had taken off her makeup. "Help me fix up your bed, Chris," she said. "I think we're both done in. And no wonder."

We pulled the couch away from the wall and tucked the sheets about it. She found me a clean towel and facecloth and took the candles and tablecloth away. I kissed her goodnight, and then, just as she was going into her bedroom, I remembered something. "Maude," I said, "why didn't you go up to see his room yesterday?"

"I don't know," she said. "I just didn't want to, somehow." She paused for a moment in the door. "You don't remember him, do you, Chris?" she asked in a low voice.

"Sure, I do," I answered. "He used to turn up every few years and we'd have lunch. You remember how he was. He even came out to the house once or twice. And before that, years ago, when we were in school, the way he'd suddenly appear sometimes. He took us to the Music Hall once."

"I don't mean that," she said. "I mean before, when he was still at home."

"I guess I don't really remember. I can remember him teaching me to swim. That sort of thing."

"Do you remember him reading aloud?"

"No."

"He read wonderfully. He could make you see everybody in the book. . . . There was no way of knowing he was going to turn out the way he did."

Long after Maude had closed her door that night, I was still kicking at the sheets that clung to my sweating legs and turning from one side to the other on the narrow, unfamiliar couch. Finally, I got up and took off my rumpled pajama top and then pulled the bottom sheet smooth and tucked it in again. I found a cigarette and an ashtray, and got back into bed. I lay on my back and smoked and stared at the lights moving across the ceiling. Sounds of cars, fragments of talk, and the tap of late walkers' heels on the sidewalk drifted into the room from the street, and once there was a man's voice, absolutely distinct, crying "Connie! Connie! Connie!" in terrible distress. Lying there with the noise of the city in my ears, I had a frightening moment of clarity when I thought I could understand why Maude and I had never wanted to talk about our common history. It seemed to me that we were like two survivors of a sudden, devastating air raid that had struck one morning when we were in different parts of the same town. We shared the experience, but meeting later, we would find that neither of us was able to understand what the other had seen and felt, so violent was the memory of our own, private disaster. She would try to tell me about the bomb that had landed on the fish store just down the street, blowing the glass from her front windows all over her at the moment when she was down on her hands and knees taking up the hem of her old green dress. And I would interrupt her: "Yes, yes, but *I* was in a barbershop when they hit the grammar school on the corner, and the power lines came down all over the street. I had to walk out through the smoke, and there were loose schoolbooks lying in the stones and dirt, and I never did get home that day."

Then, for the first time in many years, I turned myself back to France and the summer of 1933. I started with the photograph, but nothing came; I could not remember the donkey. Instead, I caught sight of a long, slope-nosed, shiny black Renault car, with my father at the wheel. He was wearing tweeds, and the four of us were driving south from Paris. We stopped in Grasse (I could see the shape of the little wooden vials of solid perfume they gave Maude and me at one of the factories), and then—instantly, in my recollection—we were at Saint-Caylus, a small fishing-village resort on the Riviera, and we had come unstuck. I cannot remember my father leaving; he was simply gone, and then, within a day or two, my mother was gone, too, taking the car, and Maude and I were left with the Cossarts. Our mother must have got their name through the hotel; almost certainly they weren't known to her until the day she realized that she had to place her children somewhere while she went off in pursuit of her husband. Perhaps she wasn't pursuing him, but why would she have left us otherwise?

I can remember the Cossarts' garden better than the house itself. There was a high wall of flaking gray stone around both the house and garden, topped all along its length by a narrow roof of tilted red tiles. Sometimes, on hot mornings, a sliver of wall would appear to come alive for an instant as a slim lizard, exactly the color of the stone, would leap for an insect. When I approached, keeping my eye on the spot, the lizard remained invisible until I had crept close enough to detect his tiny shadow pencilled on the wall beneath his pulsating ribs. He would swivel one slitted eye toward me, watching my descending hand, and then dart away, sometimes leaving the tip of his tail between my thumb and forefinger.

Mme. Cossart is only a shape to me. She has no face in my recollection, but she is tall and rather forbidding and, like so many middle-aged French women, dressed entirely in black. She might have been in mourning. I know she was French—that was why we called her Madame. But Mr. Cossart was English. We called him Herbert, and he is easier for me to visualize. He is small and red-faced, with white hair combed straight across the top of his head; his shirtsleeves are rolled up and there is a small, blurred purple tattoo—a bird, perhaps—on the inside of one forearm. I can only think of the Cossarts separately—never as a couple. Herbert would announce at breakfast that the four of us would rent a car that afternoon and drive to Nice for haircuts and ice cream; Mme. Cossart would look at him with pitying distaste and say that, *au contraire,* we would stay at home, for it was surely going to rain. Madame would pour a half glass of wine for Maude at dinner, and when Herbert protested and said that what we wanted was a glass of good fresh milk, Madame would go wordlessly to the cupboard and fetch another glass and fill it with wine for me. It seems likely that my mother hired the Cossarts because they were the only couple she could find at Saint-Caylus who could speak English to Maude and me and were willing to take us in. I think Herbert and Madame spoke French to each other, but I am not certain, for I cannot remember a single conversation between them. Where had they met and married? Why did they live in an obscure French village beside the Mediterranean? What did our mother tell them of our circumstances and needs? I shall never know.

Every afternoon after lunch, in the hottest part of the day, Madame made me lie down on a cot for a full hour's nap on a small ground-floor porch at the back of the house. I insisted that at eight I was too old for naps, but Madame said that children could not have too much sleep. I didn't sleep, of course; stripped to my underwear and dazed with heat, I would lie there waiting endlessly for the bell on the alarm clock in the kitchen to ring and terminate my sentence. I could hear the high singing of locusts in the hot garden outside and, more softly, the ceaseless small crashing of waves on the beach, just down at the end of the road. Then, almost every day, the back door would bang and Herbert would appear in the garden, wearing a dirty white panama hat and carrying garden implements. Rising and then squatting again, whistling softly to himself, he would make a slow circuit of the flower beds, leaving a trail of pulled weeds on the brick walk as he worked his way toward me. When he had finished the bed directly beneath me, he would sit down with his back resting against one of the porch pillars, dust the earth off his hands, and produce a wrinkled blue pack of Gauloises. "Well, young Chris," he would say every single time. "Thinking about your papa, I expect."

Sometime early in the summer I must have asked Herbert where my father had gone, for he took it on himself to comfort me and, after his fashion, to explain the matter. Much of the time, of course, I *hadn't* been thinking about my father (I was much more interested in my mother's absence, for instance, or whether there would be another postcard from her tomorrow, or whether we would go to the *plage* that afternoon), but Herbert's obsessive kindness infected me in time, and my father's disappearance became the central fact of my summer.

"Well now," Herbert would say, blowing a cloud of rich-smelling cigarette smoke into the warm air, "it seems to me that I read in the paper this very morning that they're having a spot of trouble over in Spain these days. Revolutions and that sort of thing. It wouldn't surprise me in the least, young Chris, if that's where your papa has gone. A secret mission for King Alfonso, I should imagine. That will be why he had to pop off like that, unexpected. Secret Service men can never explain their missions, you know. Silent as the tomb, they are. Now, you tell me your papa is a brave man, Chris? Strong? Bit of dash to him? I knew it! Not a shadow of doubt about it; that's where he is—in Spain. He'll be back one of these days. Any morning now, you'll wake up and he'll be here. Perhaps he'll bring a rifle for you and a beautiful lacework shawl for your sister. You mark my words and see."

Every three or four days, Herbert would change his story. My father was in Tripoli, he would say, putting down pirates. He was in Milan, helping distraught Italian bankers to foil a gigantic plot being hatched by a band of cunning safecrackers; he would return with a bag of gold given him for his services. He was in Africa and he would return straight across the sea, with a monkey for me riding on his neck.

Maude was the only one who might have helped me out of this confusion of exciting lies, but Maude belonged to Madame. They were together most of the morning, in the kitchen or walking to the square in Saint-Caylus to shop for groceries, and in the afternoons Madame was teaching Maude to speak French. I was convinced that my sister knew the truth, whatever it was, but I was sure that if I asked her about our father, she would look at me coldly out of those great dark eyes and tell me that I was too young to understand, or that Father was dead, or maybe only that I was being *embêtant*.

Once, I must have mentioned the then current version of my father's adventures to Herbert at the dinner table, because I can remember the angry explosion from Madame. "Listen to those two!" she said to Maude. "What stories they tell each other! Now,

in truth, Maude *chérie,* I think we have two children in this family
and not one of them is wearing skirts. *Quelle histoire!* Now you
know what men truly are—inventors and liars and those who run
away—and you can be ready for them. Beware of *ces romanciers*—
these tellers of bad tales. *Méfiez-vous."*

Our mother came back to see us from time to time. I can remember two visits, and maybe there were more. We would dine with
her at the hotel, and once she drove us to Cap d'Antibes for lunch.
On those days, Maude became herself again in my eyes—merely my
sister—and the hours went by in such a whirl of happiness and
excitement that I forgot each time that she would be someone else
altogether when we returned to the Cossarts' at night. Mother must
have been seeing our father during her absences, or at least hearing
from him, because she promised us more than once that he would
be back and that the four of us would resume our trip.

Two more events only—the last fragments I can find in me of that
long-ago summer. Both are night scenes. In the first, I wake up
suddenly, roaring with pain and fright, for a bee has blundered into
my bedroom somehow and has stung me under the jaw in my
sleep. Herbert is the first one to arrive; he wears a nightshirt and
carries an oil lamp in his hand. He examines me, discovers the
trouble, and sends Madame back to bed. He goes out and then
reappears with a mound of fresh earth from the garden in his hands.
He kneels in front of my bed and, to my astonishment, orders me
to urinate into the dirt he holds. "Go ahead, Chris," he says sternly,
"make water. Do pee-pee. What do you call it?" I protest, but he is
adamant, and at last, with some difficulty, I obey. He packs the
damp earth into a poultice and immediately claps it on my sting.
"Nothing like it, young Chris," he says cheerfully, holding the mud
pack on my neck and wiping my tears with the sleeve of his nightshirt. "Draws the sting, draws the hurt."

And then it is the end of the summer and there is a small fête
in Saint-Caylus—the celebration of a saint's day. Madame and
Herbert take us to the village square that evening, as a treat; we
see a strong man in a bathing suit lifting weights, and we eat
dinner at an outdoor café to the music of the town band. Afterward,
we jam ourselves into a cheerful crowd on a bus that drives us
around to the opposite side of the little Saint-Caylus cove, to a beach
from which we will have a fine view of the fireworks on the docks.
For a long time we sit on the beach, watching the lights across the

cove and waiting for the fireworks. It is very late, long after my
bedtime, and I fall asleep there, lying face down in the cool sand
with my head in my arms. Some time later, I awake to the sound of
cries and applause. Everyone is standing, shouting, pointing. There
is clapping and laughter all up and down the beach. Still half
asleep, I spring up and look for rockets and fires in the sky. But the
fireworks have not yet commenced. Then, following the direction
of the pointing fingers all about me, I see what is happening. In
the middle of the cove, almost halfway across from the docks, there
is a man swimming toward us through the dark water. He swims
with one arm held straight above him, and in that hand he carries
a lighted flare. Red fire spouts above him, turning the sea to scarlet,
and sparks stream over him. The arm he holds aloft is decked with
red and blue and white ribbons. The swimmer kicks mightily,
sending up showers of spray, and calls to us as he thrashes along.
I look at him for an instant and then I go mad with excitement.
"It's him!" I cry, rushing toward the water's edge. "It's him and
he's come! It's my father, it's my father! He's come for us, he's
here!" I run into the warm sea; it covers my sandals and rises to
my knees. I turn to the others, pointing and shouting. "Look,
Maude!" I call. "Look, Herbert—he's coming! That's my father!"
    There is a shocked cry from Madame, and Herbert starts forward,
but it is Maude who reaches me first. She runs into the water and
seizes my arm and yanks me back so hard that I fall down. She pulls
me up again and then slaps my face. "What's the *matter* with you?"
she says between her teeth. "What's happened to you, you little
fool? That's not our father! That's just some man." Still holding
my arm, she twists me around until her face is right over mine.
"Don't you know, Chris?" she says in an angry whisper. "Don't you
know Daddy's never coming back?"

    Four days later, our mother returns for the last time. She tells us
that we will go home without our father. She has sold the car.
Herbert accompanies us to the little Saint-Caylus station and sees
us off on the local train to Nice, where we will change for the Paris
express. A week later, the three of us sail for home on the Mauretania.

    It was cool the next morning in Maude's apartment, and I awoke
feeling rested and eager to get back to my office. I ate my breakfast
in the kitchen, while Maude washed our dishes of the night before.

She was wearing an old orange cotton bathrobe, but her new makeup and carefully arranged hair gave her a fresh, go-to-work appearance. She put the garbage pail outside the back door, along with the empty wine bottle. "The janitor will think another orgy," she said cheerfully.

I finished a second cup of coffee, and when I had repacked and closed my suitcase, Maude came out of her room wearing a handsome gray silk dress. "You go along, Chris," she said, fastening a bracelet around one wrist. "I'll just pick up your bed and finish up here. You might find a cab on Second Avenue."

We stood by the door, facing each other. She had become the elegant, efficient New York woman, a stranger to me once again. "Are you all right?" I asked.

"Of course I'm all right, Chris. I'm always all right." She gave me a quick hug. "And you're sweet. Look, can you try to forgive me for last night? Those were awful things I said to you and I didn't mean one of them. Just try to remember it as a sudden bout of female hysteria. Because that's what it was. Too much Wilmington. God, how I hate the sticks!"

"Oh, it was nothing," I said. "We were tired. It was my fault, really. I just wanted to find out more about him because— I don't know. I guess I want to be able to remember him the way a son should remember a father."

She took a cigarette from the coffee table and lit it. "Well, you know what there is to remember," she said, shaking out the match. "He was a social director in a gents' club."

"Maude," I said, "you've got to forgive him."

"I'll never forgive him!" she said, her eyes fixed on me. "Never! He was my father. I expect the best from people."

"You could try to love him."

"Oh, Chris," she said wearily. "What do we know about loving people? You've got to let me be myself. You go ahead and love him if you can. You can't make me over, so you'll just have to give up on me."

She picked up my suitcase and handed it to me. "Go along, darling," she said, smiling again. "I'm all right—just Maude. Call me someday next week, and we'll have lunch."

Descending alone in the humming elevator, I suddenly understood my sister. I knew why I had sometimes been afraid of her; her courage was greater than mine. Strong, lovely, self-destructive,

bitterly uncompromising, she had loved our father more than I ever
could.

Now another train is rolling northward at the end of a summer
day. I sit facing forward this time, on a smooth straw seat. I am
going home. My suitcase is in the rack over my head, but otherwise
everything is as always. My riddled commutation ticket is in the slot
in front of me, the corners of held evening newspapers quiver gently
to the motion of the train, the tracks make a metallic, slithering
murmur under our wheels. Outside, on my left, the Hudson slides
by, huge and white and unruffled, reflecting the sun and the empty
sky. It fills the middle distance, and by consequence there are fewer
figures in this landscape. Several fishermen flash by, sitting motionless on the bank by the roadbed. We overtake two teen-age boys
in bathing suits, very tan, riding in a rickety outboard; one of them
is sitting on the gunwales up forward, his legs straddling the bow.
Then the train slows for a stop, and the land between us and the
river widens momentarily, to make room for a dilapidated station,
an empty platform, and four empty freight cars on a siding before
a small warehouse. The train stops, releasing a few passengers, and
then, just as we start forward again, I see a man in an undershirt
holding a hose and watering a fenced patch of lawn in front of a
grimy one-story wooden house. A yellow dog darts out from behind
the house, barking at the train, and is pursued by a young girl in
a ponytail. She catches him at the open front gate and seizes him
by the collar, holding him until our train goes by. As we pass them,
gathering speed, she bends over and says something in the dog's
ear, and I find myself smiling.

At this moment, I notice the man sitting next to me, between me
and the window. He has put down his newspaper and is staring out
with a fixed, sullen expression. His eyes are cold, his smooth cheeks
rest puffily on his bulging jaw muscles, and he holds his lower lip
between his teeth. He hasn't noticed the house or the girl and the
dog; he looks past them and sees a swollen, polluted river concealing
corpses.

Uncertain now, I glance about at the other passengers near me.
But their expressions tell me nothing; they have hidden themselves
behind newspapers and tired private faces. They cannot help me.
We cannot compare notes, and none of them has the wisdom to tell
me how to live. Each of us has bought his ticket to his own destination and speeds toward it now in his own way—with eagerness,

or rage, or despair. There are no victims on this train, no unwilling deportees. The only part of the journey we cannot control is the landscape—the kind of truth we see from our separate windows—and that was arranged for us long before we left the terminal. Bathed in sunlight, our train flies through the late afternoon, rushing for the future.

THE WHITE WILD BRONCO

❖

BENEDICT KIELY

A<small>T</small> the age of five, when asked what he wanted to be when he grew up, Isaac said he wanted to be a German. He was then blond and chubby, and not at all pugnacious. Because he stuttered, he pronounced the word "German" with three, sometimes with six, initial consonants. He had heard it by his father's bedside, where, propped most of the day on high pillows, the old fusilier remembered Givenchy and Messines Ridge in the hearing of his friends: Doherty the undertaker; Mickey Fish, who sold fish on Fridays from a flat dray and from door to door, and who stopped young women—even under the courthouse clock—to ask them the time of evening; Pat Moses Gavigan, who fished pike and cut the world's best blackthorns; and Cowboy Carson, the only man in our town who lived completely in the imagination. Occasionally, the old fusilier read aloud out of one or other of the learned anthropological tomes dealing with the adventures of Tarzan the ape man, but mostly the talk was about Germans. Isaac, quiet on his creepie stool, liked the sound of the word.

Bella, the loving wife of the old fusilier, had received her husband home from the war, we were told, in a glass case, the loser by a stomach shot away when—all his superior officers dead—he, the corporal, gallantly led an action to success. He had carried the *kopje,* or whatever it was they carried in Flanders, and had stopped just short of advancing into the fire of his own artillery. Back home, stomachless in his glass case, he cheated the War Office on the delicate question of expectation of life, collected a fine pension, and lived at his ease until the world was good and ready for another war. No crippled veteran left to beg at the town's end was the old fusilier. Secure in his bed in his lattice-windowed room in his white cottage that was snug in the middle of a terrace of seven white cottages, he talked, read about Tarzan, told how fields were won, and on big British Legion days condescended to receive homage from visiting celebrities, including, once, Lady Haigh herself. On the creepie stool, chubby Isaac absorbed the wonder of half-compre-hended words, pondered the girth of the undertaker, the lean, love-less face of the fish merchant who thought that only beauty could tell him the time on a June evening, watched the hands of Moses as they cut a thorn or measured the monstrousness of an escaped pike, studied the Cowboy's eyes, which squinted—by way of two-penny paper-covered books—back to the Texas Panhandle and the old Chisholm Trail.

The undertaker, or the pike fisherman, or the fish merchant, or the Cowboy would say, "Isaac, what do you want to be when you grow up?"

Isaac would say, "I want to be a German."

Then the four visitors would laugh. His father, pale on his pil-lows, would laugh—forgetting Germans once seen in a sulphurous haze as he charged roaring through shot and shell, to become a hero. His father would read the next installment:

> "When Tarzan of the Apes realized that he was in the grips of the great jaws of a crocodile he did not, as an ordinary man might have done, give up all hope and resign himself to his fate. . . .
>
> "His body trailed out beside the slimy carcass of his captor, and into the tough armor the ape man attempted to plunge his stone knife as he was borne to the creature's horrid den. . . .
>
> "Staggering to his feet the ape man groped about the reeking oozy den. . . ."

In the moonlight, the Cowboy walked home, pulling imaginary guns and talking in admonitory tones to Wyatt Earp. "Stand there, Earp! You may be a big man, but I'll cut you down. Do I have to push you into slapping leather?"

Alone in the moonlight, on the hill that went down to the red-and-white creamery, the brook, the Cowboy's hut, the fields beyond, he pulled and whirled and fired three times. With satisfaction he listened to the echoes dying away at the town's last fringe of shabby, sleeping terraces—over the tarred iron roofs of Tansey the carter's stableyard, over the railway-engine shed and the turntable. On green-and-white moonland beyond the Dublin railway, a mystic white bronco galloped in circles, as, noiselessly, the Cowboy slipped his smoking Colt back into the holster. He turned then, and continued down the hill to Tansey the carter's, and supper. He worked, carrying bags of meal to clumsy four-wheeled drays, in the warehouse of Dale the grain merchant—nicknamed Attention—who was an amateur astronomer and had a telescope installed in a beehive-shaped structure at the back of his store. Every night, after the fusilier's reading, the Cowboy ate his supper of yellow Indian porridge and buttermilk in the huge coppery kitchen where Tansey the carter was a smiling, extrovert Buddha in the middle of his six stout sisters, who had never shown the least inclination toward matrimony.

"Every day, Cowboy, Attention's back is stiffer and stiffer," Tansey said.

"Stiff as a poker," said the third sister.

The sisters were all red-faced and brown-haired. The fourth one cooked the porridge.

"I hear he got drunk on wine gumdrops in Devlin's sweetie shop in Bridge Lane," Tansey joked. "The sergeant had to wheel his bicycle home for him."

Seriously resenting the imputation, the Cowboy, thumbs in the armholes of his patched and darned gray vest, drawled, "The Big Boss is a fast man on the draw. He never touches hard likker."

"We heard he can stare the sun in the face up in that spinning beehive of his," said the second sister.

The carter said, "It takes a good man to stare the sun in the face."

On a hook behind the broad oak door, the first sister considerately hung the Stetson that a rope juggler in a travelling circus had once given to the Cowboy.

"What goes on between himself and the sun is his own business," said the Cowboy reverently. "There was a cattleman in Wyoming had as big a spyglass. Could spot an Injun or a stray ten miles off."

"You and Wyoming," gently said the sixth sister.

"The Big Boss reaches me my wad. At the door of the bunkhouse. 'Your pay, Michael,' he says. 'Count it.' I counted one pound nineteen and elevenpence. 'A penny short, boss,' says I. 'One penny deducted, Michael, for a box of matches purchased on credit last Tuesday at 11 A.M.' He misses nothing."

"Your porridge," said Tansey the carter. "And give us another bit of the story."

"The place I was in that time," said the Cowboy. "Down Deep South. There was a river. Alligators. As plentiful as trout in the brook. This day I went for a swim. Just the way you'd go for a swim above the salmon leap by the hospital on the Camowen River."

"Showing off and strutting before the nurses," said the third sister. "For shame, Cowboy."

"And what should happen when I was out in deep water but an alligator. Silent-like, he grabs me by the arm. I could show you the marks still. But cute enough, he doesn't take the arm off. He needed it, you see, to drag me down."

"In this life you'll always get somebody to drag you down," said the second sister.

"Down to where?" asked the carter.

"Not down the town to a pub or the pictures, anyway. Down to his cave. They live in caves in that river."

"No homes to go to," said the third sister.

"Was he big?" asked the carter. "Would he be the size, now, of the last pike Pat Moses Gavigan caught at Blacksessiagh?"

" 'Size'! Ten times the size! A mouth that wide. And the growls of him. Well, there was I. My body beside the slimy carcass of my captor. But I had a knife. A stone knife. Never swam without it. Wouldn't be safe in those parts. And as I was borne to the creature's horrid den, I attempted to plunge my knife into the tough armor of the reptile."

"Cowboy," said the carter, "you're the lucky man to be alive and eating porridge there this blessed night."

" 'Lucky'! Quickness—that's what does it. An ordinary man might have given up all hope and resigned himself to his fate."

From the stables came a wild volley of hoofs on confining wood, then a second volley, then a slow thud-thud-thud and one mad, high, equine scream.

"That savage you bought," said the fifth sister. "He'll never cart."

"He'll cart," said Tansey. "More porridge, Cowboy?"

This was the time when Isaac desired—as every child, male or female, sometimes desires—a pony. It was, of course, long before he found his vocation and, in a lane above the engine shed—the town's unroofed gymnasium—learned to become the best fighter we ever had. Poise and stance, dynamite right and cunning left, footwork, speed, quick eye, cool head, and iron muscles—the fusilier's son was a natural champion. And, graduating from the green lane, he brought belts, cups, medals, honor, and glory home with him from every part of the country. We were proud of him.

But in the days of his desire for the pony, there were no blows struck but one. Where would a boy go who wanted a pony or a stable to house him but to Tansey's yard, where the great cart horses stamped with the assured gravity of savants, where the Taggarts—the horse dealers—displayed the shaggy, sullen-eyed animals they brought in droves from the mountains away to the southwest, even from tinker camps in the province of Connacht? Roosted high on the shaft of an idle dray, Isaac was there the day Tansey bought the wild white horse. In among the brown shaggy brutes he was white-limbed Tarzan among the ape people of Akut, and until he felt on his quivering flanks the confining shafts, he concealed horror in docility. Then he reared to the perpendicular, assaulted the heavens, came down again, lashed out backward, and did the rounds of the yard like a Derby winner, while old and young—Isaac among them—ran for shelter. With great Tansey swinging from the reins, the horse went round and round until the cart was in firewood and broken shafts trailed the ground.

"Powerful God," said Tansey to the Taggarts, "where did you get this one?"

"In Ballinasloe, in the County Galway," they said, as if that explained everything.

"Take him back to Ballinasloe," said Tansey. "But no, linger now," he said. "There's life in him. He'll cart. I'll coax him."

Dreaming at a safe distance, Isaac saw himself coaxing the savage with gently proffered lumps of sugar, and all through the white one's novitiate under Tansey, Isaac was in constant, reverent attendance. But no coaxing, no lump sugar, no whispers or magic hands could reconcile the untamed tinker-spirit of Ballinasloe to the base servility of the shafts of a dray.

"He has good blood in him," Tansey said. "I'll try him in a trap."

Some of the fragments of the trap, they say, were found fifty yards away on the railway line, and the great white creature stood shivering as if—if it were human—it would burst into hysterical sobs. For a whole fortnight, with Isaac perched on high walls or drays or snug on the hay in the hay shed, the wooing went on, and it was one evening in the stable that Isaac said, "Give him to me, Mr. Tansey. I'll tame him for you."

For one half second, while the carter—distracted—turned and laughed, the horse lunged and snapped, the razor teeth grazing the back of Tansey's skull and gashing the lobe of his left ear. The blood came out like a spout, and Tansey dyed his hand in it. Then, disregarding it, he looked sadly at the animal. With no sign of temper, he went to the back of the stable, picked up a crowbar from a heap of rusting metal, and with the deliberation of God struck the animal between the eyes and stunned it. When it woke up an hour later, it went—almost of its own accord—to the shafts. Isaac's sugar lumps were never needed.

By the fusilier's bedside that evening, the Cowboy was sitting straddle on a stool—knees in, feet out, hands wide—showing how he had held the reins and stayed in the saddle when lesser men had bitten the dust of the rodeo ring. Isaac chewed toffee. He said, "Tansey the carter broke a bronc today. I saw him." He told his story.

"Tansey's a brute," said Doherty the undertaker. "He'd slay his six sisters before he'd lose two pounds sterling."

"You'd benefit," said Pat Moses Gavigan. "Six coffins."

"They're six fine big girls," said Mickey Fish.

"Not a watch between them," said the fusilier. "Time doesn't count in Tansey's."

The fusilier read:

> "Screaming with terror the Maoris were dragged from their lofty perches. The beasts, uncontrolled by Tarzan, who had gone in search of Jane, loosed the full fury of their savage natures upon the unhappy wretches who fell into their clutches. . . . Sheeta, in the meanwhile, had felt his great fangs sink into but a single jugular. . . ."

Afterward, when the guests had gone, Isaac said, "Cowboy Carson had a ranch once on the Rio Grande. He told me he had seventy pinto ponies."

"Son," said the fusilier, "I hate to rob you of your fancy. But better for your father to do it than for the hard world and the black stranger. The Cowboy Carson was never out of this town except perhaps to carry Pat Moses Gavigan's bag as far as the pike water at Blacksessiagh. It all comes out of the wee books you see in the paper-shop window: 'Deadwood Dick' and 'Buffalo Bill' and 'Hit the Tuttle Trail with Hashknife and Sleepy.'"

"But he was a gun slinger, Da, in Texas."

"Guns—he never saw guns," said the fusilier, musing for a minute and remembering Flanders and the roar of the iron monsters.

In the dusk, the Cowboy walked home—spurs jingling, stiff and stilted on high heels, bowlegged from the saddle—left to right and right to left, practicing the cross draw, and remembering with affection his deceased friend Buck Duane, the Lone Star Ranger. He was light and elated. There was no pressure of crushing bags of grain on his old bony shoulders. Melodious with beeves, a freight train from the West truckled on toward Belfast. The Cowboy made his crooked way to the kitchen of Tansey the carter.

"You broke the bronc today, I'm told," he said to Tansey the carter.

"I broke the bronc, Cowboy, the only way my father taught me. If I buy a horse to cart, he has to cart. Or a woman to cook."

"He never bought a woman," said the third sister, and the six sisters laughed.

"Your porridge, Cowboy."

"Did I ever tell you about the time I was in New Zealand?"

"You never did," said Tansey the carter.

When the Americans came to our town on their way to meet Hitler, somebody told them about the Cowboy, and one of them, meeting him, said, "Haven't we encountered you before?"

"Was it in Tucson?" said another.

"More whiskey," said a third. "It was in Tombstone."

"Not there," said the Cowboy. "I guess and calculate it might have been Deadwood."

"Deadwood it was," said the three of them. "Well, we'll be doggone darned."

"Tell us about Deadwood, Cowboy," said the man behind the bar.

"I was riding shotgun at that time," said the Cowboy. "Stiff knee, you see. Couldn't mount a bronc." For corroborative purposes he displayed his stiff knee.

They listened with a little laughter. They weren't cruel. They were, in fact, kind, because the worst thing you could have done was to tell him he was never there.

By that time, the old fusilier was dead and buried by Doherty the undertaker; Attention Dale had been succeeded by a nephew, who

couldn't face the sun and sold the telescope; Mickey Fish was confined to a mental home, for chasing young girls to ask them the time
of evening; and arthritis prevented Pat Moses Gavigan from fishing
pike or cutting blackthorns. And Isaac, the fusilier's son, had realized that he would never be a German. He came like a bird as a
paratrooper into Narvik, came out again alive, and possibly helped
the three Americans who had listened to the Cowboy to storm the
French shore. Until he was killed at the Rhine crossing, he remained the best fighter our town ever had.

THE CHAMPION OF THE WORLD

❖

ROALD DAHL

ALL DAY, in between serving customers, we had been crouching over the table in the office of my filling station, preparing the raisins. They were plump and soft from being soaked in water, and when you nicked them with a razor blade the skin sprang open and the jelly stuff inside squeezed out as easily as you could wish. But we had a hundred and ninety-six of them to do altogether, and the evening was nearly upon us before we had finished.

"Don't they look marvellous!" Claud cried, rubbing his hands together hard. "What time is it, Gordon?"

"Just after five."

Through the window, we could see a station wagon pulling up at the petrol pumps, with a woman at the wheel and about eight children in the back eating ice creams.

"We ought to be moving soon," Claud said. "The whole thing'll be a washout if we don't arrive before sunset, you realize that." He was getting twitchy now. His face had the same flushed and popeyed look it got before a dog race.

We both went outside, and Claud gave the woman the number of gallons she wanted. When she had gone, he remained standing in the middle of the driveway, squinting anxiously up at the sun, which was now only the width of a man's hand above the line of trees along the crest of the ridge on the far side of the valley.

"All right," I said. "Lock up."

He went quickly from pump to pump, securing each nozzle in its holder with a small padlock.

"You'd better take off that yellow pullover," he said.

"Why should I?"

"You'll be shining like a bloody beacon out there in the moonlight."

"I'll be all right."

"You will not," he said. "Take it off, Gordon, please. I'll see you in three minutes." He disappeared into his caravan behind the

467

filling station, and I went indoors and changed my yellow pullover for a blue one.

When we met again outside, Claud was dressed in a pair of black trousers and a dark-green turtleneck sweater. On his head he wore a brown cloth cap with the peak pulled down low over his eyes, and he looked like an apache actor out of a night club.

"What's under there?" I asked, seeing the bulge at his waistline.

He pulled up his sweater and showed me two thin but very large white cotton sacks bound neat and tight around his belly. "To carry the stuff," he said.

"I see."

"Let's go," he said.

"I still think we ought to take the car."

"It's too risky. They'll see it parked."

"But it's over three miles up to that wood."

"Yes," he said. "And I suppose you realize we can get six months in the clink if they catch us."

"You never told me that."

"Didn't I?"

"I'm not coming," I said. "It's not worth it."

"The walk will do you good, Gordon. Come on."

It was a calm, sunny evening, with little wisps of brilliant white cloud hanging motionless in the sky, and the valley was cool and very quiet as the two of us began walking along the grass on the side of the road that ran between the hills toward Oxford.

"You got the raisins?" Claud asked.

"They're in my pocket."

"Good," he said. "Marvellous."

Ten minutes later, we turned left off the main road into a narrow lane with high hedges on either side, and from then on it was all uphill.

"How many keepers are there?" I asked.

"Three."

Claud threw away a half-finished cigarette. A minute later, he lit another. "It'll be a milestone in the history of poaching," he said. "But don't you go telling a single soul how we've done it, you understand? Because if this ever leaked out, we'd have every bloody fool in the district doing the same thing, and there wouldn't be a pheasant left."

"I won't say a word."

"You ought to be very proud of yourself," he went on. "There's been men with brains studying this problem for hundreds of years, and not one of them's ever come up with anything even a quarter as artful as you have. Why didn't you tell me about it before?"

"You never invited my opinion," I said.

And that was the truth. In fact, up until the day before, Claud had never even offered to discuss with me the sacred subject of poaching. Often enough, on a summer's evening when work was finished, I had seen him, with cap on head, sliding quietly out of his caravan and disappearing up the road toward the woods; and sometimes, watching him through the window of the filling station, I would find myself wondering exactly what he was going to do, what tricks he was going to practice all alone up there under the trees in the night. He seldom came back until very late, and never, absolutely never, did he bring any of the spoils with him on his return. But the following afternoon—I couldn't imagine how he did it—there would always be a pheasant or a hare or a brace of partridges hanging up in the shed behind the filling station.

This summer, he had been particularly active, and during the past couple of months he had stepped up the tempo to a point where he was going out four and sometimes five nights a week. But that was not all. It seemed to me that recently his whole attitude toward poaching had undergone a subtle and mysterious change. He was more purposeful about it now, more tight-lipped and intense than before, and I had formed the impression that this was not so much a game any longer as a sort of private war that he was waging against the famous Mr. Victor Hazel himself. Mr. Hazel was a pie and sausage manufacturer, with an unbelievably arrogant manner. He was rich beyond words, and his property stretched for miles along either side of the valley. He was a self-made man, with no charm at all and precious few virtues. He loathed all persons of humble station, having once been one of them himself, and he strove desperately to mingle with what he believed were the right kind of folk. He hunted with the hounds and gave shooting parties and wore fancy waistcoats, and every weekday he drove an enormous black Rolls-Royce past the filling station on his way to and from his factory. As he flashed by, we would sometimes catch a glimpse of his great, glistening butcher's face above the wheel, pink as a ham, all soft and inflamed from eating too much meat.

Anyway, the day before, which was Wednesday, Claud had suddenly said to me, right out of the blue, "I'll be going on up to Hazel's woods again tonight. Why don't you come along?"

"Who, me?"

"It's about the last chance this year for pheasants," he had said. "The shooting season opens Saturday, and the birds'll be scattered all over the place after that—if there's any left."

"Why the sudden invitation?" I had asked.

"No special reason, Gordon. No reason at all."

"I suppose you keep a gun or something hidden away up there?"

"A gun!" he cried, disgusted. "Nobody ever *shoots* pheasants, didn't you know that? You've only got to fire a *cap pistol* in Hazel's woods and the keepers'll be on you."

"Then how do you do it?"

"Ah," he said. There was a long pause. Then he said, "Do you think you could keep your mouth shut if I was to tell you a thing or two?"

"Definitely."

"I've never told this to anyone else in my whole life, Gordon."

"I am greatly honored," I said. "You can trust me completely."

He turned his head, fixing me with pale eyes. "I am now about to let you in on the three best ways in the world of poaching a pheasant," he said. "And, seeing that you're the guest on this little trip, I am going to give you the choice of which one you'd like us to use tonight. How's that?"

"There's a catch in this."

"There's no catch, Gordon. I swear it."

"All right, go on."

"Now, here's the thing," he said. "Here's the first big secret." He paused and took a long suck at his cigarette. "Pheasants," he whispered softly, "is *crazy* about raisins."

"Raisins?"

"Just ordinary raisins. It's like a *mania* with them. My dad discovered that more than forty years ago, just like he discovered all three of these methods."

"I thought you said your dad was a drunk."

"Maybe he was. But he was also a great poacher, Gordon. Possibly the greatest there's ever been in the history of England. My dad studied poaching like a scientist."

"Is that so?"

"I mean it. I really mean it."

"I believe you."

"Do you know," he said, "my dad used to keep a whole flock of prime cockerels in the back yard, purely for experimental purposes."

"Cockerels?"

"That's right. And whenever he thought up some new stunt for catching a pheasant, he'd try it out on a cockerel first, to see how it worked. That's how he discovered about raisins. It's also how he invented the horsehair method."

Claud paused and glanced over his shoulder, as though to make sure there was nobody listening. "Here's how it's done," he said. "First you take a few raisins and you soak them overnight in water to make them nice and plump and juicy. Then you get a bit of good stiff horsehair and you cut it up into half-inch lengths. Then you push one of these lengths of horsehair through the middle of each raisin, so that there's about an eighth of an inch of it sticking out on either side. You follow?"

"Yes."

"Now. The old pheasant comes along and eats one of these raisins. Right? And you're watching him from behind a tree. So, what then?"

"I imagine it sticks in his throat."

"That's obvious, Gordon. But here's the amazing thing. Here's what my dad discovered. The moment this happens, the bird *never moves his feet again!* He becomes absolutely rooted to the spot, and there he stands pumping his silly neck up and down, and all you've got to do is walk calmly out from the place where you're hiding and pick him up in your hands."

"I don't believe that."

"I swear it," he said. "Once a pheasant's had the horsehair, you can fire a rifle in his ear and he won't even jump. It's just one of these unexplainable little things. But it takes a genius to discover it."

He paused, and there was a gleam of pride in his eye as he dwelt for a moment upon the memory of his father, the great inventor.

"So that's Method Number One," he said. "Method Number Two is even more simple still. All you do is you have a fishing line. Then you bait the hook with a raisin, and you fish for the pheasant just like you fish for a fish. You pay out the line about fifty yards, and you lie there on your stomach in the bushes, waiting till you get a bite. Then you haul him in."

"I don't think your father was the first to invent that one."

"It's very popular with fishermen," he said, choosing not to hear me. "Keen fishermen who can't get down to the seaside as often as they want. It gives them a bit of the old thrill."

"What is Method Number Three?" I asked.

"Ah," he said. "Number Three's a real beauty. It was the last one my dad ever invented before he passed away."

"His final great work?"

"Exactly, Gordon. And I can even remember the very day it happened—a Sunday morning it was—and suddenly my dad comes into the kitchen holding a huge white cockerel in his hands, and he says, 'I think I've got it.' There's a little smile on his face and a shine of glory in his eyes, and he comes in very soft and quiet, and he puts the bird down right in the middle of the kitchen table, and he says, 'By God, I think I've got a good one this time.' 'A good what?' Mum says, looking up from the sink. 'Horace, take that filthy bird off my table.' The cockerel has a funny little paper hat over its head, like an ice-cream cone upside down, and my dad is pointing to it proudly. 'Stroke him,' he says. 'He won't move an inch.' The cockerel starts scratching away at the paper hat with one of its feet, but the hat seems to be stuck on with glue, and it won't come off. 'No bird in the world is going to run away once you cover up his eyes,' my dad says, and he starts poking the cockerel with his finger and pushing it around on the table, but it doesn't take the slightest bit of notice. And then straightaway he takes me by the arm and marches me quickly out the door, and off we go over the fields and up into the big forest the other side of Haddenham, which used to belong to the Duke of Buckingham, and in less than two hours we get five lovely fat pheasants with no more trouble than it takes to go out and buy them in a shop."

Claud paused for breath. His eyes were huge and moist and dreamy as they gazed back into the wonderful world of his youth.

"I don't quite follow this," I said. "How did he get the paper hats over the pheasants' heads up in the woods?"

"You'd never guess it."

"I'm sure I wouldn't."

"Then here it is. First of all you dig a little hole in the ground. Then you twist a piece of paper into the shape of a cone and you fit this into the hole, hollow end upward, like a cup. Then you smear the paper cup all around the inside with birdlime, and drop in a few raisins. At the same time, you lay a trail of raisins along the ground leading up to it. Now, the old pheasant comes pecking along the trail, and when he gets to the hole, he pops his head inside to gobble the raisins, and the next thing he knows he's got a paper hat stuck over his eyes and he can't see a thing. Isn't it marvellous what some people think of, Gordon? Don't you agree?"

"Your dad was a genius," I said.

"Then take your pick. Choose whichever one of the three methods you fancy, and we'll use it tonight."

"You don't think they're all just a trifle on the crude side, do you?"

"Crude!" he cried, aghast. "Oh, my God! And who's been having roasted pheasant in the house nearly every single day for the last six months and not a penny to pay?"

He walked away toward the door of the workshop. I could see that he was deeply pained by my remark.

"Wait a minute," I said. "Don't go."

"You want to come or don't you?"

"Yes, but let me ask you something first. I've just had a bit of an idea."

"Keep it," he said. "You are talking about a subject you don't know the first thing about."

"Do you remember that bottle of sleeping pills the doc gave me last month when I had a bad back?"

"What about them?"

"Is there any reason why those wouldn't work on a pheasant?"

Claud closed his eyes and shook his head pityingly.

"Wait," I said.

"It's not worth discussing," he said. "No pheasant in the world is going to swallow those lousy red capsules. Don't you know any better than that?"

"You are forgetting the raisins," I said. "Now listen to this. We take a raisin. Then we soak it till it swells. Then we make a tiny slit in one side of it with a razor blade. Then we hollow it out a little. Then we open up one of my red capsules and pour all the powder into the raisin. Then we get a needle and cotton, and very carefully we sew up the slit. Now . . ."

Out of the corner of my eye, I saw Claud's mouth slowly beginning to open.

"Now," I said. "We have a nice, clean-looking raisin with two and a half grains of seconal inside it, and let me tell *you* something now. That's enough dope to knock the average *man* unconscious, never mind about *birds!*"

I paused for ten seconds to allow the full impact of this to strike home.

"What's more, with this method we could operate on a really grand scale. We could prepare *twenty* raisins if we felt like it, and all we'd have to do is scatter them around the feeding grounds at sunset and then walk away. Half an hour later, we'd come back, and the pills would be beginning to work, and the pheasants would be up in the branches by then, roosting, and they'd be starting to feel groggy, and soon every pheasant that had eaten *one single raisin* would keel over unconscious and fall to the ground. My dear boy, they'd be dropping out of the trees like apples, and all we'd have to do is walk around picking them up!"

Claud was staring at me, rapt. "Oh, Christ," he said softly.

"And they'd never catch us, either. We'd simply stroll through the woods, dropping a few raisins here and there as we went, and even if the keepers were *watching* us, they wouldn't notice anything."

"Gordon," he said, laying a hand on my knee, "if this thing works, it will revolutionize poaching."

"I'm glad to hear it."

"How many pills have you got left?" he asked.

"Forty-nine. There were fifty in the bottle, and I've only used one."

"Forty-nine's not enough. We want at least two hundred."

"Are you mad!" I cried.

He walked slowly away and stood by the door with his back to me, gazing at the sky. "Two hundred's the bare minimum," he said quietly. "There's really not much point in doing it unless we have two hundred."

What is it now, I wondered. What the hell's he trying to do?

"This is almost the last chance we'll have before the season opens," he said.

"I couldn't possibly get any more."

"You wouldn't want us to come back empty-handed, would you?"

"But why so *many?*"

Claud looked at me with large, innocent eyes. "Why not?" he said gently. "Do you have any objection?"

My God, I thought suddenly. The crazy bastard is out to wreck Mr. Victor Hazel's opening-day shooting party.

Mr. Hazel's party took place on the first of October every year, and it was a very famous event. Debilitated gentlemen in tweed suits, some with titles and some who were merely rich, motored in from miles around, with their gunbearers and dogs and wives, and all day long the noise of shooting rolled across the valley. There were always enough pheasants to go around, for each summer the woods were methodically restocked with dozens and dozens of young birds, at incredible expense. I had heard it said that the cost of rearing and keeping each pheasant up to the time when it was ready to be shot was well over five pounds. But to Mr. Hazel it was worth every penny of it. He became, if only for a few hours, a big cheese in a little world, and even the Lord Lieutenant of the county slapped him on the back and tried to remember his first name when he said goodbye.

"You get us two hundred of those pills," Claud said, "and then it'll be worth doing."

"I can't."

"How would it be if we just reduced the dose?" he asked. "Why couldn't we divide the contents of one capsule among four raisins?"

"I suppose you could, if you wanted to."

"But would a quarter of a capsule be strong enough for each bird?"

One simply had to admire the man's nerve. It was dangerous enough to poach a single pheasant up in those woods at this time of year, and here he was planning to knock off the bloody lot.

"A quarter would be plenty," I said.

"You're sure of that?"

"Work it out for yourself. It's all done by body weight. You'd still be giving about twenty times more than is necessary."

"Then we'll quarter the dose," he said, rubbing his hands. He paused, and calculated for a moment. "We'll have one hundred and ninety-six raisins!"

"Do you realize what that involves?" I said. "They'll take hours to prepare."

"What of it!" he cried. "We'll go tomorrow instead. We'll soak the raisins overnight and then we'll have all morning and afternoon to get them ready."

And that was precisely what we did.

We had been walking steadily for about forty minutes, and we were nearing the point where the lane curved around to the right and ran along the crest of the hill toward the big wood where the pheasants lived. There was about a mile to go.

"I don't suppose by any chance these keepers might be carrying guns?" I asked.

"All keepers carry guns," Claud said.

I had been afraid of that.

"It's for the vermin mostly," he added.

"Ah."

"Of course, there's no guarantee they won't take a pot at a poacher now and again."

"You're joking."

"Not at all. But they only do it from behind—only when you're running away. They like to pepper you in the legs at about fifty yards."

"They can't do that!" I cried. "It's a criminal offense!"

"So is poaching," Claud said.

We walked on awhile in silence. The sun was below the high hedge on our right now, and the lane was in shadow.

"You can consider yourself lucky this isn't thirty years ago," he went on. "They used to shoot you on sight in those days."

"Do you believe that?"

"I know it," he said. "There wasn't a man in the whole village who didn't have a bit of shot in him. But my dad was the champion."

"Good luck to him," I said.

"I wish to hell he was here now," Claud said, wistful. "He'd have given anything in the world to be coming with us on this job tonight."

"He could take my place," I said. "Gladly."

We had reached the crest of the hill and now we could see the wood ahead of us, huge and dark, with the sun going down behind the trees and little sparks of gold shining through.

"You'd better let me have those raisins," Claud said.

I gave him the bag, and he slid it gently into a trouser pocket.

"No talking once we're inside," he said. "Just follow me, and try not to go snapping any branches."

Five minutes later, we were there. The lane ran right up to the wood itself and then skirted the edge of it for about three hundred yards, with only a little hedge between. Claud slipped through the hedge on all fours, and I followed.

It was cool and dark inside the wood. No sunlight came in at all.

"This is spooky," I said.

"Sh-h-h!"

Claud was very tense. He was walking just ahead of me, picking his feet up high and putting them down gently on the moist ground. He kept his head moving all the time, the eyes sweeping slowly from side to side, searching for danger. I tried doing the same, but soon I began to see a keeper behind every tree, so I gave it up.

Then a large patch of sky appeared ahead of us in the roof of the forest, and I knew that this must be the clearing. Claud had told me that the clearing was the place where the young birds were introduced into the woods in early July, where they were fed and watered and guarded by the keepers, and where many of them stayed, from force of habit, until the shooting began. "There's always plenty of pheasants in the clearing," he had said.

We were now advancing in a series of quick, crouching spurts, running from tree to tree and stopping and waiting and listening and running on again, and then at last we knelt safely behind a big clump of alder, right on the edge of the clearing, and Claud grinned and nudged me in the ribs and pointed through the branches at the pheasants.

The place was absolutely stiff with birds. There must have been two hundred of them, at least, strutting around among the tree stumps.

"You see what I mean?" Claud whispered.

It was an astonishing sight—a poacher's dream come true. And how close they were! Some of them were not more than ten paces from where we were kneeling. The hens were plump and creamy brown, and so fat that their breast feathers almost brushed the ground as they walked. The cocks were slim and beautiful, with long tails and brilliant red patches around the eyes, like scarlet spectacles. I glanced at Claud. His big oxlike face was transfigured with ecstasy. The mouth was slightly open, and the eyes had a kind of glazy look about them as they stared at the pheasants.

There was a long pause. The birds made a queer rustling noise as they moved about among the dead leaves in the clearing. "Ah-ha," Claud said softly a minute later. "You see the keeper?"

"Where?"

"Over the other side, standing by that big tree. Look carefully."

"My God!"

"It's all right. He can't see *us*."

We crouched close to the ground, watching the keeper. He was a smallish man with a cap on his head and a gun under one arm. He never moved. He was like a little post standing there.

"Let's go," I whispered.

The keeper's face was shadowed by the peak of his cap, but it seemed to me that he was looking directly at us.

"I'm not staying here," I said.

"Hush!" Claud said.

Slowly, never taking his eyes from the keeper, he reached into his pocket and brought out a single raisin. He placed it in the palm of his right hand, and then quickly, with a little flick of the wrist, he threw the raisin high into the air. I watched it as it went sailing over the bushes, and I saw it land within a yard or so of two hen birds standing together beside an old tree stump. Both birds turned their heads sharply at the drop of the raisin. Then one of them hopped over and made a quick peck at the ground.

I glanced up at the keeper. He hadn't moved.

Claud threw a second raisin into the clearing; then a third, and a fourth, and a fifth. At this point, I saw the keeper turn his head away to survey the woods behind him. Quick as a flash, Claud pulled the paper bag out of his pocket and tipped a huge pile of raisins into the cup of his right hand.

"Stop," I said.

But with a great sweep of the arm he flung the whole handful high over the bushes into the clearing. They fell with a soft little patter, like raindrops on dry leaves, and every single pheasant in the place must have heard them fall. There was a flurry of wings and a rush to find the treasure.

The keeper's head flicked round as though there were a spring inside his neck. The birds were all pecking away madly at the raisins. The keeper took two quick paces forward, and for a moment I thought he was going to investigate. But then he stopped, and his face came up, and his eyes began travelling slowly around the perimeter of the clearing.

"Follow me," Claud whispered. "And *keep down*." He started crawling away swiftly on all fours, under cover of the bushes.

I went after him, and we went along like this for about a hundred yards.

"Now run," Claud said.

We got to our feet and ran, and a few minutes later we emerged through the hedge into the lovely open safety of the lane.

"It went marvellous," Claud said, breathing heavily. "Didn't it go absolutely marvellous?" The big face was scarlet and glowing with triumph. "In another five minutes, it'll be pitch-dark inside the wood, and that keeper will be sloping off home to his supper."

"I think I'll join him," I said.

"You're a great poacher," Claud said. He sat down on the grassy bank under the hedge and lit a cigarette.

The sun had set now and the sky was a pale smoke-blue, faintly glazed with yellow. In the wood behind us, the shadows and the spaces in between the trees were turning from gray to black.

"How long does a sleeping pill take to work?" Claud asked.

"Look out!" I said. "There's someone coming."

The man had appeared suddenly and silently out of the dusk, and he was only thirty yards away when I saw him.

"Another bloody keeper," Claud said.

We both looked at the keeper as he came down the lane toward us. He had a shotgun under his arm, and there was a black Labrador walking at his heels. He stopped when he was a few paces away, and the dog stopped with him and stayed behind him, watching us through the keeper's legs.

"Good evening," Claud said, nice and friendly.

This one was a tall bony man of about forty, with a swift eye and a hard cheek and hard dangerous hands.

"I know you," he said softly, coming closer. "I know the both of you."

Claud didn't answer this.

"You're from the fillin' station. Right?" His lips were thin and dry. "You're Cubbage and Hawes, and you're from the fillin' station on the main road. Right?"

"What are we playing?" Claud said. "Twenty Questions?"

The keeper took a step forward. "Beat it," he said. "Go on. Get out."

Claud sat on the bank, smoking his cigarette and looking at the keeper's feet.

"Go on," the man said. "Get out." When he spoke, the upper lip lifted above the gum, and I could see a row of small discolored teeth, one of them black, the others quince and ochre.

"This happens to be a public highway," Claud said. "Kindly do not molest us."

The keeper shifted the gun from his left arm to his right. "You're loiterin'," he said, "with intent to commit a felony. I could run you in for that."

"No, you couldn't," Claud said.

All this made me rather nervous.

"I've had my eye on you for some time," the keeper said, looking at Claud.

"It's getting late," I said. "Shall we stroll on?"

Claud flipped away his cigarette and got slowly to his feet. "All right," he said. "Let's go."

We wandered off down the lane the way we had come, leaving him standing there, and soon the man was out of sight in the half darkness behind us.

"That's the head keeper," Claud said. "His name is Rabbetts."

"Let's get the hell out," I said.

"Come in here," Claud said.

There was a gate on our left leading into a field, and we climbed over it and sat down behind the hedge.

"Mr. Rabbetts is also due for his supper," Claud said. "You mustn't worry about him."

We sat quietly behind the hedge, waiting for the keeper to walk past us on his way home. A few stars were showing, and a bright three-quarter moon was coming up over the hills behind us in the east.

"Here he is," Claud whispered. "Don't move."

The keeper came loping softly up the lane with the dog padding quick and soft-footed at his heels, and we watched them through the hedge as they went by.

"He won't be coming back tonight," Claud said.

"How do you know that?"

"A keeper never waits for you in the wood if he knows where you live. He goes to your house and hides outside and watches for you to come back."

"That's worse."

"No, it isn't. Not if you dump the loot somewhere else before you go home. He can't touch you then."

"What about the other one—the one in the clearing?"

"He's gone, too."

"You can't be sure of that."

"I've been studying these bastards for months, Gordon. Honest I have. I know all their habits. There's no danger."

A few minutes later, I reluctantly followed Claud back into the wood. It was pitch-dark in there now, and very silent, and as we moved cautiously forward, the noise of our footsteps seemed to go echoing around the walls of the forest as though we were walking in a cathedral.

"Here's where we threw the raisins," Claud said.

I peered through the bushes. The clearing lay dim and milky in the moonlight.

"You're quite sure the keeper's gone?"

"I *know* he's gone."

I could just see Claud's face under the peak of his cap—the pale lips, the soft, pale cheeks, and the large eyes with a little spark of excitement dancing in each.

"Are they roosting?" I asked.

"Yes. In the branches."

"Whereabouts?"

"All around. They don't go far."

"What do we do next?"

"We stay here and wait. I brought you a light," he added, and he handed me one of those small pocket flashlights shaped like a fountain pen. "You may need it."

I was beginning to feel better. "Shall we see if we can spot some of them sitting in the trees?" I said.

"No."

"I should like to see how they look when they're roosting."

"This isn't a nature study," Claud said. "Please be quiet."

We stood there for a long time, waiting for something to happen.

"I've just had a nasty thought," I said. "If a bird can keep its balance on a branch when it's asleep, then surely there isn't any reason why the pills should make it fall down."

Claud looked at me quick.

"After all," I said, "it's not dead. It's still only sleeping."

"It's doped," Claud said.

"But that's just a *deeper* sort of sleep. Why should we expect it to fall down just because it's in a deeper sleep?"

There was a gloomy silence.

"We should've tried it with chickens," Claud said. "My dad would've done that."

"Your dad was a genius," I said.

At that moment, there came a soft thump from the wood behind us.

"Hey!" I said.

"Sh-h-h!"

We stood listening.

Thump!

"There's another!"

It was a deep, muffled sound, as though a small bag of sand had been dropped from about shoulder height.

Thump!

"They're pheasants!" I cried.

"Wait!"

"I'm sure they're pheasants!"

Thump! Thump!

"You're right!"

We ran back into the wood.

"Where were they?" I asked.

"Over here! Two of them were over here!"

"I thought they were this way."

"Keep looking!" Claud shouted. "They can't be far."

We searched for about a minute.

"Here's one!" he called.

When I got to him, he was holding a magnificent cockbird in both hands. We examined it closely with our flashlights.

"It's doped to the gills," Claud said. "It's still alive, I can feel its heart, but it's doped to the bloody gills."

Thump!

"There's another!" he cried.

Thump! Thump!

"Two more!"

Thump!

Thump! Thump! Thump!

"Jesus Christ!"

Thump! Thump! Thump! Thump!

Thump! Thump!

All around us, the pheasants were starting to rain down out of the trees. We began rushing around madly in the dark, sweeping the ground with our flashlights.

Thump! Thump! Thump! This lot fell almost on top of me. I was right under the tree as they came down, and I found all three of them immediately—two cocks and a hen. They were limp and warm, the feathers wonderfully soft in the hand.

"Where shall I put them?" I called out. I was holding them by the legs.

"Lay them here, Gordon! Just pile them up here where it's light!"

Claud was standing on the edge of the clearing with the moonlight streaming down all over him and a great bunch of pheasants in each hand. His face was bright, his eyes big and bright and wonderful, and he was staring around him like a child who has just discovered that the whole world is made of chocolate.

Thump!

Thump! Thump!

"I don't like it," I said. "It's too many."

"It's beautiful!" he cried, and he dumped the birds he was carrying and ran off to look for more.

Thump! Thump! Thump! Thump!

Thump!

It was easy to find them now. There were one or two lying under every tree. I quickly collected six more, three in each hand, and ran back and dumped them with the others. Then six more. Then six more after that. And still they kept falling.

Claud was in a whirl of ecstasy now, dashing about like a mad ghost under the trees. I could see the beam of his flashlight waving around in the dark, and each time he found a bird he gave a little yelp of triumph.

Thump! Thump! Thump!

"Mr. Victor Hazel ought to hear this!" he called out.

"Don't shout," I said. "It frightens me."

"What?"

"Don't *shout*. There might be keepers."

"To hell with the keepers!" he cried. "They're all eating!"

For three or four minutes, the pheasants kept on falling. Then suddenly they stopped.

"Keep searching!" Claud shouted. "There's plenty more on the ground!"

"Don't you think we ought to get out while the going's good?"

"No," he said.

We went on searching. Between us, we looked under every tree within a hundred yards of the clearing—north, south, east, and west —and I think we found most of them in the end. At the collecting point, there was a pile of pheasants as big as a bonfire.

"It's a miracle," Claud said. "It's a bloody miracle." He was staring at them in a kind of trance.

"We'd better just take half a dozen each and get out quick," I said.

"I would like to count them, Gordon."

"There's no time for that."

"I must count them."

"No," I said. "Come on."

"One. Two. Three. Four . . ." He began counting them very carefully, picking up each bird in turn and laying it gently to one side. The moon was directly overhead now, and the whole clearing was brilliantly illuminated.

"I'm not standing around here like this," I said. I walked back a few paces and hid myself in the shadows, waiting for him to finish.

"A hundred and seventeen, a hundred and eighteen, a hundred and nineteen, *a hundred and twenty!*" he cried. *"One hundred and twenty birds!* It's an all-time record!"

I didn't doubt it for a moment.

"The most my dad ever got in one night was fifteen, and he was drunk for a week afterward!"

"You're the champion of the world," I said. "Are you ready now?"

"One minute," he answered, and he pulled up his sweater and began to unwind the two big white cotton sacks from around his belly. "Here's yours," he said, handing one of them to me. "Fill it up quick."

The light of the moon was so strong that I could read the small print along the base of the sack. "J. W. Crump," it said. "Keston Flour Mills, London S.W. 17."

"You don't think that bastard with the brown teeth is watching us this very moment, from behind a tree?"

"There's no chance of that," Claud said. "He's down at the filling station, like I told you, waiting for us to come home."

We started loading the pheasants into the sacks. They were soft and floppy-necked, and the skin underneath the feathers was warm.

"There'll be a taxi waiting for us in the lane," Claud said.

"What?"

"I always go back in a taxi, Gordon. Didn't you know that? A taxi is anonymous. Nobody knows who's inside a taxi except the driver. My dad taught me that."

"Which driver?"

"Charlie Kinch. He's only too glad to oblige."

We finished loading the pheasants, and I tried to hump my bulging sack onto my shoulder. My sack had about sixty birds inside it, and it must have weighed a hundredweight and a half, at least. "I can't carry this," I said. "We'll have to leave some of them behind."

"Drag it," Claud said. "Just pull it behind you."

We started off through the pitch-black woods, pulling the pheasants behind us. "We'll never make it all the way back to the village like this," I said.

"Charlie's never let me down yet," Claud said.

We came to the margin of the wood and peered through the hedge into the lane. The taxi was there, not five yards away. Claud said, "Charlie boy," very softly, and the old man behind the wheel poked his head out into the moonlight and gave us a sly, toothless grin. We slid through the hedge, dragging the sacks after us.

"Hullo!" Charlie said. "What's this?"

"It's cabbages," Claud told him. "Open the door."

Two minutes later, we were safely inside the taxi, cruising slowly down the hill toward the village.

It was all over now bar the shouting. Claud was triumphant, bursting with pride and excitement, and he kept leaning forward and tapping Charlie Kinch on the shoulder and saying, "How about it, Charlie? How about this for a haul?," and Charlie kept glancing back popeyed at the huge, bulging sacks lying on the floor between us and saying, "Jesus Christ, man! How did you do it?"

"There's six brace of them for you, Charlie," Claud said.

Charlie said, "I reckon pheasants is going to be a bit scarce up at Mr. Victor Hazel's opening-day shoot this year," and Claud said, "I imagine they are, Charlie, I imagine they are."

"What in God's name are you going to do with a hundred and twenty pheasants?" I asked.

"Put them in cold storage for the winter," Claud said. "Put them in with the dog meat in the deep freeze at the filling station."

"Not tonight, I trust?"

"No, Gordon, not tonight. We leave them at Bessie's house tonight."

"Bessie who?"

"Bessie Organ."

"Bessie *Organ!*" I was completely stunned. Mrs. Organ was the wife of the Reverend Jack Organ, the local vicar.

"Bessie always delivers my game, didn't you know that?"

"I don't know anything," I said.

"Always choose a respectable woman to deliver your game," Claud announced. "That's correct, Charlie, isn't it?"

"Bessie's a right smart girl," Charlie said.

We were driving through the village now and the street lamps were still on and the men were wandering home from the pubs. I saw Will Prattley letting himself in quietly by the side door of his fishmonger's shop, and Mrs. Prattley's head was sticking out the window just above him, but he didn't know it.

"The vicar is very partial to roasted pheasant," Claud said.

"He hangs it eighteen days," Charlie said. "Then he gives it a couple of good shakes and all the feathers drop off."

The taxi turned left and swung in through the gates of the vicarage. There were no lights on in the house, and nobody met us. Claud and I dumped the pheasants in the coal shed at the rear, and then we said goodbye to Charlie Kinch and walked back in the moonlight to the filling station, empty-handed. Whether or not Mr. Rabbetts was watching us as we went in, I do not know. We saw no sign of him.

"Here she comes," Claud said to me the next morning. He was looking through the window of the filling station.

"Who?"

"Bessie—Bessie Organ." He spoke the name proudly and with a slight proprietary air, as though he were a general referring to his bravest officer.

I followed him outside.

"Down there," he said, pointing.

Far away down the road, I could see a small female figure advancing toward us. "What's she pushing?" I asked.

Claud gave me a sly look. "There's only one safe way of delivering game," he announced, "and that's under a baby."

"Yes," I murmured. "Yes, of course."

"That'll be young Christopher Organ in the pram, aged one and a half. He's a lovely child, Gordon."

I could just make out the small dot of a baby sitting high up in the pram, which had its hood folded down.

"There's sixty or seventy pheasants at least under that little nipper," Claud said happily. "Just imagine that."

"You can't fit sixty or seventy pheasants into a pram," I said.

"You can if it's got a good deep well underneath it, and if you take out the mattress and pack them in tight, right up to the top. All you need then is a sheet. You'll be surprised how little room a pheasant takes up when it's limp."

We stood beside the pumps, waiting for Bessie Organ to arrive. It was one of those warm, windless September mornings, with a darkening sky and a smell of thunder in the air.

"Right through the village, bold as brass," Claud said. "Good old Bessie."

"She seems in rather a hurry to me."

Claud lit a new cigarette from the stub of the old one. "Bessie is never in a hurry," he said.

"She certainly isn't walking normal," I told him. "You look."

He squinted at her through the smoke of his cigarette. Then he took the cigarette out of his mouth and looked again.

"Well?" I said.

"She does seem to be going a tiny bit quick, doesn't she?" he said carefully.

"She's going damn quick."

There was a pause. Claud was beginning to stare hard at the approaching woman. "Perhaps she doesn't want to be caught in the rain, Gordon. I'll bet that's exactly what it is—she thinks it's going to rain, and she don't want the baby to get wet."

"She's *running!*" I cried. "Look!" Bessie had suddenly broken into a full sprint.

Claud stood very still, watching the woman; and in the silence that followed I fancied I could hear a baby screaming.

"There's something wrong with that baby," I said. "Listen."

At this point, Bessie was about two hundred yards away from us, but closing fast.

"Can you hear him now?" I said.

"Yes."

"He's yelling his head off."

The small shrill voice in the distance was growing louder every second—frantic, piercing, almost hysterical.

"He's having a fit," Claud announced.

"I think he must be."

"That's why she's running, Gordon. She wants to get him in here quick and put him under a cold tap."

"I'm sure you're right," I said.

Claud shifted his feet uneasily on the gravel of the driveway. "There's a thousand and one different things keep happening every day to little babies like that," he said.

"Of course."

"Whatever it is," Claud said, "I wish to Christ she'd stop running."

A long lorry loaded with bricks came up alongside of Bessie, and the driver slowed down and poked his head out the window to stare. Bessie flew on, and she was so close now that I could see her big red face, with the mouth wide open, panting for breath. I noticed she was wearing white gloves on her hands, very prim and dainty, and there was a funny little white hat to match perched right on the top of her head, like a mushroom.

Suddenly, out of the pram, straight up into the air, flew an enormous pheasant.

Claud let out a cry of horror.

The fool in the truck going along beside Bessie roared with laughter. The pheasant flapped around drunkenly for a few seconds, then it lost height and landed in the grass by the side of the road. Bessie kept on running.

Then—*whoosh!*—a second pheasant flew up out of the pram.

Then a third and a fourth. Then a fifth.

"My God!" I said. "It's the pills! They're wearing off!"

Bessie covered the last fifty yards at a tremendous pace, and she came swinging into the driveway of the filling station with birds flying up out of the pram in all directions.

"What the hell's going on?" she cried.

"Go round the back!" I shouted. "Go round the back!" But she pulled up sharp beside the first pump in the line, and before we could reach her, she had seized the screaming infant in her arms and dragged him clear.

"No! No!" Claud cried, racing toward her. "Don't lift the baby! Put him back! Hold down the sheet!" But she wasn't even listening, and with the weight of the child suddenly lifted away, a great cloud of pheasants rose up out of the pram—forty or fifty of them, at least—and the whole sky above us was filled with huge brown birds clapping their wings furiously to gain height.

Claud and I started running up and down the driveway, waving our arms to frighten them off the premises. "Go away!" we shouted. "Shoo! Go away!" But they were too dopey still to take any notice of us, and within half a minute down they came again and settled themselves like a swarm of locusts all over the front of my filling station. The place was covered with them. They sat wing to wing along the edges of the roof and on the concrete canopy that came out over the pumps, and a dozen, at least, were clinging to the sill of the office window. Some had flown down onto the rack that held the bottles of lubricating oil, and others were sliding about on the bonnets of my second-hand cars. One cockbird with a fine tail was perched superbly on top of a petrol pump, and quite a number simply squatted in the driveway at our feet, fluffing their feathers and blinking their small eyes.

Across the road, a line of cars had already started forming behind the brick lorry, and people were opening their doors and getting out and beginning to cross over to have a closer look. I glanced at my watch. It was twenty to nine. Any moment now, I thought, a large black car is going to come streaking along the road from the direction of the village, and the car will be a Rolls, and the face behind the wheel will be the great butcher's face of Mr. Victor Hazel, maker of sausages and pies.

"They near pecked him to pieces!" Bessie was shouting, clasping the screaming baby to her bosom.

"You go on home, Bessie," Claud said, white in the face.

"Lock up," I said. "Put out the sign. We've gone for the day."

TERROR AND GRIEF

❖

Niccolò Tucci

THEY travelled all the time, those two. They were so dear to us,
so afraid of not having us with them all the time—and then they
left us, with the two maids and the governess, in the big apartment
in Lugano, and they had no idea how much of the world they took
with them. We lived in terror and in grief: they would never come
back. This was true even when they went to the theatre or out to
tea without us. So much more so when they were gone for months,
and sent us postcards of the Eiffel Tower, saying, "Be good. So
many kisses to our dear little birds, will be back on the ninth." And
more postcards from Venice, with the Piazza and the pigeons, and
"Be good, we miss you so, will be back on the twelfth." And in the
meantime the whole place was empty.

We looked for them but did not look for them; we were afraid
to find them where we looked for them—behind a door, at the
piano, at the desk, in their beds, in the dining room, and even in
the street, passing by and forgetting to enter, as if they did not know
us any more. We looked for them, in places where it would have
been so horrible to find them—under a bed, in a dark corner where
not even a dog would be hiding, behind the kitchen stove, in a dark
chest in which one could not breathe. (We were, in fact, forbidden
to play inside it, and also the resemblance to a casket was most
frightening.)

When the gods of the house are away, Death takes their place.
To a child, "away" *means* "death;" he gives up hope as easily as he
will give up his best toy when a new one is handed to him. Whatever he remembers is already a sad thing, for this reason: He relives
it in its absence. He will say, with great sorrow in his voice, "Remember when I saw that dog? Oh, where is that dog now?" And it
was only yesterday.

How bravely we entered that bedroom, to make sure they were in

490

Paris and not dead, and rejoiced in the emptiness that was the only cause of our despair! But then the bedroom door had to be closed again. The door was always closed when our parents were home, so, to remind us that they were not home, it should have been left open—like the stables when the horses are out. But no. The maids said it must stay closed. And the brass door handle hanging there a bit loosely, to the left, against the panelled oak—that it should have forgotten such an old lesson, and the soft order of the hand that lowered it and pulled it from the inside!

We tried never to look at the door handle when we sat in the living room, and yet it was always present to our minds. Every sound from anywhere in the apartment, from down below in the street, was first measured against the possibility that it was the handle of the bedroom door. Dogs understand these things; nurse-maids and servant girls do not. What was there to prevent our eyes from accepting the testimony of our ears and believing that they saw what they did not see? And how could we know—how could we be sure that it would not move the tiniest fraction of an inch until they came home, our dear ones, in all their glory and splendor? How could children find peace with that door handle so still and those noises so distracting?

And then the dining room, with those two chairs empty. How can you eat when your head has been cut off? The spoon goes right to your stomach, hits it, and spills the soup on your clean suit. And you are glad, because the governess shouts at you, and that is a sufficient reason to cry.

"He is not crying because you scolded him," says the visiting friend, Mme. Kondratoff, a goddess, equal to our mother in power, beauty, and fragrance, although she favors jasmine while our mother favors a perfume called Chypre Old England. "He is sad that his parents are away," she says, and the governess, Fräulein Fischer, answers, with German logic, "If he thought of his parents at all, he would not do things that will spoil their vacation. For I will have to write and tell them. I was entrusted with the house and the children by their father—by the Doctor himself. If you wish to take over, Mme. Kondratoff, this will relieve me of a great burden. But if you are not willing to do that, then I must ask you not to side with them against me. He is crying *on purpose!*"

And even she, Mme. Kondratoff, who can scare anyone among her equals when she expresses a casual opinion, yields in front of the governess, for the sake of authority and order. "Fräulein is right.

When your parents are here, you never spill soup on your clean suit. Why do it now? Fräulein is very good to you."

Fräulein was not good to us, and we knew it. And there were four of us to hold and mold and enlarge upon that knowledge: Sonia, almost twelve, and five years my elder, and the great friend of Mme. Kondratoff's daughter Tatyana; Filippo, three years my elder, and officially in love with Tatyana; myself, also in love with Tatyana, although not quite (this was a matter of prestige); and Jules Adrien, the little one, who knew nothing of love (as if we did) but said, lisping, that he, too, was in love with Tatyana. And when the rest of us denied this, he called out to the maids, "Is it true that I am in love with Tatyana?" and they said, "Yes, it is," and threatened us with punishment if we continued to tease him. So we asked him, "Jules Adrien, is it true that you are in love with Tatyana?" And he said, very seriously, "I believe so."

Tatyana, too, had a governess, an English one, who did not like our German governess, did not like us, and did not like Tatyana when she was in our company, because our admiration and our hysterical laughter at whatever she did made her completely wild. Tatyana was not like us; she never felt unhappy. Her parents left her just as frequently as our parents left us, and she hardly seemed to notice that they were gone. She amused herself with dogs and cats, with her garden, or by nailing logs and wooden boards together, using a big hammer we were never allowed even to see her use, because hammers are dangerous. When Tatyana was with us, empty rooms lost their sacredness. Nothing existed any more but dancing and singing and violence: Cushions flew through the air; beds were jumped on; chairs became soldiers, trains, automobiles; and the most solemn portraits of dead grandparents and their own dead parents and grandparents became targets for bread pellets, for mashed potatoes. But the moment she left the house, laughter and play went with her, and the silence and the fears she had displaced came back. Not even our half brother Vladimir, twelve years my elder and the great hero of all of us, could help. Besides, much of the time he was in school. We children wandered from room to room, watched like prisoners from invisible holes and followed by the sound of our own footsteps.

There was another companion we all had in those days, who helped us a great deal—the sun. His effect was not so violent as that of the presence of Tatyana. The sadness and the longing for our parents remained but were tamed by his presence. The sun entered the living room shortly after breakfast, and at a certain moment touched the bronze frills on the handle of the door that led to our parents' bedroom. Then that handle, of which I have already spoken, lost its sinister aspect and became a source of joy, because there was a halo of light around it and a new point of brightness on the ceiling. From that handle the sun moved to the side of an inlaid buhl cabinet, and then touched the pastoral scene painted on porcelain under the face of the blue-and-bronze Sèvres clock. Also various trinkets, which reacted with blinking and signalling in rainbows on the ceiling. When this happened, the ghostly marble busts of our Russian grandparents looked less pale than usual.

In its journey around the room, the sun shone on an oil painting of Sorrento, with ruins, olive groves, pine trees, Mount Vesuvius, and the blue sea. Then on the same Russian grandparents, our mother's parents, under glass, not far from their statues—Grandmother Sophie in pastel, Grandfather Vladimir in photography, a picture of his marble bust, very close to a picture of Jupiter. Then our Italian grandparents, and our Russian great-grandparents, then Mother's elder sister Adya—proud, intelligent, beautiful (locked up against her will in an insane asylum in Potsdam by her brother). Then a sinister photograph of a huge mausoleum in the cemetery in Berlin where our Russian grandparents were buried. Other paintings, too intricate to make much sense: "The Rape of Europa," Titian's "Sacred and Profane Love." Then many smaller paintings, all with thick gilded frames and placed side by side on a background of red damask. Eventually the sun arrived at "the museum" and the piano. The museum was an eighteenth-century French cabinet, in which precious objects were displayed in casual symmetry. On the top shelf, dark medieval icons stood next to enamelled Russian ashtrays, and Greek statuettes and Greek fragments next to green Pharaohs and gold bracelets from a tomb in Egypt. The lower shelves were filled with Meissen cups and saucers, Sèvres plates, and, on the bottom shelf of all, Greek and Arabic manuscripts in brown tatters and fading characters. And Chinese jades. All very depressing. But when sunshine hit the museum, revealing how much dust had settled on it, even that airless world became friendly.

Just as we always looked for our parents in the postcards they sent us, so we looked for them in the picture books on the living-room table. "Today they are in Paris. Let's try to find them." The big green book with "Vues de Paris" in gold on the cover was placed

on the carpet and opened. Sonia turned the leaves with care, Filippo
and I prone on the floor beside her, with our elbows always too close
to the book ("Get farther back or I won't turn the next page") and
our hands cupped under our chins. Up and over and down went the
slippery page, and a new image was before us—the Rue de Rivoli
taken with a camera in full daylight, the shadows quite visible and
clouds in the sky.

"Here they are, entering this car."

"No, they are *here*. See? There's Father."

"Oh, no, you are mistaken. I think they are back here, clear outside of the page. They will reach it tomorrow."

"No, they are right here in this car, and we can't see them."

This was only a game and we knew it, and yet the longing for our
parents was such that to look at those crowds in the streets of Paris
was like being close to *them*. If anyone had told me that a new person had come into a certain page, I would have believed it—or at
least I would have looked, with an absurd hope in the back of my
mind. And I did, in fact, look every morning, knowing that this was
madness. Had those been drawings and not photography, I would
never have thought of doing such a thing, but photography was real;
that was exactly what those people *had* looked like in the Rue de
Rivoli. Only one more thing was needed—that the picture go right
on developing itself after it had been taken and after it had been
printed in this book. And someday, by means of other inventions,
such as the waves in the ether, perhaps this would be possible.
Vladimir said—and also Father had said—that scientists stumbled on
discoveries. Thus the frog of Galvani, Newton's apple, the lamp of
Galileo in the cathedral of Pisa, and the latest discoveries of that
Mme. Curie who worked with her scientist husband, as our mother
was always hoping to work with hers and never did. Where normal
people saw nothing, because it would have been madness to look
for anything there, the scientist, possessed by impossible ambitions,
had found the gift of God waiting for him, right under his eyes, as a
reward for his curiosity. And would it not be wonderful if I, a child,
made such a great discovery, moved by no other urge than to see my
dear parents? So, all alone, on the carpet in our living room, with
the book open to the picture of the corner of the Rue de Rivoli and
the Place de la Concorde, I waited for Father and Mother to appear.

While Sonia practiced the piano in the morning, Filippo and I
sat on the carpet being "good" (that is, making no noise). Jules

Adrien stayed in the kitchen with the cook and the maids—their constant entertainment. We could hear his tiny voice only when Sonia paused, but their laughter we heard, and also their wet kisses, which tore like gunshots through the corridors and were at times followed by his crying. At times, the maids sang at the top of their voices, in their thick Bolognese dialect. *"Amore . . . amore!"* they yelled. *"Baciami ancora . . ."* Or *"Son fili d'oro i tuoi capelli biondi e al boccuccia d'oro . . ."* This was forbidden when our parents were home, and a deep sense of profanation ran through us; we turned to our ancestors, Jupiter well included, to assure them that we were no part of this invasion of their sacred silence.

But we had moments of great happiness in the living room, even with all the sadness of our derelict condition. There were so many of those huge picture books on the living-room table. Filippo usually looked at two volumes on Egypt, or at some thick album of family portraits. I looked at a catalogue of the Vatican Gallery, a book on Le Roi Soleil, and a book on numismatics while Sonia did her first morning exercises; then, as soon as she began her "Gradus ad Parnassum" or her "Well-Tempered Clavichord," I put these books back on the table and took a book of mythology, leafing through it slowly but impatiently, because the thin paper covering each illustration seemed to want to stick to the plate. For me this was not a book of photographs of statues of antiquity but the house of the gods. They left it every morning to go out to their former domains, with Christ's permission; came back to it in the evening; and never left it during the night. No one had told me this; it was all my invention.

I caressed the quiet stone faces. I even kissed them lightly when I was sure no one was looking. I spoke to them, and I wished they would look at me; for they seemed so absorbed in something beyond the page and out of my reach, and I did not like it. The paper was so hard that it made a noise as I turned the pages, like fresh wood in a fireplace. And yet it was almost transparent. And the smell of that book was the smell of a very noble place, unknown to me but recognizable. And I felt that the gods were away, exactly like my parents; yet I also felt they were there and knew I was touching them with clean hands, and that even the expression on my face was one of deep respect and love. Of course, I was not unobserved; my grandparents could see me. But this was not done for them; this was done for the gods in the book. I also felt that the gods in the book were listening to the clock on the mantelpiece and to the

piano. And when Sonia played Beethoven and not Czerny or Bach,
I closed the book and did something else. Romantic music was
neither for the morning nor for the Greeks. It was for afternoons
and clouds, or else for evenings, when the gods were all back and
closed in their house.

Vladimir came home from school every day when lunch was
about to be served. We were as hungry for his presence as we were
for food. The maid, alerted in the front hall (white gloves, white
lace cap, and white apron), and the cook in the kitchen (dirty apron,
red face, big wooden spoon in hand), and a third, useless maid were
all just waiting for him. They had been busy with that soup (or that
spaghetti sauce, that meat loaf) all morning; they had discussed
whether or not to have it, bought the ingredients, washed them, cut
them up, cooked them, boiled them, spiced them—always singing
or gossiping or laughing—and it was now their right to serve the
soup or the meat loaf "at its best," as if the masters were home. But
the masters were not home, and they could not do it for us children,
whom they had the right to spank and therefore could not look up
to; or for Fräulein Fischer and Fräulein Thiess (who had lunch
with us every day, and in the afternoon tutored Sonia and Filippo),
because they were Germans; so they did it for the soup. And they
said so. They, too (how children know these things!), had great sadness in their hearts, and when they shouted at Vladimir for being
two minutes late, it was because they were so lonely for their masters, whose approval was missing, whose chairs were empty.

When the two German women, who were without the dignity of
the servant or the rights of the master—when these ruling servants
praised the soup, the serving servant sneered, and commented on
that praise in a way that was so insolent that the two ruling servants
frowned and we children had to be careful not to burst into laughter. But when we children praised the soup, then the Kitchen was
happy, and *in the soup* we met.

Fräulein Thiess insulted the maids by asking for the saltcellar,
which she shook over her plate, aiming at the food from up high, as
if she wished to punish it. Even the way she cut her meat or plunged
her spoon into her soup was a way of refusing that food, of despising
those who had prepared it with so much song. In the evening, when
Fräulein Thiess was not there, Fräulein Fischer behaved like a civilized person, but at lunch she always followed Fräulein Thiess's example. And how much they ate for lunch, those two German

women! We children were always afraid there wouldn't be anything
left on the platter for us. Huge chunks of whatever it was, and then
more, and then more, and looking carefully for the best parts while
the arm of the maid shook with rage under the serving dish. "One
of these days, I shall throw everything right into her face," the maid
would tell the cook ominously, later, and we were so anxious to see
her do it, but she never kept her promise. Fräulein Fischer and
Fräulein Thiess conversed only with each other, as if they were in
Germany and we were foreigners whom they were feeding out of
charity. "You!" Fräulein Thiess said to Vladimir. "Get some wine.
But not just one bottle—two or three. I don't like to have to repeat
this every day." And Vladimir had to go and get Father's best wine.
She knew how many bottles we still had, and wanted those—not just
wine from the barrel. We always felt like spitting on her chair after
she left the dining room, but we could not. That chair was sacred—
Mother's armchair, with the two lion heads and the fringe and the
gray leather cushion. After a while, the maid took it away and put
it in a corner, replacing it with a straight chair. But it was awful,
just the same, to see that armchair being punished in a corner.

After lunch, Vladimir retired to his room to do his Greek, Sonia
and Filippo had their two hours of lessons with Fräulein Thiess,
and the governess put Jules Adrien and me to bed in her room.

Filippo suffered from convulsions, and very often, if he had been
punished in the daytime, he would have a convulsion that night.
So he slept with the governess and Jules Adrien, like a child, although he was three years older than I, and I shared Sonia's room.
But since the lessons took place there, I had to take my afternoon
nap on Filippo's bed.

Jules Adrien and the governess snored. I stayed awake and looked
at their abandoned shapes under the covers, at the green lines of
light filming the shutters on the ceiling, and listened to the world.
If there was sunshine, I could see it, of course; the film was clearer,
and shadows came and went across the whole ceiling, like the hands
of a clock gone crazy. But I could also hear that there was sunshine;
birds became more cheerful, and flew in higher and higher circles.
If there was wind, even the voices of the children playing in the park
came to me. I tried to recognize the voices, but an electric saw
whining its way through wooden boards prevented this. Iron gates
banged. Women down in the street spoke to each other *in my room.*
If clouds arrived, not only did the film fade and lose all color and

the hands of the clock become confused but birds came closer, and chirped briefly and nervously.

Noises inside the apartment were not affected by the weather. In the afternoon, table silver was thrown uncheerfully into the drawers in the dining room; the love songs of the maids became less passionate. It was no longer "Choke me, strangle me with kisses" but, rather, "Your cruelty makes me die," and other such conclusions. Fräulein Thiess asked loud questions that reached me through thick walls, but the answers could never be heard. If they were not satisfactory, the questions were repeated, in tones of mounting anger. If the answers were passable, she shouted "At long last!" and then there was a brief silence. After a while of all this, Vladimir's violin made its entry upon the scene, and the real afternoon began. The violin sobbed, uttered long lamentations, in squeaking tones, in scratching tones, in whistling tones, and always the same notes, the same mistakes, as when a nervous hand feeling a long silken robe is stopped every time by the same button. Sunshine and clouds were absorbed by that violin. It responded to sunshine with a somnolent tone that was not at all unpleasant, but when a cloud wiped all the color from the world, then the tone became offensive.

At four o'clock the governess smiled at Jules Adrien, picked him up from his crib, and greeted him like a newcomer to a world all made for him. Speaking out of the side of her mouth, in the direction of my bed and without asking my opinion, she informed me that I was rested. Aware of the coming afternoon walk with her, I felt suddenly sleepy, and even ill. With my parents away, contact with other children in the park was frowned upon because of possible contagion; Fräulein Fischer did not want to be responsible. Also, there was a good chance that Sonia and Filippo might be punished for not knowing their lessons by being made to stay home, in which case the walk was bound to be even more boring and I would rather stay home, too, listening to them discuss ways and means of murdering Fräulein Thiess.

But no. The park it must be, with or without the elder two. And the streets were full of parents who, from a distance, looked like ours. This happened also when Father and Mother were not away, but then the possibility was real: we sometimes did meet them coming home from a luncheon or going somewhere for tea. And if not, we knew we would probably find them at home, and could say, "We saw two people in the street who looked exactly like you. We ran to them and called you, but then they were not you." This mistake was now most dangerous and had to be carefully avoided; we must never forget we were unhappy, in order not to have the few seconds of mistaken happiness that would cause us in the end to suffer much more. It was all very unnatural, and like refusing to see them. Yet it had to be done. What made it harder was that the streets bore no signs of their absence. Everything was as beautiful as ever—the huge mountains surging up from the Lake of Lugano, the ancient oak trees bent over the water, the white passenger steamers full of excursionists, the canvas-covered fishing boats, the restaurants with cheerful people sitting around bright-colored tablecloths and eating pastry, the carriages waiting in line.

The return from a walk with our parents was always a pleasure. It just could not be otherwise. We would remember and go search out our toys, even those we had found boring a little while before. And then hot chocolate, and the pleasure of taking off those heavy shoes and that stiff collar and jacket and the pants we were not allowed to soil, and of putting on our dear slippers, our dear soilable pants, our gray apron with the blue ribbon all around it and the white bear embroidered on the pocket. And then dinner and bedtime, with fairy tales—always the same, for months and months—and the forbidden laugh from bed to bed in the dark before falling asleep.

But if we were returning from a walk when our parents were away, we felt a cold current of emptiness washing against us. Our chatter stopped at some distance from home, and we had a tight, choking sensation when we entered the garden. This probably explains why I so often hit my younger brother over the head just as we got home from a walk. Either he spoke about something that he knew was a secret, or he asked questions he shouldn't have asked, or he named the one thing that must forever stay unnamed. So I had to hit him.

Sonia and Filippo had a way of defending themselves against misery. They formed a twindom, walked arm in arm, and said to me, "You cannot speak to us, we are twins." After that, I was forced to walk with the governess, alongside that white-and-blue baby carriage in which Jules Adrien sat like an old lady, watching the world with tired eyes; or if he walked, then it was very slowly, and the governess spoke always to him, never to me, except to speak *of* him: He was too small to run, he was too small to understand. But I was too small to run all by myself; I was too small to understand why *he* was too small to understand. It was all very childish. I was even

too small to understand why the other two were big enough to behave like small children and pretend they were twins when they
were not.

In the meantime, Sonia and Filippo disappeared behind a tree,
then reappeared, and laughed, and disappeared behind another tree,
telling each other more and more secrets from which I was excluded.
And in this way they got home without feeling the current of
emptiness. As we took off our coats in the front hall, the governess
said to Jules Adrien, "Go to your room. There is a big surprise for
you. Your Teddy bear has been waiting for you all this time!"

I was too big for such lies, and yet too small to be left—and I was
left—like an orphan in the front hall. Had she said that my toys
were waiting for me, too, I would have gone to keep them company.
But this way I just followed my brother and took the Teddy bear
away from him, and threw it on top of a dusty cupboard, from
which it could be got down only with the help of a ladder. To justify
myself, I said, "He does not like his parents! First he cries like a
fool; then he forgets them. All he likes is his Teddy bear."

And in spite of my reasons I was punished: "No chocolate for
you!" And again they all tried to make me understand that he was
still too small to understand. "*He* loves his parents, but you don't!"
the governess said. "And I will write to them tonight. This will
make them very sad."

Jules Adrien was at once reminded of his parents, and began to
look for them. "Poor darling!" the maids would cry. "He was trying to reach the handle of that bedroom door! He wanted to see if
his Mama and Papa had gone to bed!"

I didn't blame Sonia and Filippo for not trying to defend me.
Children who live in terror very quickly adapt themselves to the
standards of terror. Whoever is not wrong in the eyes of the authorities has no reason to help those who are wrong. He enjoys the privilege of being right, for once, and wishes to stay right, so he does
nothing, even if it is clear to him that great injustice has been done.
He never knows what makes him right or wrong in the eyes of the
authorities, so he just thinks he does not know why his persecuted
brother is wrong. And out of curiosity, rather than hate, he wants to
see his brother really in the wrong. Also, it is a relief, since that
alone can put an end to his feeling that he is a witness to an injustice. The inversion of all moral standards, which causes so much
trouble later in life, is present from the very beginning. "He is
wrong because he has been punished," not "He is punished because

he has done wrong." And the victim accepts it, too. In my brother's and sister's eyes I was wrong, and in my own eyes, too. That was what made me angry. I could find peace only if I was punished, and made to suffer more than I deserved, and then, having paid my debt and plenty more, I could make the others suffer with the sight of my suffering.

There was something religious in all this—the acceptance of fate and a repayment to the gods of ten times the price, to shame them for their cruelty. But such a system—which an adult can perceive rationally without feeling a thing, while a child feels it blindly—can work only if there are gods the child can go to. When the altars are empty, who will accept his tears and who console him? Not, certainly, the maids with their red hands and their short nails and their breath charged with garlic. And not the governess with her mentholated breath and the revolting smell of perspiration all around her. Who, then? Not other victims like himself. They have no right to comfort him; they are not gods. Perhaps a half-god, if he would: Vladimir. He sometimes let me come into his room and cry, but at other times he just did not want to be bothered with the lengthy explanations of the maids and the governess's "Don't let him tell you he was punished without reason. Do you know what he did?" and the next day Fräulein Thiess scolding him for interfering with the task of the governess. So when I opened the door, he would sometimes not lift his head from his books, or he would say, "Go away, you bad boy!"

I left, gulping down my tears, and really became bad. I did all sorts of things I was not likely to be punished for if no one saw me, and they were the worst things in the world: I insulted—not my father and mother (that I reserved for the great occasions) but my maternal grandparents, but much more my grandmother than my grandfather, because he was beyond reach of even my mother's tears (he had died when she was eleven) while my grandmother was extremely close, to us and to God. She blinked from a small star. (I still see it halfway between the center of the sky and the horizon —nearer the top, though.) And when one of us misbehaved, we were told, "Your grandmother is sad now. Her star is crying." And, of course, she saw everything. Like God. So I made faces at her marble bust, first; then at various pictures of her, but not at the picture of her tomb in Berlin, for I was superstitious. I believed that if I did anything there, it would be like touching an electric wire; God, not she, would make me die at once. And I repeated, "I don't *care!* I don't *care!* I don't *care!*" Then I went to a small table and picked up a framed ivory miniature of my Aunt Adya, the madwoman in Potsdam, and shook it until I had turned her upside down. The miniature never stayed glued to its velvet background, and it was like one of those Japanese puzzles children play with.

And finally, as I grew tired of all this, I went to my book, the house of the Greek gods, and leafed through it. And the gods, walking high in the light, on soft ground, and looking sidewise, not at me, or else looking way above my head—the gods stood there in their great beauty, waiting for nothing, unwilling to judge me or to hear me, and it was they who gave me permission to live again.

This happened to me almost every day, or at least twice a week, with small variations, and yet I could never go to my Greek gods first. I first had to curse my own family gods and to upset Aunt Adya; only then did I remember where help came from, while the room grew so still that even the clock on the mantelpiece was heard again, mincing away its tiny grains of time that covered up the ruins of a bad day.

If the governess or the maids or Vladimir, surprised by that great silence, peeped in to see what I was doing, I did not turn my head, and it was not hypocrisy that made me act that way. I was finally at peace, the tears I had kept back were dry, the expression of hate was still present on my face but held, weakly, from the inside, and slowly becoming an expression of interest in outside things, no longer focussed on those images of murder and destruction that my hate had produced. I was again an onlooker, and my grandmother could see that I was good.

The daylight faded on those pages until details were hardly recognizable, but I went on feeling the presence of the gods, while from the kitchen came a smell of good food that also was a form of forgiveness. Then, as the smell grew stronger and the dark thicker, lights went on in the corridor and the best moment of the day began. Vladimir interrupted his homework, Sonia and Filippo interrupted theirs, Jules Adrien joined them from the kitchen; only I was missing. They came and called me, and at first I said no, putting back into my voice some of the hate I no longer had, for reasons of dignity. But from that moment on, I waited more and more anxiously for them to come again and tell me I must not act that way, and even to pull me by the arm and force me to go with them. And if they did, because they needed me as a partner in their games, I joined them, first as a spectator, a bit held back by shame, and then as a participant, but still with a certain restraint, turning somersaults on the carpet without laughing, as if this were a funeral with a rather exceptional ritual, not just a game. And I tried to stay far from Jules Adrien, lest I hurt him again without meaning to. Trouble seemed to emanate from me, especially in my contacts with him.

If for some reason they failed to insist enough, then I was stuck in the dark, accumulating new reason for unhappiness, hating them all, while they had a good time and I did not. And when I was called to supper, I walked into the dining room all wrapped up in my hurt dignity, with my hands behind my back, like a thinker. But the food and Vladimir usually brought me around; Vladimir was so wonderful. Also, the fact that Fräulein Thiess was not with us in the evening made things easier for him; she would never have tolerated all his stunts. "Where is Vladimir?" he would ask. And if we said "But look, he is here!" and touched his arm, his coat, his face, he would say, "No, no, this is me, this is not Vladimir. Go to his room and call him!" So we went to his room and came back and reported that he was not there. "Where has he gone?" Vladimir asked. "He must be hiding there. I'll find him." Now we all left the table; even the governess came with us. And the maids, in a procession. At his door, he turned to us, to announce what he would do to Vladimir for failing to come to supper. Then he entered quickly, closing the door behind him, and there followed a fight, with blows and groans and angry words, furniture thrown about. Finally, he emerged again, with his hair ruffled, a black eye (made with ink), marks of blows on his face, his necktie untied, his shirt torn, and a face much like mine when I was in one of my bad moods, and he marched to the dining room, followed by all of us, and sat down, his growls, as he ate, like thunder in the distance. And if we asked him "Where is Myself now?" he would tell us the most horrible stories of how Myself had been thrown out of the window and he hoped he was dead. Or he would suddenly remember that *he* was Myself, and act as if Vladimir had vanished all of a sudden. There was no end to entertainment. And though "normally" we had to be either threatened or bribed into eating, because the absence of our parents depressed us so, when Vladimir did his stunts we ate so much that the cook came into the dining room to thank us, and kissed us passionately, and called us all the most endearing names in her strange dialect. We went to bed so exhausted, yet so deliriously happy, that we still tried to laugh when our eyes had closed and the first snores came into our open mouth with the next breath.

But Vladimir was not only a clown; he was also a great scholar, a great painter, a great musician, a great toymaker, and a good and just man. No one could cut my fingernails as he did.

One day the maids, Rina and Ida, promised us that—if we were good, of course—we could go the next morning, with them, to the famous fair of San Provino, and they would buy us whistles and the Sun-and-Moon drum—a paper drum, mounted on a long stick, with the face of the sun on one side and the face of the moon on the other. I had already had one such portable Sun-Moon, but it had been punched by Filippo, and I wanted very much to get another. As I got up from my theoretical nap that afternoon, I knew there was danger ahead, and to avert it I decided to be particularly nice to Jules Adrien, and chose for my outburst of kindness the hallway next to the kitchen, where the maids could surprise me treating him just as affectionately as they did. "You are so *nice!*" I said to him. "You are the most beautiful baby in the whole world!"

I repeated this several times, because it seemed to me, from the maids' chatter in the kitchen, that they had missed this exceptional spectacle. I then tried to kiss him, but he did not want to be kissed, he wanted to go into the kitchen. I asked him whether he did not want to be carried on my shoulders, the way Vladimir carried him, making him tall enough to touch the crystal flowers of the chandelier. He did want to. So I helped him climb on a chair in the library, and I knelt down in front of it. Then I got him to put his legs around my neck, and, holding him by the hands, I slowly raised myself on my knees. But, alas, he was too heavy; I lost my balance and down we both went, flat on our faces. I cut my lip, and it bled, but he broke one of his front teeth and hit a sharp edge of a library shelf with such force that it sounded as if his skull had been split open.

At once, everyone was around us, neglecting me and taking care of him. The governess carried him, still screaming, off to her room and closed the door. After that, nothing but silence. I was aware that there would be no outing to San Provino for me now, and was resigned to that, but I wanted to know how my brother was. I was afraid I might have hurt him badly; I might even have killed him. This was my only worry. The maids saw things differently. Because this had happened to me, it was my fault, not my misfortune, and I was not to be allowed to know. I cried, "I have a right to know! I did not do it on purpose!"

"You always do these things on purpose!" Rina said.

"No!"

"Yes!"

"No!"

I went upstairs, and she followed me, and stopped me in front of the closed door.

"Get out of here or you'll be spanked!"

"I will not! I want to know!"

Rina hit me, and I hit back, with force, but missed her cheek. Instead, I scratched her eyelid, and she went wild. I ducked, she hit the doorframe with her open hand, and it hurt. "I'll get you yet," she said, nursing her hand, but in the meantime I had thrown open the door and seen that Jules Adrien was all right. The governess held him between her knees and was searching his head with a comb, looking for traces of blood under that cloud of curls. He was playing his role again—touching his head and saying, "Bad boy. He hit me."

That took care of my fears; now I must defend myself. "I did not do it on purpose and he knows it!" I shouted into the room, ready to run away at the first sign of danger.

Rina shouted at me, "He might still become an idiot! And that will be your fault!"

This made me laugh, and she chased me downstairs and as far as the front hall, where she caught me and started cuffing me. Just then the door opened and Fräulein Thiess appeared; she had forgotten her glasses. Fräulein Thiess knew very little Italian, and Rina knew no German at all. She hated Fräulein Thiess for her habit of hitting Filippo and Sonia on their fingertips with a ruler, and prided herself on the fact that she only spanked them, or, very rarely, boxed their ears.

"That boy is possessed by the Devil!" she cried now. "If he were only sorry when he has done something wrong! But you can never make him apologize. He doesn't even cry when you punish him!" This was all translated to Fräulein Thiess by Sonia and Filippo, and I was enjoying it greatly. First of all, to be known as a child that never cries had always been my greatest dream, because I did cry all the time, in secret. And, second, now I was in the hands of Fräulein Thiess.

I must explain that Fräulein Thiess had always been extremely fair in her injustice. Sonia and Filippo were her charges. All her cruelty, her hate, was concentrated on them. She never noticed my presence. Jules Adrien and I were within the field of competence of the maids and the governess, and if, instead of feeding us, they had placed us on a mantelpiece and dusted us like bronze statuettes, she would not have felt called on to interfere. Not being treated cruelly by Fräulein Thiess had its disadvantages, in terms of honor. Sonia and Filippo loved to tell me about her cruelty, and I knew that some of these stories were pure invention, but every time Fräulein really did something cruel to them, it was a matter of envy to me. What greater privilege, since I was going to be punished anyway, than to be punished by her? I would complain of the same enemy as my elder brother and sister. Perhaps I would become a twin forever.

When Sonia and Filippo confirmed the fact of my never crying, Fräulein Thiess explained, like a teacher addressing a classroom, "But that is very simple. There are ways to make a bad boy sorry. You sit there," she said to me, almost kindly, and I sat down on one of those chairs that are fated never to be sat on, because they are placed in a corridor, where there is no reason to sit down. She asked whether I was allowed to run about the house when I was being punished. Sonia and Filippo and the maid all said yes, and Fräulein Thiess shook her head disapprovingly.

"If we put him in a closet, he would break everything in it," said the maid, who did not want to see me shut up in the dark. Fräulein Thiess asked whether I played with my toys when I was being punished. They said no, and were surprised at their discovery. The fact that they were surprised made me feel superior.

"What does he do, then?"

"Nothing bad," said the maid, who was beginning to forget her anger. "He is very quiet. He becomes good again after a couple of hours."

"Where does he spend these hours?"

"Oh, in the living room."

"Doing what?"

"Looking at books."

"What books?"

"Any of those books with pictures."

"Is there one he prefers?"

No one wanted to denounce me. Sonia told me later that they would have named any book except the book of mythology. But I ruined myself by my impatience. "It's on the living-room table!" I shouted.

"All right," Fräulein Thiess said. "Now you will show me which one it is."

Acting as if under a spell, and aware of the unusual quiet, I walked into the living room, followed by everybody else. "It is *my* book," I mumbled. "My mother has left it to me in her will." Our mother had inscribed every book, every trinket in the house, to one or another of us, in order to avoid contention among the heirs.

"You seem to be hoping for your mother's death," Fräulein Thiess said.

"That is not true!"

"Remember that I am not your mother," Fräulein Thiess said. "*She* may allow you to speak that way, but I do not. Whatever I have said *is* true. Understand?"

"Yes."

"All right, now show me the book," she said gently.

I had made up my mind to resist, but her kindness again confused me and won me over.

"Forgive me for repeating my request," she said, as if I were a grown person.

"Oh," I said, and went straight to the table, touched the book, and said, "Here. It is mine. My name is in it."

She opened the book and saw my mother's inscription—"To my dear son," and so on. "Well," she said, "that can always be changed. She can inscribe it to your little brother, for example. What would you say to that? Don't you think it would be a good idea?"

"If she did that, I would burn it."

"You would? How interesting. Will you repeat that, please? What did you say you would do?"

"Scratch it."

"No, no, I heard another word before. What was it?"

Silence.

"Will you please answer my question?"

"Burn."

"Burn what?"

"That."

"That book, you mean?"

"Um."

"Very well, you may do it now." She turned to Sonia, and said, "Bring us some matches, please."

Matches, for us? That was unheard of. *"Messer, Gabel, Schere,
Licht,/Sind für kleine Kinder nicht"* was our adage: No knives, no
forks, no scissors, no light. Sonia hesitated. Filippo, who was close
to me, was pale and trembling. He kept mumbling, "You would not
dare!"—because he hoped I would. And I had never been more
scared. The maids were very worried, too; there was an atmosphere
of madness at that moment.

"Will you bring me some matches?" said Fräulein Thiess again.
"He will not do it."

And I said, "Yes, I will!"—meaning, Please believe me, and don't
ask me to actually do it.

The maids protested, and Fräulein Thiess said, "Never mind.
The police are going to take him to jail."

It never occurred to me that she was lying. Before Sonia could
bring me the matches, I scratched the red leather binding with my
nails. Filippo leaned over the book, horrified and fascinated, and
said, "Look! Look what he has done!"

Fräulein Thiess pushed him away roughly and said, "You shut
up, if you don't want to be arrested, too." Then she looked at the
scratch and said, sneering, "That's nothing. He is a coward. I knew
he had no courage!"

These words went straight to the heart of everyone of us. It was
as if she had said that all Italians are cowards. To prove to her that
Italians are not cowards, I crumpled page after page, and made a
long scratch on the face of a god, after which she took the book
away from me.

Now that I had proved what I was capable of, I could make any
claims—in fact, I had to, for the shame was too consuming.

"All right," I said, "and I am going to break everything!" I
started toward a Sèvres lamp that stood on a shaky piece of furniture next to the piano, and knew that after I had broken the lamp
my next move would be to pull the bust of my grandfather down
on me, so it would kill me.

Like a blessing from Heaven came a hailstorm of blows over my
head, and from unknown hands, and I was happy. I only hoped I
would be maimed forever, made blind or deaf, but the blows
stopped too soon, and I looked up and realized it was Vladimir,
who had stepped in and taken over the role of our father. "You
come with me," he said, squeezing my arm so that it hurt (but not
enough, never enough). Then he asked Fräulein Thiess to give him
the red book, promising her that he would take care of that, too.

"Leave it to me!" he said. "He will never see that book again." And he pushed me in front of him, all the way to his room.

After he had locked the door from the inside, he turned around and said, "What ugly things to do!"—but calmly, conversationally, as if he and I were talking about a third person, whose behavior had been shocking. At last, someone who agreed with me. How I cried in his hands, and how grateful I was that they were clean!

"Want to see something?" he said. He stood facing the door, and said, "Fräulein Thiess?" Then he made the most forbidden noises with his lips and his hands, then he repeated what she had said about taking me to jail, imitating her voice, and then more forbidden noises and gestures, but I was still so shaken that it took me a long time before I could begin to laugh.

I spent over two hours with him in that locked room. He pushed his homework aside and showed me all his best toys, which we were never even allowed to look at, even with our hands behind our backs, lest we feel tempted to touch them—toys he no longer played with but still kept, letting the echo of his childhood slowly die away in their metal. He showed me a toy steam engine of the most intricate make, mounted on his desk with screws, and it actually worked, but you had to use matches to light it; and his precious automobile, with tires, trumpets, handles, curtains, even the chauffeur and the people in their seats, looking aghast from pink porcelain faces; and a real Eiffel Tower he himself had put together, piece by piece, and never yet taken apart. He showed me his scientific instruments: the prism through which a ray of sunlight became colors; the large magnifying lens through which sunlight became fire if concentrated on a piece of paper, or even on a table. Then he told me that an ancient Greek scientist named Archimedes had used that lens (it seemed too new) to burn the ships of the Romans who were coming to take Syracuse. He got down his bound volumes of *Das Neue Universum*, a German magazine, with gold sunrays and planets on the covers, and showed me pictures: the skyscrapers of New York at night, with lightning hitting them; a tornado in America; iron foundries with white-hot iron making sparks; sea shells and strange fish deep under water; icebergs and icebreakers; wildlife. Then he taught me how to hold the violin and made me play a note, and when the squeakiest sound was heard, he said that I had talent. But no matter what he said or did, I could not help yielding to my despair again. And, in a way, I did not want to be consoled, because I knew that when Father and Mother heard what I had done to my Greek gods, there would be a most terrible scene—not accompanied by blows but marked by solemn words and the sight of my mother in tears—and I preferred to suffer right away and as much as I could. I knew that two weeks from now I wouldn't care so deeply, and so, in partial payment for that debt of remorse, I was offering Vladimir the best fruits of my sorrow now, while I had the money, so to speak. It is strange how a child will calculate these things.

Vladimir set to work on the red leather binding—first with red ink, then with brown shoe polish—and when he was finished, hardly a trace of the damage could be seen. As for the pages that had been crumpled, the plate that had scratches on it, he said he would work on them the next day, with an eraser and a hot iron. He kept assuring me that everything would be all right, and he said he would tell my father that Fräulein Thiess was a bad woman and have her chased away. In the end, just before we went down to dinner, he did the most extraordinary thing; he said to me that, on condition I stop crying, he would make me his twin. But in secret, and only as long as I deserved it.

The moment I heard this, I felt infinitely tired—so tired I could hardly keep my eyes open. The honor was too great. I felt unworthy, did not know how to behave, and was so afraid he might judge me a child after all, and take it back, when he saw my embarrassment. At dinner, I did not look at him or address a word to him, so he would realize that once I had a secret, I could act as if I did not even know it. The news, as I was being put to bed, that we would all (no exception mentioned) go to San Provino the next morning at seven left me indifferent.

A letter addressed to all of us telling us of the beauty of the Hungarian forests and plains was followed by another, in which Mother described a sunrise in the woods, with the birds singing to announce the break of day, and this, in turn, by a postcard addressed to Sonia, from which we learned, in a P.S., that our parents were not going to Greece after all but were coming home to be with us, and quite soon. This news made everything different. It was like Easter for us—a feast of Resurrection. Every single object in the house had to be polished, the curtains aired, the rugs beaten on the terrace. The floors shone like mirrors, and everything smelled clean and new and peaceful.

Then came the preparation of presents, each of us working in his room, either learning a poem by heart or making a drawing or preparing some object for their personal use—a folder for their letters, a ring for their napkin, an embroidered doily for their night table.

The maids were wild with joy at the thought that their masters were returning and they would no longer be under the surveillance of half-maids or of foreign spies (as they called any friend of the family who, on the excuse of paying us a visit, came to see how things were in the house).

Given the atmosphere of joy of those last days, there was no excuse for being bad, and, conversely, the threats of "writing to your parents" or "telling them on their return" no longer worked. Nothing would have been more unpleasant for the maids than to have to report that one of us had misbehaved. Filippo must have felt this, or he would not have chosen that moment to act as he did. Why did he have to do it? Especially when he was always so submissive, and his revolt came when everything else had worked out for the best. One day, for various crimes and misdemeanors at the lunch table, he was slapped on his wrists by the governess, rejected by us silently as a brother, and sent to his room.

Right after this incident, as we were walking out of the dining room—Sonia to prepare for her lesson, I for my nap, and Vladimir for his homework—Fräulein Thiess said, "Now, before we start our lesson, let's put my poem on your father's desk, together with the other presents." And then, forgetting that he had just been banished from the world of good children, "Where is Filippo?"

I ran to call him, and urged him to be quick, quick, or we would get there after she had already put her poem on the desk. He took such a long time buttoning his shirt and putting on his coat that I finally said, "I am not going to wait for you."

"All right, don't wait," he said. "I know the way."

"Bad boy," I said, and left the room.

They had not waited for me; they were all in the bedroom, in front of Father's desk, and Fräulein Thiess was inspecting our presents. "You cannot have the same flowers grow on trees and in the grass," she said, speaking of my portrait of Father and Mother in a forest in Hungary, in the act of caressing a deer. "And then, your parents are too small. Either make their heads smaller or their bodies much bigger."

I did not know what to say. "Must I change everything?" I asked.

"No," she said. "But next time you should remember these things. You still have a great deal to learn." She then found two mistakes

in my letter; said that Filippo should rewrite his because the calligraphy was too childish; praised Vladimir's drawing of an arch
with columns, flower capitals, statues, and an inscription to our
parents that looked as if it were written in marble; praised Sonia's
embroidery, and even the embroidery attributed to Jules Adrien
but actually the work of the maids. Only then did she allow us to
admire her own work—the perfect calligraphy, the elaborate Gothic
initials, and the spotless paper. Filippo did not seem interested at
all. He stood back, looking amused, and that disturbed me. Did he
know something about Fräulein Thiess we did not know? Was her
work really good or should we laugh at it? I asked him in a whisper,
while Fräulein Thiess occupied the whole front of the desk with
her body, and Vladimir and Sonia were giving her poem the best
place in the display, and he said, "I can do something much more
beautiful."

"What?"

"This."

He did something I prefer not to describe. I could not even ask
him not to do it; she would have heard me. But Vladimir caught
a glimpse of us and pinched his arm.

"See?" Fräulein Thiess was saying. "This is the way to write. I
did this all in India ink, without staining my hands."

We stood looking at the paper, deeply impressed—all except
Filippo.

"Well?" she asked him. "Do you like it or don't you?"

He smiled, and said nothing.

"Aha, I see. I was doing you a special favor by asking you if you
liked it or not," she said. "I don't have to ask a stupid little boy if
my writing is good." She took a deep breath and shouted, "Out of
here, now! And get your books for the lesson!"

The next day was a Sunday. We were to go to a village called
Cadro, visit a cousin of one of the maids, spend the morning there,
gathering flowers to decorate the house with, and come back in the
afternoon. The maids were worried lest Filippo ruin all our plans
and force us to stay home. They hated him already, at the mere
thought of this possibility.

I listened at the door of my room and heard Fräulein Thiess say
she would not give Sonia and Filippo any homework, provided they
did their dictation without a mistake. I ran to the kitchen to report
that everything was all right. But just as I was saying this, a yell of
indignation came from my room. "Is that an 'm'?" Silence. "Is that

an 'm'? Answer now." And Filippo still did not answer. Soon the
pounding of fists on the table was heard, and then silence again.
But a few seconds later, doors were flung open and banged, and
Sonia appeared in the kitchen, asking for lemon. Filippo had dipped
his pen into his inkwell so angrily that he had disseminated stains
of ink of all sizes on Fräulein Thiess, on himself, on the books, on
Sonia's work and his own. And again he had laughed. Sonia was out
of her wits. Now she must copy the whole page over again, and tomorrow there would be no excursion to Cadro.

Fräulein Thiess decided to give Filippo a last chance, in spite of
everything. If he copied that page he had spotted with ink blots
a hundred times that afternoon without a single mistake, she would
still let him go to Cadro with us the next day. But if he failed to
do so, then he must go all the same, carrying a big sign over his
forehead, on which she wrote the words *"Ich bin ein Esel."* That
would teach him a lesson.

But he was incorrigible. Instead of doing his homework and getting it over with, so he could go to Cadro in the morning, he sat
there writing dirty words on the pages of his notebook, on his hands,
on his shirtsleeves, on the table, even on the wall, and each time
he did one of these things, my fear and horror became greater, and
at the same time a sense of anguish gripping me at the throat made
me a part of these crimes. I felt sorry for everybody—for him, for
Fräulein Thiess, for our parents—until I needed consolation more
than he did. Now for the first time I could see myself as others saw
me in my bad moments. The amused smile on his face, his hateful
remarks, his cold acceptance of the fact that he was a born criminal
and that nothing could be done about it.

His crimes were discovered, of course, and he was punished at
once: no hot chocolate for him. Sonia and I had formed an eternal
twindom that was never going to be broken. And we no longer
bothered to notice his presence.

We were just beginning to enjoy our chocolate with yellow corn
bread, butter, and marmalade when the bell rang, and who walked
in? Mme. Kondratoff. She was back from a long trip, had seen our
parents weeks before, somewhere in Germany, and was wondering
whether they had returned or not. We were instantly around her
asking questions, and she suddenly asked why Filippo continued to
sit off by himself in a corner. So we began to tell on him, we and
the maids, and he looked rather worried now. She listened for a
while, cupping her hand around her ear (she was hard of hearing)

and seeming quite indignant. Suddenly she said, "Very well, I know, I know." And without waiting for the rest of the indictment, she marched toward him, grabbed him rudely by the shoulders, and kissed him on his eyes, on his cheeks, on his hair. Then she said to him, "Come, sit down here and have a cup of hot chocolate with me."

Two cups were brought, corn bread, butter, and marmalade were given them, and they ate while we looked on, not knowing what to think.

On the last day, every vase in the apartment was filled with flowers. The accumulation of mail was placed on Father's desk, with our presents. And then we had to decide the question of who would go to the station to meet them. Would it not be much better to wait for them at home? This debate had begun the evening before, and it went on for each of us in his dreams. Go to the station and not tell them what awaited them at home, or stay home with our presents?

Filippo had convulsions that night, I a nightmare (the two guilty ones who had something to hide). Sonia and Jules Adrien had funny dreams and told them at breakfast. Fräulein Fischer, Ida, Rina, and even Fräulein Thiess had all been visited more or less openly by that mysterious thing Good Counsel, which comes only in sleep, and to all it had said, "No one at the station." As the time of our great separation wore itself to an end, we argued, but the arguments went on only on the thinnest surface of our minds—only with words —and then even the words lost all their meaning. It became difficult for us to remember their meaning. We asked questions, and when the answer came we were surprised, because we had forgotten our own question. Images of that doorbell or that noise of the carriage in the street—auditive images intruded all the time, and charged our heart with heaviness. In the end, we were ready—just ready, nothing else, and so ready that each minute seemed a delay. And yet we knew that there was still an hour, then a half hour, then twenty-five minutes, then twenty-four. Time seemed to grow tired, sick, behind the face of the clock. What was wrong with those hands? And when it turned out that they were late—first five, then ten, then thirty minutes late—we could not speak. Why were they late? What had happened? Had this anything to do with God? And therefore with our punishment? Vladimir "directed" the train traffic from the window: "I heard a whistle. That must be a freight train. It is

waiting at the red signal, and behind it is the Paris train. . . . Yes.
. . . Did you hear it, too? There it goes again. . . . See the smoke?
No, that smoke is coming from some freight train. But that smoke
there! Wait! Hear it? Yes. That is it."

We played a similar game with the carriages that passed under
our windows. "No, that is something else. I know it cannot stop.
Wasn't I right?" "How about this one?" "I don't know." "But it
sounds as if it were to stop here." "One cannot tell. No, it won't
stop. Besides, the train has not arrived, so why should it?" When
the bell rang, neither whistles nor smoke nor carriages had been
found promising, but they were there. There could be no mistake.
The maids ran down the stairs, and we could hear their shrieks of
joy, and then words, voices, *their* voices. And now they came upstairs, yes, they came, yes, here, right here.

The wound was closed.

"How you have grown!" they said, and we stood very erect, to
exhibit every millimetre, and cheated a bit, by slightly lifting ourselves on our tiptoes. That was our first surprise—to have grown
taller without knowing it. But they, too, seemed to have grown. She
had a hat so huge and with so many feathers that it looked like the
clouds of that oncoming thunderstorm in the pastoral scene over my
father's writing desk. Gray feathers, too. And Father's neck in a stiff
collar was longer than the one he had before leaving. But otherwise
they surprised us by being all right there in front of us, collected in
their physical presence—not in ten rooms at once and outside, too,
but in one little portion of one room. And when they moved from
one place, they were gone to another. This was a second surprise.
And our impatience to exchange presents with them. In what suitcase would we find ours?

"Wait till you see what awaits you in that room!"

Entering their bedroom, they saw the stately display on the desk
and said, "Now, what *is that?*"

"Oh, nothing, nothing!"

And now the anguish. Would they appreciate every present as it
deserved? Would they know what it had cost, first in invention, then
in work?

They had just begun to read the inscriptions on their presents
when the sight of an envelope killed everything. They grabbed it—
almost tearing it from each other's hands, like children—opened it
nervously, read it together, looked at each other, making big eyes,
and then whispered to each other.

"Out of here, children! Out! Out, please!" said our father. "Your mother is very tired."

"Oh, no!" she said, suddenly tired. "I am not. What nice presents! How thoughtful of you all! Really, very, very thoughtful! We will examine everything in detail tonight. And, by the way, who forwarded the mail to us while we were away?"

Exiled to our rooms, with our governess now officially in charge, we waited and waited for it to be established who had neglected the forwarding of that important letter, and then for the endless flow of self-justification from the guilty non-forwarder to be stopped. ("Enough of this now, please! It is not important! We told you now merely so you'll remember in the future. Please! We have other worries now!") The only difference between this and their absence was that then the sacred character had abandoned the house and every single object of the house. Now that the gods were back, to us human beings was given nothing but a wise instinct to stay out of their way as long as there was thunder in the high regions.

And thunder did roll down the noble peaks, like trunks on stairways. Who had told them that Filippo went to Cadro wearing a sign on his forehead saying that he was a donkey we never knew. We suspected Vladimir, but were told by the highest authority in the house to stop guessing. Vladimir was no spy, they said. At the same time, whoever did not report everything to the highest authority in the house was guiltier even than he who had done wrong. There must be discipline and order in a loving family. "If your own brother has done wrong, who but his loving parents can right him again? Does he need your protection against those who love both you and him and who alone can tell what is best for you?"

Thus it could not have been Vladimir, though he was liable to be punished if he did not tell everything, and it was not the governess and not the maids. ("Do we, a loving family, need foreign spies or illiterate people to get the truth about our loving children? Is it not their first care and wish to confess everything? And don't you understand that if you hide your guilt from your own parents, the only people in the world who really love you, you remain guilty, you nurse the very seed of evil in your heart, and you declare yourself a better judge than those who, after God, are your only guides and judges in this world?")

So we confessed. I confessed that I had hit Jules Adrien when we came home from our walk, and Filippo confessed about the ink spots, and I forget what Sonia confessed but after she finished it

was my turn again. At first we confessed hesitantly, and then with
so much energy and enthusiasm that we confessed to things we had
never done. Confession gains momentum; you become anxious to
see the bottom of the well, to get there first; it is an open competition between you and your judges—the only form of liberty left to
man in the presence of his gods. And this confession turns out to be
an accusation (though an unwilling one) even of all those who stood
by you.

Vladimir had to explain that if he had repaired the damage to
the red book, it was not to instill into my soul the fear of those who
loved me but to console me and to repair the book—indeed, to spare
the gods one more sorrow.

In the course of the day and by these painful processes, the gods
reëstablished themselves on their true altars. And we felt clean and
happy again.

THE PARSON

❖

PENELOPE MORTIMER

H E was a short, very heavy man—obese, although oddly thin in the face and with square hands, flat-tipped fingers, no flesh between the knuckles. A narrow, flat forehead that with the years grew higher, although he never appeared to become bald; eyebrows that jutted out enormously long, curly and wiry, and small eyes beneath all this tangle as sharp as terriers', but blue. They were never tender or glazed with sentiment.

His nose became larger and bonier as his forehead grew higher. As he grew older, as his face sank away from it, this nose was like the prow of Methodism rising out of a receding sea. The eyes might blaze, the eyebrows bristle, the forehead soar ever more lofty, but the nose was of chapel and sin. Around the bridge, it had a pinched look of virtue and condemnation.

A long upper lip, which might have been taken off a comedian; and a mouth that changed with time more than any other feature, starting off wide and broad-lipped and ending as a thin line, an opening slit for food or, almost nonexistent, clamped round a cigarette.

All this head, with its contradictions and discrepancies, rode too large for the short, heavy body. His back view, in suspended gray flannels and shirtsleeves, digging, weeding, mowing a lawn, was the rear of a squat old elephant—the same vast, solid gray folds ending in short, tubular legs, the same lumbering quality.

And yet he was deft. Until he became ill and lazy and clumsy, he could make or mend most things. He played chess in a series of vicious jabs, pouncing the pieces down, grunting, puffing great blasts of smoke, and usually winning—his one intellectual achievement.

He was a clergyman for one reason only—there was nothing else he could possibly have been. As a small boy, bullied and teased by

six sisters and four brothers, he sat under the nursery table chanting, "Mama, Papa, all the children are disagreeable except me.
. . ." God shone a compassionate eye through the silk tassels on the
green serge cloth that covered the table, disregarded the ten clever
goody-goodies, and picked him out. He began preaching—a stocky,
timid, bombastic little boy shouting of Hell-fire in the front parlor
while his brothers sneered and his sisters tittered and his father
played the harmonium. As a reward, his grandmother would give
him lollipops, lovingly slipped from her tongue onto his. The only
color in the house was the white of the girls' petticoats whisking
round dark corners.

He went to various schools, but he learned nothing. He was
beaten, put in the attic, kept on bread and water. This made him
cry, convinced him that he was a sinner, but made him even more
stupid. At sixteen, hair slicked down from a center parting, stiff-
collared, in hound's-tooth check, he was taken away from school
and bound as an apprentice in his father's printing firm. The other
apprentices were disagreeable; he clung firmly to God and became
a preacher in the local Wesleyan chapel, flaying the nodding bonnets with his great new voice, guiltily and savagely in love with a
girl called Maisie. Maisie, a bobbish little rich girl of fifteen, was
frightened and ran away; she never married, but for sixty years
kept, transfixed, her startled giggle, her look of petrified alarm.

He might have gone on like this for some years, but his father
died; the printing firm collapsed. He enrolled in the Methodist
Theological College at Putney.

It was a ghastly mistake. Black-suited, forced to attend long lectures on the Roman baptismal creed, to puzzle his way through
Athanasius and Marcellus and the Cappadocians, to battle with the
theory of enhypostasia and Socinianism and kenosis, to listen to
pale young men with clammy hands discussing Theodore of Mop-
suestia and the laws of ecclesiastical polity—all this was the nearest
thing to Hell he had ever known. God moved away from him and
hid in a cloud of unknowing. For the first time in his life, with the
agony of a child who sees his father pinching the maid's bottom, he
had Doubts. He wept and prayed, but it was no good. The College
expelled him for failing all his examinations. He thought, as he
walked slowly away with his Gladstone bag and his Bible, of walking straight on into the placid river. Instead, he became a Unitarian.

He could preach again, and when he was preaching he could convince himself of anything. He shook his square hands, howled, and

whispered; his huge, resonant voice shook the corrugated-iron roofs of dismal chapels, stroked the souls of girls in village halls. But afterward, alone in his lodgings, he suffered. Preaching, although he worked as hard as he knew how to on his sermons, didn't take up much time. He had begun to read Nietzsche and, almost more furtively, H. G. Wells; he had heard, uneasily, of "Man and Superman," and the phrase "life-force" began to creep into his sermons. The idea of Life, which had nothing to do with living, had begun to take the place of God, who had shown Himself to have nothing to do with religion. "Life is Love!" he bawled to a startled congregation. Pinch-mouthed, severely buttoning their gloves, they asked him to leave. He packed his "Zarathustra" and went.

What to do with him now? He was twenty-eight, uneducated, unqualified, tormented by the sins he hadn't committed and unable to understand the ones he had, tremendously ambitious without the slightest talent for success, full of urges and yearnings and pains of the soul, frightening and frightened and altogether a mess. The family gave him a piece of land in the middle of Manitoba and sent him off, with a younger brother, to Canada. Perhaps, as the ship heaved off into the Liverpool fog, they thought they had seen the last of him.

He never found the piece of land. Perhaps he didn't really look. He took various trains in the hope of finding it, but always ended up sitting on his box in some desolate way station, waiting for a train to take him back to Winnipeg. After several of these excursions, he gave up and took a job in a printing firm. It was cold, barbaric. Everyone was disagreeable, and he spent hours every night reading Browning out loud to himself in order to keep his accent pure. Away from any form of organized religion, his doubts were calmed; the longer he stayed a printer, the firmer his faith became. After a year of it, he wrote home for his passage money. His cold, ink-stained fingers could hardly hold the pen. "I know," he wrote, "that God intends me for the Ministry."

His mother flew into one of her rages, whistled "Worthy Is the Lamb" under her breath, and sent her daughters cowering to their rooms. But she was lonely. All her sons had left her and, with this one exception, were living brash and ungodly lives, both in jail and out. One was company-promoting in Sydney, another was razing Kanaka villages to the ground for the hell of it and living with a native girl who played the mouth organ and filled his shoes with sugar, another had just killed a lumberman in an argument and temporarily disappeared. She sent the passage money.

So he came home, chilly, chastened, and full of hope. He would study, he would do what he was told. Somebody must want him; somebody must recognize his ability. As he set foot on English soil at Liverpool, he felt that one blast of his voice would be enough. "Why," bishops would ask each other, "has he been neglected so long?"

Six months later, in a tweed hat and knickerbockers, he was bicycling about the lanes of Wiltshire, his heavy head bent low over the handle bars, his stout legs numbly pedalling. He was an itinerant preacher again. Browning went with him everywhere and his text was always the same: " 'Tis not what man does that exalts him, but what man would do." He read "Saul" aloud, with great passion, in the drawing rooms of the local gentry. One of their daughters, a handsome, strong-willed, ailing woman of thirty-five, fell in love with him. They married at eight o'clock one morning in a thick fog, walking to the chapel through muddy fields and going off to a disastrous honeymoon in lodgings at Eastbourne.

Marriage, far from calming him, goaded him to a kind of fury. He had always been violently, if furtively, conscious of sex; now, legitimately sexual, he became intoxicated with the idea that the world was more or less equally divided into men and women. Free love and the life-force and the emancipation of women all whirled together in his innocent brain, causing an extraordinary chaos in which women were exactly like men and yet were at the same time accessible. His heart gave out under the strain. He became ill. His wife had a nervous breakdown. The Wesleyans turned him out. His in-laws, stern materialists who believed devoutly in success, refused to have anything to do with him. There seemed, this time, no way out.

But, of course, there was. All his life he had been beating his head against the narrow limits of Nonconformity. The Church of England, that great, placid, unshakable compromise, loomed calm and radiant over the horizon. Why had he never thought of it before? The gracious, socially acceptable vicarages; the brown, book-lined studies where even a heretic could sleep undisturbed; the great cathedrals that could ring with his reading of Isaiah, of which he was rightly proud; and, above all, the limitless scope for a man of talent.

Revived, with passionate energy and pin-bright faith, he went off
to Lambeth Palace and the Archbishop of Canterbury.

The first question he was asked was whether he had any money.
None. Oxford or Cambridge? Neither. Who would speak for him?
No one. A fortnight later, a letter came from the Palace, signed with
one spidery name; he was not, it was thought, suitable for the
Church of England.

Now it was a case of do or die. Browning was no longer any use
to him; neither was life-force. He was well into his thirties, and
God was passing him by. He badgered, he pestered, he wrote long,
impassioned letters. For the first time in his life he worked, swallow-
ing great chunks of doctrine and not daring to think how uneasily
it lay. The end—the study with its armchair and the mellow peal
of bells—was all that mattered. When at last they accepted him, he
wept for joy, although with the appearance of awful grief. Once in
the Church, he knew, nothing short of murder or flagrant adultery
would get him out.

They gave him the job of curate in a parish in the East End of
London. His residence was a little slum house next to the gasworks;
lascars prowled the streets at night and the church was a grimy
great place with a sparse scattering of old women who wanted to
take the weight off their feet and get away for an hour or two from
their drunken husbands. He found himself looking with hostile
envy at the local Catholic priest, but, of course, it was too late for
that. He applied himself to the business of visiting the sick, who
were very sick, and whom he found very disagreeable.

However, London had something to be said for it. He went,
having carefully removed his dog collar, to a private performance
of "Mrs. Warren's Profession;" he got to know a few vaguely literary personalities—the humble outer fringe of the Café Royal world;
he began to write himself, pouring out his untidy feelings on Life
and sex and God in dull, pompous sentences to which his wife
listened with an expression of hopeless martyrdom that eventually
became permanent. For her, as a curate's wife, there had begun
the lifelong task of keeping up appearances; she did this with increasing skill, but once alone with her husband she became quite
silent, an industrious shadow, locked and bolted against attack.

They were now secure. He was still fairly young, his great energy
still untapped. The ideas pullulating inside him were still unex-

pressed; an East End curacy was hardly enough. He began looking around for something more alive, something with more scope.

He was offered a village that consisted of a cozy huddle of cottages under a gentle, sheltering hill. The squire's eighteenth-century mansion faced serenely away from the church, in its wilderness of moon daisies. The vicarage stood quiet in the sun, protected by a high pink wall—a great house full of dark passages and damp stone, mellow with dust and the smell of rotting apples. There was no sound but the swing of milk pails carried on their wooden yoke, the clop of a tired horse, the hum of a fat bee in the honeysuckle. It was hard to keep awake, and a beautiful place to die in—the Church of England at its best.

He burst in like a lion, scattering teacups and raising the warm dust. For the first time in his life, he felt a sense of power. "Yes, Vicar," the villagers said. "Of course, Vicar." They pulled their forelocks, and the squire raised his hat.

" 'The voice of him that crieth in the wilderness, Prepare ye the way of the Lord, make straight in the desert a highway . . .' " He was back in form again. The church shook with Isaiah, and the moon daisies were scythed down. He had a son and two hundred and fifty pounds a year, he had a study with an armchair, and six days off a week. There was only one thing missing. He no longer believed in God.

It was a terrible realization. Not only did he not believe in God, he didn't believe in the Thirty-nine Articles, the Virgin Birth, the idea of the Trinity, the Resurrection, the sanctity of marriage, or the conception of original sin. They had all, in the security and promise of his new life, deserted him.

He began desperately to try to fill the great gap. His faith in Life became almost fanatic; loving Life and living Love—it was comprehensive, unanswerable. If anyone was foolish enough to ask him exactly what it meant, his eyes blazed more fiercely than ever, he flung his arms wide and shouted, "You ask me what Life means? Life! Life speaks for itself!"

But he had to find some more practical expression for it. The villagers seemed smugly content with their uninspired existence, and those whom he buried were undeniably dead. He persuaded the squire that what was needed was a village club, a place where they could come together as a community and live a little. He helped to build it, slapping on the cement—braces straining over his great shoulders—singing at the top of his voice. It was a very ugly building, a gabled and stuccoed monstrosity among the thatched cottages and rosy brick, but when it was finished the villagers obediently used it, playing slow games of billiards and watching with delight the children of the local gentry making fools of themselves on the overelaborate stage. It was finished, and a great hopelessness came over him as he looked at it, a great hatred of his parishioners who shambled about its clean and empty rooms. It was not enough and they were not enough. There must be something more—but what?

He was now forty-six and his wife was over fifty. His son had been followed, painfully, after five intervening years, by a daughter. In order to make ends meet, his wife had started a small residential school that she called, with a hankering after sweetness, The Little People's Garden. The vicarage was overrun with children and governesses, beans growing on blotting paper, and jam jars of catkins. He took to living in an old Army hut at the bottom of the garden, where he was waited on by a surly manservant, who occasionally took notes to the house, asking the children to tea. He began sleeping in the afternoons, waking with a start to a black world of sin and atonement, the ghostly roaring of his own voice. But the sun poured lazily down through the apple trees and there was nothing to do—hours and days of nothing to do. He had a few weeks of keeping hens, who were given incredible incubators and runs of revolutionary design. One by one, they died. Two savage dogs, whom he christened Loyalty and Verity, took over the runs. They devoured the drawing-room curtains while everyone was in church, and shortly afterward the runs were empty. Their enormous collars, together with their leads and a whistle on a leather thong, hung about for some time and then were thrown by children into the tall nettles.

He still filled the church with his voice, bellowing at the deaf squire and the old women, who had heard him a thousand times, but it was becoming an effort. He would often break off after five minutes, abruptly mutter the names of the Father, Son, and Holy Ghost, and stamp out of the pulpit. The sense of futility made him physically ill. Unable to deafen himself with ideas, he had begun to listen to the ticking of the clock, the almost inaudible snapping of decay. There was still, perhaps, time to get out.

But, of course, he couldn't get out. The Church had him trapped as effectively as if he were behind bars. He exchanged his village for an amorphous jumble of suburban streets with identical houses crammed with office girls and bank clerks. The vicarage overlooked the railway line and shuddered all night with the crash and scream of shunting cars. He started a youth club and preached his splendid, meaningless sermons to huge congregations of children—fifteen-year-old girls, who loved him, and adolescent boys with nothing better to do. "Life!" he shouted at them desperately. "Believe in Life!" He grasped the edge of the pulpit, the tears ran down his face, he laughed, he flung his spectacles into the congregation, narrowly missing his wife, who was sitting, suffering tortures of embarrassment and misery, in the front pew. When it was all over, he would go home and play the piano—loud, frustrated, unskillful chords—or shut himself in his study and sit doing nothing until, mercifully, he fell asleep.

He began toying with theosophy, anthroposophy, spiritualism. His wife, perhaps out of loneliness, had always had a very reasonable relationship with ghosts, and this, at least—the need for something mysterious in a life spent cutting up small pieces of bread for Communion, or carrying cans of water from the kitchen tap to the font, or footing the bill for sacramental wine—they had in common. For a short while, it drew them together, but whereas she was content not to believe very much, his craving for belief grew greater as the possibility of satisfying it grew less. He could by now believe ten contradictory theories at the same time, and they tossed around in his soul like dead leaves, never settling, useless, whispering in the emptiness. The day he discovered Communism, he believed, with great gratitude, that he was saved.

Once again his energy soared. Reckless, enthusiastic, he devoted a whole issue of the parish magazine to supporting the Soviet persecution of the Church. Christ, he argued, was a Communist anyway. Nobody understood it. He was amazed. At last, after so much searching, he believed he had found the true meaning of Christianity. Did the Church of England not care for Christianity? Apparently it didn't. He was advised to go north, where, it was hoped, he might sink into oblivion.

The square, gloomy house in Lancashire rose like a fortress out of a forest of dripping shrubs—laurel and rhododendron, privet and yew. The cotton mills and foundries glowed like Hell under a steel sky, and the huge church, built in memory of the Napoleonic

Wars, echoed like a tomb for the few living souls who crept inside it.

Wearily, with the resignation of a man who has been through this move many times before, he started a youth club. He was over fifty—the prime, he insisted aggressively, of life—and so heavy that it became increasingly difficult for him to move about. He went everywhere by car, hunched over the wheel, saluting his parishioners with a gesture that was half gracious, half insulting. For days at a time, he sat in his study—the same desk, the same armchair, the same glass-fronted bookshelves—speaking to no one, scribbling away at some new work that was to enlighten the world, or trying to crowd out the emptiness with bits of Bertrand Russell, a few pre-digested scraps of Einstein, populating his desert with Ethel Mannin, A. S. Neill, Rudolf Steiner, Mme. Blavatsky, Krafft-Ebing. Every Saturday, in a hushed house, he wrote what he thought was a new sermon, but they were all the same, a torment of words disgorged to a slowly dwindling congregation. His voice was still remarkable, but it had nothing to say. Like Fowler, Graham Greene's character in "The Quiet American," he longed for the existence of someone to whom he could say he was sorry. There was no one. For the first time in over twenty years, he brought the photograph of his mother out of his drawer, and set it between his watch and his collar box on the bedroom mantelpiece.

One day, while conducting a funeral service, he stumbled and fell into the open grave. Climbing out, cumbersome and horrified and ashamed, his surplice streaked with mud, he knew that everything was really over. He was not even afraid of death. It was no more than a hole in the ground, a box in the earth. He apologized, finished the service, and went home. There was nothing else he could do.

His searching now had the desperation of a man finally cornered, without sanctuary. He became a nudist. But in the colony where he went for a vacation he found nothing among the dripping trees but a group of elderly ladies dressed in spectacles, knitting scarves for their less enlightened relatives. At this time, he weighed over sixteen stone, and there was much of him to suffer. He spent one wretched night in the chalet he had booked for three weeks, and came home. The next morning, as dawn burst over the cotton mills, he was to be seen wandering naked about the shrubbery, a great, pale, disconsolate shape in the gritty light, looking for something irretrievably lost.

At the age of sixty, already an old man, he drifted west, to Somerset, setting up his desk, his armchair, his bookshelves in yet another study, laboriously climbing the stairs of a new pulpit, looking down from it on the same faces, the same bowed heads, the same expressions of patient boredom. The Church of England had fulfilled its promise; he was still alive, his children had been educated, he was sure of a pension, however small. With a sort of awkward gratitude, he tried to do his best. He started a youth club. He introduced religious film shows into the church. Some forgotten superstition, stirring again at last, prevented him from putting the screen on the altar, which, since the church was small, was the obvious place. He fixed it up between the choir stalls, and the congregation peered intently, uncomprehending, at the vast shadows, vaguely Oriental in appearance, that flickered, unfocussed, between the damp Norman pillars. The electrical part of the apparatus was unreliable, and to prevent himself from getting severe shocks he wore thick crêpe-soled shoes under his surplice. But the films disgusted him. He gave them up, and the congregation, temporarily doubled, died away. He sat longer and longer in his study, the room thick with smoke, Elgar or Sibelius blaring from the record-player, a novel from the local library propped inside a mildewed tome on psychology or ethics. He gave up writing, gave up sending his manuscripts away. He gave up composing sermons and extemporized, meandering on about Life while the children fidgeted and the two old women yawned behind gloved hands and his wife, now years younger than he, thought briskly about something else.

Sometimes, like a man stirring in his sleep, he began to think that he must move, must change, must get out of it all. But the thought was never finished. His eyes closed, Sibelius played on unheeded, soft mounds of ash fell on his darned gray pullover. When he woke, it was time for another meal. In silence, they ate scantily, shovelling in the careless food. The house crumbled and peeled round them, unmended, uncared for. He gave up having his daily bath, came down from his cold, ascetic bedroom at the top of the house to the luxurious spare room, with its great mahogany furniture and brass fire irons and little pots of dried lavender. An old, sick clergyman, he would have done better to die and be buried with honor and a rural dean in attendance. Instead, for the last time, the removal van came and took away the desk, the armchair, the bookshelves. The Church thanked him and sent him out into the world with six pounds a week and a few cordial letters of good wishes. For the first time in fifty years, Sunday became a day like any other.

He sat in a ground-floor room in North London; the room faced south and the identical rooms opposite, the identical front gardens with neat little curly girls in white socks carefully riding their tricycles on the paths. For over a year, the old man sat at his desk in this room, with the city sun pouring through the William Morris curtains.

God knows what passed through his mind. Meals came and were eaten. He was pitifully hungry, but they said he must lose weight —dandelion coffee and starch-reduced rolls—and he was beyond complaining. The days merged into months, interrupted only by the absurd celebration of sleep, when he went from the desk to the bed and sat upright, differently dressed, observing darkness.

Finally, without knowing it, he died. The nurse, to whom he was just a dead old man, bustled through her routine and left him tidy, unpillowed, slightly askew on the bed. The sun poured on through the faded linen, slanted over the leather-topped desk, with its little brass nameplate, the useless books.

The letters of condolence began to arrive. "He is passing," they said, "through the Gateway to a far, far greater happiness in that Glorious Kingdom beyond . . . truly thankful that his sufferings are over and now he knows, and has found what he longed for. . . . Perhaps he is happier now. . . . It will be a relief not to have to feel sorry for him any more, for now he has found Truth. . . ." There was no confirmation and no denial. Already he existed only as a set of ideas, shifting and fading. They could do what they liked with him. There was no way in which he could speak for himself.

I LIVE ON YOUR VISITS

❖

Dorothy Parker

THE boy came into the hotel room and immediately it seemed even smaller.

"Hey, it's cool in here," he said. This was not meant as a comment on the temperature. "Cool," for reasons possibly known in some department of Heaven, was a term then in use among many of those of his age to express approbation.

It was indeed cool in the room, after the hard gray rain in the streets. It was warm, and it was so bright. The many-watted electric bulbs his mother insisted upon were undimmed by the thin frilled shades she had set on the hotel lamps, and there were shiny things everywhere: sheets of mirror along the walls; a square of mirror backing the mirror-plated knob on the door that led to the bedroom; cigarette boxes made of tiny bits of mirror and matchboxes slipped into little mirror jackets placed all about; and, on consoles and desk and table, photographs of himself at two and a half and five and seven and nine framed in broad mirror bands. Whenever his mother settled in a new domicile, and she removed often, those photographs were the first things out of the luggage. The boy hated them. He had had to pass his fifteenth birthday before his body had caught up with his head; there was that head, in those present-ments of his former selves, that pale, enormous blob. Once he had asked his mother to put the pictures somewhere else—preferably some small, dark place that could be locked. But he had had the bad fortune to make his request on one of the occasions when she was given to weeping suddenly and long. So the photographs stood out on parade, with their frames twinkling away.

There were twinklings, too, from the silver top of the fat crystal cocktail shaker, but the liquid low within the crystal was pale and dull. There was no shine, either, to the glass his mother held. It was cloudy from the clutch of her hand, and on the inside there were oily dribbles of what it had contained.

His mother shut the door by which she had admitted him, and followed him into the room. She looked at him with her head tilted to the side.

"Well, aren't you going to kiss me?" she said in a charming, wheedling voice, the voice of a little, little girl. "Aren't you, you beautiful big ox, you?"

"Sure," he said. He bent down toward her, but she stepped suddenly away. A sharp change came over her. She drew herself tall, with her shoulders back and her head flung high. Her upper lip lifted over her teeth, and her gaze came cold beneath lowered lids. So does one who has refused the white handkerchief regard the firing squad.

"Of course," she said in a deep, iced voice that gave each word its full due, "if you do not wish to kiss me, let it be recognized that there is no need for you to do so. I had not meant to overstep. I apologize. *Je vous demande pardon.* I had no desire to force you. I have never forced you. There is none to say I have."

"Ah, Mom," he said. He went to her, bent again, and this time kissed her cheek.

There was no change in her, save in the slow, somehow offended lifting of her eyelids. The brows arched as if they drew the lids up with them. "Thank you," she said. "That was gracious of you. I value graciousness. I rank it high. *Mille grazie.*"

"Ah, Mom," he said.

For the past week, up at his school, he had hoped—and coming down in the train he had hoped so hard that it became prayer—that his mother would not be what he thought of only as "like that." His prayer had gone unanswered. He knew by the two voices, by the head first tilted then held high, by the eyelids lowered in disdain then raised in outrage, by the little lisped words and then the elegant enunciation and the lofty diction. He knew.

He stood there and said, "Ah, Mom."

"Perhaps," she said, "you will award yourself the privilege of meeting a friend of mine. She is a true friend. I am proud that I may say it."

There was someone else in the room. It was preposterous that he had not seen her, for she was so big. Perhaps his eyes had been dazzled, after the dim-lit hotel corridor; perhaps his attention had been all for his mother. At any rate, there she sat, the true friend, on the

sofa covered with embossed cotton fabric of the sickened green that
is peculiar to hotel upholsteries. There she sat, at one end of the
sofa, and it seemed as if the other end must fly up into the air.

"I can give you but little," his mother said, "yet life is still kind
enough to let me give you something you will always remember.
Through me, you will meet a human being."

Yes, oh, yes. The voices, the stances, the eyelids—those were the
signs. But when his Mother divided the race into people and human
beings—that was the certainty.

He followed her the little way across the room, trying not to
tread on the train of her velvet tea gown that slid along the floor
after her and slapped at the heels of her gilt slippers. Fog seemed to
rise from his raincoat and his shoes cheeped. He turned out to avoid
the coffee table in front of the sofa, came in again too sharply and
bumped it.

"Mme. Marah," his mother said, "may I present my son?"

"Christ, he's a big bastard, isn't he?" the true friend said.

She was a fine one to talk about anybody's being big. Had she
risen, she would have stood shoulder against shoulder with him, and
she must have outweighed him by sixty pounds. She was dressed in
quantities of tweedlike stuff ornamented, surprisingly, with black
sequins set on in patterns of little bunches of grapes. On her massive wrists were bands and chains of dull silver, from some of
which hung amulets of discolored ivory, like rotted fangs. Over her
head and neck was a sort of caul of crisscrossed mauve veiling, splattered with fuzzy black balls. The caul caused her no inconvenience.
Puffs of smoke issued sporadically from behind it, and, though the
veiling was crisp elsewhere, around the mouth it was of a marshy
texture, where drink had passed through it.

His mother became the little girl again. "Isn't he wonderful?"
she said. "This is my baby. This is Crissy-wiss."

"*What* is his name?" the true friend said.

"Why, Christopher, of course," his mother said.

Christopher, of course. Had he been born earlier, it would have
been Peter; earlier again, Michael; he had been not much too late
for Jonathan. In the lower forms of his school, there were various
Nicholases, several Robins, and here and there a Jeremy coming up.
But the members of his own class were in the main Christophers.

"Christopher," the true friend said. "Well, that's not too bad. Of
course, that downward stroke of the 'p' is bound to give him trou-

ble, and I'm never really happy about an 'r' and an 'i' together. But it's not too bad. Not too. When's your birthday?" she asked the boy.

"The fifteenth of August," he said.

His mother was no longer the little girl. "The heat," she said, "the cruel August heat. And the stitches. Oh, God, the stitches!"

"So he's a Leo," the true friend said. "Awfully big for a Leo. You want to be pretty careful, young man, from October 22nd to November 13th. Keep away from anything electrical."

"I will," the boy said. "Thank you," he added.

"Let me see your hand," the true friend said.

The boy gave her his hand.

"Mm," she said, scanning the palm. "M-hmm, m-hmm, m-hmm. Oh. Well—*that* can't be helped. Well, you'll have pretty good health, if you just watch that chest of yours. There's a long sickness in your twenties and a bad accident some time around forty-five, but that's about all. There's going to be an unhappy love affair, but you'll get over it. You'll marry and—I can't see if there's two or three children. Probably two and one born dead, or something like that. I don't see much money, any time. Well, you watch your chest." She gave him back his hand.

"Thank you," he said.

The little girl came back to his mother. "Isn't he going to be famous?" she said.

The true friend shrugged. "It's not in his hand," she said.

"I always thought he'd write," his mother said. "When he was so small you could hardly see him, he used to write little verses. Crissy, what was the one about the bumpety bunny?"

"Oh, Mother!" he said. "I don't remember!"

"Oh, you do so, too!" she said. "You're just being modest. It was all about how the bunny went bumpety, bumpety all day long. Of course you remember. Well, you don't seem to write verses any more—at least none you show to *me*. And your letters—they're like telegrams. When you write at all, that is. Oh, Marah, why do they have to grow up? And now he's going to be married and have all those children."

"Two, anyway," the true friend said. "I'm not too happy about that third one."

"I suppose I'll never see him then," his mother said. "A lonely old woman, sick and trembling, and no one to take care of me."

She picked up the true friend's empty glass from the coffee table, filled it and her own from the cocktail shaker, and returned the friend's. She sat down near the sofa.

"Well, sit down, Crissy," she said. "And why don't you take off your coat?"

"Why, I don't think I'd better, Mom," he said. "You see—"

"He wants to keep his wet coat on," the true friend said. "He likes to smell like low tide."

"Well, you see," the boy said, "I can stay just a minute. You see, the train was late and everything, and I told Dad I'd be sure to be there early."

"Oh?" his mother said. The little girl ran off abruptly. The eyelids came into play.

"It's because the train was late," he said. "If it had been on time, I could have stayed awhile. But it had to go and be late, and they're having dinner awfully early tonight."

"I see," his mother said. "I see. I had thought that you would have dinner with me. With your mother. Her only son. But no, that is not to be. I have only an egg, but I would have shared it with you so gladly. So happily. But you are wise, of course. You must think first of your own comfort. Go and fill your stomach with your father. Go eat stalled ox with him."

"Mother, don't you see?" he said. "We have to have dinner early because we have to go to bed early. We've got to get up at daybreak because we're driving to the country. You know. I wrote you."

"Driving?" she said. "Your father has a new car, I presume."

"It's the same old heap," he said. "Nearly eight years old."

"Really?" she said. "Naturally, the buses in which I am obliged to ride are all this year's models."

"Ah, Mom," he said.

"Is your father well?" she said.

"He's fine," he said.

"Why not?" she said. "What is there could pierce that heart? And how is Mrs. Tennant? As I suppose she calls herself."

"Let's not do this again, will you, Mom?" he said. "She's Mrs. Tennant. You know that. She and Dad have been married for six years."

"To me," she said, "there is only one woman who may rightfully wear a man's name; the one whose son he has sired. But that is only my humble opinion. Who is to listen to it?"

"You get along all right with your stepmother?" the true friend said.

As always, it took him a moment before he could connect the term. It seemed to have nothing to do with Whitey, with her gay little monkey's face and her flying straw-colored hair.

A laugh fell from his mother's lips, hard, like a pellet of ice. "Such women are sly," she said. "They have ways."

"Well, born on a cusp," the true friend said. "You've got to keep considering that."

His mother turned to the boy. "I am going to do something that you will agree, in any honesty, that I have never done before," she said. "I am going to ask a favor of you. I am going to ask you to take off your coat and sit down, so that for just a few poor minutes it will seem as if you were not going to leave me. Will you let me have that illusion? Do not do it out of affection or gratitude or consideration. Just in simple pity."

"Yes, sit down, for God's sake," the true friend said. "You make people nervous."

"All right, sure," the boy said. He took off his raincoat, hung it over his arm, and sat on a small, straight chair.

"He's the biggest damn thing I ever saw," the true friend said.

"Thank you," his mother said. "If you think I ask too much, I plead guilty. *Mea culpa.* Well, now that we are cozy, let us talk, shall we? I see so little of you—I know so little about you. Tell me some things. Tell me what there is about this Mrs. Tennant that causes you to rank her so high above me. Is she more beautiful than I am?"

"Mom, please," he said. "You know Whitey isn't beautiful. She's just sort of funny-looking. Nice funny."

"Nice funny," she said. "Oh, I'm afraid I could never compete with that. Well, looks aren't everything, I suppose. Tell me, do you consider her a human being?"

"Mother, I don't know," he said. "I can't do that kind of talk."

"Let it pass," she said. "Let it be forgotten. Is your father's country place attractive at this time of year?"

"It isn't a place," he said. "You know—it's just a big sort of shack. There isn't even any heat. Just fireplaces."

"Ironic," she said. "Bitterly, cruelly ironic. I, who so love an open fire; I, who could sit all day looking into its leaping golds and purples and dreaming happy dreams. And I haven't even a gas log. Well. And who is going to this shack, to share the lovely, glowing fires?"

"Just Dad and Whitey and me," he said. "Oh, and the other Whitey, of course."

His mother looked at the true friend. "Is it growing dark in here?" she said. "Or is it just that I think I am going to faint?" She looked again at the boy. "The *other* Whitey?"

"It's a little dog," he said. "Not any particular kind. It's a nice little dog. Whitey saw it out in the street, when it was snowing, and it followed her home, and so they kept it. And whenever Dad— whenever anybody called Whitey, the dog would come, too. So Dad said well, if he thought that was his name, then that was going to *be* his name. So that was why."

"I am afraid," his mother said, "that your father is not aging with dignity. To me, whimsey after forty-five is a matter of nausea."

"It's an awfully nice little dog," he said.

"The management does not allow dogs here," she said. "I suppose that will be held against me. Marah—this drink. It is as weak as the beating of my heart."

"Why doesn't he make us some fresh ones?" the true friend said.

"I'm sorry," the boy said. "I don't know how to make cocktails."

"What do they teach you, anyway, in that fancy school of yours?" the true friend said.

His mother tilted her head at the boy. "Crissy," she said, "want to be a big, brave man? Take the bowl and get some nice, cold ice out of the kitchen."

He took the ice bowl, went into the minuscule kitchen, and took a tray of ice cubes from the tiny refrigerator. When he replaced the tray, he could hardly close the refrigerator door, the shelves were so crowded. There were a cardboard box of eggs, a packet of butter, a cluster of glossy French rolls, three artichokes, two avocados, a plate of tomatoes, a bowl of shelled peas, a grapefruit, a tin of vegetable juices, a glass of red caviar, a cream cheese, an assortment of sliced Italian sausages, and a plump little roasted Cornish Rock hen.

When he returned, his mother was busied with bottles and shaker. He set the bowl of cubes beside them.

"Look, Mom," he said, "honestly I've got to—"

His mother looked at him and her lip trembled. "Just two more minutes," she whispered. "Please, oh, please."

He went and sat again.

She made the drinks, gave one to the true friend, and kept one.

She sank into her chair; her head drooped and her body looked as boneless as a skein of yarn.

"Don't you want a drink?" the true friend said.

"No, thanks," the boy said.

"Might do you good," the true friend said. "Might stunt your growth. How long are you going to stay up in this country where you're going?"

"Oh, just over tomorrow night," he said. "I have to be back at school Sunday evening."

His mother stiffened and straightened. Her former coldnesses were as tropical heat to that which took her now.

"Do I understand you to say that you will not be coming in to see me again?" she said. "Do I understand you aright?"

"I can't, Mom," he said. "I won't have a chance. We've got to drive back, and then I have to get the train."

"I quite comprehend," she said. "I had thought, in my tenderness, I would see you again before your return to your school. I had thought, of course, that if you must rush away like a mad thing today, then I would see you again, to make up for it. Disappointments —I thought I had had them all, I thought life could bring forth no new ones. But this—this. That you will not take a little bit of your time from your relatives, who have so much of it, to give to me, your mother. How it must please them that you do not want to see me. How they must laugh together. What a triumph. How they must howl in merriment."

"Mother, don't say things like that," he said. "You shouldn't, even when you're—"

"Please!" she said. "The subject is closed. I will say no more about your father, poor, weak man, and that woman with the dog's name. But you—you. Have you no heart, no bowels, no natural instincts? No. You have not. I must face the fact. Here, in the presence of my friend, I must say what I had thought never, never to say. My son is not a human being!"

The true friend shook her caul and sighed. The boy sat still.

"Your father," his mother said. "Does he still see his old friends? *Our* old friends?"

"Why, I don't know, Mom," he said. "Yes, they see a lot of people, I guess. There's almost always somebody there. But they're alone a lot of the time. They like it that way."

"How fortunate," she said. "They like being alone. Smug, content, no need— Yes. And the old friends. They do not see me. They are all in twos, they have lives, they know what they're going to be doing six months from now. Why should they see me? Why should they have memories, kindnesses?"

"Probably most of them Pisces," the true friend said.

"Well, you must go," the boy's mother said. "It is late. Late— when is it ever late for me, when my son is with me? But you have told me. I know. I understand, and so I bow my head. Go, Christopher. Go."

"I'm terribly sorry, Mom," the boy said. "But I told you how it is." He rose and put on his coat.

"Christ, he gets bigger and bigger," the true friend said.

This time, the eyelids of the boy's mother were lowered at her friend. "I have always admired tall men," she said. She turned again to the boy. "You must go," she said. "It is so written. But take happiness with you. Take sweet memories of our little time together. See—I shall show you that I bear no vengefulness. I shall show you that I wish only well to those who have wrought but evil to me. I shall give you a present to take one of them."

She rose, moved about the room, touched boxes and tables fruitlessly. Then she went to the desk, moved papers and inkstands, and brought forth a small, square box, on top of which was a little plaster poodle, sitting on its hind legs, its front paws curved endearingly, begging.

"This is a souvenir of happier times," she said. "But I need no reminders. Take this dear, happy thing to one you love. See! See what it is!"

She touched a spring at the back of the box and the "Marseillaise" tinkled forth, hesitantly.

"My little music box," she said. "That moonlit night, the ship so brilliant, the ocean so still and beckoning."

"Hey, that's cool, Mom," he said. "Thanks ever so much. Whitey'll love it. She loves things like that."

"Things like that?" she said. "There are no other things like that, when one gives from one's heart." She stopped and seemed to ponder. "*Whitey* will love it?" she said. "Are you telling me that you propose giving it to that so-called Mrs. Tennant?" She touched the box; the tinkling ceased.

"I thought you said—" the boy said.

She shook her head at him, slowly. "Curious," she said. "Extraordinary. That my son should have so little perception. This gift, from my poor little store, is not for her. It is for the little dog. The little dog that I may not have."

"Why, thanks, Mom," he said. "Thanks."

"So go," she said. "I would not hold you. Take with you my wishes for your joy, among your loved ones. And when you can, when they will release you for a little while—come to me again. I wait for you. I light a lamp for you. My son, my only child, there are but desert sands for me between your comings. I live on your visits—Chris, I live on your visits."

THE ROSE, THE MAUVE,
THE WHITE

❖

Elizabeth Taylor

I N the morning, Charles Pollard went down the garden to practice calling for three cheers. When he came to the place farthest of all from the house and near to the lake, he paused, among clumps of rhubarb and mounds of lawn clippings, and glanced about him. His voice had broken years before but was still uncertain in volume; sometimes it wavered and lost its way, and he could never predict whether it would follow his intention or not. If his voice were to come out in a great bellow or perhaps frenziedly high-pitched, people would turn toward him in surprise, even astonishment, but how, if it sank too low, would he claim anyone's attention after the boisterous confusions of "Auld Lang Syne"? He could hardly be held responsible for what his voice did, he felt, and he had often wished that he might climb to the top of a mountain and there, alone, make its acquaintance and come to terms with it. As he could not, this morning in the garden at home he put on what he hoped was an expression of exultant gaiety, snatched off his spectacles, and, waving them in the air, cried out, "And now three cheers for Mrs. Frensham-Bowater!" He was about to begin "Hip, hip, hooray" when a bush nearby was filled with laughter; all the branches were disturbed with mirth. Then there were two splashes as his little sisters leaped into the lake for safety. "And now three cheers for Charles!" they called, as they swam as fast as they could away from the bank.

If he went after them, he could only stand at the edge of the water and shake his fist or make some other ineffectual protest, so he put his spectacles on again and walked slowly back to the house. It was a setback to the day, with Natalie arriving that afternoon and likely to hear at once from the twins how foolishly he had behaved.

"Mother, could you make them be quiet?" he asked desperately, finding her at work in the rose garden.

When he told her the story, she threw back her head and laughed for what seemed to him to be about five minutes. "Oh, poor old Charles. I wish I'd been in hiding, too." He had known he would have to bear this, or something like it, but was obliged to pay the price; and at last she said, "I will see to it that their lips are sealed, their cunning chops shut up."

"But are you sure you can?"

"I think I know how to manage my own children. See how obedient you yourself have grown. I cross my heart they shall not breathe a word of it in front of Natalie."

He thanked her coldly and walked away. In spite of his gratitude, he thought, She is so dreadfully chummy and slangy. I wish she wouldn't be. And why say just Natalie when there are two girls coming? I think she tries to be knowing as well, he decided.

Two girls were coming. His sister Katie was picking sweet peas for the room these school friends were to share with her.

"You are supposed to cut those with scissors," Charles said. The ones she couldn't strip off she was breaking with her teeth. "What time are they coming?"

"In the station taxi at half past three."

"Shall I come with you to meet them?"

"No, of course not. Why should you?"

Katie was sixteen and a year younger than Charles. It is a very feminine age, and she wanted her friends to herself. At school, they slept in the same bedroom, as they would here. They were used to closing the door upon a bower of secrets and intrigue and diary-writing; knew how to keep their jokes to themselves and their conversations as incomprehensible as possible to other people. When Charles's friends came to stay, Katie did not encroach on them, and now she had no intention of letting him spoil that delightful drive back from the station; she could not imagine what her friends would think of her if she did.

So after luncheon she went down alone in the big, musty-smelling taxi. The platform of the country station was quite deserted. A porter was whistling in the office, keeping out of the hot sun. She walked up and down, reading the notices of estate agents posted along the fence, and all the advertisements of auction sales. She imagined the train coming nearer to her with every passing second;

yet it seemed unbelievable that it would really soon materialize out of the distance, bringing Frances and Natalie.

They would have the compartment to themselves at this time of the day on the branch line, and she felt a little wistful thinking that they were together and having fun and she was all alone, waiting for them. They would be trying out dance steps, swaying and staggering as the train rocked; dropping at last, weak with laughter, full-length on their seats. Then (having been here to stay with Katie on other occasions) as they came to the end of their journey, they would begin to point out landmarks and haul down their luggage from the rack—carefully, because in the suitcases were the dresses for this evening's dance.

The signal fell with a sharp clatter, making Katie jump. Now, where shall I be standing when the train stops, she wondered, feeling self-conscious suddenly and full of responsibility. Not here, right on top of the Gents' lavatory, of all places. Perhaps by the entrance . . . Nonchalantly, she strolled away.

The porter came out of the office, still whistling, and stared up the line. Smoke, bowing and nodding like a plume on a horse's head, came round a bend in the distance, and Katie, watching it, felt sick and anxious. They won't enjoy themselves at all, she thought. I wish I hadn't asked them. They will find it dreadfully dull at home, and the dance is bound to be a failure. It will be babyish, with awful things like "The Dashing White Sergeant" and "The Gay Gordons." They will think Charles is a bore and the twins a bloody nuisance.

But the moment they stepped out of the train all her constraint vanished. They caught her up into the midst of their laughter. "You can't think what happened," they said. "You'll never believe what happened at Paddington." The ridiculous story never did quite come clear, they were so incoherent with giggling. Katie smiled in a grown-up way. She was just out of it for the moment, but would soon be in the swim again.

As they drove up the station slope toward the village, they were full of anticipation and excitement. "And where is Charles?" asked Natalie, smoothing her dark hair.

Tea was such great fun, Myra Pollard told herself; though one moment she felt rejuvenated, the next minute as old as the world. She had a habit of talking to herself as to another person who was deeply interested in all her reactions, and the gist of these conversations was often apparent on her face.

They keep one young, oneself—all these young people, she thought as she was pouring out the tea. Yet the next second, her cheek resting on her hand as she watched them putting away great swags and wedges and gobbets of starch, she sighed; for she had not felt as they all felt, eager and full of nonsense, for years and years. To them, though they were polite, she was of no account, the tea pourer-out, the starch provider, simply. It was people of her own generation who said that Charles and she were like brother and sister—not those of Charles's generation, to whom the idea would have seemed absurd.

Frances and Natalie were as considerate as could be and even strove to be a little woman-to-womanly with her. "Did you ever find your bracelet, Mrs. Pollard? Do you remember you'd lost it when we were here last time? At a—dance, wasn't it?" Natalie faltered. Of course, Katie's mother went to dances, too. Indeed, why not? Grotesque though they must be. She was glad that her own parents were more sedate and did not try to ape the young.

"I wish we could go to a ball," said Lucy, one of the twins.

"Your time will come," their mother said. She laid her hand to the side of the silver teapot as if to warm and comfort herself.

"Oh, do you remember that boy, Sandy, in the elimination dance?" Katie suddenly exploded.

Frances, who was all beaky and spectacly, Mrs. Pollard thought, exploded with her.

"The one who was wearing a kilt?" Natalie asked, with more composure. She wondered if Charles was thinking that she must be older than the other girls—and indeed she was, by two and a half months.

"Will Mrs. Frensham-Bowater be there?" Lucy asked.

Her sly glance, with eyelids half lowered, was for Caroline's—her twin's—benefit.

"Of course. Mrs. Frensham-Bowater always organizes the dance," their mother said briskly, and changed the subject.

Charles was grateful to her for keeping her promise; but all the same he had had an irritating afternoon. The twins, balked in one direction, found other ways of exasperating him. When he came out of the house with his gun under his arm, they clapped their hands over their ears and fled shrieking to the house. "Charles is pointing his gun at us!" they shouted. "Don't be bloody silly!" he shouted back. "Charles swore!" they cried.

What an unholy gap between Katie and me and those little perishers, he thought. What ever did Mother and Father imagine they were up to? What can the neighbors have thought of them—at their time of life? . . . He shied away from the idea of sexual love between the middle-aged; ludicrous though it was, evidence of it was constantly to be seen.

"Did you shoot anything?" his mother asked him.

"There wasn't anything to shoot." He had known there wouldn't be and had only walked about in the woods with his gun for something to do until the taxi came.

"And the girl next door?" Frances asked. "I have forgotten her name. Will she be going to the dance tonight?"

"Oh, Deirdre," said Caroline to Lucy.

"Yes, Deirdre," Lucy said, staring across the table at Charles.

"No, she has gone to school in Switzerland," said Katie.

"Poor Charles!" the twins said softly.

"Why not try to be your age?" he asked them in a voice which would, he hoped, sound intimidating to them but nonchalant to everybody else.

"Have you had nice holidays?" Mrs. Pollard asked, looking from Frances to Natalie. Then, thinking that she was being far too hostessy and middle-aged, she said without waiting for their answer, "I do adore your sweater, Natalie."

"Jesus bids us shine, with a pure, clear light," Caroline began to sing, as she spread honey on her bread.

"Not at the table," said their mother.

"What shall we do now?" Katie asked after tea. She was beginning to feel her responsibility again. There was no doubt that everything was very different from school; Frances and Natalie seemed drawn very close together from sharing the same situation, and she was apart, in the predicament of hostess. She began to see her home through their eyes: the purple brick house looked heavy and ugly now that the sun had gone behind a cloud; the south wall was covered by a magnolia tree; there were one or two big cream flowers among the dark leaves; doves were walking about on the slate roof; some of the windows reflected the blue sky and moving clouds. To Katie, it was like being shown a photograph which she did not immediately recognize—unevocative, as were the photographs of their mothers in the dormitory at school; they seldom glanced at them from the beginning of term to the end.

They sat down on the grass at the edge of the orchard and began to search for four-leaf clovers. Their conversation consisted mostly of derogatory remarks about themselves. They were hopeless at dancing, each one said; could never think what to say to their partners; and they had all washed their hair that morning and now could do simply nothing with it.

"So lucky having red hair, Katie. How I envy you," Natalie said.

"But it's horrible. I hate it."

"It's so striking. Isn't it, Frances?"

"Well, yours is, too, in a different way," Frances said. "It's this awful mousiness of mine I can't abide."

"You can't call it mousy, it's chestnut," Katie said.

It was just a game they played, and when they had finished with their hair they began on the shape of their hands. There was never any unkindness in anything they said. They were exploring themselves more than each other.

The twins wandered about the garden, shaking milk in jars to make butter. Every few minutes they stopped to compare the curd they had collected. They had been doing this tirelessly for days but were near the time when that game would seem dull and done with and they would never play it again. They roamed about the lawn, chanting a meaningless song.

The older girls were discussing whether they would rather be deaf or blind. Frances lay on her stomach watching the children and wondering if they were not lucky to be so free of care and without the great ordeal of the dance ahead of them.

"Deaf any day," said Katie.

"Oh, no!" said Natalie. "Only think how cut off you'd be from other people—and no one is ever as nice to the deaf or has much patience with them. Everyone is kinder to the blind."

"But imagine never seeing any of this ever again," said Frances. Tears came up painfully in Katie's eyes. "This garden, that lovely magnolia tree, sunsets," Frances said. "Never to be able to read 'Jane Eyre' again."

"You could read it in Braille," Katie said.

"It wouldn't be the same. You know it wouldn't be. Oh, it would be appalling. . . . I can't contemplate it. . . . I really can't."

Anyone who reminded them that the choice might not arise would have been deeply resented.

"I suppose we had better go in and iron our frocks," Katie said. No one had found a four-leaf clover.

"Where is Charles?" Natalie asked.

"The Lord knows," said Katie.

Frances was silent as they went toward the house. She could feel the dance coming nearer to her.

But the end of it was coming, too, she comforted herself. In six hours' time it would all be over—the dreadful exposure of herself, the nakedness she felt when she set out without her spectacles, as she was determined to do, timorous and shortsighted, the mark of them still deep across the bridge of her nose. She would be committed for four hours to the confusions of a blurred and slanting room. But as the other dances had somehow come to an end, so would this, she told herself.

"The house is full of girls," Charles told his father. George Pollard left the car in the drive and went indoors. "And steam," Charles said, following him.

Natalie, Frances, and Katie had been in the bathroom for nearly an hour and could hardly see one another across the room. Bath salts, hoarded from Christmas, scented the steam, and now, still wearing their shower caps, they were standing on damp towels and shaking their Christmas talcum powder over their stomachs and shoulders.

"Will you do my back and under my arms?" asked Katie, handing to Frances the tin of Rose Geranium. "And then I will do yours."

"What a lovely smell. It's so much nicer than mine," said Frances, dredging Katie as thoroughly as if she were a fillet of fish being prepared for the frying pan.

"Don't be too long, girls!" Mrs. Pollard called, tapping at the door. She tried to make her voice sound gay and indulgent. "The twins are waiting to come in, and it's rather past their bedtime." She wondered crossly if Katie's friends were allowed to monopolize bathrooms like that in their own homes. Katie was plainly showing off, and would have to be taken aside and told so.

"Just coming!" they shouted.

At last they opened the door and thundered along the passage to their bedroom, where they began to make the kind of untidiness they had left behind them in the bathroom.

Yvette, the French mother's help, whose unenviable task it now was to supervise the twins' going to bed, flung open the bathroom window and kicked all the wet towels to one side. They will be clean, certainly, she was thinking. But they will not be chic. She had seen before the net frocks, the strings of coral, the shining faces.

She rinsed the dregs of mauve crystals from the bath and called out to the twins. The worst part of her day was about to begin.

"This is the best part of the day," George said. He shut the bedroom door and took his drink over to the window. Myra was sitting at her dressing table. She had taken off her earrings to give her ears a little rest and was gently massaging the reddened lobes. She said, "It doesn't seem a year since that other dance, when we quarrelled about letting Katie go to it."

"She was too young. And still is."

"There were girls of thirteen there."

"Well, that's no affair of mine, thank God."

"I wonder if Ronnie What's-His-Name will be sober. For the M.C. of a young people's dance I consider he was pretty high last time. He always has drunk unmercifully."

"What the devil's this?" George asked. He had gone into his dressing room and now came back with his safety razor in his hand.

"Oh, the girls must have borrowed it."

"Very hospitable guests they are, to be sure. They manage to make me feel quite at home."

"Don't fuss. You were young yourself once."

She dotted lipstick over her cheekbones, and he watched her through the looking glass, arrested by the strange sight. His incredulous expression made her smile. Eyebrows raised, she was ready to tease. He tilted her face back toward him and kissed her quickly on the mouth.

"You look absurd," he said.

As soon as she was released, she leaned to the mirror again and began to smooth the dots of color over her cheeks, until they were merged into the most delicate flush. "A clever girl," he said, finishing his drink.

The girls were still not dressed when a boy called Benedict Nightingale arrived in his father's car—and dinner jacket, George decided. Katie's first beau, he told himself, come calling for her. He felt quite irritable as he took the boy into the drawing room.

"They won't be long," he said, without conviction.

"Don't be too long, girls," Myra called again in her low, controlled, and exasperated voice. She stopped to tap on their bedroom door before she went downstairs; then, knowing that Charles would be having trouble with his tie, she went in to his rescue.

"What about a drink?" George asked Benedict reluctantly.

"No, thank you, sir."

"Cigarette?"

"No, thank you, sir."

"I don't know what they can be doing all this time. Now what the hell's happening up there?"

The twins were trying to get into Katie's bedroom to pry into adolescent secrets, and the girls, still in their petticoats, held the door against them. From the other side of it Lucy and Caroline banged with their fists and kicked until dragged away at last by Yvette.

"Now we shall be late," said Katie.

They lifted their frocks and dropped them over their heads; their talcumed armpits showed white as they raised their elbows to hook themselves at the back. Frances tied Natalie's sash, Natalie fastened Katie's bracelet.

"Is this all right?" "Does it hang down?" "You're sure?" "Am I done up?" they asked.

"Oh, yes, yes, yes—I mean no," they all answered at once, not one of them attending.

"*This* is what *I'm* allowed," said Katie, smudging on lipstick, stretching her mouth as she had seen her mother do. "So pale, I'm wasting my time."

Natalie twisted her bracelet, shook back her hair. She hummed; did a glissade across the clothes-strewn floor, her skirts floating about her. She was away, gone, in Charles's arms already. She held her scented arm to her face and breathed deeply and smiled.

Frances stood uncertainly in the middle of the room. I am the one who will be asked to dance last of all, she thought, cold with the certainty of her failure. Katie and Natalie will go flying away and I shall be left there on my own, knowing nobody, and the boy they have asked to be my partner will look glum and upset from the very beginning, and after a while will make his escape. The time will go slowly and I shall wish that I were dead. . . . She turned to the long looking glass and smoothed her frock. "I hate my bosoms," she suddenly said. "They are too wide apart."

"Nonsense, that's how they're supposed to be," Katie said, as brisk as any nanny.

"Give those girls a shout, Charles," George said and helped himself to another drink.

But they were coming downstairs. They had left the room with its beds covered with clothes, its floor strewn with tissue paper. They descended: the rose, the mauve, the white. Like a bunch of sweet peas they looked, George thought.

"What a pretty frock, Frances," Myra said, beginning with the worst.

Poor pet, she thought, and Frances guessed the thought, smiling primly and saying "Thank you."

"And such a lovely color, Natalie," Myra went on.

"But is it, though?" Natalie asked anxiously. "And don't my shoes clash terribly? I think I look quite bleak in it, and it is last year's, really."

Myra had scarcely wanted to go into all that.

"Now, Katie," she began to say, as soon as she could. "I don't think your friends know Benedict. And when you have introduced them we must be on our way. Your father and I have to go out to dinner after we've taken you to the dance. So who's to go with whom?"

That was what Frances had wondered. The worst part of being a guest was not being told enough about arrangements. One was left in a shifting haze of conjecture.

Benedict had come to attention as the girls came in, and now he stepped forward and said with admirable firmness, "I will take Katie in my car." Then he was forced to add, "I would have room for someone else in the back."

That's me, thought Frances.

"Good! Then Frances can go with you, and Charles and Natalie with us. Now, don't crush your dresses, girls," said Myra. "Gather them up—so—from the back of the skirt. Have you got everything?"

"Of course, Mother," said Katie. We aren't children, she thought.

Four hours later, Charles let go of Natalie's hand and took a pace forward from the circle of "Auld Lang Syne."

"Three cheers for Mrs. Frensham-Bowater!" he shouted. "Hip, hip, hooray!"

Myra, standing in the entrance hall with the other parents, tried to look unconcerned. She knew that Charles had been nervous all along of doing that little duty, and she was thankful that it was safely over. And that meant that the dance was over, too.

With the first bars of "God Save the Queen" they all became rigid, pained-looking, arms to their sides and heads erect; but the moment it was over, the laughter and excitement enlivened their faces again. They began to drift reluctantly toward the hall.

"How pretty the girls are," the mothers said to one another. "Goodness, how they grow up. That isn't Madge's girl, surely, in the yellow taffeta? They change from day to day at this age."

"Was it lovely?" Myra asked Katie.

"So lovely! Oh, and someone spilled fruit cup all down poor Natalie's front."

"Oh, no!" said Myra.

"She doesn't care, though."

"But her mother . . . I feel so responsible."

"Oh, her mother's awfully understanding. She won't give a damn." Unlike you, Katie's voice seemed to imply. "It was last year's, anyway."

Benedict was hovering at Katie's shoulder.

"Charles had torn the hem already, anyway," Katie said.

"But how on earth?"

"They won a prize in the River Dance."

Myra had not the faintest idea what a River Dance was, and said so.

"The boys have to run across some chalk lines carrying their partners and he tore her skirt when he picked her up. She's no lightweight, I can assure you."

"I hope it hasn't been rowdy," Myra said, but this remark was far too silly to receive an answer.

Frances had attached herself to Charles and Natalie, so that she would not seem to leave the floor alone; but she knew that Mrs. Pollard had seen her standing there by the door, without a partner, and for the last waltz, of all things. To be seen by her hostess in such a predicament underlined her failure.

"Did you enjoy it, Frances?" Myra asked. And wasn't that the only way to put her question, Frances thought, the one she was so very anxious to know—"Did you dance much?" She wanted the measure of everyone's success or lack of it made clear to her.

"We had better go back as we came," Myra said. "Have you all got everything? Well, then, you go on, Benedict dear, with Frances and Katie, and we will follow."

I wish she wouldn't say "dear" to boys, Katie thought. And she doesn't trust us, I suppose, to come on after. I hope Benedict hasn't noticed that she doesn't trust him: he will think it is his driving—or worse, that she is thoroughly evil-minded. Goodness knows what she was up to in her young days to have such dreadful ideas in her head.

The untidy room was waiting for them. Five hours earlier, they had not looked beyond the dance or imagined a time after it, although Frances had tried hard to do so.

"Well, I don't think that poor boy, Roland, will thank you much for asking him in your party," Frances said. "He was wondering how he would ever get away from me."

She thought, as many grown-up women think, that by saying a thing herself she prevented people from thinking it. She had also read a great many nostalgic novels about girls of long ago spending hours in the cloakroom at dances, and in her usual spirit of defiance she had refused to go there at all, had stuck the humiliation out, and even when she might have taken her chance with the others in the Paul Jones had stuck that out, too.

"He told me he thought you danced very well," Katie said.

This made matters worse for Frances. So it wasn't just the dancing but something very much more important: her personality, or lack of it; her plainness—what she was burdened with for the rest of her life, in fact.

Natalie seemed loath to take off her frock, stained and torn though it now was. She floated about the room, spreading the skirt about her as she hummed and swayed and shook her hair. She would not be back on earth again until the morning.

"Here is your safety pin, Katie," said Frances.

"And here, with many thanks, your necklace safe and sound."

The trinkets they had borrowed from one another were handed back; they unhooked one another; examined their stockings for ladders. Katie took a pair of socks out of her brassière.

One by one, they got into bed. Natalie sat up writing her diary but Katie thought hers could wait till morning. Benedict's amusing sayings would be quite safe till then, and by tomorrow the cloud that had been over the evening might have dispersed. The next day, when they were swimming in the lake, or cleaning out the rabbits, or making walnut fudge, surely Frances would be reëstablished among them, not cut off by her lack of success, as she now was, taking the edge off Benedict's remembered wit, making Katie's heart ache just when it was beginning to behave as she had always believed a heart should.

Turning in Benedict's arms as they danced, she had sometimes caught Frances's eyes as she stood there alone or with some other forlorn and unclaimed girl. Katie had felt treachery in the smile she had been bound to give—the most difficult of smiles, for it had to contain so much, the assurance that the dance was only a dance and nothing very much to miss, a suggestion of regret at her, Katie's, foolishness in taking part in it, and surprise that she, of all people, had been chosen. "It is soon over," she tried to signal to Frances. "You are yourself. I love you. I will soon come back."

And Frances had received the smiles and nodded. *There are other things in the world,* she tried to believe.

"Shall we have a picnic tomorrow?" Katie asked now. She snuggled down into bed and stared up at the ceiling.

"Let's have one day at a time," said Natalie. She had filled in the space in her diary, and now locked the book up with a little key that hung on a chain round her neck.

"Do put out the light before the moths come in," said Frances.

They could hear Katie's parents talking quietly in the next room. Frances thought, I expect she is saying, "Poor Frances! I'm afraid she didn't get many dances, but I am sure that Katie did what she could for her. It would really have been kinder not to have invited her." The unbroken murmuring continued on the other side of the wall and Frances longed for it to stop. She thought, She is forever working things out in her mind, and cruelly lets people guess what they are. It would be no worse if she said them out loud. . . . She had prayed that it would all be over before Mrs. Pollard came to fetch them from the dance, "God Save the Queen" safely sung and her own shame at last behind her. As the last waltz began, she had longed for someone to claim her—any spotty, clammy-handed boy would do. Benedict and Katie had hovered by her, Benedict impatient to be away but Katie reluctant to leave her friend alone at such a crucial moment. "Please go," Frances had told them, and just as they danced away, Mrs. Pollard had appeared in the doorway, looking tired but watchful, her eyes everywhere—Katie accounted for, Charles, Natalie, then a little encouraging smile and

nod to Frances herself, trying to shrink out of sight on the perimeter
of the gaiety. "As I expected," her eyes said.

Gradually, the murmurings from the other room petered out and
the house became silent. Then Natalie heard a shoe drop with a
thud on the floor in Charles's room across the landing, and presently
another. Sitting on the edge of the bed, dreaming, she thought.
She lay awake, smiling in the darkness and stroking her smooth
arms, long after the other two had fallen asleep.

REASON NOT THE NEED

❖

WALTER STONE

THE Ludlows moved into their new apartment, on the second floor of the Clover house, when the varnish was barely dry on the floor. Patience College, an enclave of elegance on the outskirts of a New England mill town, was gradually converting the commodious old houses on Faculty Row into apartments to meet the demands of an expanding faculty that had children instead of servants. Jonathan Clover, retired professor of chemistry, had died the year before; his widow had given the tall white-clapboard structure to the college on condition that she be allowed to keep an apartment on the ground floor for the rest of her life, and then had gone to stay for a while with relatives.

The college had rebuilt the house into three apartments, one on each floor and all of them unsatisfactory, but the Ludlows were used to unsatisfactory quarters. They were a family that tended to come out at the seams of their apartments; a perambulator, a tricycle, a vacuum cleaner, and a stack of magazines were likely to obtrude into their hallways, and occasionally two-year-old Mercedes would explode nude from the crowded interior, followed by their dog. The apartments always reflected Harold Ludlow himself, his pants bagging at the knees and his pockets overflowing with ungraded freshman themes and unpaid bills.

At first, the Ludlows had the whole house to themselves. There were two weeks of summer vacation left, and most of the campus was deserted, but they were haunted by two old ladies who kept dropping in to ask when Mrs. Clover would return. There was something unnaturally genteel about them, which made the Ludlows apprehensive about what Mrs. Clover, whom they had never met, would be like. Miss Stomer was a wrenlike creature with a tiny body and a large face, like a puppet's; Miss Coddle, of more normal size, had great, wet eyes and a stricken expression, recalling the face of a sheep. A neighbor explained to the Ludlows that Miss

Stomer and Miss Coddle had once roomed in the Clover house and had been present when Mr. Clover died. "They'll hang on like leeches," said the neighbor. "Mrs. Clover will come back when her family gets tired of her. They'll turn her over to Jeffrey—he's her oldest son. He can handle her." There was a stern note in the neighbor's voice.

In October, when the Ludlows had been in the house a month, they learned that Mrs. Clover was returning. Jeffrey was the first Clover they saw. One morning, a moving van arrived with Mrs. Clover's furniture, and squads of officials from the college came to see that everything was in order. Then, in the afternoon, a car drew up in front of the house, and Jeffrey Clover, with the help of his wife, maneuvered his mother out of it. She wore a black silk dress and a mourning veil, and she was small and dumpling-shaped. From behind a Venetian blind, the Ludlows watched her lurching between her son and daughter-in-law, like a child learning how to walk. It was amazing to Harold how one with so much good flesh could manage to look so dwindled by grief. Jeffrey treated her with good-natured anger, or bad-natured levity. She clung and tottered and refused to look where she was going, as though she were blind, as well as deaf. The Ludlows had been told she was deaf. Her tired, throaty voice rose to them: "It's no use, Jeffrey, I can't make it. I can't go another inch. Why don't you and Inger just leave me here on the steps? Don't bother to take me any farther. Don't tire yourselves out for me."

Harold saw Jeffrey tighten his jaw. He had a fine jaw, the kind a corporation executive, which he was, ought to have, and it went well with the rest of him. He was muscular and tan, blond and shrewd-eyed. His wife, slightly faded, and darker than he, looked almost as much the executive's wife as he looked the executive. What they seemed to have in common was an aggressive temperament linked to a short temper. "All right, Inger, you get the door," Jeffrey said. "Now, don't carry on like that, Mother. We're still on the street. The doctor said you were perfectly all right."

"Mother, do try to think about something pleasant," said Inger unpleasantly.

"Yes, Inger's right," said Jeffrey. "Get the door, Inger. U-u-up you go! That's right, Mother."

The door closed on Mrs. Clover's complaint: "I've lost my pocketbook. Have you got my pocketbook, Inger? It had my glasses in it. . . ."

Thus was Mrs. Clover ushered into the final phase of her life—almost carried like a bride across the threshold, though the bridegroom was gone forever. Once inside, she doubtless began to weep at the sight of familiar things, with all their poignant associations, but the Ludlows did not hear what went on at first in the apartment. They were having trouble enough preventing their daughter Edith from jumping rope, and controlling their daughter Mercedes, who kept trying to get out into the hallway, naked.

Later, Harold Ludlow went downstairs on his way to the basement to get a section of a bookcase he had been painting. The front door of the Clover apartment was open, and he saw that Miss Stomer and Miss Coddle had already arrived and were hovering around the widow, who was weeping. He stopped for a while uncertainly on the landing, wondering whether he should go in, but he remembered that his pants were paint-stained and his shirt dirty. Nobody noticed him.

"It gets rather chilly here, nights," Miss Stomer was saying. "I spoke to a groundsman this morning about having the steam turned on for Mrs. Clover." Her voice ran on a high, precise pitch, like a sewing machine. Her iron-gray hair was cut close about her head—bobbed in the latest fashion, though in her case the fashion had never gone out.

"Now, don't worry about it, Miss Stomer," Jeffrey said, obviously trying to keep his voice even. He had taken off his coat and opened his collar, and he was visibly perspiring; it seemed hardly likely that the room would ever get chilly. "Mother's got an electric blanket. There's nothing to worry about."

"Eh?" cried Mrs. Clover, in the midst of her tears. "What did you say?"

"Electric blanket!" shouted Inger. "You remember, we showed you how to work it."

"Eh? Blanket? Did we lose a blanket? Was it in the car?"

"No. *Electric* blanket!" Inger said. "Where's her hearing aid? Why isn't she wearing it? Oh—she *is*."

"Oh, is *that* what you're talking about?" said Mrs. Clover. "I don't want an electric blanket. I wouldn't know what to do with it. If one of you children want it, why don't you just take it? What's the good of electricity? It never works right. I spent four hundred dollars on my hearing aid and I can't hear a thing."

"I'll be glad to help her with the electric blanket this evening," said Miss Stomer.

"It's all right, Miss Stomer," said Jeffrey. "We're staying here tonight. We'll show her."

Harold descended into the cellar, aware that Miss Stomer had seen him as he crossed the doorway. He wondered whether he would dare try to go upstairs again before she left. He did, and, sure enough, she trapped him.

"Oh, Mr. Ludlow!" she cried. "Excuse me, but I don't think you've met Mrs. Clover and her family, have you?"

Harold quailed, but it was too late, and a moment later he was shaking Jeffrey's hard bronze hand and being presented to a lot of other people, among whom was Jeffrey's sister Cynthia, looking at him with a critical eye. He had heard of Cynthia; she had reputedly made money as a literary agent in New York. She had a decisive handshake, like Jeffrey's, and lines and furrows in her face.

"My father used to teach at the college, too, Ludlow," Jeffrey said. "Head of the Chemistry Department for twenty-five years, you know. We *gave* this house to the college; a lot of people might think it was foolish, because they would have had to *buy* it from us, according to the original lease of the ground—the ground belongs to the college—but we wanted Mother to be able to stay here. I'd like you to meet her. Mother! Mother!"

It was difficult to attract his mother's attention, because she was talking, and when she was talking, it was harder than ever for her to hear. "We went to Maine every summer," she was saying. "That was before those terrible hurricanes. I'm so glad my husband wasn't alive to see what the last hurricane did to the trees."

"Mother! This is Mr. Ludlow," Jeffrey said. "Sorry everything is in such a state of confusion around here, Ludlow. We've just arrived."

"Why don't I come again later?" asked Harold, beginning to back out.

"No, I want her to meet you," said Jeffrey. "It's important for her to have friends around here. Mother! This is Mr. Ludlow."

"Bloodrow?" she asked.

"Ludlow. He lives upstairs."

"Harold Ludlow," said Harold.

"Didn't we know some Bloodrows one summer in Kennebunkport?" asked Mrs. Clover.

"No, that was Woodrow," said Cynthia. "Mother's deaf, Mr. Ludlow."

"How do you do?" said Mrs. Clover. "Forgive me if I don't get up, but I'm quite sick. My legs have been bothering me. The doctor says it's arches, but I know it's my heart. They don't understand about broken hearts any more. They prefer to talk about arches."

"Now, Mother, Dr. Pease told you your heart was as sound as a dollar," Jeffrey said. "Why don't you fix her some hot milk, Inger, and maybe we can get her into bed."

"My sister died of a broken heart," announced Miss Coddle, in a hollow, miserable voice. Unlike Miss Stomer, Miss Coddle was timorous and ashamed, but she, at least, spoke normally instead of enunciating. She moved slowly, as though sleepwalking, or like a rowboat that is shipping water. Everything about her suggested drowning; even the printed flowers on her dress seemed to droop.

"Don't let's be depressing," said Miss Stomer. "I think she wants cheering up. Perhaps we should turn on the television."

Everyone turned to look at the television set, which had been looking at them with its great dead eye, waiting to be turned on and engulf them. It was the one new object in the place, and Jeffrey was evidently proud of it. Though it stood in the darkest corner of a room filled with Mrs. Clover's furniture—good furniture, all of it a bit severe and rather uncomfortable, but expensively covered, and brightened by antimacassars—it reached out into the light, into the world. It was a square blond wooden box, powerful beyond its kind, with a screen two and a half feet wide and a special attachment for a hearing aid. It rested on a hardwood swivel, and, having not a trace of aesthetic feeling in its functional lines or its electronic bowels, it dominated the living room, overwhelming the reproductions of eighteenth-century furniture, bullying the house into submission. "She'll have a life of her own here," said Jeffrey, nodding at the television set.

Meanwhile, Harold's wife, Helen, had appeared at the door, with Edith clinging to her skirt and Mercedes, now clothed, underfoot. Harold moved back to join his family and introduce them, and while he was doing so, Mrs. Clover regarded them all with earnest, sentimental eyes, through a mist of anguish. Harold began to remember that he needed a haircut, and was wondering just how dirty his shirt was, but Mrs. Clover obviously didn't have her mind fixed on such details. She was looking at the new lives that had supplanted the old, and now, as she saw Harold in the role of husband, tears began to well into her eyes again. "I wish you could have met my husband," she said, weeping. "He was such a good man. He did everything for me. He would never let me do anything. He wouldn't even let me vacuum the floor. He spoiled me."

"Now, Mother, don't carry on," said Jeffrey.

"He lived his life, and you still have yours," said Cynthia. "After all, you're only seventy-two. Cheer up." She turned to the others. "I hope she'll start painting again. It would give her something to do."

"She's a wonderful painter!" cried Miss Stomer. "Those pictures of Maine! They're so real! Why don't you put some of them up on the walls?"

"Not a bad idea," said Jeffrey. "What do you think, Cyn?"

"Sure," said Cynthia. "Some of the better ones aren't too bad."

"He always did the dishes," said Mrs. Clover. "I never had to worry about anything. If there was ever anything worrying him, he kept it to himself. I never knew what cares he had. He was such a good man. And now he's gone, and I've got nothing to live for."

"I don't know why you talk that way about Mother's pictures," said Jeffrey irritably. "Dad always thought she was pretty good."

"Oh, Dad. He thought all painters were great as long as they didn't try to do anything like Picasso." Cynthia stretched her arms and lit a cigarette.

"And now there's no way for me to tell him how much I miss him," said Mrs. Clover, and she burst into heavy sobs.

The Ludlows watched, suffering for her, while everyone else in the room continued to talk about her rather than to her, as though —it seemed to Harold—she were a thing. But *she* wasn't actually talking to *them*, either. She was addressing the universe. It was as if they were all witnessing a movie—a dramatization of the horror of bereavement. The children skipped around, the young adults quarrelled about art, the spinsters wrung their hands in pity, but the work of art itself suffered on gigantically, filling the screen before their eyes, intensely self-absorbed, indifferent to whoever watched, beyond embarrassment, beyond solace.

When the Ludlows started to go, Mrs. Clover held out her hand toward them. "I love children," she said. "I have five grandchildren of my own. I hope your children will come and see me. I always keep some candy. I never eat it myself."

"I'm sure the children will love *you*," said Helen Ludlow.

Mrs. Clover shook her head sadly, and her eyes grew wet again. She seemed to have foreknowledge of how things would be.

Jeffrey followed the Ludlows into the hall and detained Harold a moment. "Do you have a television set?" he asked. His eyes watched Harold narrowly, trying, apparently, to gauge him. Harold guessed that he was not particularly interested in people except when he was determining how much he could ask, or expect, of them.

"No," said Harold. "We thought a hi-fi would be better. We can't afford a television set, and besides it would be bad for the kids. They'd watch it all the time."

"Yes. Well, I got a pretty good one for Mother," Jeffrey said. "You folks feel free to watch it when you want to."

"It's certainly big," said Harold.

"Yes. Well, it's a special set. Has a special circuit in it. It will bring in all the Boston stations. It's the best setup you can get. Perhaps you know, I'm vice-president in charge of distribution for Gibraltar Associates—plastics—and I can get a lot of things through friends. Whenever you're ready to buy a TV, just let me know. I can get you any brand you can name for twenty-five per cent off." He paused to observe the effect of this statement.

"Gosh, that's wonderful!" said Harold, who judged that Jeffrey was expecting some show of admiration.

Jeffrey nodded, and smiled gravely. "Yes. Just let me know."

Cynthia left the next morning for New York, but Jeffrey and his wife stayed two days longer. They found a maid who agreed to come in each morning, and Jeffrey told Harold that they were looking for a student, or some other dependable young person, to occupy one of the bedrooms and keep an eye on Mrs. Clover. They finally got a girl who worked in town—attractive, but cold and haughty—and then they left.

Mrs. Clover continued grieving. The girl kept a lot of stockings drying in the bathroom all the time. Mrs. Clover did not like to have her bathroom full of damp nylons, and besides, she told Harold, the girl never talked to her, only shrugged her shoulders angrily when Mrs. Clover complained about pains in her heart. The girl never even sat in the living room with her; she was always going out on dates and coming home hours after midnight.

Mrs. Clover was afraid to be left alone. Once, she called up the Ludlows and asked Harold to come down and nail her bedroom window shut.

"Oh, that won't be necessary," he said. "I have some burglar locks."

He went down and installed them for her. She hovered near him during the process, and soon began to sob softly and pitifully. "My husband always used to do these things," she said, "and now I've got nobody. He was such a good man. You'll never imagine how kind he was to me. He spoiled me."

"Oh, no," said Harold.

"Yes, he did. He spoiled me."

Miss Stomer and Miss Coddle came to see Mrs. Clover nearly every day, but she did not seem to appreciate them. And occasionally the Ludlows would see Mrs. Clover out-of-doors, walking with a cane, at a painfully slow pace. Her face always looked drawn and tear-stained. Most people found her irreconcilable grief a little ridiculous, and one sharp-tongued neighbor said that if she had been this concerned about her husband while he was alive, he might have lived longer.

Another neighbor had Mrs. Clover to tea, and invited some of her old friends and the Ludlows as well. Mrs. Clover, with a cup of tea, which she did not touch, sitting beside her, at once began to describe the horrors of the hurricane of the preceding summer in Maine. All through the tea, she kept breaking into the conversation with further reports from the stricken area. She was apparently under the impression that there was no conversation going on around her; the hearing aid was again not functioning. One of the guests, a professor of Greek, offered to try to fix it for her. He put the button in his ear and tapped the receiver. "This thing's no good, Mrs. Clover!" he shouted. "Where did you get it?"

"Why, a salesman sold it to me. I paid four hundred dollars for it, and it never has worked."

"Maybe the batteries are dead!" the professor bellowed. "Have you any spare batteries with you?"

"My son had a boat," she replied. "The next morning it was gone. He hunted up and down that beach for a week, looking for it."

She looked pathetically immobile, sitting in a white needlepoint chair, wearing a little blue hat with a small veil, her short legs, with their swollen ankles, barely allowing her feet, in their health shoes, to touch the floor.

A few days after the tea, Mrs. Clover's roomer disappeared, taking all her nylons out of the bathroom, and Mrs. Clover went off for a

Christmas visit to one of her children. She left her key with the Ludlows, so that Edith and Mercedes could enjoy her television set. The Ludlows had never had a chance to watch television before, and because Harold was on vacation, they were able to take full advantage of the opportunity. For two weeks, they all camped in Mrs. Clover's living room, bringing down sandwiches and newspapers, Harold or his wife running upstairs for cans of beer during commercials.

They moved lamps around so that there would be less glare on the screen. Their dog lay on the Oriental rugs and sometimes climbed onto the chairs. They tried shutting him out in the hall, but he kept up a steady whining and scratching at the door, gouging the paint, so they finally gave up trying to keep him out. Soon Mrs. Clover's apartment began to look like the Ludlows', with a stack of dirty cups on the tea table, dog hair matted in the rugs and on the cushions, crumbs on the floor, newspapers lying about the room.

Harold insisted that the children be put to bed at eight o'clock, so that he and Helen could watch thereafter without being disturbed. They sat back on the couch together, jeering at the commercials, criticizing the plots of dramas, outguessing the contestants on quiz shows. Harold watched the "Late Show" and the "Late Late Show," while Helen slept on the sofa beside him. At three o'clock in the morning, he would wake her, and they would go upstairs, bleary-eyed, to face the unpleasant realities of life on the second floor. During the two weeks Mrs. Clover was away, Harold saw five Charlie Chan mysteries. He always kept his freshman themes on the sofa beside him, in case he should feel like grading them. He didn't ever feel like it, but in the two weeks he managed to make a thorough study of television, and afterward he always spoke with authority about its strengths and weaknesses.

The day before Mrs. Clover was due back, the Ludlow family cleaned and vacuumed the living room, so that Mrs. Clover's maid wouldn't be too shocked. They hadn't actually broken anything, though there were the scratched door, a torn lampshade, and a chair with a slightly cracked rung. They regretted having to give up the apartment, and thought of how cruel Mrs. Clover's children were to send her back to live by herself.

Mrs. Clover returned, again between Jeffrey and his wife, again bowed and tottering, having relapsed into her previous condition of misery. "We're getting Mother a companion," Jeffrey told the Ludlows, who had gone down to greet their neighbor. "We can't allow things to drift like this any longer. Of course, it wasn't as though she was *alone*. She has a lot of friends in town, and we're constantly phoning. But Cynthia's been busy, and my brother Ted hasn't been able to get up here at all."

The children came down the stairs. "Oh, Mama, we were going to watch 'Gunsmoke' tonight!" said Edith. She looked unhappily at the blank face of the television set.

"No, you weren't," said Harold Ludlow sharply. "That would have been way after your bedtime, anyway."

Mrs. Clover asked, "Did the children enjoy the television programs?"

"They were simply delighted with them," said Helen.

"I don't watch it much, you know," said Mrs. Clover confidentially. "I don't know how to adjust it properly. But Jeffrey likes it when he comes up to visit."

That night, Harold Ludlow turned on his radio, which was connected to his hi-fi, and started to listen to symphonic music, but at ten o'clock Mrs. Clover's electric blanket began buzzing through the loudspeaker every seven seconds, and Harold switched the set off in a rage. He had only eleven long-playing records, and was sick of all of them. His ancient collection of 78s had been ruined by thorn needles in the forties. There was no way, now, of avoiding grading papers. At eleven-fifteen, he looked in the newspaper and was relieved to discover that the "Late Show" was not worth seeing anyway.

The electric blanket became the one thing Harold Ludlow had against Mrs. Clover. If she had to come home and interrupt his study of television, she might at least not interfere with the FM reception from Boston. There was something wrong with the connections in the blanket; friends of his, to whom he reported his troubles, told him that the blanket needed to be overhauled, and new terminals installed. Apparently, Jeffrey's instinct for quality in television receivers had not extended to electric blankets. Harold seethed whenever he thought of the cut-rate merchandise under which Jeffrey's mother slept. "I thought she said she didn't like electrical gadgets," he complained to his wife. "She never turns on the TV, she never wears her hearing aid, but she always uses the electric blanket. Sometimes she forgets to turn it off all day."

Harold was assembling a short-wave kit, so that he could listen to the B.B.C., and the thought of what the electric blanket would do to reception from England was more than he could bear. But it would be impossible to talk to Mrs. Clover about the blanket. It was difficult enough to convey a simple piece of information, such as "Your telephone has been ringing for the last five minutes." How could one explain to her that connections for the electric blanket were causing electric current to arc across gaps, interfering with radio reception? The only thing to do would be to write a letter. He framed one in his mind: "Dear Mrs. Clover: Since you returned after the holidays, there has been a curious buzzing sound on my radio every night after you go to bed. I have concluded that you use an electric blanket the connections of which need repairing. Since I do not own a television set (the price is prohibitive, and it would be bad for my children to watch it all the time), I am forced to rely on radio for much of my relaxation. I'd be glad to take the blanket to a repair shop for you and pay whatever it would cost to make it noiseless. Your neighbor, Harold Ludlow."

That was one of the mild forms of the letter Harold was always planning but never got around to writing. Sometimes, when the buzzing was particularly obnoxious, the letter took on an edge of sarcasm. "Dear Mrs. Clover: Though your hearing aid happily does not interfere with my radio reception, your electric blanket does. I wish you'd start using the former and stop using the latter." As a matter of fact, Harold Ludlow's letters, however strongly put, were always harmless, because he never wrote any of them down; his letters to the *Times* about their misuse of the word "on" in head-lines, when they meant "of" or "about," his scathing letters to the college administration, his sardonic replies to letters from creditors, his harshly critical remarks to reviews and quarterlies about the decline in the quality of their poetry—all existed brilliantly in his mind but fortunately were never committed to paper.

Harold saw Mrs. Clover's blanket only once, and then under circumstances that made examination of it impossible. One morning in February, the maid rang his bell and, when he opened the door, called up the stairs, "Mr. Ludlow, would you help me pick up Mrs. Clover?"

"Pick her up?" he cried. He was wearing an undershirt and drinking his morning cup of coffee; he had just been reading an article in the paper headlined "Scientist Advises on Strontium Threat," and the "on" had disturbed his digestion. "Pick her up at the station, you mean?"

"No. Pick her up from the floor. She's on the floor."

He ran downstairs. Sure enough, she was on the floor, in the small space between her bed and her night table. She lay on her back, the electric blanket partly covering her pink nightgown. His first reaction was "Electrocuted so soon?" but she was quite normal—even crying. He took her by one shoulder and the maid took her by the other, and together they managed to bring her, at last, right side up on the edge of the bed. Her shoulders were soft, like pudding, and her nightgown, scented with perfumes, quivered all over. She was entirely inert while they lifted her, passive as a child. Her plump, ringed fingers rested quite contentedly on Harold's arm. There was nothing petulant, nothing embarrassed in the way her hands accepted her fate. He felt suddenly that the whole episode was only a rehearsal for death—that as she was getting out of bed she had thought, What would it feel like just to drop?

She did not apologize, she did not explain. The maid did the apologizing for her. "I was so sorry to disturb you, Mr. Ludlow. It won't happen again—will it, Mrs. Clover? She was trying to get out of bed by herself. She can get in all right, but she has some trouble getting out."

"Are you all right, Mrs. Clover?" asked Harold, but the hearing aid was on the night table and she did not even turn her eyes toward him.

"My son Jeffrey is in plastics," she said. "They tell me he is very distinguished. He's only forty-one, you know. Whatever he tries, he always does well. Theodore and Cynthia are more like their father. Theodore works for the government, but he's very secure there, and he has a nice family. Cynthia is in publishing. I imagine she likes her work. She's a very healthy-minded girl. They are all healthy-minded children. Theodore seems to be happier now than he used to be, when he was teaching. You understand the kind of life a teacher has, Mr. Ludlow. My husband devoted himself to the college and his family. But they tell me I'm not to cry about him any more. A year is enough, they say. I'm supposed to go on, now, like this." She looked around the room, not at Harold or the maid but at the objects on the table and the pictures on the wall. "It was my heart," she said. "It stopped beating for a minute. I've been expecting it for some time. Don't tell the children, just yet. We'll see."

"You'll be all right, Mrs. Clover," said Harold. Saying that was the only way he knew of being helpful. It was his way of comforting hurt children and sick adults, his way of counselling himself against fear and failure.

"My husband was such a good man," she said. "There was never anyone like him. They tell me a year is long enough. What do *they* know about it?"

Harold couldn't bear to watch anyone crying. He fought against a desire to throw his arms around a person who was weeping, and against a tendency to start crying himself. When her tears began again, he said impulsively "Oh, no, no!" and he held his hands tightly at his sides. There she sat, dissolving in her own tears, as though flesh were sugar, soluble in grief.

Yet if Mrs. Clover had indeed had a heart attack, she seemed much the same as ever in the succeeding weeks. A companion, a Mrs. Pinchot, came to live with her. Mrs. Pinchot, too, was in her seventies and hard of hearing, but her hearing aid worked. She was tall and stout, with regal white hair and an excellent disposition. As soon as she moved in, the Ludlows began to hear the television set, and it usually didn't go off until midnight. Sometimes it was loud, and, on the second floor, they were able to listen to quiz programs with ease.

Mrs. Pinchot understood Mrs. Clover's case immediately. "Oh, I was like that after my husband died, myself," she told Helen Ludlow. "He was a theatrical man. Oh, we knew everybody. Oh, yes, we knew all of them! But you can't just cry. You have to do something besides cry. My son's connected with Broadway. He sends me tickets to all the shows. I go and see them. Of course, they're not like the old ones. But these new musical comedies, I like them better."

The next time Mrs. Clover fell out of bed, the Ludlows heard it upstairs, for she knocked over the night table. When Harold arrived, Mrs. Pinchot had hold of Mrs. Clover's arm and was trying to tease her to her feet. "Come on, now, dearie, don't you feel silly lying there like that?" Mrs. Pinchot was saying, smiling and patting her wrist.

She and Harold helped Mrs. Clover up, and all the while Mrs. Pinchot kept talking. "Poor thing, she likes being babied. I know. I felt like that myself. But who wants to be a baby all the time? Don't you think it would be boring?"

"I never thought I'd have to live without him," Mrs. Clover said. "He spoiled me. It wasn't right. He shouldn't have taken such good care of me if he was going to die before I did."

"Yes, well, but here you are, aren't you, dearie?" Mrs. Pinchot shouted. "Now, you remember what we were going to do today? We were going to town and shop!"

"It's my heart," said Mrs. Clover—a little sharply, for she was accustomed to a more receptive audience.

"Well, suppose it is," said Mrs. Pinchot. "Might as well use it as long as you've got it. We'll take a taxi instead of a bus, if you like."

"How is her heart, anyway?" Harold asked quietly.

"Oh, I don't suppose it's too good, but then she's in her seventies and she's been wearing it out with all this crying," Mrs. Pinchot told him. "She's a lot better when she wears her hearing aid. If I could just get her to keep that on, things would be easier around here."

"I didn't think it worked."

"It doesn't, if you keep the batteries unhooked. The trouble is, she doesn't want to hear anything."

For a few weeks, Mrs. Clover refused to let the flow of her tears be staunched by Mrs. Pinchot, and there were signs that she was going to rebel—to complain to her children—but in the end she agreed to wear her hearing aid, to walk out on the street with her cane, even to watch the evening television programs. When the Ludlows, passing the door, peeked in, they could see the two of them sitting there, Mrs. Pinchot laughing heartily at the comedians, Mrs. Clover drooping sleepily but trying bleakly to concentrate.

"Come in, come in!" said Mrs. Pinchot one evening, spotting the Ludlows. They went in. "We're watching Jack Benny. Can I fix you a cup of tea? Mrs. Clover, would you like another cup of tea, too?"

Mrs. Clover shook her head glumly. Mrs. Pinchot, with spirits not in the least dampened, went to the kitchen and returned with cups and a steaming teapot. Everywhere were evidences of her occupancy. On the chair where she had been sitting lay a bag with some sewing in it, and her hat was on the mantel. The furniture had been rearranged; the more comfortable chairs had been pulled out from the walls and edged toward a semicircle facing the television set. Mrs. Clover's grief was more secret now. It appeared in furtive little lines around her mouth; it was no longer in the center of things but in the corners. She even managed to smile a little at Mrs. Ludlow, but she avoided looking at Harold.

"Why don't the children come down and see me any more?" she croaked. "I like to have them. You tell them to come and see me any time."

"My son gave me some tickets to see 'Bells Are Ringing,'" said Mrs. Pinchot. "I've been trying to get Mrs. Clover to go see it, but she says she doesn't like musicals. Do you people ever get down to New York? I think I could get you a couple of tickets from my son."

"My goodness," said Helen Ludlow. "You mustn't do that."

Mrs. Clover had turned back to watching, with some bewilderment, the complexities of the comedy on the television screen. Now her eyes strayed around the room, and her hands grew restless. She clasped her wrists, and light flashed on her diamond ring. She looked down at it, and her wrists seemed to grow tense for a moment. Then she laid her hands in her lap, and they stayed there quietly.

Early in May, Mrs. Clover had another fall—not out of bed but in the middle of the street, stopping traffic for half a block. She had just left a taxi on the far side, and was crossing to her house, carrying three packages, when suddenly she fell. Whether she had tripped on a shoelace of her health shoes or her leg muscles had forgotten to work or she had once again simply had an impulse to fall—or whether, as she claimed, her heart had stopped beating for a moment—no one ever decided. At least, she won her point for the time being, and was put to bed. The Ludlows saw the doctor hurrying up the walk, and Mrs. Pinchot did not turn the television set on at the usual time.

The next morning, Miss Stomer and Miss Coddle arrived at the front door and were let in. A few minutes later, Miss Stomer telephoned the Ludlows to ask whether Mr. Ludlow knew how to work the peculiar locks on the windows; she thought Mrs. Clover might need a little fresh air. Harold put on a tie and went downstairs just as Jeffrey, his wife, and their young son drew up outside in their new Pontiac. Harold waited for Jeffrey, who came hurrying up the walk and gripped his hand hard. "Appreciate your standing by like this, Ludlow," he said.

They entered together, Harold explaining that he was on his way to open the window locks in Mrs. Clover's room. Jeffrey seemed irritated at seeing the spinsters, but he managed to control his voice when he asked, "Where's Mother?" There was a good deal of noise at the bedroom door, what with Miss Stomer and Miss Coddle commiserating with Mrs. Clover, and Mrs. Pinchot pooh-poohing the whole thing. "Oh, the poor dear's all right," Mrs. Pinchot said. "She overdid it a little, but she's feeling better now."

"May I see her?" Jeffrey asked. He hurried past the ladies and went into the bedroom. A moment later, he came to the door and nodded to Harold, indicating that he might come in and open the locks. Harold went into Mrs. Clover's room, followed by Miss Coddle, Miss Stomer, and Mrs. Pinchot. There Mrs. Clover lay, breathing heavily, her eyes closed, her skin waxy. Jeffrey went to her and took her hand, and she opened her eyes. "I've bought a sweater for Nicholas," she whispered. "It's there on that chair. A truck splashed the package, but the damp didn't get through. Did you bring him with you? Perhaps he'd like to try it on."

"He's here," said Jeffrey. "Can you tell me what happened, Mother?"

Her lips began to tremble. "I think it was my arches."

"What did the doctor say?"

"I didn't ask him." Tears began to stream down her cheeks.

Jeffrey stared at Harold, who was trying to make a jammed burglar lock work. "Who put those things on?" he asked. "We lived here for thirty years without them."

"Your mother was afraid one night, and I happened to have them around," said Harold.

"Thanks, Ludlow, I appreciate it," Jeffrey said, "but there was no reason for her to be afraid, with all you people in the building." He took the sweater and went out of the room.

Miss Coddle now began describing the death of her great-aunt. "I have to be careful," she said. "I have the same problem she had. Heart rather high on the left side and given to fatty deposits."

"Can't we be more cheerful?" asked Miss Stomer. "Personally, I come from a rather short-lived family."

"Pish-posh," said Mrs. Pinchot. "Around here, we always bury the doctor twenty years before the patient." She turned to Mrs. Clover. "Now, here's your grandson in his new sweater. Doesn't he look nice?"

"He certainly does," said Miss Stomer. "Doesn't he look the image of your dear husband, Mrs. Clover?"

Mrs. Clover did not hear Miss Stomer's question. She began to appear a little stronger. "Where's Jeffrey?" she asked. "Has anybody told him about my attack? I hope he knows I'm all right. I don't want him to worry."

"You poor thing, how terrible it must have been, and how *dangerous,* on that awful street, with all the traffic," said Miss Stomer.

Mrs. Clover nodded contentedly. "It was terrible," she agreed. "I always used to tell my husband, 'If the college doesn't do something about those trucks, somebody's going to be killed someday.' Little did I think, in those happy days, that I was talking about myself."

"If *I* can get a word in . . ." Jeffrey called from the doorway.

"Oh, there you are!" said Mrs. Clover. "Did you hear about my attack? I fell down right in the middle of Swallow Avenue."

Jeffrey attempted to be jovial. "Why do these things always happen to you? Where was Mrs. Pinchot?"

"I was in Hartford," Mrs. Pinchot said. "I told her to stay home till I got back." She laughed. "Try to get her to go out when you're around! The minute you go somewhere, though, she's off gadding. She's a regular gadabout, but I'm glad she did it. It's a good sign. She's got nobody. She might as well learn to get along by herself."

"She has her children!" cried Miss Stomer. "And her dear grand-children. They treasure her."

"Oh, they do treasure her!" Miss Coddle echoed.

"And, of course, she has *you*," said Mrs. Pinchot.

By June, Mrs. Clover had recovered from her fall in the street, but ever afterward she seemed older and feebler. She walked bent over her cane, and her face looked less plump, her chin sharper, her eye crankier. One day, Harold Ludlow met her in the hall. Her hearing-aid wire was flopping on her net collar, and she was poking in her handbag for her key. She smiled wistfully and asked how the children were. Then, without waiting for a reply, she went on, "You know, I had a heart attack in the street. One minute I was up and the next minute I was down. You never saw anything like it. The doctor says the heart's a tricky business. He thinks *he* knows. I could have told him, last summer. Grief does it."

And whenever they met after that, she would elaborate on these themes. She would sit near the open door of her apartment, and when she saw Harold going by, she would totter out into the hall to talk to him. The weaker she grew, the happier she seemed to be. "My arches are a little better today," she said one day, "but I don't breathe right any more. My husband had the same trouble, you know. It was a symptom, but nobody paid much attention to it. He worked so hard, right to the end. Just so I wouldn't have to lift a finger." Her face began to quiver. "But, you know, my son is aw-fully good to me. That expensive television set—I don't look at it much, but he wanted me to have it. Just to make me happy. And I can visit any of the children any time I want to. I'm going to be visiting my son Theodore weekend after next. He's in Washington, you know, but he's very secure. Sometime I want you to meet his wife and children. They're very affectionate people."

Then the tears began to catch in her eyelids, and the sobs in her throat, and she wrinkled up into herself. Her weeping no longer went outward to embrace all mankind. She had learned that most people would not accept her grief as theirs. But once she had seen Harold's eyes fill with tears when hers did. That had made him her brother, if not her husband. He had become the man of the house. She used a special tone when she spoke to him, the tone of respect for one's equal. "Tell me, Mr. Ludlow," she said the following Sunday evening, "does it not seem to you that when a person dies—" She stopped; she didn't know how to finish the sentence.

He tried, though it was not satisfactory. "When a person dies, everybody dies."

"Yes," she said. "I heard the minister say that once. My son Theodore sometimes takes me to church. He explains these things to me. My husband used to do that, and now I can't do without it. I try, but I'm not well. There are a lot of things wrong that even the doctor doesn't know about. I think my husband suspected this. He used to say, 'I'll do the dishes this evening, Judith.' I want *you* to know, Mr. Ludlow, what a good man he was." Tears began to flow freely down her cheeks; her grief was moving outward, just a little, and Harold felt his customary panic.

"Oh, no, please, Mrs. Clover . . ."

Mercifully, Mrs. Pinchot appeared. "Here, here, we mustn't give way like this, must we?"

Mrs. Pinchot was very tall; Harold had never realized it before, but she was nearly as tall as he, and her great white coiffure rested on her uncreased forehead like a crown. She was a very strong woman, considering her years. She put her arm around Mrs. Clover. "Ed Sullivan is about to come on TV," she said. "Let's go look at it, and you'll be fine in five minutes."

"I suppose you're right," Mrs. Clover said. "It's time we *were* all in bed."

Mrs. Pinchot clucked. "Now, see here, you haven't got your hearing aid working. I didn't say *bed*. It's early, and I said *Ed*—Ed Sullivan. Don't you remember? We watch him every Sunday."

"Oh, that television," said Mrs. Clover. "My son Jeffrey gave it to me, bless his heart. I understand it's a very special model. He gets all kinds of favors as a result of his position."

She seemed to have forgotten that she was talking to Harold. She walked vaguely back into the apartment, and Harold never spoke to her again. He saw her occasionally in the course of that week, but when she went to visit her son Theodore, she did not come back. During late summer, it was twice rumored that Mrs. Clover had died. The first rumor was false. ("She probably started that one herself," said one of the neighbors.) But the second rumor was true.

Speculation about who would get Mrs. Clover's apartment began along Faculty Row. There was a severe housing shortage at the college, and apartments were awarded on the basis of length of service rather than of need. The Ludlows had only four years, but they felt that the house was their house, and they knew Mrs. Clover's apartment intimately. In spite of its dark living room, it was much nicer than the one on the second floor. They were bitter when they heard that within twenty-four hours of the confirmed news of Mrs. Clover's death three people, each with more than eight years seniority, had applied at the housing office for the apartment. "It's disgusting," said Harold. He proudly refrained from applying.

Weeks went by, and nothing happened. The fall semester was beginning. Nobody came to move Mrs. Clover's furniture. Mrs. Pinchot, who had left when Mrs. Clover left, didn't even come back for her things. Harold, having lost all hope of watching Mrs. Clover's television set, succumbed to the temptation he had been battling, and bought a portable set with a fourteen-inch screen, but it didn't have a very good aerial, and reception wasn't nearly as good as it was on Mrs. Clover's set. He often looked at the giant aerial rising forty feet above the roof and wondered whether the Clovers would be willing to sell it to him, to avoid having to move it.

After several urgent letters from the housing office, the Clovers finally appeared for the last time. They came in two cars, with an orange U-Haul trailer hitched on each. Jeffrey and Cynthia were in one car; their brother Ted was in the other. The Ludlows had never seen Ted before. He was taller and lankier than Jeffrey, with bushy eyebrows and a distant, melancholy look. Ted was the one their mother had liked best, though she had always been a little suspicious of his job with the government. He was no such success as Jeffrey; she had been proudest of Jeffrey. Cynthia looked drawn and edgy; she was smoking a lot, and walked around with one hand on a hip. Jeffrey was angry. When he got out of his car, he slammed the door with a great thomp. The Ludlows could hear him clumping around on the floor beneath.

The day after the Clovers came, Harold helped them load the trailers. Ted kept smiling uneasily while Jeffrey continued a tirade against the college and its housing office. "You ought to see the letter we got from them, Ludlow," Jeffrey said. "The cheapest thing I've ever seen. Why we *gave* them this house—worth twenty thousand dollars, at least—just so that Mother would have a place to stay, and she didn't even use it for two years. Then they have the nerve to order us out of our own house by the first of next week, or they'll bring legal action!" He slapped the palm of one hand against a packing crate viciously.

"They're all alike," said Cynthia. She lit another cigarette. "Well, we still have all those books to sort."

"I wish there was something I could do to get even with them," said Jeffrey. "I'd like them to know how we feel. Why, do you know my father *built* this house? Of course, he was supposed to sell it to the college, and all that, but they didn't have to do it like *this*."

"What about the pictures?" asked Ted. "I'd like some of the pictures."

"Sure," said Jeffrey.

"Help yourself," said Cynthia. "I'd like one or two."

"Yes, I guess I'll keep a couple myself," said Jeffrey. "You two can have all the rest. You know, Mother was quite a good painter, Ludlow. Have you ever looked at her paintings?"

"I've seen them," said Harold. "I really like them."

A few of them were hanging on the walnut panelling of her living room, but most of them she had hidden around corners or in back passageways, where they were like holes cut in the dark, through which one saw into summer. They were mainly New England landscapes—districts where she had spent vacations. She had painted only in the summer, and all the pictures were of simple white or yellow houses against a setting of hills or seacoast. A strange white light filled all of them. It was impossible to believe that that suffering, bereaved woman had painted such lyrical white light.

The Clovers and Harold began moving pieces of furniture out to the trailers, but whenever her children touched anything of hers, they became sad and silent. Ted looked vague and bewildered; he seemed a little like his mother—more sensitive than the rest. Cynthia and Jeffrey would glower, and occasionally Jeffrey would explode about the letter from the college. Finally, they quit trying. They all sat down—Harold with them—in the confusion of the living room and had a drink.

"It was awful," said Jeffrey. "Every time I look around here, I think of how awful it was. You know, Ludlow, she grieved herself to death. She and Dad were inseparable, and after he died, she didn't want to live any more."

"She died of a broken heart," said Ted.

"She really did," said Cynthia.

Gloom seized them, and Jeffrey frowned more fiercely than ever, to avoid tears. Cynthia looked bleakly at the burning end of her cigarette. She drank faster than the rest of them. In no time, half the bottle of whiskey was gone.

"We've got to think how we're going to do the rest of this," said Jeffrey. "Ted's taking the TV set. Right?"

"Well, we've never had one in the house," said Ted, "but maybe the kids would like it."

"Sure they'd like it. It's great. You realize what a powerful set this is? It's got a special circuit for bringing in weak signals. I thought it would make Mother happy, but she never did pay much attention to it."

Harold's heart began to thump in his throat. He had moved crates, packed dishes, drunk whiskey with them, waiting for the right moment. "What about the antenna?" he asked casually. "If you don't feel like moving it, I'd like to buy it from you."

The three of them stared at him. "You mean you *want* it?" asked Jeffrey. "I'll *give* it to you. I've been worrying about the antenna. If we left it here, the college would claim it, and I don't want them to have it. I'd go up there and take it down myself before I'd let them have it. Here—I'll sell it to you for one cent. Have to make it legal." He found a piece of paper and wrote, "Sold to Harold Ludlow for the sum of $0.01, one television antenna mounted on roof." "There," he said. "If I know this college, they'll be trying to claim the aerial is theirs, so you hang on to that."

Harold found a penny and gave it to Jeffrey. As Jeffrey slipped the penny into his pocket, he smiled, for the first time that day. "Now I feel better," he said. "Let's go."

They went back to loading the trailers. The only difficult piece to move was the television set. It took all three of the men, with

Cynthia supervising. Once that was done, the house gave up the rest of its dead easily. About noon, Mrs. Pinchot arrived to pick up her things; she had got a place to stay a block away. She was wearing the light colors that she preferred; even her coat was of light-gray wool. "When you're in New York, come and see us," said Jeffrey, trying hard to be gracious.

"Why, of course. Did you think I wouldn't?" she said. "I just wish there was something I could do. I know how you feel." She smiled at them tenderly.

"She was a wonderful woman," said Jeffrey.

"Oh, the poor thing!" said Mrs. Pinchot. "It was so hard for her. I never knew anyone to suffer so. You were very kind to her. You gave her everything she could have wanted. You mustn't feel bad."

Jeffrey bowed his head. "Well, we tried," he said.

Helen Ludlow came out of the house to talk to Mrs. Pinchot, and the rest of them went on working. In the midst of their gloomy silence, Mrs. Pinchot's light, pleasant voice fell gently, punctuated by throaty laughter, as she described the house she was living in now, and told Helen what her son had said to her over the telephone the night before. At last, Mrs. Pinchot waved goodbye to all of them and walked away, her head held high. It seemed a rather abrupt departure, but soon the reason for it was apparent. Miss Stomer and Miss Coddle were crossing the street. Miss Stomer's face was gravely composed and expressionless; Miss Coddle's eyes were red-rimmed, and her cheeks were bunched with sympathy.

This time, Miss Coddle proved to be the more articulate one. She was learned in the language of bereavement; it seemed as if she had spent her life giving and receiving condolences, and healing phrases came readily to her. "It's the saddest thing to lose a mother," she said, "but she suffered so that I'm glad for her sake, not for yours, that she has passed on."

"Oh, yes," said Miss Stomer. "It's better."

"She wanted to be with her husband," said Miss Coddle. "I know that nothing will replace her in your hearts, but time will heal your grief."

The three orphans brightened a little at these soothing words. "Thank you," said Jeffrey. "Thank you. Mother often spoke of you two. You were very kind to her. And I want to thank you for all you've done for her. I know there's no way of repaying you for what you have done, but thank you."

"She died of a broken heart," said Miss Coddle.

"You're right," said Cynthia. "Isn't it awful? They were so happy together that she just couldn't go on without him."

"You don't find people like that any more," said Miss Stomer. "So gallant and so idealistic."

"Yes," said Jeffrey. "She was a remarkable woman."

Ted looked dazed, as though he had been struck a blow. He leaned against the trailer and stared at his feet, and slowly his cheeks turned crimson. "We've always known it, haven't we?" he demanded. He looked a little angry, a little belligerent. "She was different from most people."

"Really, it's true," said Cynthia. "She was determined to die."

They looked at each other solemnly, as the awareness came home to them that they had indeed witnessed something special—the birth of a legend. They felt pride in it, pride in their family, pride in themselves.

Miss Coddle withheld her farewell as long as she could, then walked reluctantly and heavily away, as though she were walking away from life. Miss Stomer went off briskly to tea at the Alumni Club. Finally, the trailers were loaded and the ropes knotted.

"Aren't we going to sweep the place?" asked Cynthia.

"I don't feel like it," said Jeffrey. "Let the college do it." Then he remembered his mother and father; it was a matter of honor. "No," he said, jutting out his jaw. "It's going to be spotless."

Harold went back into the house with the three of them. They swept and dusted, then sat on the floor and had a last drink. "Well, it was a good house," said Cynthia cheerfully, waving her cigarette. "What are we feeling so lousy about? She had a good life."

"That's right," said Jeffrey, eager to feel that way about it.

Ted said nothing. He began to turn over the stack of paintings he had been carrying, and looked at them thoughtfully, one by one.

Harold looked at them, too. The house in the center of each pic-ture shone very clear in the delicate light that surrounded it—a work of simple geometry, neat and square, and yet luminous. How had she achieved the sense of brightness and clearness? What was there about her life that might suggest this fine peace, this clarity that transformed simple things into things of beauty? Was her power to paint light joined to her power to suffer? Perhaps so. Were they not perhaps the same thing? That small and apparently withered soul had had the capacity to feel the power of the universe, which bathes us in its light and kills us in its darkness. And when the light fades, why not weep? Why hide? Why not expect that all people will participate in tears? Is not the one who shows us light the worthiest commentator upon darkness?

Jeffrey said, "We'd like you to have one of Mother's pictures, Ludlow, if you'd care to. Something you can remember her by. You people were very kind to her, and she loved your children."

"Thank you," said Harold. "I'd like to have one."

They gave him a painting of some flowers in a vase, enclosed in a heavy wooden frame. Jeffrey shook Harold's hand, and then walked out to the car without looking back; he had accomplished a job in the most efficient way possible. Ted carried his load of pictures out and laid them carefully on the front seat of his own car. Then they all drove off, waving. The two cars turned the corner, the orange trailers bobbing easily under the weight of furniture. The street grew quiet.

Harold went back into the vacant apartment and pushed the television lead-in wire through its hole in the floor until it dropped into the basement. Next he climbed the porch roof, hauled the loose wire up the side of the house until its end emerged from the basement window, and ran it under the screen of his living-room window, and then he went in and attached it to the fourteen-inch portable set. The Ludlows gathered around the set, but the picture was only a little better than usual, and not at all like Mrs. Clover's. Radio reception, on the other hand, was now vastly improved. Never again did the sound of Mrs. Clover's electric blanket punctuate Beethoven's Ninth Symphony with buzzing noises every seven seconds. It was as though the heart of the electronic Mrs. Clover— that part of her that was composed of television set, hearing aid, and electric blanket—had stopped beating. Harold would spend evenings listening to music, and admiring the high-fidelity he had fashioned, but he would be conscious of a certain tension, a certain expectancy. He was waiting for the painful buzz, the harsh reminder of Mrs. Clover's life and death, to cut through the flow of the music. Music did not seem quite as beautiful as it had seemed when noise was interrupting it. Nor did life, without Mrs. Clover to define it by suffering.

The Ludlows were glad to have her painting of the vase of flowers, though it wasn't as good as the paintings of Maine. The flowers looked a little blurred, as if she had been looking at them through tears. The background was a muddy gray, and the identities of the flowers were ambiguous. Like Mrs. Clover herself at the end of her life, they were a little confused, a little indistinct. The Ludlows propped the picture against a wall, but they never did get around to hanging it, because it came out of its frame.

THE STREAM

❖

Arturo Vivante

IN the summer of 1941, when I was seventeen, I was released from internment and I felt like a child who has been long in bed with a fever and finds that on getting up his legs are too shaky for him to go skipping around as he wanted.

I had spent a year with four hundred other Italians in a camp near Montreal. Three years before, because of the Fascist anti-Semitic campaign, my family and I had left Italy and gone to England. In June, 1940, when Italy entered the war, all Italian men in England between the ages of sixteen and seventy were interned, regardless of their political opinions. Things were done in a hurry. There was the danger of invasion, Fifth Columnists were active in France, and there was no time to draw distinctions. A few months before, the Germans and Austrians in England, Jewish refugees included, had been interned.

I was, in June, 1940, away from home, in a boarding school in North Wales. For this reason, when the order to intern Italians came, I wasn't taken to the same internment camp as my father and elder brother. The British government's policy was to send enemy aliens away as soon as possible from what might at any moment become a theatre of war. My father and brother were sent to the Isle of Man. I was put in a batch that was sent to Canada. Another batch was shipped to Australia. Still another went down in mid-ocean aboard the Arandora Star. For a few weeks, my family thought I was on it.

After six months of internment in Canada, I was given the choice either to await release in Canada or to go back to England and be released there, by joining the Pioneer Corps (a unit of engineers made up of aliens). Three things made me decide to remain. I had a mistaken belief that my release in Canada was imminent—I spent my days writing applications declaring my anti-Fascism, and expected each day to be released on the next; my parents, who were preoccupied by conditions in England, advised me to stay; and relatives and a family friend in the United States offered to pay my expenses while I was on their side of the ocean. It was six months before I was released.

Wholly unaccustomed to freedom, like a bird just set free from a cage, I found that the beautiful, long flights I had dreamed couldn't be quite as readily accomplished as they had been in my fancy. Even the first moments of freedom weren't what I had hoped they would be. Time and again, I had imagined myself standing alone outside the gate, with walls and barbed wire behind me, at last able to choose any one of the several roads that led away from the camp to the marvellous world open to me. But that image was spoiled by having one of the camp officers accompany me in to town and, once there, take me to his home. I felt it was like having the internment prolonged. I remember something constantly urging me to leave, to go and walk alone in the city that for a whole year I had seen so tantalizingly close. I remember my impatience at last winning over my shyness, and awkwardly, very self-consciously I rose while he was insisting that I should stay a little longer. It seemed as if I were cheating my freedom of every moment that passed. I remember walking down the front steps of his house and feeling under his gaze until, having gone round a curve, I looked back, and, seeing there was no one behind me, I suddenly broke into a run that lasted till I was out of breath—and I had caught up with my freedom.

I remember wandering about Montreal a long time, climbing a hill and seeing, hardly discernible in the distance, the tiny island that had been my world for a year. I remember running down that hill and, halfway, saying to myself, "You are free—you don't have to prove it!" This thought had the effect of a brake. It sent me at a slow pace toward the boarding house where a refugee committee had arranged for me to spend a few days. It wasn't so late—half past eleven, I think—when I arrived, and yet the landlady, who had been expecting me, was worried and told me she was about to phone the police. The police . . . the police . . . Oh, but why? Just the thought of the police looking for me made me shudder and have visions of myself being taken back to the camp.

After a short stay in Montreal, I went to live in Toronto. My American relatives, learning that I would not be allowed into the

United States, had reserved a room for me in a small, out-of-the-way hotel there, owned by a man to whom they, in turn, were related. My relatives were kin to my maternal grandmother, who was an American, born in Springfield, Missouri. Her father was a minister from Syracuse, New York. In 1872, he took his family to Italy, where he founded a church. She married an Italian.

The hotel was full of old people. I remember the dead silence of the little room where I lived. It was "a nice, quiet part of town," the man who owned the hotel said. But I needed sound. If only I could have heard then even faintly the hum of New York, south of that border that, as an alien, I wasn't permitted to cross, I am sure it would have sounded like music.

I remember how impatiently I used to walk from my room to the center of Toronto, where the traffic was thickest, where the lights shone the brightest, and how, once there, I would postpone for as long as possible the time when, with an empty feeling inside and my feet aching, I would take the trolley back to the deadly parts of the town—the cemetery parts—to a hotel where a few retired people lived.

I remember returning to the room along a dark corridor, over creaky floors, opening the door, and finding the walls, the white bedcovers, and the towel all staring at me like so many blanks. I remember my image as I walked past the mirror, arresting me, and how I stood there looking at it, looking at the restlessness inside me. "Is the day really over?" I would ask myself, pulling down the bedcovers. I began to wonder if I would expend myself day after day, silently, slowly, with no outward sign and everything happening within, like champagne that has been kept too long in the bottle and, when it is opened at last, has gone flat. Would anyone know me? Would anyone see the spark that somewhere existed within me? Would I always keep it a secret? With such thoughts I would slowly get into bed and lie wondering. Often an urge to rise, to dress and go out to the center of town would overcome me. At times, I would get as far as rising from bed and switching the light on; then I would stare a long time at the glare of the lamp, which hurt my eyes and yet attracted my gaze as though I were a moth. Other times, I would get dressed and would return to bed just when I was ready to leave the room. Twice, I remember, I actually walked as far as the center of town, with the intention of going to dance in some night club where there were hostesses. The first time, I stopped in front of such a place but did not go in, and the second time I left before a waiter could get me to sit down.

I remember the meals—all paid for by my relatives—that glued me to the hotel, the dining room with its few tables, occupied by old couples who sometimes whispered but never talked to each other aloud.

It was a hesitant, lonely time, and especially lonely at seventeen, when I hadn't yet acquired the courage to approach women lonelier than I, or to talk to girls over counters; when I was too restless to read, and felt guilty about going to so many movies.

But one day a letter arrived from a distant American cousin, who wrote that she was coming to pay me a visit, and the atmosphere of depression was swept away. Her name was Jane. I had met her five years before in Italy, when she stayed at my home while on vacation. I remembered her vaguely—a girl of fourteen with red hair, who had learned Italian by reading poetry aloud with my father. I wondered what she had grown to be like at nineteen—this girl who was travelling hundreds of miles just to see me. Didn't she have anything better to do? Somehow I didn't think she would be beautiful.

But she was. She was radiant, with red hair like the setting sun and a moon-white complexion. I felt almost too shy to shake hands with her. What's more, she liked me. And that surprised me even more, because I didn't think so much of myself in those days.

Jane was the first person I had met for over a year who seemed to have warmth and affection to spare. Right away, from the moment I saw her, she treated me as if I were her favorite friend. It made me think that perhaps she also was lonely, and that she hadn't come to Toronto with purely altruistic intentions. I was glad of that, because it is much nicer to be comforted if one can comfort in return.

She was training to be a nurse in the Army. I thought of all the opportunities she had to make friends. I asked her about the doctors and the soldiers she met—hadn't someone stolen her heart? No, no one of those glorious men had. She had come to see me. And, talking to her, I came to understand that her stay at my home had left a deeper impression on her than I supposed.

I have met girls in my life who look beautiful to me but not to others, who have a beauty of expression, an inner beauty—a light, really—to which some people are blind. Jane had this kind of beauty and the other besides. She looked beautiful not just to me but to everyone. Also, she walked as if she weren't aware of her beauty, and this made her twice as beautiful. She was slightly absent-minded, given to daydreaming. One saw it in the way she moved and paused, in the way she looked at objects and people—as though she saw aspects in them that were hidden to others. Creation seemed enriched when reflected in her eyes.

"Don't thank me for coming up, it's a pleasure. It really, really is a pleasure," she said, holding both my hands and shaking them till I couldn't help laughing. That laugh swept away all my sadness and much of my shyness as well. I wanted to take her hand in mine and say, "Come, let's run down as far as the river, let's go and pick some grapes, or climb up some old trees together." But where I lived in Toronto there were only long streets and hard pavements, houses, and forbiddingly trim little lawns.

I remember that she found a letter waiting for her at the hotel. "It's from my aunt," she said, opening it. "She writes it's so good of me to come and see you. As if I were doing it as a duty! I'm not your big sister!" And she tossed the letter away, aiming at a wastepaper basket. I watched the crumpled letter's flight across the room. Amazingly, it landed where she meant it to. I clapped my hands in a burst of delight. I felt I was conspiring with her against the dutiful and dull world that her well-meaning aunt represented.

I remember going into Jane's room, and how impressed I was with her belongings; her comb and her brush, all her things had a lustre about them. When I went back to my room that evening, it seemed so dismal compared to hers, and yet they were the same kind of room; the walls and the furniture were quite the same in both.

The next morning, when I knocked at her door, she was still in bed. She asked me to come in and pull up the blinds for her. Then I remember her rising, and the long cherry-blossom nightgown she wore. Vaguely I remember her saying "Now I must get dressed, it's late. Will you wait for me in the hall?" and in the hall gazing at the blank wall as if it were a screen, and picturing something very different from what my eyes saw.

Later, I remember, she asked me for a cigarette. I didn't smoke at the time, but seeing her smoke made me want to, and that was when I started smoking.

We took many walks about town; the city looked different with her. Streets that had seemed very long while I was walking alone seemed too short. In buses, we so soon came to the end of the line.

One day, I suggested we go to the lake. It was some time before we could see it, because for a long stretch Toronto has only docks and warehouses on the lake—no esplanade. The city is built as if it were trying to avoid the one really beautiful thing nature gave it.

When we finally reached the lake, we walked along the shore. Soon we found a place where rowboats and canoes could be rented. We took a canoe, and I paddled while Jane sat facing me. We skirted the shore until we came to the mouth of a stream. We entered it and paddled upstream. The water was calm, there was hardly any current, and just one stroke was enough to send the canoe forward a long way. We had to duck our heads under two or three bridges, and then we reached an area that was quite deserted.

That stream—I can hardly believe now that it is near Toronto and that it still really exists, that if I wanted to badly enough I could even find it again and retrace its course. I remember the reeds and the sound the canoe made as we swished over them, past them. I remember the leaves of the willows—how they brushed our heads as we glided. I remember the paddle—how at each stroke it sank in the water, and my fist getting gloved in the loose, floating leaves. And I remember the banks of the stream—the woody green banks that narrowed as we went farther and farther, until they were just a few yards apart, and then just a few feet, so that the canoe was arrested and could go no farther. Above us was a green sky of willow trees; all around us were the tall, thick reeds, hiding us, holding us still. Jane, in front of me, was sitting on the floor of the canoe as in a shell.

I felt that I had finally arrived somewhere wonderful, so unexpected and beyond my plans that it seemed mythical. I felt we had arrived there not by chance, but that some secret virtue had brought us to this place. "We have arrived," I said to her.

She didn't answer; there was no need. It was as if the enchantment would suffer from any word spoken, any move made, in that stillness.

And yet it was my not making any move that turned out to be what brought an end to everything inexpressible or enchanted between us. As I looked at her, sitting within reach of my arms, canopied by that tent of green on the water, I knew there was still much to be said, far still to go; I knew there was a line that had been flung and was asking to be tightened.

But I was new to this knowledge, didn't know what she thought, dared not ask her. And so, after a while, I turned around in the canoe and began to paddle back. And the line wasn't tightened, it never closed into a knot, and I wonder what my life would have been if it had.

With her, I think the connection had been gradually tied and had never got tight enough to hurt, so that, later, it slowly loosened until it held her no longer. For me, at that period of my life, everything involved some degree of hesitation.

I remember clearly as far as I've told, but I have entirely forgotten what happened during the rest of her stay. The trip back to the lake, our return to Toronto, her departure from there have faded from my mind almost as though they never took place. I stayed four more years in Canada, going first to school, then to college, liking it better with each year that went by. In 1945, as soon as the war was over, I returned to England to join my family. A few months later, we were back in Italy. By this time Jane was married to a surgeon. When I thought of her, it was with the feeling that what we had meant to each other had ceased at the stream—or, rather, as if we had left it there, and there it had stuck, firmly tied to the place, secretly, silently living on its own, independent of us, hovering just above the surface, still perhaps seeking what we hadn't reached. For years I waited for another such setting and partner. They never came. And I was left with the feeling that I had missed my chance, and with the thought that never again would love present itself so tempting and fair.

THE INTERVIEW

❖

R. Prawer Jhabvala

I AM always very careful of my appearance, so you could not say that I spent much more time than usual over myself that morning. I trimmed and oiled my mustache, but then I often do that; I always like it to look very neat, like Raj Kapoor's, the film star's. My sister-in-law and my wife were watching me, my sister-in-law smiling and resting one hand on her hip, and my wife only looking anxious. I knew why she was anxious. All night she had been whispering to me, saying, "Get this job and take me away to live somewhere alone—only you and I and the children." I had answered "Yes," because I wanted to go to sleep. I don't know where and why she has taken this notion that we should go and live alone.

When I had finished combing my hair, I sat on the floor, and my sister-in-law brought me my food on a tray. It may sound strange that my sister-in-law, and not my wife, should serve me, but it is so in our house. It used to be my mother who brought me my food, even after I was married; she would never allow my wife to do this for me, though my wife wanted to very much. Then, when my mother got so old, my sister-in-law began to serve me. I know that my wife feels deeply hurt by this, but she doesn't dare say anything. My mother really doesn't notice things any more; otherwise, she certainly would not allow my sister-in-law to serve me. She always used to be very jealous of this privilege, though she never cared who served my brother. Now she has become so old that she can hardly see anything, and most of the time she sits in the corner by the family trunks, and folds and strokes her pieces of cloth. For years now she has been collecting pieces of cloth. Some of them are very old and dirty, but she doesn't care. Nobody else is allowed to touch them, and once, I remember, there was a great quarrel because my wife had taken one of them to make a dress for our child. My mother shouted at her—it was terrible to hear her, but then

585

she has never liked my wife—and my wife was very much afraid, and cried, and tried to excuse herself. I hit her across the face, not very hard and not because I wanted to, but only to satisfy my mother. It seemed to quiet the old woman, and she went back to folding and stroking her pieces of cloth.

All the time I was eating, I could feel my sister-in-law looking at me and smiling. It made me uncomfortable. I thought she might be smiling because she knew I wouldn't get the job for which I had to go and be interviewed that day. I also knew I wouldn't get it, but I didn't like her smiling like that, as if she were saying, "You see, you will always have to be dependent on us." It is clearly my brother's duty to keep me and my family until I can get work and contribute my own earnings to the household, so there is no need for smiling. But it is true that I am more dependent on her now than on anyone else. Lately, my sister-in-law has become more and more the most important person in the house, and now she even keeps the keys and the household stores. At first, I didn't like this. As long as my mother was managing the household, I was sure of getting many extra tidbits. But now I find that my sister-in-law is also very kind to me—much more kind than she is to her husband. It is not for him that she saves the tidbits, or for her children. She never says anything when she gives them to me, but she smiles, and then I feel confused and rather embarrassed. My wife has noticed what she does for me.

I have found that women are usually kind to me. I think they realize that I am a rather sensitive person, and that therefore I must be treated gently. My mother has always treated me very gently. I am her youngest child, and I am fifteen years younger than my brother, who is next to me. (She did have several children in between us, but they all died.) Right from the time when I was a tiny baby, she understood that I needed greater care and tenderness than other children. She always made me sleep close beside her in the night, and in the day I usually sat with her and my grandmother and my widowed aunt, who were also very fond of me. When I got bigger, my father sometimes wanted to take me to help in his stall (he had a little grocer's stall, where he sold lentils and rice and cheap cigarettes and colored drinks in bottles), but my mother and grandmother and aunt never liked to let me go. Once, I remember, he did take me with him, and he made me pour some lentils out of paper bags into a tin. I rather liked pouring the lentils—they made such a nice noise as they landed in the tin—but suddenly my mother came and was very angry with my father for making me do this work. She took me home at once, and when she told my grand-mother and aunt what had happened, they stroked me and kissed me, and then they gave me a beautiful hot fritter to eat. The fact is, right from childhood I have been a person who needs a lot of peace and rest, and my food, too, has to be rather more delicate than that of other people. I have often tried to explain this to my wife, but as she is not very intelligent, she doesn't seem to under-stand.

Now my wife was watching me while I ate. She was squatting on the floor, washing our youngest baby; the child's head was in her lap, and all one could see of it was the back of its naked legs. My wife did not watch me as openly as my sister-in-law did, but from time to time she raised her eyes to me, looking very worried and troubled. She, too, was thinking about the job for which I was going to be interviewed, but she was anxious that I should get it. I cannot imagine why she wanted us to go and live alone, when she knew that it was not possible and never would be.

And even if it were possible, I would not like it. I cannot leave my mother, and I do not think I would like to live away from my sister-in-law. I often look at her, and it makes me happy. Even though she is not young any more, she is still beautiful. She is tall, with big hips and eyes that flash. She often gets angry, and then she is the most beautiful of all. Her eyes look like fire and she shows all her teeth, which are very strong and white, and her head is proud, with the black hair flying loose. My wife is not beautiful at all. I was very disappointed in her when they first married me to her. Now I have grown used to her, and I even like her, because she is so good and quiet and never troubles me at all. But I don't think anybody else in our house likes her. My sister-in-law always calls her "that beauty," and she makes her do all the most difficult household tasks. She shouts at her and abuses her, which is not right, because my wife has never done anything to her and has always treated her with respect. But I cannot interfere in their quarrels.

I finished my meal and then I was ready to go, though I did not want to. My mother blessed me, and my sister-in-law looked at me over her shoulder, and her great eyes flashed with laughter. I did not look at my wife, who still sat squatting on the floor, but I knew she was pleading with me to get the job. Even as I walked down the stairs, I knew what would happen at the interview. I had been to

so many during the past few months, and the same thing always
happened. Of course, I know I have to work. My last position was
in an insurance office, and all day they made me sit at a desk and
write figures. What pleasure could there be for me in that? I am a
very thoughtful person, and I always like to sit and think my own
thoughts. But in that office my thinking sometimes caused me to
make mistakes over the figures, and then they were very angry with
me. I was always afraid of their anger, and I begged their forgiveness and admitted that I was much at fault. But the last time they
would not forgive me again, although I begged many times and
cried what a faulty, bad man I was and what good men they were,
and how they were my mother and my father, and how I looked
only to them for my life and the lives of my children. But when they
still said I must go, I saw that the work there was really finished, so
I stopped crying. I went into the cloakroom and combed my hair
and folded my soap in my towel, and then I took my money from
the accountant without a word and left the office with my eyes
lowered. But I was no longer afraid, because what is finished is
finished, and my brother still had work and probably one day I
would get another job.

Ever since then, my brother has been trying to get me into
government service. He himself is a clerk in government service,
and enjoys many advantages. Every five years, he gets an increase of
ten rupees in his salary. He has ten days' sick leave in the year, and
when he retires he will get a pension. It would be good for me to
have such a job, but it is difficult to get, because first there is an
interview, at which important people sit at a desk and ask many
questions. Because I am afraid of them, I cannot understand properly what they are saying, but I answer what I think they want me
to answer. But it seems that my answers are somehow not the right
ones, because they have not given me a job.

Now, as I walked down the stairs, I wished I could go to the
cinema, instead. If I had had ten annas, perhaps I would have gone;
it was just time for the morning show. The young clerks and the
students would be collecting in a queue outside the cinema now.
They would be standing and not talking much, holding their ten
annas and waiting for the box office to open. I enjoy those morning
shows, perhaps because the people who come to them are all young
men, like myself—all silent and rather sad. I am often sad; it would
even be right to say that I am sad most of the time. But when the
film begins, I am happy. I love to see the beautiful women dressed

in golden clothes, with heavy earrings, and necklaces, and bracelets covering their arms, and to see their handsome lovers, who are all the things I would like to be. And when they sing their love songs, so full of deep feelings, the tears sometimes come into my eyes, because I am so happy. After the film is over, I never go home straightway, but I walk around the streets and think about how wonderful life could be.

When I arrived at the place where the interview was, I had to walk down many corridors and ask directions from many peons before I could find the right room. The peons were all rude to me, because they knew what I had come for. They lounged back on benches outside the offices, and when I asked them, they looked me up and down before answering, and sometimes made jokes about me to one another. But I was very polite to them, for even though they were only peons, they had uniforms and jobs and belonged here, whereas I did not. At last I came to the room where I had to wait. Many others were already sitting there, on chairs drawn up against the wall all around the room. No one was talking. I found a chair, and after a while an official came in with a list and asked if anyone else had come. I got up and he asked my name, and then he looked down the list and made a tick with a pencil. "Why are you late?" he asked me very sternly. I begged pardon and told him the bus in which I had come had had an accident. He said, "When you are called for an interview, you have to be here exactly on time, or your name is crossed off the list." I begged pardon again and asked him very humbly please not to cross me off this time. I knew that all the others were listening, even though none of them looked at us. He said some more things to me very scornfully, but in the end he said, "Wait here. When your name is called, you must go in at once."

I didn't count the number of people waiting in the room, but there were a great many. Perhaps there was one job free, perhaps two or three. As I sat there, I began to feel the others all hoping anxiously that they might get the job, so I became worried and anxious, too. I stared around and tried to put my mind on something else. The walls of the room were painted green halfway up and white above that, and were quite bare. There was a fan turning from the ceiling, but it didn't give much breeze. An interview was going on behind the big door. One by one, we would all be called in there and have the door closed behind us.

I began to worry desperately. It always happens like this. When I come to an interview, I never want the job at all, but when I see all the others waiting and worrying, I want it terribly. Yet at the same time I know, deep down, that I don't want it. I know it would only be the same thing over again: writing figures and making mistakes and then being afraid when they found out. And there would be a superior officer in my office to whom I would have to be very deferential, and every time I saw him or heard his voice I would begin to be afraid that he had found out something against me. For weeks and months I would sit and write figures, getting wearier of it and wearier, and thinking my own thoughts more and more. Then the mistakes would come, and my superior officer would be angry.

My brother never makes mistakes. For years he has been sitting in the same office, writing figures, being deferential to his superior officer, and concentrating very hard on his work. But, nevertheless, he is afraid of the same thing—a mistake that will make them angry with him and cost him his job. I think it is right for him to be afraid, for what would become of us all if he also lost his job? It is not the same with me. I believe I am afraid to lose my job only because that is a thing of which one is expected to be afraid. When I have actually lost it, I am really relieved. But this is not surprising, because I *am* very different from my brother; even in appearance I am different. As I have said, he is fifteen years older than I, but even when he was my age, he never looked as I do. My appearance has always attracted others, and right up to the time I was married my mother used to stroke my hair and my face and say many tender things to me. Once, when I was walking on my way to school through the bazaar, a man called to me very softly, and when I came he gave me a ripe mango, and said, "You are beautiful, beautiful." He looked at me in an odd, kind way, and wanted me to go with him to his house, in another part of the city. I love wearing fine clothes—especially very thin white muslin kurtas that have been freshly washed and starched, and are embroidered at the shoulders. Sometimes I also use scent—a fine khas smell—and my hair oil also smells of khas. Several years ago, just after I was married, there was a handsome teen-age girl who lived in the tailor's shop opposite our house and who used to wait for me and follow me whenever I went out. But it is my brother, not I, who is married to a beautiful wife, and this has always seemed most unfair.

The big closed door opened and the man who had been in there

for an interview came out. We all looked at him, but he walked
out in a great hurry, with a preoccupied expression on his face. I
could feel the anxiety in the other men getting stronger, and mine,
too. The official with the list came, and we all looked up at him.
He read off another name, and the man whose name was called
jumped up from his chair. He started forward, but then he was
brought up short by his dhoti, which had got caught on a nail in
the chair. As soon as he realized what had happened, he became
very agitated, and when he tried to disentangle himself, his fingers
shook so much that he could not get the dhoti off the nail. The
official watched him coldly and said, "Hurry, now! Do you think
the gentlemen will wait for as long as you please?" In his confusion, the man dropped his umbrella, and then he tried to disentangle the dhoti and pick up the umbrella at the same time.
When he could not get the dhoti loose, he became so desperate
that he pulled at the cloth and ripped it free. It was a pity to see
the dhoti torn, because it was a new one, which he was probably
wearing for the first time and had put on specially for the interview. He clasped his umbrella to his chest and scurried into the
interviewing room with his dhoti hanging about his legs and his
face swollen with embarrassment and confusion.

We all sat and waited. The fan, which seemed to be a very old
one, made a creaking noise. One man kept cracking his finger joints
—*tik*, we heard, *tik*. All the rest of us kept very still. From time to
time, the official with the list came in and walked around the room
very slowly, tapping his list, and then we all looked down at our
feet, and the man even stopped cracking his fingers. A faint and
muffled sound of voices came from behind the closed door. Sometimes a voice was raised, but even then I could not make out what
was being said, though I strained hard.

My previous interview was very unpleasant for me. One of the
people who were interviewing took a dislike to me and shouted at
me very loudly. He was a large, fat man who wore an English suit.
His teeth were quite yellow, and when he became angry and shouted
he showed them all, and even though I was very upset, I couldn't
help looking at them and wondering how they had become so
yellow. I don't know why he was angry. He shouted, "Good God,
man! Can't you understand what's said to you?" It was true I could
not understand, but I had been trying hard to answer well. What
else did he expect of me? Probably there was something in my
appearance he did not like. It happens that way sometimes—they

take a dislike to you, and then, of course, there is nothing you can do.

Now the thought of the man with the yellow teeth made me more anxious than ever. I need great calm in my life. Whenever anything worries me too much, I have to cast the thought of it off immediately; otherwise, there is a danger that I may become ill. I felt now as if I were about to become very ill. All my limbs were itching, so that it was difficult for me to sit still, and I could feel blood rushing into my brain. I knew it was this room that was doing me so much harm—the waiting, silent men, the noise from the fan, the official with the list walking up and down, tapping his list or striking it against his thigh, and the big closed door behind which the interview was going on. I felt a great need to get up and go away. I *didn't* want the job. I wasn't even thinking about it any more—only about how to avoid having to sit here and wait.

Now the door opened again and the man with the torn dhoti came out. He was biting his lip and scratching the back of his neck, and he, too, walked straight out without looking at us at all. The big door of the interviewing room was left slightly open for a moment, and I could see a man's arm in a white shirtsleeve, and part of the back of his head. His shirt was very white and of good material, and his ears stood away from his head, so that one could see how his spectacles fitted over the backs of his ears. I suddenly realized that this man would be my enemy, and that he would make things very difficult for me, and perhaps even shout at me. Then I knew it was no use for me to stay there. The official with the list came back, and a panic seized me that he would read out my name. I rose quickly, murmuring, "Please excuse me—bathroom," and went out. I heard the official with the list call after me "Hey, Mister, where are you going?" so I lowered my head and walked faster. I would have started to run, but that might have caused some kind of suspicion, so I just walked as fast as I could down the stairs and right out of the building. There, at last, I was able to stop and take a deep breath, and I felt much better.

I stood still only for a minute, and then I started off again, though not in any particular direction. There were a great many clerks and peons moving past me in the street, hurrying from one office building to another, with files and papers under their arms. Everyone seemed to have something to do. In the next block, I found a little park, and I was glad to see people like myself, who had nothing to do, sitting under the trees or in any other patch of shade they could find. But I couldn't sit there; it was too close to the office blocks, and any moment someone might come up and say to me, "Why did you go away?" So I walked farther. I was feeling quite lighthearted with relief over having escaped the interview.

At last I came to a row of eating stalls, and I sat down on a wooden bench outside one of them, which was called the Paris Hotel, and asked for tea. I felt badly in need of tea, and since I intended to walk part of the way home, I was in a position to pay for it. There were two Sikhs sitting at the end of my bench, who were eating with great appetite, dipping their hands very rapidly into brass bowls. Between mouthfuls, they exchanged remarks with the proprietor of the Paris Hotel, who sat high up inside his stall, stirring a big brass pot in which he was cooking the day's food. He was chewing a betel leaf, and from time to time he very skill-fully spat the red betel juice far over the cooking pot and onto the ground between the wooden benches and tables.

I sat quietly at my end of the bench and drank my tea. The food smelled good, and it made me realize that I was hungry. I made a calculation, and decided that if I walked all the way home, I could afford a little cake. (I am very fond of sweet things.) The cake was not very new, but it had a beautiful piece of bright orange peel inside it. What I wanted to do when I got home was to lie down at once and not wake up again until the next morning. That way, no one would be able to ask me any questions. By not looking at my wife at all I would be able to avoid the question in her eyes. I would not look at my sister-in-law, either, but she would be smiling, that I knew—leaning against the wall, with her hand on her hip, and looking at me and smiling. She would know that I had run away, but she would not say anything.

Let her know! What did it matter? It was true I had no job and no immediate prospect of getting one. It was true that I was de-pendent on my brother. Everybody knew that. There is no shame in it; there are many people without jobs. And she had been so kind to me up till now that there was no reason she should not continue to be kind to me.

The Sikhs at the end of the bench had finished eating. They licked their fingers and belched deeply, the way one does after a good meal. They started to joke and laugh with the proprietor. I sat quiet and alone at my end of the bench. Of course, they did not laugh and joke with me, for they knew that I was superior to them; they work with their hands, whereas I am a lettered man who does not have to sweat for a living but sits on a chair in an office and writes figures and can speak in English. My brother is very proud of his superiority, and he has great contempt for carpenters and mechanics and such people. I, too, am proud of being a lettered man, but when I listened to the Sikhs laughing and joking, it occurred to me that perhaps their life was happier than mine. It was a thought that had come to me before. There is a carpenter who lives downstairs in our house, and though he is poor, there is always great eating in his house, and many people come, and I hear them laughing and singing and even dancing. The carpenter is a big, strong man, and he always looks happy, never anxious and sick with worry the way my brother does. To be sure, he doesn't wear shoes and clean white clothes as my brother and I do, nor does he speak any English, but all the same he is happy. I don't think he gets weary of his work, and he doesn't look like a man who is afraid of his superior officers.

I put the ignorant carpenter out of my mind, and thought again of my sister-in-law. If I were kind to her, I decided, she would really be kind to me someday. I became quite excited at this idea. Then I would know whether she is as soft and yet as strong as she looks. And I would know about her mouth, with the big, strong teeth. Her tongue and palate are very pink—just the color of the pink satin blouse she wears on festive occasions. And this satin has often made me think also of how smooth and warm her skin would feel. Her eyes would be shut and perhaps there would be tears on the lashes, and she would be smiling, but in a different sort of way. I became very excited when I thought of it, but then the excitement passed and I was sad. I thought of my wife, who is thin and not beautiful, and is without excitement. But she does whatever I want and always tries to please me. I thought of her whispering to me in the night, "Take me away to live somewhere alone—only you and I and the children." That can never be, and so always she will have to be unhappy.

Sitting on that bench, I grew more and more sad when I thought of her being unhappy, because it is not only she who is unhappy but I also, and many others. Everywhere there is unhappiness. I thought of the man whose new dhoti had been torn and who would now have to go home and sew it carefully, so that the tear would not be seen. I thought of all those other men sitting and waiting to be interviewed, all but one or two of whom would not get the job for

which they had come, and so would have to go on to another interview and another and another, to sit and wait and be anxious. And
my brother, who has a job but is frightened that he will lose it—
and my mother, who is so old that she can only sit on the floor and
stroke her pieces of cloth—and my sister-in-law, who is warm and
strong and does not care for her husband. Yet life could be so different. When I go to the cinema and hear the beautiful songs they
sing, I know how different it could be, and also sometimes when I
sit alone and think my thoughts, I have a feeling that everything
could be truly beautiful. But now my tea was finished and also my
cake, and I wished I had not bought them, because it was a long
way to walk home and I was tired.

IN THE ZOO

❖

JEAN STAFFORD

K EENING harshly in his senility, the blind polar bear slowly and
ceaselessly shakes his head in the stark heat of the July and
mountain noon. His open eyes are blue. No one stops to look at
him; an old farmer, in passing, sums up the old bear's situation by
observing, with a ruthless chuckle, that he is a "back number."
Patient and despairing, he sits on his yellowed haunches on the central rock of his pool, his huge toy paws wearing short boots of mud.

The grizzlies to the right of him, a conventional family of father
and mother and two spring cubs, alternately play the clown and
sleep. There is a blustery, scoundrelly, half-likable bravado in the
manner of the black bear on the polar's left; his name, according to
the legend on his cage, is Clancy, and he is a rough-and-tumble,
brawling blowhard, thundering continually as he paces back and
forth, or pauses to face his audience of children and mothers and
release from his great, gray-tongued mouth a perfectly Vesuvian
roar. If he were to be reincarnated in human form, he would be a
man of action, possibly a football coach, probably a politician. One
expects to see his black hat hanging from a branch of one of his
trees; at any moment he will light a cigar.

The polar bear's next-door neighbors are not the only ones who
offer so sharp and sad a contrast to him. Across a reach of scrappy
grass and litter is the convocation of conceited monkeys, burrowing
into each other's necks and chests for fleas, picking their noses with
their long, black, finicky fingers, swinging by their gifted tails on
the flying trapeze, screaming bloody murder. Even when they mourn
—one would think the male orangutan was on the very brink of
suicide—they are comedians; they only fake depression, for they are
firmly secure in their rambunctious tribalism and in their appalling
insight and contempt. Their flibbertigibbet gambolling is a sham,
and, stealthily and shiftily, they are really watching the pitiful polar

596

bear ("Back number," they quote the farmer. "That's *his* number all right," they snigger), and the windy black bear ("Life of the party. Gasbag. Low I.Q.," they note scornfully on his dossier), and the stupid, bourgeois grizzlies ("It's feed the face and hit the sack for them," the monkeys say). And they are watching my sister and me, two middle-aged women, as we sit on a bench between the exhibits, eating popcorn, growing thirsty. We are thoughtful.

A chance remark of Daisy's a few minutes before has turned us to memory and meditation. "I don't know why," she said, "but that poor blind bear reminds me of Mr. Murphy." The name "Mr. Murphy" at once returned us both to childhood, and we were floated far and fast, our later lives diminished. So now we eat our popcorn in silence with the ritualistic appetite of childhood, which has little to do with hunger; it is not so much food as a sacrament, and in tribute to our sisterliness and our friendliness I break the silence to say that this is the best popcorn I have ever eaten in my life. The extravagance of my statement instantly makes me feel self-indulgent, and for some time I uneasily avoid looking at the blind bear. My sister does not agree or disagree; she simply says that popcorn is the only food she has ever really liked. For a long time, then, we eat without a word, but I know, because I know her well and know her similarity to me, that Daisy is thinking what I am thinking; both of us are mournfully remembering Mr. Murphy, who, at one time in our lives, was our only friend.

This zoo is in Denver, a city that means nothing to my sister and me except as a place to take or meet trains. Daisy lives two hundred miles farther west, and it is her custom, when my every-other-year visit with her is over, to come across the mountains to see me off on my eastbound train. We know almost no one here, and because our stays are short, we have never bothered to learn the town in more than the most desultory way. We know the Burlington uptown office and the respectable hotels, a restaurant or two, the Union Station, and, beginning today, the zoo in the city park.

But since the moment that Daisy named Mr. Murphy by name our situation in Denver has been only corporeal; our minds and our hearts are in Adams, fifty miles north, and we are seeing, under the white sun at its pitiless meridian, the streets of that ugly town, its parks and trees and bridges, the bandstand in its dreary park, the roads that lead away from it, west to the mountains and east to the plains, its mongrel and multitudinous churches, its high school shaped like a loaf of bread, the campus of its college, an oasis of which we had no experience except to walk through it now and then, eying the woodbine on the impressive buildings. These things are engraved forever on our minds with a legibility so insistent that you have only to say the name of the town aloud to us to rip the rinds from our nerves and leave us exposed in terror and humiliation.

We have supposed in later years that Adams was not so bad as all that, and we know that we magnified its ugliness because we looked upon it as the extension of the possessive, unloving, scornful, complacent foster mother, Mrs. Placer, to whom, at the death of our parents within a month of each other, we were sent like Dickensian grotesqueries—cowardly, weak-stomached, given to tears, backward in school. Daisy was ten and I was eight when, unaccompanied, we made the long trip from Marblehead to our benefactress, whom we had never seen and, indeed, never heard of until the pastor of our church came to tell us of the arrangement our father had made on his deathbed, seconded by our mother on hers. This man, whose name and face I have forgotten and whose parting speeches to us I have not forgiven, tried to dry our tears with talk of Indians and of buffaloes; he spoke, however, at much greater length, and in preaching cadences, of the Christian goodness of Mrs. Placer. She was, he said, childless and fond of children, and for many years she had been a widow, after the lingering demise of her tubercular husband, for whose sake she had moved to the Rocky Mountains. For his support and costly medical care, she had run a boarding house, and after his death, since he had left her nothing, she was obliged to continue running it. She had been a girlhood friend of our paternal grandmother, and our father, in the absence of responsible relatives, had made her the beneficiary of his life insurance on the condition that she lodge and rear us. The pastor, with a frankness remarkable considering that he was talking to children, explained to us that our father had left little more than a drop in the bucket for our care, and he enjoined us to give Mrs. Placer, in return for her hospitality and sacrifice, courteous help and eternal thanks. "Sacrifice" was a word we were never allowed to forget.

And thus it was, in grief for our parents, that we came cringing to the dry Western town and to the house where Mrs. Placer lived, a house in which the square, uncushioned furniture was cruel and the pictures on the walls were either dour or dire and the lodgers,

who lived in the upper floors among shadowy wardrobes and chiffoniers, had come through the years to resemble their landlady in
appearance as well as in deportment.

After their ugly-colored evening meal, Gran—as she bade us call
her—and her paying guests would sit, rangy and aquiline, rocking on
the front porch on spring and summer and autumn nights, tasting
their delicious grievances: those slights delivered by ungrateful sons
and daughters, those impudences committed by trolley-car conductors and uppity salesgirls in the ready-to-wear, all those slurs and
calculated elbow-jostlings that were their daily crucifixion and their
staff of life. We little girls, washing the dishes in the cavernous
kitchen, listened to their even, martyred voices, fixed like leeches to
their solitary subject and their solitary creed—that life was essentially a matter of being done in, let down, and swindled.

At regular intervals, Mrs. Placer, chairwoman of the victims,
would say, "Of course, I don't care; I just have to laugh," and then
would tell a shocking tale of an intricate piece of skulduggery perpetrated against her by someone she did not even know. Sometimes,
with her avid, partial jury sitting there on the porch behind the
bitter hopvines in the heady mountain air, the cases she tried involved Daisy and me, and, listening, we travailed, hugging each
other, whispering, "I wish she wouldn't! Oh, how did she find out?"
How *did* she? Certainly we never told her when we were snubbed
or chosen last on teams, never admitted to a teacher's scolding or to
the hoots of laughter that greeted us when we bit on silly, unfair
jokes. But she knew. She knew about the slumber parties we were
not invited to, the beefsteak fries at which we were pointedly left
out; she knew that the singing teacher had said in so many words
that I could not carry a tune in a basket and that the sewing superintendent had said that Daisy's fingers were all thumbs. With our
teeth chattering in the cold of our isolation, we would hear her
protestant, litigious voice defending our right to be orphans,
paupers, wholly dependent on her—except for the really ridiculous
pittance from our father's life insurance—when it was all she could
do to make ends meet. She did not care, but she had to laugh that
people in general were so small-minded that they looked down on
fatherless, motherless waifs like us and, by association, looked down
on her. It seemed funny to her that people gave her no credit for
taking on these sickly youngsters who were not even kin but only
the grandchildren of a friend.

If a child with braces on her teeth came to play with us, she was, according to Gran, slyly lording it over us because our teeth were crooked, but there was no money to have them straightened. And what could be the meaning of our being asked to come for supper at the doctor's house? Were the doctor and his la-di-da New York wife and those pert girls with their solid-gold barrettes and their Shetland pony going to shame her poor darlings? Or shame their poor Gran by making them sorry to come home to the plain but honest life that was all she could provide for them?

There was no stratum of society not reeking with the effluvium of fraud and pettifoggery. And the school system was almost the worst of all: if we could not understand fractions, was that not our teacher's fault? And therefore what right had she to give us F? It was as plain as a pikestaff to Gran that the teacher was only covering up her own inability to teach. It was unlikely, too—highly unlikely —that it was by accident that time and time again the free medical clinic was closed for the day just as our names were about to be called out, so that nothing was done about our bad tonsils, which meant that we were repeatedly sick in the winter, with Gran fetching and carrying for us, climbing those stairs a jillion times a day with her game leg and her heart that was none too strong.

Steeped in these mists of accusation and hidden plots and double meanings, Daisy and I grew up like worms. I think no one could have withstood the atmosphere in that house where everyone trod on eggs that a little bird had told them were bad. They spied on one another, whispered behind doors, conjectured, drew parallels beginning "With all due respect . . ." or "It is a matter of indifference to *me* but . . ." The vigilantes patrolled our town by day, and by night returned to lay their goodies at their priestess's feet and wait for her oracular interpretation of the innards of the butcher, the baker, the candlestick maker, the soda jerk's girl, and the barber's unnatural deaf white cat.

Consequently, Daisy and I also became suspicious. But it was suspicion of ourselves that made us mope and weep and grimace with self-judgment. Why were we not happy when Gran had sacrificed herself to the bone for us? Why did we not cut dead the paper boy who had called her a filthy name? Why did we persist in our willful friendliness with the grocer who had tried, unsuccessfully, to overcharge her on a case of pork and beans?

Our friendships were nervous and surreptitious; we sneaked and lied, and as our hungers sharpened, our debasement deepened; we were pitied; we were shifty-eyed, always on the lookout for Mrs. Placer or one of her tattletale lodgers; we were hypocrites.

Nevertheless, one thin filament of instinct survived, and Daisy and I in time found asylum in a small menagerie down by the railroad tracks. It belonged to a gentle alcoholic ne'er-do-well, who did nothing all day long but drink bathtub gin in rickeys and play solitaire and smile to himself and talk to his animals. He had a little, stunted red vixen and a deodorized skunk, a parrot from Tahiti that spoke Parisian French, a woebegone coyote, and two capuchin monkeys, so serious and humanized, so small and sad and sweet, and so religious-looking with their tonsured heads that it was impossible not to think their gibberish was really an ordered language with a grammar that someday some philologist would understand.

Gran knew about our visits to Mr. Murphy and she did not object, for it gave her keen pleasure to excoriate him when we came home. His vice was not a matter of guesswork; it was an established fact that he was half-seas over from dawn till midnight. "With the black Irish," said Gran, "the taste for drink is taken in with the mother's milk and is never mastered. Oh, I know all about those promises to join the temperance movement and not to touch another drop. The way to Hell is paved with good intentions."

We were still little girls when we discovered Mr. Murphy, before the shattering disease of adolescence was to make our bones and brains ache even more painfully than before, and we loved him and we hoped to marry him when we grew up. We loved him, and we loved his monkeys to exactly the same degree and in exactly the same way; they were husbands and fathers and brothers, these little, ugly, dark, secret men who minded their own business and let us mind ours. If we stuck our fingers through the bars of the cage, the monkeys would sometimes take them in their tight, tiny hands and look into our faces with a tentative, somehow absent-minded sorrow, as if they terribly regretted that they could not place us but were glad to see us all the same. Mr. Murphy, playing a solitaire game of cards called "once in a blue moon" on a kitchen table in his back yard beside the pens, would occasionally look up and blink his beautiful blue eyes and say, "You're peaches to make over my wee friends. I love you for it." There was nothing demanding in his voice, and nothing sticky; on his lips the word "love" was jocose and forthright, it had no strings attached. We would sit on either side of him and watch him regiment his ranks of cards and stop to drink as deeply as if he were dying of thirst and wave to his animals and say to them, "Yes, lads, you're dandies."

Because Mr. Murphy was as reserved with us as the capuchins were, as courteously noncommittal, we were surprised one spring day when he told us that he had a present for us, which he hoped Mrs. Placer would let us keep; it was a puppy, for whom the owner had asked him to find a home—half collie and half Labrador retriever, blue-blooded on both sides.

"You might tell Mrs. Placer—" he said, smiling at the name, for Gran was famous in the town. "You might tell Mrs. Placer," said Mr. Murphy, "that this lad will make a fine watchdog. She'll never have to fear for her spoons again. Or her honor." The last he said to himself, not laughing but tucking his chin into his collar; lines sprang to the corners of his eyes. He would not let us see the dog, whom we could hear yipping and squealing inside his shanty, for he said that our disappointment would weigh on his conscience if we lost our hearts to the fellow and then could not have him for our own.

That evening at supper, we told Gran about Mr. Murphy's present. A dog? In the first place, why a dog? Was it possible that the news had reached Mr. Murphy's ears that Gran had just this very day finished planting her spring garden, the very thing that a rampageous dog would have in his mind to destroy? What sex was it? A male! Females, she had heard, were more trustworthy; males roved and came home smelling of skunk; such a consideration as this, of course, would not have crossed Mr. Murphy's fuddled mind. Was this young male dog housebroken? We had not asked? That was the limit!

Gran appealed to her followers, too raptly fascinated by Mr. Murphy's machinations to eat their Harvard beets. "Am I being farfetched or does it strike you as decidedly queer that Mr. Murphy is trying to fob off on my little girls a young cur that has not been trained?" she asked them. "If it were housebroken, he would have said so, so I feel it is safe to assume that it is not. Perhaps cannot *be* housebroken. I've heard of such cases."

The fantasy spun on, richly and rapidly, with all the skilled helping hands at work at once. The dog was tangibly in the room with us, shedding his hair, biting his fleas, shaking rain off himself to splatter the walls, dragging some dreadful carcass across the floor, chewing up slippers, knocking over chairs with his tail, gobbling the chops from the platter, barking, biting, fathering, fighting, smelling to high heaven of carrion, staining the rug with his muddy feet, scratching the floor with his claws. He developed rabies; he bit a child, two children! Three! Everyone in town! And Gran and her poor darlings went to jail for harboring this murderous, odoriferous, drunk, Roman Catholic dog.

And yet, astoundingly enough, she came around to agreeing to let us have the dog. It was, as Mr. Murphy had predicted, the word "watchdog" that deflected the course of the trial. The moment Daisy uttered it, Gran halted, marshalling her reverse march; while she rallied and tacked and reconnoitred, she sent us to the kitchen for the dessert. And by the time this course was under way, the uses of a dog, the enormous potentialities for investigation and law enforcement in a dog trained by Mrs. Placer, were being minutely and passionately scrutinized by the eight upright bloodhounds sitting at the table wolfing their brown Betty as if it were fresh-killed rabbit. The dog now sat at attention beside his mistress, fiercely alert, ears cocked, nose aquiver, the protector of widows, of orphans, of lonely people who had no homes. He made short shrift of burglars, homicidal maniacs, Peeping Toms, gypsies, bogus missionaries, Fuller Brush men with a risqué spiel. He went to the store and brought back groceries, retrieved the evening paper from the awkward place the boy had meanly thrown it, rescued cripples from burning houses, saved children from drowning, heeled at command, begged, lay down, stood up, sat, jumped through a hoop, ratted.

Both times—when he was a ruffian of the blackest delinquency and then a pillar of society—he was full-grown in his prefiguration, and when Laddy appeared on the following day, small, unsteady, and whimpering lonesomely, Gran and her lodgers were taken aback; his infant, clumsy paws embarrassed them, his melting eyes were unapropos. But it could never be said of Mrs. Placer, as Mrs. Placer her own self said, that she was a woman who went back on her word, and her darlings were going to have their dog, softheaded and feckless as he might be. All the first night, in his carton in the kitchen, he wailed for his mother, and in the morning, it was true, he had made a shambles of the room—fouled the floor, and pulled off the tablecloth together with a ketchup bottle, so that thick gore lay everywhere. At breakfast, the lodgers confessed they had had a most amusing night, for it had actually been funny the way the dog had been determined not to let anyone get a wink of sleep. After that first night, Laddy slept in our room, receiving from us, all through our delighted, sleepless nights, pats and embraces and kisses and whispers. He was our baby, our best friend, the smartest, prettiest, nicest dog in the entire wide world. Our soft and rapid blandishments excited him to yelp at us in pleased bewilderment, and then we would playfully grasp his muzzle, so that he would snarl, deep in his throat like an adult dog, and shake his head violently, and, when we freed him, nip us smartly with great good will.

He was an intelligent and genial dog and we trained him quickly. He steered clear of Gran's radishes and lettuce after she had several times given him a brisk comeuppance with a strap across the rump, and he soon left off chewing shoes and the laundry on the line, and he outgrew his babyish whining. He grew like a weed; he lost his spherical softness, and his coat, which had been sooty fluff, came in stiff and rusty black; his nose grew aristocratically long, and his clever, pointed ears stood at attention. He was all bronzy, lustrous black except for an Elizabethan ruff of white and a tip of white at the end of his perky tail. No one could deny that he was exceptionally handsome and that he had, as well, great personal charm and style. He escorted Daisy and me to school in the morning, laughing interiorly out of the enormous pleasure of his life as he gracefully cantered ahead of us, distracted occasionally by his private interest in smells or unfamiliar beings in the grass but, on the whole, engrossed in his role of chaperon. He made friends easily with other dogs, and sometimes he went for a long hunting weekend into the mountains with a huge and bossy old red hound named Mess, who had been on the county most of his life and had made a good thing of it, particularly at the fire station.

It was after one of these three-day excursions into the high country that Gran took Laddy in hand. He had come back spent and filthy, his coat a mass of cockleburs and ticks, his eyes bloodshot, loud *râles* in his chest; for half a day he lay motionless before the front door like someone in a hangover, his groaning eyes explicitly saying "Oh, for God's sake, leave me be" when we offered him food or bowls of water. Gran was disapproving, then affronted, and finally furious. Not, of course, with Laddy, since all inmates of her house enjoyed immunity, but with Mess, whose caddish character, together with that of his nominal masters, the firemen, she examined closely under a strong light, with an air of detachment, with her not caring but her having, all the same, to laugh. A lodger who occupied the back west room had something to say about the

fire chief and his nocturnal visits to a certain house occupied by a
certain group of young women, too near the same age to be sisters
and too old to be the daughters of the woman who claimed to be
their mother. What a story! The exophthalmic librarian—she lived
in one of the front rooms—had some interesting insinuations to
make about the deputy marshal, who had borrowed, significantly,
she thought, a book on hypnotism. She also knew—she was, of
course, in a most useful position in the town, and from her authoritative pen in the middle of the library her mammiform and azure
eyes and her eager ears missed nothing—that the fire chief's wife
was not as scrupulous as she might be when she was keeping score
on bridge night at the Sorosis.

There was little at the moment that Mrs. Placer and her disciples
could do to save the souls of the Fire Department and their families,
and therefore save the town from holocaust (a very timid boarder
—a Mr. Beaver, a newcomer who was not to linger long—had sniffed
throughout this recitative as if he were smelling burning flesh), but
at least the unwholesome bond between Mess and Laddy could and
would be severed once and for all. Gran looked across the porch at
Laddy, who lay stretched at full length in the darkest corner,
shuddering and baying abortively in his throat as he chased jack
rabbits in his dreams, and she said, "A dog can have morals like a
human." With this declaration Laddy's randy, manly holidays were
finished. It may have been telepathy that woke him; he lifted his
heavy head from his paws, laboriously got up, hesitated for a moment, and then padded languidly across the porch to Gran. He stood
docilely beside her chair, head down, tail drooping as if to say,
"O.K., Mrs. Placer, show me how and I'll walk the straight and narrow."

The very next day, Gran changed Laddy's name to Caesar, as
being more dignified, and a joke was made at the supper table that
he had come, seen, and conquered Mrs. Placer's heart—for within
her circle, where the magnanimity she lavished upon her orphans
was daily demonstrated, Mrs. Placer's heart was highly thought of.
On that day also, although we did not know it yet, Laddy ceased to
be our dog. Before many weeks passed, indeed, he ceased to be
anyone we had ever known. A week or so after he became Caesar,
he took up residence in her room, sleeping alongside her bed. She
broke him of the habit of taking us to school (temptation to low
living was rife along those streets; there was a chow—well, never
mind) by the simple expedient of chaining him to a tree as soon as

she got up in the morning. This discipline, together with the stamina-building cuffs she gave his sensitive ears from time to time, gradually but certainly remade his character. From a sanguine, affectionate, easygoing Gael (with the fits of melancholy that alternated with the larkiness), he turned into an overbearing, military, efficient, loud-voiced Teuton. His bark, once wide of range, narrowed to one dark, glottal tone.

Soon the paper boy flatly refused to serve our house after Caesar efficiently removed the bicycle clip from his pants leg; the skin was not broken, or even bruised, but it was a matter of principle with the boy. The milkman approached the back door in a seizure of shakes like St. Vitus's dance. The metermen, the coal men, and the garbage collector crossed themselves if they were Catholics and, if they were not, tried whistling in the dark. "Good boy, good Caesar," they carolled, and, unctuously lying, they said they knew his bark was worse than his bite, knowing full well that it was not, considering the very nasty nip, requiring stitches, he had given a representative of the Olson Rug Company, who had had the folly to pat him on the head. Caesar did not molest the lodgers, but he disdained them and he did not brook being personally addressed by anyone except Gran. One night, he wandered into the dining room, appearing to be in search of something he had mislaid, and, for some reason that no one was ever able to divine, suddenly stood stockstill and gave the easily upset Mr. Beaver a long and penetrating look. Mr. Beaver, trembling from head to toe, stammered, "Why —er, hello there, Caesar, old boy, old boy," and Caesar charged. For a moment, it was touch and go, but Gran saved Mr. Beaver, only to lose him an hour later when he departed, bag and baggage, for the Y.M.C.A. This rout and the consequent loss of revenue would more than likely have meant Caesar's downfall and his deportation to the pound if it had not been that a newly widowed druggist, very irascible and very much Gran's style, had applied for a room in her house a week or so before, and now he moved in delightedly, as if he were coming home.

Finally, the police demanded that Caesar be muzzled and they warned that if he committed any major crime again—they cited the case of the Olson man—he would be shot on sight. Mrs. Placer, although she had no respect for the law, knowing as much as she did about its agents, obeyed. She obeyed, that is, in part; she put the muzzle on Caesar for a few hours a day, usually early in the morning when the traffic was light and before the deliveries had started, but the rest of the time his powerful jaws and dazzling white sabre teeth were free and snapping. There was between these two such preternatural rapport, such an impressive conjugation of suspicion, that he, sensing the approach of a policeman, could convey instantly to her the immediate necessity of clapping his nose cage on. And the policeman, sent out on the complaint of a terrorized neighbor, would be greeted by this law-abiding pair at the door.

Daisy and I wished we were dead. We were divided between hating Caesar and loving Laddy, and we could not give up the hope that something, someday, would change him back into the loving animal he had been before he was appointed vice-president of the Placerites. Now at the meetings after supper on the porch he took an active part, standing rigidly at Gran's side except when she sent him on an errand. He carried out these assignments not with the air of a servant but with that of an accomplice. "Get me the paper, Caesar," she would say to him, and he, dismayingly intelligent and a shade smart-alecky, would open the screen door by himself and in a minute come back with the *Bulletin,* from which Mrs. Placer would then read an item, like the Gospel of the day, and then read between the lines of it, scandalized.

In the deepening of our woe and our bereavement and humiliation, we mutely appealed to Mr. Murphy. We did not speak outright to him, for Mr. Murphy lived in a state of indirection, and often when he used the pronoun "I," he seemed to be speaking of someone standing a little to the left of him, but we went to see him and his animals each day during the sad summer, taking what comfort we could from the cozy, quiet indolence of his back yard, where small black eyes encountered ours politely and everyone was half asleep. When Mr. Murphy inquired about Laddy in his bland, inattentive way, looking for a stratagem whereby to shift the queen of hearts into position by the king, we would say, "Oh, he's fine," or "Laddy is a nifty dog." And Mr. Murphy, reverently slaking the thirst that was his talent and his concubine, would murmur, "I'm glad."

We wanted to tell him, we wanted his help, or at least his sympathy, but how could we cloud his sunny world? It was awful to see Mr. Murphy ruffled. Up in the calm clouds as he generally was, he could occasionally be brought to earth with a thud, as we had seen and heard one day. Not far from his house, there lived a bad, troublemaking boy of twelve, who was forever hanging over the fence trying to teach the parrot obscene words. He got nowhere, for she spoke no English and she would flabbergast him with her cold eye and sneer, *"Tant pis."* One day, this boorish fellow went too far; he suddenly shot his head over the fence like a jack-in-the-box and aimed a water pistol at the skunk's face. Mr. Murphy leaped to his feet in a scarlet rage; he picked up a stone and threw it accurately, hitting the boy square in the back, so hard that he fell right down in a mud puddle and lay there kicking and squalling and, as it turned out, quite badly hurt. "If you ever come back here again, I'll kill you!" roared Mr. Murphy. I think he meant it, for I have seldom seen an anger so resolute, so brilliant, and so voluble. "How dared he!" he cried, scrambling into Mallow's cage to hug and pet and soothe her. "He must be absolutely mad! He must be the Devil!" He did not go back to his game after that but paced the yard, swearing a blue streak and only pausing to croon to his animals, now as frightened by him as they had been by the intruder, and to drink straight from the bottle, not bothering with fixings. We were fascinated by this unfamiliar side of Mr. Murphy, but we did not want to see it ever again, for his face had grown so dangerously purple and the veins of his forehead seemed ready to burst and his eyes looked scorched. He was the closest thing to a maniac we had ever seen. So we did not tell him about Laddy; what he did not know would not hurt him, although it was hurting us, throbbing in us like a great, bleating wound.

But eventually Mr. Murphy heard about our dog's conversion, one night at the pool hall, which he visited from time to time when he was seized with a rare but compelling garrulity, and the next afternoon when he asked us how Laddy was and we replied that he was fine, he tranquilly told us, as he deliberated whether to move the jack of clubs now or to bide his time, that we were sweet girls but we were lying in our teeth. He did not seem at all angry but only interested, and all the while he questioned us, he went on about his business with the gin and the hearts and spades and diamonds and clubs. It rarely happened that he won the particular game he was playing, but that day he did, and when he saw all the cards laid out in their ideal pattern, he leaned back, looking disappointed, and he said, "I'm damned." He then scooped up the cards, in a gesture unusually quick and tidy for him, stacked them together, and bound them with a rubber band. Then he began to tell us what he thought of Gran. He grew as loud and apoplectic as he had been that other time, and though he kept repeating that he knew *we* were innocent and he put not a shred of the blame on us, we were afraid that he might suddenly change his mind, and, speechless, we cowered against the monkeys' cage. In dread, the monkeys clutched the fingers we offered to them and made soft, protesting noises, as if to say, "Oh, stop it, Murphy! Our nerves!"

As quickly as it had started, the tantrum ended. Mr. Murphy paled to his normal complexion and said calmly that the only practical thing was to go and have it out with Mrs. Placer. "At once," he added, although he said he bitterly feared that it was too late and there would be no exorcising the fiend from Laddy's misused spirit. And because he had given the dog to us and not to her, he required that we go along with him, stick up for our rights, stand on our mettle, get up our Irish, and give the old bitch something to put in her pipe and smoke.

Oh, it was hot that day! We walked in a kind of delirium through the simmer, where only the grasshoppers had the energy to move, and I remember wondering if ether smelled like the gin on Mr. Murphy's breath. Daisy and I, in one way or another, were going to have our gizzards cut out along with our hearts and our souls and our pride, and I wished I were as drunk as Mr. Murphy, who swam effortlessly through the heat, his lips parted comfortably, his eyes half closed. When we turned in to the path at Gran's house, my blood began to scald my veins. It was so futile and so dangerous and so absurd. Here we were on a high moral mission, two draggletailed, gumptionless little girls and a toper whom no one could take seriously, partly because he was little more than a gurgling bottle of booze and partly because of the clothes he wore. He was a sight, as he always was when he was out of his own yard. There, somehow, in the carefree disorder, his clothes did not look especially strange, but on the streets of the town, in the barbershop or the post office or on Gran's path, they were fantastic. He wore a pair of hound's-tooth pants, old but maintaining a vehement pattern, and with them he wore a collarless blue flannelette shirt. His hat was the silliest of all, because it was a derby three sizes too big. And as if Shannon, too, was a part of his funny-paper costume, the elder capuchin rode on his shoulder, tightly embracing his thin red neck.

Gran and Caesar were standing side by side behind the screen door, looking as if they had been expecting us all along. For a moment, Gran and Mr. Murphy faced each other across the length of weedy brick between the gate and the front porch, and no one spoke. Gran took no notice at all of Daisy and me. She adjusted her eyeglasses, using both hands, and then looked down at Caesar and matter-of-factly asked, "Do you want out?"

Caesar flung himself full-length upon the screen and it sprang open like a jaw. I ran to meet and head him off, and Daisy threw a library book at his head, but he was on Mr. Murphy in one split second and had his monkey off his shoulder and had broken Shannon's neck in two shakes. He would have gone on nuzzling and mauling and growling over the corpse for hours if Gran had not marched out of the house and down the path and slapped him lightly on the flank and said, in a voice that could not have deceived an idiot, "Why, Caesar, you scamp! You've hurt Mr. Murphy's monkey! Aren't you ashamed!"

Hurt the monkey! In one final, apologetic shudder, the life was extinguished from the little fellow. Bloody and covered with slather, Shannon lay with his arms suppliantly stretched over his head, his leather fingers curled into loose, helpless fists. His hind legs and his tail lay limp and helter-skelter on the path. And Mr. Murphy, all of a sudden reeling drunk, burst into the kind of tears that Daisy and I knew well—the kind that time alone could stop. We stood aghast in the dark-red sunset, killed by our horror and our grief for Shannon and our unforgivable disgrace. We stood upright in a dead faint, and an eon passed before Mr. Murphy picked up Shannon's body and wove away, sobbing, "I don't believe it! I don't *believe* it!"

The very next day, again at morbid, heavy sunset, Caesar died in violent convulsions, knocking down two tall hollyhocks in his throes. Long after his heart had stopped, his right hind leg continued to jerk in aimless reflex. Madly methodical, Mr. Murphy had poisoned some meat for him, had thoroughly envenomed a whole pound of hamburger, and early in the morning, before sunup, when he must have been near collapse with his hangover, he had stolen up to Mrs. Placer's house and put it by the kitchen door. He was so stealthy that Caesar never stirred in his fool's paradise there on the floor by Gran. We knew these to be the facts, for Mr. Murphy made no bones about them. Afterward, he had gone home and said a solemn Requiem for Shannon in so loud a voice that someone sent for the police, and they took him away in the Black Maria to sober him up on strong green tea. By the time he was in the lockup and had confessed what he had done, it was far too late, for Caesar had already gulped down the meat. He suffered an undreamed-of agony

in Gran's flower garden, and Daisy and I, unable to bear the sight
of it, hiked up to the red rocks and shook there, wretchedly ripping
to shreds the sand lilies that grew in the cracks. Flight was the only
thing we could think of, but where could we go? We stared west at
the mountains and quailed at the look of the stern white glacier;
we wildly scanned the prairies for escape. "If only we were something besides kids! Besides girls!" mourned Daisy. I could not speak
at all; I huddled in a niche of the rocks and cried.

No one in town, except, of course, her lodgers, had the slightest
sympathy for Gran. The townsfolk allowed that Mr. Murphy was
a drunk and was fighting Irish, but he had a heart and this was
something that could never be said of Mrs. Placer. The neighbor
who had called the police when he was chanting the "Dies Irae" before breakfast in that deafening monotone had said, "The poor guy
is having some kind of a spell, so don't be rough on him, hear?" Mr.
Murphy became, in fact, a kind of hero; some people, stretching a
point, said he was a saint for the way that every day and twice on
Sunday he sang a memorial Mass over Shannon's grave, now marked
with a chipped, cheap plaster figure of Saint Francis. He withdrew
from the world more and more, seldom venturing into the streets at
all, except when he went to the bootlegger to get a new bottle to
snuggle into. All summer, all fall, we saw him as we passed by his
yard, sitting at his dilapidated table, enfeebled with gin, graying,
withering, turning his head ever and ever more slowly as he maneuvered the protocol of the kings and the queens and the knaves.
Daisy and I could never stop to visit him again.

It went on like this, year after year. Daisy and I lived in a mesh
of lies and evasions, baffled and mean, like rats in a maze. When we
were old enough for beaux, we connived like sluts to see them, but
we would never admit to their existence until Gran caught us out
by some trick. Like this one, for example: Once, at the end of a long
interrogation, she said to me, "I'm more relieved than I can tell
you that you *don't* have anything to do with Jimmy Gilmore, because I happen to know that he is after only one thing in a girl,"
and then, off guard in the loving memory of sitting in the movies
the night before with Jimmy, not even holding hands, I defended
him and defeated myself, and Gran, smiling with success, said, "I
thought you knew him. It's a pretty safe rule of thumb that where
there's smoke there's fire." That finished Jimmy and me, for afterward I was nervous with him and I confounded and alarmed and

finally bored him by trying to convince him, although the subject had not come up, that I did not doubt his good intentions.

Daisy and I would come home from school, or, later, from our jobs, with a small triumph or an interesting piece of news, and if we forgot ourselves and, in our exuberance, told Gran, we were hustled into court at once for cross-examination. Once, I remember, while I was still in high school, I told her about getting a part in a play. How very nice for me, she said, if that kind of make-believe seemed to me worth while. But what was my role? An old woman! A widow woman believed to be a witch? She did not care a red cent, but she did have to laugh in view of the fact that Miss Eccles, in charge of dramatics, had almost run her down in her car. And I would forgive her, would I not, if she did not come to see the play, and would not think her eccentric for not wanting to see herself ridiculed in public?

My pleasure strangled, I crawled, joy-killed, to our third-floor room. The room was small and its monstrous furniture was too big and the rag rugs were repulsive, but it was bright. We would not hang a blind at the window, and on this day I stood there staring into the mountains that burned with the sun. I feared the mountains, but at times like this their massiveness consoled me; they, at least, could not be gossiped about.

Why did we stay until we were grown? Daisy and I ask ourselves this question as we sit here on the bench in the municipal zoo, reminded of Mr. Murphy by the polar bear, reminded by the monkeys not of Shannon but of Mrs. Placer's insatiable gossips at their postprandial feast.

"But how could we have left?" says Daisy, wringing her buttery hands. "It was the depression. We had no money. We had nowhere to go."

"All the same, we could have gone," I say, resentful still of the waste of all those years. "We could have come here and got jobs as waitresses. Or prostitutes, for that matter."

"I wouldn't have wanted to be a prostitute," says Daisy.

We agree that under the circumstances it would have been impossible for us to run away. The physical act would have been simple, for the city was not far and we could have stolen the bus fare or hitched a ride. Later, when we began to work as salesgirls in Kress's, it would have been no trick at all to vanish one Saturday afternoon with our week's pay, without so much as going home to say goodbye. But it had been infinitely harder than that, for Gran, as we now see, held us trapped by our sense of guilt. We were vitiated, and we had no choice but to wait, flaccidly, for her to die.

You may be sure we did not unlearn those years as soon as we put her out of sight in the cemetery and sold her house for a song to the first boob who would buy it. Nor did we forget when we left the town for another one, where we had jobs at a dude camp—the town where Daisy now lives with a happy husband and two happy sons. The succubus did not relent for years, and I can still remember, in the beginning of our days at the Lazy S 3, overhearing an edgy millionaire say to his wife, naming my name, "That girl gives me the cold shivers. One would think she had just seen a murder." Well, I had. For years, whenever I woke in the night in fear or pain or loneliness, I would increase my suffering by the memory of Shannon, and my tears were as bitter as poor Mr. Murphy's.

We have never been back to Adams. But we see that house plainly, with the hopvines straggling over the porch. The windows are hung with the cheapest grade of marquisette, dipped into coffee to impart to it an unwilling color, neither white nor tan but individual and spitefully unattractive. We see the wicker rockers and the swing, and through the screen door we dimly make out the slightly veering corridor, along one wall of which stands a glass-doored bookcase; when we were children, it had contained not books but stale old cardboard boxes filled with such things as W.C.T.U. tracts and anti-cigarette literature and newspaper clippings related to sexual sin in the Christianized islands of the Pacific.

Even if we were able to close our minds' eyes to the past, Mr. Murphy would still be before us in the apotheosis of the polar bear. My pain becomes intolerable, and I am relieved when Daisy rescues us. "We've got to go," she says in a sudden panic. "I've got asthma coming on." We rush to the nearest exit of the city park and hail a cab, and, once inside it, Daisy gives herself an injection of adrenalin and then leans back. We are heartbroken and infuriated, and we cannot speak.

Two hours later, beside my train, we clutch each other as if we were drowning. We ought to go out to the nearest policeman and say, "We are not responsible women. You will have to take care of us because we cannot take care of ourselves." But gradually the storm begins to lull.

"You're sure you've got your ticket?" says Daisy. "You'll surely be able to get a roomette once you're on."

"I don't know about that," I say. "If there are any V.I.P.s on board, I won't have a chance. 'Spinsters and Orphans Last' is the motto of this line."

Daisy smiles. "I didn't care," she says, "but I had to laugh when I saw that woman nab the redcap you had signalled to. I had a good notion to give her a piece of my mind."

"It will be a miracle if I ever see my bags again," I say, mounting the steps of the train. "Do you suppose that blackguardly porter knows about the twenty-dollar gold piece in my little suitcase?"

"Anything's possible!" cries Daisy, and begins to laugh. She is so pretty, standing there in her bright-red linen suit and her black velvet hat. A solitary ray of sunshine comes through a broken pane in the domed vault of the train shed and lies on her shoulder like a silver arrow.

"So long, Daisy!" I call as the train begins to move.

She walks quickly along beside the train. "Watch out for pickpockets!" she calls.

"You, too!" My voice is thin and lost in the increasing noise of the speeding train wheels. "Goodbye, old dear!"

I go at once to the club car and I appropriate the writing table, to the vexation of a harried priest, who snatches up the telegraph pad and gives me a sharp look. I write Daisy approximately the same letter I always write her under this particular set of circumstances, the burden of which is that nothing for either of us can ever be as bad as the past before Gran mercifully died. In a postscript I add: "There is a Roman Catholic priest (that is to say, he is *dressed* like one) sitting behind me although all the chairs on the opposite side of the car are empty. I can only conclude that he is looking over my shoulder, and while I do not want to cause you any alarm, I think you would be advised to be on the lookout for any appearance of miraculous medals, scapulars, papist booklets, etc., in the shops of your town. It really makes me laugh to see the way he is pretending that all he wants is for me to finish this letter so that he can have the table."

I sign my name and address the envelope, and I give up my place to the priest, who smiles nicely at me, and then I move across the car to watch the fields as they slip by. They are alfalfa fields, but you can bet your bottom dollar that they are chockablock with marijuana.

I begin to laugh. The fit is silent but it is devastating; it surges and rattles in my rib cage, and I turn my face to the window to avoid the narrow gaze of the Filipino bar boy. I must think of something sad to stop this unholy giggle, and I think of the polar bear. But even his bleak tragedy does not sober me. Wildly I fling open the newspaper I have brought and I pretend to be reading something screamingly funny. The words I see are in a Hollywood gossip column: "How a well-known starlet can get a divorce in Nevada without her crooner husband's consent, nobody knows. It won't be worth a plugged nickel here."

THE ROSE GARDEN

❖

MAEVE BRENNAN

MARY LAMBERT, an Irish shopkeeper, was left a widow at the age of thirty-nine, after almost ten years of marriage. She was left with two children—Rose, seven, and Jimmy, two. As far as money was concerned, she was no worse off than she had been, since it was she who supported the family, out of the little general shop she kept.

Her husband, Dom, first showed his illness plainly in the month of October, but he lingered on, seeming to grow stronger at Christmas time, and died early in February, at about seven in the morning. Mary and a young priest of the parish, Father Mathews, were in the room with him when he died. Mary had Dom's comb in her hand, because he had asked her, one time during the night, to comb the hair back off his forehead. The comb was broken in half. She was accustomed to use the coarse-toothed half for her own hair, which was long and black. The fine-toothed half had been suitable for his lifeless invalid's hair. Even in health his hair had been fine and lifeless, but now it just looked dusty against the pillow. Father Mathews, who was anxious to get away, asked Mary if she would like him to send the woman next door up to see her, but she shook her head violently, and said that she'd be forced to make an exhibition of herself soon enough, at the wake and the funeral, and that for the time being she'd just as soon be left alone.

She sat down beside the bed, on the chair she had carried up from the parlor the morning she first had to send for the doctor. It was a straight-backed mahogany chair with a black horsehair seat. Ordinarily there would be no chair in the bedroom. She had expected the doctor to sit on it, but instead he had put his black bag down on it. She stared at the room. The room, its walls, its dull color, its scarce furniture, its dust, its faded holy pictures, its bad, sick aspect, disgusted her, and the body on the bed was a burden she

could not bear. The seat of the little parlor chair was hard under
her. There was no rest in the room. Her legs were tired. One leg
was shorter than the other, so that she had to walk crookedly, leaning forward and sideways. The exertion she had to make gave her
great power in her right leg. She wore long skirts, and tall black
boots laced tightly in but leaving her knees free. The laced boots
were very solid and hard-looking, as though the feet inside them
were made of wood. The feet inside were not made of wood. She
had a great feeling in them, and in all parts of her body.

She was big, with a narrow nose, and a narrow-lipped mouth too
small for the width of her face. She was well aware that she was
ugly and awkward, especially from the back. She said that the
crookedness in her legs came from climbing up and down the
twisted stairs of this house, in which she was born. The house was
really two corner houses that had been knocked into one. The
houses had been thrown together, and the staircase twisted determinedly from one house up into the other, although it was impossible to tell whether it had been built from the first floor up or
from the second floor down, the construction of it was so ungainly
and uneasy. The stairs thrust its way, crooked and hard, up through
the house, and some of its steps were so narrow it was difficult to
find a foothold on them, and some started wide and narrowed to
nothing at the other side, so that they could not be depended on
going down as they could going up. It was a treacherous stairs, but
no one had ever been known to slip on it, because it forced respect
and attention, and people guarded themselves on it.

Mary knew it very well. She knew where the hollows were, and
the worn places, and where it turned, and where it thinned off. It
changed appearance as the hours of the day went by, and looked
entirely different at night, in lamplight or candlelight. In the
wintertime the bottom step was always slippery with wet feet in
from the street. In the summertime the top step was warmed by sun
from a stray window, and when Mary was a child she often sat there
for hours, because her father spent all his time in the shop downstairs. Her mother had died at Mary's birth. Her father, a retired
policeman, was sixty when she was born. In his shop, in what had
once been the parlor of one of the houses, he sold bread, sugar,
milk, tea, cigarettes, apples, penny sweets, and flour. The milk
stood in a big tin can on the counter, with a dipper hanging from
the side of it, to measure out the customers' pints. The same farmer

who brought the milk brought eggs and butter. There was a sack of potatoes slumped open against the wall in one corner.

From the time she could walk, Mary hung around the shop. Because of her crippled leg, she often was allowed to miss school. Sometimes her father would sit her up at the window, which was filled with sweets, pencils, and cigarettes, and she would play with the sweets, and eat them, and look at the other children playing in the street or looking in at her. She grew fat, and by the time she was twenty she had settled into a wide, solid fatness. She developed a habit, in the street, of whirling around suddenly to discover who was looking at her ungainly back, and often she stood and stared angrily at people until they looked away, or turned away. Her rancor was all in her harsh, lurching walk, in her eyes, and in the pitch of her voice. She seldom upbraided anybody, but her voice was so ugly that she sounded rough no matter what she said.

She was silent from having no one to talk to, but she was very noisy in her ways. When she was left in charge of the shop, she would push restlessly around behind the counter, and move her hands and feet so carelessly that by the time her father got back, half the stock would be on the floor. There would be cigarettes, spilt sugar, toffees, splashes of milk, and even money down there by her boots. Her father would get down on his knees and scramble around, picking up what could be picked up, and cursing at her. She cared nothing for what he said. She had no fear of him, and he was not afraid of her, either. He had forgotten her mother, and she had no curiosity about her mother.

The counter in the shop was movable, and when she took charge, she made her father help her shove it forward from where she sat, to give her legs plenty of room. She always went to early Mass, when the streets were deserted, so that no one would have a chance to see her awful-looking back and perhaps laugh at her. During the whole year, there was only one occasion, apart from Mass time, when she willingly went outside the door, and that was in June, on the Feast of the Sacred Heart, when the nuns of the Holy Passion, who occupied a convent on a hill over the town, opened their famous rose garden to the public.

These nuns lived and had their boarding school in a stately stone building surrounded by smooth green lawns and spiky boxwood hedges, and hidden from the world by towering walls and massive iron gates. Except for the one day of the year when they threw open their garden, they had very little to do with the daily life of the

town. Their rose garden was very old. An illustrious family had
once owned these grounds, and it was they who had marked out
the garden, and dug it, and planted it, and enjoyed it, long ago,
years before the nuns came. Surrounded by its own particular wall,
and sealed by a narrow wooden door, the garden lay and flourished
some distance behind the convent, and it could only be reached
by a fenced-in path that led directly out of the back door of the
convent chapel. Only the nuns walked there. It was their private
place of meditation, and because of its remoteness, and also because
of the ancient, wild-armed trees that dominated the old estate, it
could not be viewed from any window of the convent.

All during the year the nuns walked privately in their garden,
and only opened it to ordinary people the one day. It is a pity that
everyone in the world could not be admitted at one time or another
to walk in that garden, best of all to walk there alone, it was so
beautiful in the sun. The nuns walked there undisturbed, apparently, and still it was altogether a stirring place, warm red, even
burning red, the way it filled the nostrils and left a sweet red taste
in the lips, red with too many roses, red as all the passionate instruments of worship, red as the tongue, red as the heart, red and dark,
in the slow-gathering summertime, as the treacherous parting in
the nuns' flesh, where they feared, and said they feared, the Devil
yet might enter in.

Even if there wasn't much of a summer, even if the sun was thin,
what heat there was somehow collected itself inside the high stone
walls of the garden. The walls should have been covered by a
creeper, a red leaf or a green leaf, but instead they were bare and
clean, warm under the hands. The tall walls of the garden were
uncovered and stony under the sun, except for one, the end wall,
that was covered by forsythia, yellow at its blooming time, on or
about Christmas Day. Then the forsythia wall would stand up overnight in a brilliant tracery of true yellow, a spidery pattern of yellow, more like a lace shawl than a blanket, but none the less wonderful for that. Of course, the forsythia showed to great advantage
then, with the rest of the garden a graveyard.

When word came of the yellow blooming, the nuns would come
out together in twos and threes, with their black wool shawls
around their shoulders, to witness the miracle. It was a great pleasure to them, confused in their minds with the other joys of Christmas, and they compared the delicate golden flowers to "baby stars
in the canopy of heaven" and "tiny candles lighted to honor the

coming of Our Lord." All of their images were gentle and diminutive, and they spoke in gentle excited voices, crying to each other across the frosty air, "Sister, Sister, did you hear what Sister just said?" "Sister, have you noticed how clear and silent the air is this morning?"

But with the coming of June the roses arrived in their hundreds and thousands, some so rich and red that they were called black, and some so pale that they might have been white, and all the depths between—carmine, crimson, blush, rose, scarlet, wine, purple, pink, and blood—and they opened themselves and spread themselves out, arching and dancing their long strong stems, and lay with lips loose and curling under the sun's heat, so that the perfume steamed up out of them, and the air thickened with it, and stopped moving under the weight of it.

Mary loved that burning garden. From one summer to the next, she never saw the nuns, nor did she think of them. She had no interest in them, and there was not one among them who as much as knew her name. It was their urgent garden she wanted. She craved for her sight of the roses. Every year she made her way up the hill, alone, and went into the garden, and sat down on a stone bench, covering the bench with her skirt so that no one would offer to share it with her. She would have liked to go in the early morning, when few people would be there and she would have a better look at the garden, but she was afraid she would be too much noticed in the emptiness, and so she went in the middle of the afternoon, when the crowd was thickest.

Once she had seen the garden in the rain. That was the year she remembered with most pleasure, because the loitering, strolling crowd that usually jammed the narrow paths between the rose beds was discouraged by the weather. She had the garden almost to herself, that time. Wet, the roses were more brilliant than they ever had been. Under the steady fine rain the clay in the beds turned black and rich, and the little green leaves shone, and the roses were washed into such brightness that it seemed as though a great heart had begun to beat under the earth, and was sending living blood up to darken the red roses, and make the pink roses purer.

Another year, the day turned out cold, and all the roses stood distinctly away from each other, and each one looked so delicate and confident in the sharp air that Mary thought she could never forget one of their faces as long as she lived. She had no desire to grow roses herself, or even to have a garden. It was this red garden, walled, secret, and lost to her, that she wanted. She loved the garden more than anyone had ever loved it, but she did not know about the forsythia that came in December to light up the end wall. No one had ever told her that the forsythia bloomed, or how it looked. She would have liked the forsythia very much, although it could not have enveloped her as the roses did. All during the year, she thought backward to her hour in the garden, and forward to it. It was terrible to her, to think that the garden was open to the nuns and closed to her. She spoke to no one about her longing. This was not her only secret, but it was her happiest one.

Mary's father used to take in lodgers—one lodger at a time because they only had one room to spare. The lodgers were men who visited the town from time to time, commercial travellers. Sometimes a man would take a job in the town, and stay with them for a few months or so. Once they had a commercial traveller who made a habit of staying with them every time he came to town, and then he got a job selling shoes in a local shop, and stayed almost a year. When he left for good, to take a better-paid job with a brother-in-law who had a business in Dublin, Dom Lambert came, and moved into the lodger's room.

Dom was a meek and mild little draper's assistant, with wide-open, anxious blue eyes and a wavering smile. He was accustomed to watch his customers vacillate between two or more rolls of cloth, and his smile vacillated from habit. He had small, stained teeth that were going bad. When they ached, he would sit very quietly with his hands clenched together and ask for hot milk. He told Mary that his skull was very thin. He said it was as thin as a new baby's, and that a good crack on it would be the finish of him. He was always stroking his skull, searching for fissures. He was afraid a roll of cloth might tumble down on him off a shelf and he would die with customers in the shop. Even a spool of thread, he said, might do considerable damage.

Dom dressed neatly, in dark draper's suits. He was most particular about the knot of his tie, and he wore a modest stickpin. He was proud of his small feet, and polished his shoes in the kitchen every morning, assuming various athletic positions according to whether he was wielding the polish brush, the polishing cloth, or the soft finishing brush. He brushed his suits, too, and did his nails with a finicky metal implement he carried in his pocket. He tidied his own room, and made his bed in the morning. Every morning he left the house at eight-thirty, and he returned at six-thirty. He liked to

read the paper at night, or play a few games of patience, or go for
a stroll. He went to bed early, and in the morning descended looking brisk and ready to do his day's work. Still, his color was bad,
and he often had to hammer his chest to dislodge a cough that
stuck there.

When Dom had been living nine years in the house, Mary's father
died very suddenly, one night. Mary was lying awake in the dark,
and she heard her father's voice calling loudly. She found him
hanging half out of bed, holding the little white stone holy-water
font, that he had dragged off its nail in the wall.

"The font is dry," he cried to her. "Get me the priest."

He waved his dry fingertips at her, that he had been feeling in
the font with, and died. Dom helped her to raise him back against
the bolster. She lifted the dry font from the floor and upended it
over her father's forehead.

"There might be a drop left in it," she said, but there was nothing. The font was sticky and black on the inside, and when she put
it to her nose it smelled like the room, but more strongly.

"He went very quick," Dom said. "Are you going to call the
priest?"

"I don't know what I'm going to do," she said. "I meant to fill
the font with holy water this coming Sunday."

"Are you going to shut his eyes?" Dom asked, pressing his hands
painfully together, as though he already felt the cold man's lids
resisting him.

"No," she said. "They'll be closed soon enough."

She took up her candle and walked back to her room, her white
flannel nightdress curved and plunging around her large body. She
got into bed and pulled the clothes up around her.

"Good night now," she said to Dom. "There's no more to be done
till morning."

She raised herself on her elbow to blow out the candle.

Dom said, "Are you not afraid to be in here by yourself, with
him dead in there like that?"

"He can't do anybody any harm now," she said. "What ails you,
Dom? Are you trying to tell me you're afraid of a poor dead man?"

"I'm afraid of my life," Dom said. His shirt, which was all he had
on, shivered in the leaping candlelight.

"Let me stay in here a minute," he said.

"Are you afraid he'll come after you, or what?"

"Let me kneel up here against the bed till it gets light!" he begged. "I'm not able to go back into that room by myself, and pass his door. Or put on your clothes, and we'll go together to call the priest."

"I'll do nothing of the sort," said Mary. "If you won't go back to bed, throw that skirt there around your shoulders, or you'll catch your death."

She dragged her great black skirt from where it hung over the end rail of the bed, and flung it to him. Then she blew out the candle and fell asleep, although she had intended to stay awake. As the room grew light, she woke up, to find Dom huddled against her in sleep. He was lying outside the covers, with his nose pressed against her shoulder, and her skirt almost concealing his head. As she watched him, he opened his eyes and gazed fearfully into her face. He started to close his eyes again, to pretend he was asleep, but thought better of it.

"I only wanted to get in out of the cold," he said.

"That's all very fine," said Mary, "but don't go trying to get on top of me."

"Oh, God, I wouldn't do the like of that!" Dom said.

"I don't know, now, there was a man lodged here before you came. He weighed a ton, it seemed like."

"A great big man!" said Dom, who was shocked.

"The same size as yourself. Maybe not even as big, but he was like lead. He came in here two nights running, just before he went off for good. The first night he came in, it was black dark. I thought for a minute it was my father getting in the bed with me, and then didn't I realize it was the commercial traveller. The next night, in he came again. I let on in the morning nothing had happened, and so did he."

"And did you not tell your father?"

"Why would I tell him?"

"Maybe it was your father all the time."

"It wasn't him. It was the commercial traveller, all right. If nothing else, I'd have known him by the feel of the shirt he had on him. Anyway, my father hadn't that much interest in me."

"Lord have mercy on him—your poor father, I mean," said Dom, who was growing uncomfortable and ashamed as the increasing light disclosed them to each other.

Mary had run out of small talk, but because she wanted him not to go, and because she had as much ordinary courage as any other human being, she spoke up. "I'll move over," she said, "and you

lie in here beside me. As long as you're here, you may as well settle
yourself."

The bed in which they lay, like all the beds in that house, was
made with only one sheet, the undersheet. There was no top sheet
—only the rough warm blanket, and then another blanket, a thinner
one, and on top of all a heavy patchwork quilt. The beds were high
up off the floor, and made of brass, and all the mattresses sagged.
The floors sagged, too, some sliding off to the side, and some sinking gently in the middle, and all of the rooms were on different
levels, because of the way in which the two houses had been flung
together. There were no carpets on the floors, and no little mats
or rugs. The bare old boards groaned disagreeably under the beds,
and under Mary's feet, and under Dom's feet.

Mary and Dom got married as quickly as they could, because
they were afraid the priest might come around and lecture them,
or maybe even denounce them publicly from the pulpit. They
settled down to live much as they had lived before Mary's father
died. Most of their life was spent in the kitchen. This was a large,
dark, crowded room set in the angle where the two houses joined,
and irregular because it took part of itself from one house and part
from the other. The only window in the kitchen was small and
high up, and set deep in the thick old wall. It looked out on a tiny,
dark yard, not more than a few feet square, in which there was an
outhouse. In this window recess Dom kept his own possessions—his
playing cards, a pencil, a bottle of blue-black ink, a straight pen,
a jotter, a package of writing paper with matching envelopes, and
the newspapers. After Rose got big enough to be with him, he
began to keep a tin box of toffees there, and he liked to play a game
of coaxing with her, with a toffee for a prize. The toffees were not
of a kind sold in Mary's shop, which offered only cheap loose
sweets, sold five for a penny, or even eight or ten for a penny. Rose
liked those sweets, too, but she liked the tin-box toffees in the bright
twists of paper best of all.

Rose was her father's girl. Everyone said so. Mary said so, more
often than anyone else. She said it bitterly to Dom, and mockingly
to Rose, but once she had said it she shut up, because it was not to
start a quarrel that she said it but only to let them know that she
knew.

Jimmy, the little baby, was Rose's pet. Dom liked him, but Rose
clung to him, and when he fretted she would hang over the side of

his cradle and talk to him, and dangle toys in front of him, and try to make him laugh.

Mary and Dom were not long married when Mary began to nag at him to give up his job at the draper's. Her reason for doing this, which she could not reveal to him, was that she could not bear to let people see him smile. She was unsmiling herself, as her father had been, and she believed that people only smiled in order to curry favor. People like herself, at any rate. "People like us," she was always saying, "people like us," but she did not know what she meant, unless it was that the rest of the people in the world were better off, or that they had some fortunate secret, or were engaged in a conspiracy in which she was not included.

Dom's smile did not disturb her until one afternoon she went over to the draper's to buy the makings of a dress for herself. She did not want him to wait on her, because she was ashamed to let him know how many yards it took to go around her, but she watched him with a customer, and it was then, against his own background of trying to sell and trying to please strangers, that she saw the history of his hopeful, uncertain smile, as he eagerly hauled down rolls of cloth and spread them out for inspection. After that day she gave him no peace till she got him out of his job. She told him that he could take over the running of her shop, and Dom liked that idea, because he had always wanted to be his own man, but he was just as anxious-faced behind her counter as he had ever been, and she gradually edged him back into the kitchen, out of sight.

She only wanted to take care of him, and protect him from people. She had known from a child that if she asked she would get, because of her deformity. She had always seen people getting ready to be nice to her because they pitied her and looked down on her. Everyone was inclined to pity her. How could they help themselves? She was an object for pity. The dead weight of her body, that she felt at every step, was visible to all the world. She almost had to kneel to walk. Even her hair was heavy, a dense black rug down her back. She was always afraid people might think she was asking for something. She always tried to get away from people as quickly as she could, before they got it into their heads that she was waiting for something. What smile could she give that would not be interpreted as a smile for help? In fact, that is what she thought, herself—that if she smiled at them it would only be to ingratiate herself, because she had no other reason to smile, since she hated them all. If she had said out loud why she hated them, she would have said it was because they were too well off, and stuck up, and too full of themselves. But she never would give them an opening for their smiles and greetings, and she came to feel that she had defeated them, and shut them all out. To have rescued Dom's weakness from their sight, and from their scornful pity—that was a triumph, although she was unable to share it with him, since she did not know how to explain to him that while she thought he was good enough, other people would never think him good enough, and therefore she had to save him from them, and hide him behind herself.

To pass the time, Dom began to do odd jobs around the house. Once in a while he took a broom and swept the upstairs rooms. Sometimes he got a hammer and some nails and wandered around, trying to tighten the floor boards or the stair boards, but the rigid, overstrained joints and joinings of the house rejected the new nails and spat them back out again before the tinny glitter had even worn off their heads. He often spent the whole day at a game of patience, and when Mary came back out of the shop to see about their middle-of-the-day meal, he would be sitting hunched over the kitchen table, with the cards spread out in front of him and a full cup of cold tea, left over from his breakfast, at his elbow. When Rose got to be big enough, he liked to tell her about the days when he was a draper, and he collected a few reels of thread, and some needles and pins, and bound some pieces of scrap cloth into neat rolls, and the two of them would play shop for hours.

Before Rose was born, Dom scrubbed out the old cradle in the kitchen, and polished it till it shone. The cradle had been there for Mary, and after she grew out of it it was used as a receptacle for old and useless things of the house. Before Dom scrubbed it, Mary cleared it out. It was a huge wooden cradle, dark brown and almost as big as a coffin, but seeming more roomy than a coffin, and it had a great curved wooden hood half covering it, that made the interior very gloomy. It stood on clumsy wooden rockers. There was no handle to rock it by. Mary remembered her father's hand on the side of it, and the shape of his nails. She had slept in the cradle, in the kitchen, until she was four, or nearly five. Her father had looked after her himself, so the cradle was left within easy distance of the shop. She could well remember her father looking in at her. Sometimes a woman would look in at her, but her father did not encourage visitors. He had the idea that all women were trying to marry him, or to get him to marry again, and he kept them out.

If Mary made a sudden movement, or jumped around, the cradle would rock far to the left and far to the right on its thick, curved rockers, and she knew that no power on earth could stop it until in the course of time it stopped itself. If she tried to clamber out, the cradle would start its deliberate plunging, right, left, right, left, and she would cower down with her face hidden in the bottom until the cradle was still under her again. She was always afraid alone in the dark bottom of the house. Her father slept upstairs. At night she would see his face, darkened by the candle he held aloft, and then the very last thing she would see was his shadow falling against the shallow, twisting staircase.

In the cradle, when she set about emptying it, Mary found a dark-red rubber ball with pieces torn, or rotted, out of it, and some folded, wrinkled bills, and a new mousetrap, never used, and a pipe of her father's, and two empty medicine bottles with the color of the medicines still on the bottoms of them, and a lot of corks, big and little, and a man's cloth cap, and a stiff, dusty wreath of artificial white flowers from her own First Communion veil, and a child's prayer book, her own, with the covers torn off.

When they were first married, Dom used to walk to early Mass with Mary on Sunday, but after a while he began making excuses, and they got into the habit of attending different Masses. She continued to go to the early Mass, and he would go later. When Rose started to walk, he took her with him. He would wash her, and do her hair, and see that her shoes were polished, and then she would give Mary a kiss goodbye and run off down the street after him.

One weekday morning, about a year before he died, Dom gave Mary the shock of her life. Instead of lying on in bed, as he usually did, he got up at seven-thirty, and shaved himself, and did himself up the way he used to in the days when he was at the draper's. When she saw him go out, she said nothing, but after a few minutes she locked the shop door, and went back and sat down at the kitchen table. People came knocking, but Mary paid no attention, and when Rose came to stand beside her she pushed her gently away. At three in the afternoon, she told Rose to mind the baby, and she put on her hat, and her Sunday coat, and went out looking for Dom. There was no sign of him on any street. At the draper's she stood and looked in, but he was not there. The man who had taken his place was only a youngster, very polite and sure of himself, she could see that. It occurred to her that even if she met Dom, she'd hardly know what to say, so she turned around and went home. Dom was sitting in the kitchen by the stove, warming his hands.

"Oh, I thought I would never see you again!" Mary cried.

Dom did not look up, but Rose looked up from her bead box. Dom asked, "What put that idea in your head?"

"I thought you'd gone off on me."

"Can't a man even go for a walk now, without the house being brought down around him?"

"I was full sure you were gone for good, when I saw you walking out of the door this morning. I didn't know what to do. I didn't know what I was going to do."

"Where would I go, will you tell me that?"

"Is that all you have to say to me, after the fright you've given me—that you have no place to go to? Is that the only reason you came back?"

"Rose," he said, turning from the stove. "Give us a look at the little necklace you're making there."

Mary got the tea ready. When they were all sitting at the table, she said loudly, "I suppose it was on Rose's account you came back. You were afraid I wouldn't take good enough care of her, I suppose?"

"That's a nice thing to say in front of the child," he said.

"You take her part against me."

"Somebody has to take her part."

"And who's to take my part?"

"Aren't you able to look after yourself?"

"I wish to God she'd been born crooked the way I was. There'd have been no pet child then."

"God forgive you for saying the like of that!" he shouted, and he jumped up out of his chair and made for the stairs.

"God has never forgiven me for anything!" she screamed after him, and she put her head down against the edge of the table.

Rose slipped around the table and put her arm around Mary's neck. "I'll mind you, Mammy," she said.

Mary looked at her. Rose had her father's uncertain smile, but on her face it was more eager. Mary saw the smile, and saw the champion spirit already shining out of Rose's eyes.

"Who asked you to mind me?" she said. "Go on and run after

your father. You're the little pet. We all know that. Only get out
of my sight and stay out."

Rose got very red and ran upstairs. Mary got to her feet and
lumbered up after her. Dom was lying on the bed with Rose alongside him.

Mary cried, "Nobody's asking you to stay here! Nobody's keeping
you. What's stopping you from going off—and take her with you.
Go on off, the two of you."

"I wish to God I could," Dom said. "I declare to God I wish I
could, and I'd take her with me, never fear."

That night, as they lay in bed, Dom said, "Mary, I'm terrible
sorry about what I said to you today. I don't know what got into
me."

"Oh, Dom, never mind about it," she said. "I gave you good
reason."

Encouraged by these words, she put her arms around him. With
his body in her arms, she was comforted. That is what she wanted—
to be allowed to hold him. She thought it was all she wanted—to be
allowed to hold a person in her arms. Out of all the world, only he
would allow her. No one else would allow her. No one else could
bear to let her come near them. The children would allow her, but
their meagre bodies would not fill her arms, and she would be left
empty anyway.

As Dom fell into sleep, his body grew larger and heavier against
her. Holding him, she felt herself filled with strength. Now if she
took her arms from him and stretched herself out, she would touch
not the bed, and not even the floor or the walls of the room, but
the roofs of the houses surrounding her, and other roofs beyond
them, far out to the outer reaches of the town. She felt strong and
able enough to encircle the whole town, a hundred men and
women. She could feel their foreheads and their shoulders under
her hands, and she could even imagine that she saw their hands
reaching out for her, as though they wanted her.

In all her life, there was no one had ever wanted her. All the
want was hers. She never knew, or wondered, if she loved or hoped
or despaired. It was all the one thing to her, all want. She said every
day, "I love God," because that is what she had been taught to say,
but the want came up out of herself, and she knew what she meant
by it. She said, "I want the rose garden. I want it," she said, "I

want to see it, I want to touch it, I want to feel it, I want to hide myself in it, I want it for my own." She could not have said if it was her hope or her despair that was contained in the garden, or about the difference between them, or if there was a difference between them. All she knew was what she felt. All she felt was dreadful longing.

When Father Mathews found that Mary wouldn't allow him to get one of the neighbors up to take his place at the bedside, he didn't know what to do. It seemed unchristian and unfeeling to leave her alone, but he was dying to stretch his legs and get a breath of fresh air, and above all he wanted to get away out of the room. He decided that the most likely thing would be to talk his way out, and so he said again what he had said before—that Dom's fortitude was an example to the whole parish, and that he had left his children a priceless legacy of faith and humility, that the priest and the teachers at the school would have a special interest in the bereaved little ones, and that Dom's soul was perhaps even at this instant interceding for them all before the throne of the Almighty.

"What about me, Father?" Mary asked.

"What was that?" asked Father Mathews.

"What about me, Father? That's all I'm asking you."

"Oh, Mrs. Lambert, your heart is heavy now, but have no fear. God will comfort you in His own time and in His own way."

"I might have known you wouldn't give me a straight answer, Father."

"Mrs. Lambert, Our Blessed Lord enjoins us to have *faith*," Father Mathews said gently.

He was developing a headache out of the endless talk, in this airless room, with no sleep all night, and he was beginning to wonder if he hadn't already done more than his duty.

Mary stared indifferently at him, and he hesitated to speak for fear of provoking her into some further rigmarole. After a few seconds the rising silence in the room pushed him to his feet almost in spite of himself, but at the door he turned and whispered that he would speak to Father Dodd immediately about the arrangements for the funeral, which would probably be on Thursday. He then said that he would call back later in the day to see how she and the children were getting along, and he added that Father Dodd himself might even find time to come—just for a few minutes, of course, because he was greatly taken up at this time of the year, between Christmas and Easter.

As he felt his precarious way downstairs, he couldn't help rehearsing a question that he knew he would never ask, because it would seem uncharitable. The question was what sort of a woman is it could sit beside her husband's body, with her unfortunate children in the next room, and think only about herself?

THE BUBBLE

❖

NANCY HALE

Now when Eric was born in Washington, D.C., I was eighteen, and most people thought I was too young to be having a baby.

I went down there two months before it was going to come, to stay at my mother-in-law's house. She was crazy for the baby to be born in Washington, and I was just as glad to get away from New York. My father had been divorced from my mother, and she had gone abroad, and he was getting married to Estrella, so I couldn't go *there,* and I had got so I couldn't stand that first awful little apartment, with the ivory woodwork and a red sateen sofa; I didn't know how to make it look attractive, and it depressed me. Tom, Eric's father, stayed on in it after I went to his mother's; I remember he used to work in a bond house.

It felt strange, staying with my mother-in-law. She had a big house, right opposite to the old British Embassy. That makes you realize how long ago this was, and yet I am still, all these years later, wondering about why it was the way it was. Mrs. Tompkins' house was a real house, with five stories and four servants, and meals at regular times and a gong that the colored butler rang to call you to them. I had never lived in a real house. My father always had apartments with day beds in them, so we could open the whole place up for parties, and we ate any time. My father was an art critic on the *Tribune.* Nobody remembers who he was any more; everybody forgets things so fast.

My room in Washington was in the front, on the top floor, looking out at the rambling, old, mustard-yellow Embassy. Sometimes at night I would lean on the window sill and watch the cars draw up and the people in evening dress get out and walk up the strip of crimson carpet they rolled out across the sidewalk for the Embassy parties. And I would weep, up there on the fourth floor, because I was so big and clumsy, and I felt as if I would never, never go dancing again, or walk along a red carpet, or wear a low-cut dress. The last time I had was one night when I went dancing at the old Montmartre with Tom and Eugene—I was in love with Eugene—and I had seen myself in a long mirror dancing and realized how fat I looked, and that was another reason I wanted to get away from New York and go and have it in Washington. I had two black dresses— one plain wool and the other with an accordion-pleated crêpe skirt —and one velours hat, and I wore them and wore them and wore them all those last weeks, and I swore to myself that when it was born I would burn them in the fireplace in my room there. But I never did.

I used to live in a kind of fever for the future, when the baby would have come and I would look nice again and go back to New York and see Eugene. I took regular walks along the Washington streets—N Street, and Sixteenth Street, and Connecticut Avenue with all the attractive people going into restaurants to lunch—in my shapeless black dress and my velours hat, dreaming of the day when I would be size 12 and my hair would curl again and I would begin to have fun. All those days before Eric was born were aimed frontward, hard; I was just getting through them for what it would be like afterward.

My mother-in-law was the one who was really having the baby; she was full of excitement about it, and used to take me to Washington shops to buy baby clothes. Looking back all these years later, I remember those sunny afternoons in late winter, and the little white dresses and embroidered caps and pink sweaters spread out on the counter, and stopping to have tea and cinnamon toast at the Mayflower, with the small orchestra playing hotel music, and they seem beautiful and tranquil, but in those days I was just doing any old thing she suggested, and I was living to get back to New York and begin having fun again.

I remember she gave a ladies' luncheon for me, to meet some of the young mothers she thought I would like to know. I suppose they were a couple of years older than I, but they seemed middle-aged to me and interested in the stupidest things; I wanted to cry because nobody was anything like me.

But now I remember that the luncheon was really beautiful. The dining room was big and long, and on the sideboard was Mrs. Tompkins' silver *repoussé* tea service. The table was laid with a huge white damask cloth, and the napkins had lace inserts. It was a real ladies' lunch party, with twelve ladies and a five-course luncheon; I had never been to one before in my life, and I seldom have since. I remember the first course was shrimp cocktails in glasses set in bowls filled with crushed ice. And for dessert there was a special confection, which had been ordered from Demonet's, the famous Washington caterer; it was a monument of cake and ice cream and whipped cream and cherries and angelica. But all I could think about was how food bored me and how I wanted to get back and begin living again. I felt in such a hurry.

Later that day, Mrs. Tompkins gave me a lot of her linens. It was before dinner. We used to sit in the small library and listen to Amos and Andy every night at seven. And this night she brought in a great armful of linens to show me, and everything I admired she would give me. There were damask tablecloths with borders of iris and borders of the Greek key, and round embroidered linen tea cloths, and dozens and dozens of lace and net doilies to go under finger bowls, and towels of the finest huck with great padded monograms embroidered on them. "Dear child," she said, "I want for you to have everything nice." I ended up with a whole pile of things. I wonder what ever became of them. I remember imagining what my father would have thought if he could have seen me with a lot of tablecloths and towels in my lap. "The purchase money of the Philistines," he might have said. But I have no idea what happened to all that linen, and my father is dead long ago and nobody remembers him any more. I remember when I went up to my room to change into my other dress for dinner I wept, because I was so big and ugly and all surrounded with lace doilies and baby clothes and Eugene might fall in love with somebody else before I could get back to New York.

That was the night the baby started to come.

It began about ten o'clock, just before bedtime, and when I told my mother-in-law her face lit up. She went and telephoned to the doctor and to the nurse, and then came back and told me the doctor said I was to rest quietly at home until the pains started to come every fifteen minutes, and that the nurse, Miss Hammond, would be right over. I went up to my room and lay down. It didn't hurt too much. When Miss Hammond arrived, she stood by my bed and smiled at me as if I were wonderful. She was tall and thin with sallow hair, an old-maid type.

About one o'clock, Mrs. Tompkins telephoned the doctor again, and he said to take me to the hospital. Mrs. Tompkins told me she had wired Tom to take the midnight down, but I didn't care; I was having pains regularly, and the difference had begun, the thing I have always wondered about.

We all got in a taxi, Mrs. Tompkins and Miss Hammond and I, there in the middle of the night, and drove through the dark Washington streets to the hospital. It was portentous, that drive, significant; every minute, I mean every present minute, seemed to matter. I had stopped living ahead, the way I had been doing, and was living in right now. That is what I am talking about.

I hadn't worn my wedding ring since I fell in love with Eugene. I'd told my mother-in-law that I didn't like the feeling of the ring, which was true. But in the taxi, in the darkness, she took off her own wedding ring and put it on my finger. "Dear child," she said, "I just won't have you going to the hospital with no ring." I remember I squeezed her hand.

I was taken at once to my room in the hospital, where they "prepared" me, and then almost immediately to the delivery room, because they thought the baby was coming right away. But then the pains slowed down, and I stayed in the delivery room for a long time, until the sun began to stream through the east window. The doctor, a pleasant old man with a Southern accent, had come, and he sat in the sunshine reading the morning newspaper. As I lay on my back on the high, narrow delivery cot, the pains got steadily harder, but I remember thinking, There's nothing scary about this. It just feels natural. The pains got harder and harder.

There was the doctor, and a nurse, and my own Miss Hammond, whom I felt I had known forever; occasionally she would wipe my forehead with a cool, wet cloth. I felt gay and talkative. I said, "I know what this pain feels like. It feels as if I were in a dark tunnel that was too small for me, and I were trying to squeeze through it to get to the end, where I can see a little light."

The doctor laughed. "That's not what you're doin'," he said. "That's what that baby's doin'."

But that was the way it felt, all the same.

"Let me know when you need a little somethin'," he said.

After a while I said, "This is *bad.*" And instantly he was at my side with a hypodermic needle, which he thrust into my arm, and the pain was blunted for a time.

"Let me know when you need a little somethin'," he said again.

But I was feeling very strong and full of power. I was working my way down that long, dark tunnel that was too tight for me, down toward the little light that showed at the far end. Then I had a terrible pain. That's all I'm going to stand, I thought calmly. Deliberately I opened my mouth and screamed.

At once, they put a mask over my face, and the doctor's voice said, "Breathe deeply."

And I was out.

I would come back into the brilliant sunshine of the room and the circle of faces around me, and smile up at them, and they would smile back. And then a fresh pain would approach, and I would say, "Now."

"Bear down," the doctor's voice said as the mask covered my face and I faded away from the room. "Bear down."

So I would bear down, and be gone.

Back into the sunny room and out again, several times, I went. And then, on one of the returns, to my astonishment, I heard a small, high wail that I nevertheless knew all about. Over to one side of me stood a crib on stilts; it had been standing there all along, but now above its edge I could see two tiny blue things waving faintly.

"It's a boy," I heard my darling Miss Hammond's voice saying. "You've got a beautiful boy, Mrs. Tompkins."

And then I felt a fearful pain coming. They put the mask over my face for the last time, and I went completely out.

When I woke up, it was in my own room. Mrs. Tompkins was there, and Miss Hammond, and Tom. They kissed me, and beamed at me, and Tom kept pressing my hand. But I was immune from them all.

I was inwardly enthroned. Seated on a chair of silver, sword in hand, I was Joan of Arc. I smiled at them all, because I might as well, but I needed nobody, nothing. I was the meaning of achievement, here, now, in the moment, and the afternoon sun shone proudly in from the west.

A nurse entered bearing a pale-blue bundle and put it in my arms. It was Eric, of course, and I looked down into his minute face with a feeling of old familiarity. Here he was. Here we were. We were everything.

"Your father's come," Mrs. Tompkins said.

My father's head appeared round the door, and then he came in, looking wry, as he did when people not his kind were around. He leaned down to kiss me.

"Brave girl," he whispered. "You fooled 'em."

That was right. I had fooled them, fooled everybody. I had the victory, and it was here and now.

Then the nurse took the baby away, and Miss Hammond brought a big tray of food and cranked my bed up for me to eat it. I ate an enormous dinner, and then fell asleep and did not wake up for fifteen hours.

When I woke, it was the middle of the night, and the hospital was silent around me. Then, faintly, from somewhere down the corridor, although the month was February, someone began to sing "Silent Night." It was eerie, in my closed room, to hear singing in the darkness. I looked at where the window showed pale gray and oblong. Then I realized what the tune was that was being sung, and felt horribly embarrassed. I could hear my father saying, "These good folk with their sentimental religiosity." Then the sound of the singing disappeared, and I was never sure where it had come from, or, indeed, whether I had really heard it or not.

Next morning, bright and early, a short, thin man with gray curly hair walked into my hospital room and said, "What's all this nonsense about your not wanting to nurse your baby? I won't have it. You *must* nurse your child." He was the pediatrician, Dr. Lawford.

Nobody had ever given me an order before. My father believed in treating me as if I were grown-up. I stared at the strange man seating himself by the window, and burst into tears.

"I tell you what, my dear little girl," he said after a few moments. "I'll make a bargain with you. I believe you have to go back to New York and take up your life in six weeks. Nurse your baby until you have to go, and then you can wean him."

I nodded. I didn't know anything about any of it—only what older women had said to me, about nursing ruining your figure— and all of that seemed in another life now.

Flowers began to arrive, great baskets of them from all Mrs. Tompkins' friends, and they filled my room until it looked like a bower. Telegrams arrived. A wire came, late one day, from Eugene. It read, "AREN'T YOU SOMETHING." But Eugene no longer seemed quite real, either.

I would lie in that hospital bed with the baby within my arm, nursing him. I remember it with Dr. Lawford sitting in the chair by the window and tall, old-maidish Miss Hammond standing beside my bed, both of them watching me with indulgent faces. I felt as though they were my father and my mother, and I their good child.

But that was absurd, because if they were taking care of anybody, it was Eric.

I stayed in the hospital ten days. When we went home to Mrs. Tompkins', it was spring in Washington, and along every curb were barrows of spring flowers—daffodils and hyacinths and white tulips.

Miss Hammond and Eric had the room next to mine on the fourth floor. Miss Hammond did what was called in those days eighteen-hour duty, which meant she slept there with the baby and went off for a few hours every afternoon. It was Mrs. Tompkins' delight, she said, to look after the baby while Miss Hammond was out. Those afternoons, I would take a long nap, and then we would go out and push the baby in his father's old perambulator along the flower-lined streets, to join the other rosy babies in Dupont Circle, where the little children ran about in their matching coats and hats of wool—pink, lavender, yellow, and pale green.

It was an orderly, bountiful life. Breakfast was at eight, and Mrs. Tompkins dispensed the coffee from the silver *repoussé* service before her, and herself broke the eggs into their cups to be handed by the butler to Miss Hammond and me. We had little pancakes with crisp edges, and the cook sent up rich, thick hot chocolate for me to drink, because I had not yet learned to like coffee. In those days, a thing like that did nothing to my figure. When we had gone upstairs, I would stand in front of the mahogany mirror in my bedroom, sidewise, looking at my new, thin shape, flat as a board again, and then I would go in to watch Miss Hammond perform the daily ceremony of the baby's bath—an elaborate ritual involving a rubber tub, toothpicks with a cotton swab on the end of them, oil, powder, and specially soft towels—and the whole room was filled with the smell of baby. Then it would be time for me to nurse Eric.

I used to hold him in my arm, lying on my bed, and it was as though he and I were alone inside a transparent bubble, an iridescent film that shut everything else in the world out. We were a whole, curled together within the tough and fragile skin of that round bubble, while outside, unnoticed, time passed, plans proceeded, and the days went by in comfortable procession. Inside the bubble, there was no time.

Luncheon was at one-thirty, Amos and Andy was at seven, dinner was at seven-thirty, bedtime was at ten-thirty, in that house. The servants made excuses to come up to the fourth floor and look at the baby, and lent unnecessary helping hands when the butler lifted the perambulator down the steps to the street for our after-

noon walk among the flowers. The young mothers I had met came
to see the baby, and Mrs. Tompkins ordered tea with cinnamon
toast served to us in the drawing room afterward; they talked of
two-o'clock feedings, and the triangular versus square folding of
diapers, and of formulas, and asked me to lunch at the Mayflower,
early, so that I could get home for the early-afternoon feeding. But
the young mothers were still strangers to me—older women. I did
not feel anything in common with their busy domestic efficiency.

The spring days passed, and plans matured relentlessly, and soon
it was time for me to go home to New York with the baby, to the
new apartment Tom had taken and the new nurse he had engaged
that Mrs. Tompkins was going to pay for. That was simply the way
it was, and it never occurred to me that I could change the plans.
I wonder what would have happened if a Dr. Lawford had marched
in and given me an order. . . . But after all, I did have to go back;
New York was where I lived; so it's not that I mean. I really don't
understand what I do mean. I couldn't have stayed at my mother-
in-law's indefinitely.

I don't remember starting to wean Eric. I remember an afternoon
when I had missed several feedings, and the physical ache was hard,
and Mrs. Tompkins brought the baby in for me to play with.

I held him in my arms, that other occupant of the fractured
bubble, and suddenly I knew that he and I were divided, never to
be together again, and I began to cry.

Mrs. Tompkins came and took the baby away from me, but I
could not stop crying, and I have never again cried so hard. It never
occurred to me that anything could be done about it, but we were
separated, and it was cruel, and I cried for something. I wish I
could remember exactly what it was I did cry for. It wasn't for my
baby, because I still had my baby, and he's grown up now and works
in the Fifth Avenue Bank.

After that, time changed again for me. It flowed backward, to the
memory of the bubble and to the first high moment in the hospital
when I was Joan of Arc. We left Washington on a morning with
the sun shining and barrows of flowers blooming along the curb as
we went out the front door and the servants lined up on the steps
to say goodbye. Eric was in a pink coat and a pink cap to match,
with lace edging. But he didn't really belong to me any more—not
the old way. I remember Mrs. Tompkins had tears in her eyes when

she kissed us goodbye in the Union Station. But I felt dry-eyed and unmoved, while time flowed backward to that night we drove to the hospital in the middle of the night and she put her ring on my finger.

Of course, when we got back, New York looked marvellous. But even while I was beginning to feel all its possibilities again, time still flowed backward for me. I remember when it was that it stopped flowing backward. I was in someone's room in the St. Regis, where a lot of people were having a drink before going on to dance. I sat on the bed. A young man I had never seen before sat beside me. He said, "Where have you been all my life?"

And I said, "I've been having a baby."

He looked at me with the shine gone out of his eyes, and I realized that there were no possibilities in a remark like mine. I laughed, and reached out my glass to whoever the host was, and said something else that made the young man laugh, too. And then time stopped flowing backward and began once more, and for always, to hurry forward again.

So that is what I wonder about, all these years later. What it is that makes time hurry forward so fast? And what it is that can make it stop, so that you can live in now, in here? Or even go backward? Because it has never stopped or gone backward for me again.

It isn't having a baby, because I've had four, God help me—two by Tom, counting Eric, and two by Harold, not to mention that miscarriage, and although I hoped it would, time never did anything different again, just hurried on, hurried on.

It isn't, as it occurred to me once that it might be, getting free of men in your life as I was free of them long ago with Mrs. Tompkins. Here I am, rid of my husbands, and the younger children off to school now, in this apartment. It isn't big, but I have day beds in the bedrooms so that every room looks like a sitting room for when I have a party. I'm free, if you want to call it that, and my face isn't what it was, so that I'm not troubled with *that* kind of thing, and yet, when you might think life would slow down, be still, time nevertheless hurries on, hurries on. What do I care about dinner with the Deans tonight? But I have to hurry, just the same. And I'm tired. Sometimes I imagine that if Mrs. Tompkins were still alive, or my father, even . . . But they're dead and nobody remembers them any more, nobody *I* see.

MORE FRIEND THAN LODGER

❖

Angus Wilson

As soon as Henry spoke of his publishing firm's new author, Rodney Galt, I knew that I should dislike him. "It's rather a feather in my cap to have got him for our list," Henry said. The firm, of which he is a junior partner, has offices in Bloomsbury, and is called Brodrick Layland—which, as a name, is surely a feather in no one's cap, but that by the way. "I think Harkness were crazy to let him go," Henry said, "because although 'Cuckoo' wasn't a great money spinner, it was very well thought of indeed. But that's typical of Harkness. They think of nothing but sales."

I may say, for those who don't know my husband Henry, that this speech was very typical of *him,* because, first, I should imagine most publishers think a lot about sales, and if Brodrick Layland don't then I'm sorry to hear it, and, second, Henry would never naturally use expressions like "a great money spinner," but since he's gone into publishing he thinks he ought to sound a bit like a business-man, and he doesn't really know how. The kind of thing that comes natural to Henry to say is that somebody or something is "very well thought of indeed," which doesn't sound like a businessman to anyone, I imagine. But what Henry is like ought to emerge from my story, if I'm able to write it at all. And I must in fairness add that my comments about him probably tell quite a lot about me; for example, he isn't by any means mostly interested in the money in publishing but much more in "building up a good list," so his comment on Harkness wasn't hypocritical. As his wife, I know this perfectly well, but I've got into the habit of talking like that about him.

Henry went on to tell me about "Cuckoo." It was not either a novel (which one might have thought) or a book about birds or lunatics (which was less likely, although it's the kind of thing I might have pretended to think in order to annoy him). No,

"Cuckoo" was an anthology, and a history of cuckolds famous in fact and fiction. Rodney Galt, it seemed, had a great reputation—not as a cuckold, for he was single, but as a seducer—and although his book's title might suggest otherwise, his victories were not only, or even mainly, among married women. He was particularly successful, as a matter of fact, at seducing younger daughters and debs. Henry told me all this in a special, offhand sort of voice intended to suggest that at Brodrick Layland they took that sort of thing for granted. Once again, I'm being bitchy—because, of course, if I had said "Come off it, Henry," or words to that effect, he would have changed his tone immediately. But I did not see why I should, because among our acquaintances we do number a few, though not many, seducers of virgins, and if I made Henry change his tone it would suggest that he was *quite* unfamiliar with such a phenomenon. Fairness and truth are my greatest difficulties in life.

To return to Rodney Galt—Henry said that the book he was going to write for Brodrick Layland was to be called "Honour and Civility," and, again, it was not to be a novel. Rodney Galt used the words "Honour" and "Civility" in a special sense—some would say an archaic sense, but he did not see it that way, because he preferred not to recognize the changes that had taken place in the English language in the last hundred years or so. "Honour," for him, meant "the thing that is most precious to a man," but not in the sense that the Victorians meant by saying that honour was the thing most precious to a woman. Rodney Galt, from what I could gather, would have liked to see men still killing each other in duels for their honour, and offering civilities to one another in the shape of snuff and suchlike before they did so. He believed in "living dangerously" and in what is called "high courage"—exemplified preferably in sports and combats that were of long standing. He was, therefore, against motor racing, and even more against "track," but in favor of bullfighting and perhaps pelota; he was also against dog racing but in favor of baccarat for high stakes. The book, however, was not to be just one of those books that used to be called things like "Twelve Rakes," or "Twenty Famous Dandies." It was to be more philosophical than they were, involving the author's whole view of society, and explicating what, in Mr. Galt's view, constituted the patrician life.

I told Henry that I did not care for the sound of Mr. Galt. Henry only smiled, however, and said, "I warn you that he's a snob, but on such a colossal scale and with such *panache* that one can't take exception to it."

I told Henry firmly that I was not the kind of woman who could see things on such a large scale as that, and also that if, as I suspected from his saying "I warn you," he intended to invite Rodney Galt to the house, only the strictest business necessity would reconcile me to it.

"There *is* the strictest business necessity," Henry said, and added, "Don't be put off by his matinée-idol looks. He's indecently good-looking."

Henry giggled when he said this, for he knew that he had turned the tables on me. He used to believe—his mother taught him the idea—that no women like men to be extremely good-looking. He knows different now, because I have told him again and again that I would not have married him if he had not been very handsome himself. His mother's code, however, dies hard with him, and even now I suspect he thinks that if his nose had not been broken at school, I should have found him too perfect.

Reading over what I have written, I see that it must appear as though Henry and I live on very whimsical terms, gilding the pill of our daily disagreements with a lot of private jokes and "sparring" and, generally, rather ghastly arch behavior. We do it with no conscious intent, however. Henry and I have reasonable proportions of sense of humor, but no more. He gets his, which is dry, from his mother. My parents had no vestige of humor; my father was too busy getting rich, and my mother was too busy unsuccessfully trying to crash county society. But it *is* true that Henry and I, in our five years of marriage, have built up a lot of private joking and whimsical talking, and I can offer what seem to be some good reasons for it. First, there is what anyone would pick on—that our marriage is childless—which, I think, is really the least of the possible reasons; it certainly is with me, although it may count with Henry more than he can say. The second is that everything counts with Henry more than he can say. "Discerning" people who know Henry and his mother—and, indeed, all the rest of the Ravens— usually say that they are shy beneath their sharp manner. I don't quite believe this; I think it's just that they find it easier to be sharp, so that other people can't overstep the mark of intimacy and intrude too far on their interior lives. You can tell from the way Henry's mother shuts her eyes when she meets people that she has an interior life, and actually she is a devout Anglican. And Henry has an interior life, which he has somehow or other put into his publishing. Well, anyhow, Henry's manner, shy or not, makes me shy, and I've got much more whimsical since I knew him.

But also there's my own attitude to our marriage. I can only sum it up by saying that it's like the attitude of almost everyone in England today toward almost everything. I worked desperately hard to get out of the insecurity of my family—which in this case was not economic, because they're fairly rich and left me quite a little money of my own, but social—and when I married Henry, I loved every minute of it, because the Ravens are quite secure in their own way, which Henry's mother calls "good country middle-class, June dear, and no more." And if that security is threatened for a moment I rush back to it for safety, but most of the time, when it's not in danger, I keep longing for more adventure in life, and a wider scope and more variety, and even greater risks and perils. Well, this feeling about our marriage makes me uneasy with Henry, and I keep him at a humorous distance. And he, knowing it, keeps me at one all the more.

To return once again to Rodney Galt—Henry did, in fact, invite him to dinner a week after our conversation about him. He was not, of course, as bad as Henry had made out—that is to say, as I have sketched above—because that description was part of Henry's ironical teasing of me. However, he was pretty bad. He said ghastly things in an Olympian way—not with humor, like Henry and me, but with "wit," which is always rather awful. Still, I must admit that even at that first dinner I didn't mind Rodney's wit too much, partly because he had the most lovely speaking voice (I don't know why one says "speaking voice," as though most of one's friends used recitative), very deep and resonant, which always "sends" me, and partly because he introduced his ghastly views in a way that made them seem better than they were. For example:

Henry said, "I imagine that a good number of your best friends are Jews, Galt."

And Rodney raised his eyebrows and said, "Good heavens, why?"

And Henry answered, "Most anti-Semitic people make that claim."

And Rodney said, "I suppose that's why I'm not anti-Semitic. I can't imagine knowing any Jews. When would it arise? Oh, I suppose when one's buying pictures or objects, but then that's hardly *knowing*. It's simply one of the necessities. Or, of course, if one went to Palestine, but then that's hardly a necessity."

And I said, "What about Disraeli? He made the Tory party of today." (I said this with a side glance at Henry, because he used, then, to describe himself as a Tory Democrat, although since Suez he has said that he had not realized how deeply Liberalism ran in his veins.)

Rodney said, "What makes you speak of such unpleasant things?"

And I asked, "Aren't you a Tory, then?"

And he answered, "I favor a return to the wise policies of King George the Third, if that's what you mean."

Henry said, "Oh! But what about the Suez Canal and the British Empire? Disraeli made those."

And Rodney looked distant and remarked, "The British Empire, even at its height, was never more than a convenient outlet for the middle-class high-mindedness of Winchester and Rugby. The plantations and the penal colonies, of course, were a different matter." Then he went straight on and said, "The thing that pleases me most about coming to Brodrick Layland is your book production, Raven. I do like to feel that what I have written, if it is worth publishing at all, deserves a comely presentation."

This, of course, was very gratifying to Henry. They talked about books—or, rather, the appearance of books—for some time. It appeared that Rodney was a great collector of books, as he was of so many other things—porcelain, enamels, Byzantine ivories, and Central American carvings. He was quick to tell us that, of course, with his modest income he had to leave the big things alone, and that—again with his modest income—it was increasingly difficult to pick up anything worth having, but it could be done. He left us, somehow, with the impression that he would not really have cared for the big things anyway, and that his income could not be as modest as all that. "Heaven defend me," he said, "from having the money to buy those tedious delights of the pedants—incunables. No, the little Elzevirs are my particular favorites—the decent classical authors, charmingly produced. I have a delightful little Tully, and the only erotica worth possessing, Ovid's 'Amores.'"

It was in talking of Ovid that Rodney said something that gave me a clue to my feelings about him.

"I know of no more moving thing in literature than Ovid's lament, as an exile, for Rome," he said. "It's just how any civilized Englishman today must feel when, chained to his native land, he thinks of the Mediterranean—or almost anywhere else outside England, for that matter." He smiled as he said it. Of course, it was the most awful, pretentious way of talking, but I do so often feel I would rather be almost anywhere than in England that he made me feel guilty for not being as honest as he was.

It seemed, however, that, after a great deal of travel in a great many places, he *was* now for some time to be chained to his native land. He had, he said, a lot of family business to do. He was looking out for a house something like ours. He even hinted—it was the only hint of his commercially venturesome side that he gave that evening —at the possibility of his buying a number of houses, as an investment. Meanwhile, he was staying with Lady Ann Denton. I ventured to suggest that this might be a little too much of a good thing, but he smiled and said that she was a very old friend—which, although it rather put me in my place, gave him a good mark for loyalty. Henry scolded me afterward and told me that Rodney was having an affair with Lady Ann. This surprised and disconcerted me. Lady Ann is old—over forty—and very knocked-about and ginny. She has an amusing, malicious tongue and a heart of gold. Sometimes I accept her tongue because of her heart, and sometimes I put up with her heart because of her tongue. Sometimes I can't stand either. But, as you will have already seen, my attitude toward people is rather ambiguous. Still, Henry is very fond of her. She makes him feel broadminded, which he likes very much.

Rodney and I had it out, a little, about snobbery, that evening. "Heavens! I should hope so," he said when I accused him of being a social snob. "It's one of the few furies worth having that are left to us—little opportunity though the modern world allows of finding anyone worth cultivating. There still do exist a few families, however, even in this country. It lends shape to my life, as it did to Proust's."

I said that though it had lent shape to Proust's work, I wasn't so sure about his life.

"In any case," Rodney said, with a purposeful parody of a self-satisfied smile, "art and life are one." Then he burst out laughing, and said, "Really, I've excelled myself this evening! It's your delicious food."

Looking back once more at what I have written, I see that I said Rodney wasn't as bad as Henry made out, but everything I have reported him as saying is quite pretentious and awful. The truth is that it was his smile and his good looks that made it seem all right. Henry had said that he was like a matinée idol, but this is a ridiculous expression for nowadays (whatever it may have been in the days of Henry's mother), because no one could go to a matinée, with all those gray-haired old ladies up from the country rattling tea trays, and feel sexy about anything. But Rodney was like all the best film stars rolled into one, and yet the kind of person it wasn't surprising to meet—and these, taken together, surely make a very sexy combination.

It was clear, that evening, that Henry liked him very much, too. Not for that reason, of course; Henry hasn't ever even thought about having feelings of that kind, I'm glad to say. As a matter of fact, Henry doesn't have sexy feelings much, anyway. No, that's quite unfair and bitchy of me again. Of course he has sexy feelings, but he has them at definite times, and the rest of the time such things don't come into his head. Whereas I don't ever have such strong sexy feelings as he has, but I have some of them all the time. This is a contrast that tends to make things difficult.

No, I could see at once the reason Henry liked him, and as soon as Rodney had left, I said, "Well, he's quite your cup of tea, isn't he? He's been everywhere and knows a lot about everything." I said the last sentence as if it were in quotation marks, because it's one of Henry's favorite expressions of admiration, and I often tease him about it. It isn't very surprising he should use it, because he went to Charterhouse, and then, in the last two years of the war, he went to Italy, and then he went to The Queen's College, Oxford, and then he went into Brodrick Layland. So *he* hasn't been every-where. As a matter of fact, he does know quite a lot about quite a number of things, but as soon as he knows something, he thinks it can't be very important.

We agreed, then, that Rodney Galt was quite awful in most ways but that we rather liked him all the same.

In the weeks that followed, Henry seemed to see a good deal of Rodney Galt. He put him up for his club. I was rather surprised that Rodney should want to be a member of Henry's club, which is rather dull and literary. I had imagined him belonging to a great many clubs of a much grander kind already. Henry explained that he did, in fact, belong to a lot of others, but that he had been abroad so much he had lost touch with them and their worlds. I thought that was very odd, too, because I imagined that the point of clubs was that no matter how often you went round the world, and no matter how long it took you, when you came back, the club was there. However, as I only knew about clubs from the novels of Evelyn Waugh, I was prepared to believe that I was mistaken. In any event, it seemed that Rodney wanted particularly to belong to this literary sort of club, because he believed very strongly that one should do everything one did professionally, and as he was now going to write books, he wanted to belong to that sort of place. "He's a strange fellow in many ways," Henry said. "A mass of contradictions."

Rodney's contradiction in this case seemed odd to me. I had imagined that the whole point of his books would be that they would be thrown off in the midst of other activities—that they would be amateur productions that proved to be more brilliant than the professional. However, his new attitude, if less romantic, was more creditable, and certainly more promising for Brodrick Layland. I decided, indeed, that he had probably only made this gesture to please Henry, which it did.

We dined once or twice with Rodney and Lady Ann. She has rather a nice house in Chester Square, and he seemed to be very comfortably installed—more permanently than his earlier talk of buying houses suggested. But this may have been only the appearance that Lady Ann gave to things, for she made every effort short of absurdity to underline the nature of their relationship. I really could not blame her for this, because she had made a catch that someone a good deal less battered and ginny might have been proud of, and I had to admire the manner in which she did avoid absurdity, because, looking at him and at her, it *was* very absurd, even apart from the large gap in their ages—fifteen years, at least, I decided.

Lady Ann, as usual, talked most of the time. She has a special way of being funny; she speaks with a drawl and a very slight stutter, and she ends her remarks suddenly with a word or expression that isn't what one expects she is going to lead up to. Well, of course, one does expect it, because she always does it, and, like a lot of things, it gets less funny when you've heard it a few times. For example, she said she quite agreed with Henry—she wouldn't have missed the Braque exhibition for anything, but then she got a peculiar pleasure, almost a sensual one, from being jammed really tight in a crowd. Henry always laps up Lady Ann. She's a sort of tarty mother-substitute for him, I think, and, indeed, if he wanted a tarty mother, he had to find a substitute. I thought that perhaps

Rodney would be bored with her carrying on, but if he was, he didn't show it. This, of course, was very creditable of him, but made me a little disappointed. Occasionally, it is true, he broke into the middle of her chatter, but then she interrupted him, sometimes just as rudely. They might really have been a perfectly happy pair, which I found even more disappointing.

I can't help thinking that by this time you may have formed some rather unfavorable views about the kind of woman I am. Well, I've already said that I often have very bitchy moods, and it's true, but at least I know it. But if you ask me *why* I have bitchy moods, it's more difficult to say. In the first place, life is frightfully boring nowadays, isn't it? And if you say I ought to try doing something with my time—well, I have. I did translations from French and German for Brodrick Layland for a while, and I did prison visiting. They're quite different sorts of things to do, and it didn't take long for me to get very bored with each of them. Not that I should want wars and revolutions; whenever there's an international crisis, I get a ghastly pain in my stomach, like everybody else. But, as I said, like England, I want security and I don't. However, what I was trying to explain about was my bitchy moods. Well, when I get very bored and depressed, I hate everyone, and it seems to me everyone hates me. (As a matter of fact, most people do like Henry better than me, although they think I'm more amusing.) But when the depressed moods lift, I can't help feeling that people are rather nice, and they seem to like me, too. I had these moods very badly when I was sixteen or so, and now, in these last two years (since I was twenty-five), they've come back, and they change much more quickly. When I talked to Henry about it once, he got so depressed and took such a "psychological" view that I've never mentioned it again. In any case, it's easy to take "psychological" views, but I'm by no means sure that it isn't just as true to say, like my old nurse, "Well, we all have our ups and downs"—and certainly that's a more cozy view of the situation.

But enough about me, because all this is really about Rodney Galt. Well, in those few times I saw him with Lady Ann (it seems more comic always to call her that) I began to have a theory about him, and when I get theories about people I get very interested in them. This time, I was especially interested, because if my theory was right, Lady Ann and Henry and Brodrick Layland, and no doubt lots of other people, were liable to be sold all along the line, or up the river, or whatever the expression is. On the other hand (if my theory was right), it only made *me* feel that he was more *fascinating*—the best sort of theory to have.

One thing I wanted to know about was Rodney's family. In such cases, I always believe in asking directly, so I said, "Where are your family, Rodney?"

He smiled, and said, "In the Midlothian, where they've been for a sufficient number of recorded centuries to make them respectable. They're the best sort of people, really," he added. "The kind of people who've always been content to be trout in the local minnow pond. I'm the only one who's shown the cloven hoof of fame-seeking. There must be a bounderish streak somewhere, though not in Mother's family, who were all perfectly good dull country gentry. Of course, there was my great-great-great-uncle the novelist. But his was a very respectable, middling sort of local fame, really."

Well, there wasn't much given away there, because, after all, there are minnows and minnows—and even "country gentry" is rather a vague term. It was a bit disingenuous, that about Galt the novelist, because even I have heard of him, and I know nothing of the Midlothian. And that was the chief annoyance—I knew absolutely no one with whom I could check up. But it didn't shake my theory.

Now we come to the most important point in this story: when Rodney Galt became our lodger. But first I shall have to explain about the "lodger battle" that Henry and I had been waging for over a year. This means explaining about our finances. Henry had some capital, and he put that into Brodrick Layland, and really, all things considered, he gets quite a good income back. But the house we live in is mine—it was left to me by my Aunt Agnes—and it's rather a big house, situated in that vague area known as "behind Harrods." And in this big house there is only me and Henry, and one or two foreign girls—servants. They change usually every year, and at the time I'm speaking of—about six or seven months ago—there was just one girl, a Swiss called Henriette Vaudoyer. Henry had long been keen that we should have a lodger, who could have a bedroom and sitting room and bathroom of his own. He said he didn't like my providing the house and getting nothing back from it. He thought that at least I ought to get pin money out of it. This was absurd, because Daddy left me quite a little income—a great deal more than would be required even if I were to set up a factory for sticking pins into wax images. I think Henry had at least three

real reasons for wanting this lodger: one, he thought it was wrong
to have so much space when people couldn't find anywhere to live,
and this, if I had thought of it first, I would have agreed with,
because I have more social conscience, really, than Henry; two, the
empty rooms (empty, that is, of human beings) reminded him of
the tiny feet that might have pattered but did not; three, he had an
idea that having a lodger would give me something to do, and
would help with the moods.

The last two of these reasons annoyed me very much and made
me unwilling to have a lodger. So Henry was rather shy about suggesting that we should let the top floor to Rodney Galt. He only
felt able to introduce the subject by bringing up the brilliant first
chapter of Rodney's new book. Henry, it seemed, had been bowled
over by this chapter when Rodney submitted it, and even Henry's
senior partner, Mr. Brodrick, who had his feet pretty firmly planted
on the ground, rocked a little. Nothing must get in the way of the
book's completion.

Well, it seemed that living at Lady Ann's did. Henry pointed
out that, wonderful friend though Lady Ann was, she could be
difficult to live with if you wanted to write, because she talked so
much. I said yes, she did—and drank so much, too. Then I asked
about the house that Rodney was going to buy. Henry said that
Rodney hadn't seen the one he really wanted yet, and that he didn't
want to do too much house hunting while he was writing the book,
which would require a lot of research. Above all, of course, he did
not want to involve himself with a house that might turn out to be
a white elephant. With this I thoroughly agreed, and, to Henry's
surprise and pleasure, I said yes, Rodney could come as a lodger.

I was a little puzzled about Lady Ann. I made some inquiries,
and, as I suspected, Rodney had thrown her over, and now he was
said to have taken up with Susan Mullins—a very young girl but
almost as rich as Lady Ann. However, Lady Ann was putting a
good face on it before the world. I was glad to hear this, because
the face she usually put on before the world, although once good,
was now rather a mess. But I didn't say anything to Henry about
all this, because he was so fond of Lady Ann and I was feeling very
friendly toward him for making such a sensible suggestion about a
lodger.

Hardly had the lodger idea taken shape when it almost lost its
shape again. All because of Mr. Brodrick. I should tell you that
Henry's senior partner was one of the many people about whom

my mood varied. He was a rather handsome, gray-templed, port-flushed old man of sixty-five or so—more like a barrister than a publisher, one would think. Anyway, what would one think a publisher looked like? He was a determinedly old-fashioned man—but not like Rodney, except that both of them talked a bit too much about wine and food. No, Mr. Brodrick was an old-world-mannered, "dear lady" sort of man—a widower gallant to the fair sex is how he saw himself, I think. He had a single eyeglass on a black ribbon, and he ate mostly at his club. Sometimes I thought he was rather a sweet old thing, and sometimes I thought he was a ghastly old bore and a bit common to boot. At first, it seemed, he'd been delighted at Henry's capturing Rodney for their list, mainly because he was rather an old snob and Rodney apparently knew well a lot of people whom he himself had only met once or twice but talked about a good deal. So when Rodney came to Brodrick Layland, Mr. Brodrick patted Henry on the back—literally, I imagine, though not heartily—and saw him even more than ever as "a son, my dear boy, since I have not been blessed with any offspring myself." (I often wondered whether Mr. Brodrick didn't sometimes say to Henry "When's the baby coming along?," he was so keen on heirs for Brodrick Layland.) But suddenly it seemed that, one day, Mr. Brodrick was talking to Mr. Harkness, of Harkness & Co., and Mr. Harkness said that the reason they hadn't gone on with Rodney as an author was, they'd had a lot of financial trouble with him—loans not repaid, and so on. Mr. Brodrick didn't care for the sound of that at all, and he thought that he and Henry should do what he called "keeping a very firm rein on Master Galt's activities." And since he saw Henry as a son, and perhaps me as a daughter-in-law (who knows?), he was very much against our having Rodney as a lodger. The more strictly commercial the relations with authors, the better, he said.

Henry was upset by all this and a good deal surprised at what Mr. Harkness had said. I was not at all surprised, but I did not say so. I said that Harkness had no right to say such things or Mr. Brodrick to listen to them. In any case, I said, how did we know that Mr. Harkness had not just made them up out of sour grapes? And as to commercial relations, I pointed out that Rodney's being a lodger was commercial, and anyway the rent was being paid to me. So Mr. Brodrick knew what he could do. But Henry still seemed a little unhappy, and then he told me that he had, himself, lent Rodney various sums. I saw right then that there was nothing for it but to play the brilliant first chapter for all it was worth. Did Henry, I said, expect that anyone capable of that brilliant first chapter was going to fit in with every bourgeois maxim of life that people like Harkness and Mr. Brodrick laid down in their narrow scheme of things? I was surprised, I said, that Henry, who had a real flair for publishing because he cared about books, should be led into this sort of "business is business" attitude, which, if persevered in, would mean confining one's list to all the dullest books produced. Anyway, I made it clear that I was determined Rodney Galt should come, if only as a matter of principle. When Henry saw that I was determined, he decided to stand on principle, too, and on the great coup he had made for Brodrick Layland, as forecast by that brilliant first chapter. So Rodney moved in.

What with all the research Rodney needed to do for his book, and what with Susan Mullins, you may think that I had got unduly excited about nothing. But if you have jumped to that conclusion —well, then, I think you can't have a very interesting mind, and you certainly don't understand *me*. When I say that I had become interested in Rodney, that's exactly what I mean, and "being interested," with me, comes to this—that I don't know really what I want, or, indeed, if I want anything at all, but I know for certain that I don't want to let go. So, for the first week or so, Rodney went to the British Museum and read books about civility and honour, of which they have lots there—intended, when they were published, in the seventeenth and eighteenth centuries, for people who were on the social make, I think. I used to rather like to reflect that, after all this time, they were being read again by Rodney. When he was not at the British Museum, he was with Susan Mullins, or on the telephone talking to her.

The British Museum fell out of Rodney's life before Susan Mullins did. After only a fortnight, he decided to borrow books from the London Library, which, as he had a sitting room, seemed only sensible. Then came a period when Susan did not telephone so often, and once or twice Rodney telephoned to her and spoke, instead, to her mother—who was not called Mullins but Lady Newnham, because she had been divorced and married again to a very rich Conservative industrialist peer—and then high words were exchanged. And finally, one day when he rang, he spoke to Lord Newnham, and *very* high words were exchanged, and that was the end of that. It became difficult then for Rodney to keep his mind on the books from the London Library, let alone go to the British

Museum. It seemed, somehow, that his mind was diverted more by financial schemes than by study. None of this surprised me much, but I thought I would not worry Henry by telling him, in case he began to be afraid that there would only be a brilliant first chapter and no more.

So Rodney and I used to go out in his M.G. (and perhaps it would have been more in keeping if he had refused to use any kind of motorcar later than a De Dion Bouton, but I was glad that he didn't). We went here, there, and everywhere, and all over the place. We saw a great number of lovely houses—a lot in London, but gradually more and more outside London. Rodney came very near to taking some of them, he said. And then, since he proposed to turn some of the houses, when he bought them, into furnished rooms or flats, we looked at a great number of antiques. The antiques we looked at were rather expensive to use as furnishings of flats or rooms, but Rodney said that only good things interested him, and what was the good of his *expertise* if he never used it? It was quite true—that he had *expertise,* I mean.

We had a lot of very good luncheons, too. According to my theory, Rodney would pay for these during the first phase, but later I would have to pay. I was determined to make the first phase last as long as possible. We suddenly took to going to places like Hampton Court, and Cambridge, and Hatfield House, and Wilton. We did not go to see any friends, though—partly because it wouldn't have done but mostly because we really were very content to be alone together. However, often when we passed great parks or distant large houses, Rodney told me which of his friends they belonged to, and this was nice for him.

In fact, we both had a wonderful time, although Rodney's time would have been more wonderful, he said, if I'd agreed to go to bed with him. Sometimes he cajoled, or at least he made himself as attractive and sweet as he could, which was a lot, and this, I imagine, is what "cajole" means. But often he took a very high-handed line, because in Rodney's theory of seducing there was a lot about women wanting to be mastered, which fitted into his general social views. Then he would tell me that unless I let myself go and accepted his mastery, which was what I really wanted, I would soon become a tight little bitch. I had, he said, all the makings of one already, at twenty-seven. "It's happening already, with your bitter humor, and your whimsey, and your melancholy moods!" he cried. "You're ceasing to be civilized."

Civilization seemed to be his key to seduction; at least, he made light of my married position on the same ground. "In any civilized century," he said, "the situation would be sensibly accepted." And then he talked of Congreve and Vanbrugh, and Italian society. But I didn't care to decide too easily, because Vanbrugh and Congreve were no longer alive, and this was not Italy of the *cicisbei,* and affairs of this kind aren't easy to control, and even if life was often boring, it was secure. Also, I quite enjoyed things as they were, even the violent things he said about my becoming a bitch, but I wasn't sure that I would like all that masterfulness on a physical plane.

So we went on as I wished, and I enjoyed managing the double life, and if Rodney didn't exactly enjoy it, he was very good at it. For example, one morning an absolutely ghastly thing happened. Henry's mother suddenly arrived as Rodney and I were about to set off for Brighton. I have often said of Henry's mother that you can feel two ways about her; I think that I would be prepared to feel the nicer way more often if she didn't seem to feel so consistently the nastier way about me. As it is, our relations are not very good, and since, like most people, we find it easier to fight battles on our home grounds, we don't often meet.

Henry's mother doesn't bother much about dress, and, that day being a rather cold summer day, she was wearing an old squirrel-skin coat over her tweeds. As to her hats, you can never tell much about these, because her gray hair gets loose so much and festoons all over them. It is said in the Raven family that she should have been allowed by her father to go to the University, and that she would then have been a very good scholar, and happy to be so. As it is, she has lived most of her life in a large red brick Queen Anne house in Hampshire, and the only way you can tell that she is not happy, like all the other ladies, is that, as well as gardening and jam-making and local government, she does all the very difficult crossword puzzles very quickly, and, as well as reading the travel books and biographies recommended in the Sunday papers, she reads sometimes in French, and even in German. She closed her eyes when she saw me, but this was no special insult, because she always does this when she speaks.

"You shouldn't live so close to Harrods, June dear, if you don't want morning callers" was how she greeted me. As Rodney and I

were both obviously about to go out, there was not much to answer
to this. But the Ravens have a habit of half saying what is on their
minds, and it immediately seemed certain to me that she had only
come there because she'd heard about the lodger and wanted to
pry. I said, "This is Rodney Galt, our lodger. This is Henry's
mother."

Rodney must have formed the same conclusion, for he immediately said, "How do you do? I'm afraid this is a very brief meeting,
because I'm just off to the London Library."

"Oh?" Henry's mother said. "You must be one of those new members who have all the books out when one wants them. It's so difficult being a country member. Of course, when Mr. Cox was
alive . . ." And she sighed, putting the blame onto Rodney but
also making it quite clear to me that he was what she wanted to
investigate.

I thought it would be wise to deflect her, so I said, "You'll stay
and have a coffee or a drink or something, won't you?"

But she was not to be deflected. "What strange ideas you have
about how I spend my mornings, June dear," she answered. "I
haven't come up from the suburbs, you know. I'm afraid you're
one of those busy people who think everybody idle but yourself.
I just thought it would be proper, since I was so close at Harrods,
that we should show each other that we were both still alive. But
I don't intend to waste your time, dear. Indeed, if Mr. Galt is going
to the London Library, I think I shall ask him if he will share a
taxi with me. I'm getting a little old to be called 'duckie,' as these
bus ladies seem to like to do now."

So Rodney was caught good and proper. However, I needn't
have worried for him. When Henry came home, I learned that his
mother had been round to Brodrick Layland and had spent her
time singing Rodney's praises. It appeared that he'd been so helpful
in finding her the best edition of Saint-Simon that she had offered
him luncheon, and that he had suggested Wheeler's. His conversation must have been very pleasing to her, for she made no grumble
to Henry about the bill. She had only said, "I can't think why you
described him as a beautiful-looking young man. He's most pre-
sentable, and very well informed, too." So we seemed to have got
over that hurdle.

But Rodney was a success with all our friends—for example, with
les jeunes filles en fleurs. This is the name that Henry and I give

to two ladies called Miss Jackie Reynolds and Miss Marcia Railton, and the point about the name is that although they are Lesbian ladies, they are by no means *jeunes filles* and certainly not *en fleurs*. Henry is very fond of them, because, like Lady Ann, they make him feel broadminded. They are generous, and this is particularly creditable because they do not make much money out of their business of interior decoration. They have lived together for a great many years—since they were young, indeed, which must be a great, great many years ago—and Henry always says that this is very touching. Unfortunately, they are often also very boring, and this seems to be all right for Henry, because when they have been unusually boring he remembers how touching their constancy to each other is, and that apparently compensates him. But it doesn't compensate me. When the *jeunes filles* met Rodney, Jackie, who is short and stocky, with an untidy black-dyed shingle, put her head on one side and said, "I say, isn't he a smasher!" And Marcia, who is petite rather than stocky, and altogether dainty in her dress, said, "But of a beauty!"

This is the way they talk when they meet new people; Henry says it's because they are shy, and so it may be, but it usually makes everybody else rather shy, too. I thought it would paralyze Rodney, but he took it in his stride and said, "Oh, come! I'm not as good-looking as all that."

That was when I first realized that I preferred Rodney on his own, and this in itself is a difficulty, because if one is going to be much with somebody you are bound to be with other people, too, sometimes. However, the evening went swimmingly. Rodney decided that although he would always have really *good* objects in his *own* house, when he got it, the people to whom he would let furnished flats would be much happier to be interior-decorated— and who better to do it than *les jeunes filles en fleurs?* Well, that suited Marcia and Jackie all right. They got together, all three, in a huddle, and a very funny huddle it was. Rodney already knew of some Americans, even apart from all the people who would be taking furnished flats from him, who might be interested in having interior decoration done, and the rest of the evening was spent in discussion of deals. Henry said afterward he'd never felt so warm toward Rodney as when he saw how decent he was to *les jeunes filles.*

The truth was that, much though I was enjoying Rodney's company, I was beginning to get a little depressed by the suit he so ardently urged and the decision that this ardor was forcing upon me. It would be so much nicer if there were no cause and effect in life—no one thing leading inevitably to another but just everything being sufficient in itself. Yet I could see that Rodney was not the kind of person to take life in this way, and quite suddenly something impressed this realization upon me rather strongly.

I have not said much about our Swiss, Henriette Vaudoyer, and I don't propose to say much now, because nothing is more boring than talk about foreign domestics. I have to put up with it at three-quarters of the dinners we go to. Henriette was a very uninteresting girl, but quite pretty. There were only four of us in the house— Henry and me in one bedroom, and Rodney and Henriette in two bedrooms. Well, no one can be surprised that Rodney and Henriette began to be in one bedroom, sometimes, too. I wasn't surprised, but I was upset; it gave me a pain in my stomach. Clearly, there were only two things I could do about that pain—get rid of Rodney or get rid of Henriette. The brave thing would have been to get rid of Rodney before I got worse pains, but already the pain was so bad that I was not brave enough. I gave Henriette notice. She said some very unpleasant, smug, Swiss sort of things to me, and she began to say them to Henry, which was more worrying.

Luckily, one of Henry's great virtues is that he never listens to talebearing, and he did what is called "cutting her short." However, he was a bit worried lest I should decide to do without a foreign girl, because we'd always had one, and sometimes two. But I explained that we had Mrs. Golfin coming in to do the heavy chores, and that she was only too pleased to come in even more— and, for the rest, having more to do would be wonderful for my moods, about which I was getting worried. So Henry saw the necessity, and Henriette went. But I saw clearly, too, that I would have to decide either to accept Rodney's importuning or not, because soon he would take no answer to be the same as "Answer—No."

I think maybe I might have answered no, except that, at the time, Henry annoyed me very much over the holiday question. This is an old and annoying question with us. Every year since we were married, Henry has said, "Well, I don't know why we shouldn't manage Venice [or Madrid, or Rome] this year. I think we've deserved it."

First, I want to say that people don't deserve holidays—they just take them—and, second, I want to point out that we're really quite rich, and there's no question of our not being able to "manage"

Venice or Rome. I long, in fact, for the day when he will say, "Well, I don't know why we shouldn't manage Lima this year, taking in Honolulu and Madagascar on the way home." But if he can't say that—and he can't—then I would prefer him to ask, "Shall we go to Italy or Spain or North Africa this year, June? The choice is yours."

However, just about the time Henriette left, he came out with it: "Well, I don't see why we shouldn't manage Florence this year."

So I said, "Well, I do, Henry, because I don't bloody well want to go there."

And then he was very upset, and as I was feeling rather guilty anyway, I apologized, and said how silly my moods were, and Florence would be rather enchanting.

Henry cheered up a good deal at this. "If that is so," he said, "I'm very glad, because it makes it much easier for me to tell you something. It's been decided on the spur of the moment that I'm to go to New York on business. It's only for a fortnight, but I must leave next week."

Now, I wouldn't really have wanted to go to New York on a rush visit for Brodrick Layland, but somehow everything conspired to make me furious, and I decided then and there that what I wanted was what Rodney wanted, physical mastery or no. And actually, when the time came, the physical mastery wasn't such a trial. I mean there was nothing "extra," or worrying, about it. And, for the rest, I was very pleased.

So when Henry set off for New York, I was committed to a new course of life, as they say. But the weekend before Henry left he insisted on running me down to a country hotel in Sussex and making a fuss over me. I suppose I should have felt very bad about it, because really he did his best to make the fuss as good as possible. But all I could think of was that I did hope cause and effect, and one thing following another, wasn't going to make life worse, instead of better. After all, I had made this committal to a new course in order to make life *less* boring, but if it meant that there were going to be more decisions and choices in front of me, it would be much *more* boring. One thing I did decide was that I would try not to talk about Rodney to Henry, even if I did have to think of him. After all, talking about Rodney would not have been a very kind return for the fussing.

In the end, it was Henry who raised the subject of Rodney. It

seemed that Lady Ann had not been able to put a good face on *all*
the time. One day, at a cocktail party, when even she had found
the gin stronger than usual, she had dropped her face in front of
Henry. She'd said that the money she had spent on Rodney nobody
knew (this I thought was hypocritical, because she was just telling
Henry how much it was), and the return he'd made had been
beneath anything she'd ever experienced. I must say she couldn't
have said worse, considering the sort of life she's led. Henry was
very upset, because although he liked Rodney, Lady Ann was such
a very old friend. But I said that age in friendship was not the
proper basis for judgment, and I also reminded him that hell had
no fury. I succeeded in pacifying him, because he didn't want his
fussing to be spoiled, but I could see that things would never be
the same between Rodney and Henry—as now, indeed, they were
not between any of the three of us.

Well, there we were—Rodney and me alone for ten days. And
Rodney did exactly the right thing; he suggested that we spend
most of the time in Paris. How right this was! First, there was the
note of absurdity—adultery in Paris. "That," said Rodney, "should
satisfy your lack of self-assurance—your passion to put all your
actions in inverted commas." It must be said that Rodney under-
stands me very well, for someone only my age, because I do feel less
troubled about doing anything when I can see it as faintly absurd.
Of course, the reasons he gives don't satisfy me. So when I asked
him why I was like that, he said, "Because you're incurably middle-
class, June darling."

On the whole, though, by this time, Rodney was giving me less
of his "patrician" line. However, things had not yet reached the
point where I could tell Rodney my theory about him. This theory,
you will already have guessed, was that he was little better or little
worse, or whatever, than an adventurer, not to say a potential crook.
I did indeed know that his affairs had reached a serious state, because of some of the telephone conversations that I overheard, and
because of the bills that kept arriving. The nicest thing was that
Rodney paid the whole of the Paris trip. It is true that he hadn't
paid his rent for some weeks; it is also true that his trip to Paris
was intended as an investment. Nevertheless, I think it was very
lovely of him to have paid the Paris trip when he was up to his eyes
in debts. Let me say that until the last day or so the Paris trip was
everything I could have asked or that money could buy. Also,
though I don't think Rodney realized this, it was a great relief

to me not to be committing adultery in Henry's house (for, in a sense, it *was* Henry's, although it belonged to me).

It was only on the last day but one of our trip, when we were sitting at a café looking at the Fontainebleau twiddly staircase and drinking Pernod, that Rodney began to press his further suit. I had been expecting it, of course; indeed, it was the choice that lay ahead—the inevitable decision, and all the other things that I had so hoped would not happen but that I knew would. He asked me, in fact, to leave Henry for him. At first, he just said it was what we both wanted. Then he said he loved me too much to see me go on living with Henry in such a dead pretense life, getting more bitterly whimsical and harder every year. Then he said I was made like him, to use life up and enjoy people and things, and then pass on to others. It was all very unreal, but if he had only known, it was exactly this confidence-trick part of him that attracted me. I could quite clearly see the life of travel and hotels we should have on my money, and the bump there would be when we got through my money, which I think Rodney would have done rather quickly. But it was the bogusness, the insecurity, and even, perhaps, the *boue* beneath for which I had such a nostalgia.

Somehow, Rodney didn't grasp this, or perhaps he was too anxious about securing his aims. For he suddenly changed his tone and became a pathetic, dishonest little boy pleading for a chance. He was desperate, he said, and it must look as though he was after my money. This I had to admit. "Well," he said, "then you know the worst." But he begged me to believe that if he could have me with him, it would be different. He had real talent, and he only needed some support to use it. Did I understand, he asked me, exactly what his life had been? And then he told me of his background—his father was a narrow, not very successful builder in a small Scotch town—and described to me most movingly his hatred of it all, his hard, if dishonest, fight to get into a different world, the odds against him. It was I, he said, who could get him onto the tramlines again.

I don't think I'm very maternal, really, because I didn't find myself moved; I only felt cheated. If I hadn't been sure that, whatever he said, life with Rodney would in fact have been much more like what I imagined than like what he was promising, I should have turned him down on the spot. As it was, I said I must think about it. He must leave me alone in London for at least a fortnight, and then I would give him an answer. He accepted this because, anyway, he had business in France, so I returned to London alone.

Henry was glad, on his return, to find Rodney absent, I think. And in a short while he was even more glad. Or, at any rate, I was, because if Rodney had been in our house, I think that Henry would have hit him. This, of course, might have fitted into Rodney's ideas of the violence of life, even if not into his view of civilization, and probably, Rodney being much younger, he would have won the fight, which would have made me very angry because of Henry. But it is just possible that Henry would have won, and this would have made me very sad, because of my ideal picture of Rodney. What put the lid on it for Henry was a visit he made to his mother shortly after his return, when he discovered that Rodney had borrowed money from her. I could only think that if Rodney could get money from Henry's mother he had little to fear about the future (and maybe if my future was joined to his, though precarious, it would not founder). But Henry, of course, saw it differently—and so did I when I heard of the sum involved, which was only fifty pounds, a sum of money insufficient to prevent foundering.

Hardly had Henry's mother dealt Henry's new-found friendship a blow from the right when up came *les jeunes filles* and dealt it a knockout from the left. It seemed that they had busily decorated and furnished two flats for American friends of Rodney's—one for Mrs. Milton Brothers, and one for Robert J. Masterson and family —and, as these American people were visiting the Continent before settling in England, the bills had been given to Rodney to send to them. The bills were quite large, because Rodney had told *les jeunes filles* not to cheesepare. Now Mrs. Brothers and Mr. Masterson and family had arrived in London, and it seemed that they had already given the money for *les jeunes filles* to Rodney, plus his commission. Jackie said "You can imagine what it makes us look like!" and Marcia said "Yes, really it *is* pretty grim."

Then Jackie said, "We look such awful chumps," and that, I think, was what I agreed with most.

Henry said he felt sure that when Rodney returned he would have some explanation to offer. I didn't think this likely and I didn't think Henry did.

"Well," said Jackie, "that's just it. I'm not sure that Rodney *ought* to return, because if Mrs. Brothers goes on as she is now, I think there'll be a warrant out for him soon."

I felt miserable when they had gone, and so did Henry, but for different reasons. All I could find to do was to pray that Mrs. Brothers should die in her bath before she could start issuing warrants. Henry said, "I only hope he doesn't come near this house again, because I'm not sure what my duty would be."

Then, the very next morning, at about eleven o'clock, the telephone rang and it *was* Rodney. I told him what Henry had said, and we agreed that it was most important that he should come to the house when Henry was out. He came just before lunch. I had expected him to look a little hunted, the way Humphrey Bogart sometimes used to look in fugitive films. He did look a little hunted, but it wasn't quite like the films—less to my taste—and I suddenly thought of something. I made an excuse and ran upstairs and hid my jewel box. I would have hated to be issuing warrants for Rodney. Then we had a long chat and something more. About that, I will only say I have rather "a time and a place" view, and so it ended things, as far as I was concerned, with a whimper rather than a bang. As for the chat, I said that I had thought things over and the answer was no, very reluctantly.

When people say, "You don't know what it cost me," I think it's rather stupid, because they could always tell you. So I will tell what this answer cost me—it cost me the whole of a possible different life with someone very attractive. I shall always regret it when the life I am leading is particularly boring, which it often is. But that, after all, is the nature of decisions. The answer had to be no. And I do not despair of other chances. But life is indeed a cheat. What Rodney said after my negative answer was a pity. He went on again about how soon I would become a hard little bitch and rather depressing, with all *my* "amusing" talk. He even said, "I should think you might go off your head. People who get the idea that they can make a game of other people's lives often do." I must say I thought that, everything about Rodney's own life considered, this was a bit too much. And so I changed the conversation to the warrant that might be out at any moment. Rodney was well aware of it, he said, and he had almost enough, but not quite, to get abroad that night. I said I would see what I could find in ready cash, because obviously checks would be no good. He didn't seem sure about this, but I stuck to my point, emphasizing how little he understood money matters, as evidenced in his life. While I was looking for what cash I had, he went upstairs to the lavatory and I heard him walking about in my bedroom, so I was glad, for his sake, that I had hidden my jewel box. And I did find enough to help him overseas, because I had put some aside in case he turned up, although I did not tell him this. And anyway, looking rather hunted but still very handsome, he went, out of my life.

Everything was an anticlimax without Rodney, although his name was kept alive, what with Henry's mother, and *les jeunes filles,* and the Americans, and Mr. Brodrick furious at having only a first chapter, however brilliant, after paying so much as an advance. But all this was not the same for me as Rodney's physical presence —not at all the same.

It was only a month later that it got into the papers, in quite a small column, that he'd been arrested for stealing some money at the house of the Marchesa Ghirlandini, in Rome, where he was a guest. The column also mentioned Mrs. Brothers' warrant.

Well, I did miss the excitement of life with him, and so I got talking a little about it to an old friend of mine—Mary Mudie, who writes a long, gossipy column in a Sunday newspaper. And, sure enough, there was a featured bit about him the very next Sunday— all about the well-known people he'd dined with, and about Lady Ann Denton, and how he was one of "the many fortunate young men of talent and charm who had profited by her friendship," and how valuable she was as a bridge between her generation and the young. Then, there was a bit about Rodney's great brilliance as a writer, saying how few who knew him in this capacity realized his double life. It told with what expectancy connoisseurs of the fresh and original in modern writing had awaited his new book and how ironic its title, "Honour and Civility," now seemed. So brilliant was the first chapter of this book that an old, established publishing firm, famed for its cautious policy, had gone to unusual lengths to assist the young author. Realizing the supreme importance to a writer of congenial surroundings in which to work, the enterprising junior partner of the firm, Mr. Henry Raven, had even installed their brilliant protégé as a tenant in his own house. Then came a block heading, "More Friend Than Lodger," which was followed by a bit about me: " 'I can hardly believe that Rodney was leading this double life,' said almond-eyed, brunette June Raven, well-known young London hostess, and wife of publisher Raven. 'He was more of a friend than a lodger as far as I was concerned. He was not only clever and witty but he had the rare gift of easy intimacy.' "

Dear Mary followed this up immediately with a mention of Rodney's first book, " 'Cuckoo'—a study of married infidelity in history's pages, as witty as it was scholarly." The paragraph then went on to a little interview with Rodney's parents. " 'Rodney never took to the building trade,' his father told me in the front parlor of his typical, unpretentious little Scots 'hame.' 'He always wanted big things out of life.' " And then Mary ended on a moral note: "Rodney Galt got his big things—bigger, perhaps, than he imagined, when an Italian court on Monday last sentenced him . . ."

It was a sad little article, but I did think it was clever of Mary to have made so much of what I told her.

I'm afraid Rodney will be very upset by the piece about his parents, but he did say very nasty things to me. And I was afraid, too, that Henry wouldn't like the "more friend than lodger" part, but Henry ought to pay for my being faithful to him, too, I think. At least, that's how I feel after life has presented me with such awful choices.

Sure enough, Henry read Mary's article and got into a terrible rage. "I'm pretty sure it's actionable," he said.

So I looked very nonchalant, and said, "I don't think so, darling, because I supplied Mary with all the information."

Then he looked at me, and said, "I think you should be very careful, June. This sort of mischievous behavior is frequently a danger signal. It may seem a strange thing to say to you, but you'd only have yourself to blame if you went off your head." He was trembling when he went out of the room, so I think it likely that he'd known about me and Rodney for some time.

Well, there you are—both Henry and Rodney take a "psychological" view of me. But, as I said earlier, I often think that common-sense views are wiser. I spoke before of my old nurse, and what she used to say of me was "Miss June wants to eat her cake and have it." Well, so do most people one meets nowadays. But I think perhaps I want it more than the rest, which makes me think that, in the end, I'll get it.

RETURN

❖

ROBERT M. COATES

C ARTER JOHNSON was hurrying across Sixth Avenue near the corner of Tenth Street when he noticed the water tower. He was
in that place because he was on his way to his bank, and he was
hurrying because it was close to bank-closing time and the check
he had in his wallet, for three hundred and seventy-six dollars, from
a client of his out in Albion, Ohio, meant the difference between
being able to meet his payroll that week out of funds and having
to try, perhaps unsuccessfully, to borrow.

That was how tight things were with Carter at the moment, as
indeed they had been for some time; and yet, despite the pressure
that was on him, the instant that he saw the water tower, rearing up
proudly before him, he stopped dead in his tracks and stared at it.
It was on the near corner of a corner building just a couple of
blocks or so down the avenue from him, and though the building
itself wasn't really tall—seven or eight stories high at the most, he'd
have judged if he'd bothered to judge it—it was tall for the neighborhood; nothing else of that height was anywhere near it, and the
result was that the tower stood out sharp and clear, high and iso-
lated. It was a water tower much like any other, round and squat
and capacious-looking, standing on a stiltlike framework of beams
and uprights, and with an iron ladder leading up one side of it to
the tip of its cone-shaped roof. But there was nothing beyond or behind it but the clean, clarion sky, almost cloudless, and still cool
with the coolness of early summer. And the clean, bright sun struck
down, just right, and the air had just the right promise of breezi-
ness: against the blue there, in that matchless atmosphere, it was
hard to think of its being attached to anything—the tower looked
carefree and invulnerable, like a balloon getting ready to soar.

It seemed to Carter, standing staring at it, that if a man could
only get up to the top of that tower and sit there, looking around him,

he'd be carefree and invulnerable, too. He would have the world at his feet and yet have no bother from it. He would be away from everything and also above it. He would be just about the happiest man on earth.

Less than twenty minutes later, Carter Johnson was sitting on top of the water tower, and though afterward he didn't remember a great deal about how he had got there, it was in fact a good deal easier than he might have expected. The building turned out to be an old one, largely given over to lofts and small manufactories. There was a square, bare hall, dim and dusty and with a plain pine floor that was very much scuffed, which served as entrance hall, and as Carter came in, he was just in time to see the broad, heavy doors of what looked like a freight elevator sliding lazily shut in the wall that was facing him.

Otherwise, the hall was empty. But there was a stairway leading up, in a sort of rectangular spiral around the elevator well, and without a moment's hesitation Carter started up it—up and up and up, as it turned out, till he reached the roof. No one stopped him. When he reached the third-floor landing, a door opened on a chatter of what sounded like linotype machines (the door itself said, "Yerkes & Bonding Job Printing"), and a man in greasy black coveralls came out, crossed the landing, and, opening a door on the same clatter on the other side, disappeared within.

But he walked past Carter as Carter walked past him, unnoticing. Halfway up to the next floor, Carter heard the clanking wheeze of the elevator descending. And on the floor above that, the next-to-the-last floor, there was a man standing as if waiting in an open doorway. He was a short, chunky, dark-haired man in vest and shirtsleeves, with a half-smoked but unlit cigar in his mouth, and Carter, mounting the stairs toward him, regarded him with both interest and detachment—as a climber, scaling a mighty mountain, might regard a peasant he encountered on the way.

To his surprise, as he reached the landing, the man spoke. "You from Schmidt's?" he wanted to know, and—with no desire to confuse; actually, he was a little bit apprehensive—quickly, Carter replied: "No. No, I'm from nowhere." Then, as the man stared ("Huh?" he said, or something like that) and as Carter brushed past, he added, with a bright smile, pointing up, "I'm just going there." And hurried on.

But even he, though he stared at Carter suspiciously, made no effort to stop him; and it was as well that he hadn't, Carter thought a second later as he spiralled the last flight up. "I'd have *killed* him!" he told himself then, and though actually he knew there was little likelihood that he would ever have done anything as violent as that—for throughout his whole life he had lived peaceably, and people don't change quite so radically, even in crisis—there's no question, either, but that something desperate would have resulted if at that late moment anyone had attempted to bar him from his desire. And the thought settled in his mind and remained there, coming up, obliquely, to the surface later.

The top floor, luckily, was deserted. There was a door, labelled "Excelsior Appliances," swinging half open on a bare room rowed with dusty windows, but Carter wasted no time on that. There was a stairway still, iron-runged and steel-railed now, and narrower, but leading up, to a kind of squared cupola with a door, hooked shut, at the top of it: it took no more than a moment to run up the stairs and, the door unhooked, step out onto the roof—grimly tar-and-gravelly, strewn with odd bits of rubbish, and indented with ancient puddles, but free-aired and devoid of smells (Lord! What smells he had climbed through, now that he thought of it!) and sunlit, sunlit at last.

A moment more, and he was up the tower. It could have been minutes or it could have been hours—Carter now was in a mood where time scarcely existed—before one man's head and then another's came peering out of the cupola doorway below. Then the two men themselves—one a short, wiry, black-haired fellow, probably an Italian, in brown work pants and an old blue sweater, the other larger, solider, older, in vest, shirtsleeves, and baggy gray pants—walked slowly out onto the roof.

They came out cautiously, looking this way and that before they advanced, and Carter knew somehow, immediately, that they were looking for him. Even so, it was a while before they found him; and Carter, sitting there silently watching them (he hadn't quite reached the peak of the water tower, but he was near it: he was perched, his knees hunched under him, on the very last rungs of the ladder that lay along the roof of it), felt that mixture of slyness, amusement, and vague triumph that a boy perched high up in a tree and half hidden by its branches might feel, looking down on the world below. In the end, it was he who gave them the clue.

For he just couldn't help it. "Excelsior!" he called down, deliberately making his voice sound high and ringing, and as the idea took hold of him he jumped to his feet and held his arms out stiffly before him, like a man carrying a banner. "Excelsior!" It was a nice-sounding word, and he repeated it, though already the two heads had swivelled up toward him—two melons fitted with features. They stared as Carter posed valiantly before them, and the smaller one was so startled that he even let out a little yelp. Bowing graciously, Carter sat down.

"Didn't I tell ya? I told ya, Frank, didn't I? Didn't I tell ya?" the smaller man cried excitedly, and the older one, but without turning his head—he was still staring steadily at Carter—nodded soberly.

"Yeah, but Jesus! You know, you read about these things—" he said. Then, raising his voice, he directed it suddenly at Carter. "Listen, pal, man to man now," he demanded, it seemed almost angrily. "What the hell do you think you're doing up there, anyway? Don't you know you're just gonna make trouble for yourself?"

Carter, however, was ready for him. "You're so childish," he told the man pityingly. And he meant it; it *was* childish. It had been a mistake, and a sad one, to bring these two into the thing in the first place. For the truth was these men didn't fit in; whatever his plan was, they didn't belong at all.

"Otherwise, it's the cops," the other persisted. "The cops, and maybe the loony bin. You don't want that, do you?"

And there was more talk, more talk. Sometime, in the interval, the littler fellow had vanished; but at the same time, or somewhere around then—time, like everything else, was a little confused—other people had come straggling out onto the roof to join him: a pack of young girls, some of them in work smocks, and all squealing and chattering; the two men that he'd passed on the stairway, and whom he recognized briefly, as if in a lightning flash, and then lost in the pack of others, others. . . . Though they talked, for the most part, among themselves, that still made a hubbub of voices, and Carter, even when he was answering that other, the baggy-pantsed one, felt as if he were addressing a multitude.

It made him feel at once flighty and exasperated, and when someone from the crowd cut in—as a tall, almost freakishly thin man did once: "For God's sake, Frank, leave him stay there! Leave him stay till the cops come!" he called loudly, suddenly—it only confused, and at the same time excited, Carter the more. There were times when he just sat down, hid his head between his knees (but no fool he! still watching, waiting), and said nothing.

For the other, the one in the baggy pants, still persisted. "Come on

down, pal," he kept saying wheedlingly; and when the cops came
—for they did come; Baggy-Pants had been right about that—their
talk followed the same pattern. "What you got to gain by staying
up there?" (This, later, from a cop—or was it?—halfway up the
ladder; there was a while when they talked quite amicably together.) "Come on down. Come on down, get it over with. What
you got to lose, coming down?" That was the pattern. And there
was more talk, more talk: once, to mock them (this was at a moment when he was conscious of their being a multitude, and all
staring at him: he must look like a weather vane), he flapped his
arms against his sides and crowed. "Cock-a-doodle-*doo!*" he crowed,
as loudly and defiantly as he could. But all that happened was that
it set some of the girls to chattering, and when he leaned out over
them from his ladder and said bitterly "How silly can you get!" it
only made a couple of them chatter the more.

Carter never was angry, though. Once, because there was so much
talk about who was he, where did he come from—"What's your
name, Mac?" someone was asking, again from part way up the
ladder—he reached into his coat pocket for his wallet and tossed it
down to them. He knew his own name, of course; it was Thomas
Carter Johnson. But it seemed simpler, at the moment, more dignified, really, to do it that way.

"Look in there if you don't believe me," he called down to the
swarm of them; and then, since the two seemed to belong together,
he took off his coat and threw it down after the wallet. "Take that,
too, if you want it," he told them. Or rather, he told the other, the
big, baggy-pantsed, saggy-bodied first one that he'd at first despised
and now almost liked, and he was glad that the wallet, and the
jacket, too, fell just about at his feet, so he was able to reach them
before any of the others: it made Carter feel that his things were
in good hands.

And that, too, was at a time when the roof was full of people;
Baggy-Pants was the only one that he knew there. It was at a time
when he felt at his most capricious. He was in a wonderful mood
then: a mood, really, that he'd never had at all before, unless it had
been sometime too far back to remember, and this might have been
true, too, for now he had that tree-climbing, up-to-the-summit feeling of being a boy again—really being a boy again: a mood of confidence, too. It was a mood, strange to him for years, when he felt
that anything, everything, that he did would be, automatically,
right. And when the new man, round-faced, round-eyed, brown-

haired, climbed up to him, up the ladder—or up, anyway, near him —Carter told him about it.

But that came later, and anyway, his moods alternated. There were times when he just sat down, sullenly, sadly—knowing he was capricious, but still glorying in it: after all, who, up here, was to dictate to him?—and just sat there, contemplating confusion.

For it was confusion. And it had been a mistake, getting even the other one into it; things, otherwise, had been so simple, or they would have been. To be sure, there had been a few seconds, at first, when the height distressed him. The tower itself, when he got to the top of it, was higher than he had thought, and barer, too; easier to fall from. Even the roof of the building seemed a good two- or three-story drop, straight below him, while the street below that, crawling and twinkling with traffic, and with a crowd now gathering along the curbing, staring melon-faced, seed-faced, up at him —the street, seen past the edge of the nearer cornice, seemed a fall like a plummet's fall, dizzying. He had reeled, at first sight, or the street had reeled, wavelike, rising and falling; but like a sailor mounting a mast, he had clung, he had hung, and now (like the sailor, in his crow's nest) all he felt was a kind of easy swaying-awayness.

Or he *had* felt it, for a moment—who could be sure? For there had been a moment, too, those first moments, when he'd felt that if he wanted to dive, he could make the divingest dive that had ever been heard of, right straight down to that street below. But that had passed. He had felt, after that—even, inside that—a peace, in those first few cheerful moments, a real peace, an upliftedness. It was this, mainly, that he was trying to recapture now, and if at times he sat down silently and said nothing, it was not entirely from sullenness, or from spitefulness, either. It was more to remove himself from the turmoil and confusion that had somehow grown up around him, and when the man climbed up the ladder and tried to talk to him, Carter told him so.

"I can't seem to get away," he said. He felt foolish, then and later, about bringing out his private problems for public examination. But his position, up there on the tower, seemed to demand it; in a way, he was a public figure up there. He was the focus, the center about which everything seemed to be revolving, from the tower itself to the street below, and so he felt that, like Joe DiMaggio or Secretary Dulles, he had to go with it, he had to live up to what was expected of him. But the man—he was a priest, or a minister, from his collar, but he had a long, hangdog face, and Carter didn't like him—the man didn't seem really to understand.

"Get away from what?" he asked. And then, unctuously, "Man, man, don't you realize it? What you're trying to get away from is yourself. And you can't do that." He had climbed, Carter noticed, halfway up the ladder, only up to the roof edge, and had stopped there. "No matter how high you go, you've still got yourself to contend with. You've still got yourself along with you," he said. But he had stopped, Carter noticed. He had stopped where the others had stopped.

Everybody, now, he had noticed, was being very careful not to get too close to him. He had warned them off once. "Keep away from me, damn you!" he had yelled, away back there, when someone— was it the priest again? No, maybe a policeman—had tried to swarm right up beside him and get hold of his hand.

"We're going down now," the man had said, talking to him as if he were a child, giving emphasis to every syllable. "We're going down now." And Carter, for the first time, feeling power, the power of his altitude, his position: "Keep away from me, damn you! Don't touch me!" he had cried. And, by God, he had made it stick —the man had retreated!

But now— Well, it was more confused. Someone, someone, meanwhile, had told him that Clara, Clara, his wife was coming over to talk to him. "She'll be here any minute now," the man had said. "And she said just to wait, wait, wait. She'll be here any minute. She wants to talk to you."

But that was one thing, and here was the other man, asking, asking. "Get away from what?" he was asking, and that made things all the more confused. Because, really, at that moment, Carter didn't, actually, know.

"Get away from *them*," he said, and he pointed, tentatively, at the clumps of people on the rooftop and the crowd in the street below. "Them, down there," he added, a bit petulantly; after all, anyone ought to know what he was talking about.

The man, though, was jovial. "You're not worried about *them?* Who are they, anyway?" the man asked, in his briskest manner.

"I don't know," Carter had to admit. It was in his mind to say, too, that he didn't know *him*. But politeness delayed him, and by that time the other was speaking.

"Well, then—"

"Well, then. Well, then! Well *then!*" The fact that he hadn't said quite what he'd wanted to say lent force to his way of talking. "Well, then, why're they here? What are they waiting for?" And then, since things seemed to be forcing themselves into a pattern (for why, after all, did one climb to a high place, and why did others worry about his climbing, unless he was meaning to use it as a place to jump from), "Are they waiting to see me jump?"

"Jump!" the priest cried. Or was it another? People came and went; it seemed he had been talking endlessly, but maybe some of them had been the same.

The roof was bare now, except for a few people here and there, and a group of men in uniform, spreading a sort of canopy, or was it a net, around the base of the tower; he, for one, missed the squealing and talking that had gone on before. The crowd in the street below, though, was growing steadily. Night was falling, too, or the day was waning; anyway, there had been a change in the angle of the sunlight, and the street was barred across with shadow now. But the light struck in strongly still, though slantingly, on the rooftop, and its very slantingness added to his feeling of isolation —statuesqueness, even, set off there, lit up there, to be stared at, on the water tower.

But there was something, too, about the light, and the lateness, that disturbed him. And the trouble was that people kept climbing up and interrupting him. "You love your wife, don't you? She loves you. And you wouldn't want to be the means of bringing sorrow and grief to her, would you?" someone was saying, and then talking and talking. And Carter, meanwhile, was trying to figure out something; it was the crowd below that had brought it into his mind. For they, obviously, had all been hurrying somewhere; nowadays, everyone was hurrying. And now there they all were down there, stopped dead in their tracks, and here *he* was, and hadn't he been hurrying somewhere, too? The image of a marbled interior, with lines of people standing before brass-barred windows, appeared momentarily before him, and he thought: the bank?

But the thought brought no connotation, and he let it vanish. "Just another day wasted" was all he got out of it, and he said this as much to himself as to whoever was there at the moment. "She will never forgive me for this," he added, meaning Clara—for hadn't they been talking about her? And he was almost certain, too, that he'd heard the man, this or some man, say that Clara was coming over—that Clara was coming over. But he was afraid to ask, to make sure.

"Not Clara. She don't condone things," he went on, instead, and more or less as a stopgap, but still following his own line of thought, and when the man asked jovially "Wanna bet?" Carter just stared at him and went on as before. "You condone things, don't you?" he asked. "I condone things." In a way, the very sound of the words appealed to him. "I mean, if you did something that was wrong, or I did—well, you know what I mean. You'd *condone* things. But Clara—" There were hundreds of things that came into his mind—about the dishes, the dog, the way he handled his affairs, the time she'd blasted at him about that old shirt of his in the closet—but he was too tired now to go into them. He was really, suddenly, getting tired.

And besides, he felt shamefaced, somehow, talking like this about his wife to a total stranger. When the man said something about "not wanting to hurt her," Carter snapped back at him. "I have never hurt anyone in my life," he told him, and he noticed that the man changed his tack immediately.

"What you need is a rest," he kept saying now; you had to admit that he was persistent. "You know, you said so yourself, a while back. You said you wanted to get away, think things over. And, Lord knows, here's your chance, if you want to take it. Stop and think of it, man—what's keeping you? What you got to lose? You got money. You got over five hundred dollars in that wallet," he said, and at that Carter perked up a little. He had forgotten about the wallet.

"Have I?" he asked, almost timidly; there seemed to be so much that he had forgotten.

"Sure, you have. You come down and we'll show it to you, we'll give it to you." And though he, and the others, had done the same thing dozens of times before, and got the same reaction: "Come on, fella, come on down right now. Give me your hand and I'll help you," he said, and when Carter pulled back, he went on imperturbably. "You see, man, you don't know what's good for you. What you want to do is to take that money and take your wife and go off somewhere, take a rest, take some time off and think things over. Get some relaxation. God! I wish I was in your shoes, man! Ever seen Niagara Falls? The Bahamas?" he was asking when someone shouted up from below.

"Frank, she's here!" the man shouted. "Let *her* talk to him," and the man on the ladder turned, and Carter looked, and there, sure enough, was Clara! Carter never had been more surprised in his life.

She had just come out the door of the little cupola, with its stairs leading up, up, up—he had almost forgotten that up-ness—from the streets below; two men who had come with her were standing beside her, and she stood there a moment, staring up at him. "Oh, Carter, *Carter!*" she called then, suddenly, and he could tell from the very tone of her voice that she was upset. "Carter, what are you doing? Come down," she cried. But she didn't seem angry; and indeed, seeing her, so small down there, so small down there, her voice coming up to him only faintly, he thought she seemed frailer, gentler—younger, even, fairer haired—than he had seen her looking in years.

And she really *was* there; that alone was enough to wring him. "Clara, why did you come?" he called down to her. She had only her housecoat on, and that somehow made him sorrier—sorry not only for her but for him and for everyone.

"Carter, why wouldn't I?"

"Well, but still . . . I didn't want you to see me like this" was all he could say, though he meant it the other way, with the housecoat and all. In a way, he was quoting her.

"I want to see you *safe,*" she said. "Come *down.*" She was almost strident; and there was something in the way she said it, stalwartly — Well, it reminded him of times in the past when she had been stalwart, too, stalwart for both of them. Up there, all alone, he felt himself softening.

Suddenly, too, everything that the man said began to make sense. For he, too, had kept on talking, in a kind of running accompaniment, even while Clara was talking. "See? See? You see? Didn't I tell you?" he kept saying, insinuatingly. "Man, man, it's just like I told you, you've got nothing to worry about. With a wife like that to stick by you. Money in your pocket . . ."

"I've got bills, though," Carter put in, but tentatively. He was ready to be convinced.

And the man convinced him. "Bills can wait!" he said. "What you need is a little rest and relaxation, and you'll be right back in there pitching. Listen, man, why'n't you hop off someplace—Niagara Falls, Atlantic City," he was saying, and always so coaxingly; though Carter didn't really like him, he had to admit that everything he said made sense.

"Listen, Clara," he called out suddenly. He was bypassing the

man on the ladder, and he knew it. But he couldn't help it. It was
what the man himself had said that had made him think of it.
"Clara, listen. Do you want to go see the Natural Bridge?" he called
down, and at first she looked startled; he could understand that.
After all, it was something she'd wanted to do years before, in their
happier times. Even he had forgotten it, till this other had started
talking about other places.

"What?" she called back.

"The Natural Bridge. You know, in Virginia?" he called down,
and she still seemed a little unsettled; one of the men standing with
her had to nudge her before she answered.

"Sure. Sure. Anything you want. Anywhere. Only just come
down." And then, suddenly, she burst out weeping. She was weeping, there, right in front of everyone, and it was that that decided
him. "Well, I will, Clara. Yes, I will," he said. He couldn't hear, he
couldn't see, but he could almost feel the sigh of relief—it was like
an exhalation—that followed.

And then, bustling. "Here, here, man. Let's have your hand. Let
me help you," from the man that had been talking.

"No, no. Give him time," from the voice down below. "Don't
hustle him."

In the midst of it, Carter had his own timetable to follow. "Wait.
Wait. Wait," he said, and they waited. He was standing now at the
top of the ladder leading down the tower's side, and they were all,
near below or far away, silent, watching him. It was a moment of
power, and he knew that he held it, though he knew also that he
had no right to it. It was the power of his own life or death. He
could turn, if he wanted to, this way, and dive, and they'd have
their fulfillment—or *they* would, down in the street below.

Or he could walk right down, down the ladder, down the stairs.
"I want my wallet," he said, and they listened; he could hear them
talking among themselves.

"Of course, man. We've got it right here. Come on down and
we'll hand it over to you," they said. But that didn't satisfy him, and
he told them so. If a man had power, he might as well use it.

"No, I want it here," he told them. "I want the man I gave it to,
too," he added, and that seemed to trouble them. Since he didn't
know the man's name, it troubled him, too. "The baggy-pantsed
one. The man that came up to talk to me first. I think he must be
the superintendent," he told them, carefully, and that seemed to
clear things; there was a rushing about among the people below.

("You just stay there. He'll be right along," whispered someone close at hand.)

And he was, of course; sure enough, soon enough, he was. He came climbing up, looking heavy, and hard-worked, and solemn—and worried now, too—but easygoing and companionable, just as Carter remembered him, and as he neared the top, he reached into his vest pocket and fished out the wallet and handed it over. "Here's your wallet," he said, as easy as that. "You coming on down?"

"Yes, indeed. Right now," Carter said, and he smiled to reassure him. "Just don't hustle me."

And come down he did, step by step, with the baggy-pantsed one climbing down ahead to guide him. He came down as he said he would, but still it was strange. "You can't lose," some one of them had said; had it been the jovial one? But the thing was, he *did* lose: every step down he took he lost purpose, he lost importance.

He was moving down now into a different air, darker, heavier. Baggy-Pants was there to guide him, not too far ahead, not too near, not too careful nor too easygoing, and Carter followed him. And yet still, going down, step by step, confidence forsook him; when he reached the hard, gravelled roof—and below that, six or seven more stories down to, well, what would you call it, reality? When he made that contact— "Clara!" he cried.

She was standing there before him, but it was she and yet not she; she as he had known her, not as he had hoped she would be, and when—even, still, hoping—he started toward her, she jumped back quickly, almost affrightedly, and that told him, oh, that told him. At the same time, the two men who were standing beside her moved forward. Carter turned, and this time it was the baggy-pantsed one he confronted—and so, oddly, it was to him he voiced his protest.

"You! You let me down, too!" he cried out, and then he was engulfed in a storm of struggling.

THE CHILDREN'S GRANDMOTHER

❖

SYLVIA TOWNSEND WARNER

LOOKING westward under the dusky winter skies, which had a russet tinge, as though the color of the Cornish moor were reflected in the low-hanging clouds, one saw along the horizon a band of pale light, and that was the sky above the Atlantic.

"You say Roses is five miles from the sea?" my sister Anne had commented. "Why, the children will grow up little sea monsters. You can whisk them there in a moment, before the old lady has time to say no." In fact, it was not so easy. The children's grandmother could not imagine the car—a large, old Daimler, a car for carrying dowagers to court rather than children to the sea—being driven by anyone but Job. Job understood it. We lived at Roses for nearly three years before I was allowed to drive the Daimler to the sea, and even then Job came, too. Job also understood the tides, and as my children's Aunt Madeleine had been drowned off the beach where they paddled, I could not gainsay the importance of Job's understanding the tides. By then, I had become so much a piece of life at Roses that I was not sorry to have Job in the back of the car, representing, for he was an immensely heavy and solemn old man, the rightful dowager. Graciously rising and sinking, bowing to a nonexistent populace at every jolt in the narrow lane, Job accompanied us to the sea, and sat down on the flat rock that was called Job's Rock, as other rocks were called the Castle, the Maiden, and the Churn, and took out his knitting. He sat on his rock and watched the sea, and his needles clicked and flicked, gathering the wool into socks and scarves and jerseys for the children, and at some mysteriously indicated moment he would cry out, in his foghorn bellow, that the current was flowing past the Churn, that swimmers and paddlers must return to the beach. We obeyed him, knowing that he was our friend. We must have known it by intuition, for he hardly ever spoke, his face was as expressionless as the moon, and his eyes were like two large iron nails driven deep into it and fastened by rust.

There were two other coves, both within much the same distance from Roses, but we were forbidden to go to them. To reach them, one had to pass through a village called St. Keul, where, the children's grandmother said, there was always fever. At first, this prohibition was merely a mercy to me, and St. Keul a place where I need not be paraded in my widow's dress, or repeat the story of the car accident in which my husband had been fatally injured, and I scarcely injured at all, to listeners whose code of manners spared me no questions and whose loyalty to the old family inscribed very clearly on their severe countenances a loyally unspoken opinion that the wrong one had survived. Their sympathy, naturally enough, went to my husband's mother, who would oversee these conversations almost as a mother oversees her child's performance at the dancing class, sternly attentive that I should not omit a single pirouette in the elaborate ritual of courtesy between high and low. As time went on, and I became better trained in these formalities, and saw her skilled and scrupulous observance of them, I found that I could not reconcile the ban on St. Keul with the reason she gave for it. Any outbreak of sickness, any sickbed, childbed, deathbed, among our poor neighbors became her affair—not, I think, that she liked doing good but simply because she could not conceive herself not doing it. No danger or loathsomeness could turn her aside from a purpose. The Daimler swayed and sidled down chaseways and field tracks to carry her and her chest of homeopathic medicines anywhere and everywhere—except to St. Keul. Whatever the reason for her ban, it could not be fever—unless (the surmise darted upon me and darkened into belief) it was from St. Keul that the infection had reached out to Guy and Everard, the twin sons who had died, one at midnight, the other before day, as though they had died in a ballad. No doubt I could have known the truth for the asking, but I could not bring myself to ask. There was something so hysterically ludicrous in the story of this doomed nursery that I dreaded to hear it consecutively told. Such narratives are more tolerable in the city, where, indeed, they can be a social asset, and people dine out on them: "Max, Max, tell us that appalling story, that 'Seven Little Niggers' story of the family at Roses!" But at Roses one was a long way from any city.

My husband, the last of my mother-in-law's children, and born a long interval after the others, was the only one who lived to grow up, his childhood intimidated by the presence, which was also an absence, of Madeleine, Guy, Everard, Lucas, Alice, and Noel. He

grew up an only child, in the middle of this shadowy band of
brothers and sisters who his father and the servants assured him
were angels in Heaven, who his mother told him were dead. Unable to reconcile a discrepancy, he yet felt himself confronted with
a choice between becoming another angel or another dead child at
the feet of the white marble angel that showed up so embarrassingly
among the wooden and small iron crosses in the village graveyard.
Meanwhile, he lived among their vestiges—riding Guy's bicycle,
filling the blank pages in Lucas's scrapbook, or giving tea parties
under the weeping ash to the dolls of Madeleine, Alice, and Noel.
Twice a year, he stood to be measured against the nursery door,
where their heights were recorded in his mother's handwriting,
creeping up among and through them like a shoot of this year making its way through last year's thicket, until at last he surmounted
them all and still remained alive. Their initials and his—a C for
Charles—were still legible when I came to Roses with his four
fatherless children and the measuring began again, the children's
grandmother writing the new initials and the dates of the twentieth
century in the same calm, cursive hand. Age for age, the new meas-
urements all fell below the old. She never remarked on it, but I
supposed that to herself she commented on the stocky, inelegant
stature inherited from a mother born of the sturdy middle class.
She never remarked on my children's sturdy-middle-class health,
either. Beyond a few prohibitions—St. Keul, bathing in the current
that drowned Madeleine, eating chocolates after teeth had been
brushed for bedtime—she had no trace of grandmotherly fuss or
grandmotherly fondness. During our first years at Roses, while I was
still capable of town-bred speculation and analysis, I used to wonder if her detachment sprang from a contained and despairing diffi-
dence—if, having failed so pitiably to rear her own children, she
had made some violent vow not to meddle with mine. Later, seeing
her detachment persisting, quite unchanged, under her grandchildren's affection, I came to suppose her dislike of her son's marriage perpetuated in a stoical disapproval of the fruits of it—for she
was completely a stoic; in all the years I lived under her roof, I
never heard her utter a regret or an aspiration. And at other times
I had the simple and sentimental thought: She has lost all her
children; she dare not love again. In spite of this detachment—or
perhaps because of it—her relationship with her grandchildren was
as easy as the relationship of sea and seaweed. We think of children
as being our dependents; at best, this is only a half-truth. The child

is a social tyrant, imposing on its elders an obligation to conform, to be in keeping, and as a rule the elderly, being on the outermost and most provincial rim of the child's society, transform themselves the most slavishly, and climb downward, so to speak, in a headlong flurry to be accepted. The children's grandmother was as equalitarian among my children as though she were another child. She spoke to them, even to the youngest, without a change of voice or manner, and bargained with them in such matters as winding her wool or stripping the gooseberry bushes as sternly as though they were horse dealers. They, in turn, bargained with her and, by measuring their wits against hers, came to know her as confidently as Job understood the Daimler and the tides. In spite of her threescore years and ten, she was as active as a hound. It was an extraordinary sight to see them playing hide-and-seek in the orchard—the tall old woman running, with her gray head stooped, under the lichened boughs, or folded away in some narrow hiding place, her eyes blazing with excitement. With a fickleness that matched the fickleness of a child, she would say curtly "That's all" and walk out of the game without a trace of fatigue, for she played to please herself, not them. Even in that most grandmotherly role of storyteller, she retained an egoism of artistry. It was she who chose the stories; it was to her own ear they were addressed, or perhaps to the ghost of her unsurmisable childish self, seated among my children, who listened with critical ease to her narratives, as a cultured audience listens to a first-rate performer. "Nothing too much." It is, I believe, a Stoic maxim; at any rate, it is a canon of classical performance. I never heard her carried away into overdramatization or false emphasis. Her ghosts appeared without those preliminary warnings, lowered tones that say "Here comes the ghost," as stentoriously as the major-domo announces "His Grace the Duke of So-and-So;" the squeals of the little pigs were related, not mimicked; her bears growled as a matter of course. Listening one evening to the dignified inflections of the Wolf Grandmother replying to the inquiries of Little Red Riding Hood, I realized that this was, in fact, the lot of my children: They had a Wolf Grandmother. a being who treated them with detached benignity, who played with them and dismissed them and enjoyed them without scruple, and would, at a pinch, defend them with uncontaminated fury. Her eyes were large the better to see them with, her ears long the better to hear them, her claws sharp the better to tear—by an accident of kinship—not them but the village of St.

Keul, the malevolence of the sea, the Jesuitry of the bedtime chocolate.

They loved her with an unjaded love—as they love her memory
to this day. They throve in her as they throve in the climate of moor
and sea. What she felt for them I could not determine. Unless there
is a kind of love that can exist without a breath of tenderness, it
was not love. It was too passionate for affection. It had nothing in
common with the wistful doting of old age. It had a quality, at once
abstract and practical, that made it seem like some deeply felt
bargain, as though, perhaps, she accepted them as the remission of
her own tragedy, an indulgence of a maternal feeling that in her
own maternity had been deformed by constant blasts of fate, as the
thorn trees on the moor were blown out of shape by the wind from
the sea. But she never made any move to take them from me or set
them against me. Circumstances—my loneliness, my poverty, my
husband's perplexing injunction that his children should grow up
at Roses—all made it easy for her to avenge herself on me for a marriage she had disapproved; but, having brought herself to swallow
me, she had, it appeared, no further wish than to make a good digestion of me.

Once only did I see her exhibit an unequivocal force of feeling—
and the exhibition left me baffled as ever as to the nature of the
feeling itself. There were vipers on the moor, and Job had taught
the children how to handle them safely, since it was too much to
expect that they would not handle them at all. The length of a
viper lashing below the small brown fist that held it firmly just
below the head, the smell of the viaticum chloroform on the wad of
cotton wool, and, later, the stink of a dissection had become familiar
to me, and not even very alarming. But on this occasion Paul's hand
was still greasy from helping to lubricate the Daimler. The viper
writhed out of his grasp and fell at Caroline's bare feet, and bit her
in the toe. For several days, she was dangerously ill. During that
time, I had a horrible leisure in which to observe my mother-in-law.
Under her reserve, I saw a wildcat fury at this misadventure, a rage
so intense that I was afraid to leave Paul in the same room with her,
for it seemed possible that in some self-contained trance of resentment she would turn and rend him to pieces. Her anxiety appeared
to have carried her beyond the fact of a child in danger of dying; it
was harsh and abstracted, akin to the anxiety of the speculator who
has staked everything, future as well as fortune, on a coup and sees

the market wavering against him; and when the doctor pronounced Caroline out of danger, she gave vent to a shuddering, astonished "Whew-w!," as though it were she herself who had escaped a mortal peril.

While he was still congratulating her, she quitted him to unlock the wine cellar, bringing out bottle after bottle of Burgundy, rum, and Sauterne. Standing in the kitchen like some descended Juno, she brewed a vast bowl of punch, from which we must all drink to celebrate Caroline's recovery, and the kitchen maid was sent pelting off to summon the outlying people of the estate: the bailiff, the shepherds, the furze cutters. It was a cold evening, for though the month was August, a sea fog was coming in. Fetched out of the chilly dusk into the blazing kitchen and given mugfuls of punch, the celebrants became very drunk. It was alarming to see the familiar and sombre faces of everyday acquaintance smeared with looks of vinous beatitude, and though the congratulations they gave me were sincere, I felt as though I were hemmed in by a throng of sheepish satyrs. Perhaps I was a little drunk myself, though I had managed to spill out half my tumblerful. As soon as I could, I got my tipsy children away. I went to sit by Caroline's bed, hearing the shouts and songs of the retiring guests and the hubbub of the household folk still at it in the kitchen. Till this evening, I had never seen the children's grandmother anything but abstemious. Now I watched her drinking glass after glass, drinking enough to put any man under the table. I was worried about her, concerned for her credit, and for her health. The noise died out at last, but still she did not come to bed. I had nerved myself to go in search of her when I heard her foot on the stair, the firm, unhurried tread exactly as usual. She paused at the door, and I thought she would enter. Seized by an unaccountable sense of danger, I stood myself in front of the child's bed, as if to protect her. But the door did not open, and presently I heard a calm, fragile sound—concluding some train of satisfied thought, the old lady had clicked her tongue against the roof of her mouth—and then the footsteps went evenly on.

Apparently my children had inherited her knack for hard drinking. On the morrow, they were none the worse for having gone drunk to bed, and clamored for another occasion for punch. On her eightieth birthday, she said, and with Wolf Grandmother dexterity boxed back their endeavors to ascertain the happy date. The possibility that she might die before then occurred to none of us. She proceeded through old age as infallibly, as vitally, as my children grew from childhood to youth.

In our small world, where she and they moved through time like mowers through a field, scything down the years and leaving them prone behind them, I alone seemed unable to grow older. My middle-aged body showed few changes; my circumstances even enforced on me a sort of retrogression into girlishness. I had my four children, and the wedding ring on my finger, yet when the young chauffeur who came after Job's death persisted in calling me "Miss," the error was felt to be natural, and even fitting; a newcomer, he rightly discerned and proclaimed the accomplishment of a process that the others had for a long while been inattentively forwarding. Interpolated as a daughter-in-law, I was now a daughter of the house, the faithful, negligible daughter who has never left home.

Such daughters are usually scorned by their mothers. Soon after my reclassification by Martin (the new chauffeur was called Martin), the children's grandmother broke her severe procedure and was rude to me. We were bound on one of her errands of mercy, and Martin, who piqued himself on already knowing his way everywhere, was settling us in the car. "High Grange," he said confidently. "That's through St. Keul, and then left."

"No," I answered. "You turn left at the crossroads, and then—"

Her voice cut through mine. "Idiot!" she exclaimed. "Woolgathering as usual! Martin is perfectly right. Drive through St. Keul, Martin."

There is a moment when, still conscious under the anesthetic, one crosses a frontier between a known and an incalculable world. That is how I felt when the car held on over the crossroads and I saw a landscape typically familiar but in fact strange, unassimilated, and raw, and because St. Keul did not immediately start up before us, like some conjurer's castle, I had the impression that we were endlessly going nowhere, or perhaps were dead. Martin, his ears still scarlet with embarrassment, was driving faster than she approved, but she made no move to check him. She sat upright and silent in an Egyptian gravity, clad in her smooth, dark tweed as though in basalt, her hands laid in rigid composure along her thighs. Only an occasional flick of her fingers, disquieting as the undulation that brings the heather root to life as a snake, escaped her self-control.

She had gratuitously insulted me, I had failed to defend myself, and now I was falling back on the private retaliation of pity—pitying her for being so old, and for the barren stubbornness that was forcing her to flout a superstition of so many years' observance. The watery sunlight lit up some slate roofs clotted about a narrow church with a slated belfry. I saw her hands relax. Very softly, she began to whistle. It was a jigging little tune of a few notes, the sort of tune one learns in the nursery; and Guy, my younger son, would whistle in just the same manner on the way back from the dentist. Absorbed in the whistling soliloquy, she was driven through St. Keul. The infection of her odd merriment gained on me, and I began to feel meaninglessly merry myself.

"There!" she exclaimed as we left it behind us. "So much for St. Keul!"

Recklessly, dancing to the tune of her whistling, I asked, "But what was the fever at St. Keul? What kind of fever?"

"Only young children died of it," she replied. "I don't give a rap for it now. Yours have outgrown the danger. You really need not fuss about it any longer."

I did not say that it was she, not I, who had laid the ban on St. Keul. I was thinking of a different peril. It seemed to me that the passage of our unmistakable Daimler had roused unfavorable attention in the slighted village, and that on our return we should very probably be stoned. But at High Grange she learned that two sons of a fisherman's family had been drowned, and after visiting the bereaved household we went home by a different route.

It was on this return journey that Martin ran into a cow—a contributory reason for his dismissal a few weeks later. He did not understand the Daimler. But he understood my true status at Roses, and stayed long enough to see me established in it. I suppose there is an inherent servility in my nature. The barter of an unspoken for an outspoken censure did not seem to me too high a price to pay for the relief of being on easier terms with the children's grandmother, of having some claim on her affection, if only as her drudge. It was as though she would at last allow me to live again, after the long years during which I had been compelled to exist merely as a cipher. I took up my new life, and with the departure of my children to their boarding schools I became almost the unmarried daughter. Living at her beck and call, submerged in busy economies that were to pay for the children's education, assenting to her opinions and listening to her stories (told with as much spirit as ever, and for her own entertainment), I had no time for the speculations and ruminations of my cipher days. St. Keul, that Dark Tower, was now the place where we bought sardines, and the problem of the reserve and detachment qualifying her love for the children—the problem, even, as to whether she loved them at all—was not even a problem. At first, she had disliked us, and gradually her dislike had been overcome—that, and no more, was the explanation.

It was not the explanation. I did not arrive at the truth until the day she lay dying, whirled away like a dandelion clock by a brief pleurisy. She had lain for some hours without speaking, and only from time to time stirring her hand. I sat beside her, grieving perhaps, or perhaps grieving that I could not grieve more, and straining my ears for the noise of the car that might bring Paul home from college in time to do his part as the elder male of the family. Becoming aware that I was being looked at, I turned and saw her glance dwelling on me. Her eyes gleamed in their sockets; her lips were forming painfully into a smile of contempt. She struggled to raise herself, and writhed across the bed toward me.

"Heh! You poor creature!" she said, taking hold of my chin in a violent, shaking grasp. "Heh! You poor, luckless creature! You have not lost one of your children, not one!"

I thought she was raving, but her tone steadied, and there was the force of years of rational consideration in her voice as she continued, "So when you are old, you will not have a single child left you. Nothing but strangers!"

Those were the last words she spoke. Then it was the disclosure of her hoarded malice that appalled me. Now I am appalled for a different reason. I am beginning to think that her words are coming true.

SIX FEET OF THE COUNTRY

❖

NADINE GORDIMER

M Y wife and I are not real farmers—not even Lerice, really. We
bought our place, ten miles out of Johannesburg on one of
the main roads, to change something in ourselves, I suppose; you
seem to rattle about so much within a marriage like ours. You long
to hear nothing but a deep satisfying silence when you sound a
marriage. The farm hasn't managed that for us, of course, but it
has done other things, unexpected, illogical. Lerice, who I thought
would retire there in Chekhovian sadness for a month or two, and
then leave the place to the servants while she tried yet again to get
a part she wanted and become the actress she would like to be, has
sunk into the business of running the farm with all the serious
intensity with which she once imbued the shadows in a playwright's
mind. I should have given it up long ago if it had not been for her.
Her hands, once small and plain and well-kept—she was not the sort
of actress who wears red paint and diamond rings—are hard as a
dog's pads.

I, of course, am there only in the evenings and on weekends. I am
a partner in a luxury-travel agency, which is flourishing—needs to
be, as I tell Lerice, in order to carry the farm. Still, though I know
we can't afford it, and though the sweetish smell of the fowls Lerice
breeds sickens me, so that I avoid going past their runs, the farm is
beautiful in a way I had almost forgotten—especially on a Sunday
morning when I get up and go out into the paddock and see not the
palm trees and fishpond and imitation-stone bird bath of the
suburbs but white ducks on the dam, the lucerne field brilliant as
window dresser's grass, and the little, stocky, mean-eyed bull, lustful
but bored, having his face tenderly licked by one of his ladies.
Lerice comes out with her hair uncombed, in her hand a stick
dripping with cattle dip. She will stand and look dreamily for a
moment, the way she would pretend to look sometimes in those

plays. "They'll mate tomorrow," she will say. "This is their second day. Look how she loves him, my little Napoleon." So that when people come out to see us on Sunday afternoon, I am likely to hear myself saying as I pour out the drinks, "When I drive back home from the city every day, past those rows of suburban houses, I wonder how the devil we ever did stand it. . . . Would you care to look around?" And there I am, taking some pretty girl and her young husband stumbling down to our riverbank, the girl catching her stockings on the mealie-stooks and stepping over cow-turds humming with jewel-green flies while she says, ". . . the *tensions* of the damned city. And you're near enough to get into town to a show, too! I think it's wonderful. Why, you've got it both ways!"

And for a moment I accept the triumph as if I *had* managed it— the impossibility that I've been trying for all my life—just as if the truth was that you could get it "both ways," instead of finding yourself with not even one way or the other but a third, one you had not provided for at all.

But even in our saner moments, when I find Lerice's earthy enthusiasms just as irritating as I once found her histrionical ones, and she finds what she calls my "jealousy" of her capacity for enthusiasm as big a proof of my inadequacy for her as a mate as ever it was, we do believe that we have at least honestly escaped those tensions peculiar to the city about which our visitors speak. When Johannesburg people speak of "tension," they don't mean hurrying people in crowded streets, the struggle for money, or the general competitive character of city life. They mean the guns under the white men's pillows and the burglar bars on the white men's windows. They mean those strange moments on city pavements when a black man won't stand aside for a white man.

Out in the country, even ten miles out, life is better than that. In the country, there is a lingering remnant of the pretransitional stage; our relationship with the blacks is almost feudal. Wrong, I suppose, obsolete, but more comfortable all round. We have no burglar bars, no gun. Lerice's farm boys have their wives and their piccanins living with them on the land. They brew their sour beer without the fear of police raids. In fact, we've always rather prided ourselves that the poor devils have nothing much to fear, being with us; Lerice even keeps an eye on their children, with all the competence of a woman who has never had a child of her own, and she certainly doctors them all—children and adults—like babies whenever they happen to be sick.

It was because of this that we were not particularly startled one night last winter when the boy Albert came knocking at our window long after we had gone to bed. I wasn't in our bed but sleeping in the little dressing-room-*cum*-linen-room next door, because Lerice had annoyed me and I didn't want to find myself softening toward her simply because of the sweet smell of the talcum powder on her flesh after her bath. She came and woke me up. "Albert says one of the boys is very sick," she said. "I think you'd better go down and see. He wouldn't get us up at this hour for nothing."

"What time is it?"

"What does it matter?" Lerice is maddeningly logical.

I got up awkwardly as she watched me— How is it I always feel a fool when I have deserted her bed? After all, I know from the way she never looks at me when she talks to me at breakfast the next day that she is hurt and humiliated at my not wanting her—and I went out, clumsy with sleep.

"Which of the boys is it?" I asked Albert as we followed the dance of my torch.

"He's too sick. Very sick, *Baas*," he said.

"But who? Franz?" I remembered Franz had had a bad cough for the past week.

Albert did not answer; he had given me the path, and was walking along beside me in the tall dead grass. When the light of the torch caught his face, I saw that he looked acutely embarrassed. "What's this all about?" I said.

He lowered his head under the glance of the light. "It's not me, *Baas*. I don't know. Petrus he send me."

Irritated, I hurried him along to the huts. And there, on Petrus's iron bedstead, with its brick stilts, was a young man, dead. On his forehead there was still a light, cold sweat; his body was warm. The boys stood around as they do in the kitchen when it is discovered that someone has broken a dish—uncoöperative, silent. Somebody's wife hung about in the shadows, her hands wrung together under her apron.

I had not seen a dead man since the war. This was very different. I felt like the others—extraneous, useless. "What was the matter?" I asked.

The woman patted at her chest and shook her head to indicate the painful impossibility of breathing.

He must have died of pneumonia.

I turned to Petrus. "Who was this boy? What was he doing here?" The light of a candle on the floor showed that Petrus was weeping. He followed me out the door.

When we were outside, in the dark, I waited for him to speak. But he didn't. "Now, come on, Petrus, you must tell me who this boy was. Was he a friend of yours?"

"He's my brother, *Baas*. He come from Rhodesia to look for work."

The story startled Lerice and me a little. The young boy had walked down from Rhodesia to look for work in Johannesburg, had caught a chill from sleeping out along the way, and had lain ill in his brother Petrus's hut since his arrival three days before. Our boys had been frightened to ask us for help for him because we had never been intended ever to know of his presence. Rhodesian natives are barred from entering the Union unless they have a permit; the young man was an illegal immigrant. No doubt our boys had managed the whole thing successfully several times before; a number of relatives must have walked the seven or eight hundred miles from poverty to the paradise of zoot suits, police raids, and black slum townships that is their *Egoli*, City of Gold—the Bantu name for Johannesburg. It was merely a matter of getting such a man to lie low on our farm until a job could be found with someone who would be glad to take the risk of prosecution for employing an illegal immigrant in exchange for the services of someone as yet untainted by the city.

Well, this was one who would never get up again.

"You would think they would have felt they could tell *us*," said Lerice next morning. "Once the man was ill. You would have thought at least—" When she is getting intense over something, she has a way of standing in the middle of a room as people do when they are shortly to leave on a journey, looking searchingly about her at the most familiar objects as if she had never seen them before. I had noticed that in Petrus's presence in the kitchen, earlier, she had had the air of being almost offended with him, almost hurt.

In any case, I really haven't the time or inclination any more to go into everything in our life that I know Lerice, from those alarmed and pressing eyes of hers, would like us to go into. She is the kind of woman who doesn't mind if she looks plain, or odd; I don't suppose she would even care if she knew how strange she looks when her whole face is out of proportion with urgent uncertainty. I said, "Now I'm the one who'll have to do all the dirty work, I suppose."

She was still staring at me, trying me out with those eyes—wasting her time, if she only knew.

"I'll have to notify the health authorities," I said calmly. "They can't just cart him off and bury him. After all, we don't really know what he died of."

She simply stood there, as if she had given up—simply ceased to see me at all.

I don't know when I've been so irritated. "It might have been something contagious," I said. "God knows?" There was no answer.

I am not enamored of holding conversations with myself. I went out to shout to one of the boys to open the garage and get the car ready for my morning drive to town.

As I had expected, it turned out to be quite a business. I had to notify the police as well as the health authorities, and answer a lot of tedious questions: How was it I was ignorant of the boy's presence? If I did not supervise my native quarters, how did I know that that sort of thing didn't go on all the time? Et cetera, et cetera. And when I flared up and told them that so long as my natives did their work, I didn't think it my right or concern to poke my nose into their private lives, I got from the coarse, dull-witted police sergeant one of those looks that come not from any thinking process going on in the brain but from that faculty common to all who are possessed by the master-race theory—a look of insanely inane certainty. He grinned at me with a mixture of scorn and delight at my stupidity.

Then I had to explain to Petrus why the health authorities had to take away the body for a post-mortem—and, in fact, what a post-mortem was. When I telephoned the health department some days later to find out the result, I was told that the cause of death was, as we had thought, pneumonia, and that the body had been suitably disposed of. I went out to where Petrus was mixing a mash for the fowls and told him that it was all right, there would be no trouble; his brother had died from that pain in his chest. Petrus put down the paraffin tin and said, "When can we go to fetch him, *Baas?*"

"To fetch him?"

"Will the *Baas* please ask them when we must come?"

I went back inside and called Lerice, all over the house. She came down the stairs from the spare bedrooms, and I said, "*Now* what am I going to do? When I told Petrus, he just asked calmly when they could go and fetch the body. They think they're going to bury him themselves."

"Well, go back and tell him," said Lerice. "You must tell him. Why didn't you tell him then?"

When I found Petrus again, he looked up politely. "Look, Petrus," I said. "You can't go to fetch your brother. They've done it already—they've *buried* him, you understand?"

"Where?" he said slowly, dully, as if he thought that perhaps he was getting this wrong.

"You see, he was a stranger. They knew he wasn't from here, and they didn't know he had some of his people here, so they thought they must bury him." It was difficult to make a pauper's grave sound like a privilege.

"Please, *Baas*, the *Baas* must ask them?" But he did not mean that he wanted to know the burial place. He simply ignored the incomprehensible machinery I told him had set to work on his dead brother; he wanted the brother back.

"But, Petrus," I said, "how can I? Your brother is buried already. I can't ask them now."

"Oh, *Baas!*" he said. He stood with his bran-smeared hands uncurled at his sides, one corner of his mouth twitching.

"Good God, Petrus, they won't listen to me! They can't, anyway. I'm sorry, but I can't do it. You understand?"

He just kept on looking at me, out of his knowledge that white men have everything, can do anything; if they don't, it is because they won't.

And then, at dinner, Lerice started. "You could at least phone," she said.

"Christ, what d'you think I am? Am I supposed to bring the dead back to life?"

But I could not exaggerate my way out of this ridiculous responsibility that had been thrust on me. "Phone them up," she went on. "And at least you'll be able to tell him you've done it and they've explained that it's impossible."

She disappeared somewhere into the kitchen quarters after coffee.

twitched their ears against the flies. Petrus, Franz, Albert, and the old father from Rhodesia hoisted it on their shoulders and the procession moved on, on foot. It was really a very awkward moment. I stood there rather foolishly at the fence, quite still, and slowly they filed past, not looking up, the four men bent beneath the shiny wooden box, and the straggling troop of mourners. All of them were servants or neighbors' servants whom I knew as casual, easygoing gossipers about our lands or kitchen. I heard the old man's breathing.

I had just bent to pick up my club again when there was a sort of jar in the flowing solemnity of their processional mood; I felt it at once, like a wave of heat along the air, or one of those sudden currents of cold catching at your legs in a placid stream. The old man's voice was muttering something; the people had stopped, confused, and they bumped into one another, some pressing to go on, others hissing them to be still. I could see that they were embarrassed, but they could not ignore the voice; it was much the way that the mumblings of a prophet, though not clear at first, arrest the mind. The corner of the coffin the old man carried was sagging at an angle; he seemed to be trying to get out from under the weight of it. Now Petrus expostulated with him.

The little boy who had been left to watch the donkeys dropped the reins and ran to see. I don't know why—unless it was for the same reason people crowd round someone who has fainted in a cinema—but I parted the wires of the fence and went through, after him.

Petrus lifted his eyes to me—to anybody—with distress and horror. The old man from Rhodesia had let go of the coffin entirely, and the three others, unable to support it on their own, had laid it on the ground, in the pathway. Already there was a film of dust lightly wavering up its shiny sides. I did not understand what the old man was saying; I hesitated to interfere. But now the whole seething group turned on my silence. The old man himself came over to me, with his hands outspread and shaking, and spoke directly to me, saying something that I could tell from the tone, without understanding the words, was shocking and extraordinary.

"What is it, Petrus? What's wrong?" I appealed.

Petrus threw up his hands, bowed his head in a series of hysterical shakes, then thrust his face up at me suddenly. "He says, 'My son was not so heavy.'"

Silence. I could hear the old man breathing; he kept his mouth a little open, as old people do.

"My son was young and thin," he said at last, in English.

Again silence. Then babble broke out. The old man thundered against everybody; his teeth were yellowed and few, and he had one of those fine, grizzled, sweeping mustaches that one doesn't often see nowadays, which must have been grown in emulation of early Empire builders. It seemed to frame all his utterances with a special validity, perhaps merely because it was the symbol of the traditional wisdom of age—an idea so fearfully rooted that it carries still something awesome beyond reason. He shocked them; they thought he was mad, but they had to listen to him. With his own hands he began to prize the lid off the coffin and three of the men came forward to help him. Then he sat down on the ground; very old, very weak, and unable to speak, he merely lifted a trembling hand toward what was there. He abdicated, he handed it over to them; he was no good any more.

They crowded round to look (and so did I), and now they forgot the nature of this surprise and the occasion of grief to which it belonged, and for a few minutes were carried up in the delightful astonishment of the surprise itself. They gasped and flared noisily with excitement. I even noticed the little boy who had held the donkeys jumping up and down, almost weeping with rage because the backs of the grownups crowded him out of his view.

In the coffin was someone no one had ever seen before: a heavily built, rather light-skinned native with a neatly stitched scar on his forehead—perhaps from a blow in a brawl that had also dealt him some other, slower-working injury, which had killed him.

I wrangled with the authorities for a week over that body. I had the feeling that they were shocked, in a laconic fashion, by their own mistake, but that in the confusion of their anonymous dead they were helpless to put it right. They said to me, "We are trying to find out," and "We are still making inquiries." It was as if at any moment they might conduct me into their mortuary and say, "There! Lift up the sheets; look for him—your poultry boy's brother. There are so many black faces—surely one will do?"

And every evening when I got home, Petrus was waiting in the kitchen. "Well, they're trying. They're still looking. The *Baas* is seeing to it for you, Petrus," I would tell him. "God, half the time

I should be in the office I'm driving around the back end of the town chasing after this affair," I added aside, to Lerice, one night.

She and Petrus both kept their eyes turned on me as I spoke, and, oddly, for those moments they looked exactly alike, though it sounds impossible: my wife, with her high, white forehead and her attenuated Englishwoman's body, and the poultry boy, with his horny bare feet below khaki trousers tied at the knee with string and the peculiar rankness of his nervous sweat coming from his skin.

"What makes you so indignant, so determined about this now?" said Lerice suddenly.

I stared at her. "It's a matter of principle. Why should they get away with a swindle? It's time these officials had a jolt from someone who'll bother to take the trouble."

She said, "Oh." And as Petrus slowly opened the kitchen door to leave, sensing that the talk had gone beyond him, she turned away, too.

I continued to pass on assurances to Petrus every evening, but although what I said was the same and the voice in which I said it was the same, every evening it sounded weaker. At last, it became clear that we would never get Petrus's brother back, because nobody really knew where he was. Somewhere in a graveyard as uniform as a housing scheme, somewhere under a number that didn't belong to him, or in the medical school, perhaps, laboriously reduced to layers of muscle and strings of nerve? Goodness knows. He had no identity in this world anyway.

It was only then, and in a voice of shame, that Petrus asked me to try and get the money back.

"From the way he asks, you'd think he was robbing his dead brother," I said to Lerice later. But as I've said, Lerice had got so intense about this business that she couldn't even appreciate a little ironic smile.

I tried to get the money; Lerice tried. We both telephoned and wrote and argued, but nothing came of it. It appeared that the main expense had been the undertaker, and after all he had done his job. So the whole thing was a complete waste, even more of a waste for the poor devils than I had thought it would be.

The old man from Rhodesia was about Lerice's father's size, so she gave him one of her father's old suits, and he went back home rather better off, for the winter, than he had come.

KIN

❖

EUDORA WELTY

"Mingo?" I repeated, and for the first moment I didn't know what my aunt meant. I had been telling her and my cousin Kate a little, just a beginning, of my news when the cook, Rachel, brought in the one letter.

My aunt was bridling daintily at the unopened envelope in her hand. "Of course, you'll have to ride out there Sunday, girls, and without me."

"Mingo!" I said. "It's still in existence."

"Open it—what does she say now?" said Kate to her mother. Aunt Ethel still frowned very slightly at the sealed letter. Kate said, "Ma'am? If Uncle Felix—"

"Uncle Felix! Is _he_ still—?" I had arrived only day before yesterday, and we had had so much to catch up with, besides, necessarily, going to parties. They expected me to keep up in spite of being gone almost my whole life; I was taken away from Mississippi when I was eight and my last visit was years and years ago. I was the only one in Aunt Ethel's downstairs bedroom neither partially undressed nor, to use my aunt's rather persuasive word, "reclining."

"Of course he is," said Aunt Ethel, tearing open the envelope and bringing out an old-fashioned "correspondence card" filled up on both sides with a sharp, jet-black hand, and reading the end. My little aunt, for her heart's sake, had to lie propped up. There, inside her tester bed, she sometimes looked out as if, I thought, she were riding in some old-fashioned carriage or litter. She had to rest the greater part of each day, even during my visit, brief though it was, when perhaps I would never get a chance afterward to come back. "He is," she said to Kate.

"_Still_ this, _still_ that," murmured Kate, looking at me sidelong. She was upon the bed, too. She leaned lightly across her mother, who was in pink negligee, read ahead of her for an instant, and plucked the last piece of the city candy I had brought from the big shell dish Rachel had seen fit to put it in.

I rocked. However, I did see I must stop showing what might be too much exuberance in Aunt Ethel's room, since she was old and not strong, and take things more as they came. Kate and I were double first cousins. Aunt Ethel was my mother's sister, and Kate's father and my father were brothers. I was the younger, and neither of us was married yet, but I was not going to be an old maid! I was already engaged, up North, though I had not yet come to setting a date for my wedding. Kate, though, as far as I could tell, didn't have anybody.

My aunt had drawn that card and its envelope both to her pillowed face. She was smelling them. Mingo was the home place. It was miles from anywhere, and I saw that she was not to go there any more.

"Look at the gilt edge," she said, shining it. "Isn't it *remarkable* about Sister Anne? I wonder what drawer she went into to find *that* to favor us with? . . . 'Had to drop'—'watch'?—no, 'water on his tongue—yesterday so he could talk. . . . Must *watch* him—day and night,' underlined. *Poor* old man. She insists, you know, Dicey— that's what she does."

"Who," I sighed, for I thought she had said "Sister," and there was no sister at all left of my Aunt Ethel's. But my mind had wandered for a moment. It was two-thirty in the afternoon, after an enormous dinner, at which we had had company—six girls, chattering almost like ready-made bridesmaids—with wonderful black, bitter, moist chocolate pie under mountains of meringue, and black, bitter coffee. We could hear Rachel now, off in the dis- tance, peacefully dropping the iced-tea spoons into the silver drawer in the pantry.

In this little courthouse town, several hours by inconvenient train ride from Jackson, even the cut grass in the yards smelled different from Northern grass. And the spring was so much farther advanced—the birds so busy you turned as you would at people as they plunged by. Bloom was everywhere in the streets, wisteria just ending, Confederate jasmine beginning. And down in the gardens!—they were deep-colored as old rugs, in the morning and evening shade. Everybody grew some of the best of everybody else's flowers. Everywhere we went calling, Kate brought me out saying, "Here she is! Got off the train talking, and hasn't stopped yet."

And everywhere the yawning, inconvenient, and suddenly familiar rooms were as deep and inviting and compelling as the yawning big roses opening and shattering in one day in the baking gardens. At night, the moths were already pounding against the screens.

Aunt Ethel and Kate, and everybody I knew here, lived as if they had never heard of anywhere else—even Jackson—in houses built in the local version of the eighteen-eighties, tall and spread out at the bottom with porches, and winged all over with awnings and blinds. As children, Kate and I were brought up across the street from each other. From Aunt Ethel's front window I could see our chinaberry tree, which Mother had always wanted to cut down on account of its litter, standing in its slowly realized bloom. Our old house was lived in now by a family named Brown, who were not very much, I gathered—the porch had shifted, and the screens looked black as a set of dominoes.

Aunt Ethel had gone back to the beginning of her note. "Oh-oh. Word has penetrated even Mingo, Miss Dicey Hastings, that you're in this part of the world! The minute you reached Mississippi, our little paper had that notice you laughed at, that was all about your mother and me and your grandmother, so of course there's repercussions from Sister Anne. 'Why didn't we tell her!' But honestly she might be the remotest kin in the world, for all you know when you're well, but let yourself get to ailing and she'd show up in Guinea, if that's where you were, and stay. 'A year if need be' is the way she put it about precious Uncle Felix."

"She'll be coming to you next if you don't hush about her," said Kate, sitting bolt upright on the bed. She adored her mother, her family. What she had was company excitement. And I guess I had trip excitement—I giggled. My aunt eyed us and tucked the letter away among the pillows.

"But who is she, pure and simple?" I said.

"You'd just better not let her in," said Aunt Ethel to Kate. "That's what. . . . Sister Anne Fry, dear heart. Declares she's wild to lay eyes on you. I *should* have shown you the letter. Recalls your sweet manners toward your elders. Sunday's our usual day to drive out there, you remember, Dicey, but I'm inclined to think—I feel now—it couldn't be just your coming brought on this midweek letter. Uncle Felix was taken sick on Valentine's Day and she got there by Saturday. . . . Katee, since you're not working this week —if you're going, you'd better go on today."

Kate had told them at the bank that she was not working while I was here. "Oh, curses!" she cried to me. Of course, we had planned something.

"Mama, what is she?" asked Kate, standing down in her cotton petticoat with the ribbon run in. She was not as tall as I. "I may be as bad as Dicey but I don't intend to go out there today without you and not have her straight."

Aunt Ethel looked patiently upward, as if she were reading now from the tester, and said, "Well, she's a remote cousin of Uncle Felix's, to begin with. Your third cousin twice removed, and your Great-Aunt Beck's half sister, my third cousin once removed and my aunt's half sister, Dicey's—"

"Don't tell me!" I cried. "I'm not that anxious to claim kin!"

"She'll claim *you!* She'll come visit you!" cried Kate.

"I won't be here long enough." I could not help smiling.

"When your mother was alive and used to come bringing you, visits were different," said my Aunt Ethel. "She stayed long enough to make us believe she'd fully got here. There'd be time enough to have alterations from Miss Mattie, too, and transplant things in the yard if it was the season, even start a hook rug—do a morning-glory, at least, even if she'd never really see the grand finale. . . . Our generation knew more how to visit, whatever else escaped us—not that I mean to criticize one jot."

"Mama, what do you *want?*" said Kate, in the middle of the floor. "Let me get you something."

"I don't want a thing," said her mother. "Only for my girls to please themselves."

"Well, then, tell me who it was that Sister Anne one time, long time ago, was going to marry and stood up in the church? And she was about forty years old!" Kate said. I'd dropped my hat down on the little chair some time, and now she lightly, excitedly lifted it to her own head—without a mirror, bare feet, petticoat, and all. She made a face at me.

Her mother was saying, "Now, *that* is beyond me at the moment, perhaps because it didn't come off. Though he was some kind of off-cousin, too, I seem to recall. . . . I'll have it worked out by the time you girls get back from where you're going. Very becoming, dear."

"Kate," I said, "I thought Uncle Felix was old beyond years when I was a child. And now *I'll* be old in ten years, and so will you. And he's still alive."

"He *was* old!" cried Kate. "He *was!*"

"Light somewhere, why don't you," said her mother.

Kate perched above me on the arm of my chair, and we gently rocked.

I said, "He had red roses on his suspenders."

"When did he ever take his coat off for you to see that?" objected my aunt. "The whole connection always went out there for *Sundays,* and he was a very strict gentleman all his life, you know, and made us be ladies out there, even more than Mama and Papa did in town."

"But I can't remember a thing about Sister Anne," I said. "Maybe she was too much of a lady."

"Foot," said my aunt.

Kate said, prompting, "She fell in the well."

I cried joyously, "And she came out! Oh, I remember her fine! Mournful! Those old black drapey dresses, and plastered hair."

"That was just the way she looked when she came out of the well," Kate said.

" 'Mournful' isn't exactly the phrase," said my aunt.

"Plastered black hair, and her mouth drawn down, exactly like that aunt in the front illustration of your 'Eight Cousins,' " I told Kate. "I used to think that was who it was."

"You're so bookish," said my aunt flatly.

"This is where all the books *were!*" And there were the same ones now—no more, no less.

"On purpose, I think she fell in," continued Kate. "Knowing there were plenty to pull her out. That was her contribution for Cousin Eva's wedding celebrations, and snitching a little of *her* glory. . . . You're jiggling me, the way you're rocking."

"There's such a thing as being unfair, Kate," said her mother. "I always say, *poor* Sister Anne."

"*Poor* Sister Anne, then."

"And I think Dicey just *thinks* she remembers it, because she's heard it."

"Well, at least she had something to be poor about!" I said. "Falling in the well and being an old maid, that's two things!"

Kate cried, "Not so headlong!"

"Maybe she even knew what she was about. Eva's Archie Fielder got drunk every whipstitch for the rest of his life," said Aunt Ethel.

"Only tell me this, somebody, and I'll be quiet," I said. "What poor somebody's Sister Anne was she, to begin with?"

Then I held the rocker still and leaned against my cousin. I was terrified that I had brought up Uncle Harlan. Kate had warned me again since I arrived not to mention her father. Ever since his death seventeen years ago, Aunt Ethel could not bear to hear the name of her husband spoken, or to speak it herself.

"Poor Beck's, of course," said Aunt Ethel. "She's a little bit kin on both sides. Since you ask, Beck's *half* sister—that's why we were always so careful to call her Sister."

"Oh, I thought that was just for teasing," said Kate.

"Well, of course the teasing element is not to be denied," said Aunt Ethel.

"Who began—" My hat was set, not at all rightly, on my own head by Kate—like a dunce cap.

The town was so quiet the doves from the river woods could be heard plainly. In town, the birds were quiet at this hour. Kate and I went on bobbing slowly up and down together as we rocked very gently by Aunt Ethel's bed. I saw us in the pier glass across the room. Looking at myself as the visitor, I considered myself as having a great deal still to confide. My lips opened.

"He was ever so courtly," said my aunt. "Nobody in the family more so." Uncle Felix was her uncle, only my great-uncle.

Kate pulled a little hair, with a tiny sting, from my neck, where it had always grown too low. I slapped at her wrist.

"But this last spell," Aunt Ethel said, "when I couldn't get out, and he's begun failing, what I remember about him is what I used to be told as a child, isn't that strange? When I knew him all my life and loved him. For instance, that he was a great one for serenading as a young man."

"Serenading!" said Kate and I together.

"I didn't know he could sing," said Kate.

"He couldn't. But he was a remarkable speller," said my aunt. "A born speller. I remember how straight he stood when they called the word. You know the church out there, like everything else in the world, raised its money by spelling matches. He knew every word in the deck. One time—one time, though!—I turned Uncle Felix down. I was not so bad myself, child though I was. And it isn't—"

"Ma'am?" Kate said.

"It just isn't fair to have water dropped on your tongue, is it?"

"She ought not to have told you, the old buzzard!"

"The word," said my Aunt Ethel, "the word was knick-knack. K-n-i-c-k, knick, hyphen, k-n-a-c-k, knack; knick-knack."

"She only writes because she has nothing else to do, away out yonder in the country!" Kate said.

"She used to get *dizzy* very easily." Aunt Ethel spoke out in a firm voice, as if she were just waking up from a nap. "Maybe she did well—maybe a girl might do well sometimes *not* to marry, if she's not cut out for it."

"Aunt Ethel!" I exclaimed. Kate, sliding gently off the arm of my chair, was silent. But as if I had said something more, she turned around, her arm raised, in a saluting, mocking way.

"Find me her letter again, Kate. Where is it?" said Aunt Ethel, feeling under her solitaire board and her pillow. She held that little gilt-edged card, shook it, weighed it, and said, "All that really troubles me is that I can't bear for her to be on Uncle Felix's hands for so long! He was always so courtly, and his family's all, all in the churchyard now. But us!—Or New York!"

"Mama, let me bring you a drink of water."

"Dicey, I'm going to *make* you go to Mingo."

"But I want to go!"

She looked at me, uncomprehending. Kate gave her a glass of water with ice tinkling in it. "That reminds me, whatever you do, Kate, if you do go today, take that fresh Lady Baltimore cake out to the house; little Di can sit and hold it while you drive. Poor Sister Anne can't cook and loves to eat. She can *eat* awhile. And make Rachel hunt through the shelves for some more green-tomato pickle. Who'll put that up next year!"

"If you talk like that," said Kate, "we're going to go right this minute, right out into the heat. I thought this was going to be a good day."

"Oh, it is! Grand! Run upstairs, both, and get your baths, you hot little children. You're supposed to go to Suzanne's, I know it."

Kate, slow motion, leaned over and kissed her mother, and took the glass.

"Kate! If only I could see him one more time. As he was. And Mingo. Old Uncle Theodore. The peace. Listen, you give him my love. He's *my* Uncle Felix. Don't tell him why I didn't come. That might distress him more than not seeing me there."

"What's Uncle Felix's trouble?" I asked.

Aunt Ethel smiled, looked for a minute as if she would not be allowed to tell me, and then said, "Old age. I think Sister Anne's lazy, *idle!*" she cried. "You're drawing it out of me. She never cooked nor sewed nor even cultivated her mind! She was a lily of the field." Aunt Ethel suddenly showed us both highly polished little palms, with the grave gesture a girl uses toward a fortune-teller—then looked into them a moment absently and hid them at her sides. "She just hasn't got anybody of her own, that's her trouble. And she needs somebody."

"Hush! She *will* be coming here next!" Kate cried.

"She has no inner resources," confided my aunt, and watched to see if I was too young to guess what that meant. "How you girls do set each other off! Not that you're bothering me, I love you in here, and wouldn't deprive myself of it. Yes, you all just better wait and go Sunday." She shut her eyes.

Rachel came in Aunt Ethel's room bearing a vase full of roses.

"Look-look!" chanted Kate.

Rachel believed in cutting roses in the heat of the day—and nobody could prevent her now, since we had forgotten to cut them ourselves. Aunt Ethel's roses were at their height. The look of satisfaction on Rachel's face was like something nobody could interrupt. To our sighs, for our swooning attitudes, she paraded the vase through the room and around the bed. Then she set it on the little table and marched back to her kitchen.

"*Rachel* wants you to go. All right, you tell Uncle Felix," said Aunt Ethel, turning toward the roses, spreading her little hand out chordlike over them, "—of course he must have these—that *that's* Souvenir de Claudius Pernet—and *that's* Mermaid—Mary Wallace —Silver Moon—those three, of course, Etoiles—and oh, Duquesa de Penaranda—Gruss an Aachen's his cutting he grew for me a thousand years ago—but there's my Climbing Thor! Mercy!" She sighed, looking at it. "How fresh!" Still looking at the roses, she waited a moment. Pressing out of the vase, those roses of hers looked heavy, drunken with their own light and scent, their stems, just two minutes ago severed with Rachel's knife, vivid with pale thorns through cut glass. "You know, Sundays always *are* hotter than any other days, and I tell you what: I do think you'd better go on to Mingo today, regardless of what you find."

Circling around in her mind like old people, she got back to where she started—which Aunt Ethel never used to do; she never used to get back!

"Yes'm," said Kate.

"Aunt Ethel, wouldn't it be better for everybody if he'd come in town to the hospital?" I asked, with all my city seriousness.

"He wouldn't consider it. So give Sister Anne my love, and give

Uncle Felix my dear love. Will you remember? . . . Go on, naked,"
said my aunt to her daughter. "Take your cousin upstairs in her
city bonnet. You both look right feverish to me. Start in a little
while, so you can get your visit over and come back in the cool of
the evening."

"These nights now are so bright," said my cousin Kate, with a
strange stillness in her small face, transfixed, as if she didn't hear
the end of the instructions and did not think who was listening to
her, either. Standing with bare white arms pinned behind her head,
with the black slick hair pinned up, she said, "These nights are so
bright I don't mind, I don't care, how long any ride takes or how
late I ever get home!"

I jumped up beside her and said pleadingly to them both, "Do
you know I'd *forgotten* the Milky Way!"

My aunt didn't see any use answering that, either. But Kate and
I were suddenly laughing and running out together, as if we were
going to the party after all.

Before we set out, we tiptoed back into Aunt Ethel's room and
made off with the roses. Rachel had darkened it. Again I saw us in
the mirror, Kate pink and me blue, both our dresses stiff as boards
(Kate's dresses—I had gone straight into Kate's clothes) and creaking
from the way Rachel starched them, our teeth set into our lips, half
smiling. I tried my hat, but Kate said, "Leave that, it's entirely too
grand for out there. Didn't you hear Mama?" Aunt Ethel stayed
motionless, and I thought how she was bound to look pretty, even
asleep. I wasn't quite sure she was asleep.

"Seems mean," said Kate, looking between the horns of the
reddest rose, but I said, "She meant us to."

"Negroes always like them full-blown," said Kate.

Out in the bright, she said, "Look! Those crazy starlings have
come. They always pick the greenest day!"

There they were, feeding at our feet, all over the yard and every
yard, iridescently black, bound for the North. As we climbed into
the car, I saw Rachel looking out from the back hall window, with
her cheek in her hand. She watched us go, carrying off her cake
and her flowers, too.

I was thinking, If I always say "still," Kate still says "always," and
laughed, but would not tell her what I was laughing about.

Mingo, I learned, was only nine miles and a little more away.
But it was on an old road, in a part the highway had deserted long

ago, lonely and winding. It dipped up and down, and the hills felt high, because they were bare of trees, but they probably weren't very high; this was Mississippi. There was hardly ever a house in sight.

"So green," I sighed.

"Oh, but poor," said Kate, with her look of making me careful of what I said. "Gone to pasture now."

"Beautiful to me!"

"It's clear to Jericho. Looks like that cake would set heavy on your knees, in that old tin Christmas box."

"I'm not ever tired in a strange place," I said. And then "Banks and towers of honeysuckle hanging over that creek!" We crossed an iron bridge.

"That's the Hushamingo River."

We turned off on a still narrower, bumpier road and began to see gates.

Near Mingo, we saw an old Negro man riding sidesaddle—except there was no saddle at all—on a slow black horse. He was coming to meet us—that is, making his way down through the field. As we passed, he saluted by holding out a dark cloth cap stained golden.

"Good evening, Uncle Theodore." Kate nodded. She murmured to me, "Rachel's his daughter, did you know it? But she never comes back to see him."

"Everybody's kin," I said, and sighed into the sweet air.

On the last turn, up and down the road we saw cars and horses and wagons and one yellow wooden school bus, standing empty and tilted to one side. "Oh, Lordy, we're too late!" Kate exclaimed. She stared back for a moment toward where Uncle Theodore had been riding so innocently away. Primroses were blowing along the ditches and between the wheel spokes, and in the wagons empty cane chairs sat in rows, and some of the horses were eating the primroses. That was the only sound as we stood there. No, a chorus of dogs was barking in a settled kind of way.

From the gate, we could look up and see the house, at the brow of the slope. It looked right in size and shape but not in something else; it had a queer intensity for afternoon. Was every light in the house burning, I wondered. Of course: on the high and sloping porch, sitting on the railing between the four remembered pale, square cypress posts, or standing, very quietly, was stationed a crowd of people.

"The whole countryside's turned out," Kate said, and gritted her teeth. The night before, in her sleep, she had done that.

What I could not help thinking as we let ourselves through the gate was that I'd either forgotten or never known how *primitive* the old place was.

Immediately, my mind remembered the music box up there in the parlor. It played large, giltlike metal discs, pierced with holes —eyes, eyelets, slits, mysterious as the symbols in a lady's dress pattern, but a whole world of them. When the disc turned in the machine, the pattern of holes unwound a curious, metallic, depthless, cross music, with silences clocked between the notes. Though I did not like especially to hear it, I used to feel when I was here I must beg for it, as you should ask an old lady how she is feeling.

"I hate to get there," said Kate. She cried, "What a welcome for you!"

I said, "Don't say that."

She fastened that creaky gate. We trudged up the straight but uneven dirt path, then the little paved walk, toward the house. We shifted burdens; Kate took the cake and I took the flowers, the roses going like headlights in front of us. The solemnity on the porch was overpowering, even at this distance. It was serene, imperturbable, gratuitous; it was the look of "good countrypeople" at such times.

On either side of us were Uncle Felix's roses—hillocks of bushes set in hillocks of rank grass and ragged robins and hung with roses the size of little biscuits; indeed, they already had begun to have a baked look, with little carmine edges curled. Kate dipped on one knee and came up with a four-leaf clover. She could always do that, even now, even carrying a three-layer cake.

By the house, wisteria had taken the scaffolding where a bell hung dark, and gone up into a treetop. The wisteria trunk, sinews raised and twined, like some old thigh, rose above the porch corner, above roof and all, where its sheet of bloom, just starting to go, was faded as an old sail. In spite of myself, I looked around the corner for that well: there it was, squat as a tub beneath the overpiece, and a tiger cat asleep on its cover.

The crowd on the porch, mostly old, some young, and some few children, were dressed in their best dark clothes—hot dark blue, dark brown, vaguely powdered over with the golden dust of their arrival here in midafternoon. As we approached, they made no motion; even the young men sitting on the steps did not stand up.

Then an old man came out of the house and a lady behind him, the old man walking with the help of canes and the lady tiptoeing. Voices were murmuring softly all around.

Viewing the body, I thought, my breath gone—but nobody here's kin to me.

The lady had advanced to the head of the steps. It had to be Sister Anne. I saw her legs first, and her feet were set one behind the other, like an "expression" teacher's, while the dress she had on was rather girlish, black taffeta with a flounce around it. To my rising eyes, she didn't look half so old as she did when she was pulled back out of the well. Her hair was not black at all. It was rusty brown, soft and unsafe in its pins. She didn't favor Aunt Ethel and Mama and them, or Kate and me, or any of us in the least, I thought —with that short face.

She was beckoning, a gesture that went with her particular kind of uncertain smile. "What do I see? Cake!" She ran down the steps. "You *surprised* me!" Sister Anne cried at Kate. She took the cake-box out of her hands and kissed her. Two spots of red stabbed her cheeks. I was sorry to observe that the color of her hair was the very same I'd been noticing that spring in robins' breasts—a sort of stained color.

"Long-lost cousin, ain't you!" she cried at me, and gave me the same kiss she had given Kate—a sort of reprisal kiss. Aunt Ethel's roses smothered between our unequal chests.

"Monkeys!" she said, leading us up, looking back and forth between Kate and me, as if she had to decide which one she liked better before anything else in the world could be attended to. She had a long neck and that short face, and round, brown, jumpy eyes with little circles of wrinkles at each blink. "Step aside for the family, please?" she said next, in tones I thought rather melting.

Kate and I did not dare look at each other. We did not dare look anywhere. As soon as we had moved through the porch crowd and were arrived inside the breezeway—where, however, there were a few people, too, standing around—I looked and saw the corner clock was wrong. I was deeply aware that all clocks worked in this house, as if they had been keeping time just for me all this while, and I remembered that at picking time the bell in the yard was rung every day at straight-up noon, to bring them in out of the fields. And I had once supposed they rang it at midnight, too.

Around us, voices sounded as they always did everywhere in a house of death, soft and inconsequential, and tidily assertive.

"I believe Old Hodge's mules done had an attack of the wander-lust. Passed through my place Tuesday headed east, and now you seen 'em in Goshen."

Sister Anne was saying bodingly to us, "You just come *right* on *through*."

Kate burst into tears. I held her to me, to protect her from more kisses. "When, when?" she gasped. "When did it happen, Sister Anne?"

"Now, when did what happen?" Sister Anne lifted her brow and fixed her eye on the parlor doorway. The door into that room was open, but the old red curtain was drawn across it, with bright light, looking red, too, streaming out around it. Just then, there was a creaking sound inside there, like an old winter suit bending at the waist, and a young throat was cleared.

"Little bit of commotion here today, but I *would* rather you didn't tell Cousin Felix anything about it," said Sister Anne.

"Tell him! Is he alive?" Kate cried wildly, breaking away from me, and then even more wildly, "I might have known it! What sort of frolic are you up to out here, Sister Anne?"

Sister Anne suddenly marched to the other side of us and brought the front bedroom door to with a good country slam. That room—Uncle Felix's—was full of people, too. The overflow from outside was sitting in there.

"I beg your pardon," said Kate, in a low voice. We were still just inside the house—in the breezeway, which was almost as wide as the rooms it ran between from front porch to back. It was a hall, really. Open at the beginning, it had long been enclosed, and papered like the parlor, in red. But when I was a child, it was still called the breezeway.

"Why, Kate. You-all would be the first to *know*. Do you think I'd have let everybody come, regardless of promises, if Cousin Felix had chosen *not* to be with us still, on the day?"

While we winced, a sudden flash filled the hall with light, changing white to black, black to white. I saw the roses shudder and charge in my hands, Kate with white eyes rolled, and Sister Anne with the livid brow of a hostess and a pencil behind one ear.

"That's what you mean," said Sister Anne. "That's a photographer. He's here in our house today, taking pictures. He's *itinerant*," she said, underlining in her talk. "And he *asked* to use our parlor —we didn't ask *him*. Well—it *is* complete."

"What is?"

"Our parlor. And all in shape, curtains washed—*you know*."

Out around the curtain came a very young man, dressed in part in a soldier's uniform not his, looking slightly dazed. He tiptoed out onto the porch. The bedroom door opened on a soft murmuring again. Then out the door came an old lady with side combs, in an enormous black cotton dress. An old man came behind her, with a mustache discolored like an old seine. Sister Anne pointed a short strict finger at them.

"We're together," said the old man.

"I've got everything under control," Sister Anne called over her shoulder to us, leaving us at once. "Luckily, I was always able to be in two places at the same time, so I'll be able to visit with you back yonder and keep things moving up front, too. Now, what was your name, sir?"

At the round table in the center of the breezeway, she leaned with the old man over a ledger opened there, by the tray of glasses and the water pitcher.

"But where could Uncle Felix be?" Kate whispered to me. As for me, I was still carrying the roses.

Sister Anne was guiding the old couple toward the curtain, and then she let them into the parlor.

"Sister Anne, where have you got him put?" asked Kate, following a step.

"You just come right on through," Sister Anne called to us. She said, behind her hand, "They've left the fields, dressed up like Sunday and Election Day put together, but I can't say they all stopped long enough to bathe, ha-ha! April's a pretty important time, but having your picture taken beats that! Don't have a chance of that out this way more than once or twice in a lifetime. Got him put back out of all the commotion," she said, leading the way. "The photographer's name is—let me see. He's of the Yankee persuasion, but that don't matter any longer, eh, Cousin Dicey? But I shouldn't be funny. Anyway, travelled all the way from some town somewhere since *February*, he tells me. Mercy, but it's hot as churchtime up there, with 'em so packed in! Did it ever occur to you how vain the human race can be if you just give 'em a chance?"

There was that blinding flash again. Curtain or not, it came right around it and through it, and down the hall.

"Smells like gunpowder," said Kate stonily.

"Does," agreed Sister Anne. She looked flattered, and said, "May be."

"I feel like a being from another world," I said all at once, just to the breezeway.

"Come on, then," said Sister Anne. "Kate, leave her alone. Oh, Cousin Felix'll eat you two little boogers up." Kate was steering me by the elbow.

"Now, how could she have *moved* him away back here," Kate marvelled. Her voice might even have been admiring with Sister Anne not there.

"Hold your horses while I look at this cake," said Sister Anne, turning off at the kitchen. "What I want to see is *what kind*."

She squealed as if she had seen a mouse. She took a lick of the icing on her finger before she covered the cake again and set it on the table. "My favorite. And how is Cousin Ethel?" Then she reached for my roses.

"Your ring!" she cried—a cry only at the last second subdued. "Your ring!"

She took my face between her fingers and thumb and shook my cheeks. She could do this because we were kin to each other.

With unscratchable hands, she began sticking the roses into a smoky glass vase too small for them, into which she'd run too little water. There was plumbing. The well must be abandoned.

"Well," she said, poking in the flowers, as though suddenly we had all the time in the world, "the other morning I was looking out at the road, and along came a dusty old-time Ford with a trunk on the back, real slow, then stopped. It was a man. I wondered. And in a minute knock, knock, knock. I changed my shoes and went to the door with my finger to my lips." She showed us.

"He was still there, on the blazing porch—eleven-fifteen. He was a middle-age man all in hot black, short, but reared back, like a stove handle. He gave me a calling card with a price down in the corner, and leaned in and whispered he'd like to use the parlor. He was an itinerant! That's almost, but not quite, the same thing as a gypsy. I hadn't seen a living person in fourteen days, except here, and he was an itinerant photographer with a bookful of orders to take pictures. I made him open and show me his book. It was chock-full. All kinds of names of all kinds of people from all over everywhere. New pages clean, and old pages scratched out. In purple indelible pencil. I flatter myself I *don't get* lonesome, but I felt sorry for *him*.

"I first told him he had taken me by surprise, and then thanked him for the compliment, and then said after persuasion like that he *could* use the parlor, *providing* he would make it quiet, because my cousin here wasn't up to himself. And he assured me it was the quietest profession on earth. That he had chosen it because it *was* such quiet, refined work, and also so he could see the world and so many members of the human race. I said I was a philosopher, too, only I thought the sooner the better, and we made it today. And he borrowed a bucket of water and poured it steaming down the radiator, and returned the bucket, and was gone. I almost couldn't believe he'd been here. You know how it is.

"Then, here today, right after dinner, in they start pouring. There's more people living in and around Mingo community than you can shake a stick at, more than you would ever dream. Here they come, out of every little highroad and byroad and cover and dell, four and five and six at the time—draw up or hitch up down at the foot of the hill and come up and shake hands like Sunday visitors. Everybody that can walk, and two that can't. I've got one preacher out there brought by a delegation. Oh, it's like Saturday and Sunday put together. The rounds the fella must have made! It's not as quiet as all he said, either. There's those mean little children —he never said a word about them, the spook.

"So I said, 'All right, Mister, I'm ready for you. I'll show them where they can sit and where they can wait, and I'll call them.' I says to them, 'When it's not your turn, please don't get up. If you want anything, ask me.' And I told them that any that had to could smoke, but I wasn't ready to have a fire today, so mind out.

"And he took the parlor right over, and unpacked his suitcase, and put up his lights, and unfolded a campstool, until he saw the organ bench with the fringe around it. And shook out a big piece of scenery, like I'd shake out a bedspread, and hooked it to the wall, and commenced pouring that little powder along something like a music stand. 'First!' he says, and commenced calling them in. I took over that. He and I go by his book and take them in order, one at a time, all fair, honest, and aboveboard."

"And so what about Uncle Felix!" cried Kate, as if now she had her.

"The niggers helped to get him back there, but it was mostly my fat little self," said Sister Anne. "Oh, you mean how come he consented? I expect I told him a story." She led us back to the hall, where a banjo hung, like a stopped clock, from a high nail, and some small, white-haired children were marching to meet each other, singing "Here Comes the Duke A-Riding, Riding" in flat, lost voices. I, too, used to think that breezeway was as long as a tunnel through some mountain.

"Get!" said Sister Anne, and clapped her hands at them. They flung to the back, off the back porch into the sun, and scattered toward the barn. With reluctance, I observed that Sister Anne's fingers were bleeding from the roses. Off in the distance, a herd of black cows moved in a light of green, the feathery April pastures deep with the first juicy weeds of summer.

There was a small ell tacked on to the back of the house, down a turn of the back porch, leading, as I knew, to the bathroom and the other little room behind that. A young woman and a little boy were coming out of the bathroom.

"Look at that." Sister Anne shuddered. "Didn't take them long to find out what *we've* got."

I never used to think that other little room was to be taken seriously as part of the house, because apples were kept in it in winter and because it had an untrimmed, flat board door, like a shed door, where you stuck your finger through a rough hole to lift up the latch.

Sister Anne stuck in her finger, opened the door, and we all three crowded inside the little room, which was crowded already.

Uncle Felix's side and back loomed from a feather bed, on an old black iron frame of a bedstead, which tilted downward toward the foot with the sinking of the whole house from the brow of the hill toward the back. He was white-headed as one of those escaping children, but not childlike—a heavy bulk, motionless, in a nightshirt, facing the window. A woven cotton spread was about his knees. His hands, turned under, were lying one on each side of him, faded from outdoor burn, mottled amber and silver.

"That's a nigger bed," said Kate. I turned and looked straight into her eyes.

"*It—is—not*," said Sister Anne. Her whole face shook, as if Kate could have made it collapse. Then she bowed her head toward us— that we could go on, now, if that was the spirit we had come in.

"Good evening, sir," said Kate, in a changed voice.

I said it after her.

Uncle Felix's long, mute, grizzly head poked around his great shoulder and, motionless again, looked out at us. He visited this gaze a long time on a general point among the three different feminine faces—if you could call Sister Anne's wholly feminine—but

never exactly on any of them. Gradually, something left his eyes.
Conviction was what I missed. Then even that general focus altered,
as though by a blow, a rap or a tap from behind, and his old head
swung back. Again he faced the window, the only window in the
house looking shadeless and shameless to the west, the glaring west.

Sister Anne bore the roses to the window and set them down on
the window sill in his line of sight. The sill looked like the only
place left where a vase could safely be set. Furniture, odds and ends,
useless objects were everywhere, pushed even closer together by the
bed. There were trunks, barrels, chairs with the cane seats hanging
in a fringe. I remembered how sometimes in winter, dashing in
here, we would snatch an apple from the washed heap on the floor
and run out slamming the door before we froze to death; that window always stayed open, then as now propped with a piece of stove-
wood. The walls were still rough boards with cracks between. Dust
had come in everywhere; rolls of dust or lint or cottonwood fuzz
hung even from the ceiling, glinting like everything else in the unfair light. I was afraid there might be dirt daubers' nests if I looked.
Our roses glared back at us as garish as anything living could be,
almost like paper flowers, a magician's bouquet that has exploded
out of a rifle to shock and amaze us.

"We'll enjoy our sunset from over the pasture this evening, won't
we, Cousin Felix!" called Sister Anne, in a loud voice. It was the
urgent opposite of her conspiratorial voice. "I bet we're fixing to
have a gorgeous one—it's so dusty! You were saying last week,
Cousin Felix, we already need a rain!"

Then, to my amazement, she came and rested her foot on a stack
of mossy books by the bed—I was across from her there—and leaned
her elbow on her lifted knee and looked around the room with the
face of a brand-new visitor. I thought of a prospector. I could look
if she could. What must have been a Civil War musket stood, like a
forgotten broom, in the corner. On the coal bucket sat an old bread
tray, split like a melon. There was even a dress form in here, rising
among the trunks, its inappropriate bosom averted a little, as
though the thing might still be able to revolve. If it were spanked,
how the dust would fly up!

"Well, he's not going to even know *me* today," said Sister Anne,
teasing me. "Well! I mustn't stay away too long at a time. Excuse
me, Cousin Felix! I'll be right back," she said, taking down her
foot. At the door, she turned to look at us sadly, and closed the door
after her.

Kate and I looked at each other across the bed.

"Isn't this just—like—her!" said Kate, with a long sigh. She pulled open the door suddenly. From the other part of the house came the creakings of that human tiptoeing and passing going on in the breezeway.

A flash of light travelled around the bend. If these couldn't be exactly seen from here, they could be felt each time they happened, like lightning at night when the head is beneath the cover. Very close by, a child cried. Kate shut the door on it.

Back came Sister Anne—she really was back in a minute—saying, "I know you didn't mean it, Kate." She looked across at me. "Speak! Tell him who you are, child, if you want to."

Instead—without knowing I was going to do it—I stepped forward, and my hand moved out of my pocket with my handkerchief, with some magnolia-fuscata flowers in a knot in the corner, and I put it under Uncle Felix's heavy brown nose.

He opened his mouth. I drew the sweet handkerchief back. The old man said "Hide," with dreadful difficulty, and left his mouth open with his tongue out for anybody to see.

Sister Anne backed away from us all and kept backing, to the front of the paper-stuffed fireplace, as if she didn't even know the seasons. I almost expected to see her lift her skirt a little behind her. She gave me a playful look, instead.

"Hide," gasped the old man. "And I'll go in. Kill 'em all. I'm old enough I swear you, Bob. Told you. Will for sure if you don't hold me, hold me."

Sister Anne winked at me.

"Surrounded. . . . They're inside." On this word, he again showed us his tongue, and rolled his eyes from one of us to the other, whoever we were.

Sister Anne had produced a thermometer. With professional motions, she was shaking it down. "All right, Cousin Felix, that's enough for now! You pay attention to that sunset, and see what it's going to do! . . . Listen, that picture made twenty-six," Sister Anne murmured.

Uncle Felix held his mouth open and she popped the thermometer straight in, and he had to close it. It looked somehow wrong, dangerous; it was like daring to take the temperature of a bear.

Before I knew it, his hand raked my bare arm down. I felt as if I had been clawed, but when I bent toward him, the hand had fallen inert again on the bed, where it looked burnished with hundreds of country suns and today's on top of them all.

"Please, Ma'am," said a treble voice at the door. A towheaded child looked in solemnly; his little red tie shone as his hair did, as with dewdrops. "Miss Sister Anne, the man says it's one more and then you."

"Listen at that. My free picture," said Sister Anne.

For whom! I wondered.

"Don't you think I need to freshen up a little bit?" she said. "My hair's been combed since four o'clock this morning."

"You go right ahead," said Kate. "Right ahead."

Sister Anne bent to sight straight into Uncle Felix's face, and then took the thermometer out of his lips and sighted along it. She read off his temperature to herself; that was *hers*, what he gave *her*.

Uncle Felix made a hoarse sound as she ran out again. Kate moved to the trunk, where, on a stack of old books and plates, was a water pitcher that did not look cold, and a spoon. She poured water into the spoon, and gave the old man some water on his tongue, which he offered her. But already his arm had begun to stir, to swing, and he put the same work-heavy, beast-heavy hand, all of a lump, against my side again and found my arm, which this time went loose in its socket, waiting. He pulled me all the way down. On my knees, I found a pencil lying in the dust at my feet. He wanted it.

My Great-Uncle Felix, without his right hand ever letting me go, received the pencil in his left. For a moment, our arms crossed, but it was not awkward or strange; more as though we two were going to skate off, or dance off, out of here. Still holding me, but without stopping a moment, as if all the thinking had already been done, he knocked open the old hymnbook on top of the mossy stack at the bedside and began riding the pencil along over the flyleaf; though none of the Jerrolds that I ever heard of were left-handed, and certainly not he. I turned away my eyes.

There, lying on the barrel in front of me, looking vaguely like a piece of worn harness, was an object that I slowly recognized as once beloved to me. It was a stereopticon. It belonged in the parlor, on the second shelf on the round table in the middle of the room, with the Bible on top. It belonged to Sunday and to summertime.

My held hand pained me through the wish to lift that old, beloved, once mysterious contraption to my eyes and dissolve my sight, all our sights, in that. In that delaying, binding pain, I re-

membered Uncle Felix; that is, I remembered the real Uncle Felix,
and could hear his voice, respectful again, asking the blessing at the
table. Then I heard the cataract of talk, which I knew he engen-
dered; that was what Sunday at Mingo began with.

I remembered the house, the real house, always silvery, as now,
but then cypressy and sweet, cool, reflecting, dustless. Sunday dinner
was eaten from the table pulled to the very head of the breezeway,
almost in the open door. The Sunday air poured in through it, and
through the frail-ribbed fanlight and side lights, down on the island
we made, our cloth and our food and our flowers and jelly and ourselves, so lightly enclosed there, as though we ate in pure running
water. So many people were gathered at Mingo that the Sunday
table was pulled out to the limit, from a circle to the shape of a race
track. It held my mother, my father and brother—Aunt Ethel; Uncle
Harlan, who could be persuaded, if he did not eat too much, to take
down the banjo later; my Jerrold grandmother, who always spoke
of herself as "nothing but a country bride, darling," slicing the
chicken while Uncle Felix cut the ham; Cousin Eva and Cousin
Archie; and Kate, Kate everywhere, like me. And plenty more besides; it was eating against talking, all as if nobody would ever be
persuaded to get up and leave the table: everybody, we thought, that
we needed. And some were so pretty!

And when they were, the next thing, taking their naps all over
the house, it was then I got my chance, and there would be, in lieu
of any nap, pictures of the world to see.

I ran with the stereopticon straight for the front-porch steps, and,
sitting there, stacked the slides between my bare knees in the spread
of my starched skirt. The slide belonging on top was "The Ladies'
View, Lakes of Killarney."

And at my side sat Uncle Felix. With his coat laid folded on the
porch floor on the other side of him, sitting erect in his shirtsleeves,
he would reach grandly for the instrument as I ran bringing it out.
He saddled his full-size nose with the stereopticon and said, "All
right, Skeeta." And then as he signalled ready for each slide, I
handed it up to him.

Some places took him a long time. As he perspired there in his
hard collar, looking, he gave off a smell like a cut watermelon. He
handed each slide back without a word, and I was ready with the
next. I would no more have spoken than I would have interrupted
his blessing at the table.

Eventually, they—all the rest of the Sunday children—were awake and wanting to be tossed about, and they hung over him, pulling on him, seeking his lap, his shoulders, pinning him down, riding on him. And he, with his giant size and absorption, went on looking his fill. It was as though while he held the stereopticon to his eye, *we* did not see *him*. Gradually, his ear went red. I thought all the blood had run up to his brain then, as it had to mine.

I suppose all of us did a little looking in the stereopticon. But it was he and I who mostly passed it back and forth.

I remember Uncle Felix loving the stereopticon, for the reason that he wouldn't let me have it for so long. I had to plead with him on the strength of fairness to let me take my turn.

We passed each other those sand-pink cities and passionate fountains; a waterfall, which rocks snuffed out like a light; islands in seas; red Pyramids, and sleeping towers; checkered pavements on which curious strollers had come out (with shadows that seemed to go farther each time we looked, as if the strollers had moved) and where the statues blushed; volcanoes; the Sphinx, and Constantinople; and again, again the Lakes, like starry fields—brought forward each time so close that it seemed to me the tracings from the beautiful hard face of a strange coin were being transferred to my brain. Yet there were things also that I did not see, which could make Uncle Felix pucker his lips as for a kiss.

"Now! Dicey! I want you to tell me how I look!" Sister Anne stepped in, to a flash from the front. A low growl from the bed filled the room, following the flicker, almost companionably.

Sister Anne had put on a hat—a hat from no telling where, what visit, what year, but it had been swashbuckling. It still was; it was a sort of pirate hat—black, of course.

"You look mighty dressed up," said Kate, for me.

"Thank you. Oh! Everything comes at once if it comes at all!" she cried, looking from one to the other of us. "So you can't turn around fast enough! You come on Mr. Do-lollie's day! Now what will I do for Sunday!"

Under her cry was a slow, delicate noise. Uncle Felix had torn out the leaf of the book he had worked over. Now he let me go, and took both swollen fists and over the lump of his body properly folded his page. He nudged it into my tingling hand.

"*He'll* keep you busy!" said Sister Anne, nodding. "*That* table looks ready to go to market!" Her eyes were so bright, she was in such a state of excitement and suspense, that she seemed to lose for that moment all ties with us or the house and all remembrance where anything was. The next minute, she was gone.

I had slipped the torn page from the book, still folded, into my pocket, working it down through the starch-stuck percale. Now I leaned down and kissed Uncle Felix's long, unshaven, unbathed cheek. He didn't look at me—Kate stared, I felt it—but in a moment his eyes shut.

I went to stand by Kate at the window. She had turned her back to the room, and was looking out. The light was burrowing into the roses, their heads hung. Out there was the pasture. The small, velvety cows had come up to the far fence and were standing there looking toward the house. They were little, low, black cows, soot-black, with their calves among them, in a green that seemed something to drink from more than something to eat.

Kate touched my hand and groaned under her breath. "Come on. I've *got* to see her do it."

We approached the bed. Again Uncle Felix's head poked forward and held still, the late western light full on him now. "We'll be back, Uncle Felix. Listen to me. We'll both be back," Kate said. "It's nothing—it's all nothing."

I felt that I had just showed off a good deal in some way. She bent down, hands on knees, as to a child, but his face did not consult us again, although his eyes had opened. We left him by himself. In his bleached gown, he looked like the storybook picture of the Big Bear, the old white one with star children on his back and other star children following, in triangle dresses, starting down the Milky Way.

Sister Anne had got clear ahead of us. We saw her in her sweeping hat at the table, over the ledger. The front bedroom door was open again, and we stepped in there before she saw us.

Thick around the room, on the rocking chair, on parlor chairs and the numerous cane chairs from the dining-room set, our visitors were visiting. A few were standing or sitting at the windows to talk, or leaning against the mantel. The four-poster held, like a paddock, a collection of cleaned-up little children, mostly girls, some of them mutinous and tearful, one little girl patiently holding a fruit jar with something alive inside.

"Writing herself in, signing herself out—all in one," Kate whispered, watching.

When Sister Anne went into the parlor, Kate gripped my wrist wickedly, and we tiptoed back out, crossed the breezeway, and stood there by the parlor curtain until Kate lifted it. Sister Anne was shaking out her skirt, and crumbs scattered on the rug. She had managed a slice of that cake. The parlor in its plush was radiant in the spectacular glare of multiplied lights brought close around the organ bench. The wallpaper now had a cinnamon cast. Its design had gone into another one—it, too, faded and precise, ringed by rain and of a queerly intoxicating closeness, like an old trunk that has been opened still again for the children to find costumes. White flags and amaryllis in too big a vase, where they parted themselves in the middle and tried to fall out, were Sister Anne's idea of what completed the mantel shelf. The fireplace was banked with privet hedge, as for a country wedding. I could almost hear a wavery baritone voice singing "Oh, Promise Me." But there we stood.

One with his camera and flash apparatus, the photographer stood with his motionless back to us, bent down under the cloth. It was he that was standing still. Sister Anne sat one way, then the other. A variety of expressions travelled over her face—pensive, eager, wounded, sad—and, yes, what I thought of then as "professional."

"I don't know why she can't make up her mind," I said. "She's done nothing but practice all afternoon."

"Wait, wait, wait," said Kate. "Let her get to it."

What would show in the picture was none of Mingo at all, but the itinerant backdrop—the same old thing, a scene that never was, a black and white and gray blur of unrolled, yanked-down moonlight, weighted at the bottom with the cast-iron parlor rabbit doorstop, just behind Sister Anne's restless heel. The photographer raised up with arms extended, as if to hold and balance Sister Anne just exactly as she was now, with some special kind of semaphore. But Sister Anne was not letting him off that easily.

"Just a minute—I feel like I've lost something!" she cried, in a voice of excitement. "My handkerchief?"

I could feel Kate whispering to me, sidewise along my cheek. "Do you suppose she told him there was a Yankee in the house? He might mean Yankees." Kate slanted her whisper into my hair. It was more feeling than hearing, what she said. "But he was almost too young for killing then. Of course, he wasn't too young to be a drummer boy."

I shrugged.

"Mama can tell us! What did the note say? Did it go on just warning us?"

I shook my head. But she knew I had looked at it.

"Tell you when we get out," I whispered, stepping forward a little and moving the curtain better.

"Oh, wait!" Sister Anne exclaimed again.

I couldn't have cared, or minded, less how Sister Anne looked. I had thought of what was behind the photographer's backdrop. It was the portrait in the house, the one painting on the walls of Mingo, where pictures were considered frivolous. It hung just there on the wall that was before me, crowded between the windows, high up—the romantic figure of a young lady seated on a fallen tree under brooding skies: my Great-Grandmother Jerrold, who had been Evelina Mackaill. The painter had called at the door (taken the family off guard, I was sure of it) with a ready-made portrait that had a blank circle of canvas where the head was to be fitted in —the head of this black-haired, black-eyed lady who always looked the right mysterious age to be my sister. The yellow skirt spread fanlike, straw hat held ribbon in hand, orange beads big as peach pits (to conceal the joining at the neck); or the forest scene so unlike the Mississippi wilderness (that density she had been carried to as a bride, when the logs of this house were cut, exposed, where she'd died of yellow fever); or the melancholy clouds obscuring the sky behind the passive figure with the small, crossed feet—none of that, world or body, was really hers. Yet here it was hers. *She* had eaten bear meat, seen Indians, and slaves had died in her arms, to what unknown feelings. And still those eyes—not quite level in the otherwise careful, conscientious face—opaque, all pupil, belonged to Evelina: they saw out, as mine did; weren't warned and didn't warn, as mine weren't and didn't—and I had claimed her long ago. I, her sister, knew who had endured and was enduring back there. As she had pushed her head once straight through that early cloth, she might now through the next push her head again.

I returned the touch of Kate's hand. This time, I whispered, "What he wrote was 'River—Daisy—Midnight—Please.' "

" 'Midnight'!" Kate exclaimed aloud. Then " 'River daisy'? His mind has quit, the poor old man."

"Daisy's a girl's name," I whispered impatiently.

Then Kate whispered, "You must mean Beck, Dicey—that was his wife, and he meant her to meet him in Heaven. Look again. *Look* at Sister Anne!"

Sister Anne had popped up from the organ bench. Whirling around, she flung up the lid—hymnbooks used to be stuffed inside

—and extracted something. To our amazement and delight, she rattled open a little fan, somebody's black one; it even *sounded* rusty. As she sat down again, she drew that fan, black and covered over with a shower of forget-me-nots, negligently across her bosom.

The photographer wasted not another moment.

The flash ran wild through the house for Sister Anne, singeing our very hair in the door, filling our lungs with gunpowder smoke. I had a little fit of coughing.

"Now let her try forgiving herself for this," said Kate, and almost lazily folded her arms there.

"Did you see me?" cried Sister Anne, running out crookedly and catching on to both of us to stop herself. "Oh, I hope it's good! Just as the thing went off, I blinked!" She laughed, but I believed I saw tears start out of her eyes. "Look! Come meet Mr. Puryear. Come have your pictures taken! It's only a dollar down and you get them in the mail!"

And for a moment I wanted to—wanted to have my picture taken against that absurd backdrop, having a vain, delicious wish to send it in the mail to someone, to torment someone with it, then have something to laugh about together afterward.

Kate drew on ladylike white cotton gloves, which I had not noticed her bringing. Whatever she had been going to say turned into "Sister Anne? What have you been telling Uncle Felix?"

"What I *didn't* tell him," replied Sister Anne, "was that people were getting their pictures taken. I didn't want him to feel left out. It was just for one day. Mr. Alf J. Puryear is the photographer's name—there's some Puryears in Mississippi. I'll always remember his sad face."

"Thank you for letting us see Uncle Felix, in spite of the trouble we were," said Kate, in her clear voice.

"You're welcome. And come back. But if I know the signs," said Sister Anne, "we're losing him fast, ah me. Well! I'm used to it, I can stand it, that's what I'm for. But, oh, I can't stand for you all to go! Stay—stay!" And she turned into our faces that outrageous, yearning smile she had produced for the photographer.

I knew I hadn't helped Kate out yet about Sister Anne. And so I said, "Aunt Ethel didn't come today! Do you know why? Because she just can't abide you!"

The bright lights inside just then went off. As Kate and I turned and ran down the steps, a voice out of the porch shadow said, "It seems to me that things are moving in too great a rush." It sounded sexless and ageless both to me; it sounded dead. And a voice just like it said, "I would thank Mr. Jerrold if he'd fix his road, so's we could get over it a little better. I don't think it would make anybody mad at him."

Sister Anne's picture, the free one, had been the last one. But nobody seemed to be leaving. Children were the only ones flying loose. Maddened by the hour and the scene, they were running barefoot and almost silent, skimming around and around the house. The others sat and visited on, in clouds of dust, all holding those little tickets or receipts that I had noticed wilting in their hands; some of the old men had them stuck in their winter hats. At last, maybe the Lady Baltimore cake would have to be passed.

"Sister Anne, greedy and all as she is, will cut that cake yet, if she can keep them there a little longer!" said Kate, in answer to my thought.

"Yes," I said.

"She'll forget what you said. Oh, the sweet evening air!"

I took so for granted once the old soft airs of Mingo as I knew them—the interior airs that were always kitchen-like, carrying the odor of oil lamps, wood ashes, and that golden scrapement off cake papers, and outside, beyond the just-watered ferns lining the broad, strong railing, the fragrances winding up through the lustre of the fields and the dim, gold screen of trees and the river beyond, so rich I could almost see them, untransparent and Oriental. In those days, fresh as I was from Sunday school in town, I could imagine the Magi riding through, laden.

At other times—perhaps later, during visits back from the North —that whole big congregated outside smell, like the ripple of an animal's shining skin, used suddenly to travel across and over to my figure standing on the porch, like a marvel of lightning, and by it I could see myself, by myself, a child on a visit to Mingo, hardly under any auspices that I knew of, but wild myself, at the mercy of that touch.

"It's a wonder she didn't let the niggers file in at the back and have theirs taken, too. If you didn't know it was Sister Anne, it would be past understanding," Kate said. "It would kill Mama. We must spare her this."

"Of course!" Sparing was our family trait.

We were going down the walk, measuredly, like lady callers who had left their cards, in single file. That was the one little line of cement laid down out here in miles—narrow as a ladder.

"But listen, who was Daisy, have you thought? *Daisy*," said Kate, in front. She looked over her shoulder. "I don't believe it."

I smoothed out that brown page of the hymnbook with the torn edge, that purple indelible writing across it where the print read, "Round & Shaped Notes." Coming around, walking in the dampening uncut grass, I showed it to Kate. You could still make out the big bold "D" with the cap on.

"'*Midnight.*' But they always go to bed at dark out here."

I put the letter back inside my pocket.

Kate said, "Daisy must have been smart. I don't understand that message at all."

"Oh, I do," I lied. I felt it was up to me to lie. I told Kate, "It's a kind of shorthand." Yet it had seemed a very long letter—didn't it take Uncle Felix a long time to write it!

"Oh, I can't think even out here, but mustn't Daisy be dead? Not Beck?" Kate ventured, then was wordless.

"Daisy was Daisy," I said. It was the "Please" that had hurt me. I put the old iron ring over the gate and fastened it. Two Cape jessamine bushes hid the gateposts entirely, and they were all in bud, and for a moment, just at the thought, I seemed to reel from a world too fragrant, as I suspected Aunt Ethel had reeled from one too loud.

"I expect by now Uncle Felix has got his names mixed up, and Daisy was a mistake," Kate said.

She could always make the kind of literal remark, like this, that could alienate me, even when we were children—much as I love her. I don't know why yet, but some things are too important for a mistake even to be considered, ever. I was sorry I had showed Kate the message, and said, "Look how we've left him by himself."

We stood looking back, in our wonder, until out of the house came the photographer himself, all packed up—a small, hurrying man, black-coated as his subjects were. He wore a pale straw summer hat, which was more than they had. It was to see him off, tell him goodbye, reassure him, that they had waited.

"Open it again! Look out, Dicey," said Kate. "Get back."

He did not tarry. With paraphernalia to spare, he ran out between the big bushes ahead of us with a strange, rushing, fuselike, Yankee sound—out through the evening and into his Ford, and was gone like that.

And then Kate and I were both excruciated by our terrible desire, and, catching each other at the same moment with almost fierce hands, we did it—we laughed. We leaned against each other and on the weak open gate, and gasped and choked into our handkerchiefs, and finally we cried. "Maybe she kissed him," cried Kate, at random. Each time we tried to stop ourselves, we sought each other's faces and started again. We laughed as though we were inspired.

"She forgot to take the pencil out of her hair!" gasped Kate.

"Oh, no! What do you think Uncle Felix wrote with! He managed—it was the pencil out of Sister Anne's head!" That was almost too much for me. I held on to the gate.

I was aware somehow that birds kept singing passionately all around us just the same, and hurling themselves like bolts in front of our streaming eyes.

Kate tried to say something new, to stop us disgracing ourselves and each other, our visit, Aunt Ethel, everything. Not that anybody, anything in the world could hear us, reeled back in those bushes now, except ourselves.

"You know Aunt Beck—she never let us leave Mingo without picking us our nosegay on the way down this walk, every little thing she grew that smelled nice—pinks, four-o'clocks, verbena, heliotrope, bits of Nicotiana. She grew all such little things, just for that, Di. And she wound their stems, round and round and round, with a black or white thread she would take from a needle in her collar, and set it all inside a rose-geranium leaf, and presented it to you at the gate—right here. That was Aunt Beck," said Kate's positive voice. "She wouldn't *let* you leave without it."

But it was no good. We had not laughed together that way since we were too little to know any better.

With tears streaming down my cheeks, I said, "No! No! I don't remember her."

"But she wouldn't *let* you forget. She'd fuss at you!"

Then we stopped.

There was the house, floating on the swimming dust of evening, its gathered, safe-shaped mass darkening. A dove in the woods called its five notes—two and three—at first unanswered. The last gleam of sunset could be seen going on behind the threadbare curtain of wisteria. The cows were lowing. The dust was in windings, the roads in their own shapes in the air, the exhalations of where the people all had come from.

"They'll all be leaving now," said Kate. "It's first-dark, almost."

But the grouping on the porch still held, that last time we looked back, posed there along the rail, as quiet and obscure and never known as passengers on a ship already embarked to sea.

Something moved. The little girl came out to the front, holding her glass jar, like a dark lantern, outward. Kate and I turned, wound our arms around each other, and got down to the car.

It was all one substance now, one breath and density of blue. Along the back where the pasture was, the little, low, black cows came in, in a line toward the house, with their sober sides one following the other. Where each went looked like simply where nothing was. But across the quiet we heard Uncle Theodore talking to them.

Across the road was Uncle Theodore's cabin, where clumps of privet hedge in front were shaped into a set of porch furniture, god-size, table and chairs, and a snake was hung up in a tree.

We drew out of the line of vehicles, and turned back down the dark blue country road. We neither talked, confided, nor sang. Only once, in a practical voice, Kate spoke.

"I hate going out there without Mama. Mama's too nice to say it about Sister Anne, but I will. You know what it is: it's in there somewhere."

Our lips moved together. "She's common. . . ."

All around, something went on and on. It was hard without thinking to tell whether it was a throbbing, a dance, a rattle, or a ringing—all louder as we neared the bridge. It was everything in the grass and trees. Presently, Mingo church, where Uncle Felix had been turned down on "knick-knack," revolved slowly by, with its faint churchyard. Then all was April night. I thought of my sweetheart, and wondered if he were writing to me.

THE CLASSLESS SOCIETY

❖

Elizabeth Hardwick

WILLARD NESBITT marked his place in "The Power Elite" with a matchstick and put the book on the table beside his reading chair. Nesbitt was a handsome man, with a brisk, trim, lecturing air about him both in and out of his classroom. He was a professor of American history at the University of Chicago and well known beyond that for his books, his round-table discussions, his articles in the Sunday *Times*. He was clever, had easy, rather flippant manners, and treated the academic world as if he were just passing through on his way to, perhaps, the State Department or the United Nations. Hidden in his sensible heart was the desire to run sometime for the Senate, like Paul Douglas.

Nesbitt put down his book with an ambiguous sigh. He found it very difficult to like anything with his whole mind. He was always being disappointed, even in the best. Laurence Olivier's Hotspur turned out to be not quite as vigorous as he had heard it was; David Oistrakh's violin playing left him with a sense of imperfection hard to define; he had expected there would be a lot more in Dr. Jones' biography of Freud than he found; and he thought there might well be a lot less on every subject from Arnold Toynbee. Professor Nesbitt rejoiced in his failure to concur with the common opinion; he cherished his dissents and worked to refine and elaborate them as if they were a piece of historical composition always going to press. When he said, hesitating and smiling slyly, that de Tocqueville's "Democracy in America" was immensely readable and would cause less trouble if thought of as a sort of poem, his students were charmed by his impudence. The theme that went the campus rounds, year in and year out, about Nesbitt was that whether one liked him or not, he was at least alive.

Henrietta, Willard's wife, looked up from the crossword puzzle in the *New Statesman & Nation*. The Nesbitts were expecting guests for dinner—Henrietta's cousin Dodo Babcock, and a colleague of Willard's, Clarence Anderson. The Nesbitts had known Anderson for five or six years. They invited him every year to several cocktail parties and small dinners, and yet they did not especially like him. The invitations were sometimes to be laid at the door of Clarence's condition of bachelorhood but more often to something demanding and disturbing in the man himself. Willard, if a number of months had passed without his making any special effort over Anderson, would begin to experience a feeling of unease, of neglectfulness vaguely dangerous to his own well-being. Anderson's themes were a devotion to academic life and a claim to be a nature molded by the habit of idealism and disinterestedness. He played upon these themes gently enough, but with assurance, leaving his auditors with the feeling of having been accused of something less than perfection.

"I dread seeing Dodo tonight, somehow," Henrietta said.

"All that branch of your Babcock relations fills me with gloom," Willard answered. "They have suffered the most fantastic collapse. The strain seems to have undergone a queer fatigue, as even metals are said to do. Or so I've heard."

"Metals?" Henrietta said sharply.

Willard went on, in a musing tone, "There is an element of mystery about this generation of Babcocks. They present with a good deal of clarity the ancient debate between environment and heredity. Their parents were so gay and rich, and the children are so melancholy and undistinguished. They haven't even got money."

"Yes, they do seem rather languid," Henrietta agreed. "John and Evelyn have tried them all and given them up, though I think they admit that young Perry is good fun upon occasion." John and Evelyn were Henrietta's brother and sister-in-law.

"But they think Perry's wife is awful. I distinctly remember Evelyn's saying that," Willard offered.

"I believe she thought it was *Dudley* Babcock's wife who was so awful," Henrietta said.

"Each in her own way, perhaps."

Henrietta Nesbitt had been born a Babcock. In Chicago, the name of this family rang out with a clear and beautiful glory. The founder of the family had made a fortune in the copper mines of the West; copper sons had married Chicago meat-packing daughters. Henrietta's branch of the family had never been as rich as Dodo Babcock's branch. Now both branches were of unexceptional means, though among the more distant cousins there were still Babcocks of large fortune.

Willard Nesbitt took pride in making no use of Henrietta's connection with the great and famous Babcock family. This was not the act of spiritual renunciation he sometimes imagined, since there was not a great deal of personal advantage to be gained from the connection; the advantage, such as it was, was purely aesthetic. Willard, straining to keep the proper degree of faith with what he described as his own "fabulously simple" beginnings, felt that the absence of material benefit from his marriage gave him the right—even the duty—to make creative use of his special knowledge, through Henrietta, of the decline of certain members of what he liked to call "the ruling class." On an intimate and yet ironic note, he sometimes declared he was less fascinated by the living Babcock fortune than by the dead one—those riches gone like a dear person, or buried by destiny like a once thriving village crushed by disaster. The financial decay of some of Henrietta's relatives served Nesbitt as fresh fact from which theories might be drawn.

"It's damned risky having Clarence Anderson to meet poor Dodo Babcock," Willard said, with a sigh.

"Do you suppose he'll be wearing his black loafers with the tassels on them?" Henrietta said.

"Of course, and God knows what to match. These English teachers are all Cockneys at heart, secretly in love with Princess Margaret."

"Poor Dodo," Henrietta said. "She has a faded regality, but her housekeeping is like a Puerto Rican's."

" 'Faded regality'—monstrous phrase. Probably accurate."

"Don't you like Clarence Anderson *at all?*" Henrietta asked lazily. "If not, why do you see him?"

"I always expect him to be something like Thorstein Veblen. You know, he's Norwegian, and from one of those states out there—Nebraska, I think."

"He probably does go in for 'pecuniary emulation'—or whatever Veblen called it," Henrietta said, with a smile. Nesbitt had been educating Henrietta for all the years of their marriage, but he did this without earnestness, because he was proud of his wife's somewhat destructive natural brightness and not ashamed of her ignorance. The frightfully poor education of the well-bred society lady was a topic they often discussed. If Henrietta thought, as Zola is said to have thought, that Charlemagne lived and flourished around the fifteenth century—well, that was amusing. With her frightening gift for mockery, her disarming self-confidence, she at least did not have to talk cant, and that was worth all the education in the world. Or usually worth it. Willard had had occasion to feel Henrietta's bite sink into some sensitive spot of his own being.

"It certainly is hard to make the grade with you," Henrietta said, after a pause.

"Well, some few do at last succeed with me, but rare is the bird that meets with your unqualified praise," Willard answered in his most affectionate voice.

"Don't be ridiculous. . . . Please don't be over Dodo's head to-night. It's bad manners."

"But it is impossible not to be over Dodo's head. I thought manners was the art of the possible—or is that politics?"

"It can be cow-milking, for all I know. Dodo has her own peculiar backwardness—that I admit, since one must. But she's not stupid."

"I like old Dodo," Willard said, retreating hastily. (Henrietta did not like to be pushed the whole way in her condemnation of her family. Sometimes, if they drank too many Martinis before dinner, she would turn upon Willard and say, with profound intent, "You know nothing whatsoever about people with money and power. That you can go about all over the country, and on television, sounding off on the subject completely amazes me!")

"Do you think Dodo will be annoyed that we haven't asked some-one more fancy than Clarence?" Henrietta wondered. "It's been such a long time since we've had her over I feel a little stingy not to be making it more of an occasion. One of the ways in which Dodo is absolutely unique is that you can't flatter her by intellectual ap-peal, so Clarence *as a mind* won't mean a thing to her. She's an old-fashioned girl—money and position speak louder to her than all the artistic or cultural honors in the world. Mother, for instance, is quite different. When we asked her to our cocktail party for that dull friend of Albert Schweitzer's, she was beside herself with joy and excitement."

"Actually, there is no one in Chicago fancier than Clarence An-derson when you come right down to it."

The Nesbitts had a four-room walkup apartment near the univer-sity. The place was brownish, shabby, comfortable, stuffed with books and periodicals—all of which indicated, like a workman's toolbox in a hallway, the life of the occupant. At the Nesbitts', there

were also a few surprises, the most surprising and important of
which was a huge abstraction done in the manner of Jackson Pollock. "By a very gifted young Chicago painter, a friend of ours,"
Willard would say by way of identification. The Jackson Pollock
disciple had turned out to be a disappointment to the Nesbitts. He
seemed to be becoming less known rather than more, but they did
not take down the picture and store it in the basement, as the mu-
seums do. To be snobbish about Chicago painters seemed to them
ludicrous and dull, like protesting about baseball or television.
Among their other possessions were a magnificent silver tray, nearly
as large as the abstraction, and a badly restored portrait of "Aunt
Mag Pierce," by Sully, which hung with careful negligence in a not
very light corner of the dining room, flanked on one side by a
Medici print of Uccello's "Cavalry Battle" and on the other side by
a disc of hammered copper brought from Istanbul.

Just after Henrietta went to the bedroom to smooth her hair, the
street doorbell rang. "There they are!" she called out. "Or at least
there Clarence is. Dodo is probably still at home looking for her
change purse or coloring her nails."

Willard opened the door and saw that Clarence had arrived first,
but Dodo was just behind him on the stairs, calling up to him wistfully, "We are both going to the same place. Of course, I couldn't
have known."

Clarence had a rather controlled and faraway expression on his
face. He loathed being patronized by the Nesbitts. He thought himself much more popular, serious, and clever than they; in his opinion, Willard was something of a charlatan, and Henrietta came
under his suspicion as impertinent and shallow. Since he harbored
these disparaging thoughts, the feeling he had that the Nesbitts,
even at their friendliest, were somehow snubbing him made him
rage with irritation and resentment. His dream was that he might
get the jump on the Nesbitts—in some subtle, fascinating, and
morally plausible way soar above them. That was the desperate
hope behind his cool and stiff expression when the door opened.

Willard, seeing that Clarence *was* wearing his black loafers with
the tassels on them, smiled and bowed. An amused and condescending look came involuntarily over his face—just the look that Clarence detested, and called "the hard-hearted Nesbitt smile."

When Dodo joined them, Willard said, "I don't know whether
Henrietta told you that her cousin Dodo Babcock was dining with
us tonight. And here she is."

"How do you do?" Dodo said, calmly inspecting Clarence. "I came by taxi for fear of being late. I hope I'm not."

"You're in perfect time," Willard said. Dodo was impressive in a dress of purple silk and a little cape of black broadtail. She did not look smart—the cape was worn in spots and the dress was not new —but she did have, resting upon the solid foundation of her privileged childhood, an awesome tranquillity, a quaintly pure and steadfast self-confidence. Her gaze was fresh, open-eyed, and self-esteeming, in the manner of a family portrait.

Clarence felt tricked and uncertain when he recognized the clear tremble of interest that flowed through him as he was presented to Dodo. He had not expected a relative of Henrietta's, an unmarried lady, clearly near his own age of thirty-eight. His mind, always painfully alerted by piercing longings, and his flirtatious heart leaped up to greet the complications and possibilities of the situation. He smiled, carefully measuring his gallantry.

"Dodo, darling, how are you!" Henrietta said gaily, coming out of her bedroom in a hurry as her guests entered, acting as if she had not expected them so soon. Henrietta hated to give the impression of being ready and waiting for anyone, and this led her to assume a flustered and brightly rushed air when guests arrived, even though she was, behind the busyness, prompt, efficient, and quite prepared to receive them. "You two have been introduced, I gather," she added, smiling brilliantly at Clarence and giving him her hand.

"You're looking awfully well," Clarence said, deciding to pay Henrietta, rather than Dodo, his first quietly uttered compliment.

"I wish I could believe you," Henrietta replied, smiling mischievously at Clarence's way of feeling out a situation, as if he were a diplomat among an inscrutable, tricky people.

Clarence Anderson was not a lighthearted man, and when he took a notion to denounce someone, his nature forced him to assume a moralistic tone. This tone was quite in contrast to the way of the Nesbitts, who went in, simply and indefatigably, for the kind of impudence and gossip they judged to be amusing. Clarence never mentioned the defect of an acquaintance without clearly showing the poor, faulty person's character to be morally inferior to his own. When he used the word "dull," he did not mean to lament a lack of sprightliness so much as to expose a sluggish, self-loving soul, remarkably different from his own vigorous, light openness of feeling. With his impatient, moralizing bent, Clarence was a powerful enemy. Clarence's enmity was, like the Nesbitts' insults, purely verbal. He did not wish to effect a deterioration in his antagonist's circumstances so much as to cause everyone to think of his victim precisely as he did. If he thought someone charmingly foolish or harmlessly inane, he was not satisfied until the whole world acknowledged this foolishness or inanity. It was an agony to him that there might exist an intelligent person who knew his circle of friends and yet saw the various members of it in a light opposed to his own. To insist on his own view was, to his mind, "telling the truth." Stubbornly he repudiated the tolerant, careless opinion, and with a great show of idealism and objectivity he corrected it. This readiness to speak out led Clarence to imagine that others spoke out also, and when he was praised, as he often was by timid, well-mannered people, he took the praise as genuine and unmixed, and found much pleasure in it.

"I'll go first. I'd love a Martini, pet," Henrietta said, leading the way into the living room. She sat down, crossing her long, handsome legs, of which she was very vain. She wore high heels, which would have been painful if her delight in the way they showed her legs to advantage had not mysteriously made her nearly unconscious of any such pain. For the rest, she was passable in appearance—round nose, brown face, good teeth, and graying brown hair, difficult to manage.

"I'm very fond of gin myself," Dodo said thoughtfully. "I suppose one shouldn't say a thing like that, but I do think a gin drink is awfully good before dinner. God himself wouldn't drink it afterward."

"And what about you, Anderson?" Willard said abruptly. "You aren't to feel committed by the ready Martini pitcher."

"I don't feel committed, but I'll take one nevertheless. It would be a great deprivation to have to forgo what I really prefer."

Clarence was as clerical-suited as Nesbitt was brown-tweeded. This evening, Willard was dressed with even more than his usual sportiness: he was wearing an old jacket with suède patches on the elbows. Clarence immediately analyzed the patched jacket as a form of condescension toward himself. He marked it down against Willard as inverted snobbery. Clarence had, by his quickness to spot pretension, succeeded in turning quite a few people against the Nesbitts. He had made Willard's intellectual arrogance appear flimsy and ersatz. "What, in the long run, has Nesbitt written?" often passed Clarence's lips. As for Henrietta's connection with the Babcock family, Clarence sometimes made its very existence seem open to question, or, if admitted, a peculiar and interesting handicap, a disqualifying affliction.

When Willard saw Clarence's red bow tie and inky sack suit, he felt a gush of irritation, even though he knew that this was the way Clarence would and did dress, with a reasonable sort of up-to-dateness and appropriateness, as economically and neatly achieved as a little suburban house, with its breezeway, utility room, and dining area. Nesbitt wanted Clarence, as he said, to be, like Thorstein Veblen, a radical from the Western plains, and Clarence, in turn, thought Nesbitt should go around with a sign on his back that read, "Born in Akron, Ohio, of simple, decent stock. Undergraduate at Wayne, connection with Harvard on graduate level *only,* wife from minor branch of well-known Chicago family—the poor side."

Clarence smiled quietly at Dodo Babcock, and she returned his smile with equal quiet and composure. Dodo tended toward redness, even down to the girlish flush of her cheeks. Her hair was touched with auburn lights, her eyebrows were a scanty reddish brown, and her hands, pink as a shell, lay beautifully and languidly in her purple silk lap. In her face, there was the mark of a charming immaturity, of expectation still to be fulfilled, and a suggestion of hurt feelings—proud, disdainful chagrin, such as one finds in those for whom history is fully dramatized in the story of their own fate. A reactionary, of course, Clarence thought, but amiably, forgivingly.

"Well," Willard said, with a short laugh, waiting for the conversation to begin.

After a pause, Clarence said, "Did you know that idiot G. B. Cooper was being sent to Baghdad by the Ford Foundation? I have no doubt scholars, even bone-lazy ones like Cooper, can benefit from the advantages of foreign travel, but—"

"Baghdad. That's pretty foreign indeed," Dodo said vaguely.

"Exactly," Clarence said. "There is something exorbitant—monstrous—about these foundation affairs. They go beyond what anyone would expect. In the long run, I am most bothered by the details—the luxurious, preposterous details. Wife and children and Chevrolet all sent, free of charge, to Baghdad!"

"G. B. Cooper? I can't quite place him," Willard said.

"He's the most slavish follower of T. S. Eliot in America—perhaps in the world, for all I know. The whole—the whole, mind you —of his professional attitude comes out of 'Tradition and the Individual Talent.' I doubt he has read a critical work before or since."

"That doesn't seem quite enough baggage, somehow," Henrietta suggested.

"Wife, children, and car sent to Baghdad," Clarence repeated. "It's an unnerving thought. For quantity, lavishness, excess, trust our dear, huge America!"

"I bet they wish they had some quantity in Baghdad," Dodo said, nodding coquettishly.

Everyone smiled. "Have you ever applied for Baghdad yourself, Clarence?" Henrietta asked.

"God, no!" Clarence replied with heat.

"Or some more plausible place?" Willard added.

"To be perfectly frank," Clarence said, delighted to be able to state his position, "I have not applied for Baghdad, or Istanbul, or even London, the love of my life. I can't feel deeply needed in the Near East. I am astonished at those who can, and full of admiration for them. Trucking over the world with only my treasured Victorian prose to offer the fellahin—Cardinal Newman and Ruskin in the Garden of Allah? One must keep some sense of what is fitting. As for London, I am too full of gratitude and private feelings of reverence to want to go dashing over there, my pockets full of money, to tell them what they already know, or to do work they've already done."

"That's excessive. Your conscientiousness is out of control," Henrietta said, with a clear trace of ill-humor.

One of Clarence's "positions" was a refusal to apply for grants, fellowships, easy posts. Whether this attitude came from a fear of failure, even Willard, an inveterate and successful getter of grants, project funds, and endowments, was uncertain. Clarence had a way of suggesting that since he could never be entirely sure his researches would be of clear value to the world, it would be personally fraudulent for him to accept—indeed, to seek—generous sums. He preferred to let his lonely little bark move under its own sail.

Clarence continued, "When I was at Oxford in '54, there was quite a bit of fun poked at American scholars and their foreign studies and lectures and cushy positions. It is easy enough to dismiss that as envy, but I think it is more serious—or less serious. I mean I truly believe one can maintain that all manner of stupid, incompetent, repetitive work is being done by our American scholars, and at an expense that staggers the imagination!"

Willard poured a second Martini for everyone. Then he settled back in his chair and, smiling maliciously at Clarence's flushed, eager face, said, "What you people never seem to realize is that these foundations literally—*literally,* mind you—have more money than they can spend. To look upon the few thousand one may get for teaching as something that must in the purest, most competitive sense be earned is sheer conceit!" With a modest, self-deprecating laugh, he added, "This thing is bigger than any of us. Of course, you aren't married, Anderson, and so perhaps you are allowed more perfection and chastity than the rest of us. Without undeserved honors and unearned foundation funds, how on earth could I keep my son Clark at Groton, where he is dreadfully and expensively out of place?"

Clarence knew well that Willard Nesbitt did not think of himself as the recipient of undeserved honors and unearned funds. It was enraging that by this insincere show of cynicism Nesbitt could make him seem to be guilty of false piety and pretentious scrupulosity.

"Groton?" Dodo said vaguely. "I wonder if Clark sees anything of Babcock Van der Veen, who is also there. You remember—he's old Cousin Jimmy's nephew."

"That I couldn't possibly say, dear," Henrietta answered. "Boys of Clark's age are very odd. They seem to fear nothing so much as their blood relations." Henrietta's smile for Dodo was just a little too brilliant, too sweet. All of Henrietta's pride and her habit of condescension came together in the smile. Her arrogance was of the enduring, comfortable kind, and came from her sheer and bold delight in being who she was. She felt she and Dodo had something no deprivation or failure could erase; beyond that, everything was trimming, superstructure. It was a pleasure to feel herself clever, to be married to a well-known man, but these were truly to be described as pleasure, not as the very foundation of her personal well-being or her belief in herself. Henrietta's tendency to patronize was just as real and unmanageable as her family pride. She was tolerant of Dodo as a fellow-Babcock but also superior to her cousin's helpless pale eyes, her innocence of intellect, her bald and uncomplicated assumptions. She felt that Dodo's imagination declined to supply the facts relating to her true situation.

Turning suddenly to Clarence, Dodo asked, in her thrilling and beautiful voice, "Did you admire Adlai Stevenson terribly?"

Clarence blushed. He longed to resent Dodo as a foolish woman, but when his intense powers of observation revealed to him the ambivalence of the Nesbitts' presentation of their cousin, the way they at once displayed and gently mocked her, he felt hopelessly drawn to her—allied even to her complacency and childishness.

"Yes, yes, I must say I did—quite a lot. He seemed to me a remarkable man," Clarence answered. "And I am not ashamed to admit that I cherished his literacy. It is a mistaken notion that one can think without words." He did not smile, he did not adopt his moralizing, rebuking tone. He treated, or pretended to treat, Dodo's question with deep and puzzling seriousness. Also, he was curious to know how this creature might express herself on the subject of politics and whether she might not discomfit her hosts. Clarence secretly suspected Willard and Henrietta of political dishonesty. He believed they were more conservative than they appeared, more willing to compromise with the status quo than they admitted.

"I dislike Adlai Stevenson terribly," Dodo offered. Willard laughed indulgently, but she appeared unaware of the meaning of this laugh, which was designed to stop the free expression of her political notions. "I know quite a few people who know him personally. The idea seems to be that he is very superficial."

"Are you a great partisan of Eisenhower, then?" Clarence said, bending politely toward Dodo and waiting gallantly for her reply.

"I am indeed. I love him. Terribly," Dodo said, with her great, pale-eyed earnestness.

Henrietta coughed. "A perfectly atrocious dinner is awaiting us," she said. "I have my part-time maid here this evening. She was a short-order cook—for the White Tavern or some such place."

At that moment, a moon-faced colored woman appeared and said, "O.K."

They went into the dining room and settled themselves under the Sully portrait of "Aunt Mag Pierce" and the disc of hammered copper. Willard had trouble with the wine bottle, but when the cork was at last extracted, he said, "The wine is not superb, that I grant you. But it is just good enough to resent being on the same program with the overdone lamb that is as sure to follow as the night the day."

"Do you remember Hélène, Mummy's wonderful Swiss cook?" Dodo said wistfully. She was incorrigibly reminiscent. The disposition came upon her with the regularity of a stutter.

"I do remember her, dear, and a painful memory it is, at the moment," Henrietta replied.

During the meal, Clarence observed Dodo—trained the heavy

ammunition of his mind upon her, as if he were a general besieging an undefended shepherdess on her lonely hill. At the same time, he was careful to conceal the wild unruliness of his natural curiosity. Dodo was, he saw, of a savage invincibility and bitter composure. She lived, waiting patiently and proudly, like an old deposed tribal chieftain indolently dreaming of a hopeless return to power and dignity. "I passed our old house recently," she said, accepting a second potato. "Can you imagine, the old red draperies—the velvet ones with gold braid—are still hanging, even after all these years! It's an awful thought—insulting, somehow. I felt, looking at those dingy curtains behind the smeared windows, as if some part of my past were still in the house, rotting away. It's a rooming house, or so I gather from the looks of the place. Milk cartons on every window ledge, miserable faces peering out of the windows, dirty, torn shades in the room that used to be mine. Do you remember the dressing table with the pink brocade skirt I was so fond of, Hennie?" Dodo coughed, reproaching fate and adversity. Henrietta gave a melancholy sigh in honor of the old, decaying red brick mansion and the memory of gold service plates, four butlers, and the little Babcocks, pale and fair and spoiled.

"Let it all go! I couldn't care less!" Dodo suddenly exclaimed. "I miss having someone to wash out my underwear more than I miss our marble entrance hall. Money, not beauty, is what I mourn." To her, it was more tedious to have to wash a coffee cup than to be forced to wear a tattered dinner dress. In these preferences Dodo showed a clear and terrifying grasp of reality. She understood that the dirty coffee cup represented an effort. A frayed dress was simply itself. It did not ask anything of her except the nerve to wear it, and that nerve Dodo had in abundance.

Clarence did not speak during this nostalgic moment. His silences were ordinarily well considered; there was a lurking, impressive withholding of approval in them. He knew when to let other people worry for fear they might be making fools of themselves; with a deep and greedy sense of drama he could sit nodding attentively and send a chill of apprehension through the speaker. In this case, though, his silence was not malicious, for, in truth, Clarence found Dodo endlessly engaging. His sensibility, his scholarly discipline, his obstinacy—it was almost a form of genius the way he could bring all these to bear upon the thin, reddish woman sitting across from him. He felt, somehow, a vague but genuine sympathy with this frayed and yet luxurious person. Already he was busily informing

his conscience that Dodo had an honesty, a candor, and a rigid simplicity of emotion that he found more elegant and admirable than
Henrietta's cleverness. Dodo was certainly not smart, and she was
not kind. She was profoundly incapable of that greatness of sacrifice or purity of feeling at whose throne Clarence worshipped and in
whose name he criticized and sighed over most of his acquaintances.
But Clarence decided to find Dodo majestically produced, gloriously
out of date, even historically significant. No, not that, not significant, he amended his thoughts, but socially expressive in a small and
interesting way. She was ridiculous, like many a genuine article;
she was a Chicago Babcock, helpless, proud, paralyzed by her self-
esteem and bemused by the decline of her fortunes. Her clear
eyes and pink skin reminded him of portraits of German princesses.
Her long, pale fingernails were adorned with coral polish; on one
haughty finger there was a splendid emerald ring, telling of days
past and lost treasure hoards. There was a runner in her stocking, an
affecting thinness to her ankles, a whiff of sachet clinging to the
dress of purple silk.

Clarence was, he liked to say, "some kind of a Socialist." Still, he
did not approve of what he called "Socialist provincialism;" he
freely admitted the possibility of charm, the capacity for suffering,
in all classes. Thus, it was almost to his credit, he believed, to take a
tolerant, worldly view of Dodo.

As a young girl, Dodo had spent several years in Italy, living in an
expensive *pensione* in Florence. She never managed to meet the
eligible Englishman who should have entered her life, conquering
her with his vanity and his pedigree. She did not even manage to
return to America with an attractive, penniless Italian of noble
birth. It was not that she sought and did not find. She did not seek
and was not found. Dodo had studied singing, but her interest in
singing had gradually declined, leaving as a mark of its previous
existence only a quantity of vehement opinion. As her passion for
the art and the hopes of her youth diminished, they had been replaced by dissatisfaction with other voices and with modern music.
Now, at dinner at the Nesbitts', she found her days as a voice student another topic for reminiscence. "I was a mezzo," she explained,
giving to the middle register in which nature had placed her voice
a romantic, elusive significance. Then, with the authority of a retired diva, she turned and said to Clarence with dazzling irrelevance,
" 'The Rake's Program,' or whatever that phony concoction was

called—I couldn't, and never shall, find the courage to hear it through. Nowadays you can put anything over by a little publicity in the right places. The Russians, in my opinion, have no feeling for the voice. They understand only the violin."

Clarence listened, and allowed an expression of gentle amusement to pass over his features. He thought there was considerable beauty in the clarity of Dodo's chagrined countenance.

"Dodo, dear," Willard said as they left the table, "your intransigence in this other-directed world we live in is a delightful curiosity."

"I can't imagine what you mean," Dodo said, smiling girlishly. "I simply state my opinion. Nothing very original about that."

Willard Nesbitt did not like to offer his guests alcohol after dinner, and so at his parties there was always this period of pause and hesitation, and even a bit of discomfort, because his guests were likely to wonder suddenly if Nesbitt did not regret the whole affair. And he did, indeed, often give the clearest indication that he wished the evening were over. By not drinking after dinner, Willard managed to avoid dull, headachy mornings and lazy, worthless days. His ambitions were limitless; there was not enough time for all he wanted to do. His abrupt seizures of boredom and restlessness were symptoms of his ambition and of his sense that time was running out and fame fickle and hard to command. He enjoyed social life, and yet he felt himself best suited to the formal occasion, to the meetings and councils of public life, to an existence of decisions, addresses, cameras, and microphones. He had had all too much of the unbuttoned, cozy, secure little world of the university.

Nesbitt's restlessness, as the evening went on, offended Clarence, who took it for what it was, since he understood his colleague very well, and yet felt an exception should be made in his own case. His sense of personal affront was quickly translated into a generalization: Nesbitt's longing for the world stage was an example of the increasing commercialization and superficiality of academic life.

Clarence, a bachelor and only thirty-eight, was nevertheless a lover of things as they once were. Everything seemed to him to have been subtly degraded, from the quality of bread to the high-school curriculum. Violent feelings of disappointment, exhausting worries about the future of culture, had a fierce dominion over Clarence's existence. He was so fully and abjectly under the tyranny of these feelings that the feelings themselves were in his own mind mistaken for "work." When he was angry with a colleague, defeated in a committee meeting, dismayed by the poor preparation of the students, these experiences seemed to him to be his job. They were much too devastating and severe for him to take lightly. In judging his extremity of emotion, he found it simply an example of his greater diligence and dedication, his superiority to the mechanics being turned out by the graduate schools. Clarence cared, he suffered, he worried. Nesbitt's Under-Secretary of State airs and his desire to be an important figure in the intellectual world seemed to his critic, Clarence, to be a slighting of the great career of education.

Across the room, cool and smiling, sat Dodo Babcock. That schizophrenic, dangerous serenity, Clarence thought. Childishness, indifference, greed, and empty vanity; Clarence counted them off on his fingers—the faults of upper-class women. Yet out of nowhere came the answer that he had the opposite qualities in superabundance. He was careful, liberal, idealistic, and so the arrogant, self-loving, little-girl character of Dodo appealed to him. He tilted his head so that he might overhear what she was saying to Henrietta without interrupting his own conversation with a drowsy-looking Willard.

"This heavy reliance on Freud may prove embarrassing a few decades from now—even one decade from now," Clarence was saying. "I don't think people quite realize the extent of this influence. It is like a gas that has mixed into the natural atmosphere. Of course, a great mind and great work would make incalculable differences in special fields—in this case, in psychology and character analysis. But history, sociology, religion, architecture! I am reminded of the seriousness with which the Victorians took phrenology."

"You can't honestly mean to imply the two things are comparable in any sense," Willard said, languidly taking a cigarette from a Chinese box on the table.

"No, I certainly do not. I think Freud is immense, don't mistake me. But still, some of the details, some of the literalness, the use to which he has been put, disturbs me. Even the greatest intellectual events are often distorted by overearnest followers. There are fashions, exaggerations, mistakes here, as elsewhere. We don't know exactly what will remain, after all, of Freudianism—what its real contribution will turn out to be."

"Naturally, naturally," Willard said, without enthusiasm.

Clarence heard Henrietta say to Dodo, "Your parents were truly glamorous, and I am not one to use that word lightly."

"Daddy was the most wonderful person I have ever known," Dodo said. "He was strong, clever, good-natured. He knew how to have a good time, how to be gay, how to give people pleasure." It seemed to Clarence that Dodo blushed when she saw him looking at her.

"Who are you?" Dodo suddenly said to him. "Are you terribly brilliant, and all that?"

"Yes, I must confess I am," Clarence replied, with an elaborate flourish of self-mockery. "I am very frightening with my great brilliance."

Dodo did not laugh. She was as free of irony as a doll. A mind like that, Clarence thought giddily, lives by sheer superstition. Dodo's eyes remained upon him. She was archaic, quaint, and yet not really eccentric. Clarence decided it would be agreeable if she turned out to love Jane Austen, or even Trollope. But his sanity soon returned and he sullenly reminded himself that privileged persons no longer had hobbies like Jane Austen. Daddy Babcock would never have spent an evening—or an hour—with Roman history. The Babcocks' culture, such as it was, was thin and vulgar, and prodigiously indolent. Clarence's irritation mounted, but it did not center on Dodo so much as on her group—or what was once her group. Dodo's haughty, grim helplessness saved her. The old purple dress and the runner in her stocking somehow brought her back to the possible. At least she was a failure! And at the same time a challenge, subtly touching the vein of competition that throbbed in Clarence's soul. The smile Dodo gave him was sweet, hesitant, wondering. He observed that he and she were not at ease with each other, and this signified to him the possibility of sexual drama—the painful and promising period of courtship and discovery. Clarence felt bold. He said, in a harsh, uncaring voice, "Do you like chamber music, Miss Babcock?"

"I adore it," Dodo said, clasping her hands and looking at Willard and Henrietta as if she had scored a triumph and meant to be congratulated. They gave no sign of encouragement, but Dodo let the disappointment pass. She did not know that though she had been asked with Clarence for the evening, she was not particularly asked to admire him.

"Would you like to go with me to hear three fine instrumentalists perform some trios next week?" said Clarence. "The 'Archduke,' for one, and some Mozart, I think. The full program escapes me."

"I'd adore it," Dodo said.

"Good!" Clarence said.

Henrietta looked at him with a twisted grin. Willard coughed. Clarence now felt he could leave the Nesbitts to their post-mortem conversation. He could leave dramatically, on his own terms, giving as fit payment for the evening's invitation the little bit of confusion, wonder, and mystery that his determination to continue the friendship with Dodo meant for the Nesbitts. Looking at his watch, he exclaimed gaily that it was a quarter to eleven. With great gentleness and delicacy, he offered Dodo a taxi ride, which she accepted. The Nesbitts were quiet.

At the door, Clarence took his time. He paused reflectively, to round out his conversation with Willard. "There is certainly a question of just how much encouragement we want to give the new era in education, which I have called the Divinity School Era," he said slowly. "I, for one, am not absolutely certain that it is an advance on the Teachers College Age."

"Perhaps not," Willard said limply. "The only thing that can be said for it is that a lot of persons will be forced to take New Testament Greek."

"Some comfort but not enough," Clarence said, giving his arm to Dodo and disappearing down the stairs.

Alone, the Nesbitts were crestfallen. "That was sort of boring," Henrietta said. She poured herself a brandy and shrugged when Willard refused one.

"Clarence is terribly irritating," Willard said savagely. "Somehow, I keep forgetting just how provoking his personality can be. He's too cold and at the same time too intense—a tiresome, disturbing combination. I don't know why I ever had the dull idea of having him here. We didn't even *owe* him! Of course, no one owes him, because he never invites anyone."

"What did you think of Dodo?" Henrietta said, dreamily sipping her brandy. "She seemed delighted with Clarence—at least delighted for *her*. She's not very demonstrative, but the poor girl is susceptible. *Quite,* I can tell you."

"I thought Dodo was the same," Willard said crossly. "But I must say that if she is attracted to Clarence, then she has deteriorated since the last time I saw her. She used to have more sense. It would be absolutely unbearable if that ass Anderson started to escort Dodo about. I thought it was very speedy of him to make the engagement for that damned concert right here, the first meeting."

"I don't know that I agree," Henrietta said, her eyes glinting mischievously. The brandy was having its effect. "Dodo is lonely. She must be. And Clarence is plausible to a degree that is positively frightening."

"He'd only be using that foolish Dodo to vex us. I know him! I don't relish the idea of Clarence as a part of the family, let me tell you—not even as a part by nothing more than friendship with Dodo. Not even that! The whole thing is exasperating!"

"Just exactly why, pet?" Henrietta insisted, with a bit of hoarseness, giving her husband that look of bone-and-blood superiority he had learned to dread. "Dodo is not likely to marry anyone—at least so far as I can predict. You can never tell about what are called the middle years, though. Of course, she turned down a number of quite soundly eligible persons in her very young days. And don't you forget it!"

"Why should I forget it?"

"Well, I mean her situation, her single blessedness, is due to a certain overreaching of ambition and expectation at an earlier date. It is not that she was unmarriageable, by any means. You never know what odd person—what shy girl—will turn out to be difficult to please in the most outrageous and inexplicable way. Her sister Jeannine, a great beauty and wildly popular, was not like that at all. She married at twenty-one, and while Emory is perfectly sweet, he's nothing to write home about so far as money, birth, personal charm, or even achievement is concerned!"

"Poor Emory!" Willard said. He was extremely annoyed with Henrietta. If anything, she disliked Clarence more than he did!

"I'd loathe having Clarence Anderson seeing a lot of Dodo. Simply loathe it," Henrietta continued, gathering steam. "He is not a bijou. Not for my money."

"Maybe that is exactly what he is, at least to some people. Ugh!" Willard said.

"But, loathe it as I would," Henrietta went on briskly, "I think, from their point of view, they might have a pleasant time together occasionally. Concerts, little dinners, a play. Not too frequently, just once in a while."

"You've got it all worked out. Anyone would think you were directing them in a movie."

Henrietta was hardly listening. "I always think of poor Dodo in the theatrical way I last saw her on her own ground, in that dreary, soiled little flat of hers. It's a frightful place, and somehow made all the worse because of bits of heavenly things here and there, all chipped and dusty and battered. The final tableau was wonderful: there was Dodo in an ancient wrapper eating a sandwich of canned meat, sitting under the portrait of Grandfather Perry Babcock, who made three million out West before he was twenty-five—all those years ago."

"Clarence will adore that note, I assure you. Nothing will escape him, and his additions to the scene will be epical. If he chooses to do so, he can manage to turn Dodo's poverty into a great spiritual principle. A sort of Christian Socialist impulse will be found to lie behind the waste and poor management."

"Darling," Henrietta interrupted, "there's one thing I believe should be cleared up. By your standards and Clarence's, Dodo isn't poor! She has, unearned, at least three or four thousand dollars a year. Unearned and for life, bar the revolution. That isn't *poor*, really. It's just poor to Dodo."

"Yes, I suppose she has something," Willard conceded irritably. "But, with her, what is unearned is all there is. She couldn't *earn* her carfare. That three or four thousand is all she'll ever have. With taxes, and so on, I can imagine Dodo feels pretty strapped and worries quite a bit about the future."

"How do you know that's all she'll ever have? You have much less imagination than our dear Clarence."

"How do you know Clarence has imagination about what Dodo will have—or has, for that matter?"

Henrietta lit a cigarette and resumed with a knowledgeable air, "At least, Clarence wouldn't be so positive about a thing like that. He wouldn't consider Dodo or her prospects mummified. Don't forget, Mr. Professor, rich people, well-connected people, are always inheriting a little bit here and there. Sometimes more than a little bit will come from an utterly unexpected source—and a greater delight human society cannot offer. Yet sometimes from an expected source nothing comes, or much less than might have. That scars your very soul, believe me. . . . But don't count out any Babcock while a single branch of the family is as filthy rich as Uncle Wink!"

Henrietta was soaring into her most lofty sphere. "In the thirties, when all the so-called clever people were making so much fun of Ford and Rockefeller and Uncle Wink, I felt, without daring to utter it, that times would change, the swing would come. Right now, I don't know a single damned sociologist who wouldn't be beside himself with joy at the thought of dining with Uncle Wink and Aunt Bea! And the conversation would be a lot more diverting than what one hears at the Faculty Club, I can assure you. I don't deny that it would be different—lighter—but that light sort of thing can, in its own way, be original and interesting. And, above all, gay! God, the charm of a sense of gaiety!"

These aggrieved moods appalled Willard. He felt defenseless, embarrassed, accused. Henrietta struck this note only when she had had too much to drink, and the mood and the language—even the feelings—vanished with the return to full sobriety. And yet how distressing the words were, how resentful, how disappointed and unpredictable! Just beneath the surface of Henrietta's amiable, witty, and nervous temperament lay this sewer of narrowness and disillusion. Willard shrank from the moments when it was exposed to him. He hated himself for having clumsily allowed himself to be somehow paired with Clarence Anderson in Henrietta's intoxicated dialogue. Her grudging, preaching, outlandish statements seemed to be meant for both men alike. It was a relief to know that in the morning she would mercilessly make fun of Clarence and praise her husband.

Henrietta was reaching her big scene. She began, as usual, to repeat her refrain. "I find myself overcome with admiration for you academic people—"

"Really, dear?" Willard injected in a vanishing voice.

"Yes, utter admiration. How you talk about things with such godlike assurance! How you give forth on matters you have never experienced! Ideas flow like wine—everything out of books and other people's lectures, nothing from actual life! People write *books* on the psychology of the upper classes who have only read other books on the upper classes, or on the peasants—it's all the same—or on Negroes, any subject you like. There is always someone with the courage to talk or write on any topic under the sun. The brave teacher is always to be found!" Her voice dropped. "And now I suppose our good friend Clarence will join you in the fascinating analysis of the great Middle Western fortunes—in the authoritative statement on the Chicago robber barons!"

Willard shivered. He picked up his book, kissed Henrietta on the cheek, and retired to his bedroom. Thoughts and dreams of Clarence Anderson tormented his sleep.

FIRST MARRIAGE

❖

St. Clair McKelway

WHENEVER I start writing seriously about myself (he said) a small ground force composed of the kind of men who fought at Thermopylae makes an effort to surround and contain me. These men are not equipped with the weapons I carry. I am facing them alone, but I have, so to speak, a shoulder holster in which is lodged a .45. In the pockets of my jacket are two grenades. And in my briefcase is an automatic rifle that can be assembled and put to use as easily as a fishing rod. There are no shells in the .45 or in the automatic rifle, and the grenades do not have any high explosive in them. Mine are empty weapons, but my antagonists don't know this. Not looking at them—but aware that they are looking at me— I put on a silent demonstration. I set up the automatic rifle, I take the .45 and twirl it once or twice, I juggle the grenades from hand to hand. And soon I am left alone. Then I cease to be a prestidigitator and go on writing about myself. There is no further interference. I usually write in the study of my home, in North Stamford. I mean to say that on the extremely rare occasions when I write about myself I usually do it there. My monthly reports as chief trust officer of the bank, my annual reports to the board of directors, my public speeches, my business correspondence—and even most of my personal correspondence—are written or dictated at the main office downtown, of course. What I'm talking about are these things I sometimes write in my study at home. When I finish them, I read them once, tear them up, and burn them in the fireplace. We've got this long trip to Chicago ahead of us, and you're my second-in-command, my first assistant at the bank, so I'm your superior, so to speak. After a while, you'll go to your roomette and go to sleep and I'll stay in this drawing room and go to sleep, but right now I want to tell you about what I wrote the other evening in my study on the general subject of my first marriage. Some of what

I've already told you is exactly the way I wrote it down. But mostly I'll be telling you *about* what I wrote that evening, not *what* I wrote. In any case, I have the floor, as you might say, and we don't need to talk any more about how to handle the deal tomorrow. We can't fail if we play it safe, and that's what we're going to do. We've been over the whole thing. The hell with it until tomorrow.

I was twenty and she was twenty. We were precocious, and we thought we were experienced. I had gone to work for the bank and she had been to Goucher, but hadn't graduated, and had come to New York to start learning how to be a fashion designer. She was determined to be a fashion designer. I didn't know why then and I still don't know why. The other evening, I wrote down a great deal about her mother and father and sisters and the one brother, and I wrote a lot about my family, but none of it seems pertinent now. Suffice it to say that we both came from what used to be called the genteel poor. That meant our fathers made around five thousand a year and were thinking about getting a motorcar when we were in the Boy Scouts or the Camp Fire Girls, before this country got into the First World War. Anyway, I didn't turn out as I then thought I would turn out, and she didn't go on with the plans she had when I first met her. I run into her once in a great while these days, at some big party or in some restaurant—once in two or three years, maybe. We never really quarrelled, you see.

Needless to say, we have both changed a lot. We've changed almost as much as the building in which we had our first apartment. It was on Sheridan Square, down in Greenwich Village. It was a four-story brick building, an old private residence, wide enough to have three windows across the front on the upper floors. On the ground floor was a cafeteria. Our newest branch office opened there a few weeks ago, as you know—or at least you know we opened the new branch on Sheridan Square a few weeks ago. The branch bank is on the ground floor now, and the trust department of that branch is on the second floor. The bookkeeping department is on the third floor. I don't know what's on the top floor.

The building wasn't torn down when the bank decided to take it over. It was remodelled. The shell or skeleton or whatever you call it is the same as it always was. As you know, I haven't visited every single one of our branch offices in Manhattan. I haven't had time to, and there was no need for it. I didn't even know this new branch was in that building until I saw it out of a taxicab window the other day—last Tuesday—when I was riding down Seventh Avenue after the convention lunch at the Astor. But I recognized it. A couple of blocks after I'd recognized it, I told the cabdriver to pull over to the curb. I paid him off and walked back and went up in an automatic elevator to the second floor. There wasn't any elevator in the place when we lived there, of course. Some young fellow I've met at annual meetings spoke to me when I got out at the second floor, and I told him I'd just happened to be passing by and thought I'd drop in and see the new branch's trust department. He was very pleased, and showed me around, talking a blue streak all the time. I have no idea what he said.

The building wasn't very deep from front to back, and it isn't any deeper now. Where the trust department is—that was where our first apartment was. On the second floor. The woodwork is all gone, and the marble fireplace is gone. The fireplace was in the living room. In addition to the living room, there was a kind of alcove, where our bed was—a studio couch, double-size—and there was a bathroom and a kitchen, both very small. When we moved in, the woodwork had at some time in the past been painted white and it needed repainting. We painted it ourselves—the heavy doors, the wide window frames and window seats, the built-in bookcases on either side of the fireplace, the arch between the living room and the alcove. And the floors, of course. We painted the floors black and the heavy old doors black, and we painted all the rest of the woodwork orange. The walls were in good enough shape and didn't need to be painted. They were covered with stuff of a grayish, brownish shade known in those days as oatmeal wallpaper. It had a rough texture and was very durable. The walls didn't seem very important anyway. The woodwork was what was important, and the way we painted it I suppose I'd think it was fantastic now, but it looked fine then. It was very satisfactory. She thought the whole place looked beautiful. I didn't use that word much. I often told her she was beautiful, and she was, but otherwise I didn't use that word much. All this, you understand, was quite some years ago. To be exact, it was in 1925.

One reason we didn't think it necessary to paint the walls was that the bookcases covered one main wall of the living room and on the other main wall, opposite the fireplace and the bookcases, we tacked up a large piece of batik. B-a-t-i-k, but pronounced as if it were spelled b-a-t-e-e-k. That was a kind of cloth material. It was supposed to come from India or Ceylon or the Dutch East Indies or somewhere out there. This material was woven in its natural color, of course—cream-colored, I guess. Then the natives out there would dye it. The way they did that, they would brush wax over the part or parts of the material they didn't want to be colored by the dye in the first tub of dye, and then they would dip the whole piece in. Then, after it had dried out, they would get the wax off the undyed parts with boiling water, and then they'd put some wax on the parts that had been dyed in the first tub of dye and dip the whole thing in the second tub of dye—except that, before doing that, they'd have put wax on some of the undyed parts as well as the parts already dyed. Then, in the same way, they'd use a third and maybe a fourth tub of dye. This process gave batik an interesting design when they were all through dyeing it. She told me all about how it was done. Our batik that we tacked on the wall opposite the fireplace and the bookcases was mostly a terra-cotta shade of red, with some yellow and some dark brown or black here and there. She thought it was beautiful and I liked it, too. In fact, I was extremely fond of it. The orange and black woodwork made the room gay, and the batik made it warm and soft. It was a very popular material. Everybody we knew in the Village had a piece of it on at least one wall of their living room. Then, as now, of course, a great many people who were neither artists nor writers lived down there. We knew two or three people who said they were artists and one chap who said he was a writer and another who said he was a poet, and we knew several newspaper reporters, both male and female, but most of our friends were young men who worked in Wall Street or in advertising agencies—or in the bank, of course—and young girls who worked in Wanamaker's or somewhere like that, or were still studying at Columbia, or ran little shops or something. We hadn't known anybody in New York very long at the time of our marriage, because she was brought up in Rochester and my family came from around Trenton, and I'd been brought up there, of course. As a matter of fact, most of the people we knew were people we'd met in speakeasies—except for a couple of chaps I'd become friends with at the bank. From any number of different aspects, it must have been an entirely different sort of thing, being in the Village in 1925, than what it must be like now. But, on the other hand, I don't really know anything about what it's like now. To be twenty, I mean—down there or anywhere else. My oldest daughter's only seventeen, and besides, she and the two boys live in North Stamford, naturally. You've met my present wife, of course.

In the Village in those days, as I say, we met most of the people we knew in speakeasies, but we weren't particularly interested in knowing other people, no matter where we met them. We were always talking to each other about ourselves, about our thoughts and ambitions, about our dreams. Or so I wrote the other night. We talked a lot to each other about our pasts—all sorts of details, the smallest details, things that had happened to us before we met. We didn't exactly talk like married people. We talked like very young people, and yet we were married. Her face was young and bright and I guess mine was, too, and we were always laughing or looking very solemn. We would laugh, for example, at things in a book called "Crome Yellow," by Aldous Huxley, or at something H. L. Mencken had written in the *American Mercury*. And we would look solemn when she read aloud to me, or I read aloud to her, the poems of Rupert Brooke or Edna St. Vincent Millay. I hadn't thought of those names for years, and I would have sworn I didn't remember them, but the other night when I was writing in my study they came to my mind as easily as the hours of departure of express trains to Stamford from Grand Central. We laughed and looked solemn at all the wonderful things we discovered together, and we never thought of ever being old or of ever being dead. There were just the two of us in all the world, and we were neither for it nor against it, we were just going through it together. We talked as I imagine a couple of very serene philosophers might talk to each other when they sit together on a terrace overlooking a mountain valley. We never argued. We discussed. And neither of us tried to come out ahead, neither of us tried to win, because our hearts were full of truth, and the truth in our hearts was the same truth.

This writing seriously about myself is a very peculiar thing, and that's the reason why I always tear up what I've written and burn it, after I've read it through once. But some of it stays in my mind. When I am writing in this fashion, I put things down I don't know the meaning of, don't even pretend to know the meaning of. Walking around that second floor of the branch bank on Sheridan Square last Tuesday, looking for something that had moved away, I knew I'd be writing that evening in my study about this first marriage. What I told you about the men at Thermopylae is exactly what I wrote when I first sat down to write that evening, and that's an example of what I mean when I say these things I write on these rare occasions are peculiar, very strange.

Something just comes out, like the Thermopylae men and all that stuff. I don't know anything about who fought at Thermopylae, whether they were Spartans or Athenians or what, but it popped out of my ball-point pen, and so did a lot of other things I don't know the meaning of. And a lot of these things I can't remember again now, and I suppose I will never be able to remember them again. I felt solemn when I was writing that evening, but not what I'd call sad. I felt something like the way we used to feel when we looked solemn because of things we'd seen or done together. I haven't told you a fraction even of what I remember now of what I wrote then, and what I wrote then was only a fraction of everything that happened, but it's getting late, and I guess we'd better have one for the road and call it a night. One for the road. One for the railroad, the New York Central Railroad.

Of course, I set down a good many pages concerning the end of our marriage and why we thought we'd better get the divorce, and I remember all that now, but when you come right down to it none of it makes any real sense. There wasn't anything embarrassingly personal about it or anything like that, but it just seems to have no significance, whereas some of the other things I put down and have forgotten and even some of the things I remember now and have told you about seem to mean something. Of course, almost everybody we knew in those days got a divorce, sooner or later, one way or another, and I wouldn't be surprised if most of those divorces were as foolish, really, as ours was. It was the fashion in those days, and I guess it's gotten to be something more than a fashion in these days. Or maybe conditions are improving in that direction now. I don't know. Our marriage lasted not quite three years, and we didn't have any children, although she had some later on and so did I.

I used to tell her there was nobody like her in the whole wide world, and she used to tell me the same thing, and, you know, I think in a way we were both right? At that time, in that place, there were just the two of us. And each of us was unique as far as the other was concerned. For a long time, there was nobody else in my life and there was nobody else in her life. When other people got into my life later on, it wasn't the life I had then that they were getting into. That life had moved on. When it was there, on Sheridan Square, nobody else could possibly have gotten into it. I think it was the same with her. We danced on rooftops. All over New York, and even at the Bossert, on Brooklyn Heights, there were bands on the tops of hotels, playing music for us to dance to. And we were married. Although, as I said, I wrote all the facts down along with everything else the other evening, I don't know what happened to that marriage. She used to quote a poem by a Frenchman, and one line of it was "Where are the snows of yesteryear?" She used to say the beautiful thing about that line was that the poet wasn't saying the snows of yesteryear had melted or disappeared, he was saying that the snows of yesteryear are still somewhere—unchanged, just as they were—and he's asking only to be told where they can be found. That was the first thing I remembered when I stepped off the elevator on the second floor of that building on Sheridan Square last Tuesday. She had bobbed hair and bangs that curled over her forehead and she had a mischievous smile along with her other smiles. Mildred Hastings. Milly.

THE COUNTRY HUSBAND

❖

JOHN CHEEVER

To begin at the beginning, the airplane from Minneapolis in which Francis Weed was travelling East ran into heavy weather. The sky had been a hazy blue, with the clouds below the plane lying so close together that nothing could be seen of the earth. Then mist began to form outside the windows, and they flew into a white cloud of such density that it reflected the exhaust fires. The color of the cloud darkened to gray, and the plane began to rock. Francis had been in heavy weather before, but he had never been shaken up so much. The man in the seat beside him pulled a flask out of his pocket and took a drink. Francis smiled at his neighbor, but the man looked away; he wasn't sharing his painkiller with anyone. The plane had begun to drop and flounder wildly. A child was crying. The air in the cabin was overheated and stale, and Francis' left foot went to sleep. He read a little from a paper book that he had bought at the airport, but the violence of the storm divided his attention. It was black outside the ports. The exhaust fires blazed and shed sparks in the dark, and, inside, the shaded lights, the stuffiness, and the window curtains gave the cabin an atmosphere of intense and misplaced domesticity. Then the lights flickered and went out. "You know what I've always wanted to do?" the man beside Francis said suddenly. "I've always wanted to buy a farm in New Hampshire and raise beef cattle." The stewardess announced that they were going to make an emergency landing. All but the child saw in their minds the spreading wings of the Angel of Death. The pilot could be heard singing faintly, "I've got sixpence, jolly, jolly sixpence. I've got sixpence to last me all my life . . ." There was no other sound.

The loud groaning of the hydraulic valves swallowed up the pilot's song, and there was a shrieking high in the air, like automobile brakes, and the plane hit flat on its belly in a cornfield and shook them so violently that an old man up forward howled, "Me kidneys! Me kidneys!" The stewardess flung open the door, and someone opened an emergency door at the back, letting in the sweet noise of their continuing mortality—the idle splash and smell of a heavy rain. Anxious for their lives, they filed out of the doors and scattered over the cornfield in all directions, praying that the thread would hold. It did. Nothing happened. When it was clear that the plane would not burn or explode, the crew and the stewardess gathered the passengers together and led them to the shelter of a barn. They were not far from Philadelphia, and in a little while a string of taxis took them into the city. "It's just like the Marne," someone said, but there was surprisingly little relaxation of that suspiciousness with which many Americans regard their fellow-travellers.

In Philadelphia, Francis Weed got a train to New York. At the end of that journey, he crossed the city and caught, just as it was about to pull out, the commuting train that he took five nights a week to his home in Shady Hill.

He sat with Trace Bearden. "You know, I was in that plane that just crashed outside Philadelphia," he said. "We came down in a field . . ." He had travelled faster than the newspapers or the rain, and the weather in New York was sunny and mild. It was a day in late September, as fragrant and shapely as an apple. Trace listened to the story, but how could he get excited? Francis had no powers that would let him re-create a brush with death—particularly in the atmosphere of a commuting train, journeying through a sunny countryside where already, in the slum gardens, there were signs of harvest. Trace picked up his newspaper, and Francis was left alone with his thoughts. He said good night to Trace on the platform at Shady Hill and drove in his second-hand Volkswagen up to the Blenhollow neighborhood, where he lived.

The Weeds' Dutch Colonial house was larger than it appeared to be from the driveway. The living room was spacious and divided like Gaul into three parts. Around an ell to the left as one entered from the vestibule was the long table, laid for six, with candles and a bowl of fruit in the center. The sounds and smells that came from the open kitchen door were appetizing, for Julia Weed was a good cook. The largest part of the living room centered around a fireplace. On the right were some bookshelves and a piano. The room was polished and tranquil, and from the windows that opened to the west there was some late-summer sunlight, brilliant and as clear as water. Nothing here was neglected; nothing had not been burnished. It was not the kind of household where, after prying open a stuck cigarette box, you would find an old shirt button and a tarnished nickel. The hearth was swept, the roses on the piano were reflected in the polish of the broad top, and there was an album of Schubert waltzes on the rack. Louisa Weed, a pretty girl of nine, was looking out the western windows. Her younger brother Henry was standing beside her. Her still younger brother, Toby, was studying the figures of some tonsured monks drinking beer on the polished brass of the wood box. Francis, taking off his hat and putting down his paper, was not consciously pleased with the scene; he was not that reflective. It was his element, his creation, and he returned to it with that sense of lightness and strength with which any creature returns to its home. "Hi, everybody," he said. "The plane from Minneapolis . . ."

Nine times out of ten, Francis would be greeted with affection, but tonight the children are absorbed in their own antagonisms. Francis has not finished his sentence about the plane crash before Henry plants a kick in Louisa's behind. Louisa swings around, saying, "*Damn* you!" Francis makes the mistake of scolding Louisa for bad language before he punishes Henry. Now Louisa turns on her father and accuses him of favoritism. Henry is always right; she is persecuted and lonely; her lot is hopeless. Francis turns to his son, but the boy has justification for the kick—she hit him first; she hit him on the ear, which is dangerous. Louisa agrees with this passionately. She hit him on the ear, and she *meant* to hit him on the ear, because he messed up her china collection. Henry says that this is a lie. Little Toby turns away from the wood box to throw in some evidence for Louisa. Henry claps his hand over little Toby's mouth. Francis separates the two boys but accidentally pushes Toby into the wood box. Toby begins to cry. Louisa is already crying. Just then, Julia Weed comes into that part of the room where the table is laid. She is a pretty, intelligent woman, and the white in her hair is premature. She does not seem to notice the fracas. "Hello, darling," she says serenely to Francis. "Wash your hands, everyone. Dinner is ready." She strikes a match and lights the six candles in this vale of tears.

This simple announcement, like the war cries of the Scottish chieftains, only refreshes the ferocity of the combatants. Louisa gives Henry a blow on the shoulder. Henry, although he seldom cries, has pitched nine innings and is tired. He bursts into tears. Little Toby discovers a splinter in his hand and begins to howl. Francis says loudly that he has been in a plane crash and that he is tired. Julia appears again, from the kitchen, and, still ignoring the chaos, asks Francis to go upstairs and tell Helen that everything is ready. Francis is happy to go; it is like getting back to headquarters company. He is planning to tell his oldest daughter about the airplane crash, but Helen is lying on her bed reading a *True Romance* magazine, and the first thing Francis does is to take the magazine from her hand and remind Helen that he has forbidden her to buy it. She did not buy it, Helen replies. It was given to her by her best friend, Bessie Black. Everybody reads *True Romance*. Bessie Black's father reads *True Romance*. There isn't a girl in Helen's class who doesn't read *True Romance*. Francis expresses his detestation of the magazine and then tells her that dinner is ready—although from the sounds downstairs it doesn't seem so. Helen follows him down the stairs. Julia has seated herself in the candlelight and spread a napkin over her lap. Neither Louisa nor Henry has come to the table. Little Toby is still howling, lying face down on the floor. Francis speaks to him gently: "Daddy was in a plane crash this afternoon, Toby. Don't you want to hear about it?" Toby goes on crying. "If you don't come to the table now, Toby," Francis says, "I'll have to send you to bed without any supper." The little boy rises, gives him a cutting look, flies up the stairs to his bedroom, and slams the door. "Oh dear," Julia says, and starts to go after him. Francis says that she will spoil him. Julia says that Toby is ten pounds underweight and has to be encouraged to eat. Winter is coming, and he will spend the cold months in bed unless he has his dinner. Julia goes upstairs. Francis sits down at the table with Helen. Helen is suffering from the dismal feeling of having read too intently on a fine day, and she gives her father and the room a jaded look. She doesn't understand about the plane crash, because there wasn't a drop of rain in Shady Hill.

Julia returns with Toby, and they all sit down and are served. "Do I have to look at that big, fat slob?" Henry says, of Louisa. Everybody but Toby enters into this skirmish, and it rages up and down the table for five minutes. Toward the end, Henry puts his napkin over his head and, trying to eat that way, spills spinach all over his shirt. Francis asks Julia if the children couldn't have their dinner earlier. Julia's guns are loaded for this. She can't cook two dinners and lay two tables. She paints with lightning strokes that panorama of drudgery in which her youth, her beauty, and her wit have been lost. Francis says that he must be understood; he was nearly killed in an airplane crash, and he doesn't like to come home every night to a battlefield. Now Julia is deeply committed. Her voice trembles. He doesn't come home every night to a battlefield. The accusation is stupid and mean. Everything was tranquil until he arrived. She stops speaking, puts down her knife and fork, and looks into her plate as if it is a gulf. She begins to cry. "Poor Mummy!" Toby says, and when Julia gets up from the table, drying her tears with a napkin, Toby goes to her side. "Poor Mummy," he says. "Poor Mummy!" And they climb the stairs together. The other children drift away from the battlefield, and Francis goes into the back garden for a cigarette and some air.

It was a pleasant garden, with walks and flower beds and places to sit. The sunset had nearly burned out, but there was still plenty of light. Put into a thoughtful mood by the crash and the battle, Francis listened to the evening sounds of Shady Hill. "Varmits! Rascals!" old Mr. Nixon shouted to the squirrels in his bird-feeding station. "Avaunt and quit my sight!" A door slammed. Someone was playing tennis on the Babcocks' court; someone was cutting grass. Then Donald Goslin, who lived at the corner, began to play the "Moonlight Sonata." He did this nearly every night. He threw the tempo out the window and played it *rubato* from beginning to end, like an outpouring of tearful petulance, lonesomeness, and self-pity—of everything it was Beethoven's greatness not to know. The music rang up and down the street beneath the trees like an appeal for love, for tenderness, aimed at some lonely housemaid— some fresh-faced, homesick girl from Galway, looking at old snapshots in her third-floor room. "Here, Jupiter, here, Jupiter," Francis called to the Mercers' retriever. Jupiter crashed through the tomato vines with the remains of a felt hat in his mouth.

Jupiter was an anomaly. His retrieving instincts and his high spirits were out of place in Shady Hill. He was as black as coal, with a long, alert, intelligent, rakehell face. His eyes gleamed with mischief, and he held his head high. It was the fierce, heavily collared dog's head that appears in heraldry, in tapestry, and that used to appear on umbrella handles and walking sticks. Jupiter went where he pleased, ransacking wastebaskets, clotheslines, garbage pails, and shoe bags. He broke up garden parties and tennis matches, and got

mixed up in the processional at Christ's Church on Sunday, barking
at the men in red dresses. He crashed through old Mr. Nixon's rose
garden two or three times a day, cutting a wide swath through the
Condesa de Sastagos, and as soon as Donald Goslin lighted his
barbecue fire on Thursday nights, Jupiter would get the scent.
Nothing the Goslins did could drive him away. Sticks and stones
and rude commands only moved him to the edge of the terrace,
where he remained, with his gallant and heraldic muzzle, waiting
for Donald Goslin to turn his back and reach for the salt. Then he
would spring onto the terrace, lift the steak lightly off the fire, and
run away with the Goslins' dinner. Jupiter's days were numbered.
The Wrightsons' German gardener or the Farquarsons' cook would
soon poison him. Even old Mr. Nixon might put some arsenic in
the garbage that Jupiter loved. "Here, Jupiter, Jupiter!" Francis
called, but the dog pranced off, shaking the hat in his white teeth.
Looking in at the windows of his house, Francis saw that Julia had
come down and was blowing out the candles.

Julia and Francis Weed went out a great deal. Julia was well
liked and gregarious, and her love of parties sprang from a most
natural dread of chaos and loneliness. She went through her morning mail with real anxiety, looking for invitations, and she usually
found some, but she was insatiable, and if she had gone out seven
nights a week, it would not have cured her of a reflective look—the
look of someone who hears distant music—for she would always
suppose that there was a more brilliant party somewhere else.
Francis limited her to two week-night parties, putting a flexible
interpretation on Friday, and rode through the weekend like a
dory in a gale. The day after the airplane crash, the Weeds were
to have dinner with the Farquarsons.

Francis got home late from town, and Julia got the sitter while
he dressed, and then hurried him out of the house. The party was
small and pleasant, and Francis settled down to enjoy himself. A
new maid passed the drinks. Her hair was dark, and her face was
round and pale and seemed familiar to Francis. He had not developed his memory as a sentimental faculty. Wood smoke, lilac,
and other such perfumes did not stir him, and his memory was
something like his appendix—a vestigial repository. It was not his
limitation at all to be unable to escape the past; it was perhaps his
limitation that he had escaped it so successfully. He might have
seen the maid at other parties, he might have seen her taking a

walk on Sunday afternoons, but in either case he would not be searching his memory now. Her face was, in a wonderful way, a moon face—Norman or Irish—but it was not beautiful enough to account for his feeling that he had seen her before, in circumstances that he ought to be able to remember. He asked Nellie Farquarson who she was. Nellie said that the maid had come through an agency, and that her home was Trénon, in Normandy—a small place with a church and a restaurant that Nellie had once visited. While Nellie talked on about her travels abroad, Francis realized where he had seen the woman before. It had been at the end of the war. He had left a replacement depot with some other men and taken a three-day pass in Trénon. On their second day, they had walked out to a crossroads to see the public chastisement of a young woman who had lived with the German commandant during the Occupation.

It was a cool morning in the fall. The sky was overcast, and poured down onto the dirt crossroads a very discouraging light. They were on high land and could see how like one another the shapes of the clouds and the hills were as they stretched off toward the sea. The prisoner arrived sitting on a three-legged stool in a farm cart. She stood by the cart while the mayor read the accusation and the sentence. Her head was bent and her face was set in that empty half smile behind which the whipped soul is suspended. When the mayor was finished, she undid her hair and let it fall across her back. A little man with a gray mustache cut off her hair with shears and dropped it on the ground. Then, with a bowl of soapy water and a straight razor, he shaved her skull clean. A woman approached and began to undo the fastenings of her clothes, but the prisoner pushed her aside and undressed herself. When she pulled her chemise over her head and threw it on the ground, she was naked. The women jeered; the men were still. There was no change in the falseness or the plaintiveness of the prisoner's smile. The cold wind made her white skin rough and hardened the nipples of her breasts. The jeering ended gradually, put down by the recognition of their common humanity. One woman spat on her, but some inviolable grandeur in her nakedness lasted through the ordeal. When the crowd was quiet, she turned—she had begun to cry—and, with nothing on but a pair of worn black shoes and stockings, walked down the dirt road alone away from the village. The round white face had aged a little, but there was no question but that the maid who passed his cocktails and later served Francis his dinner was the woman who had been punished at the crossroads.

The war seemed now so distant and that world where the cost of partisanship had been death or torture so long ago. Francis had lost track of the men who had been with him in Vésey. He could not count on Julia's discretion. He could not tell anyone. And if he had told the story now, at the dinner table, it would have been a social as well as a human error. The people in the Farquarsons' living room seemed united in their tacit claim that there had been no past, no war—that there was no danger or trouble in the world. In the recorded history of human arrangements, this extraordinary meeting would have fallen into place, but the atmosphere of Shady Hill made the memory unseemly and impolite. The prisoner withdrew after passing the coffee, but the encounter left Francis feeling languid; it had opened his memory and his senses, and left them dilated. He and Julia drove home when the party ended, and Julia went into the house. Francis stayed in the car to take the sitter home.

Expecting to see Mrs. Henlein, the old lady who usually stayed with the children, he was surprised when a young girl opened the door and came out onto the lighted stoop. She stayed in the light to count her textbooks. She was frowning and beautiful. Now, the world is full of beautiful young girls, but Francis saw here the difference between beauty and perfection. All those endearing flaws, moles, birthmarks, and healed wounds were missing, and he experienced in his consciousness that moment when music breaks glass, and felt a pang of recognition as strange, deep, and wonderful as anything in his life. It hung from her frown, from an impalpable darkness in her face—a look that impressed him as a direct appeal for love. When she had counted her books, she came down the steps and opened the car door. In the light, he saw that her cheeks were wet. She got in and shut the door.

"You're new," Francis said.

"Yes. Mrs. Henlein is sick. I'm Anne Murchison."

"Did the children give you any trouble?"

"Oh, no, no." She turned and smiled at him unhappily in the dim dashboard light. Her light hair caught on the collar of her jacket, and she shook her head to set it loose.

"You've been crying."

"Yes."

"I hope it was nothing that happened in our house."

"No, no, it was nothing that happened in your house." Her voice was bleak. "It's no secret. Everybody in the village knows. Daddy's an alcoholic, and he just called me from some saloon and gave me a piece of his mind. He thinks I'm immoral. He called just before Mrs. Weed came back."

"I'm sorry."

"Oh, *Lord!*" She gasped and began to cry. She turned toward Francis, and he took her in his arms and let her cry on his shoulder. She shook in his embrace, and this movement accentuated his sense of the fineness of her flesh and bone. The layers of their clothing felt thin, and when her shuddering began to diminish, it was so much like a paroxysm of love that Francis lost his head and pulled her roughly against him. She drew away. "I live on Belleview Avenue," she said. "You go down Lansing Street to the railroad bridge."

"All right." He started the car.

"You turn left at that traffic light. . . . Now you turn right here and go straight on toward the tracks."

The road Francis took brought him out of his own neighborhood, across the tracks, and toward the river, to a street where the near-poor lived, in houses whose peaked gables and trimmings of wooden lace conveyed the purest feelings of pride and romance, although the houses themselves could not have offered much privacy or comfort, they were all so small. The street was dark, and, stirred by the grace and beauty of the troubled girl, he seemed, in turning in to it, to have come into the deepest part of some submerged memory. In the distance, he saw a porch light burning. It was the only one, and she said that the house with the light was where she lived. When he stopped the car, he could see beyond the porch light into a dimly-lighted hallway with an old-fashioned clothes tree. "Well, here we are," he said, conscious that a young man would have said something different.

She did not move her hands from the books, where they were folded, and she turned and faced him. There were tears of lust in his eyes. Determinedly—not sadly—he opened the door on his side and walked around to open hers. He took her free hand, letting his fingers in between hers, climbed at her side the two concrete steps, and went up a narrow walk through a front garden where dahlias, marigolds, and roses—things that had withstood the light frosts—still bloomed, and made a bittersweet smell in the night air. At the steps, she freed her hand and then turned and kissed him swiftly. Then she crossed the porch and shut the door. The porch light went out, then the light in the hall. A second later, a light went on upstairs at the side of the house, shining into a tree that was still covered with leaves. It took her only a few minutes to undress and get into bed, and then the house was dark.

Julia was asleep when Francis got home. He opened a second window and got into bed to shut his eyes on that night, but as soon as they were shut—as soon as he had dropped off to sleep—the girl entered his mind, moving with perfect freedom through its shut doors and filling chamber after chamber with her light, her perfume, and the music of her voice. He was crossing the Atlantic with her on the old Mauretania and, later, living with her in Paris. When he woke from this dream, he got up and smoked a cigarette at the open window. Getting back into bed, he cast around in his mind for something he desired to do that would injure no one, and he thought of skiing. Up through the dimness in his mind rose the image of a mountain deep in snow. It was late in the day. Wherever his eyes looked, he saw broad and heartening things. Over his shoulder, there was a snow-filled valley, rising into wooded hills where the trees dimmed the whiteness like a sparse coat of hair. The cold deadened all sound but the loud, iron clanking of the lift machinery. The light on the trails was blue, and it was harder than it had been a minute or two earlier to pick the turns, harder to judge—now that the snow was all deep blue—the crust, the ice, the bare spots, and the deep piles of dry powder. Down the mountain he swung, matching his speed against the contours of a slope that had been formed in the first ice age, seeking with ardor some simplicity of feeling and circumstance. Night fell then, and he drank a Martini with some old friend in a dirty country bar.

In the morning, Francis' snow-covered mountain was gone, and he was left with his vivid memories of Paris and the Mauretania. He had been bitten gravely. He washed his body, shaved his jaws, drank his coffee, and missed the seven-thirty-one. The train pulled out just as he brought his car to the station, and the longing he felt for the coaches as they drew stubbornly away from him reminded him of the humors of love. He waited for the eight-two, on what was now an empty platform. It was a clear morning; the morning seemed thrown like a gleaming bridge of light over his mixed affairs. His spirits were feverish and high. The image of the girl seemed to put him into a relationship to the world that was mysterious and enthralling. Cars were beginning to fill up the parking lot, and he noticed that those that had driven down from the high land above Shady Hill were white with hoarfrost. This first clear sign of autumn thrilled him. An express train—a night train from Buffalo or Albany—came down the tracks between the platforms, and he saw that the roofs of the foremost cars were covered with a skin of ice. Struck by the miraculous physicalness of everything, he smiled at the passengers in the dining car, who could be seen eating eggs and wiping their mouths with napkins as they travelled. The sleeping-car compartments, with their soiled bed linen, trailed through the fresh morning like a string of rooming-house windows. Then he saw an extraordinary thing; at one of the bedroom windows sat an unclothed woman of exceptional beauty, combing her golden hair. She passed like an apparition through Shady Hill, combing and combing her hair, and Francis followed her with his eyes until she was out of sight. Then old Mrs. Wrightson joined him on the platform and began to talk.

"Well, I guess you must be surprised to see me here the third morning in a row," she said, "but because of my window curtains I'm becoming a regular commuter. The curtains I bought on Monday I returned on Tuesday, and the curtains I bought on Tuesday I'm returning today. On Monday, I got exactly what I wanted—it's a wool tapestry with roses and birds—but when I got them home, I found they were the wrong length. Well, I exchanged them yesterday, and when I got them home, I found they were still the wrong length. Now I'm praying to high Heaven that the decorator will have them in the right length, because you know my house, you *know* my living-room windows, and you can imagine what a problem they present. I don't know what to do with them."

"I know what to do with them," Francis said.

"What?"

"Paint them black on the inside, and shut up."

There was a gasp from Mrs. Wrightson, and Francis looked down at her to be sure that she knew he meant to be rude. She turned and walked away from him, so damaged in spirit that she limped. A wonderful feeling enveloped him, as if light were being shaken about him, and he thought again of Venus combing and combing her hair as she drifted through the Bronx. The realization of how many years had passed since he had enjoyed being deliberately impolite sobered him. Among his friends and neighbors, there were brilliant and gifted people—he saw that—but many of them, also, were bores and fools, and he had made the mistake of listening to them all with equal attention. He had confused a lack of discrimination with Christian love, and the confusion seemed general

and destructive. He was grateful to the girl for this bracing sensation of independence. Birds were singing—cardinals and the last of
the robins. The sky shone like enamel. Even the smell of ink from
his morning paper honed his appetite for life, and the world that
was spread out around him was plainly a paradise.

If Francis had believed in some hierarchy of love—in spirits
armed with hunting bows, in the capriciousness of Venus and Eros
—or even in magical potions, philtres, and stews, in scapulae and
quarters of the moon, it might have explained his susceptibility and
his feverish high spirits. The autumnal loves of middle age are well
publicized, and he guessed that he was face to face with one of these,
but there was not a trace of autumn in what he felt. He wanted to
sport in the green woods, scratch where he itched, and drink from
the same cup.

His secretary, Miss Rainey, was late that morning—she went to a
psychiatrist three mornings a week—and when she came in, Francis
wondered what advice a psychiatrist would have for him. But the
girl promised to bring back into his life something like the sound
of music. The realization that this music might lead him straight
to a trial for statutory rape at the county courthouse collapsed his
happiness. The photograph of his four children laughing into the
camera on the beach at Gay Head reproached him. On the letter-
head of his firm there was a drawing of the Laocoön, and the figure
of the priest and his sons in the coils of the snake appeared to him
to have the deepest meaning.

He had lunch with Pinky Trabert, who told him a couple of dirty
stories. At a conversational level, the mores of his friends were
robust and elastic, but he knew that the moral card house would
come down on them all—on Julia and the children as well—if he got
caught taking advantage of a baby-sitter. Looking back over the
recent history of Shady Hill for some precedent, he found there was
none. There was no turpitude; there had not been a divorce since
he lived there; there had not even been a breath of scandal. Things
seemed arranged with more propriety even than in the Kingdom of
Heaven. After leaving Pinky, Francis went to a jeweller's and
bought the girl a bracelet. How happy this clandestine purchase
made him, how stuffy and comical the jeweller's clerks seemed,
how sweet the women who passed at his back smelled! On Fifth
Avenue, passing Atlas with his shoulders bent under the weight of
the world, Francis thought of the strenuousness of containing his
physicalness within the patterns he had chosen.

He did not know when he would see the girl next. He had the bracelet in his inside pocket when he got home. Opening the door of his house, he found her in the hall. Her back was to him, and she turned when she heard the door close. Her smile was open and loving. Her perfection stunned him like a fine day—a day after a thunderstorm. He seized her and covered her lips with his, and she struggled but she did not have to struggle for long, because just then little Gertrude Flannery appeared from somewhere and said, "Oh, Mr. Weed . . ."

Gertrude was a stray. She had been born with a taste for exploration, and she did not have it in her to center her life with her affectionate parents. People who did not know the Flannerys concluded from Gertrude's behavior that she was the child of a bitterly divided family, where drunken quarrels were the rule. This was not true. The fact that little Gertrude's clothing was ragged and thin was her own triumph over her mother's struggle to dress her warmly and neatly. Garrulous, skinny, and unwashed, she drifted from house to house around the Blenhollow neighborhood, forming and breaking alliances based on an attachment to babies, animals, children her own age, adolescents, and sometimes adults. Opening your front door in the morning, you would find Gertrude sitting on your stoop. Going into the bathroom to shave, you would find Gertrude using the toilet. Looking into your son's crib, you would find it empty, and, looking further, you would find that Gertrude had pushed him in his baby carriage into the next village. She was helpful, pervasive, honest, hungry, and loyal. She never went home of her own choice. When the time to go arrived, she was indifferent to all its signs. "Go home, Gertrude," people could be heard saying in one house or another, night after night. "Go home, Gertrude." "It's time for you to go home now, Gertrude." "You had better go home and get your supper, Gertrude." "I told you to go home twenty minutes ago, Gertrude." "Your mother will be worrying about you, Gertrude." "Go home, Gertrude, go home."

There are times when the lines around the human eye seem like shelves of eroded stone and when the staring eye itself strikes us with such a wilderness of animal feeling that we are at a loss. The look Francis gave the little girl was ugly and queer, and it frightened her. He reached into his pocket—his hands were shaking—and took out a quarter. "Go home, Gertrude, go home, and don't tell anyone, Gertrude. Don't—" He choked and ran into the living room as Julia called down to him from upstairs to hurry and dress.

The thought that he would drive Anne Murchison home later that night ran like a golden thread through the events of the party that Francis and Julia went to, and he laughed uproariously at dull jokes, dried a tear when Mabel Mercer told him about the death of her kitten, and stretched, yawned, sighed, and grunted like any other man with a rendezvous at the back of his mind. The bracelet was in his pocket. As he sat talking, the smell of grass was in his nose, and he was wondering where he would park the car. Nobody lived in the old Parker mansion, and the driveway was used as a lovers' lane. Townsend Street was a dead end, and he could park there, beyond the last house. The old lane that used to connect Elm Street to the riverbanks was overgrown, but he had walked there with his children, and he could drive his car deep enough into the brushwoods to be concealed.

The Weeds were the last to leave the party, and their host and hostess spoke of their own married happiness while they all four stood in the hallway saying good night. "She's my girl," their host said, squeezing his wife. "She's my blue sky. After sixteen years, I still bite her shoulders. She makes me feel like Hannibal crossing the Alps."

The Weeds drove home in silence. Francis brought the car up the driveway and sat still, with the motor running. "You can put the car in the garage," Julia said as she got out. "I told the Murchison girl she could leave at eleven. Someone drove her home." She shut the door, and Francis sat in the dark. He would be spared nothing then, it seemed, that a fool was not spared: ravening lewdness, jealousy, this hurt to his feelings that put tears in his eyes, even scorn—for he could see clearly the image he now presented, his arms spread over the steering wheel and his head buried in them for love.

Francis had been a dedicated Boy Scout when he was young, and, remembering the precepts of his youth, he left his office early the next afternoon and played some round-robin squash, but, with his body toned up by exercise and a shower, he realized that he might better have stayed at his desk. It was a frosty night when he got home. The air smelled sharply of change. When he stepped into the house, he sensed an unusual stir. The children were in their best clothes, and when Julia came down, she was wearing a lavender dress and her diamond sunburst. She explained the stir: Mr. Hubber was coming at seven to take their photograph for the

Christmas card. She had put out Francis' blue suit and a tie with some color in it, because the picture was going to be in color this year. Julia was lighthearted at the thought of being photographed for Christmas. It was the kind of ceremony she enjoyed.

Francis went upstairs to change his clothes. He was tired from the day's work and tired with longing, and sitting on the edge of the bed had the effect of deepening his weariness. He thought of Anne Murchison, and the physical need to express himself, instead of being restrained by the pink lamps on Julia's dressing table, engulfed him. He went to Julia's desk, took a piece of writing paper, and began to write on it. "Dear Anne, I love you, I love you, I love you . . ." No one would see the letter, and he used no restraint. He used phrases like "heavenly bliss," and "love nest." He salivated, sighed, and trembled. When Julia called him to come down, the abyss between his fantasy and the practical world opened so wide that he felt it affect the muscles of his heart.

Julia and the children were on the stoop, and the photographer and his assistant had set up a double battery of floodlights to show the family and the architectural beauty of the entrance to their house. People who had come home on a late train slowed their cars to see the Weeds being photographed for their Christmas card. A few waved and called to the family. It took half an hour of smiling and wetting their lips before Mr. Hubber was satisfied. The heat of the lights made an unfresh smell in the frosty air, and when they were turned off, they lingered on the retina of Francis' eyes.

Later that night, while Francis and Julia were drinking their coffee in the living room, the doorbell rang. Julia answered the door and let in Clayton Thomas. He had come to pay her for some theatre tickets that she had given his mother some time ago, and that Helen Thomas had scrupulously insisted on paying for, though Julia had asked her not to. Julia invited him in to have a cup of coffee. "I won't have any coffee," Clayton said, "but I will come in for a minute." He followed her into the living room, said good evening to Francis, and sat awkwardly in a chair.

Clayton's father had been killed in the war, and the young man's fatherlessness surrounded him like an element. This may have been conspicuous in Shady Hill because the Thomases were the only family that lacked a piece; all the other marriages were intact and productive. Clayton was in his second or third year of college, and he and his mother lived alone in a large house, which she hoped to sell. Clayton had once made some trouble. Years ago, he had stolen some money and run away; he had got to California before they caught up with him. He was tall and homely, wore horn-rimmed glasses, and spoke in a deep voice.

"When do you go back to college, Clayton?" Francis asked.

"I'm not going back," Clayton said. "Mother doesn't have the money, and there's no sense in all this pretense. I'm going to get a job, and if we sell the house, we'll take an apartment in New York."

"Won't you miss Shady Hill?" Julia asked.

"No," Clayton said. "I don't like it."

"Why not?" Francis asked.

"Well, there's a lot here I don't approve of," Clayton said gravely. "Things like the club dances. Last Saturday night, I looked in toward the end and saw Mr. Granner trying to put Mrs. Minot into the trophy case. They were both drunk. I disapprove of so much drinking."

"It was Saturday night," Francis said.

"And all the dovecotes are phony," Clayton said. "And the way people clutter up their lives. I've thought about it a lot, and what seems to me to be really wrong with Shady Hill is that it doesn't have any future. So much energy is spent in perpetuating the place —in keeping out undesirables, and so forth—that the only idea of the future anyone has is just more and more commuting trains and more parties. I don't think that's healthy. I think people ought to be able to dream big dreams about the future. I think people ought to be able to dream great dreams."

"It's too bad you couldn't continue with college," Julia said.

"I wanted to go to divinity school," Clayton said.

"What's your church?" Francis asked.

"Unitarian, Theosophist, Transcendentalist, Humanist," Clayton said.

"Wasn't Emerson a transcendentalist?" Julia asked.

"I mean the English transcendentalists," Clayton said. "All the American transcendentalists were goops."

"What kind of a job do you expect to get?" Francis asked.

"Well, I'd like to work for a publisher," Clayton said, "but everyone tells me there's nothing doing. But it's the kind of thing I'm interested in. I'm writing a long verse play about good and evil. Uncle Charlie might get me into a bank, and that would be good for me. I need the discipline. I have a long way to go in forming my character. I have some terrible habits. I talk too much. I think

I ought to take vows of silence. I ought to try not to speak for a week, and discipline myself. I've thought of making a retreat at one of the Episcopalian monasteries, but I don't like Trinitarianism."

"Do you have any girl friends?" Francis asked.

"I'm engaged to be married," Clayton said. "Of course, I'm not old enough or rich enough to have my engagement observed or respected or anything, but I bought a simulated emerald for Anne Murchison with the money I made cutting lawns this summer. We're going to be married as soon as she finishes school."

Francis recoiled at the mention of the girl's name. Then a dingy light seemed to emanate from his spirit, showing everything—Julia, the boy, the chairs—in their true colorlessness. It was like a bitter turn of the weather.

"We're going to have a large family," Clayton said. "Her father's a terrible rummy, and I've had my hard times, and we want to have lots of children. Oh, she's wonderful, Mr. and Mrs. Weed, and we have so much in common. We like all the same things. We sent out the same Christmas card last year without planning it, and we both have an allergy to tomatoes, and our eyebrows grow together in the middle. Well, good night."

Julia went to the door with him. When she returned, Francis said that Clayton was lazy, irresponsible, affected, and smelly. Julia said that Francis seemed to be getting intolerant; the Thomas boy was young and should be given a chance. Julia had noticed other cases where Francis had been short-tempered. "Mrs. Wrightson has asked everyone in Shady Hill to her anniversary party but us," she said.

"I'm sorry, Julia."

"Do you know why they didn't ask us?"

"Why?"

"Because you insulted Mrs. Wrightson."

"Then you know about it?"

"June Masterson told me. She was standing behind you."

Julia walked in front of the sofa with a small step that expressed, Francis knew, a feeling of anger.

"I did insult Mrs. Wrightson, Julia, and I meant to. I've never liked her parties, and I'm glad she's dropped us."

"What about Helen?"

"How does Helen come into this?"

"Mrs. Wrightson's the one who decides who goes to the assemblies."

"You mean she can keep Helen from going to the dances?"

"Yes."

"I hadn't thought of that."

"Oh, I knew you hadn't thought of it," Julia cried, thrusting hilt-deep into this chink of his armor. "And it makes me furious to see this kind of stupid thoughtlessness wreck everyone's happiness."

"I don't think I've wrecked anyone's happiness."

"Mrs. Wrightson runs Shady Hill and has run it for the last forty years. I don't know what makes you think that in a community like this you can indulge every impulse you have to be insulting, vulgar, and offensive."

"I have very good manners," Francis said, trying to give the evening a turn toward the light.

"Damn you, Francis Weed!" Julia cried, and the spit of her words struck him in the face. "I've worked hard for the social position we enjoy in this place, and I won't stand by and see you wreck it. You must have understood when you settled here that you couldn't expect to live like a bear in a cave."

"I've got to express my likes and dislikes."

"You can conceal your dislikes. You don't have to meet everything head-on, like a child. Unless you're anxious to be a social leper. It's no accident that we get asked out a great deal. It's no accident that Helen has so many friends. How would you like to spend your Saturday nights at the movies? How would you like to spend your Sundays raking up dead leaves? How would you like it if your daughter spent the assembly nights sitting at her window, listening to the music from the club? How would you like it—" He did something then that was, after all, not so unaccountable, since her words seemed to raise up between them a wall so deadening that he gagged: He struck her full in the face. She staggered and then, a moment later, seemed composed. She went up the stairs to their room. She didn't slam the door. When Francis followed, a few minutes later, he found her packing a suitcase.

"Julia, I'm very sorry."

"It doesn't matter," she said. She was crying.

"Where do you think you're going?"

"I don't know. I just looked at a timetable. There's an eleven-sixteen into New York. I'll take that."

"You can't go, Julia."

"I can't stay. I know that."

"I'm sorry about Mrs. Wrightson, Julia, and I'm—"

"It doesn't matter about Mrs. Wrightson. That isn't the trouble."

"What is the trouble?"

"You don't love me."

"I do love you, Julia."

"No, you don't."

"Julia, I do love you, and I would like to be as we were—sweet and bawdy and dark—but now there are so many people."

"You hate me."

"I don't hate you, Julia."

"You have no idea of how much you hate me. I think it's sub-conscious. You don't realize the cruel things you've done."

"What cruel things, Julia?"

"The cruel acts your subconscious drives you to in order to ex-press your hatred of me."

"What, Julia?"

"I've never complained."

"Tell me."

"You don't know what you're doing."

"Tell me."

"Your clothes."

"What do you mean?"

"I mean the way you leave your dirty clothes around in order to express your subconscious hatred of me."

"I don't understand."

"I mean your dirty socks and your dirty pajamas and your dirty underwear and your dirty shirts!" She rose from kneeling by the suitcase and faced him, her eyes blazing and her voice ringing with emotion. "I'm talking about the fact that you've never learned to hang up anything. You just leave your clothes all over the floor where they drop, in order to humiliate me. You do it on purpose!" She fell on the bed, sobbing.

"Julia, darling!" he said, but when she felt his hand on her shoul-der she got up.

"Leave me alone," she said. "I have to go." She brushed past him to the closet and came back with a dress. "I'm not taking any of the things you've given me," she said. "I'm leaving my pearls and the fur jacket."

"Oh, Julia!" Her figure, so helpless in its self-deceptions, bent over the suitcase made him nearly sick with pity. She did not un-derstand how desolate her life would be without him. She didn't understand the hours that working women have to keep. She didn't understand that most of her friendships existed within the framework of their marriage, and that without this she would find herself alone. She didn't understand about travel, about hotels, about money. "Julia, I can't let you go! What you don't understand, Julia, is that you've come to be dependent on me."

She tossed her head back and covered her face with her hands. "Did you say that *I* was dependent on *you?*" she asked. "Is that what you said? And who is it that tells you what time to get up in the morning and when to go to bed at night? Who is it that prepares your meals and picks up your dirty closet and invites your friends to dinner? If it weren't for me, your neckties would be greasy and your clothing would be full of moth holes. You were alone when I met you, Francis Weed, and you'll be alone when I leave. When Mother asked you for a list to send out invitations to our wedding, how many names did you have to give her? Fourteen!"

"Cleveland wasn't my home, Julia."

"And how many of your friends came to the church? Two!"

"Cleveland wasn't my home, Julia."

"Since I'm not taking the fur jacket," she said quietly, "you'd better put it back into storage. There's an insurance policy on the pearls that comes due in January. The name of the laundry and the maid's telephone number—all those things are in my desk. I hope you won't drink too much, Francis. I hope that nothing bad will happen to you. If you do get into serious trouble, you can call me."

"Oh my darling, I can't let you go!" Francis said. "I can't let you go, Julia!" He took her in his arms.

"I guess I'd better stay and take care of you for a little while longer," she said.

Riding to work in the morning, Francis saw the girl walk down the aisle of the coach. He was surprised; he hadn't realized that the school she went to was in the city, but she was carrying books, she seemed to be going to school. His surprise delayed his reaction, but then he got up clumsily and stepped into the aisle. Several people had come between them, but he could see her ahead of him, waiting for someone to open the car door, and then, as the train swerved, putting out her hand to support herself as she crossed the platform into the next car. He followed her through that car and halfway through another before calling her name—"Anne! Anne!"—but she didn't turn. He followed her into still another car, and she sat down in an aisle seat. Coming up to her, all his feelings warm and bent in her direction, he put his hand on the back of her seat—even this touch warmed him—and, leaning down to speak to her, he saw that it was not Anne. It was an older woman wearing glasses. He went on deliberately into another car, his face red with embarrassment and the much deeper feeling of having his good sense challenged; for if he couldn't tell one person from another, what evidence was there that his life with Julia and the children had as much reality as his dreams of iniquity in Paris or the litter, the grass smell, and the cave-shaped trees in Lovers' Lane.

Late that afternoon, Julia called to remind Francis that they were going out for dinner. A few minutes later, Trace Bearden called. "Look, fellar," Trace said. "I'm calling for Mrs. Thomas. You know? Clayton, that boy of hers, doesn't seem able to get a job, and I wondered if you could help. If you'd call Charlie Bell—I know he's indebted to you—and say a good word for the kid, I think Charlie would—"

"Trace, I hate to say this," Francis said, "but I don't feel that I can do anything for that boy. The kid's worthless. I know it's a harsh thing to say, but it's a fact. Any kindness done for him would backfire in everybody's face. He's just a worthless kid, Trace, and there's nothing to be done about it. Even if we got him a job, he wouldn't be able to keep it for a week. I know that to be a fact. It's an awful thing, Trace, and I know it is, but instead of recommending that kid, I'd feel obliged to warn people against him—people who knew his father and would naturally want to step in and do something. I'd feel obliged to warn them. He's a thief . . ."

The moment this conversation was finished, Miss Rainey came in and stood by his desk. "I'm not going to be able to work for you any more, Mr. Weed," she said. "I can stay until the seventeenth if you need me, but I've been offered a whirlwind of a job, and I'd like to leave as soon as possible."

She went out, leaving him to face alone the wickedness of what he had done to the Thomas boy. His children in their photograph laughed and laughed, glazed with all the bright colors of summer, and he remembered that they had met a bagpiper on the beach that day and he had paid the piper a dollar to play them a battle song of the Black Watch. The girl would be at the house when he got home. He would spend another evening among his kind neighbors, picking and choosing dead-end streets, cart tracks, and the driveways of abandoned houses. There was nothing to mitigate his feeling—nothing that laughter or a game of softball with the children would change—and, thinking back over the plane crash, the Far-quarsons' new maid, and Anne Murchison's difficulties with her drunken father, he wondered how he could have avoided arriving at just where he was. He was in trouble. He had been lost once in his life, coming back from a trout stream in the north woods, and he had now the same bleak realization that no amount of cheerfulness or hopefulness or valor or perseverance could help him find, in the gathering dark, the path that he'd lost. He smelled the forest. The feeling of bleakness was intolerable, and he saw clearly that he had reached the point where he would have to make a choice.

He could go to a psychiatrist, like Miss Rainey; he could go to church and confess his lusts; he could go to a Danish massage parlor in the West Seventies that had been recommended by a salesman; he could rape the girl or trust that he would somehow be prevented from doing this; or he could get drunk. It was his life, his boat, and, like every other man, he was made to be the father of thousands, and what harm could there be in a tryst that would make them both feel more kindly toward the world? This was the wrong train of thought, and he came back to the first, the psychiatrist. He had the telephone number of Miss Rainey's doctor, and he called and asked for an immediate appointment. He was insistent with the doctor's secretary—it was his manner in business—and when she said that the doctor's schedule was full for the next few weeks, Francis demanded an appointment that day and was told to come at five.

The psychiatrist's office was in a building that was used mostly by doctors and dentists, and the hallways were filled with the candy smell of mouthwash and memories of pain. Francis' character had been formed upon a series of private resolves—resolves about cleanliness, about going off the high diving board or repeating any other feat that challenged his courage, about punctuality, honesty, and virtue. To abdicate the perfect loneliness in which he had made his most vital decisions shattered his concept of character and left him now in a condition that felt like shock. He was stupefied. The scene for his *miserere mei Deus* was, like the waiting room of so many doctors' offices, a crude token gesture toward the sweets of domestic bliss: a place arranged with antiques, coffee tables, potted plants, and etchings of snow-covered bridges and geese in flight, although there were no children, no marriage bed, no stove, even, in this travesty of a house, where no one had ever spent the night and where the curtained windows looked straight onto a dark air shaft. Francis gave his name and address to a secretary and then saw, at the side of the room, a policeman moving toward him. "Hold it, hold it," the policeman said. "Don't move. Keep your hands where they are."

"I think it's all right, Officer," the secretary began. "I think it will be—"

"Let's make sure," the policeman said, and he began to slap Francis' clothes, looking for what—pistols, knives, an icepick? Finding nothing, he went off, and the secretary began a nervous apology: "When you called on the telephone, Mr. Weed, you seemed very excited, and one of the doctor's patients has been threatening his life, and we have to be careful. If you want to go in now?" Francis pushed open a door connected to an electrical chime, and in the doctor's lair sat down heavily, blew his nose into a handkerchief, searched in his pockets for cigarettes, for matches, for something, and said hoarsely, with tears in his eyes, "I'm in love, Dr. Herzog."

It is a week or ten days later in Shady Hill. The seven-fourteen has come and gone, and here and there dinner is finished and the dishes are in the dishwashing machine. The village hangs, morally and economically, from a thread; but it hangs by its thread in the evening light. Donald Goslin has begun to worry the "Moonlight Sonata" again. *Marcato ma sempre pianissimo!* He seems to be wringing out a wet bath towel, but the housemaid does not heed him. She is writing a letter to Arthur Godfrey. In the cellar of his house, Francis Weed is building a coffee table. Dr. Herzog recommended woodwork as a therapy, and Francis finds some true consolation in the simple arithmetic involved and in the holy smell of new wood. Francis is happy. Upstairs, little Toby is crying, because he is tired. He puts off his cowboy hat, gloves, and fringed jacket, unbuckles the belt studded with gold and rubies, the silver bullets and holsters, slips off his suspenders, his checked shirt, and Levis, and sits on the edge of his bed to pull off his high boots. Leaving this equipment in a heap, he goes to the closet and takes his space suit off a nail. It is a struggle for him to get into the long tights, but he succeeds. He loops the magic cape over his shoulders and, climbing onto the footboard of his bed, he spreads his arms and flies the short distance to the floor, landing with a thump that is audible to everyone in the house but himself.

"Go home, Gertrude, go home," Mrs. Masterson says. "I told you to go home an hour ago, Gertrude. It's way past your suppertime, and your mother will be worried. Go home!" A door on the Bab-

cocks' terrace flies open, and out comes Mrs. Babcock without any
clothes on, pursued by her naked husband. (Their children are away
at boarding school, and their terrace is screened by a hedge.) Over
the terrace they go and in at the kitchen door, as passionate and
handsome a nymph and satyr as you will find on any wall in Venice.
Cutting the last of the roses in her garden, Julia hears old Mr.
Nixon shouting at the squirrels in his bird-feeding station. "Rap-
scallions! Varmits! Avaunt and quit my sight!" A miserable cat
wanders into the garden, sunk in spiritual and physical discomfort.
Tied to its head is a small straw hat—a doll's hat—and it is securely
buttoned into a doll's dress, from the skirts of which protrudes its
long, hairy tail. As it walks, it shakes its feet, as if it had fallen into
water.

"Here, pussy, pussy, pussy!" Julia calls.

"Here, pussy, here, poor pussy!" But the cat gives her a skeptical
look and stumbles away in its skirts. The last to come is Jupiter. He
prances through the tomato vines, holding in his generous mouth
the remains of an evening slipper. Then it is dark; it is a night
where kings in golden suits ride elephants over the mountains.

INDEX

❖